GREAT CAPTAIN

Three Novels of

Abraham Lincoln

❧ ☙

FOREVER FREE

WITH MALICE TOWARD NONE

THE LAST FULL MEASURE

GREAT CAPTAIN
Three 'Lincoln' novels
by
HONORÉ MORROW

Forever Free
With Malice Toward None
The Last Full Measure

William Morrow and Company
Publishers   *New York*

FOREVER FREE
© 1927 by Honoré Willsie Morrow

WITH MALICE TOWARD NONE
© 1928 by Honoré Willsie Morrow

THE LAST FULL MEASURE
© 1930 by Honoré Willsie Morrow

Forever Free

CONTENTS

CHAPTER I

AFTER the inaugural ceremonies which inducted Lincoln into office, that fine noon of March, 1861, the Lincoln family moved from Willard's Hotel to the White House.

The removal was watched by a crowd consumed with more than even the usual vast curiosity displayed over the movements of a new Chief Executive. And the crowd contained many persons who, normally, would have considered such inquisitiveness beneath their dignity. Such a person was the hostess at a small dinner party given that evening in a house on Ninth Street, near F.

It was an attractive house to the guests who crossed the tiny Georgian portico and flagged hall leading to a back parlor, which was small but handsomely furnished. A soft coal fire burned in the English grate. The marble mantel held a beautiful collection of Dresden figures, shepherds and shepherdesses, herding their fairy sheep toward a white marble clock in a glass cover. The Chippendale furniture; the gray and green Brussels carpet, with its design of morning glories; the tidies, knitted in intricate designs of birds, that hung over each chair back; the hassocks with hand-embroidered covers; the green velvet window draperies, formed a quite perfect background for the young hostess, standing before the fire.

She was very tall, nearly six feet, and about twenty-eight years of age, —tall and handsome,—with chestnut curls hanging over her ears, and violet eyes of unforgettable depth and luster. She wore a green silk gown over an enormous crinoline. It was cut very low, displaying a splendid whiteness of bust and arms. She opened and closed a tiny sandalwood fan as she talked.

Dinner was over, and the trio composing the party had returned to the parlor before beginning the conversation that brought in the crowd around Willard's.

"I yielded to my curiosity," she said, "and joined the evil-smelling mob before Willard's to catch a glimpse of the new Queen, and the young royalties."

"Not so evil-smelling, either, as you insinuate, my dear," smiled the man who stood beside the center table, thoughtfully twirling his half-filled liqueur glass. He was tall, taller than the young woman, lean and blond, with a smooth-shaven, aquiline face. "I was there myself, and I saw Mr. Russell, the correspondent of the London *Times*, and Thurlow Weed, and Mrs. Eames, and Mrs. Greenhow."

"There were any number of Southern women, Tom!" exclaimed Miss

Ford. "I suppose Mrs. Greenhow went hoping to see the Queen as-sassinated."

The third member of the party spoke. He was old enough to have been the father of the other two, a gray-bearded man, in evening clothes that added to the extraordinary dignity of his bearing. He bowed to the hostess.

"Miss Ford, pardon, I beg of you, the presumption of a gray head, but will you not be seated, so that I may yield to the temptation offered by this arm chair? I am very tired."

"Oh, how thoughtless I am, my dear Judge!" cried Miss Ford, sinking to the ottoman beside the table, and leaning one arm on the polished mahogany surface, where the lamplight gleamed on her flawless skin. "You must be tired, indeed, after your long trip."

The judge sank into the arm chair. "Part of my weariness was due to my standing in this same vulgar crowd for a look at Mrs. Lincoln," he said with a sigh. "It is a more astute face than gossip had led me to suspect. The woman is not a fool, even if she is ill-bred."

"A common sort of a shrew, I reckon she is." Miss Ford spoke thought-fully. "She has complete control of Lincoln. What a monstrosity that man is!"

"Fittingly so, Lady!" exclaimed Taylor who still stood with his liqueur glass. "Seward ought to put him to chopping wood for the Cabinet fire-place. From all I can gather, it's his chief qualification for his position."

"Seward plans to do just about that, I fancy," said the judge. "Mrs. Lincoln is a Kentuckian, I hear, and a pro-slavery sympathizer. Also she is socially ambitious, and utterly ignorant of the most ordinary social usages."

"Then, if she has complete control of Lincoln,—" Miss Ford paused. "Judge Campbell," she began again, abruptly, "what is it you want of me? What can I do? There must be something portentous afoot, or you would not have spared me all this time, old friend though you are."

"I come to you from a friend of equally long standing." The judge leaned forward and looked at her, keenly. "I come to you from the President of the Confederacy, Jefferson Davis. He asks for your help. He believes you will not deny it to him."

"He is my father's dearest friend!" exclaimed Miss Ford. "It will be difficult for me to deny him anything."

"Close the door, Tom," directed Justice Campbell. "I am about to give you two the full confidence of the Confederacy. Sit down beside Miss Ford, I pray, Tom. Your restlessness is disconcerting." He paused, fitted his finger tips carefully together, gazed at them a long moment, then said:

"The provisional government of the Confederacy desires to avoid war. It is eager to establish the Confederacy by negotiation with Congress, if possible. To that end, three commissioners have been sent by President Davis to Washington for the purpose of feeling out the temper of the Lincoln Administration. I am one of those commissioners. We are working with as much secrecy as possible."

Taylor spoke suddenly. "Sir, have you talked with the hot heads in Richmond and Charleston? You can't have, or you'd realize that they are already on a war basis there. Why, Governor Pickens of South Carolina is urging Beauregard to attack Fort Sumter, *now*."

The justice raised his hand. "I know! I know! But that is not the South at its best. We want no war. We want peaceable secession, not a military dictatorship. Now, as I understand the situation, William Seward, the new Secretary of State, is the actual head of the Administration. He also declares for peace. But what Lincoln wants, we do not know. If, as gossip has it, he is under the control of Seward and his own wife, our problem is with them, not with the President."

"Not altogether," interrupted Miss Ford. "If Lincoln is as weak as that, what will prevent Charles Sumner and the Abolitionists from getting control of him, or what will prevent the commissioners from using him?"

"Exactly!" agreed Campbell. "You have come to the point with your usual perspicacity, Miss Ford. Lincoln will belong to the party first on the ground, to the party that keeps its representatives closest to him. Properly manipulated, he can be enormously useful in obtaining official recognition of the Confederacy."

"The manipulation must be extremely agile," Taylor smiled, "to get action before Sumter is taken."

"What if Fort Sumter is taken, sir?" asked Justice Campbell, somewhat irascibly. "The North did not take action when seven States were taken by the Confederacy. Why should one fort cause even a ripple in its complacency?"

"Abe Lincoln said in his inaugural address this noon," replied Taylor, "that he proposed to hang on to what Buchanan had left him. If he meant it, he might feel peevish over the loss of Fort Sumter and Charleston harbor."

"Don't you know any one who really understands that great, shambling simpleton?" cried Miss Ford. "Everybody knows Seward wrote the inaugural speech, and Seward is a political weathercock."

"No one seems to know Lincoln," replied Justice Campbell, "that is, no one in public life. But, unless I misread the astute look on Mrs. Lincoln's face, she knows her husband. And thus we arrive at the point, Miss Ford, where you can help."

"I?" asked the young woman, her face kindling. "But why and how, *I?*"

"Yours was the first name mentioned by President Davis," said Campbell, "and after three hours of discussion of many names, it was you to whom he returned. Your long social experience, your tact, your high degree of intelligence, but above all, his knowledge of the intense devotion of your father and yourself to the cause of slavery; these were the qualities the President named again and again. It is known—pardon my seeming bad taste—it is known in Washington and New York that your father has lost a great deal of money in the present financial crisis."

Miss Ford smiled. "We still are able to exist. But father is spending his time on the plantation, and we are going to close this house."

"Good!" cried the judge. "Dear Miss Ford, let it seep out that you are in such financial straits that you must seek pecuniary aid. Find some one who can recommend you to the Lincolns, then proceed to procure a position as Mrs. Lincoln's social companion, or as governess to the two young boys—then teach us how to handle Abe Lincoln."

Miss Ford had flushed a deep red. "You ask a Ford of Virginia to earn her living?"

"Worse than that," replied Justice Campbell with deep earnestness, "I ask you to earn it in a family that, both socially and politically, must be abhorrent to you, or to any other lady of the South. Miss Ford, on the character of this backwoodsman, this rail splitter, rests the future of the Confederacy. We *must know* him. If you can make us know him, you will accomplish a task not second in importance to any that can be done for our sacred institutions."

"A spy!" exclaimed the Virginian, lifting her chin. "Me, a spy."

"Lady," Taylor leaned toward her, anxiously, his blond skin pale with intensity of feeling, "Lady, don't do this thing, I beg of you!"

"What do you mean, sir?" exclaimed Campbell. "Are you treasonable to our cause?"

"No, Judge Campbell," replied Taylor, "but Miss Ford and I grew up on adjacent plantations. She represents all the loveliness, all the splendor of ladyhood to me. I cannot bear the thought—"

"Sir!" thundered Campbell, "had this been the moment to think of personal honor, would I have stooped to use the prestige of my high office in the Federal courts to further the cause of Secession? I, sir, have such loyalty to our social institutions and rights—"

"Just a moment, Judge," interrupted Miss Ford, "I'm afraid I'm a little cold blooded. If I go into this thing, I shall do so for just one reason. I believe that the institution of slavery is seriously menaced. I want to keep my slaves, and all that slavery gives to the South. If I undertake this dreadful work, I shall do so with no illusion of splendor connected with it, and I'd admire you and Mr. Davis, and all the others of you whom I know so well, if you'd be equally candid."

Taylor laughed. "She has us there, Mr. Justice!"

"Do you mean, Miss Ford," asked Campbell, ignoring Taylor's thrust, "that you will undertake the work?"

The Virginian rose, and paced splendidly in sweeping crinoline up and down the room, finally coming to pause beside the fire which she eyed thoughtfully, for some moments.

"Either you are very wise," she said at last, "in choosing so conspicuous a type as mine for this work, or else you are dangerously foolish. Hoping that you are the former, I'll agree to undertake it for just two months."

Campbell rose and solemnly shook hands with her. Then he turned to the younger man.

"Mr. Taylor, Mr. Davis asked me, in case Miss Ford agreed to this

great sacrifice, to invite you to undertake to act as direct messenger between himself and this lady."

Taylor's pale face blazed. But before he could reply, Miss Ford put her
hand on his arm. "Think, Tom dear!"

He stared at her, his eyes softening. "Do you want me, Lady?"

"I want you, I need you. Two months are nothing, considering the tremendous stakes."

"I'll help, with one understanding," ejaculated Taylor. "When war is
declared, I want a commission."

"You shall have it." Justice Campbell held out his hand. "Your grateful
country will one day thank you both. Now, then, let us work out some
details."

An hour later, Justice Campbell left the little house on Ninth Street,
and Miss Ford and Taylor, after seeing him to the door, returned to the
fire in the back parlor.

"Do you care to take a look in at the Inaugural Ball, Lady?" asked
Taylor.

She gave him a glance half scornful, half humorous. "Don't force me to
meet the wild animals till the new business requires it, Tom. When do
you start for—what is Judge Campbell's phrase?—'The provisional capital
at Montgomery, and His Excellency, the President of the Confederacy'?"

"To-morrow or the next day," replied Taylor, smiling at Miss Ford's
mimicry of Justice Campbell, but sobering quickly, as he said, "I can't
help feeling a little tragic about it, Lady. After all, our ancestors did as
much about establishing the Federal government as did the most ardent
of these Northerners—"

Miss Ford tossed her fine head. "I have no sentimentality about governments, I can tell you, Tom. I've lived too close to Washington all my
life. There's nothing high or fine about governing. It's all intrigue, crooked-
ness, selfish grabbing—with the lowest types of minds succeeding best. My
political litany is very simple: I believe in slavery because I think it produces the finest type of white civilization. I wish to keep my slaves because they make it possible for me to live beautifully. I shall be fiercely
loyal to Jefferson Davis and his crowd because they are fighting the slavery
fight."

"You always have seen life without shadings of meaning," mused Taylor.
"I suppose it's that decisiveness that makes your nature so irresistibly attractive to my everlasting quibbling over motives.—Will your father fall in
with the idea of buying the tavern at Fairfax Courthouse?"

"With the Davis crowd supplying the money? Why not, my dear Tom?"
drawled Miss Ford. "Who is this man Mosby who will head the information bureau there?"

"I don't know him," replied Tom, "except by reputation. A very clever
fellow, I've been told. Where are you going, Lady?" as she rose and moved
toward the door.

"Both you and I are going to drop in on Mrs. Eames. She'll be sure to have a crowd there, this evening, all of them gossiping about the Lincolns. I want to hear what I can, and if Charles Sumner is there, make him some casual suggestions."

A few moments later, the two Virginians were on the way to the Eames home, one of the social centers of Washington.

March, in the city of Washington, can be as genial as April in Chicago, and the windows of Lincoln's bedroom, looking south to the Potomac were open to a soft wind that smelled, not too unpleasantly, of the flats and marshes that lay between the White House grounds and the river.

The bedroom, in the southwest corner of the Executive Mansion, was handsomely furnished with a great mahogany bedstead, with bureaus, tables, and chairs of rosewood, and with a thick-piled red carpet, somewhat worn, as were the heavy red hangings and the upholstering; but they were not the less pleasant and ease-inviting, for that.

The gas had been turned low in the jet beside the bureau, and Mr. Lincoln, in a faded blue dressing gown, walked slowly toward the arm chair that stood by one of the windows. Even the dressing gown could not conceal much of his fine length of six feet, four inches, nor could it soften his stoop, or the disproportionately great length of arms and legs, of hands and feet; nor did it conceal the fact that he was thin through the chest, from front to back, and narrow across the shoulders. What it did conceal, however, was the fact that his excessive thinness,—he weighed but a hundred and sixty pounds,—did not make a weak man of him. He was all steel muscle and sinew, a man of astounding physical strength and endurance.

He dropped into the arm chair, put his feet upon the window ledge and leaned his head against the cushioned back of the chair. Seen in profile, his head was unusually high above his ears,—those outstanding ears that *Punch* and *Harper's* and *Leslie's Weekly* so delighted to accent for the amused and contemptuous public! Seen from the front, the forehead, the dome of the head, covered by thick black hair, was magnificent, as was the architecture of the eye socket and the bold firmness of the nose and the granite chin.

Those who knew him best, as for example his secretary, John Hay, insisted that Lincoln was not ugly, but homely,—to an American, a subtle, and vastly significant distinction. Those who knew him least, as for example, the correspondent of the London *Times*, spoke of Lincoln's awkward height, his too prominent ears, his shambling gait, his huge feet and hands, of his too large mouth and too heavy lower lip; and he spoke of the striking beauty of his gray eyes, full, deep, penetrating and ineffably tender; and ended by saying that Lincoln's was a face of infinite sagacity, his personality such that something quite other than his physical peculiarities would make it impossible for the most indifferent observer to pass him in the street without notice.

Lincoln watched the far starlit gleam of the river, without actually seeing it. He was grave, but not sad. The day had gone better than he had dared hope. Not that he had shared the general fear among his supporters, that he would be assassinated during the inaugural ceremonies. All General Scott's precautions,—the heavily guarded barouche, the sharpshooters stationed on the roofs along Pennsylvania Avenue, the soldiers with cocked guns at the Capitol,—had amused and irked him.

"Nothing on earth, I reckon, can keep a man from shooting me," he had told his wife that morning, "if he really has set his tooth for it. Besides, it's not common sense to fence me in with guns all day, then turn me loose at a public ball at night."

No, his apprehensions had not been for his own safety. They had been lest the South would choose to embarrass him by some act of such sinister fury, that the "irrepressible conflict" would be precipitated before he could be installed in the White House. The North was not ready for war, could not be until it had found its master. That, as Lincoln saw it, was his task,—to focus all the quarreling or indifferent forces of the North on one purpose,—that of saving the Union.

There was a murmur of voices in the next room,—Mary and her sisters putting on the finishing touches for the Inaugural Ball. Mary, he told himself, was happy at last. Thank God for that! She had earned happiness. A child's voice now, in staccato exclamations,—Taddie asking for something. Bobbie, the oldest boy, had gone back to Harvard an hour before, glad, he said, as his father recalled with a chuckle, to be snubbed in Cambridge, after the sickening licking of his boots in Springfield and Washington.

The door between the two rooms suddenly swung open, admitting a burst of light, eight-year-old Taddie, and a violent smell of Florida water. The boy, resplendent in a purple velvet suit, flung himself upon his father's great knees.

"Papa day! Papa day! Can't I go to the pa'ty? Willie's going and I didn't fight when motha made me get into this nasty suit! I've got myself all pe'fumed up fo' it."

"You smell like Al Herbert's barber shop on a Saturday night," said Lincoln, kissing the child's quivering lips several times. Taddie was the baby of the family, and appeared even younger than his years, because of the impediment in his speech that blurred all his R's. "Who says you can't go, precious Tadpole, after getting rigged out in these ice cream clothes?"

"Motha said so. I told he' I'd as soon die as not go and I would. That ball will be betta' than fo'ty ci'cuses! Old Edwa'd, the doo'man told me so. I'll die if I can't go, Papa day!"

The child's blue eyes were turned up to his father's gray ones in an agony of pleading. Every nerve in his little body was tense with excitement. His father patted the velvet shoulder and turned toward the open door.

"Mary! O Mary! Can you come here a moment?"

"Sorry but I can't, Abra'm," returned a clear voice. "It's a critical moment."

"Then warn the girls that two men are coming in!" called Lincoln, putting Tad down and rising. There was a muffled shriek and the sound of fleeing feet, as father and son appeared in Mrs. Lincoln's room.

Mary Lincoln stood before the pier glass that was set into the door of the wardrobe, and, for a long moment, Lincoln paused, staring at her, heedless of Tad's impatient jerking at his hand. Mary always had been pretty, but now she seemed to him to be actually beautiful. She was of a little less than medium height, inclined to plumpness, with a wonderful fair skin, and masses of brown hair, braided about a well-shaped head. Her forehead was full and high, her eyes large, blue, set well apart under straight, fine brows. Her eyes, Lincoln said, were the kindest in the world. Her nose was straight and a little long, her lips were too thin for beauty, but sensitive and wistful in expression. Her skin and her round, full throat were lovely.

It was a face of penetrating intelligence.

Lincoln drew a long breath of admiration, partly for the new dress, partly for the glow in Mary's vivid face. She wore white satin, over an enormous crinoline. Lincoln hated crinolines, but he thought the lace that draped the skirt and bodice was exquisite, and that the pearl necklace and bracelets were iridescent as dewdrops on her fair skin. Twining a wreath of jessamine and violets in her hair, she smiled at him in the mirror, then frowned.

"You ought to be dressed, Abra'm!"

"All set, but my jacket, wife! Why not let Taddie go, as long as Willie's going?"

"He ought to be in bed this minute," replied Mary. "It's after ten o'clock and he's worn out with excitement. He's been half hysterical, all day. He hasn't Willie's calm temper, and he'll be down with a bilious attack, next!"

Lincoln looked down at the small boy whose scowl so ludicrously duplicated his mother's. He was a very pretty child, and his father doted on his cherub-like features. "Meaning," smiled Lincoln, "that Tad's your mental legatee and Willie's mine!"

"No," returned Mary, trying the effect of the wreath with head turning now this way, and now that. "I don't mean so at all. Taddie has your soft heart and my nerves, and a smaller replica of your brain. Willie has my hard heart, your nerves, and more than my brain."

Her blue eyes twinkled. Lincoln gave a low chuckle in response, and then said, earnestly, "Please let Taddie go! He'll be as calm as Willie. Can't you promise that, son?"

"Yes, Motha, yes! Yes! Yes! Yes!" shrieked Tad.

"There, you see?" exclaimed his mother, turning round to look disapprovingly, first at her husband, then at her young son. "No! You must go to bed, Tad."

With a scream as of mortal pain, Tad threw himself on the floor. Lincoln picked him up, kissed him, then said in a voice of unmistakable firmness, "One more scream like that, young man, and I'll put you to bed, myself."

Tad instantly became silent. His father crossed the room, and standing before Mary, his hands in his dressing gown pockets, looked down at her without smiling, as he said, gently,

"If I beguile you into believing how handsome I think you're looking, will you let the boy go?"

"Oh, that's not fair, Abra'm! No! No! No! He mustn't go."

"I'll go his security for good behavior. Better let him go, Mary!"

"No! No!" repeated Mary with more emphasis than the case would seem to warrant, to one who did not know how badly Lincoln spoiled his children.

"I reckon he'll have to go, Mary," said Lincoln, still gently.

She looked up into the deep-set, gray eyes. Back of their tenderness she saw the granite, and a look of helplessness came into her face. It was all too familiar an experience for both husband and wife, and Mary had not the gift of patience, persistent as she was. She knew only too well, however, when she was worsted.

"Have your own way, Abra'm," she said, sadly, and turned back to her toilet. "Taddie, go wash your face and find Willie."

With a whoop of joy, the child flew from the room.

Lincoln took an eager stride that carried him between his wife and the mirror. He caught her fingers in his big, warm palms.

"Now, I've offended you again! But he wants things so that it actually gripes him, just like I did when I was little, and I never had them. That's why I interfere. You don't know what that kind of punishment is, Mary."

"Don't I?" Mary looked up and Lincoln saw the look in her blue gaze that never failed to fill him with contrition. He realized, whenever he had time to think about it, that he neglected Mary in many little ways. He put a great hand on either side of her face and stooped toward her, but she moved back from him.

"You're putting the boys in the way of losing their hunger for anything, Abra'm. You are satiating them now, and later, when life has no zest for them, they'll blame you."

Lincoln nodded. "My head's in perfect accord with your statement, my dear, but my heart isn't." His beautiful white teeth flashed in a whimsical smile.

"If only you could learn to say 'No'!" sighed his wife.

"It's an awful weakness," groaned Lincoln, then with his irresistible twinkle, "I've often wondered what would have become of me if I'd been a girl. With this incapacity for saying 'No,' nothing but my ugliness could have saved my virtue! That's why the Almighty made me a man, I'm sure!"

Mary burst into helpless laughter, suddenly kissed one of the great hands that lay on her shoulders, and gave him a little push. "Go along, you great child, and put on your proper coat! And *please* don't forget the white gloves! They're in your little upper bureau drawer."

Lincoln's shout of laughter ended in a comical groan. He kissed Mary, very tenderly, and slowly returned to his own room. There, he turned up the gas, pulled off the dressing gown, and put on the black broadcloth frock coat that lay on the bed. It had been made for him by an excellent New York tailor, and he scrutinized his reflection in the mirror with whimsical satisfaction. He was searching in the wrong drawer for his gloves when a knock sounded at the outer door.

"Come in! Come in!" shouted Lincoln.

A young man entered. He was of medium height, and did not look his twenty-two years, in spite of a small, black mustache. His face was as round as Tad's, with blunt features and high color. His eyes were a brilliant black, beneath heavy brows that lifted at their outer edges, giving him a perpetually quizzical expression that was very attractive. He wore impeccable broadcloth evening clothes. This was John Hay, assistant to the President's private secretary, George Nicolay.

"What's the trouble, John? House on fire?" asked Lincoln.

"In a way, yes, Mr. Lincoln," answered young Hay. "Nicolay thought you ought to have this letter, at once. It's from the Acting Secretary of War."

"Is it more important to these United States than my getting into white gloves?" asked the President, continuing his search in the bottom bureau drawer.

"I think so. Major Anderson sent word from Fort Sumter to-day," replied Hay, his eyes snapping with excitement, "that his food supplies won't last much longer, and that he must be reënforced, or the fort evacuated, within the next month. The Acting Secretary thought you ought to have this information in case anything came up, to-night."

Lincoln ceased his search for his gloves. "Hand over the note, John."

Very deliberately he put on his spectacles, read the missive through, folded it, and put it into his hip pocket.

"John, what do you think of my new clothes? My wife says this is the first time she's ever got me into a decent fitting suit."

"They look very well, sir. But," his cheeks flushing, "do you get the significance of that letter, Mr. President? If we reënforce Sumter, the South will take it as an excuse for precipitating a fight. If we don't reënforce, our only toe-hold on Charleston is gone."

"I might get the significance," said Lincoln mildly, "frontier town politician though the newspapers say I am! As I recall, there was considerable discussion of Fort Sumter even back Springfield way, John."

"I beg your pardon, sir!" exclaimed Hay.

"That's all right!" smiled Lincoln. "Nobody knows better than I that I can stand a heap of educating. My wife has been currying me for twenty years, haven't you, Mary?" as Mrs. Lincoln swept into the room, closely followed by Tad and Willie.

Mary smiled and turned to young Hay. "How well your evening clothes become you, John! No wonder the girls buzz round you so!"

The young secretary made a profound obeisance. "But no one will look at me if I stand near you, Madam President! You are regal to-night! What a wonderful dress!"

"It's thirty steps around the bottom of the skirt," said Willie solemnly. He was a slender boy of eleven, with a strong resemblance to his father.

The three grown people laughed, and under cover of this, John Hay bowed himself out of the room.

"I like that boy!" said Mary Lincoln. "He's a little highty-tighty now, with excitement and his elevation to grandeur, but he has a brain. After he understands you, he'll in many ways be more valuable to you than Nicolay."

"Socially, perhaps," agreed the President. "But for steady chewing of the cud of hard detail, thank heaven for George Nicolay. Mary, where did you put those gloves? Have I got to wear them?"

"You most certainly must!" snapped his wife. She sailed like a full-rigged vessel across the great room, took the gloves from the drawer, and with the boys beside her, watched the President, sternly, while he worked his great hands into the white kids.

The clock on the mantel ticked loudly for many minutes, during the process. Tick! Tock! Tick! Tock!—Lincoln's mind took a long stride. Food supplies running low,—whose carelessness, or worse, was that? What had old General Scott been thinking and doing? A fine soldier, the General-in-Chief of the army, but weakened now by senility, and an interest in politics. The old man must ease himself into retirement. Then whom could Lincoln get adequately to head up the pitiful excuse for an army? All the months since his nomination, Lincoln had been gathering information about the Federal military resources, and sweating blood over Buchanan's inadequacy. Who would head up the army until he knew enough to head it up, himself— Tick! Tock! Tick! Tock!

"Papa day!" plaintively from Taddie. "The hack has been waiting fo' us, fo' a long time."

"You mean the carriage, Taddie," corrected his mother.

"It's a hack, just like we'd go to the depot in, in Sp'ingfield," insisted Taddie.

"If you rush papa, he'll tear his gloves," said Willie, breathing hard in sympathy with his father's struggles.

"Almost done, boys!" exclaimed Lincoln. "Here, fasten this button, Willie, and then both hands will be jailed for the evening."

With a chuckle, Willie complied, and Lincoln offered his arm to his wife. But to the boys' great delight, although he made a valiant effort, the President could not pass through the broad doorway, beside the crinoline, and was obliged to follow at a respectful distance. So, in a gale of laughter, the family set off for the Inaugural Ball.

Outwardly, the ball was only a larger edition of the many political functions the Lincolns had attended, or had staged, themselves, in Illinois. But Lincoln knew that the crowd was not made up of folk from all sections of the country, as it normally should have been. The South was absent. Social Washington, which prided itself on belonging to the Southern aristocracy, was absent. And the President, shaking hand after hand, was never for a moment unconscious of the fact that, while the Marine Band boomed and shrilled quadrille, waltz, and polka, the nation was sick, and that it was like dancing in the parlor while one's mother fought for life in the room adjacent.

Hand after hand in his own, he watched the faces keenly, towering above the crowd, bending his head now and again to say a special word to one who would pause for special greeting, listening to Marshal Lamon's never-ending comments on the personages filing by, and never for a moment ceasing to hear the choking struggle for existence in the room adjacent.

As the hours wore on, the noisy gayety about him grew increasingly distasteful to him, and he was casting about in his mind for an excuse to go home, when, about one o'clock, a small hand caught Lincoln's left thumb, and he looked down into Willie's solemn gray eyes. "Papa, Taddie's pretty sick in there behind that bank of ferns. I found a kind-looking man standing alone in a corner, and got him to hold Tad while I got you."

"Jings!" exclaimed his father. "Your mother was right as usual! Go find your aunts or your Uncle Todd. I'm busy."

"They're all dancing. Besides Taddie says he'll yell if anybody but you comes for him. If you'll come round through the passage behind you, there won't many folks notice you."

Lincoln glanced about him. His mentor, Marshal Lamon, was giving his attention, for the moment, to a tall, handsome woman, with three great ostrich plumes protruding from the top of her head.

"Lead quickly, son," said Lincoln.

A moment later he was stooping over Taddie, who was reclining across the knees of a rubicund gentleman in immaculate evening attire. The President lifted the child, holding him easily across his chest with one great arm.

"He'll do now, I think, Mr. President," said the gentleman.

"All my fault!" exclaimed Lincoln. "I always was, and will be, the prize fool! You've moved into a warm place in my heart, sir, without needing to knock at the door."

"I hope I may not be moved out, Mr. President," returned the rubicund gentleman, with something earnest in his smile, and scrutinizing Lincoln closely, as he spoke. "You and I may have need of a firm sympathy with each other, sir. I am William Russell of the London *Times*."

"I know the London *Times*," said Lincoln. "I suspect it's one of the greatest powers in the world. In fact, I don't know of a greater, except, perhaps, the Mississippi. Come and see me, Mr. Russell."

"Thank you, Mr. President, I will," returned the Englishman, gravely.

Taddie opened his eyes. "You'd betta get me home befo' I'm sick again," he said in a warning tone.

Lincoln shook Russell's hand, both men laughing, then fled into the passageway, where he met the outraged Lamon, who growled, savagely:

"Look here, Lincoln, there's no call for you to play nurse, at this particular moment. I want to tell you—"

"It's no time now for a report from the subcommittee," interrupted Lincoln, coolly. "Get our hack, Hill, and call my wife. I'm taking Tad home."

The Marshal groaned, but strode off as he was bidden.

With unusual self-control, Mary said nothing on the ride home, regarding Tad's share in cutting the party short, but after both boys were in bed, in the rooms across the hall from their parents, she came into her husband's room to brush her hair. Lincoln, once more in the blue dressing gown, was slowly pacing the floor.

Mary in a long, pink flannel boudoir sacque took a vehement stroke at her shining brown locks.

"Abra'm, I've held off for an hour, but I'm going to tell you now that this thing can't be repeated. You must promise to let me control the boys' doings, or they'll not only make our lives miserable, but they'll be known as public nuisances. It was bad enough in Springfield, but, after all, every one there knew us and the children, and, I hope, made allowances. Here, misbehavior on their part will raise more enemies for you than you're willing to believe. You must make up your mind to say 'No!' Good heavens, are you going to be as weak as this with that ravening horde of office seekers? I can't understand how a man of your really remarkable judgment of human beings can be so spineless in his actions toward them."

Lincoln watched the brush following the bright waves of hair. That horde of office seekers! All week, they had packed the corridors of Willard's Hotel. They pursued him like the creatures of a nightmare. Tomorrow, they would descend upon the White House. Nicolay would help. There was a man, young as he was, who could say "No," so that even a job seeker understood it. Yes, Nicolay must take the initial shock tomorrow, while he extracted what he could from old General Scott.

"Abra'm!" cried Mary. "You aren't listening to me at all! Stop pacing the floor, and give me an answer."

Lincoln paused before her. "My dear Mary, what answer is there to give? I know my shortcomings as well as you do. I'll husk out the office-seeking job somehow, I reckon. As for the boys,—Mary, if my life depended on it, I couldn't deny them a pleasure it was possible for me to give them. We've worried the thing over between us a hundred times. It's no use. I know my limits."

No one knew better than Mary that it was no use, and, having given vent to her irritation, she sighed and acknowledged defeat by saying, with an air of general interest:

"No, you have no illusions about yourself or any one else. You are a man without illusions. There lies the basis of your great strength."

"And weakness," added Lincoln.

Mary nodded, and neither spoke, while she finished brushing and braiding the long, beautiful strands. When she had finished, she followed her husband in a turn up and down the room, then she brought him to pause and, looking earnestly up into his face, she said:

"I'm not going to nag you, Abra'm, one bit, if I can help it. You know how abominably quick my tongue is! I fight it as hard as you do your own loving heart. I shall leave you alone as much as I possibly can, and still take proper care of you."

Lincoln returned her look. "Don't you worry about nagging me, Mary. I need nagging. Nobody but you and I know what I owe to that same nagging of yours. They'd laugh me out of the White House if I had the manners now that I had when you married me, twenty years ago. All I want to warn you of is this: Confine your nagging to me and the household help. Let the President's help alone."

"I'll try. Good night, Abra'm. God keep you and help you."

"I guess He will, if I do my share," replied her husband, cheerfully, and as she went into her own room, he resumed his tramping from fireplace to window and back again.

CHAPTER II

LINCOLN went down to breakfast, the next morning, at eight o'clock. He had difficulty, even at that early hour, in eluding the crowd that packed the main hall on the first floor and the public staircase. Old Daniel, the assistant doorkeeper, held the mob at bay by a rope across the stairhead. He was addressing the foremost gentlemen in a wheedling manner:

"For Gawd's sake, gentlemen, use the cuspidors! Use 'em! Polished for this very occasion." Lincoln smiled, as he fled down the hall, and closed the door of the family dining room after him.

And it looked for a time as if even this room were not safe, for three gentlemen thrust their heads through a north window, and begged in unison for post office appointments in Iowa, Vermont, and Ohio. Marshal Lamon, who was breakfasting with Lincoln, ejected them without wasting a word on them, and locked the windows as well as the door into the room.

The President made no comment, nor did he do more than nod when Lamon outlined his plans for the Presidential Levee, to be held on March 8. When he had finished his meal under Mary's eye,—he would have eaten nothing had she not kept plate and cup filled,—Lincoln went upstairs to the President's office.

He entered it slowly and glanced around, with the thought that he ought to give attention to the details of its furnishings, since so large a part of the next four years was to be spent here. He noted the marble fireplace with its brass fenders and bright wood fire, the south windows with their view of the half-finished Washington monument, protruding from the acres of rubbish, the shining Potomac, and the red hills of Virginia beyond. He noted the huge oak Cabinet table in the middle of the room, a smaller table near one of the windows, which would be his own desk, a shabby sofa on either side of the east door into the secretaries' office, maps and dull portraits on the walls. A sweeping glance gave him all this before George Nicolay, followed by young Hay and Stoddard, came forward to greet him.

William Stoddard, a friend of John Hay, was a charming, slender youth, of even more the scholar type than Hay. He was destined to have first handling of all the President's mail. Lincoln's choice of two young men of this character, Mary wrote her sister that day, was, to her, one more proof of his fine judgment of men. Lincoln put a cordial arm over Stoddard's shoulders.

"You've got a tough job, Billy,—clearing stumpage for the rest of us to plow. And it'll get worse instead of better. Think your nerve will hold?"

Stoddard blushed with pleasure, and stuttered with embarrassment and Lincoln, wearing a friendly grin that showed his even, white teeth, turned to Nicolay as to an old friend. And though Nicolay had been with Lincoln only since the beginning of his election campaign, he already had earned the standing of an old friend. He was a Hanoverian by birth, and, as Thurlow Weed said after bumping against him in Springfield, somewhat bilious of temperament,—a compliment, coming from a politician of Weed's ilk! All that a man of firm character and deep loyalty could do to stand between Lincoln's kindliness, and the politician's rapacity, George Nicolay was to do. All that a keen student of American history and politics, a fluent writer, an adept at handling detail, could give to Lincoln, through four exhausting years, he was to give.

As for externals, he looked older than his twenty-eight years. He was of middle height, with a cool, penetrating dark eye, and a short mustache and goatee that concealed a firm, not unhumorous mouth.

"Well, Nicolay," said Lincoln, "are we ready to fire the salute?"

"We are, sir," replied Nicolay with a smile. "General Scott is waiting for you in the reception room."

"Good!" The President nodded. "Stoddard, shunt the folks waiting on the stairs directly into the secretaries' office. I want you boys to do what you can to weed them out before they reach me. Give each one a fair hearing, but keep them moving."

"Shall we send them to the heads of the departments in which they want jobs?" asked Hay.

"Not at first," replied Lincoln. "The heads haven't been inducted into office yet, and anyhow, I want to get a line on the problem myself. A new party,—they look for the spoils to be tremendous. We've got to give out offices enough to keep the influential men in line. On the other hand, our problems are going to be strange enough without adding to them by crippling the regular Federal business with green hands. By the way, John, when you have a free moment, I wish you'd buy me Halleck's book on military strategy. Have it put in my bedroom. Get the money from Mrs. Lincoln."

Young Hay gave the President a bright, curious look as he answered promptly, "I will, Mr. Lincoln."

The President nodded dismissal and, striding across the room, put his head into the reception hall.

"Come in, General! Come in!"

A handsome old gentleman, smooth-shaven, save for sideburns, wearing a blue broadcloth uniform with sash and gold epaulets, greeted the President with a stiff bow, and, obviously hampered by age and great lameness, followed into the office, where both men seated themselves before the fire.

"General," asked Lincoln, without preliminaries, "Major Anderson says he's got to have bread down there at Fort Sumter. What are you going to do about it?"

The old General sat stiffly erect. "That, Mr. President, cannot be decided without much study."

"Well, I suppose you've been studying, as you say, for a good many months. Go ahead and tell me just what the conditions are in Charleston harbor! I'm a willing learner, General."

General Scott cleared his throat, and began an elaborate description of the fortification and defense of the harbor. He spoke, as was his wont, in sounding phrases, embellished with classic anecdotes.

Lincoln, sitting with his hands clasped about his left knee, listened patiently until the old man finished, and then, without changing his posture, he said: "General, there's a story out in my neck of the woods of a man whose cabin burned down, and the neighbors all contributed something to start him over again. They were so liberal that he found himself better off than he'd ever been before, and he grew proud and particular. One day, a neighbor brought him a bag of oats, but the man who'd been burned out refused it. 'No, friend!' said he, 'I'm not taking oats now. I'm taking nothing but money.'"

The General stared at the President, puzzled and half offended. "What am I to understand by that, sir? Surely this is no moment for levity!"

"Certainly it's not," agreed Lincoln, "but we each speak in our own tongue. I can't point my remarks from the classics, so I use the illustrations that're familiar to me. What I mean is this: My neighbors have put me in a position where I can demand something of real value. I want the military facts in the Fort Sumter crisis, General, not the sort of evasions you hand out to the folks under you."

The fine old soldier rose painfully, and with every aspect of outraged dignity. Before he could speak, however, Lincoln thrust him gently into his chair, and patted him on the shoulder.

"There! There, General! You mustn't take offense at me! If I promise to endure your Greek heroes, you must promise to put up with my worthies from the Sangamon. I understand your position, how you've been thwarted by the Congress in all attempts to put the army on a war basis, how you've been imposed on and harassed by politicians, and how your great talents—"

"Tut! Tut!" puffed General Scott, suddenly smiling, "all this is unnecessary! I'm a soldier and enjoy fights of every kind. I have every sympathy for your difficulties, sir. Command me!"

"Are you sure you understand what my difficulties are, General?" asked Lincoln, anxiously. "You and I must see single-eyed, for we're destined to tackle this together."

"My vision perhaps has military restrictions, sir," replied Scott.

Lincoln looked into the glowing fire, and spoke slowly: "This Government has been handed over to me, not in its original integrity, but humbled, diminished, and threatened. I'm going to restore it, but I look to exhaust all peaceful means first. I know that delay works in the interest of rebellion, but how can I threaten force until I'm in a position to use it?

Our military strength is almost nothing. But that's not the worst. The North is torn by dissension, where it's not completely indifferent. Of just one thing I'm sure. I shall give up nothing that Buchanan hasn't already let slip. You must plan to reënforce Sumter, at once."

The General's reply was prompt. "To supply or reënforce the fort, sir, would require a fleet of vessels and transports that would take four months to collect, also 5000 regulars and 20,000 volunteers, which would require new acts of Congress to authorize, and from six to eight months to raise, organize, and discipline. The rebels at Charleston are in a position of enormous strength, sir."

The President jerked his head, ran his fingers through his black hair until it stood on end, then asked abruptly:

"What about Fort Pickens at Pensacola?"

"We still hold it, but it should be reënforced without delay."

"Get at that job at once," said Lincoln, "and try to work out a better plan for Fort Sumter. In the meantime, I'll send some one to Charleston to see if there's any truth in the rumor that there are many Unionists still there. Well," with his sudden smile, "I reckon I've given you a mean job of knitting, General. Something like turning the heel of the sock, eh?"

The old man, who had been eyeing the President keenly, replied with a gallant attempt to speak in the vernacular: "Many soldiers are expert knitters, sir," and rose once more.

Lincoln nodded, and putting his great arm around the General's waist, much disarranging the yellow sash, thereby, he assisted him to the door.

"Louis," he said to the waiting messenger, "go down to the General's carriage with him, then find out how Tad is this morning."

"He's fine, sir," replied Louis with a grin, as he took the old soldier gently under the arm. "He and Willie have just been fighting in the hall, and their mother had some trouble pulling Tad off his brother."

The President laughed and returned to his desk, where Nicolay was waiting with a list of persons whom he thought Lincoln ought to see.

The next few hours were like a nightmare to Lincoln, with men filing in and out of his room, at the shortest possible intervals, all of them with their demands made in terms of highest possible urgency on their part, and implying the greatest possible obligation to them on Lincoln's part. Just as he had reached the point where he felt he could endure no more, he was rescued by young Stoddard, who announced that the foreign diplomats were awaiting him in the Blue Drawing Room. He remained chatting with the diplomats for an hour, then, as the last Minister, M. Mercier of France, bowed himself out, Mary burst in from the Red Room.

"I thought they'd never leave," she groaned. "I'm trying to check over the list of necessary repairs. This house looks like a shabby hotel on the point of failure! It's absurd, this attempt to keep it on such simple lines. The President's wife must consult every morning with the darky cook, and plan all the meals for the day. I don't mind the work, but it seems as if my time ought to be more valuable. When the mob thins out of the

East Room, I want you to look at the carpet in there. It has no pile left."

The President looked down at her with the same expression of amused tenderness that he gave the children, and Mary was quick to note it.

"You think I don't recognize the importance of your work? I do. But I consider the carpet in the East Room quite as much a matter for the President's attention as the post master in Soap Creek."

"I've got to understand the problem—" began Lincoln.

"Nonsense!" interrupted Mary. "You haven't the cold blood to turn them out, just as you can't tell me to stop wasting your time!"

She left abruptly, closing the door of the East Room behind her.

Lincoln rumpled his hair, then pulled the bell rope. To the colored servant who answered he said:

"What's your name, young man?"

"James, Mr. President, sir."

"Well, James, how am I to get back up to my office without the coat and breeches being pulled off me by my constituents?"

James grinned broadly, and scratched his head. "Well, Mr. President, sir, you kin work round to the help's stairs, sir, and then—and then—there you is, sir! Don't do you no good, nohow! You'd have to cross upstairs, where they're swarming thickest."

Lincoln chuckled. "Go find Marshal Lamon, and send him to me, here. Tell him I need help, and need it quick."

He turned to throw a stick of wood on the fire, then waited, motionless, his eyes on the flames, his thoughts on Fort Sumter, until Lamon's imposing figure in blue-checked trousers and fawn-colored, long-tailed coat, appeared in the doorway.

"Lamon," said the President, "I want you to get the job-hunters moved out into the yard, or somewhere. I've got so I don't feel as if I was master in my own house. You might pass the word around that I can't do anything until the members of the Cabinet take office, later in the week, and that, after they're in, I'll do as little as I can."

"That's the idea!" agreed the Marshal. "You'd better stay here while I call off all bets. They'll all be mad."

"One moment, Lamon!" Lincoln drew the Marshal near him and said in a low voice, "I've just been thinking that the hatred and rancor out there on the staircase, the greed and confusion, are typical of the whole country. Confusion worse confounded! I must understand! I must have facts! I must *know* before I act. For instance, what's the real temper of Charleston? Look here; I'm going to send you down there to inspect the Post Office, though, by jings, you're better fitted to inspect the race tracks! And I'm going to ask my old friend Hurlbut to go down with you, to visit his sister who lives in Charleston. You'll draw the fire, as representing me, while Hurlbut gets the facts. Start as soon as you can."

"Shall I go before the levee?" asked the Marshal.

"Lamon, shall we stand shaking hands at the front door while fire rages in our cellar?"

"Right again!" ejaculated the Marshal. "I'll find Hurlbut, to-night."

Lincoln nodded. "I'm not sure what the duties of a Marshal are, are you, Lamon? Struck me, when they told me we had to have one, that he would be about as useful to me as that cane my wife made me carry at the inaugural ceremonies."

"I'd come to the conclusion about an hour ago," replied Lamon, "that I was supposed to be something like a cross between a time-keeper and a tout; and I was going off behind the woodshed for a good cry. But the thought of Charleston steadies my nerves."

"Well," chuckled the President, "you might try to earn part of your keep by helping to get me back to my office again!" He looped his arm in that of his friend and together they made the difficult journey to the upper floor.

Seward was ill for a day or so after the inauguration, but on the evening of the sixth of March he strolled into the President's office, accompanied by William Russell. Lincoln was glad to see the famous war correspondent. He had taken an instant liking to him, but, more than that, it was highly important that England obtain a just view of America's burning problem. This man, unless Lincoln's keen judgment of men was at fault, would probe to the bottom, and report only on what he actually brought to light.

"Well, sir," Lincoln patted him on the back, "you're as welcome as the first batch of buckwheat griddle cakes. Ever eat any?"

Russell smoothed his dark mustache with a manner that might have indicated a touch of embarrassment, but his voice was unperturbed.

"Never, Your Excellency!"

"Come to breakfast here along next November, sir, and we'll see what my wife can do to lift your ignorance. In the meantime, draw up to the fire and tell me what England will do if war visits this unhappy country." Lincoln pulled out a chair as he spoke.

"We'll have no war, and my prophecy is that the seceding states will shortly begin to return at the rate of one a month," exclaimed Seward, as he eased his frail figure into a chair.

"There, Mr. Russell, from his own lips! And any one in these United States'll tell you that Seward knows more about the matter than I do," said Lincoln.

Russell turned from his scrutiny of the President to Seward, who made no attempt to deny Lincoln's statement. Seated, Seward was far more impressive than standing, for his marked stoop, and his careless habit of dress were thus made inconspicuous, and his finely shaped head, with his thin, smooth-shaven face, the secret, penetrating eyes, the aquiline nose and humorous mouth, were given their full value.

"The report is true, I suppose," said Russell, "that Jefferson Davis issued a call this morning for 100,000 volunteers for three years?"

Seward gasped. "Good God! I didn't hear that! Is it authentic, Russell?"

"I believe that it is," replied the war correspondent.

Seward jumped to his feet. "Welles and Cameron must know this, at once. Excuse me, Russell!" He rushed from the room.

The two men left before the fire looked at each other, and Lincoln smiled. Russell seemed puzzled. "Mr. Welles is Minister of the Navy and Mr. Cameron of War, are they not?"

"Secretaries, we call 'em."

"But surely they must have the report?"

"Just to make sure, I sent it to them an hour ago," replied the President, dryly. "Seward will find one at his house or office."

There was a pause, during which the Englishman pondered heavily, and Lincoln turned over in his mind the questions on the theory of democracy he would like to discuss with him. But before he could frame the first query Russell broke the silence.

"Mr. Seward is a very important figure in your country."

"None more so," replied the President. "It was fully expected that he'd be Republican nominee for this job, and he deserved the nomination far more than I did. In fact, I'm a good deal like the fellow who wandered out in his pasture during a storm to find his cows, put up an umbrella, and the lightning struck him! I've held almost no office. Seward, on the other hand, has been Governor of one of our greatest States, and is our foremost party manager. He has been a Senator, and is a distinguished lawyer. He, rightly, has enormous weight in this country."

"Are you to be quoted on this, Mr. President?" asked Russell.

"I suppose I've said nothing that couldn't be printed," replied Lincoln, carefully, "but I reckon we'd better agree right here that you quote me to no one. I'd like to have you get the English people started right on Seward, though. He's going to kick over the traces a bit, and have trouble sticking near the starting post. But if he strikes his possible stride, no one can beat him in his job."

Russell was again eyeing Lincoln keenly and thoughtfully. "Perhaps, Mr. President, you'd be interested in hearing the opinion of Seward I've sent to the *Times?*"

"Yes, I'd like to hear it!" exclaimed Lincoln.

Russell pulled out his notebook and began to read: "Seward, a subtle, quick man, rejoicing in power, given to perorate and to oracular utterances, fond of badinage, bursting with the importance of state mysteries, and with the dignity of directing the foreign policy of the greatest country,— all Americans think,—in the world."

He put up the notebook, but before Lincoln could speak, Mrs. Lincoln burst into the office. Her face was flushed, her eyes dark, and she spoke breathlessly:

"Mr. Lincoln, I must have your ear for a moment!"

Russell rose, bowing to Mary as she said, "Pardon me, sir! But I've received such an especially insulting letter that I can't put off showing it to Mr. Lincoln."

"I'll withdraw, at once, Madam President," murmured the Englishman.

"No, you won't, sir!" declared Lincoln. "I want to thresh out several matters with you. Mary, let me introduce Mr. Russell of the London *Times,* and let me see that letter."

Mary offered her hand with a quick smile that did not, however, quench the anger in her blue eyes. "Mr. Hay told me that you were in Washington. We shall hope to see you at the White House frequently."

"You are very gracious—" began Russell.

He was interrupted by an angry snort from Lincoln. "Here, Russell, look at this gush of sewage! What can a man in my job do when his wife receives that kind of an insult?"

The Englishman read, his ruddy face turning a slow purple as he did so. Having finished, he dropped it to the floor, as though the slime it contained were tangible. He and Lincoln looked at each other.

"How about giving it to your police?" asked Russell. "It's unsigned, you see."

"Right!" nodded Lincoln, "I'll do that, to-night."

"But what I want to know," cried Mary, "is this! Leaving out the nastiness, is the letter true? Is there a cabal formed here in Washington strong enough to wreck any social efforts I make as mistress of the Executive Mansion?"

"Mary, I'm afraid they're going to try," replied Lincoln, sadly. "It's one of the prices you pay for being my wife."

"But have you facts, Mr. Lincoln?" demanded Mary.

The President turned to the reporter. "You've only been in Washington a short time. What have you heard?"

Russell looked at Mary apologetically. "The women of secession sympathies are vehement, active, and extraordinarily venomous. Much of their venom seems to be aimed at Mrs. Lincoln."

Mary sank into the chair Seward had vacated. "It doesn't seem possible!" She looked from her husband to the Englishman. "You know a good deal about the society of capitals, I'm sure, Mr. Russell. Give me some advice."

"Ask the President to require the secretary who opens his mail to open yours also. You should never see such letters," replied Russell promptly. "As for the others, I'd devote all my thoughts and talents to the President's constituents."

"Never!" cried Mary. "I mean—as to the matter of the letters, your advice is excellent. The letters shall go to young Stoddard. But as to the rest of it,—give in weakly to those hussies? Cease at the behest of this vile anonymity to hold my levees and balls? Why, the idea is preposterous! I'll fight them with my last breath!"

"Bravo!" exclaimed Russell. "Command me to help you in any possible way, Madam President."

Mary laughed excitedly. "I shall, indeed. We'll see! Fort Sumter and I are both flying the flag. We shall—" The door from the family sitting room slammed, and the three before the fire turned to behold Willie clinging to the knob.

"Mamma, I want the arnica bottle," he said.

"Willie, what have you been doing? Come into the light where I can see you!" exclaimed his mother.

Willie came slowly forward. His black hair was disheveled, his lower lip was bleeding, his collar torn, and his trousers mud stained. He paused beside his father, who pulled him gently to his great knees, and began to staunch the dribble of blood with a red cotton handkerchief. The firelight flickered unevenly on the group, and Russell regarded it, with sudden tenderness in his cynical eyes.

"What's been troubling you, sweetheart?" asked Lincoln.

"Out on Pennsylvania Avenue, just now, I went to the little refreshment stand to buy some pop," replied Willie, his boyish voice unhurried, like his father's. "A lady was there buying some for her boy. I guess he's about fourteen. And this lady said to the other lady that yonder was the White House, where the Illinois gorilla and his ape wife were setting up their menagerie. I couldn't hit the lady, so I licked jelly out of the boy. I hate Washington."

"Oh, that's not right for a child to hear such things! How can they! What have we ever done?" cried Mary, dropping to her knees before Willie, and kissing his grimy hand.

"Don't be too troubled, wife," begged Lincoln. "You and Willie can't fight my battles. And that's all it is. Just trying to hurt me through you."

Willie suddenly blinked back tears. "I'll always fight 'em! With my last breath, I'll fight 'em!"

"Look here, old chap," said Russell, suddenly, to Willie, "if you'll show me where to get some ice, I'll show you how to take the swelling from that lip, quite in the manner of the best prizefighter."

"Do you know any prizefighters?" asked Willie, eagerly.

"I've seen all the best of them and know them, too," said Russell, rising.

Willie left his father and slipped his fingers into Russell's. "I like English men better than American ladies," he volunteered. "You helped me out when Tad vomited the other night. Come on, we'll find James. And Tad will want to see the blood."

He was still chattering, in his unhurried voice, as the door into the sitting room swung behind him and his guest. Mary and her husband stared at each other in a silence too pregnant for speech.

CHAPTER III

TO Lincoln, the levee on the eighth of March was not an unamusing affair, primarily because of Seward. He thought of Russell's characterization of the Secretary of State a number of times during the evening, and chuckled as he thought. For, while the President and Mrs. Lincoln received the endless stream in the Blue Room, Seward established himself in the Green Room, within the President's line of vision, and there received tribute from a stream, which, though not so long, was in many ways more brilliant, and certainly more deferential, than that which passed by Lincoln.

In a momentary lull in the handshaking ordeal, Mary touched her husband's arm. She was wearing a magenta, brocaded silk dress and looked, Lincoln thought, as though she belonged in the elaborately furnished drawing room, with its candelabra, its carved cabinets, its gilt and satin furnishings.

"Getting tired, Mary?" he asked.

She shook her head. "Have you observed Governor Seward? What stupid fools make up our public!"

"I'm more grateful to him every minute for taking up some of my slack," declared the President, rubbing his aching hand.

"Look; who's that with him now?" asked Mary. "What a wonderful looking man! Is it another Englishman? Lord Lyons?"

"That's Charles Sumner, Senator from Massachusetts," replied Lincoln. "He and Seward will have many a tussle before the crop's husked out. Sumner's now Chairman of the Senate Committee on Foreign Relations."

A man of Lincoln's own great height towered high above little Seward's white head. For a moment, Mary could see him clearly, then the crowd closed in, and only her husband could observe the face of the Senator from Massachusetts. It was a face familiar enough to the President, one that he thought again, as he had many times before, was the most winning in expression he ever had seen. The broad, massive forehead, from which was tossed back thick, brown hair, only lightly touched with gray, although Sumner was fifty, the deep blue eyes, the well cut lips were the fine embodiment of the essentially noble spirit of the man.

Over the heads of the milling crowd, President and Senator caught each other's gaze, and for a moment gray eyes held blue. A little later, Sumner, with a lady on his arm, came to a halt before the Presidential party, and the crowd, willy-nilly, was deflected, as though a great boulder had dropped into a current, thrusting it from its course.

"I'm glad to see you, Sumner," said Lincoln.

"And I you, Mr. Lincoln. May I present my friend, Miss Ford, from the red hills of Virginia, one of the social leaders of the old South in Washington?"

Lincoln made his quick, quaint bow over the languid hand of the tall, striking-looking young woman in green silk.

"I'm not sure that is a tactful recommendation to a Republican administration," exclaimed Miss Ford, in her curiously clear and penetrating, though drawling, voice.

"But my wife would say you were the more welcome as a Virginian, to a Republican levee, I reckon," said the President, presenting the Senator and Miss Ford to Mary.

"This is the first time in six years that I've entered the White House portals, Madam President," said Sumner. "I regard this as one of the most privileged moments of my life."

"Mary," Lincoln's hand was on Sumner's shoulder, "take a good look at this fellow. Seward told me once that Sumner was his ideal of a cosmopolitan, but I disagree with Seward. Sumner's my ideal of a bishop, though I never met one."

Mary, who had been exchanging greetings with Miss Ford, looked up into the Senator's face. She liked Sumner instantly and warmly. And Sumner, keen observer of women, perceived in the President's wife that intellectual vitality and acumen which he told himself could be little appreciated by the type of men and women with whom her lot was cast.

"After all," said Mary, "I don't see why one ideal is necessarily incompatible with the other."

"When you know me better," Sumner was smiling, "I think you'll discover I'm nothing so unhuman as either."

"Come, Senator, do give me an opportunity to admire Mrs. Lincoln's dress!" protested Miss Ford. "You have the most perfectly monopolistic manner I've ever seen. I suppose you acquired it in London drawing rooms. It's not American, I assure you."

"What must I do?" asked Sumner. "Am I not to keep you sheltered from the mob?"

Mary gave Miss Ford a second keen look, which took in the beautiful chestnut ringlets, the flashing violet eyes, the clear cut mouth and chin. She at once discovered that out of all the hundreds of women's faces that had moved before her vision that night, this one alone roused her interest. She drew Miss Ford a little back of the receiving line. Charles Sumner followed, glancing from one woman to another, his blue eyes amused and keen.

"It was charming of you to come to-night," began Mary.

"Not at all," protested Miss Ford, handing her huge ostrich feather fan to Sumner, who immediately began to wave it with the skill of long usage. "I've heard so much gossip about you, Madam President, that frankly, I came to see for myself."

Mary flushed a little as she smiled. "Ah! You are frank, indeed! May I be equally frank, and ask you what your report to your friends will be?"

"That you have a charming taste in dress!" sweeping Mary with a glance. "As for the rest, I am sure they must be mistaken."

Senator Sumner gasped at this exchange of feminine amenities. "But, my dear Miss Ford—!"

"Don't bother, Senator!" exclaimed Mary. "I understand. Miss Ford is giving me a chance. The rest are condemning me unseen and unheard. I am grateful to her."

"You are keen, Madam President," drawled the Virginian. "You see, I've always been a friend of the White House, and mighty proud of the privileges I possessed here. Of course, of political necessity, those days are gone. I myself am retiring to our plantation near Fairfax Courthouse. I don't expect to live in Washington again till our family fortunes have been retrieved. But when that time comes, if you all are still here, I'd like to feel I still could drop in for a cup of tea at the White House, as of old. Politics should not prejudice social habits."

Mary's blue eyes brightened with each of Miss Ford's slow spoken sentences. "When are you leaving for the plantation, Miss Ford?" she asked, eagerly.

"As soon as I can rent our house here, Madam President."

"Before you go, say to-morrow afternoon, will you not revive your old custom by taking tea with me? You are so frank! I am, if you will come, going to presume upon your frankness by asking you questions about the social problems I am meeting here."

The Virginian laughed. "That might be interesting, might it not, Senator?"

"No one could help Mrs. Lincoln more than you, Miss Ford, if you will bury animosity," he replied, seriously.

"Animosity? I am no Secessionist, Senator!" exclaimed Miss Ford. "I'm a pro-slavery Unionist."

"I don't care what you are!" declared Mary. "Come and have tea with me."

The Virginian hesitated for a moment, then with a sudden stretching of her hand to Mary, she exclaimed, "Well, thank you; I reckon I can't resist your cordiality, Madam President. I'll come! Senator, if you'll see me to my carriage, I'll relieve you of that fan."

With a swirl of billowing silk skirts, she made her bow and moved away.

Late the following afternoon, Miss Ford arrived at the White House. She was accompanied by a negro maid, who bore in her arms two squirming pups. Mary received her guest in the family sitting room, upstairs, for it was the only spot in the house outside of the bedroom safe from office seekers.

"The hound dogs are for your two boys," drawled the Virginian. "Our old Sally littered in Washington, and I can't bother taking six pups out to the plantation, when we already have sixty of 'em. Put them on the hearthrug, Jinny, and wait for me in the carriage."

"And ask the doorman to send my two sons here at once, please, Jinny," added Mary with an apprehensive eye on the rug and the puppies.

"Of course I know they'll become an intimate scourge in your household," continued Miss Ford, seating herself with a careless and graceful adjustment of her crinoline. "But the only thing I know for sure about boys is that they like dogs."

"You're wonderfully kind," exclaimed Mary, really touched. "Ah, here they are!" as the two boys burst into the room. "Willie and Tad, come here before you touch the dogs, and meet Miss Ford; then thank her for the gift."

With the hasty casualness of childhood, the boys shook hands, then leaped together for the hearthrug.

"The one with the black patch on his eye is mine!" shouted Taddie.

"He's not! He's the biggest so he's mine!" in Willie's unhurried tones.

"You di'ty skunk—" began Tad.

Mary made no futile comment or gesture. She crossed the room, put a pup under either boy's arm, took each boy by an ear, and marched them to the hall door. "Out you go, gentlemen all," she said and closed the door firmly after them.

"Are they often like that?" drawled Miss Ford, as Mary, a little breathless, returned to her chair before the window.

"That was mild. They are real boys," replied Mary, "so admonition is wasted on them. They'll crowd till they come up against something firm."

"And you are that something firm, I imagine," said the Virginian, fine, violet eyes fixed on Mary with interest.

"I try to be," replied Mary. "I suppose they appear rude and unattractive to you, as you don't know boys. But really, lads of their age are very lovable, and it's not always easy to be harsh with them as one must be."

"Shall you send them to school?" asked Miss Ford.

"We think not. In a school they'd be both spoiled and insulted. We shall have tutors."

"Insulted?" Miss Ford pulled off her long black gloves, and adjusted the wide lace collar that fell over her sloping shoulders.

Mary's eyes blazed as she nodded. "I'll explain to you what I mean," and she told of the letter she had received and of Willie's fight.

"What fools people are!" exclaimed the Virginian when Mary had finished. "I love your young Willie. He should have been a Virginian."

"He is one, remotely, on both his father's and my side." Mary looked out the window to the hills that rolled beyond the Potomac. "I am a Kentuckian, myself, though, and as proud of that as you are of being a Virginian."

"How could you marry a Republican, then?" cried Miss Ford.

"I didn't marry a Republican," declared Mary, stoutly. "I married"—she paused thoughtfully, then she lifted her chin—"I married an intellectual and spiritual giant—hidden for the sins of some other life in the casings of a backwoodsman."

If Miss Ford felt an inclination to sneer, she hid it under an admirable show of sympathetic interest.

"I've helped him a little," Mary went on, "but not much. He's unique, predestined. I've given him the normal life of a husband and father without which he might have grown awry. That's all."

There was a moment's silence, after which Miss Ford asked gently, "Is it your plan to introduce the President to social Washington?"

Mary laughed. "Thrust a full grown oak into a tiny garden of annuals? But I'm really not the fool you think me, my dear! I am the member of the family with social ambitions."

Miss Ford put more sugar in her tea, and stirred it gracefully, while she studied the shabby Brussels carpet with its design of an upset basket of roses.

"Ah," she sighed, at last, "I understand how intriguing it must have been to marry such a giant, even though it was a bitter dose for a Kentuckian to marry a man with Mr. Lincoln's partiality for niggers."

Mary's small figure in the huge padded arm chair drew itself erect. "You are mistaken on two counts, Miss Ford. Though I am a Kentuckian, I don't support slavery. Mr. Lincoln has no partiality for niggers, as such."

"You see," drawled the Virginian, "I own that black girl, Jinny, and some twenty other niggers, in my own right. My father owns about a hundred field hands and a dozen house niggers. I haven't any desire to be stripped of my property by this administration or any other."

"But how could we strip you?" exclaimed Mary, impatiently. "All Mr. Lincoln desires is to keep the Union together. He knows he has no right to destroy slavery."

Miss Ford's occasional dimple came into play. "I am so relieved! As long as you and the President are not Abolitionists, I am yours to command."

"Abolitionist! I abhor the thought!" cried Mary. "Do have a fresh cup of tea and tell me, what can I do to overcome this dreadful cabal that has been raised against me in Washington. You see," as Miss Ford's eyebrows arched, "I am taking the bull by the horns, if you'll pardon the figure."

"Can you endure straight facts, Madam President?" asked Miss Ford.

Mary compressed her lips for a moment before replying. "I must endure them, if my life here is not to be a social fiasco. If I understand conditions, perhaps I can combat them."

"I believe that you can!" exclaimed the Virginian. "And if I can help you otherwise than by what I am about to tell you, I am yours to command. I certainly do admire spunk."

Thereupon, Miss Ford gave a good half hour to instructing Mary Lincoln with regard to the ramifications of Washington society. She spoke with a sardonic deliberation that fascinated her hearer, who realized that she was being given an invaluable cross section of the social intrigues of the women of the Capital.

It was twilight, and the boys had brought the puppies back to visit their former mistress, before Miss Ford left the White House.

CHAPTER IV

MISS FORD

LINCOLN brought all three of his secretaries to the supper table that evening in an endeavor to catch up with the hundred matters he had been obliged to overlook during the day. Mary did not intrude on the business at hand. She devoted herself to the boys' table manners.

But for a hurried moment, as her husband left the dining room she caught his hand.

"Miss Ford is going to help at my first levee, Abra'm!" she began.

"Yes! Yes, dear Mary!" stooping to kiss her. "You call on young Stoddard to help you with your invitations. I'm on my way to the Cabinet meeting."

And he was gone, leaving Mary and young Stoddard smiling at each other in bewilderment.

This first official Cabinet meeting had cost Lincoln much thought. His desire had been to deal with his secretaries separately, until he and they had the routine of business well in hand. But the machinations of the Secessionists were forcing him out of his leisurely pace. His difficult assistants would have to learn to pull together at once, and not after they had adjusted themselves to office.

He looked about the long table for a moment before speaking, at these faces, none of which he believed looked on his with actual friendliness. Then he gave the reason that had forced him to what he felt was a premature session.

"Gentlemen, General Scott told me, to-day, that he wants us to evacuate Fort Sumter."

For a moment there was shocked silence.

Seward was the first to speak. "Evacuate, then, by all means! We'll soon have South Carolina back in the Union. What does it matter?"

Chase, the Secretary of the Treasury, and the handsomest man in the Cabinet, leaned toward Lincoln, and said in the voice one would use to an ignorant child:

"Don't you know that giving up Fort Sumter will finally convince the South that we are all supine cowards?"

Bates, the Missourian, banged on the table. "Never! Reënforce, if it requires fifty thousand men."

Lincoln's face was inscrutable. The three men of his Cabinet who had been his chief rivals for the Presidency had spoken.

Montgomery Blair, a Blair of Maryland, jumped to his feet, overturning his chair. "By the living God, Mr. President, I'd not only reënforce, but I'd send fifty thousand men into South Carolina to bring her to her senses, as Andrew Jackson threatened to do when that traitorous State attempted nullification."

"I'd like further information," said Welles, cautiously. The white-bearded Secretary of the Navy from Connecticut was a Democrat, and out of sympathy with every one in the room.

Before Lincoln could reply, Seward began an elaborate explanation of general conditions. Maryland was probably hostile to the Union. Virginia, as well as Tennessee, was wavering. Still, under his own careful manipulations, he was sure they would be saved. Let force be used to take Fort Sumter, and these States surely would join the so-called Confederacy. He could save the country from actual war he was sure, but he must have time, time.

"Time! Time!" sneered Blair. "You parade your office, Seward, while treason thrives on your intrigues."

"Come, Blair, isn't that a little strong?" protested Seward, with fine good nature.

"You talk too much, Mr. Seward," snapped Welles. "You'll chatter us into war, yet."

Bates and Smith began to whisper together. Seward rapped on the table. "Gentlemen, you ask for information. How can I give it to you unless you favor me with your undivided attention?"

Welles turned angrily to the President, who sat with a leg flung carelessly over one arm of his chair.

"Is ex-Governor Seward chairman of this meeting, sir? Is he privy to your information? Is it fair to the rest of us that he should be so?"

"Seward has been seeing a lot of folks, Mr. Welles," replied Lincoln. "Let's get his report on 'em. Go ahead, Governor. What do you reckon you'll do if you have time?"

"This must be unofficial," said Seward, "but the Secessionists have sent three commissioners up here, and I'm in constant communication with them."

"That's not proper," exclaimed Smith, the Secretary of the Interior.

"What about?" demanded Blair.

"Who are they?" asked Chase.

"They have come to treat with the Administration for the recognition of the Confederacy," was Seward's unperturbed reply. "I hope to gain time by offering to negotiate with them."

"And you permit this, Mr. President?" gasped Welles.

"I?" Lincoln smiled. "I do not recognize the existence of a Confederacy! Now, then, friends, you have all the facts I have regarding Fort Sumter. Within the next two weeks I hope to have more. In the meantime, I shall take all your opinions under advisement. Please give me at any time, any facts or ideas that may come to your minds."

"Mr. President, when shall you call the next Cabinet meeting?" asked Welles.

The President hesitated. Seward replied for him. "I'll undertake to let you know, Mr. Welles."

"You?" exclaimed the Secretary of the Navy. "Thank you! But I know of no reason that prevents my dealing directly with the President."

Lincoln spoke soberly. "Meetings must be irregular until the confusion of office seekers, and our newness to the routine of the jobs subside. I certainly shall not fail to take direct counsel with each or all of you when need arises."

"But what is to be done about Sumter?" insisted Blair.

Again Seward attempted to reply, and again Welles and Blair raised their voices in violent protest against what they styled his officiousness.

Lincoln watched and listened with absorbed interest. A Cabinet of brilliant men he had desired, and had procured. But also it appeared he had gathered together men of violent feelings, deep egotism, childish antipathies, and each one as personal in his reactions as Mary, in her most personal moments.

So far, Lincoln had known these men only in their public capacities—as Democrats and Republicans, as Radicals or Conservatives, as Senators, Judges, Governors. Before he could hope to head up this alarmingly accomplished group, he must know them as human beings. A few more sessions like this, he told himself, and their characters would be exposed as no number of individual conferences would expose them. Jealousy is a pitiless betrayer of the weak and sordid in human desires. Ever since boyhood, Lincoln had been a close and practical student of local politicians. These men differed little, he thought, from those with whom he long had had intimate contacts.

It was late when the meeting ended, and it ended with no policy formulated for the handling of the fort in Charleston harbor. For a long time after the meeting had adjourned, the President sat before the fire, passing in review each of the seven men he had asked to help him through the impending crisis. His mind remained longest with Seward. Of all the men in the Cabinet, Seward was the most nearly essential for the success of the task Lincoln had set himself. And yet, he was the most dangerous to the welfare of the country. For, as Lincoln had discovered in the past few weeks, Seward was not a statesman but a politician; he was a profound egoist and a busybody. Controlled and directed to a great single purpose, no man in the United States could be more useful. Uncontrolled, he would waste his great talents and the resources of his office on a thousand abortive alarms and excursions.

The clock on the mantel struck eleven as the door opened. Lincoln was expecting Nicolay to bring him a report on possible legal methods of forcing the collection of internal revenue in the seceded States. He held out his hand without turning his head.

"All right, Nicolay! You must be tired, boy. Go to bed."

"Mr. President!" said a woman's voice.

Lincoln came slowly to his feet. Miss Ford, in a green velvet riding habit, was standing near the door, which she had closed suddenly behind her.

"How did you get here, Madam?" exclaimed the President.

"Nothing could be simpler, my dear Mr. Lincoln," tossing her riding crop on the table, and seating herself before the fire. "Your doorman was asleep, as the rest of your household seems to be. I was belated in a ride into the country, and on sudden impulse, I stopped here. I am a creature of impulse."

"I see," said Lincoln, thinking, as he looked at her deep-set eyes and firm, curved lips, that he never had seen a face more brilliantly and coolly calculating. "What can I do for you?"

"Mr. Lincoln," leaning toward him, eagerly, "I know how irregular this proceeding is—but—well, Mrs. Lincoln has made a tremendous impression on me. I want to help her."

It seemed to Lincoln that he never had seen a handsomer woman, and he told himself, whimsically, that she was more dangerous to unprotected men than all of old General Scott's militia.

"What makes you think my wife needs help?" he asked.

"Two things. First, as a Virginian who leads an active social life, I know how bitterly the women of Washington are going to wage war on her. Second, because she showed me this afternoon that she intended to make an aggressive little war of her own. She is an extremely able person. I think if she receives the right kind of advice for a few weeks, she will work wonders. But if she goes on in the recalcitrant spirit in which she is beginning, she will fail, ignominiously."

Lincoln nodded. "You think you could give her that advice?"

"I certainly do. But I shall need your backing."

"Mine? My dear Miss Ford, I never make suggestions to Mrs. Lincoln about her tea fights and such. I'm not fitted for it. Out home she managed things fine. I realize, of course, that she's got a very different nut to crack here, but I don't see where my backing will help." He rose to lean against the mantel. He was tired, and, for all his desires to make Mary happy, social intrigues were the last things that could touch his interest. "You fix up any arrangement you like with my wife. Don't bother me about it," with a little smile.

Miss Ford's expression was bewildered. "But the suggestion I had to make involves the outlay of money."

"All right! The Madam holds the purse strings in our family," suppressing a yawn.

She took the hint and rose. "But, Mr. President, this involves you. Young Stoddard is no help to Mrs. Lincoln. I want you to appoint me as one of the White House secretaries, and allow me to manage the social end for both of you. Don't let your lack of social experience blind you to the importance of your entertaining adequately and elegantly."

"Have you mentioned this to Mrs. Lincoln?" asked the President.

"Yes, this afternoon, and she said I'd have to speak to you. I got to thinking about it, on my ride, and as I'd heard that the only chance to catch you alone was late at night, here I am." She smiled at him, as though to say that she was throwing herself on his mercy.

Lincoln sighed. He liked women, but he knew that he was no judge of them. Even as a lawyer, he was hopelessly sentimental in handling them. Some thought of this made him unwontedly cautious.

"All my secretaries are recommended by folks I know and trust," he said. "Who will recommend you, if my wife and I should agree that such an arrangement is such as she might like."

"Mercy!" making a little face, "how important you make it sound. Well, Senator Sumner is my friend and—"

"Sumner would be enough, in case Mrs. Lincoln takes a notion to carry the idea through," the President interrupted. "I'll talk it over with her. I'll call young Hay or Stoddard to see you home, if you wish, Miss Ford."

"No, please! Old Uncle Ben, my butler-groom, is outside with my horse."

"Then I'll see you to the door, myself," offering her his arm with the comical, snapping bow that already was one of Washington's jokes.

They paced slowly along the dimly lighted halls, to the lobby, where old Edward, his lined, Irish face relaxed in sleep, sat bolt upright inside the door. Lincoln, smiling like a boy in mischief, tiptoed past him and opened the door. The Virginian slipped out into the March wind.

The President returned to the second floor, and put his head quietly into the door of the secretaries' office. Hay was not to be seen. Nicolay sat at his desk, his head on his arms, fast asleep. Lincoln crossed the room, and put his hand on the young man's shoulder. Nicolay bounded to his feet, blinked and apologized.

The President slipped an arm around him. "Come with me, George. There's something I want you to do."

He led Nicolay out of the office and into the bedroom next door, where, with the light dimmed, young Hay already lay fast asleep. Lincoln led the young man up to the bedside.

"Here!" he exclaimed. "Is a hint enough, or do I have to undress you myself, George?"

Nicolay laughed. "You're too good to me, sir. I haven't finished the report."

"But you've finished yourself! Can't have you done up before the race begins. Look at John, there! Doesn't look a day over eighteen. Nice boy! Good big funny-bone!" Lincoln pulled the quilt over young Hay's shoulders and tiptoed out.

He did not return to his office, but with a lighted candle, which he took from the hall table, he entered one of the bedrooms opposite his and Mary's. Willie lay with a pillow over his head and a puppy curled up against his back. Lincoln removed the pillow, kissed the boy's moist forehead, and went into Tad's room. Tad's covers were on the floor. Tad's feet were on his pillow on which also lay a whimpering little hound. Lin-

coln chuckled, turned the boy skillfully around to share the pillow with
the pup, and lifted the covers over him. Then, shading the candle, he
gazed down at the child.

"Pretty boy! Pretty little fellow! Wonderful to think of anything with
that beauty coming from my loins," he thought. Then he crossed the hall
into his wife's room.

She was propped up in bed reading, with a candle at her elbow. She
looked up at her husband with a smile.

"Glad you're awake!" he exclaimed, putting his candle beside her, and
sitting down on the bed. "I'm having trouble to ease myself to bed, to-
night, somehow."

"Overtired, poor dear!" murmured Mary. "Shall I read you to sleep?"

"I guess not, Mary. I just dismissed a lady visitor."

"For goodness' sake!" ejaculated Mary, her eyes twinkling. "Have they
begun, already?"

"Seems like!" with a broad grin that quickly faded into a scowl of
concentration. "It was that Miss Ford. Let me tell you."

He gave the details of the conversation.

Mary listened intently. "She went further than I meant," she said when
Lincoln had finished, "but, if Charles Sumner recommends her, what do
you think of the idea?"

"I can't put her on my official pay roll," replied the President. "If you
want to pay her out of my salary, it's all right with me. You know what
you want. I'll talk to Sumner to-morrow."

Mary nodded. "Let me know what he says. Where is Artemus Ward's
latest effusion? I'll read you to sleep."

"No, save yourself for later, when the hard times come. I'll drowse off
nicely. Good night, dearest Mary."

He lifted her in his great arms for a moment, then tucked her in as
tenderly as he had Tad, took up his candle and went to bed.

CHAPTER V

BREAD FOR ANDERSON

CHARLES SUMNER appeared in Lincoln's office, the next day, to consult with him concerning the appointment of Charles Francis Adams as ambassador to England. The matter of Miss Ford had slipped from the President's mind, but Sumner, as the conference ended, paused with one huge, white hand on the door knob, and said:

"Miss Ford tells me that she hopes I will recommend her as a fourth secretary to the White House, Mr. President."

"Jings! I'd forgotten the lady!" exclaimed Lincoln. "What's she like, Senator? Anything back of this sudden spasm of helpfulness she evidences?"

"Indeed, I'm sure not!" Sumner's voice was a little indignant. "I've known her for years. She is altogether a charming and cultured lady, that is, as culture is rated in this country. Her father has met with heavy losses, and it's understood that she is financially much embarrassed. It must have taken an exceedingly great effort of will, to bring her petitioning to you. For not only is she a Virginian, but also she is a slave owner."

"What would be said if my wife employed a person of her political persuasions?" asked Lincoln.

"All Southerners would be pleased. Politically, I'd say that a more adroit motion could not be made." Sumner nodded sagaciously.

"Then I reckon I'll give Mary her head on the matter," Lincoln's voice expressed relief, "and forget it myself."

He was vaguely conscious, a week later, that Miss Ford's trunks were moved into the room next to that occupied by the little boys. But he was so irregular in his attendance at meals, his one opportunity to meet family guests, that it was a long time before the Virginian actually rose on his horizon.

By nature a man of most careless and casual habits, he was finding it exceedingly difficult to systematize his work, so that chaos should not completely hamper his efforts.

He managed after a few weeks to direct the great bulk of the office seekers to the various departments, but this seemed only to give greater opportunity to the self-appointed saviors of the nation, who thronged the White House and the Capitol, and all of the saloons and hotels of Washington.

As if to off-set the overactivity of those officious persons, there was every day more apparent an extraordinary inertia on the part of those who Lincoln had hoped would act most quickly. Old General Scott was dilatory in carrying out his orders. Seward ignored his suggestions. He even went so far as to hint, in a written memorandum, that Lincoln turn the reins of government over to the Secretary of State.

The President took all these manifestations of contempt for his ability with outward calm. Actually, he was deeply perturbed, but his unparalleled capacity for self-control enabled him to keep from making a move until he understood the natures of the men about him. His sense of proportion was rarely at fault. The point in Seward's insolent memorandum that really troubled him was not its insolence, but the fact that Seward showed a lack of common sense, when he suggested that the best way to prevent war breaking out in America was for America to find some pretext to declare war on Spain, France and England, in turn. A foreign war, declared the Secretary of State, would unite the North and South against a common enemy.

He squelched Seward's wild aspirations easily enough, in a return memorandum, then stood by the window of his office, looking, in a troubled way, at his family below. Young April was flushing over the White House garden. Mary was talking to the gardener. Tad and Willie were racing their hound dogs. Miss Ford was walking slowly along the paths, reading a letter. As the President looked out on the pleasant scene, a large man in riding clothes appeared in the garden. He bowed over Mary's hand, then over Miss Ford's.

"That's William Russell," murmured Lincoln. He suddenly leaned from the window. "Hey, Russell! come up here a moment, will you?" he called.

The Englishman looked up, bowed and started for the house. A moment later he entered the office.

"You're very scarce with your society as far as I'm concerned, Russell," exclaimed the President, crossing the room to greet him, and feeling again the sense of liking and admiration for the dark-faced war correspondent. "I hear you're going to make a trip South, and up the Mississippi valley."

"Yes, Mr. President. Miss Ford has been giving me a letter to friends in Alabama."

"I suppose she knows the best kind of folks," nodded Lincoln. "It doesn't take you long to get acquainted, does it? Miss Ford, for instance!"

Russell, a tall man, himself, looked up at Lincoln with a questioning expression, then looked out the window and back again before he replied:

"I did not meet her in the White House, Your Excellency, although I believe she is by way of being one of the White House under-secretaries. I met her, last night, at a dinner a Mrs. Greenhow was giving to the three commissioners sent here, I believe, by Mr. Jefferson Davis. When I learned that Miss Ford was an intimate friend of Mr. Davis', I asked her to give me a card of introduction to him."

"And I wonder what Charles Sumner would say to that!" exclaimed Lincoln. "Oh, well, why shouldn't she know him! And what if she does! She's not my secretary, Russell. She makes social war dances for my wife. What I called you up here for was to ask you what you think of Charles

Francis Adams as our Minister for St. James. I suppose you've met him, too, by now?"

"Yes, Mr. President, I've had the pleasure of dining with him a number of times."

"Good! Draw up here by the window and give me your idea of what England would like to get from us in the shape of an ambassador. Jings, tall as you are, Russell, I can rub my nose on the top of your head." He was leading the Englishman by the arm toward an arm chair, as he spoke.

"I've been in certain wild parts of this globe, sir, where, if I'd had your inches, the natives would have made a god of me," smiled Russell. "If ever you grow dissatisfied with a mere presidency, I'll give you the address of my savage friends."

Lincoln laughed, and the conference was begun with the utmost good feeling on both sides. It ended abruptly, an hour later, when Tad rushed, shrieking, into the office. He would not stay to be comforted, and Lincoln looked after him uneasily, as the child fled through the private passage to the sitting room.

"I wonder if he's really hurt," he exclaimed.

Russell got to his feet. "Shall I go after him, Mr. President, or call his governess?"

"Our talk is over, I reckon," said Lincoln, whose heart was always torn when Taddie wept, "so I'll go, myself. Let me see you again before you start South," and he hurried into the sitting room.

Tad was not there, but his shrieks led the President on into his own bedroom. Tad had flung himself on his father's bed. Lincoln stooped over him.

"Get off! Away off, Papa day!" shrieked Tad. "I hate you! I hate Willie! Most of all I hate Miss Fo'd!"

"Come over here and tell me all about it," said his father, seating himself in his favorite chair by the window.

"No! No! No!" screamed the child.

The door from the hall opened and admitted Willie. He wore his best clothes, a dark green velvet round-about and long trousers of the same shade of broadcloth. A wide, white collar with a flowing green tie gave the final touch of festivity to his costume. The boy looked scornfully at his brother, and appealingly at his father.

"Something's got to be done about Taddie," he announced. "He says nobody can marry Miss Ford but him, then he— Hey, shut up that racket, Tad, so's I can tell Papa day!"

Tad suddenly sat erect, face sodden with tears. He, too, was dressed for a party. His was a wine-colored velvet suit, the coat edged about with silk braided scollops, a lace collar finishing the neck.

Immensely interested and edified, the President looked from one boy to the other.

"You tell it the way it was then," sobbed Tad.

"Don't I always?" drawled Willie. "Well, Papa, Tad can believe what-

ever he wants to about who is going to marry Miss Ford. I think myself
that if I don't, John Hay will. But Tad oughtn't to get mad at one of
mother's parties about it, so's everybody says the Lincolns don't know how
to bring up children. Seems to me they're saying enough stuff, without
Tad's handing 'em something more."

"Well, I asked he'," Tad wiped his eyes on his sleeve, "and—"

"Wait a moment, boys. Willie, run in and get me a needle full of
black linen thread out of your mother's basket. I pulled a suspender button off my new suit last night, and I forgot to tell Mamma. I'll sew it on
while you fellows talk."

Willie flew on his errand, and Tad continued to sob, but softly now,
and with constant repetitions of his last statement, "I asked he'—"

There was no coaxing him in one of his tantrums, so his father took
his best trousers out of the wardrobe, put on his spectacles and, as Willie
returned with the needle, seated himself, saying:

"Get on with the story before I'm interrupted, Willie."

"Well—" the older boy began, feet apart, head thrust forward in amusing imitation of his father's habitual position, as Lincoln observed with a
chuckle, "well, mother was having tea in the Blue Room, and Mr. Mercier
was there, and Miss Ford and two or three other ladies, like Mrs. Welles,
and some of the Cabinet wives that don't amount to much."

"Who said that last?" interrupted Lincoln.

"I heard Miss Ford tell mother. And John Hay came in from some
errand he'd been on, and asked for a cup of tea, and Mr. Sumner was
there, and he'd been talking French with mother, and he said she spoke
it wonderfully, and she said she'd been obliged to speak nothing else in
the school where she went for four years, and I thought to myself, if
everybody only knew how much mother did know it might make 'em
ashamed, and just then Tad had to make a fool of himself."

"Tell what you did! Tell what you did!" shrieked Tad.

"Well, John Hay had been standing and talking to Miss Ford, holding
a cup in one hand, with his little finger stuck out, like this, and his mouth
all minced up polite, like this . . ." Lincoln gave a sudden shout of
laughter, as he recognized John at his social best.

Willie gave his father an indignant look. The President became ab-
normally serious, and thrust his needle vigorously through the broadcloth.
Willie proceeded.

"I'm not trying to be funny, I'm just telling you. Well, Miss Ford was
looking up into John's face, like this." A lady, eyes rolled adoringly, was
suggested. Lincoln choked, but said nothing. "Now you know, Papa day,
Miss Ford is us boys' friend first. She gave us the pups. She didn't give
John Hay anything. And I know him, how all the girls out in Springfield
got crazy about him, and I decided I'd interfere. So I went out in the
hall, like some one had beckoned, and came back and told John you
wanted him. And he went. And before I could move, Tad, he climbs into
Miss Ford's lap and jams her crinoline thing, and I just gave him a little

pull, like that, and he goes crazy right off and yells that I'm a dirty skunk, and Miss Ford's his girl. And he knocked her tea cup over."

"You knocked it you'self, di'ty skunk," shouted Tad.

"I did not! And everybody looked shocked, and mother put us right out."

"Then what happened?" asked Lincoln.

"Well, I suppose you heard Tad come roaring up here. I walked a piece with Mr. Mercier, just to show I didn't care."

"And was Miss Ford burned with the tea?"

"Not to hurt. She passed Mr. Mercier and me in the hall, she and Mr. Sumner, and she smiled at us. I can make a bow just like Mr. Mercier's." An imaginary hat pressed against his heart, Willie made a profound obeisance.

"I like the way Mr. Sumner does it best," exclaimed Tad, jumping from the bed, lifting his father's high hat from the table to his head, then sweeping it through the air, and holding it at arm's length, before returning it to eclipse his flushed little face.

"This is the way Chevalier what-you-may-call-him, the Italian Minister, does it," proclaimed Willie, taking the hat.

Lincoln watched them from smiling, reminiscent eyes, eyes that saw a shadowy figure behind the little velvet-clad bodies—the figure of a boy in battered jeans, barefoot, destitute of the necessities of life. It was but a fleeting shadow, however, for the never long absent tap sounded on the door, and John Hay came in.

"I wanted a moment alone with you, sir," he said soberly.

"I suppose to announce your impending marriage." Lincoln spoke seriously.

John gasped. "God forbid! What do you mean, sir?"

"You've almost broken Tad's heart, coming between him and Miss Ford," replied Lincoln. "And it's not a laughing matter," he added hastily.

"I see," gulped John, looking from one boy to the other. "They both admit her charm. Why shouldn't I respond to it as well as they?"

"I asked he' fi'st," cried Tad.

"You may have her," declared John, "with one stipulation. If I promise not to become engaged to her, may I talk to her when she talks to me? She knows a great deal about Southern politics."

"Yes, you may do that," agreed Willie, with a generous air.

"What business you got saying that?" demanded Tad, belligerently, then turned to John. "Be polite to he', John, and I'll be satisfied with you' p'omise."

"That being settled, boys, scuttle to your room and get hands washed for supper," ordered their father, and for once they obeyed without protest.

The two men smiled at each other, then young Hay said, "Mr. Lincoln, what attitude are we to take toward the newspaper men? I mean those who we know are deliberately circulating lies about you? Don't we issue any contradictions at all?"

"Not unless I tell you to," replied the President. "I suppose something extra ornery has come up! Greeley calling names as usual?"

"Nothing so simple as that!"

"Chicago papers say I was drunk at my own table last night? They've said that so many times, I'd almost believe it myself if I read all the reports."

Young Hay shook his good-looking black head. "It's not the published lie that's hard to scotch—! There's a newspaper man from New York, one of the hail-fellow, well-met type who claims to be rather an intimate of yours. You've never met him, and if I have my way you never shall. His special claim to fame is that you tell him your obscene stories."

"My what?" exclaimed the President.

John Hay flushed but went on steadily. "Nothing is more current in the country than the idea that you have a choice collection of dirty jokes that you spring on all occasions. This reporter has told a number that he claims you whispered in his ear. To-day, one reached Nicolay and me—a joke you are said to have perpetrated on a member of the Cabinet. It's so indecent that I can't repeat it. But it will make you infinite trouble when it reaches that Cabinet member's ear. I want you to authorize me to go to that reporter and flay him alive."

Lincoln looked at the excited young face with real affection. "John, you and George both know I don't tell obscene stories. And I know it. Before long, the Cabinet will recognize that fact. That's enough."

"I realize you can't authorize anything like that," blazed John, "but now you know, and I warn you that if I hear that beast repeating any of his filth, I shall knock him down."

"You can't knock him down, John. You aren't in a position to waste time scratching flea bites, when a cyclone is about to strike the house—but your loyalty warms my dried old heart. John, this man Russell—what do you think of him?"

"He knows more about war than any one in this country. He doesn't get on well with American reporters, because the London *Times* wants facts, and our papers want scare heads. He's insulted a lot of distinguished politicians, because he won't let them spit tobacco juice on the floor of his room, like they do on the White House floors. He's a remarkably fair and keen observer. I tell you, sir, I hope to write one day, and I'd like to learn my trade from him. I'm dropping in on him all I can."

"That's right. Keep in touch with him. And this Miss Ford. What does she want?"

John flushed ever so slightly. "Nothing, I think, sir, except a little social excitement."

"Hum!" murmured Lincoln. "What's that book sticking out of your pocket, John?"

"Walt Whitman's 'Leaves of Grass.' Oliver Wendell Holmes says there's all kinds of leaves in it except fig leaves, but I don't see anything in it to shock anybody. Care to take a look at it?"

"I know pages of it by heart," said the President, rising to pull off his coat and vest. "There was a copy around the office at Springfield. That fellow Whitman isn't a poet, but he's the prophet of democracy. He's helped me a good deal when I've got bilious wondering if any government which is not too strong for the liberties of the people can be strong enough to maintain itself."

He sat down on the edge of the bed and removed his boots, displaying the gray wool socks he wore without regard to season or place. Slowly, his fine, wistful eyes on John's eager face, he removed his snuff-colored trousers, and began to draw on the black broadcloth.

"That's the eternal problem of America," he went on. "The Fathers thought they'd solved it in the Constitution. Whitman thinks what he calls 'the indissoluble love of comrades' is inherent in democracy, and will give it eternal life." He pulled his suspenders over his shoulders and tested the strength of the button he had sewed on.

"And does Whitman's answer satisfy you, Mr. Lincoln?" asked young Hay.

"One side of me," replied the President. "He's a man, is Whitman. I'd like to know him. . . . Wish you'd go out and buy me some white gloves, John. I can't remember where I put my last pair. That is, if you can spare the time. Going out to supper?"

"I've plenty of time," replied John. "I'm dining late at M. Mercier's, with Russell, Lord Lyons, and lesser lights. M. Mercier threatens to call on me for a toast to Russell."

"Good! That portion of the show won't be dry, I know!" The President, donning a fresh collar, smiled at the young man.

John paused with his hand on the door knob. "Hay that is green, sir, can never be dry," he chuckled, and was gone.

CHAPTER VI

THE QUALITY OF MERCY

THIS night of April first, the initial State dinner took place. It was a tedious affair, followed by an informal session of the Cabinet, during which Lincoln tried to beguile the members into agreeing on some policy toward the relief of Fort Sumter.

While the prolonged wrangling that followed the President's first suggestions was going on, a quite different type of conference on the same subject was in progress in a not far distant part of Washington.

Miss Ford's house was boarded up as to windows, and linen draped as to furniture. None the less, a fire crackled in the back parlor grate, and Miss Ford herself sat in its blaze, talking with Justice Campbell.

At the moment Lincoln was making his first gently expressed pronouncement on the urgency of this Sumter problem, Miss Ford was saying to the Justice:

"I have seen almost nothing of the President, so far, Judge, but I have access as I wish to his papers. I never saw so careless a man in my life. He trusts every one. He's reading a book on military science—Halleck's, I think, whoever that may be. He left it lying in the sitting room to-night, with these two papers in it as markers. I borrowed them for the evening."

She passed to Campbell Seward's memorandum and a copy of Lincoln's reply. The justice read them with avidity. He returned Seward's proposals with the remark, "The man's a cheap jingoist." Lincoln's answer he studied for several moments, before laying it on his knee, and looking up to say slowly to the Virginian:

"Whoever wrote this has produced a state document that no ruler ever excelled in astuteness. If Lincoln wrote it, the whole Secession party is acting on a wrong theory."

"Lincoln wrote it," said Miss Ford. "I heard Nicolay tell John Hay that 'the old man has written a scorcher to Seward. Wouldn't let me make a suggestion—'"

Campbell stared anxiously at the fire, then asked, "What about Mrs. Lincoln?"

"I am under the impression that she has a profound influence on her husband, but, frankly, I've seen so little of them together, and Mrs. Lincoln is for the moment so engrossed in planning how to cope with the female dragons of Washington, that I can't give you concrete evidence. By the way, isn't the Fort Sumter situation getting rather out of hand with Mr. Davis? Can't he control the Charleston crowd until you and the other commissioners have had your full opportunity? I believe that you underestimate the importance of the taking of Sumter on the attitude of the administration."

"Horace Greeley said yesterday, in an editorial, to let the South go. That he, for one, refused to live in a nation pinned together with bayonets," was Campbell's reply.

"But Greeley is an enemy to Lincoln's crowd," protested Miss Ford. "Read those notes on the back of Seward's memorandum. They are in Lincoln's handwriting."

The justice hastily turned the sheet indicated. Written in the President's cramped hand were several terse statements.

"Fort Sumter: Lamon and Hurlbut report no Union feeling in Charleston.

"Captain Fox's plan much simpler than Scott's for provisioning the fort. General Scott admits Fox navy plan of attack might be successful.

"The Secessionists need war to whip up general Southern enthusiasm for secession.

"If we give up Sumter, it will be to admit to the world that the Republic has fallen apart, that humanity's greatest experiment in democracy is a failure.

"If we move on Sumter, the war party, heading up in Charleston, will use the first move as an excuse for war.

"The Cabinet is divided, the decision rests with me."

Justice Campbell jumped to his feet and shook the paper before Miss Ford's intelligent eyes. "I've told them so! I've warned my colleagues, I've warned President Davis, that Pickens and his crowd would rush us into war!"

Miss Ford looked calmly up into his agitated face. "Why do you take it for granted that Lincoln will order Captain Fox to move?"

"Don't you think that he will?" demanded Campbell.

"No, I don't. We've probably underestimated his intelligence, but of his sentimental softness there can be no doubt. He can't say 'No' to an office seeker. His servants impose on him shamefully. His children tyrannize over him. He is utter mush in his Cabinet. He, as you see, takes an insult from Seward as most men would take a compliment."

"You say you've had no contacts with him in these two weeks. What have you been doing with your opportunities?" cried the justice, fretfully.

The Virginian drew herself up. "Sir, I have given you invaluable information, this evening. I dislike my work, exceedingly. I resign from this moment."

Campbell threw up his hands. "Oh, my dear Miss Ford, do permit me the luxury of relieving my frayed nerves by scolding! Surely that should not be too great a strain on our friendship. I am truly sorry. Will you not forgive me? You are not the only one doing distasteful work."

Instantly mollified, the Virginian rose to put her hand on the justice's arm. "I'm sorry too! My hasty temper hasn't improved in the fortnight. I've made copies of those papers, Judge. I'll leave the copies with you. I must return these with all speed. You can get the copies to President Davis at once? Tom Taylor hasn't returned from his trip to Montgomery."

"I'll take charge of them, Miss Ford," replied the justice, buttoning the papers into an inside pocket. "Now then, how can we sound out Lincoln? How can we make sure that that decision will be moving in our direction?"

Miss Ford looked thoughtfully at her finger nails. "Can't we give him some alleged secret information to the effect that Davis, if given a certain amount of time, can get control of the Charleston crowd?"

"Yes! Yes! But can we get any sort of guarantee from Governor Pickens and Beauregard, there in Charleston, that they will wait for Lincoln to make the first move?" cried Campbell.

"It's your business, isn't it, to reassure Lincoln first and get the guarantee from Pickens, afterward?" asked the Virginian.

"I'll reach Lincoln, as I have before, through Seward. He's very easy to handle!" mused the justice. "Then I'll go to Charleston, myself. In the meantime, go to Lincoln, Miss Ford, to-morrow, and give him an inkling."

Miss Ford shook her head as she handed her mantua to the justice. "I must not rouse his suspicions. Or, if not his, those of his secretaries. They are decidedly on the *qui vive*, those lads. You see Seward early in the morning."

"Yes! Yes!" adjusting the mantua over the Virginian's beautiful shoulders. "You are quite safe to return to the White House by yourself?"

"Quite!" replied Miss Ford, somewhat dryly, as she bowed to Campbell, and removed her enormous yardage of skirts from the room with the deliberate grace habitual to her.

She took a closed carriage to the main entrance of the Executive Mansion, then undulated up the curving driveway to the portico. She arrived a few moments after the Cabinet members had dispersed. Old Daniel, who already was devoted to her,—she was that rare bird, a perfect lady, he said,—asked her if she had had a pleasant evening. Young Stoddard, meeting her on the staircase, begged for a flower from the wreath of roses in her hair, and told her that the family, including Hay and Nicolay, had gone to bed.

She fastened the rose in the boy's buttonhole, and traversed the deserted upper half with silent tread. Mrs. Lincoln's door was closed. That of the President was slightly ajar. She could hear him pacing the length of the room. Then she heard Mrs. Lincoln's voice.

"Aren't you going to bed, Abra'm? Here's the last *Petroleum Nasby*? Shall I read to you?"

"No, darling Mary. I'm going to climb into bed at once, and let friend Halleck on the Military Art and Science drowse me to sleep. Good night to you."

A short silence, then the click of the door into Mrs. Lincoln's room. Miss Ford took an irresolute step nearer to the gleaming crack. She caught a glimpse of the President in his nightshirt, and, turning quickly, she hastened into the sitting room, then into her own quarters.

Lincoln picked up the copy of Halleck, turned toward the bed, hesitated, then stood long in thought, going over in his mind the fruitless bickering of the Cabinet session just passed. It was ghastly to think of the uncertainty that ruled these men, when certainty was so essential to save the country. He fluttered the pages of the book in his hand where he remembered leaving his notes on Fort Sumter. They were not there. Perhaps one of the boys had taken them. Perhaps they'd dropped out on the sitting-room table.

He drew on his faded dressing gown, thrust his feet into his slippers, and made his way to the deserted room, still warm with firelight that showed him his papers, lying on the floor beside the huge center table. He shook his head over his own carelessness and with remarkable quietness returned to his bedroom.

He held the notes on the back of Seward's memorandum close to the candle to review them, then dropped them and began to pace the floor.

The decision more certainly than ever, after to-night's session with Chase, Seward, Welles, and the rest of the oak-table crowd, was his to make. Very well, before he slept, he would make it.

Up and down, he paced, up and down. His own body, the objects in the candle- and fire-lighted room, the starlit views from his windows, receded from his consciousness. He was alone in a universe of the spirit.

Mary came in at about two o'clock. She stood in silence by the window a long half hour. Lincoln did not see or hear her until she put her arm through his, and with eyes that told of her consuming anxiety, pressed her palm against his cheek, and forced him to look down at her.

"It is Sumter. It is war or dissolution," she said in a low voice.

"Yes!" replied Lincoln. "That's what slavery has brought the nation to; yet North and South tell me not to touch slavery."

"The North would not fight to set the slaves free," said Mary quickly.

"Not yet," agreed the President. "People don't understand yet." He resumed his slow pacing.

"Curiously," said Mary, keeping step with him, "if this were a decision concerning one of the children, or one of your clients or friends, I'd know your answer would be on the soft and easy side. But in this, which does not concern your affections, I know that your conclusion will be made with the ruthlessness that's the reverse side of your sweetness and patience."

Lincoln looked down at her. Her understanding seemed at the moment the one solid rock in the void where his spirit was wandering. He kissed her with lingering tenderness.

"Go to bed and rest, my darling Mary," he said.

"But I cannot sleep, Abra'm," humbly.

"You'll be resting and I must husk this out with my own hands."

Without another word, she left him, and he continued his solitary march. Bit by bit, he was placing his facts in their logical sequence. Not only contemporary and local facts, but world facts. He could see Europe gloating over the failure of the Union, and watching for an excuse to rush in and despoil the combatants.

If he relieved Sumter, war would come. Call it a war to save the Union. Aye, it would be a war for that purpose. But, basically, it would be a war caused by human slavery, and it was unthinkable that the Union and slavery should be saved together, that endless blood be shed, the war won, the South whipped back into the Union, with the viper still hanging to her breast.

This must not be.

If war came, it must come because the time had arrived when humanity must make another great stride in the struggle for freedom. The Magna Charta had guaranteed the freedom of those already free. Had the time come when a war could be fought in order to guarantee freedom to the bondman?

Up and down, up and down, mile after mile paced off over the shabby carpet. Could he make the awful resolve—the death-dealing, agony-bringing decision, and could he hold the decision thus made through months and years of carnage? Could he, in the name of freedom, deliberately turn America into hell on earth?

Solitary, foreordained, he wandered in profundity of thought that took no cognizance of time.

At dawn he paused, shivered, deadly pale. He glanced unseeingly around the room, realized with surprise that a new day had come, then crossed to his table where there were writing materials. He wrote a telegram and rang his bell. After a long wait, old Daniel appeared, blinking and startled. Lincoln gave him the message and asked for some coffee. Then he began to dress for the day's work.

The telegram bade Captain Fox proceed to the relief of Fort Sumter not later than the 6th of April.

CHAPTER VII

WHILE Lincoln was at breakfast that morning, Seward rushed into the dining room, his vest unbuttoned, his tie flying.

"Mr. President," he panted, "news of unprecedented importance has just reached me. You must give me a private conference immediately."

"Must be unprecedented, Seward," said Lincoln, dryly, "if you want advice from me on it."

Seward flushed, started to speak, then, as if conscious for the first time of Mrs. Lincoln, Miss Ford, and the two little boys, he greeted them, before saying to the President,

"I'm afraid I deserve that, sir. I received your reply to my memorandum, yesterday. After a night spent in pondering on its contents, I wish to say that I bow to the superior view."

Lincoln eyed the Secretary of State closely. No one knew how much it would mean to him if Seward would give over his dreams of leadership, and subordinate himself to his proper position. He rose from the table, took the smaller man by the arm, and led him into the State dining room.

"Here's the only private spot I can think of on the spur of the moment, Seward. What's on your mind?"

Seward hesitated for a moment. He moved away from Lincoln, in order to look up into the President's weary gray eyes. Suddenly Seward's face twitched. "Mr. Lincoln, as to my memorandum—I have underestimated your abilities. Will you accept my apology?"

Lincoln grasped the ex-Governor's hand, dropped it, and seized the frail little man in a great bear hug. "And now, by jings, let it rain!" he cried. "Our umbrella is raised!"

Seward tried to laugh, but was too much moved. "Your decision was right, Mr. President," he said, tremulously.

"Well," chuckled Lincoln, still holding Seward before him, "I hope I'm as right as Pat was. I was tramping to court when I was a young lawyer, too poor for a rig, when the judge came along in a closed carriage, and invited me to ride. I was mighty glad to climb aboard. But my happiness didn't last long. The judge's driver was sending the carriage from one side of the road to the other without aim or reason, and every moment seemed like we'd turn turtle. The judge was reading papers, not seeming to notice what was happening, so I said nothing until we careened over a log, and I cracked my head on the carriage top. Then I kicked. The judge grunted and put his head out the window, and roared at the driver,

" 'You scoundrel! You're drunk this morning!'

"Pat turned round to look at the judge. 'Be gorra, your Honor,' he said, 'and that's the first rightful decision ye've handed down for a year.'"

Lincoln burst into a great roar of laughter, and, a little hysterically, Seward joined him. But after a moment of this, the President pulled himself up, abruptly.

"What was the unprecedented news, Seward?"

The Secretary of State sobered instantly. "I was waited on before my breakfast this morning by Justice Campbell of Alabama. I have told you of him and his business in Washington."

"His alleged business—" interpolated Lincoln. "Any federal judge who will use his high office to cloak his political intrigues has a streak of yellow in his hide."

"At least," replied Seward, "he's sincere in his desire to prevent war. Jefferson Davis has agreed to move the capital of the Confederacy to Charleston, and to make Governor Pickens Secretary of State, if he will give Davis and the commissioners two more months in which to establish the rebellion pacifically. He begs of us to hold Fox back until he, Campbell, can get down to Charleston, and make his offer to Pickens."

"How did he learn about Captain Fox?" asked Lincoln, in dismay.

"He says it's common talk," replied the ex-Governor. "What does that matter? You will give the necessary assurances to Campbell, will you not, sir?"

"Seward," replied the President, "I want to impress on you that private intrigues will never get the United States out of the trouble into which she's worked herself. I'll have nothing to do with Campbell and his machinations. I don't trust him, or any man of his ilk. My earnest advice to you is that you refuse to meet these fellows who wear gum shoes."

The godfather of the new Republican party bestowed on Lincoln a glance of injured dignity that gave way immediately to one of bewilderment.

"But what are we to do?"

"We'll relieve Sumter," replied Lincoln. "I sent a telegram to Fox at dawn, telling him to get going not later than the 6th of April."

Seward fell back against the great hall table. "You—you—you did that, sir?"

"I did that, sir," replied the President grimly. "God help me and this country."

"But you can undo the message. It's not too late!" eagerly, from the Secretary of State.

Lincoln stood for a moment, going back in his mind to his soul-gripping ordeal of the night. He still was smiling grimly, when he shook his head and repeated,

"It is too late. You gather up the Cabinet about noon, Governor, and I'll have it out with them and you too."

Seward went from the room, with his head bowed on his breast. Lincoln would have gone directly to his office, but Mary caught him on the stairs, and prevailed on him to return to his unfinished breakfast.

He had formulated no very clear idea of how to win his Cabinet to support him in his decision. He followed, perhaps, the only method that could have brought them into even a half-hearted acquiescence. He made his statement, listened for an hour to their protests and vituperations, and when they had exhausted themselves, restated his unalterable purpose and left the room.

Taddie had come into the Cabinet room during the last of the discussion. Much to the annoyance of the secretaries, he began to tease his father for a dollar, but he did not gain Lincoln's attention until the latter, white and spent, had made his way to the sitting room. Then Lincoln gave the child the money, and strode on to his bedroom. Tad ran to find his brother, asking Miss Ford, whom he met in the hall, for Willie's whereabouts.

"I'll tell you where Willie is, if you'll tell me where your father is," replied Miss Ford. "I have a message for him from your mother."

"You'd betta' not botha' Papa day," Tad shook his little head wisely. "He wouldn't hea' you if you yelled at him. He has one of his deaf spells on, that he gets when he has to do something he don't like."

"Mercy!" exclaimed Miss Ford. "I hope it's nothing he has to do to you or Willie or mother or me!"

"It's not! I was in the Cabinet meeting with him. Papa day has told some one to start with b'ead and meat fo' Ande'son, and they've been telling him he mustn't, and he says he al'eady has. So don't you botha' him."

"I won't!" Miss Ford pretended to shudder, to the child's great amusement. "Willie is in the garden," she said, and turned into her room.

The immediate events that followed the sending of the telegram to Captain Fox were, in a sense, anti-climax to Lincoln. In the vigils of his night of pacing, he had lived through all the shocks, the passions, the agonies that the Civil War could offer. He had foreseen, of course, that for a few days he would be terribly alone in his singleness of purpose. He was a good prophet.

He was obliged to use the most urgent measures to force General Scott into such active preparations for the impending struggle as could be made without authority from Congress. The treasury was bankrupt. There was no war feeling in the North. Commercial interests were entirely hostile to any action that would seem to coerce the seceding states; nothing must interrupt cotton trading. During the days that followed the sending of the telegram, Chase and Seward did not cease to harp on these conditions.

Lincoln remarked grimly that he believed patriotism was dead in the North; then he deliberately turned a deaf ear to their comments, and concentrated every effort of his mind on getting the relief fleet started toward Charleston harbor.

Slow as he was in some aspects of his executive work, General Scott surprised Lincoln by his activity in others. As soon as the President apprised him of the orders he had given to Fox, Scott organized an army Secret Service that began to function immediately. The first fruits of this Service was an intercepted telegram from Jefferson Davis to Justice Campbell. The message stated that Campbell's information regarding Captain Fox's orders having been received, Beauregard had been ordered to demand the evacuation of Fort Sumter by its commander, Major Anderson.

Lincoln read the telegram on the evening of April 8th, and again urged Fox to make all possible speed. But it was too late to save the fort. On the 12th of April, at 4:30 in the morning, the stillness was broken by the sound of a mortar shot from a Secession battery in Charleston harbor. The shell rose high against the starlit heavens, curved gently in its course, and burst over Fort Sumter.

CHAPTER VIII

"ON TO RICHMOND!"

IT was on Sunday afternoon, April 14th, that word reached the White House that Anderson had evacuated Fort Sumter. Lincoln had been enveigled into the garden by Mary, who was deeply concerned over his long work hours. All day, the White House had been thronged as though a public reception were in progress. The Lincolns escaped into the garden by passing through the basement kitchen.

Mary was scolding the President, when John Hay appeared in the offing.

"You'll break down, Abra'm. I talked to Dr. Stone about you yesterday. He's certain that you have a consumptive tendency. He says that I must force you to eat and sleep properly."

Lincoln laughed. "I reckon Dr. Stone is barking up the wrong tree, this time. Why, Mary, my whole backwoods life has been preparing me for just such strains as this. It will take something more than the siege of Sumter to break down these muscles. Look!"

He slipped his great hands under her arms and swung her into the air as he would swing Taddie. Mary shrieked, and struggled to hold down the great sails of her skirts.

"There's John Hay! Quick, Abra'm! Oh, you are disgusting! This is not a husking bee on the Sangamon!"

Lincoln set her down calmly, and turned to his secretary. "News from Sumter, John?"

"Yes, sir," handing the President a memorandum from General Scott.

Lincoln read it, but without the sinking of the heart which he had anticipated. He was fully prepared for the giving up of the fort.

"The next thing is to issue the call to arms we worked out this morning, John," he said. "We'll get right at it."

Mary turned white. "War! Is that what it means, Abra'm?"

He nodded and started toward the house, which he entered again by way of the basement.

Mary remained standing by a rose bush, trembling a little, and she was still standing there when, five minutes later, Miss Ford in a pale green moiré antique came quickly down the path.

"Fort Sumter has fallen, Mrs. Lincoln!" she exclaimed.

"Yes! My poor husband!" ejaculated Mary.

"Do you think it means war?" asked the Virginian, turning to pick a tulip, which she tucked into her chestnut curls.

"What else can it mean? Mr. Lincoln is not Mr. Buchanan, content to sit as if paralyzed, while the South robs the nation," cried Mary.

"He seemed so gentle," murmured Miss Ford.

"So he is, where his affections are concerned, or mere personal interest," replied Mary. "But in his patriotism, he's flint. That's where a great many people are misunderstanding him."

"But war!" drawled the other, trying the effect of another tulip in the draperies of her skirt. "Does he realize that if he brings on war, in three months' time he'll be taking you all back to Illinois, while Jefferson Davis sits in the White House?"

Mary's blue eyes flashed. "Don't talk nonsense, Miss Ford."

"I reckon three months from now it won't seem nonsense, unless you can use your influence on the President to hold his hand, and refuse to declare war."

"My influence!" Mary smiled. "You flatter me, my dear! I can influence his manners, I can rouse his ambition, I can sometimes make him change his opinions of people. But, in twenty years, I have never been able to get him to revise a moral decision, once made."

There was silence for a moment. Mary looked up at the white pile of the house. It had taken her many years to make herself mistress of that beautiful roof tree. It seemed that she was to rule in it only under the shadow of national tragedy. She sighed, and the Virginian echoed the sound.

"I was thinking, dear Madam President," she smiled ruefully, "that all our beautiful and elaborately laid plans will now go for nothing. You will be expected to give up all formal entertaining—if there is war. And that means that my usefulness to you is ended. You see, I'm selfish, after all."

"Nonsense!" cried Mary. "I'll need you more than ever! If these Southern women are nasty to me now, what will they be if Mr. Lincoln uses soldiers to put down the Secessionists! Certainly you can help me to make them see—" She suddenly paused, gave Miss Ford a keen look, and went on, "I'm just remembering that you are a Virginian and a slaveholder, and that you may feel that you cannot be loyal to me and to Virginia, too."

"I'm going to tell you quite cold bloodedly," said Miss Ford, with a lowering of her voice to confidential notes, "that all I want is my slaves. If no one takes them away from me, they can have their old Union or their cunning little brand new Confederacy or any other sort of idiotic political arrangement these grown up boys like to play with."

"Well, that is rather a cynical way to look at it." Mary's tone held an edge of disapproval. "But after all how else can an honest person look at slavery?" She was thoughtful for a moment. She liked Miss Ford, and admired her. Even in the scant three weeks she had known the Virginian she had grown to depend on her. The previous week at least a dozen members of the innermost Southern circle had attended her teas—women who if Miss Ford had not urged them, Mary knew, would never have consented to meet the wife of the Republican President.

"Don't go, Miss Ford," she exclaimed, with her sudden, charming smile. "I need your help and I need—your friendship."

A quick and unaccustomed flush touched the Virginian's oval face to exaggerated beauty. "Thank you, Madam President," she said. "I'll try to give you both. But"—hesitating—"if I come to you will you be able to give me frequent absences, without pay, of course. That poor plantation of ours needs more than my dear old father's attentions, now."

"Certainly, my dear, certainly," agreed Mary.

Miss Ford did not return to the house a moment later, when her employer did, but strolled slowly among the shrubs and trees that bordered the south lawn. Taylor met her there, just as the early spring dusk settled among the syringa bushes.

"I've been waiting a long hour, Lady," he said, lifting her fingers to his lips.

"I'm sorry, Tom, but I've only now learned what we wished to know. I am to stay on at the White House. The President is issuing a call for militia. Mrs. Lincoln or no one else can stop him. It's war, Tom. Pray God a short one."

"It's bound to be, with a military fool like Scott, and a backwoods orator like Lincoln attempting to meet Beauregard and Davis," declared Taylor, squaring his fine shoulders as he spoke. "Davis owes me a commission, I reckon."

"Don't be too sure that Lincoln is only a backwoods politician," retorted Miss Ford. "Didn't Judge Campbell tell you about his reply to Seward?"

"Yes, he showed it to me. Astute, I'll admit, but legal astuteness doesn't necessarily make an efficient commander-in-chief of an army and navy. The folks in Montgomery nearly burst with laughter, when any one mentions Lincoln in that capacity."

"I don't much blame them." Miss Ford smiled as she spoke. "Nevertheless, he's no fool, and Mrs. Lincoln says herself that she can't influence him on matters of moral principle—so I'm about to undertake that job, myself!"

"You! What are you up to now, Lady?" peering at her through the dusk.

"If I can win the confidence of Charles Sumner, of Jefferson Davis, of William Seward, is there any reason why Abraham Lincoln can hold out against me?" She gave him a little green silk mantle which he adjusted over her shoulders. "And having won his confidence, I shall give him mine, and tell him to what men to give the job of running his absurd little war for him."

Taylor did not speak for a moment.

"Don't you approve?" demanded the Virginian.

"I'm going over in my mind the list of men who are proud to call themselves your friends," replied Taylor. "I'm sorry for Abraham! But—it's hateful work, Lady."

She tossed her head. "Oh, I laid my conscience away in rose leaves when I undertook this job. As a matter of fact, I can't see why it's worse to shoot a fellow citizen, as you plan to do, than to spy on him and use him, as I plan to do."

Taylor sighed. "Perhaps you're right. But I always shall hate it for you. When do you wish to see me again?"

"In a week, unless something urgent happens. Then I'll send Jinny to you. I must go in now, Tom."

"Oh, Lady, what is the hurry! Let's stroll and talk of something sweeter than war politics." He put a pleading hand on her arm.

She laughingly removed it. "I must go to watch my prey! Moreover, that dreadful river damp is rising. Dr. Stone says breathing that is what keeps typhoid going in Washington. Good night, Tom dear." And she was gone.

But, however concrete were her plans for becoming a close friend to Lincoln, she was able to execute none of them that night, or for many days and nights that followed. Quite literally, until he dropped exhausted into bed, the President never was alone. His call for 75,000 men for three months to repossess the forts and places seized from the Union had broken the lethargy that had paralyzed the North. The country was roused to a fury of war enthusiasm as difficult to control and direct as had been its inertia. For the first two or three weeks after the fall of Fort Sumter, it seemed to Lincoln that he could never bring order out of the chaos. His days were frenzied, never free from the exhausting pressure of interviews, of the demands for his authority to be used in the thousand different matters he controlled as President and as Commander-in-Chief.

At this time Nicolay helped him more than any one else. The secretary had all the orderliness of habit that Lincoln lacked. Mary called her husband's attention to this several times, and, finally, one hot May morning, when Lincoln entered his office at seven in the morning to find it already packed with important personages, he fled to Nicolay's office.

"George," he pleaded, "I'm drowning! Can't you send me a raft?"

Nicolay looked up from the letters Stoddard was handing him, with hurried résumés of their contents.

"What's the trouble, Mr. Lincoln?"

"My room's so full of folks I can't reach my desk. Have I got to see all of them?"

"You should not see any of them, sir. But—"

Lincoln interrupted, "I reckon I've been a fool. Shoo them out for me, George. Fix it so I can scratch the back of my neck without opening the window for space to do it in."

"If you will permit Hay and Stoddard and myself to order your day for you, sir," Nicolay spoke with earnestness based on anxiety, "you will do better work for the country."

"Do it, boy, do it!" urged the President, with the sense of gratitude and relief he always experienced when Nicolay put a shoulder under his burdens.

His days went better after that, though he still found it infinitely difficult to deny himself to any one who wished to see him. But he was realizing more clearly every hour, that only by educating himself thoroughly in the theory of war, could he hope to place men fit to carry on the war, in places of responsibility. He could train himself only in solitude and this knowledge, quite as much as Nicolay's urging, helped him to tear himself away from his visitors, and to remain, for long hours, in his room with his war maps, his reports from the War and Navy departments, and his books on the military art.

He was at work thus, late one evening in May, seated before a huge map of the United States, hung on the wall opposite his head. On this map, with different colored pins, he had outlined General Scott's plan for the conduct of the war, which Lincoln had dubbed the "Anaconda."

It seemed to him that the General's basic theory was sound. Scott's idea was to envelop the seceding states with a cordon of military posts down the Ohio and the Mississippi, by a blockade of all ports on the Atlantic and the Gulf of Mexico, and by a military line, thrown from the Potomac to the Ohio.

Sound, thought Lincoln, as far as the military end went. Its weak side lay in the fact that it would take an enormous amount of time to develop military leaders and armies fitted to undertake the task. And time was exactly what the North would not grant the administration. Across the Potomac, on Arlington Heights, were encamped thirty thousand of the "three months' men," under General McDowell. They were as yet, with all the good will in the world, only what William Russell said of them— an untrained, unequipped rabble.

Yet Northern newspapers and politicians already were urging Lincoln to send to take Richmond McDowell's host, which they characterized as a "magnificent army of 100,000 men, fit to wipe the Rebels off the face of the earth."

Horace Greeley led the pack shrilly, with the slogan "On to Richmond!" and "On to Richmond!" echoed a million lesser voices.

It was of this slogan that Lincoln was thinking, shortly after midnight, when Mary came in, candle in hand.

"Bedtime, dear," she said. "Shall I read to you?"

He did not hear her.

"Abra'm, do answer me!" she begged.

It was not Mary's voice that reached his ears but Greeley's, insistent as a gadfly's. "On to Richmond!" Where, he asked himself, once more, was he to find a man who could make an army out of a mob in a few weeks' time? How long could he hold off the battle that Greeley and his fellow politicians were forcing on him?

"You ought to go to bed, Abra'm!" Mary raised her voice. Her husband's capacity for concentration was undoubtedly a great intellectual asset to himself, but it was decidedly trying, at times, to other people. She pulled her wrapper more closely about her, and stood hesitating. Then in a still louder voice, she repeated, "You ought to go to bed, Abra'm!" and with this, she suddenly turned off the gas, leaving only the candle in her hand to light the room.

Lincoln, startled, raised his head. "That won't do, Mary. I can't see the map clearly."

"I don't mean you to," she retorted. "You must go to bed, or you will be ill."

The President sighed. If only he could make Mary understand that his great strength was in little danger of being impaired, that this was what he had to give to his country, the strength acquired during his laborious youth. He rose, and taking the candle from her hand, he lighted the gas from its flame.

"Go back to your bed, Mary dear. I've a hard nut to crack, to-night." He sat down, and carefully removed a green headed pin from Mobile to Cairo.

His face was ghastly with weariness, and, as she observed its deepened pallor, the fear that would not leave her, clutched Mary's heart again.

"I'm trying to keep you from galloping consumption!" she cried, her voice rising hysterically, "and you sit as if it were some childish mania of mine you were trying to thwart. You shall go to bed! Go, I tell you, go!"

She screamed the last words at him, at the same time raising her hand again toward the gas jet. But before she could carry out her purpose, the door into the hall, which had been left ajar, was pushed open, and Miss Ford rushed in.

"What's the matter! Shall I call the guard?"

Mary turned on her, furiously. "What do you mean by intruding in this room, Madam?"

The Virginian wrapped the folds of her pale green peignoir more closely about her tall figure. "I'm very sorry, Mrs. Lincoln," she replied, frigidly. "I was reading in my room, and when I heard you scream, I thought some one was annoying you and the President, and that perhaps I could call the guard to eject the intruder."

"You remind me, Miss Ford," Lincoln's voice was urbane, "that I've meant all day to talk to you. Come in and sit down."

"Mr. Lincoln!" shrilled Mary. "Have you no sense at all? It's one o'clock, and Miss Ford is in her night clothes."

"Are those night clothes?" with a chuckle. "She's lots better covered than you were at supper, to-night, Mary."

"I can dress in a moment or two, sir," said Miss Ford gently, "if Mrs. Lincoln doesn't mind waiting for me."

"Please do wait until morning, Miss Ford," urged Mary, less stridently, but none the less urgently.

"Mary, you take that chair by my bed and tend to your knitting for a moment." Lincoln spoke in a tone of unmistakable authority and Mary obeyed him. He pushed forward a cushioned ottoman for Miss Ford. "What I have to say won't take long. I gather from what Charles Sumner told me about you, Miss Ford, that you didn't secede when the rest of Virginia did."

"No, Mr. President, I am pro-slavery, but I still belong to the Union."

"Then, I take it, you're in sympathy with this movement of the folks in the western part of Virginia around Wheeling, to set up housekeeping for themselves as a separate State?"

"Oh, decidedly in sympathy," replied Miss Ford.

Lincoln watched her. She looked extraordinarily intelligent, but he wondered if Sumner, talking to him about her discretion and high sense of honor, might not be mistaken. Yet this was only a vague surmise, one of those unreasoning intuitions he often got about men—seldom, if ever, about women. Perhaps he ought to have talked this over with Mary before broaching it to Miss Ford. Mary was the one who knew folks. But time pressed so unrelentingly!

"I want you to do for me an errand that a tactful woman can do better than a man," he said, "because she would be less observed. Sumner says you have relatives at Wheeling."

"Yes, Mr. President, a married brother," Miss Ford nodded, "a Union slaveholder, like my father and me."

"Good. Now, I have reason to believe that a very pretty counter-revolution is being planned by the Secessionists up around Wheeling. They're going to try to lick these western Virginians into the Confederacy. I want to know just how strong that movement is, and what chance it has for success. Will you go up for a visit to your brother, and find out for me?"

"Gladly!" exclaimed Miss Ford. "I'll start in the morning."

"I'll be much obliged to you." The President rose as he spoke. "You see Nicolay, and he'll get the money for you and arrange for your pay. And I'll give you a letter to General McClellan. He's a promising officer, heading up the Ohio three months' men."

"I know George McClellan, Mr. Lincoln!" exclaimed Miss Ford. "As a West Point cadet, he used to visit our plantation."

"Seward didn't exaggerate your wide acquaintanceship," smiled the President.

"You can spare me, can you not, Mrs. Lincoln?" asked Miss Ford.

"Why consult me!" exclaimed Mary, with a smile that did not entirely counteract the bitterness in voice and eye.

Lincoln turned to her apologetically, and Miss Ford made her escape from the room.

"You don't really mind me picking up whatever tool comes to hand, Mary? I hadn't time—"

His wife interrupted with an hysterical laugh. The strain of the past two months had brought her to the breaking point, and this appeared to be the proverbial last straw.

"Mind! Mind! Who am I to mind? A lay-figure called the Mistress of the White House! You don't condescend to speak to me once in a week. You ignore my presence and now, without bothering to consult me, you take my one companion, the one person who—"

Lincoln took a step toward the door. "I'll recall the mission, Mary. I'm so sorry you take it this way."

"Come back!" cried Mary, bursting into tears. "Do you want her to think I'm jealous—? Can't you be anything but dense in your conception of me and my needs?"

For five minutes, she lashed him with all the fury of her hysterical temper.

Lincoln did not speak. Sometimes her hysteria wore itself out, and ended in contrition as unreasoning as her temper. But not to-night. He watched her,—sadly,—realizing as he did so, that the hostility of Washington, the vile innuendoes against her character that were finding their way into newspapers were biting deeper into her sensitive soul than he had thought.

At last he crossed to her side, put his arm around her shoulders, and placed his great hand gently over her mouth. She struggled to free herself, but not until she had become quite still did he release her. Then she fled with a sob to her own room.

Very slowly he placed Halleck back on the table near the head of the bed, and prepared himself for rest. He lighted the candle on the night stand, got into bed, and opened his Bible. These outbursts of Mary's upset him.

Lincoln read slowly through several of the Psalms, then closed the book, and lay staring at the bedpost. He was thinking, not about the war, not about slavery, or the friction in his Cabinet. He was thinking about Mary. No one of all the human beings that he knew, he told himself, had finer possibilities than his wife, or less chance for happiness.

All her generosity of spirit, all her brilliancy of mind, all her managing ability, must be blocked continually by her inability to control her tongue.

He sighed deeply and closed his eyes. As he did so the door from Mary's room opened, and his wife flung herself on her knees by his bedside, and laid her forehead on his hand.

"Oh, Abra'm! Abra'm! Forgive me, for I can't forgive myself!"

He raised himself on his elbow and kissed the back of her bowed head. "I'm not much good to you, wife," he said humbly. "There's nothing for me to forgive. It's only yourself you harm. I was just lying here, thinking that, and how, if you repeat to-night's tantrums in front of folks, all the Miss Fords in the world can't help you to off-set the gossip."

Mary raised her tear-stained face. She had been thinking only of her relation to her husband. "What do I care about that—" she began impetuously.

Lincoln touched her lip with a forefinger. "There it goes again, that tongue you can't break to harness! You care about it a whole lot, just as I care about it for you."

Mary swallowed a great sob. "Yes, I care," she admitted, "but it has no importance at all, in comparison with what I care for your admiration. I want your love! Oh, Abra'm!—and little by little, I'm killing it."

"Pshaw!" exclaimed Lincoln. "You talk as if I didn't know all about folks, and what to expect of 'em, even women!" His white teeth gleamed for a moment, then he added, sadly, "Can't I help you, somehow, to get a grip on yourself?"

"You help me every day of your life by the example of your patience." Mary clasped his great hand with both her own and laid her cheek against it.

The gesture was so like Taddie's in his moments of remorse, she was so like a child, huddled in her pink wrapper at the bedside, shivering from spent nerves, that her husband's eyes filled with tears. With a sudden movement of his powerful body he lifted her, and gathered her warmly in his arms.

"Poor girl!" he murmured. "Poor Mary! I reckon they couldn't have chosen two folks with stronger weaknesses than you and me for this job! It'll take more than Miss Ford and Seward to pull us through. Guess the Almighty will have to keep us on His mind most of the time."

"I know He will you!" whispered Mary, brokenly, "*I* don't matter."

CHAPTER IX

MASSA LINCUM'S NIGGER

THINKING the matter over, as she journeyed from Washington to Wheeling, Miss Ford decided that this errand was devised in Heaven to give her the much sought opportunity to win the President's confidence. She believed herself to be only one of several acquaintances that Lincoln was employing in this same search for news. It was possible, she told herself, that he was testing her, was planning bigger work for her, and would have her watched while in Wheeling. It behooved her, then, to act with complete honesty toward him, to conduct herself, until the errand was completed, consistently as a friend he was justified in trusting. She made a wry face at herself as she realized that she had reached this conclusion with a keen sense of satisfaction.

"Either I'm not a born spy," she told herself as she watched the beautiful Staunton turnpike corkscrew through the hills ahead of the station wagon Uncle Ben was driving for her, "or else I'm beginning to have a vague sympathy for that misplaced, ugly rail-splitter."

She was still complacent when she returned to Washington a week later. She walked firmly past the protesting Billy Stoddard into the President's office.

Lincoln was deep in a conversation with William Russell on England's frank partiality toward the Confederacy. He was so keenly interested in the Englishman's explanation of the British ideals of diplomacy that, for a moment, as the tall woman in her flowing draperies appeared suddenly at his desk, he wondered what she wanted of him. Then, with an effort, he returned to his anxieties regarding western Virginia, and jumping to his feet he exclaimed,

"Did you bring home the bacon?"

"I hope so," she replied, shaking hands first with the President, then with the war correspondent.

Russell excused himself at once, and Miss Ford, sinking into his chair, untied the strings of her green bonnet, and smiled at Lincoln. She then proceeded to give him a succinct account of the Union organization existing in most of the counties lying between the Allegheny and the Ohio rivers. She showed him that Confederate recruiting officers were making very little headway in these counties, while Union recruiting was highly successful.

"If," she ended, "you will order General McClellan, as the Wheeling Unionists have asked you, to send armed regiments of the Ohio militia up to Wheeling, the moral effect of that move will undoubtedly crystallize the new State into being."

"That's been my impression," commented Lincoln. "Your report presents real evidence, which is what I lacked. I'm greatly obliged to you, Miss Ford. Did you hear much about McClellan up that way?"

"He's on everybody's lips," replied Miss Ford. "He has a remarkable personality. He's done little so far, yet you feel his presence very keenly. I think he's going to be a great military leader, Mr. Lincoln."

"I hope he will be!" Lincoln's voice was hearty. His judgment had not been at fault. Tested by other reports, the Virginian had done an accurate job, and had talked with more people than his three other investigators put together. He was glad on two counts, first, to have fairly conclusively proved to him that an important portion of Virginia could be saved to the Union, second, that this woman for whom Mary and the boys had such a liking was proving herself loyal,—loyal and intelligent enough, he thought, to be sent, a little later, to Kentucky, to help beguile that wavering State into remaining with the Union.

"You've done a good job. I'm going to give you a bigger and harder one, next time." He showed his white teeth in an approving smile.

"I'm so glad! What is it?" exclaimed Miss Ford, leaning one elbow on his desk, and returning his smile.

"I can't tell you that in one sitting. You've got to be educated piecemeal to it. You watch your chance, and when you can, buttonhole me, look me in the eye, and say 'Kentucky' to me. I'll tell you all I can at that particular moment."

The Virginian laughed as she rose. "What fun! I begin to feel as important as I'm sure Secretary Seward does with all his little mysteries."

Lincoln drew a pile of letters toward him and began to sign them. "I dare you to tell Seward that," he chuckled.

"I dare!" she cried, as she left him.

Had Lincoln not been absorbed most of the twenty-four hours in looking for light to lead himself and the country through the military chaos, the national bankruptcy, the foreign and domestic insolences, that now submerged the unhappy Union, he might have been struck by the number of times a day he was exchanging a few moments of conversation with the Virginian.

When he thought of Kentucky, he was conscious of the fact that one of his many plans for helping the Blue Grass State was progressing well, but, outside of that, Miss Ford did not actually catch his full attention again until the latter part of June.

One beautiful afternoon, at this time, accompanied by John Hay and William Russell, the British war correspondent, Lincoln descended the steps under the north portico to enter his carriage. He was going to visit McDowell's camp across the river.

"John, you'll ride backward, being young and easy to impose on, and I'll—" The President stopped abruptly as he roused from his concentration on his companions. Mary and Miss Ford were seated in the barouche.

"We, too, wish to inspect the famous Army of the Potomac!" exclaimed Mary, with a smile.

"Some one will have to stay at home," drawled Miss Ford.

"I reckon it can't be any one of the masculine persuasion," returned Lincoln. "You ladies are very ornamental, but Russell and Hay are useful on an expedition like this."

"I can sit with the driver," suggested John Hay, with his usual tact. "Mr. Russell's too big from every angle—"

Russell smiled. Lincoln's lips were a little grim. He didn't want the women along, but neither did he want to risk a temper fit on Mary's part. He stood with one foot on the step, addressing himself to Miss Ford.

"You know," he said, "I've got to take a look at McDowell's troubles. And I can't do it riding backward, or chatting with beautiful ladies. If you and my wife insist on going, I'll have to ask you to allow Russell and me to use the seat you're in now, and you'll have to be inconvenienced by riding backward."

"Mr. President!" protested Russell, "I'll get my horse!"

"You'll do nothing of the sort. I need your ear and eye close at hand," said the President.

"My dear Mr. Lincoln," exclaimed Miss Ford, gracefully moving to the opposite seat, and arranging the silk dust coat that covered her crinoline, "so long as you don't send us back to our rooms, as we should be sent, we're glad to sit anywhere, even postilion fashion. We knew we risked that, didn't we, Mrs. Lincoln?"

Mary's eyes twinkled as she crowded her billowy skirts and dust coat in beside the Virginian's. "He'd better be thankful we didn't bring the boys."

"And the pups!" added John Hay.

The President chuckled as he doubled his long body on the rear seat.

The carriage passed rapidly down the dusty road toward Long Bridge, past the fields in which were piled the stones for completing the Washington monument, past squalid cottages beyond which lay a fine view of the richly wooded Virginia shore, to the ancient wood and brick structure, part causeway and part drawbridge which spanned the Potomac, here a mile wide.

A sentry sitting on a stump, at the bridgehead, his gun in his lap, was reading a newspaper. He looked up as the carriage halted.

"Where do you folks think you're going?" he demanded, without rising.

"Keep quiet, John," said the President, as he saw his young secretary's profile turn purple. "I'm Mr. Lincoln," turning to the sentry. "I'm going to call on General McDowell."

"Yes, I knowed it was you, Mr. Lincoln, by your picture, but I don't know all the folks with you."

"I have a pass from General Scott." Russell gravely produced the document.

"So have I!" John's sense of humor was returning.

"How about the women folks?" demanded the sentry. "They make more trouble than the men."

"Don't they!" agreed Lincoln, genially. "Well, these ladies have passes, I suppose. At least I found 'em in my carriage and they refused to be turned out, so I suppose they're all equipped for the trip."

"Mr. Lincoln!" exclaimed Mary. She leaned forward to smile at the sentry. "I'm Mrs. Lincoln, and this is my friend, Miss Ford."

Russell moved uneasily. The President chuckled. "Might as well get used to our lack of pomp, Russell! It'll take us a long time to stiffen our backs to carrying war weapons."

"Can't help it, ma'am, if you ain't got passes, you can't cross," declared the sentry.

"Mr. Lincoln, fix it for us!" implored Mary. "You've punished us enough for our presumption."

Still chuckling, the President produced two cards, scribbled on them with pencil, and Mary showed them to the sentry, who nodded grudgingly, and, at a word from John Hay, the driver started the horses across the bridge.

The soldiers on duty at the other end nodded informally at the President, and permitted the barouche to pass without stopping. The party immediately entered a maze of camps scattered among the magnificent trees that lined the shore to the crest of Arlington Heights, a mile or so beyond. The horses trotted smartly along the road to Arlington House, formerly the home of the Confederate, General Lee, but now confiscated by the Union, and in use as McDowell's headquarters.

They wound through the beautiful park that surrounded the mansion, to the carriage porch. An orderly led them through the wide hall to the great portico in front, with its wide and lovely view of the Potomac and the city.

A group of officers hastily left a map-covered table at the far edge of the porch, and, led by McDowell, a stocky, bearded man, came forward to greet the President and his party. At Lincoln's suggestion, two of the officers took the ladies off for a look at the house and grounds. As the crinolines undulated away under tiny sunshades, he turned to McDowell.

"Well, General, when do we have that battle?"

McDowell smiled ruefully. "What has Horace Greeley decided, sir?"

"Immediately, General! This exact moment! I reckon that this perfect army of yours,—by the way, it's not possible that those several thousand un-uniformed and otherwise fellows we saw drilling in squads on our way up here are an essential part of the fighting force?" Lincoln's smile was more rueful than the officer's.

"They *are* the fighting force, sir!" replied McDowell.

There was a moment's silence, during which Lincoln stared across the shimmering blue Potomac. John Hay looked at Russell, whose military opinion he respected even more than he did the war correspondent's literary ability. Russell, leaning against a white pillar, with arms folded across his broad chest, eyed a shambling soldier who, in a rumpled and dirty uniform, and with still dirtier accouterments, was doing guard duty on the terrace before the house.

"Let's see if my information is correct," said Lincoln, finally. "You have about thirty thousand men, and the Confederates have an equal number. A good part of your military is made up of three months' men, whose time is about expired. Thirty miles south of here, the Confederates have thrown up heavy batteries—near Manassas. How are their lines disposed near here, and how can you best reach them?"

"I don't know, sir," replied McDowell, "for certain. There is no such thing procurable as a decent map of Virginia. I can be sure only of the direction of the main roads. I can get no geographical information because the enemy is in full force along my front, and I have no cavalry officer capable of conducting a reconnaissance through the dense woods."

"Yet our constituents must have a battle, they say," murmured Lincoln.

McDowell's gray eyes snapped with sudden fury. "Damn the politicians!" he said. "They'll wreck us before we begin."

John Hay flushed. "War and politics, campaigns and statecraft," he exclaimed, "are Siamese twins."

"So you see, General, I am of some importance, even to the military," smiled the President. "You must remember this, that the enemy is in no better shape than yourself."

"But nothing decisive is to be gained by such an engagement, sir," pleaded McDowell. "General Scott agrees as to that. By fall we'll be in shape to give decisive battle."

"I know! I know!" murmured Lincoln. He took a turn or two round the table, unbuttoned his vest and tightened his suspender strap, buttoned the vest, then stood absolutely motionless, one hand on William Russell's broad shoulder, while he gazed unseeingly at the Potomac. Some day, he thought, he'd look at this view when his mind was not overwhelmed with responsibility.

"Is there anything I can do for you, in particular, General?" he finally asked.

"Hold that battle off until we at least have some sort of transportation for our ammunition, Mr. President," replied McDowell with a grim little smile. "What is it?" as an orderly approached and saluted.

"A rebel officer, General, under a flag of truce, wishes to give a letter to the President."

McDowell glanced inquiringly at Lincoln who nodded.

"Bring him up," ordered the General.

From the trees to the left emerged a tall, gray figure, with a figure in blue on either side. As the trio moved toward headquarters, Mary and Miss Ford, each on the arm of an officer, crossed the terrace from the right front. Midway just before the portico the two parties met.

"Oh! Oh!" cried Miss Ford, dropping her escort's arm. "It's Tom Taylor! My dear Tom!" flying toward the Confederate officer and clasping his hand in both of hers. "What has happened! Don't tell me you are a prisoner!"

"Why, howdy, Lady Ford!" drawled Captain Taylor. "Don't tell me you're consorting with the Yankees!"

"Ah, but such wonderful Yankees!" smiled Miss Ford, turning to introduce Mary, to find, however, that Mary had withdrawn behind her husband. As if greatly confused, the Virginian fled to Mary's side.

Captain Taylor saluted the President. "I have the honor, sir, to request that you receive a letter from His Excellency, Jefferson Davis, President of the Confederacy."

Lincoln looked down into the man's handsome, half insolent eyes.

"Did you come far with that letter, Captain Taylor?" he asked.

"I came from President Davis, sir," replied Taylor, promptly.

"Quite some distance," said Lincoln, gently. "Too bad for you to have had so much trouble for nothing."

The Confederate flushed. "How am I to understand that, sir?"

"As a refusal to receive your letter." Then, with a sudden feeling of bitterness, Lincoln added, "How can you so insult my high office, Taylor, as to ask me to receive a message from a man presuming what Davis has presumed? Has he not insulted his flag enough but he must add this affront?" Lincoln turned on his heel. "Time we were heading for home," he said, calmly. "Have you and my wife satisfied your curiosity, Miss Ford?"

"Entirely, sir," replied the Virginian.

"How about you, Russell?" turning to the Englishman. "Are there any questions you'd like to ask the General that he can properly answer?"

McDowell raised his eyebrows. "I don't know anything about Mr. Russell's sense of propriety, Mr. President, so there is nothing personal in my remark, that if he possesses one he's unique among the reporters in the United States."

The Englishman laughed. "After all, General, I fancy your reporters are controlled by the law of demand."

"I'm afraid that's true," agreed McDowell. "What can I do for you, sir?"

"May I ask for permission to study the methods of your drill officers? I am keenly interested in the study of citizen soldiery."

McDowell thought for a moment before he replied, "Come here to headquarters, Mr. Russell, whenever you have time for such study, and I'll see what I can do to accommodate you. I'm going to suggest, sir," turning to the President, "that you permit the ladies to drive on slowly in your carriage, while you gentlemen accompany me in an inspection of the camp."

"Oh, but we wish to see the camp too, do we not, Mrs. Lincoln?" cried Miss Ford.

"Certainly we do!" agreed Mary, taking her husband's arm.

"All right! Lead ahead, McDowell!" Then, as they followed the General around the mansion, and entered a company street, among the trees to the east, he looked back with a smile to Miss Ford, who was walking between John Hay and Russell. "I suspect you of wanting to look over the darkies we saw as we drove up. What is it Butler has named the runaway niggers down at Fortress Monroe?—contraband of war. Let us hope these are not contrabands, General."

"I'm asking them no awkward questions, Mr. President," replied McDowell, falling back beside Mrs. Lincoln. "They are very useful around the camp, I assure you. See those fellows cleaning up underbrush?" The group paused to watch several negroes at work with axes behind a line of tents.

"What is the difference between the contraband and stolen property!" asked Miss Ford, indignantly.

"Depends on where you are, I reckon," replied Lincoln. "Around here, I'm insisting that the Fugitive Slave Law be enforced, and all slaves be returned to their masters—if their masters call for 'em. You back me in that, don't you, General?"

"Certainly, sir. There was an owner came here this morning and got back three of his slaves. Name of Ford, Sylvester Ford. Perhaps a relation of yours, Madam?" smiling at the Virginian.

She did not smile. Instead she lifted her handsome head angrily. "My father, sir. I hope he had no trouble with the black fools."

"None in particular. An Uncle Tom's cabin touch, that was all. Niggers weeping, overseer cursing, owner with knitted brows."

Lincoln looked at the Virginian with astonishment. The entire expression of her face had changed. She looked like a handsome termagant.

"Touching their slaves," he thought, "is to set loose a secret poison in them."

"Must have been a scalding comedy," sneered Miss Ford. "A hard fate, indeed, for them to leave this crude camp for the comforts of my father's plantation! My heavens!" suddenly pointing a graceful hand toward a young negro who came out of a near-by tent, with a gun he was polishing. "There's another of our niggers. Zeb, come here!"

The negro, a stalwart young fellow in faded cotton pants and a new red army shirt, was cleaning a gun. He grinned widely, and shook his head.

"Can't order me no more, little Miss! I'se a Lincum nigger now. I'se in a Lincum camp. I'se white, all but ma cola!"

Curiously enough, no one laughed. By this time, the audience was large, and the street was thronged with listening soldiers. The July sun burned through the shade of the giant sycamores. There was no wind. The shrilling of locusts rose even above the noises of the camp. Miss Ford, in her yellow frock and cloak, her little yellow hat lying coquettishly on the mass of her chestnut curls, was a brilliant and intensely feminine figure despite her extreme height.

"Come here, Zeb!" she repeated.

Zeb put one great hand against the pale trunk of a sycamore, as if he needed its well-rooted support.

"I ain't going back to the plantation no mo', little Miss! They got Nap and Courty and Mattie this morning. But I'se no field hand. I learned to read and write from old Miss. I was her body servant. I makes claim to my rights. I'se a Lincum nigger." This with a flash of his eyes toward the President.

Lincoln stood in characteristic attitude, hands clasped behind him, head thrust forward. Something in the young negro's words and pose,— that huge, finely shaped black hand clinging to the tree,—moved him unbearably. He could conduct himself with perfect logic and consistency, he thought, on this fugitive slave question, so long as he did not actually see a fugitive! A Lincoln nigger! It was a new phrase to the President and stirred him profoundly.

Miss Ford turned abruptly to Lincoln.

"Will you kindly exercise your authority, sir?"

General McDowell interrupted hastily. "It's neither necessary nor proper for you to appeal to the Chief Executive in these circumstances, Madam. If you wish to take the negro away with you, I'll see that he moves."

"Massa Lincum! Massa Lincum!" cried Zeb. "Tell 'em not to tech me; I ain't going back to slavery. Nebba, Massa Lincum." The darkey's beautiful, mellow voice was incredibly appealing.

The President looked down at the Virginian. Her eyes were black with that strange not-to-be-controlled passion, which he had observed to obsess all slaveholders, when their authority over the blacks was impugned or questioned.

"Will you sell this darkey, Miss Ford?" he asked, miserably, "I can get some one to buy him and set him free."

"Abra'm; Abra'm!" murmured Mary, but no one heard her.

"He's not for sale!" replied the Virginian. "Will you give the necessary orders, General?"

"Massa Lincum!" pleaded Zeb.

The President's lips quivered and he gave a great sigh. "Zeb," he said, his voice rising clearly—"I reckon you'll have to go back, boy, while we fight this thing out."

"Ain't never going back!" reiterated Zeb. "If I can't be a Lincum nigger, I'll jes go up along to Mass' Jesus." And with overwhelming suddenness he put his mouth over the barrel of the gun he'd been polishing, touched the trigger with his bare toe, and blew off the top of his head.

Russell and McDowell prevented Lincoln by force from running to help pick up what was left of Zeb. For a few moments, after he had reached the barouche, whither McDowell hastened the party, the President said nothing. Then he looked at Miss Ford, sitting opposite him, still with that look of the termagant in her violet eyes.

"That is reality! While we play with words, Zeb gives us truth. I don't see how God Almighty can forgive us."

"Only a fool Yankee would put arms in the hands of a nigger, in the present state of things," declared the Virginian. Then with a curious note of triumph in her voice, she added, "You'd better take it, Mr. President, as a warning from the Almighty that you will be playing with all the fires of hell, if you allow your struggle to preserve the Union to touch slavery."

Lincoln looked at her curiously. "Have you no regrets, Miss Ford, for having driven a human being to suicide?"

"I regret losing a thousand dollars' worth of nigger," retorted the Virginian.

"Oh, my dear Miss Ford!" protested Mary. "I'm a native of a slave State but, really, one oughtn't to speak so of the slaves! That tone is what feeds the fury of the Abolitionists."

Miss Ford's face softened as she looked down at the pale-faced little lady at her side. "I reckon I do sound too brutal for good manners," she said, "but you must admit, Madam President, that I've never made any attempt to deceive you on my feeling about slavery. Come! Why let the incident spoil a lovely afternoon? Mr. Russell, say something enlivening for the ladies and gentlemen!"

The Englishman who had witnessed the tragedy and listened to the conversation following, with most intense interest, responded at once. "I cannot say that something enlivening occurs to me, at the moment. I am wondering how the Secession party can hope to secede, on the plea that it must have the right to keep slaves if it wishes, and, at the same time, keep the slavery issue out of the war which it is waging, to make that secession good."

"Of course, it can't be done!" declared Lincoln.

Miss Ford gave him a quick glance, but before she could speak, John Hay made an effort to turn the subject. "That was quite a coincidence, Miss Ford, your meeting an old friend on the terrace of Arlington House! Are many Southerners as heavily friended as you?"

The Virginian showed her dimples. "There is an opportunity for you to turn one of your neat compliments, Mr. Hay, but I won't press you! As a matter of fact, the larger slaveholders of the South do have a very broad acquaintanceship among themselves, much like that which obtains among the landed aristocracy, perhaps I might say the feudal aristocracy, of England."

"Nothing small or American about your Southern estimation of your-selves, eh?" chuckled young Hay.

Miss Ford turned to Russell. "You had an exceptional opportunity to observe the South at its best, on your recent trip, sir. You visited our finest families, our most extensive plantations. Do I overestimate our right to claim aristocratic kinship with the British?"

Lincoln looked with amused eyes at the Englishman. Russell's urbanity, however, was unshaken. "Their hospitality robbed me of power or desire to judge them, Miss Ford. I was prepossessed, like most of my countrymen, in their favor, before I began my tour."

"And what of your prepossession after the tour—?" asked the Virginian, eagerly.

"In spite of it," replied Russell with a slight deepening of the voice, "I came away with the conviction that human slavery is essentially wrong."

"If slavery is not wrong, nothing is wrong!" exclaimed Lincoln.

Miss Ford threw up both her hands. "But we are no longer discussing slavery!" she protested.

"You asked for my opinion of your Southern aristocracy," said Russell, "an aristocracy built on slave labor. How can we fail to consider slavery in expressing an opinion of it?"

"You are a Northern sympathizer!" ejaculated Miss Ford.

"I am a neutral," replied Russell, "and sincerely so. But I'm going to free my mind of this statement, in questionable taste though it may be. This war will never end, until the slavery issue enters and is fought to a conclusion. Until North and South faces that fact squarely, both are showing themselves to Europe as afraid to face the results of their own political policies."

"Right!" shouted Lincoln, so fiercely that the horses plunged, "and I am the biggest coward of us all!"

He sank back in the carriage, his head on his breast, and there was that in his silence which held his companions quiet until the ride was finished.

CHAPTER X

PERHAPS poor Zeb, himself, would have been reconciled to leaving a life which had brought him so little joy, had he known the effect his suicide was to have on "Massa Lincum."

The press of duties absorbed the President after the return from Arlington until midnight. But when he at last won to the quiet of his bedroom, he dropped into his chair by the window and entered into one of those long wrestling matches of the spirit that were the milestones of his magnificent, but eminently human, growth through the war.

He began by reproaching himself for not pressing his offer to buy Zeb, feeble as that remedy for a nasty situation had been. Then he grunted in disgust as he told himself that the offer was typical of his own softness. Was that softness affecting his stand on slavery in general? He could not answer that query, but, after a moment, he told himself that his sentimentality, his horror of others' suffering, was effecting his stand on the conduct of the war.

The North, clamoring for battle, could be made to understand how stupid were its demands only by witnessing the disaster sure to follow a premature action. Zeb's method! Could he use it? Could he allow Greeley and his screaming fellows to egg on McDowell and himself to send the army to certain and bloody failure?

And, from every point of view, was not failure at this time best? Early triumphs would not end the war, as Russell had said, because they would not settle the slavery issue— Defeat on defeat for the North, humiliation on humiliation, loss on loss, until the saving of the Union became all too meager a cause—that would be the moment to suggest that ultimate abolishment of slavery alone could justify the dreadful carnage—

Toward dawn, some one took his hand. He raised his head for a moment to smile at Mary, then dropped it again, though he clung to her warm, firm, little fingers.

Dawn gave way to sunlight. Flies buzzed on the ceiling. Doors slammed. The boys took their dogs into the garden. Voices sounded in Mary's room, then subsided. A little later, Miss Ford spoke from the hall, in her peculiarly clear drawl.

"Mrs. Lincoln, may I not send you all in some breakfast?"

"Don't bother just now, Miss Ford. I'll be out soon."

Ordinarily, Mary's voice alone had power to pierce through one of Lincoln's black fogs. But as the Virginian's slow tones penetrated through the door, he heard them.

"Just the same tones that said 'Zeb, come here!'" he exclaimed. "Mary, what's the matter with that woman?"

"She owns many slaves. All her property is in slaves," replied Mary.

"I was beginning to like and admire her," he murmured.

"She was very unpleasant yesterday, but still, I can't help liking her," Mary nodded her head. "And I can't say your absurd offer to buy the nigger impressed me as admirable. You weren't exactly a brilliant spectacle as Chief Executive, yesterday, Abra'm."

"I reckon I was at my least brilliant point when I let you two women intrude yourselves in the party." Lincoln sat erect with a sigh. "I wonder if her meeting Taylor there wasn't a little too pat?—Still, I don't quite see—"

Mary interrupted. "Oh, she's no spy! Don't let her peculiarities as a slaveholder inoculate you with spy fever, Abra'm!"

"Oh, very well!" sighed Lincoln, too weary for argument. "Somehow I don't feel very brisk, this morning."

"Humph! Strange!" snapped Mary. "You ate practically no supper last night. No food since yesterday noon. No sleep last night. I have a devil's temper, Abra'm, but you have the habits of an imbecile." Very gently, she began to undo his tie and collar. "Let's get some clean things on you, dear, before your breakfast."

Lincoln caught her fingers, kissed them and rose. "I've got to send a message to the war office, right off."

Tie trailing, collar unbuttoned, he strode out of the room.

Two hours later, McDowell received his orders to move his ill-trained, badly equipped army toward Manassas Junction.

Perhaps nothing was so typical of Washington, those summer days, as dust. It rolled in clouds up and down Pennsylvania Avenue, which, as a favorite route for marching troops, had been ground, knee deep, into powder. It turned the red, white and blue that draped the shops and boarding houses of the main thoroughfare to a universal gray. It obscured the foliage of the young trees struggling for existence at the curb, and it rolled in ceaseless fog-like waves over the White House gardens, where Mary loved to work in the early morning. Even the fountain below the south portico, despite the earnest efforts of the gardener, sprayed mud into a basin of mud.

The day after the visit to Arlington Heights was a Saturday, and the weekly concert of the United States Marine Band in the White House grounds was due. Mary had planned on this day to move the family out to the cottage at the Soldiers' Home, which Buchanan had used as a summer residence. But, unexpectedly, a flag raising was scheduled at the close of the concert, at which she and the President were obliged to be present. She was tired after the night of strain, and would be doubly so after the afternoon's ceremonies, so she decided to postpone the migration until the following week.

Miss Ford had begged off sitting on the dais, erected below the south portico for the ceremonies. The dust, she said, was too thick for her patriotism. She was going to spend the afternoon in a much needed beauty sleep. When therefore, Willie found her, late in the afternoon, seated with a tall, blue-eyed man in the shade of a clump of ailanthus trees, that observing youth chided her frankly for her seeming deception.

"It was too hot in my room," she explained smilingly.

"Thought you hated dust," he said, disengaging his lips from a pop bottle. "And you're right where it and the folks are thickest," looking with distaste at the close packed crowds milling over the lawns. "Soldiers and crinolines, crinolines and soldiers," he muttered. "Gosh, they crowd everything! Going to get closer to see my father raise the flag?"

"Willie," Miss Ford caught his grubby hand languidly, "you look very nice in that brown linen suit."

"It's meant to be white, you know!" grinned Willie.

Miss Ford returned the smile. "This is a very old friend of mine, and I want you to go fetch Pensacola and Sumter for him to see. He gave me the mother of the pups."

"All right! Reckon I'll have to make Tad help me."

When the boy had disappeared, the Virginian turned to the man, who had been eyeing him keenly:

"His father must have been exactly like him at his age, though bigger and more awkward, Tom," she said.

"His father wasn't ever as clever as that lad, Lady Ford," said Taylor.

"Not so clever I agree. That's the mother in Willie. But Lincoln must have been far more intelligent. That's where Jeff Davis and his crowd are making their mistake, Tom. That's where I made my mistake, when I agreed to the present campaign."

The man dusted off his linen trousers with his broad brimmed straw hat, and listened for a moment to the band. "Invitation to the Dance," he murmured. "Wish we had that music at the plantation, with only you and me to dance to it. Had any new evidence of his intellectual prowess, Lady?"

"Yes, Tom, I have. In the first place, after fumbling for a short time, he's become master and overseer, both, of this plantation. Seward takes orders like a lamb. Cameron mutters, but under his breath, and does what he's told. Chase is nasty, but he's left off his patronizing manner." She paused and laughed reminiscently. "The family sitting room is sort of an overflow office, and Lincoln pays no more attention to the presence of the children or Mrs. Lincoln or myself than to so many chairs. Sometimes it annoys strange callers, but the 'regulars' are now as indifferent as he. Two or three nights ago I was sitting in the twilight, waiting for Mrs. Lincoln and the boys to get ready for the theater.

"Lincoln came in without seeing me, threw himself down in a chair, unbuttoned his vest, put his feet on the mantel, and groaned as if he were weary beyond words. A second after, the door from his office burst open, and a huge, bald-headed man half sidled, half loped into the room.

He looked about until he caught sight of the President. Then he shouted, 'See here, Lincoln, we've got to finish, so's I can get back to New York. More light! Must have more light!' He lighted the gas and shuffled over to the President and stood by his chair as if he wanted to bite him.

"The President showed those nice white teeth of his. They always surprise me so in his sallow face. 'Greeley,' he said, 'why don't you read Artemus Ward when your nerves get bad?'

"Greeley,—yes, that's who it was—was furious. 'Have you no sense of decency?' he shrieked.

"'I never asked myself that,' said Lincoln and you should have seen his gray eyes twinkle. 'But at least, I've never followed you into the privacy of your sitting room to tell you how little you know.'

"Greeley stuck out his lower lip like a child that's had its hands smacked. But the President didn't seem to notice. He went right on with what he had to say. 'Didn't it ever strike you as interesting, Greeley, that a couple of pretty poor sticks like you and me should have reached positions of such power? Came up from about the same conditions, both of us from poor folks, starved for an education, both of us,—sort of pulled ourselves up by our boot straps. Never'll lose the marks of the fight, either of us. No manners, no enjoyment of lots of the fine things better educated folks admire. But here we are, trying to lead millions of people who've been better trained than either of us. Reckon we're tarred with the same stick, Greeley. Now you go home to the *Tribune* and try to get off my back long enough for me to try to get far enough ahead of the people so's they won't trample me to death!'

"Well, do you know, Tom, Greeley stood there bursting to talk, and he didn't dare do so! He gasped and puffed, and he turned round, and went out of the room without a word."

Tom chuckled, then said, thoughtfully, "Common sense, Lady, but not what I've been raised to call intellectuality. What happened next? Did the old boy see you? Aren't getting a little sentimental about the log splitter, are you, my dear?"

Miss Ford gave a disdainful sniff and passed her sunshade to her companion to raise. The lowering sun was creeping under the trees. "Mrs. Lincoln happened next, and with her pushed in a delegation of clergymen. They throng the White House day and night. It may interest you to know that they were Abolitionists and they demanded of the President that he issue at once an edict of freedom to the slaves."

"Ha!" ejaculated Tom. "Here's first-hand information on that point! What did he say?"

"After they'd finished explaining to him that it was the Almighty's wish that he wipe slavery from the land, Lincoln asked them if it didn't strike them as curious that when he was carrying the responsibility the Lord should give them the special information and never a word to him. Then he walked off! a way he has of ending an argument." She wiped her face delicately with her handkerchief. "If you are seen here, Tom, there'll be trouble."

"Safest place to hide is in a crowd. No one will bother us except the Lincoln boys, thanks to you," replied Tom.

"Willie won't be back before you leave. Only an Alpine glacier moves more imperceptibly than Willie on an errand. But I have more direct evidence of his feeling about slavery and the war." She told him at length of the episode at Arlington. "Mark my words, Tom, Lincoln is going to work the slavery issue into the war and that at no very distant date. The South will have to hurry, if it is to win the war before that time."

"Is he influenced by Sumner?" asked Taylor.

"If Sumner influences him in anything vital, it's more than any member of his Cabinet has done," replied the Virginian.

"Curse the fool!" muttered Taylor.

"That's just the point. He's turning out not to be a fool," exclaimed Miss Ford.

The two sat brooding for a moment. The sun turned the fog of dust to a golden glory. A drunken soldier gravely offered Taylor a chew of plug tobacco. The Confederate brushed him aside as though he were an importunate fly. The band passed from "Autumn Leaves" to "Believe Me If All Those Endearing Young Charms."

"You recall my telling you about meeting McClellan again when I took the trip to Wheeling?"

Captain Taylor nodded.

"I've not been able to put him out of my mind. He's as fascinating as ever. I'm only a mild sample of what he can do to the stern, as well as the fair sex. He's really sincere in his belief that slavery should be left alone. I wish he were Secretary of War instead of Cameron."

"Why not Secretary of State instead of Seward," returned Taylor with an amused smile, "or President instead of Lincoln?"

Miss Ford gave him a quick look. "Laugh, if you please, but McClellan in the White House would be a godsend to the South. He'd preserve the Union and slavery both." She paused to think, then went on. "Unless the South wins quickly, a dictator is not an unthinkable solution. Greeley has suggested it already in his impatience with Lincoln, and Greeley's following and influence is immense. Listen, Tom! It may not be McClellan, but Jefferson Davis's job is to watch the Northern forces for the right military man to make dictator."

"It all seems unreal and remote," Taylor moved a little uneasily, "but perhaps we can't have too many strings to our bow. I'll certainly pass on your ideas to Davis. Can't say that I seem to hanker for plot and counter-plot as you do."

"All women love it," said the Virginian. "Weren't you delighted with the practical effect of my embracing you yesterday at Arlington?"

"You mean the pass! Yes, it is worth its weight in gold. Ought to carry me through the war. How did you get it?"

"Mr. Lincoln wrote it in the carriage, yesterday, to get me past the sentry. I was frightened to death lest he use my name, and I almost screamed with relief when he wrote 'Pass bearer.' I knew that espionage was going to be stricter and stricter in the city, and I maneuvered a week before I finally worked out the scheme. Of course, I didn't realize the fates would permit me to meet you at Arlington. When do you return to Davis?"

"This report from you is my last chore; Jeff had only a half hope Lincoln could be bluffed into receiving a letter. He's trying anything to get him to acknowledge there is a Confederacy. Is all well at Fairfax Courthouse?"

"Working smoothly, I think. Captain Mosby is in charge under J. E. B. Stuart. Stuart sent me word he would give me a commission as an aide to him if I wished one. We'll see—Ah, the flag raising, at last! You must go now, Tom. The crowd will be breaking."

The man did not stir for a moment, as high above the crowd an enormous flag slowly ascended the pole below the portico, urged by the invisible arms of Lincoln. As the lazy folds whipped out under the dust-laden wind, Taylor rose, silently, his eyes on the flag.

"You are regretful?" asked Miss Ford.

"Always," he replied, "but not the less a firm believer that right is on our side. Good-by, my dear Lady!"

"Take good care of yourself, Tom," she replied, and looked after him until he was lost among the shrubs near Pennsylvania Avenue. Her solitude was not allowed to remain long uninterrupted, however, for Taylor had scarcely reached Pennsylvania Avenue when Willie and Tad appeared, each dragging a pup. Both the boys were dirty and disheveled, and both the pups were barking excitedly. John Hay followed them.

"Where's the man?" demanded Willie.

"He had to go. There didn't seem much hope that you'd be back before Christmas. So sorry, for he'd loved to see the puppies!" Miss Ford looked at the boy's flushed face with a quizzical smile.

"It was an engagement with me, and he'd ought to have kept it," said Willie, in the deliberate voice that always made his remarks impressive. "I brought John Hay along, too, because he seems to like to know the men that know you."

John Hay sighed dramatically and dug into the pocket of his linen trousers. "Hush money again in order, I see. Here you are!" bringing up a handful of pennies. "The popcorn man was making delicious smells as I came by. Divide equally, and take the impregnable fastnesses with you," indicating Sumter and Pensacola, the puppies.

When they were alone, John turned uneasy, black eyes on the Virginian. "Wasn't that Captain Taylor with you? I caught just a glimpse of him through the trees as I came up."

"Mercy, no!" exclaimed Miss Ford. "He's a hundred or a thousand miles away from here by now, I pray. You're not catching spy fever, I hope, Mr. Hay."

"No, I'm not," replied John. "At least, I don't think that's what they call my affliction. It's a curious ailment. Never had it, at least, not seriously, until I met you."

"Indeed! Well," with a provocative little laugh, as her eyes met his levelly, "let's hope that the affliction will not assume serious proportions. Perhaps it will cure itself."

John returned her look. "It will cure itself if it becomes complicated by spy fever."

"Mercy, what a revolting idea! If you'll give me your arm, Mr. Hay, I think I'll join Mrs. Lincoln. It looks as though one could pass through the crowd now without having one's clothing rent from one's body."

They made their way in silence to the house. John left Miss Ford at her door, then went rather unhappily into the secretaries' office. George Nicolay looked up from his writing.

"You have an air of pain, Johnny. Confide in me, do!"

"Miss Ford was holding a confab in the garden just now with the Captain Taylor of yesterday's fame. Then she lied to me about it."

"What else could she do, if you were fool enough to ask her the direct question?" Nicolay dropped his pen and relighted his cigar.

"I wish she weren't so devilish good looking," grumbled Hay. "Do you think I ought to warn the President?"

"He needs no warning. You might tell Mrs. Lincoln about it," said Nicolay.

"Well, I may at my first opportunity." John pulled off his coat, and settled himself at his desk. "I wish she wasn't so devilish good looking," he repeated.

Nicolay laughed.

CHAPTER XI

THE following week, the family, with Miss Ford, moved out to the Soldiers' Home, which lay about four miles north of the White House. Here, in the little brick house so reminiscent of the simple home in Springfield, set high on the tree-covered hill, Mary hoped that her husband would find a certain amount of relief, not only from the humid heat of the city, but from visitors as well.

Certainly the nights that Lincoln spent at the Soldiers' Home were cooler than the White House nights, but he experienced far too few of them. His associates felt uneasy when the Chief Executive was out of immediate reach. He himself wanted to be able to wander into the war office at any hour of the night, particularly now that the Army of the Potomac was on the move. Lincoln felt as if the magnificent trees that made a paradise of the park around the brick house were an insuperable barrier between himself and his job. So poor Mary spent a large portion of her time traveling into the city, in the vain attempt to fetch her husband back with her.

When, on July 19th, the first news of McDowell's disaster at Bull Run was brought to the Soldiers' Home by a dusty aide, Mary and Miss Ford immediately left for the Executive Mansion. Nor during the feverish days that followed, when the North seemed to have gone mad with amazement and chagrin, and to be intent on crucifying Lincoln and McDowell—could they be persuaded to return to the country. Willie and Tad, on ponies, with a soldier detailed to guard them, drifted back and forth between the two establishments, enjoying the disorder and excitement quite as much as did Pensacola and Sumter, who had a "chasing" acquaintance with every chicken and cat along the route.

Lincoln was vaguely conscious that his family had returned, and that Mary was extraordinarily tactful and tender with him. He told her, one day, when she had sent his supper up to the Cabinet room without waiting to be asked, that she was as grateful to him as dry socks and a shirt would be to a man working in a tornado. But this was his sole remark to her for several days.

He had bowed his back patiently enough to the outcry following Bull Run. Even the stupidity of the attacks from high places did not surprise him into a retort. General Scott, who was, as may be supposed, deeply chagrined, and yet in an I-told-you-so state of mind, was exceedingly bitter over the criticisms of Edwin M. Stanton, who had been a prominent member of Buchanan's cabinet.

To Lincoln, sitting on the desk in the war office, the old General-in-

Chief said, "Stanton is an able man, sir, with a considerable understanding of military problems, and I learned to rely on him before you came in power. But he is not only stupid, sir, but ridiculous when he accuses you, Mr. President, and me of appointing only Republicans to the army."

"Shucks, General," replied Lincoln, patting the old gentleman gently on the shoulder, "you must harden yourself. What Stanton says of you is nothing to what he says of me. He says I'm an imbecile. He lays 'the irretrievable misfortune and national disgrace' of Bull Run directly on my shoulders. And he's quite correct in so doing. I'm going, however, to heed only one point in his or anybody else's hollering. I reckon, as he says, we've got to get a new man in McDowell's place. Too bad, for McDowell's an excellent soldier, competent people like you and William Russell tell me. But the public has lost faith in him. And they are shaky on me too. But," with a chuckle, "I'm not so easy to kill."

"I seriously object to replacing General McDowell!" cried Scott, placing a shaking old hand on his sword.

"I know! It is tough. But it will have to be done, General. What would you say to moving McClellan down here? His victories in West Virginia have put him in high favor, and, as near as I can judge, the young fellow has all the makings of a first class military leader."

Lincoln spoke as tentatively as he could, for Scott was extremely sensitive, but, having the night after Bull Run made up his mind to put McClellan at the head of the Army of the Potomac, he found it a little difficult to show his usual deference in leading the old man to make the decision he, Lincoln, desired.

"Think it over, General," he said, "and let me know what you conclude, within the week. I've had reports from many reliable folks, both male and female, and they all have come under McClellan's charm. You know as well as I do that charm is just about the rarest bird in and about Washington to-day, General."

He shook hands with Scott and returned to his office.

Stanton, though brilliant and hostile, was not in the position to frustrate Lincoln's plans as could Greeley. That very able editor was in an obvious state of funk which he displayed, not only in the New York *Tribune*, but in passionate letters to the President, pleading with him: ". . . You are not considered a great man, and I am a hopelessly broken one. You are now undergoing a terrible ordeal, and God has thrown the gravest responsibilities upon you. Do not fear to meet them. If the Union is irretrievably gone, there should be an immediate disbandment of forces. . . . If it is best for the country and mankind that we make peace with the rebels at once and on their own terms, do not shrink even from that—"

"Greeley ought to uphold my hands better than this," was the only comment Lincoln thought necessary to make on this extraordinary appeal, as he gave the letter back to Nicolay to file, and he turned to his making of a new memorandum on what he designated at the top of the paper "As To The Whole Anaconda Movement."

A few days after the battle of Bull Run, Miss Ford borrowed from Mary the pass which Lincoln had given his wife on the day of the visit to Arlington. She had lost her own pass, said the Virginian, and she wished to go out to Fairfax Courthouse to see if there was anything left at all of the plantation, and to discover, if possible, the whereabouts of her father. Mary, all sympathy, suggested that they get the President to give her an escort through the chaotic Union lines that stragglingly embraced Fairfax Courthouse and its environs.

"Go back with Yankee soldiers? The home folks would lynch me!" declared Miss Ford. "No, dear Mrs. Lincoln, Jinny and I will make our way through quietly, and be back to-morrow night."

The conversation took place in Mary's bedroom, where Lizzie Keckley, a colored mantua maker, was at work. She was a negress of considerable intelligence, who had bought her own freedom, and was in great demand among the fashionables of Washington. After Miss Ford had left the room, Lizzie re-pinned the sleeve she was trying on Mary's graceful white arm.

"You are awkward with this fitting, Lizzie. Aren't you well, this morning?"

"Yes, Madam, but I was listening to Miss Ford, I guess, instead of thinking about my work. Madam, if you'll excuse me for saying so, I don't think you should have let her have that pass. Jinny tells me she writes letters all the time to Jefferson Davis, and that they're sent from the tavern at Fairfax Courthouse."

Mary whirled away from the deft, brown fingers. "You're saying she's a spy, Lizzie Keckley! You ought to be ashamed of yourself!"

"Madam!" Lizzie drew herself up proudly. She was a finely built woman of middle age, with the dignity often seen in the better type of negro. "Madam, I am no more ashamed than you would be to report a spy. That's why I'm working here, to-day, instead of for other ladies who would pay me better and be less impatient. I want to uphold Mr. Lincoln's hands."

"Lizzie!" exclaimed Mary, with that childish catch of repentance in her voice that endeared her to those who knew her best. "It's I who should be ashamed! But I'm so fond of Miss Ford, and she's been so good to me and the children! I'm sure you must be mistaken!"

The mantua maker laid the flowing sleeve aside, and lifted a billowy drift of pink tartan skirting. "I am not mistaken, Madam President." She smoothed the tartan over the cutting board, which she had laid on the bed, and lifted her shears, hesitated a moment with eyes first on one edge of the material, then on the other, and finally made a great slash as she said:

"Jinny says that Miss Ford wrote a letter last night telling Jefferson Davis that she heard Mr. Lincoln tell Mr. Seward that he was going to bring Major McClellan to Washington to look him over, and that she was going to have a talk with McClellan and size him up."

"But can Jinny read?" asked Mary, fatuously.

"She's as well educated as I am, and you can judge me by my good English. She's a smart nigger, and she's going to help Mr. Lincoln set all niggers free. The word's gone round that he'll bring the day of glory if he can."

Mary stood in her chemise and petticoat, staring first at the mantua maker, then at the new crocheted lace pillow shams Miss Ford had made for her. She was convinced that Lizzie Keckley was telling the truth, and her first impulse was to fly to her husband with the information. But she feared he'd only shrug his shoulders. Surrounded by intrigue in his very Cabinet, by disloyalty in his party, by hatred and deceit from those on whom he must depend to carry on the war, what would secondhand information about a spy mean to him? And what was the use of going to him, or to any one else, until she had checked up Lizzie's statement?

"I suppose, Lizzie," she said, suddenly, through set teeth, "that you think I ought to send Miss Ford away, right now. But I'm going to do nothing of the sort."

The colored woman straightened her back and stood with her scissors poised over the dress material, while she looked at Mary with an expression of singular intelligence. "Why not, Madam?"

"Because, Lizzie, here's my first chance to do something for the war, for my country. The newspapers are always insinuating that I'm giving information to the Secessionists. I think some of the members of Mr. Lincoln's Cabinet believe that my sympathies are Southern. If I catch Miss Ford, it will prove I'm not. See!" She looked eagerly at the colored woman. "I'm so lonely, Lizzie. Now that Mr. Lincoln has reached the White House, my occupation's gone."

"The war has upset everything," Lizzie nodded.

"Well, call it that if you wish," the Mistress of the White House mused sadly for a moment, then said, energetically, "I shall find out what her little game is and beat her at it. I need her, socially. She probably thinks she needs me to get information from me. Very well, dog eat dog, as Mr. Lincoln would say. You'll see that I'm just as clever as Miss Ford."

"You have as much brain, and are better educated. That's just the way I hoped you'd take it!" A sudden smile lighted the colored woman's habitually tragic eyes. "And you've got Jinny and me to help you."

"You haven't mentioned this to any one else, have you, Lizzie?"

"No, Madam President, certainly not."

"Then don't, until I tell you to. . . . So that's why—" Mary suddenly felt hurt and lonely. . . . "I'm just realizing another angle, Lizzie. I thought she liked me,—and I do so need a companion."

"She must like you," declared Mrs. Keckley, stoutly. "Any one who gets to know you real well does. But Miss Ford or any other old-time Southerner isn't going to lose her slaves without fighting for 'em, tooth and claw."

Miss Ford returned in time for tea, the following afternoon. This was a function the Virginian herself had established in the family sitting room. Hither, from four to six o'clock, repaired many members of the exhausted official family, and any Congressman or other caller whom the young secretaries, collaborating with Mrs. Lincoln or Miss Ford, thought worth the attention.

During the early summer, the tea hour had become an essential part of the day's routine. Lincoln liked the idea. He loved any informal opportunity to play host. He strolled in and out of the room, as mood and opportunity permitted. He seldom came alone. Sometimes he brought in a distracted woman, weeping over son or husband caught by the war, and turned her over to his wife for tea, and the kindly word she knew so well how to give. Frequently he dragged forward by the arm a bashful soldier. Once, his guest was a Fox Indian in full regalia, and at another time a festive, white haired and illiterate old tramp, who claimed to have known the President as a boy. Several times he was accompanied by the suave M. Mercier, the French Minister, or Lord Lyons, a little condescending.

On the afternoon of Miss Ford's return there was a violent thunderstorm that thinned the throng which usually filled the house, and permitted a fuller attendance at tea, than usual, of the President's associates.

Standing in one of the windows was Seward, arguing violently with Charles Sumner on the matter of Seward's last exchange of insolences with Great Britain. Sumner knew the men then governing England, personally and intimately, and was often in despair, he frequently told Lincoln, over Seward's ignorant tactlessness.

"Father" Welles was seated before the flower-filled fireplace, pulling at his white beard, as he listened to John Hay's opinion of the battle of Bull Run.

Mr. Chase, seated on a couch with his pretty daughter Kate on one side of him, and William Russell on the other, was laying down the law concerning the abilities of John Frémont, whom Lincoln lately had appointed to head up the military department of the West, with headquarters at St. Louis. His sonorous phrasing did not entirely silence the rest of the room, until he was heard to say suddenly to Russell:

"My dear sir, I hear that a Union soldier fired at you when he read your name on your pass yesterday."

All conversation ceased as every one waited for Russell's reply. The Englishman replied coolly. "Yes, it appears that telling the truth is a crime, in this country."

"What did you really do, Mr. Russell?" cried Mary from the tea table. "I've heard that people are saying worse things about you than about me. I can't imagine what vocabulary they are drawing from!"

"I did the usual thing for war correspondents, I fancy, Madam President! I rode out into Virginia with the idea of getting as close as possible to the battle supposed to be raging at Manassas Junction. I was still several miles from the scene of the main action at Bull Run, when I was stopped by fleeing Union soldiers and officers. They literally clogged the roads. Then I wrote to my paper, the London *Times*, what I observed, no more and no less. Last week, the New York *Times* copied my account. Other papers immediately followed suit, branded me as a liar, as having maliciously maligned your glorious troops, as having questioned their bravery. It appears now that the whole country is in full cry against me. I have been christened Bull Run Russell and I have no friends left except—"

He paused, and, with the others, rose as Mr. Lincoln led an officer into the room.

The newcomer was about thirty-five years of age. He was under middle height, but powerfully built, square shouldered, thick throated, with slightly bowed legs. His head, which was covered with heavy auburn hair, was well set, his features regular, with a remarkably determined jaw beneath a reddish brown mustache. His forehead was furrowed. His eyes, a beautiful deep blue, were a little wistful in expression. His whole personality was one of extraordinary charm.

"Mrs. Lincoln," said the President, "this is the new commander of the Army of the Potomac, General McClellan. Miss Ford, I think you said you knew the General. And this is Senator Sumner and here's England, in the shape of Russell. By jings, Russell, you'd better not repeat your opinion of our glorious troops to McClellan, or he'll refuse you a correspondent's privilege."

McClellan looked up into the big Britisher's broad face. "You ought to know something about soldiers if you're the Russell I think you are," he said courteously.

Russell bowed. "I saw you last in the Crimea, sir."

"When you loaned me the only decent horse I'd ridden in a month, sir!" McClellan turned to Lincoln. "That was in 1855, when Jefferson Davis was Secretary of War. He sent three of us to study the operations in the Crimea. . . . So your opinion of my new army is not high? Well, I'm in agreement with you. Come to my headquarters, and I'll tell you how I plan to make a real fighting machine of it."

"There was an officer in, to-day," said Lincoln, sinking into a chair beside Miss Ford, "who told me I was all wrong, that Bull Run wasn't a defeat for the North. As near as I could make out, from his report, our men had licked the Rebels and then had run away."

A general laugh greeted this and the various broken conversations were taken up again. McClellan smiled at Miss Ford, as he took a chair near her. "I recall your telling me that you were keeping strange company, for a Ford of Virginia!" he exclaimed. "Just what are you doing, Lady? I forget details!"

"Earning my living as Mrs. Lincoln's social assistant, and incidentally trying to influence the President on the side of not dealing too harshly with us poor slaveholders," replied the Virginian, with a little smile at Lincoln.

The President returned the smile as he accepted a cup of tea from Mary. "She's influencing all of us, McClellan, one way or another. John Hay writes poetry to her, don't you, John?"

Young Hay blushed but showed no other sign of confusion. "The competition between Russell and myself is very sharp, sir. Russell has every advantage save that of poetic genius."

"So you admit your genius!" exclaimed Mary.

"Certainly!" retorted Hay. "But I've a notion, if Miss Ford continues to be so cold, to get a commission as a major-general."

Everybody laughed, McClellan adding, "Come to me for your training, Hay. I'll see that you're made regimental poet. A minstrel in uniform ought to outrank Russell at every point."

"I see I've got to revise my strategy," declared Russell, looking at Miss Ford with an enigmatic expression in his keen eyes.

"I'm quite sufficiently entranced by your present tactics," drawled the Virginian. "I reckon the ladies in the Crimea, if there were any, must have given you a wonderful schooling, Mr. Russell."

John Hay groaned, and again every one laughed. Russell turned to McClellan. "I shall be glad to avail myself of your invitation, General. When is one apt to find you least busy?"

"Never!" smiled McClellan. "So come when you will. The amount of work to be accomplished is stupendous, but I glory in the thought of it. As if the military details were not enough, the President has been impressing me with the political significance of my work. I find myself in a new and a strange position here! President, Cabinet and General Scott all deferring to me. By some strange operation of magic, I seem to have become the power of the land."

Miss Ford, who had been leaning toward him over the tea table, drinking in his every word, gave a little sigh. Mary exchanged a look with William Russell. Charles Sumner, who had broken off his conversation with Seward to listen to the conversation round the tea table, rose abruptly. "There's certainly been a grave mistake made in this hasty choice," he said in a low voice to the Secretary of State.

"Lincoln seldom misjudges his man," replied Seward, in the same tone.

Sumner shrugged his shoulders, and took his leave.

McClellan, after a short exchange of Fairfax Courthouse memories with Miss Ford, rose also. Lincoln took him by the arm.

"Mustn't work too hard, my boy! Too much depends on you. Before you leave, let me show you my map."

He led McClellan into his bedroom, and brought him to pause before the war map which showed by the pins both the ideal "Anaconda" plans, and the actual campaign in progress.

McClellan's blue eyes swept the map intelligently, but cursorily. "Scott's plan has an essential weakness," he said. "As long as we are so heavily outnumbered by the enemy, the coils of the snake will be ineffectual. We must have men, more men, training, and more training. Then I propose to carry this thing *en grand* and crush the Rebels in one campaign."

Lincoln moved uneasily, picked up "Halleck" and laid it down, then quoted good humoredly, "If it were done when 'tis done—then 'twere well it were done quickly."

"Aphorisms won't make an army move," rather contemptuously from the young General, Lincoln thought. "You'll really have to excuse me now, sir. I have some immensely important matters to attend to, to-night."

"Of course you have," agreed the President gently. "Good night, my boy. God speed you in your great task."

Lincoln felt a real sense of relief, with McClellan actually heading the demoralized Army of the Potomac, and after the tea party he yielded to Mary's pleas and consented to spend the night at the Soldiers' Home. He asked William Russell to come along, so, with Mary and Miss Ford, the barouche was full.

The country road was beautiful in the twilight, and for a time there was silence while each of the four enjoyed, in his or her own way, the surcease from the turmoil of the Capital. It was not until the stars were shut out by the great branches of oak and tulip trees that Mary said thoughtfully:

"I wonder what Mrs. McClellan's honest opinion is of her husband."

Russell laughed. "My dear Mrs. Lincoln, what a terrible thought!"

"Not at all!" retorted Mary. "I assure you that my honest opinion of my husband is a very pleasant thing to contemplate."

She was sitting beside Lincoln, and at her stout declaration, he dropped his great hand on her knee.

"We're not going to give you any praise for that," exclaimed Miss Ford. "Are we, Mr. Russell?"

"Certainly not," replied the Englishman. "I claim to be able to pass a very creditable examination myself on the pleasant opinion side. I might go further than you, even, Madam President, having had a wider experience with men."

"Hear! Hear!" chuckled the President. "What a delightful evening I'm having!"

"Well, Mr. Russell, with your wider experience of men, what do you think of General McClellan?" asked Mary.

"A man of most felicitous social gifts," replied the correspondent.

"Oh, don't be irritating!" urged Mary. "No one is going to quote you."

"Let's have it, William!" said Lincoln, abruptly, realizing suddenly that there was no one whose opinion he'd rather have.

"William! Mercy, how familiar!" commented Mary.

"Please!" protested Russell. "I can't tell you how complimented I felt—if it means what I hope it means."

"It means I look on you as one of the few disinterested friends I possess, if you want plain truth, by jings!" Lincoln lifted his hand from Mary's tiny knee and banged it down on the Englishman's mighty one. "Now, boy, let's have it."

"His appointment is bound to be popular. He has the points that make for personal popularity. But all he's done to gain his exalted position is to have some skirmishes with bands of Confederates in West Virginia. Is he your best bet, Mr. Lincoln, as you Americans say?"

"Yes," answered the President, thinking of the long hours spent in reviewing all the available material.

"What of Frémont, sir?" asked Russell. "He is at least a more picturesque figure for popular purposes, after his western explorations. He's quite the rage in England."

"Well, I'll tell you one single fact about Frémont," replied Lincoln. "Blair and other of my Cabinet members, and General Scott, were all positive that Frémont, with the Senator Benton following in St. Louis, would do wonders at cleaning up the mess out West. I gave him his appointment the first of July. He stayed in New York three weeks, fussing over some private matters, and Blair and the rest of his backers never got him started for St. Louis until yesterday. He did so with every hour as important to the North out there as a century of ordinary time! Poor Blair got so he squirmed himself out of excuses, when I'd ask him, night and morning, 'Frémont launched yet?' " Lincoln laughed dolefully.

"And what was your opinion of General McClellan, Miss Ford?" asked Mary.

"He's a delightful person. Also, I would guess, a fine executive. My cousin knows of his work for the Illinois Central."

"Humph!" sniffed Mary. "Well, I'll tell you what I think of him."

"Don't, Mary!" protested Lincoln. "You have an awful gift for prophesying the truth about folks."

Mary gave no heed. "George McClellan is already too conceited to see straight, and he's a coward. I know the way his lips quirk and shake."

"He's no coward. I've known him since his West Point days," contradicted Miss Ford.

"Humph!" replied Mary, impolitely.

The carriage turned up the driveway to the house, the boys and the pups tumbled noisily to meet the visitors, and no one spoke of McClellan again that evening.

CHAPTER XII

LIZZIE KECKLEY

LIZZIE KECKLEY, cutting out a red merino cloak for the Mistress of the White House, had a few words to say about Miss Ford's trip to Fairfax Courthouse, a day or so after the Virginian's return to Washington.

"Jinny says," relieving her mouth of half a dozen pins, "that Miss Ford met an old friend named Captain Taylor out at the Ford's plantation. Jinny listened under the window. She says they were rejoicing over the turn things took at Bull Run, but mostly they were conjecturing about how the President stands on interfering with slavery. They'd heard that General Frémont had said to Horace Greeley, up in New York, that when he got out to St. Louis he was going to pronounce all the slaves in Missouri free, and they were wondering what Mr. Lincoln would do if that happened. Miss Ford, she said Frémont would be assassinated if he tried that foolishness."

Mary turned white. "Don't talk assassination ever in my presence, Lizzie. I live in a bloody shadow. The President constantly is threatened with that!"

"I'm sorry, Madam. I won't again. It seems Miss Ford didn't go out so much to give as to get news. She wanted to hear all about how soon Bull Run made the Secesh leaders feel they would end the war. She kept saying if it didn't end quick, Mr. Sumner would get the slavery issue into it."

"Lizzie," asked Mary, "why has Jinny turned against her mistress, like this?"

"You remember that day you all saw Zeb shoot himself? Well, Zeb was Jinny's husband."

"Ah!" Mary shook her head thoughtfully. "Slavery *is* a wicked thing."

There was little here, Mary felt, to rouse further suspicions regarding the Virginian. Certainly, that astute person was behaving admirably, during these feverish August days. With the letdown of social activities that followed McDowell's disaster, she began to give time to the two little boys, taking walks with them, joining them in games of croquet, reading Peter Parley to Tad and to Willie, Scott's "Lay of the Last Minstrel." The children liked her.

Lincoln had not forgotten his thought of sending Miss Ford to Kentucky, but the stress of trying to force action on the part of his military leaders, thrust the thought into the background during August. Even the pertinacity of the Virginian was unable to break through the absorption with which the President studied the prosecution of the war, until chance permitted her to catch him, one moonlit evening, returning from the war office.

She waylaid him under the trees near the north portico. "Kentucky!" she exclaimed, laughingly.

"Jings! You're right! Kentucky!" he replied. "If I fail in my military harvest, I ought to try the harder to bring in political sheaves, eh!"

"Well, Mr. President, August yielded the Union forts, Hatteras and Clark!" suggested Miss Ford.

"Mere flea bites and you know it, Miss Ford!" protested Lincoln, moving toward the door, with the Virginian on his arm. "So you really still want to help me about Kentucky?"

"What should change me?" she inquired, looking archly up into his face, as they entered the hall.

Lincoln smiled, but perfunctorily. She was beautiful and likeable, he told himself, but whenever she actually entered his consciousness, he saw Zeb's poor blasted face over her shoulder. Nevertheless, he believed she might give him real help in Kentucky.

"Come up to my office for a few moments," he said. "I can give you your instruction right now, and you can get going, to-morrow or next day."

The heat was extraordinary. The President's office was full of mosquitoes and great moths, buzzing around the lights. Miss Ford set her fan to work the moment she had settled her white organdy ruffles on the little sofa. Lincoln unbuttoned his white linen coat and vest, ran his fingers through his wet black hair, and sank slowly to his desk chair.

"Kentucky worries me," he sighed. "I reckon part of my withered old heart never will leave my native state. It will hurt me forever if she doesn't come over grandly to the Union side. I've sent a pair of good Kentuckians out there. Major Anderson, who's recruiting for me—"

"His name spells magic, since Sumter, of course," interrupted Miss Ford.

Lincoln nodded. "The other emissary is Navy Lieutenant William Nelson! You've seen him playing about here with John Hay. He has the social gifts Kentucky appreciates. I've given him leave of absence and sent him to Kentucky, without instructions. Then, there's my dear friend James Speed of Louisville. He is—"

Lincoln suddenly paused. Something in the deep violet eyes, looking so clearly into his, tore his thoughts for the moment from the spheres of influence he was establishing in Kentucky. For the first time in the course of his acquaintanceship it occurred to him that Miss Ford liked him, that her scorn, her earlier patronizing manner, had been replaced by respect and almost, he might have sworn, affection. If this were the case, he need not guard his statements, limiting them to facts all the world knew, as he had been doing. If she now respected and liked him, her loyalty would not be so open to question,—always, of course, remembering that she was a slaveholder.

"What is troubling you, sir?" asked the Virginian, in her soft, slow tones.

"Well, I was thinking that your attitude had changed toward me. That you weren't looking on me so much as the toy jumping jack, jerked by Seward and Sumner, as you did at first, and in that case, I'd tell you something more about conditions out yonder."

"Why should you think I could look on you so?" exclaimed the Virginian, indignantly.

"Oh, come, Miss Ford," Lincoln smiled at her. "I can see through a stone fence as far as any one! I'd like to possess McClellan's ways, or young Nelson's, and I know just how you ladies feel toward me."

"If you knew how I felt toward you, you'd be ashamed of your last three or four statements," retorted Miss Ford.

"That's good! I'm obliged to you, Miss Ford," feeling that, for once, she was showing him the side most remote from her devotion to slavery. "This being so, I'll talk to you about Frémont. Kentucky has its eye on the General. If he keeps on fooling with emancipation of the slaves, Kentucky will kick over the traces, and secession will get her. If he does go very far in that direction, I'll abrogate whatever he does!"

The Virginian smiled. "Good! There's where your hard common sense speaks."

"There's where I'm trying to soothe your slavery qualms," thought the President. Aloud, he said, "Of course, Frémont may listen to my warnings, that is, if Mrs. Frémont will back me. She's old Benton's daughter and ought to have been a man. She's handsome as they make 'em, and she's Frémont's boss. Now, then, didn't I hear you say that you'd met her?"

"For once, I must fail you on an acquaintance, sir," shaking her head, "but we have many mutual friends. I know that she knows me, very well."

"Good! You go out to St. Louis and make Mrs. Frémont make her spouse see sense about emancipation in its effect on Kentucky, to say nothing of Missouri."

"I like that errand. Like the other one, I can do it with perfect honesty!" cried Miss Ford.

"It's the sort of errand I aim to give people," said Lincoln, rising with a weary sigh.

Miss Ford swept slowly toward the door, where she paused to say, with convincing sincerity,

"I hope nothing will ever happen to prevent my doing such constructive work as this." The door swung gently after her, and Lincoln went to bed.

Acting on her usual plan of confiding nothing of her personal affairs to any woman, Miss Ford merely asked Mrs. Lincoln for permission to have a two weeks' leave of absence, for business reasons, and she was gone before it occurred to the President that Mary should have been consulted. When, the evening after the Virginian's departure, Mary said at supper, with a sigh,

"Poor Miss Ford had to go off again. I do miss her so!" Lincoln, with the guilty adroitness of a long-married husband, looked sympathetic, shook his head and asked Mary how her garden was coming along.

It was Lizzie Keckley with a letter from Jinny in St. Louis who roused Mary's slumbering suspicions. Not that the report told of Miss Ford's being engaged in any but loyal activities, but it stated that Mrs. Frémont's maid had heard Mrs. Frémont speak of Miss Ford as Mr. Lincoln's unofficial emissary.

Mary's quick temper flared. She tore the letter in half and, with the pieces in her hands, flew to find her husband. John Hay, looking up from his shabby desk, in the still shabbier secretaries' office, looked troubled as he saw the fury in Mrs. Lincoln's eye.

"The President is in conference with Mr. Seward and Mr. Cameron," he said. "They are in great trouble. Word has just reached us that General Frémont has issued a proclamation freeing all the slaves belonging to rebels in the State of Missouri. Looks as if we'd lose the border states to secession, in spite of the way the President has been nursing them along."

"Yes, and do you realize that Miss Ford is out there,—as one of Mr. Lincoln's nurses,—that he's trusted that spy! That's what comes of his ceasing to confide in me." Mary shook the torn letter before John's anxious and abashed gaze.

"Oh, do you think that, too," he exclaimed.

"Too!" cried Mary. "What do you mean, John Hay? Don't try to soothe me!"

"I want to soothe you just enough so that you'll let me confide in you about Miss Ford, dear Madam President," retorted the young man. "But if you frighten me to death, the confidences, of course, will be lost to you and the world forever!"

In spite of herself, Mary's blue eyes twinkled. "I'm glad I'm formidable to some one!" she exclaimed.

"Formidable! My poor knees are clacking together like the clapper bones in a minstrel show. When you came in, I thought I was to be beheaded. Now I hope for nothing worse than forty years in the Tower!" He was leading her slowly toward Nicolay's empty chair, as he chattered. "How lovely that purple dress is! Have I seen it before? What is it made of, poplin?"

"It's a lavender print, goose. Come, John, I'm sorry I showed temper, but really—that man—"

"What's the poor old Tycoon done now?" asked John, looking at her with an affectionate smile. "How do you like my new name for him? We are corresponding at present with the Tycoon of Japan, concerning treaty ports. Nicolay and I think the title just suits our blessed War Chief."

"You ought to watch him more closely than you do, John, or he won't be a Tycoon long. Now listen to me! I must tell this or burst."

She gave him a concise account of Lizzie Keckley's and Jinny's reports on Miss Ford. She was a remarkable raconteur and John Hay, in spite of an anxious scowl, chuckled many times during the recital. When the story was done, he told her of the seemingly trivial incidents that had made him uneasy regarding the beautiful Virginian.

"And what's more, I think William Russell shares my suspicions," he ended.

"But I thought you both were more or less in love with her!" exclaimed Mary.

Hay grinned. "So we are, in a comfortable sort of way. She's quite a perfect object to which to devote verses."

"Oh! That!" Mary shrugged the plump shoulders across which the lavender print was draped so gracefully. "Will you tell Mr. Lincoln, or shall I, John? I don't relish the job, now I'm cooled down. He does trust his friends so!"

John sighed. "I'll tell him, of course, but he'll wish to follow it up with you and Lizzie."

"I suppose so," echoing his sigh, as she left the office.

She got her moment with the President, just before he started for a tour of inspection of the fortifications McClellan was throwing up around the city. He listened to her intently, shaking his head in a troubled way.

"I've been uneasy about her, ever since the Zeb episode. I thought she was actually growing friendly, though, I still was a little uneasy. I fixed this job in St. Louis so if she wasn't playing fair, she'd be pretty sure to stub her toe and show her petticoat."

"What are you going to do about it?" urged Mary, anxiously.

"Wait for her to show her petticoat," he replied, stooping to kiss the troubled face. "There's going to be several folks talk too much, shortly. I sent a letter to Frémont to-day, abrogating his freeing of the slaves."

"Well, Abra'm, even after twenty years, you do beat me!" exclaimed his wife. "I thought I had to protect you from her!—You keep out of the sun all you can, this afternoon."

"Yes, ma'am," replied the President, meekly.

There was, indeed, a flood of talk set loose by Lincoln's abrogation of Frémont's act. All the Abolitionists in Congress immediately were about the President's ears. Charles Sumner could not contain himself for indignation. He was in New York when he heard of Lincoln's action, but the moment he returned to Washington he called his carriage and galloped to the White House. That it happened to lack but a half hour to midnight made no impression on him.

Lincoln was in his bedroom, in his nightshirt and slippers,—the night was stifling,—reading *Petroleum Nasby* on War. He was shrieking with laughter, as Sumner burst unceremoniously in at the door.

"Mr. Lincoln! How could you?" groaned Sumner, dramatically casting his high hat and the newspaper report of Lincoln's letter together on the table.

"Jings! Listen to this, Charles! How does the fellow think of such gags?"

While Sumner walked the floor, groaning, the President read aloud the paragraph which he had so enjoyed. Then he pulled off his spectacles, and placed them in the pamphlet. "If I didn't laugh at least once a day, Charles, I'd cut my throat. What's on your mind?"

Sumner tossed his great arms into the air, and replied, with a voice that shook the chandelier: "How idle to possess the power of a god, and not to use it godlike! A vain masquerade of battles, a flux of blood and treasure and nothing done! This was your great moment, and you cast it back in the teeth of the man who gave it to you!"

"Meaning John Frémont? I've had a lot of trouble with that fellow." Lincoln thrust a long, bare leg over the arm of his chair, and shook his head. He was sorry that Sumner had come to him at such a weary moment of the day, but, since he was here, it would be best to arrive at a clear understanding with the great Abolitionist.

"Frémont's proclamation," he said, "is simply dictatorship. It assumes that a general may do anything he pleases, political as well as military. Frémont's proclamation was not an act of military necessity, but based on his own political desires. Did I not abrogate this act, I should be surrendering the government by permitting a general to make permanent rules of property."

"Quibbling!" cried the Senator. "Legal quibbling that every day gives moral support to the rebellion!"

"Charles, use a little Yankee sense along with your oratory. The Kentucky legislature wouldn't budge in our favor until I modified Frémont's proclamation. To lose Kentucky was to lose Missouri and Maryland, and the job on our hands would be too large for us. We would as well consent to separation at once, including the surrender of this Capital. But the revocation of Frémont's decree has saved Kentucky to the Union, and placed forty thousand soldiers in the Union Army."

"I have no patience with the undue influence the border states are having on this administration—" Sumner was interrupted by the sudden opening of the hall door.

A fine looking woman in a sweeping black silk dress, her dark hair looped over her ears, a gray veil thrown back over her tiny bonnet, swooped into the room. Miss Ford in a green silk traveling cloak, and a broad green hat with sweeping plume followed her. Sumner gave an agonized glance at Lincoln's nightshirt. With astounding quickness, he tossed the dressing robe from the bed to the President's knees, while Miss Ford performed a breathless introduction:

"Mr. Lincoln, may I present Mrs. John Frémont who—"

Mrs. Frémont interrupted. "Who has come from St. Louis, without rest or sleep, to demand an immediate explanation of your brutality to her husband. Why have you dared—"

"Just a moment, Madam!" protested Lincoln. "A man in his nightshirt is at a disadvantage in an interview of this sort, as my friend Sumner has tactfully suggested. But if the general public insists on using my bedroom as a reception hall, I'm the last man in these United States to protest."

He pulled on the robe slowly as he continued, "Mrs. Frémont, this is Senator Charles Sumner."

Mrs. Frémont bowed, but the rush of her anger could not be checked or diverted, and, with a sigh, Lincoln, long trained in the symptoms of feminine hysteria, gave her her way.

"You have dared to send Montgomery Blair out to St. Louis to spy on John Frémont—A *Blair!* Not fit to black my husband's boots. Isn't that true, sir?"

"The Blairs, when the war began," replied Lincoln, mildly, "could think of nothing but Frémont. At their earnest recommendations and solicitations, he was made a general and sent to St. Louis."

"I don't believe it! I don't believe they've ever been anything but his enemies," cried Mrs. Frémont.

"One moment, Mrs. Frémont!" Miss Ford put a firm hand on the older woman's arm. "You forgot yourself when you broke into this room at midnight. You are still further forgetting yourself when you give Mr. Lincoln the lie. He's not only President of the United States, but he's also not the kind of a man you speak so to!"

"Abe Lincoln?" cried Mrs. Frémont. "From the backwoods on the Sangamon? This is his kind of language!"

"I'll not tolerate this!" ejaculated the Virginian, drawing herself to her fine height, and looking extraordinarily handsome in the flickering candle-light. "When you asked me to introduce you to the President, I did not agree to acquiesce to your insulting him."

"Don't worry, Miss Ford," said Lincoln. "I'm a hard person to insult. Give her her head for a little. Sometimes it cures 'em."

Mrs. Frémont who had been nervously ransacking the little silk bag she carried, now shook a letter in Lincoln's face, and demanded of him, in exchange for it, any letters he may have had from Frank or Montgomery Blair concerning her husband.

The room was poorly lighted. Lincoln had been reading by a single candle, the light of which flickered on his hollow cheeks, his tender lips, the shadowed gray eyes daily growing more shadowed. Sumner looked from this beautiful and ugly face, at which so shortly before he himself had glared in anger, to the quivering, half-maddened features of John Frémont's wife, and, even in the dim candle glow, one could see him flush. His own great egotism melted as it had melted many times before in Lincoln's presence.

"Whatever the President has done at least has been done properly, and I for one—" He tried to be heard above Mrs. Frémont, but failed.

The door from Mary's room opened and Mary, in her pink boudoir gown, appeared. She was carrying her candle. She placed it on the reading table, then stood beside Sumner, listening.

For perhaps five minutes Mrs. Frémont rushed on, reciting the history of her husband's course, denouncing his accusers, demanding retractions, apologies and new commissions. No one interrupted her, until, with eyes filled with tears of weariness and indignation, she declared:

"You are merely jealous. You know that if John C. Frémont wished, he could have your place here in the White House." There Mary took a step toward her.

"Madam!" she began.

Lincoln touched his wife on the shoulder. "Mary, be silent!" he said, giving her what she called his "look of granite." She subsided. But Miss Ford did not recognize the look, or at least she refused to apply it to herself.

She seized Mrs. Frémont by both wrists and shook her, vigorously. She was furiously angry, herself.

"Do you mean to say, Mrs. Frémont, that that weak, vacillating man of yours could ever hope to hold the reins here? Don't you know that it would require a man of twice General Frémont's mental stature, and ten times his military skill? And don't you realize by now that Lincoln is a consummate politician, that he's never going to alienate the Southern Unionists by setting the slaves free?"

Mrs. Frémont whirled so impetuously on the Virginian that her crinolines knocked *Petroleum Nasby* off the table. The President rescued his spectacles and the pamphlet, giving the latter a little pat as he laid it down.

"If you were so sure of that, Madam," shrieked Mrs. Frémont, "why did you try by every sly method to encourage my husband to issue that edict of freedom?"

"Your insinuations are utterly false, Madam Frémont!" cried the Virginian, furiously.

"You shall not give me the lie! I was bred in politics and I understand political intrigue, even when it's far more cleverly handled than yours, Miss Ford," ejaculated Mrs. Frémont. "But whatever is your motive, your scheming will fail. No one can be the head of this government who will not before long agree to free the slaves if the Union forces win."

"Your husband will never be that head, notwithstanding the machine you are building in Missouri, to that end," drawled Miss Ford.

"Nor will George McClellan, in spite of your favor, Madam," retorted Mrs. Frémont. "No one can become a real leader of this Union who is afraid to free the slaves."

"No man can attempt to free the slaves in this country and not be assassinated," drawled Miss Ford.

There was a moment of appalled silence, broken by Sumner. "Miss Ford, dare you so to malign your countrymen? Dare you?"

The Virginian tossed him a haughty look, in which sparkled a considerable degree of contempt. "Your fanaticism is as absurd, Charles, as Horace Greeley's. The only difference is that you thunder in the open, where any one can come back at you, while Greeley screams his invectives and then runs to hide under the bed. But both of you are alike in mistaking the temper of this country as regards the freeing of slaves. Am I not right, Mr. Lincoln?"

But Jessie Frémont was not to be permanently turned from her quarry. Startled into silence for a moment by Miss Ford's abrupt suggestion, she revived and returned with renewed vigor to her attack on the President. He watched her with weary patience, until she threw the letter from her husband in his face. He picked this up, and thrust it into the pocket of his dressing gown. Then he shook his finger before Mrs. Frémont's eyes so suddenly that she caught her breath. He quickly made his statement:

"Madam, you have taxed me so violently with many things that I've had to exercise all the awkward tact I have to avoid quarreling with you. I will answer the general's letter by mail. Kindly make no attempt to prolong or repeat this interview. And now, good night, everybody. I'm going to bed."

He picked up his candle, nodding his head at Mary. She at once lifted hers, made a sweeping bow and left the room. Charles Sumner took one of Mrs. Frémont's arms, Miss Ford, the other, and thus they forced the protesting, half weeping woman out the door. Lincoln listened to her voice receding down the hall, then he blew out his candle and got into bed.

LINCOLN'S waking thought, the next morning, was that if he was in for an unpleasant session with Miss Ford, he'd better have done with it as soon as possible. The Virginian, apparently, was at one with him as to the value of speed, for she met him in the garden, whither he slipped for a breath of air before breakfast. She wore the green traveling suit and carried a little reticule filled with papers.

Lincoln, standing under a copper beech, hands clasped behind his back, watched her sweep up the path, her poise unassailable, he thought.

"Good morning, Mr. President! That was a horrid scene you were inflicted with, last night. I tried my utmost to persuade her to leave it till morning. But all I could do was to follow her and try to protect you from the worst."

"Can't blame Mrs. Frémont for fighting for her General," replied Lincoln. "You were the one I needed protection from!"

"I?" raising her eyebrows.

"Why did you try double dealing in St. Louis, Miss Ford?" laying a great hand on her shoulder and looking into her fine eyes. "Do the slaves mean more to you than honor?"

She flushed painfully but returned his look. "I was not double dealing in St. Louis. I gave you the chance to show your stand on slavery and thus save Kentucky. Didn't it swing the legislature immediately for the Union?"

Lincoln gazed at her with a curious sort of admiration. If her influence had counted with Frémont, she had done just that! But what was her motive? He dropped his hand from her shoulders, and bowed his head in thought. The Virginian watched him with a smile half wistful, half determined, touching her lips.

His suspicions were thoroughly roused about her, now, but he did not think it would be wise summarily to dismiss her. She was a person of distinguished friendships. She was herself a personage. He proposed to know exactly what her business in the White House might be. He was convinced that this was no ordinary spy case, such as the chief of the National Detective Police might handle successfully.

"Perhaps it helped," he agreed, reluctantly. "Suppose you give me the report on your work out there."

"I have written it out for you," she said, "because I have to go immediately to our plantation. My father is ill. I hope to be back in a couple of days."

"Very well," replied the President. "I'll go over the whole matter with

you, on your return." He shook hands with her, with a distinct sense of
relief. Jinny and Mrs. Keckley were as competent as Baker to watch the
Virginian, outside the White House.

He read her report at breakfast, handing it over afterward to Mary. It
was a remarkably keen diagnosis of the whole complicated situation in
Missouri, where not only was North contending with South, but where conservative and radical Northerners, as the pro-slavery and anti-slavery forces
were called, fought bitterly one with the other. Lincoln, for months, had
been obliged to interfere personally, in an endeavor to force sufficient
harmony to save the people of the State from the lawlessness and crime
that prevailed.

Miss Ford passed lightly over these facts, long known, of course, to the
President. But she gave details that the President had not heard as yet,
of the bitter personal quarrel between Frémont and the highly influential
family of Blairs, who were loyal to the administration, intensely eager to
hold their much loved Missouri to the Union. The blame for this, Miss
Ford laid squarely on the shoulders of Frémont. This was important information if true. But still more important for the President's attempt to
analyze Miss Ford's obscure motives, was the suggestion that closed her
report.

She thought that General McClellan should be sent to Missouri for a
month, to clean up the civil as well as the military chaos that reigned in
the State.

"I wonder," was Lincoln's comment as he gave the document to John
Hay, when he reached his office, "just how far-reaching her friendship for
George McClellan is."

Young Hay took the paper with a look of interest. "I heard that she
was back, Mr. President, very much so!" with a grin. Then he nodded toward the reception room. "There's a group of reporters out there, sir,
champing on the bit and snorting. General McClellan has issued another
of his mad, sad statements, and they want your opinion on it. Among
others, is the fellow I ordered last spring not to come here again, the
one that accredited a vile joke to you about one of your Cabinet members.
I told him you wouldn't see him, but he showed me a glowing letter
from Miss Ford, introducing him to you."

Lincoln flushed. That evil pun had made him infinite trouble with
Secretary Chase, who had refused to believe Lincoln's repudiation of its
authorship.

"It makes me just as mad to be accused of telling smutty stories as it
would be if they called me a bawd, out and out," he declared, angrily.

Young Hay took an eager step toward his chief. "You see, sir, you have
the reputation, already passing into legend, of being incapable of losing
your temper, even of feeling righteous indignation. A fellow like this
Gordon trades on that reputation, or he'd never dare to come near you.
Now I've seen you hopping mad, several times, and it has a most salutary
effect on every one."

"Bring him in here to me, John," said Lincoln. "They can accuse me of drunkenness, of treachery to my party, they may call me an ape and a clodhopper and a fool, and I can keep silence. But when it comes to saying I deal in smut—well, we can't stop the spread of the poison now, but I can show one of the carriers what I think of it. Bring Mr. "Obscene" Gordon in here."

John rushed from the room and returned at once, followed by a young-ish man, handsome in a florid, loose-lipped fashion, dressed in the most immaculate of gray linen suits.

"This, Mr. President," said Hay, "is the reporter of whom I spoke to you last spring."

Gordon nodded his head familiarly to the President. "Say, Lincoln, what is your comment on the report that McClellan has said, 'I would cheerfully take the dictatorship and agree to lay down my life when the country is saved'?"

"Have you credentials, Mr. Gordon, giving your title to my con-fidences?" asked Lincoln.

"Oh, didn't think you were particular. I'm from the New York *World* and here's a letter from a friend of yours and the Madam's." The young man handed the President a note which he took and very deliberately putting on his spectacles, read:

"Dear Mr. Lincoln: All my friends are not Southerners. Some of them belong to New York and Boston. Mr. Gordon's father and mine have been business associates in a remote way. Mr. Gordon's brother carries on his father's business. Mr. Ethan Gordon, who presents this to you, is a brilliant newspaper writer who has a large following of readers. May I presume to suggest that his friendly understanding of your Administration would be of great political value to you.

I am, dear Mr. Lincoln, with most respectful and humble salutations, the least of the secretaries,

ANNABEL FORD."

Lincoln passed the letter to Hay. "Keep that with her report, John." Then he turned to Gordon. "About that nasty pun on Mr. Secretary Chase, you spread abroad as coming from me. I don't like it, Mr. Gordon. It is not an open sesame to my confidence."

Gordon laughed. "But it was witty, you'll admit, Lincoln. You ought to be glad to have it believed you fathered it. I'll never give you away, if that's the angle of it you don't like."

Lincoln's great hands twitched. "Open the door, John," he ordered. With astounding quickness, one of his long arms shot out. He seized Gordon by the coat collar, and twisted him toward the door. Then he lifted his long leg in the enormous carpet slipper, and a second later Gordon catapulted into the midst of the astounded reporters milling about Billy Stoddard's desk.

"There," sighed Lincoln, "that didn't do him a might of harm, and it did me a lot of good. Let the others in now, John."

It was after he had finished a pleasant ten minutes with the newspaper men that one of McClellan's aides, who had witnessed Gordon's hasty departure from Lincoln's presence, came in and ventured a comment.

"Mr. President, that fellow Gordon is in a position to do you a lot of harm, if he wants to. He's a popular war correspondent."

"You know him well?" inquired Lincoln. "Like his stories?"

"I've never met him, sir, though I suppose I shall. He's a great friend of General McClellan's, and has free entrance to his councils."

"I'm sorry to hear that," was Lincoln's comment. "What can I do for you, Captain?"

"General McClellan wishes me to say, sir, that the forward movement of the troops which you ordered for Monday week is impossible. The enemy has at Manassas 130,000 troops while we number less than 85,000. He earnestly desires that you send him at least 50,000 more men."

"My report from General Scott, yesterday," replied Lincoln, quickly, "shows 155,000 of our troops on the other side of the Potomac. Every line of transportation into Washington is clogged with soldiers, and there are more to come. McClellan feels that he has a lien on the best troops, the best officers in the country. I have given them to him. He has begged me to detach no troops or officers from his command, no matter what the emergency elsewhere, or the pressure brought to bear on me. I have acceded to his request. He told me a week ago that he was ready to destroy Beauregard. Now he asks for more troops."

"And he must need them, if he says so, sir," said the officer, earnestly. "He knows his business."

"I am banking the resources of this country on the people's faith in him," returned Lincoln, running his hands through his hair. "God give him strength," he thought, "to learn his business and give me patience to uphold his hands while he does so." Then aloud, "Very well, he shall have his men with what dispatch I can urge on General Scott."

The Captain saluted, and turned briskly on his heels. Lincoln, alone for a moment, brought his fist down on his desk.

"By jings, some one has got to move! If none of our generals can, I'll learn how, myself. . . . Hello, Governor," as Seward came in, hands full of papers.

"Did I catch you talking to yourself, Mr. Lincoln?" smiling as he dropped wearily into a chair. "Sure sign of senility, I've heard."

"Guess you've got me, Governor. I was cussing out our military men. Looks like you and I would have to shoulder a gun ourselves."

"We'd make a fine pair of old vultures, Lincoln! But, speaking of senility, that's really what's the matter with our armed forces, east and west. Old Scott is doddering. Why not get rid of him and put McClellan in his place. By the gods, he is a young Napoleon! Scott is jealous of him and one can scarcely blame him!"

"George has got his hands full, I reckon, with the Army of the Potomac, Governor. Let's see some results with that before we boost the boy again."

"Nonsense! Boy! He's reached his full stature now."

"Governor, what's he done besides train the green hands? Why doesn't he move? Is he going to let the fall rains interfere; and his campaign for the year end before it's begun?" Lincoln, who had risen, took a seat on the Cabinet table and caught Seward by his shoulders as he passed. "Seward, I'm oppressed with evil foreboding this morning. I am backing, and shall back, McClellan to the uttermost limits. Am I right?"

The Governor put both his hands affectionately on the President's knees and gave him a clear look from his fine, blue eyes.

"You are absolutely right, Lincoln. Wise in your choice and in your patience as you always are. Make McClellan General-in-Chief, find him a Secretary of War in whom he has confidence, and the war is won."

Lincoln hesitated as he was learning to hesitate over Seward's impulsive suggestions. He said slowly, "Scott has already urged me to accept his resignation. McClellan has affronted him needlessly, I fear—I'll think about it. Yes—yes, I'll think about it."

The two men remained staring at each other, then Stoddard brought a message to Seward and he left. But it was several moments before the President turned to his waiting desk. Even then, for many minutes he sat pondering on all he knew about George McClellan.

CHAPTER XIV

BALL'S BLUFF

LINCOLN, that evening, sat long on the edge of Mary's bed, discussing Miss Ford with her. He was much relieved when Mary agreed with him that the time had not yet arrived for turning the detective police on the Virginian's trail. Mary was very sure that, given time, she, with Lizzie and Jinny, could trace Miss Ford's motives to their source. And thus the matter was left.

When after three days, the Virginian returned from the plantation and settled with great apparent happiness to her light duties in the White House, Mary did not find it difficult to treat her with friendliness. She liked Miss Ford, and, as she admitted to herself, a little ruefully, the Virginian knew how to play on her pet weakness, social ambition.

Moreover, while Jinny's report was puzzling, it was not particularly disquieting. Her mistress had met Captain Taylor at the plantation. Miss Ford had chattered to him at some length on the political situation in Missouri and Kentucky, but most of their talk had been about McClellan and the possibility of persuading Lincoln to make the proposed visit to St. Louis, "where," Miss Ford had said, "he will all unconsciously sow the seeds for the great harvest."

Mary talked Jinny's story over with John Hay, and they agreed to wait for the Virginian's next move, before troubling the President again with the matter. What that move might be, they did not guess until later in the autumn. And then it was made with such frankness that they were utterly disconcerted.

In October, Miss Ford induced the mistress of the White House to resume her weekly semi-public teas in the Blue Room. Her scheme, she told Mary quite frankly, was to entice the lion and the lamb to break bread together.

"If word percolates to the influential centers of the South," she said, "that Mrs. Lincoln has no anti-slavery predilections, as she shows by the fact that she invites some of the most rabid pro-slavery wives to take a dish of tea with her, it will do more to dissipate the horrid gossip about you, in Washington, than anything I can think of."

Mary, who was still suffering acutely under the derision and insults of social Washington, was only too ready to agree with the Virginian, and so the weekly teas flourished. They were attended by a carefully chosen, but incongruous crowd. Ladies who paraded their slaves in the shape of negro maids in the very drawing rooms, rubbed shoulders with ladies from Boston, who smiled at the maids, and scowled at their mistresses. Ladies from New York affected the large cosmopolitan manner toward both factions, and ignored certain ladies from the Lincolns' home town, who refused to be patronized by any one, particularly by New Yorkers.

Mary found these teas immensely amusing and inspiriting. In fact, every one seemed to be complacent about them, except Lizzie Keckley. She, vigorously attacking the exquisite materials for which Mrs. Lincoln had made a trip to New York, made no bones about expressing her disapproval.

"You're giving those slavery folks exactly what they want, Mrs. Lincoln," she said, one October afternoon, when she was helping her mistress to dress for the weekly tea pouring.

"What is it they want?" asked Mary, trying the effect first of a black lace scarf on her red velvet frock, then of a crimson India shawl.

"They want to influence General McClellan, without him or any other Northerner realizing it. He comes two or three times a month to the teas, with his handsomest officers. Then Miss Ford, and any lady from Virginia or South Carolina or Alabama can flatter him just the way they've been told to flatter him, and give him any ideas about himself and Mr. Lincoln they want him to get. Madam, you just watch and see if it isn't the day after these tea parties that the President has the hardest time with McClellan."

"I have no way of learning that." Mary shrugged her shoulders impatiently under the India shawl, on which she finally had settled. "Even if what you say is true, I don't see how my stopping these teas will keep them from reaching McClellan. They'd just go about it another way. And, Lizzie, you've no idea how much these affairs have helped me, personally. Why, it's been weeks since I've had an anonymous letter, Stoddard says, with a Washington or Southern postmark. And it's only rarely that I'm yelled at in the streets, never any more by well dressed women."

If the pathos of this plea struck Lizzie Keckley, she gave no sign. She rose from her knees,—she had been tying Mary's sandals,—and gave her an appraising look from her dark eyes. "Just as soon as you told me about the things Miss Ford and Mrs. Frémont said, that night, I felt that General McClellan ought to be guarded against these—these—" suddenly her dark face purpled—"these Southern witches. He's a mighty good soldier they tell me, and you certainly ought to help protect him, Mrs. Lincoln."

"Oh, you are too officious, Lizzie!" exclaimed Mary, swishing from the room.

Nevertheless, her conscience smote her that afternoon, as she watched the handsome young general surrounded by the usual group of vivacious women. She, herself, had never changed her first impression of McClellan. She did not believe in the disinterestedness of his motives. She feared his ambition. She was convinced that he was afraid to fight. But her husband trusted him, and his country idolized him. She had no right, she told herself, to permit her social ambitions to lay him open to undue influence. Troubled by these thoughts she was impatient with Tad, when he came marching into the drawing room in the uniform of an officer of the 71st

Pennsylvania which Baker, the former Senator from Oregon, now in the Army of the Potomac, had had made for the child.

"Run out, Taddie," she exclaimed. "No, you can't have even a tea-spoonful of tea."

Tad's nerves jangled in response to hers. "You must give an officeh whateveh he asks fo'," he screamed, stamping his foot. "Colonel Baka'll have you locked up. He told me no one could boss me in these clothes."

"Colonel Baker is our much loved friend," said Mary, with a little smile, for the benefit of the listening women, "but he mustn't put absurd ideas into your little head. Run out, Taddie!"

Tad made a grab at the cream jug and upset it on Mary's red India shawl. He began to cry hysterically and his mother rose hastily to take him from the room. She was furious with the child. But she managed to control herself until she had dragged Tad to the sanctuary of her own room, then she spanked him soundly, sent him to bed, and felt the better for it.

His screams brought Lincoln into the room, pen in hand.

"Yes, I whipped him," exclaimed Mary in response to his inquiring look, "and I'll thank you not to go coddling him. He's a saucy, disobedient boy, and you're the one that makes him so. Look at this shawl!"

She held it up, giving as she did so a succinct history of Tad's sins.

"Is McClellan down there?" asked the President abruptly, when she had finished.

"Yes, surrounded by the usual bouquet of Southern beauty," replied Mary.

"He sent me word that he was too busy to come to a Cabinet conference, this afternoon," mused Lincoln. "Funny!"

"Not funny at all," snapped Mary. "Quite in line with his condescending manner to you. He's completely spoiled too. I don't see why you endure it."

"Mary, I'd hold McClellan's horse for him, if he'd win this war for me. Nothing else matters." He looked at her with grave sweetness.

Mary dropped her shawl to the floor and threw her arms about him. "Oh, Abra'm! Abra'm! You shame me, utterly! I'm so trivial. But love me, dearest, love me in spite of it! Love me for my big love for you, if for nothing else."

Lincoln picked her up as if she had been Taddie, and, holding her against his heart, he looked down into her eyes.

"You know that I love you," he said, tenderly.

"But not as I love you! Not with the feeling I have for you." She hid her face against his heart.

An expression of acute pain tightened the muscles of the President's face, but he said nothing. He wondered if he were capable any more of feeling toward any human being in the world as Mary felt toward him,— if this ghastly weight of responsibility could crowd out of his life forever all intimate personal relations. Some day, he thought, when there was more time, he would try to explain this to Mary. But now, he must return to his rewriting of Seward's message to France on the cotton blockade. Seward was too hasty in issuing ultimatums but, by jings, he knew law!

He set Mary gently to her feet, and would have hurried away, but she caught one finger in a buttonhole of his vest.

"Abra'm, let me go downstairs and send McClellan up to you! I'd like nothing better than a chance to do so! Two can play at this errand-boy game.—What McClellan needs is what I just gave poor little Taddie."

Lincoln smiled and shook his head. "No, thanks. I'll look him up later in the evening. Let me go, dear Mary."

"Just one thing more, Abra'm! I never get a moment alone with you. At these teas of mine, there are, I think and believe, emissaries of Jeff Davis,—women who seek to flatter McClellan into believing that he's a slave Unionist. Do you wish me to cut off those affairs?"

"You get a lot of pleasure out of these tea fights, don't you, Mary?"

"Yes, I do, but if you say stop, they stop, with no recriminations."

"I know of no better way to give McClellan his chance than to give him all the rope he wants, Mary. After he's had his fling, I think the real stuff in him will come out. Russell says there's no better hand that he's ever seen at licking an army into shape."

Mary jerked firmly at the buttonhole. "Abra'm, I don't care what William Russell or any one else says. McClellan is small potatoes. You'll be able to win the other members of your Cabinet, excepting possibly Chase, as you have Seward. But you'll never win McClellan. You'll have to break him. And you'll never win this war until all the men in power, civil and military, recognize you as leader. What's that ode of Horace's— 'You must have a heart thrice bound with bronze'—chill your heart, dear Abra'm."

He listened carefully. Mary, at her best, possessed acumen that he dared not question. She dropped her hand from his buttonhole. He nodded and turned away. Mary returned to the Blue Room.

The beautiful October days marched steadily toward the rains of November. Washington was so packed with the military, that, to the casual observer, it would seem that the political significance of the sprawling, half-built little city was entirely submerged. It seemed so, in very fact, to Lincoln as he strove in vain to move McClellan toward the Rebels.

Day after day slipped by,—the wonderful clear days of Potomac autumn, with the sound of northing geese at night, sailing high under the frosty stars,—but not until the 31st of the month, with the first November rain softening the clay roads of Maryland and Virginia, did McClellan send word to the President that he was about to make a strong reconnaissance up the Potomac toward Leesburg.

It was not much, but better than nothing, thought Lincoln, and set himself patiently to await results. Perhaps, perhaps the Rebels would face McClellan in battle. But in spite of the President's hopes, the reconnaissance would have been only a reconnaissance had not General Stone, in crossing the river, stumbled upon a fight. A light engagement followed in which 49 Union men were killed, with 200 wounded and missing. There was about an equal loss on the Rebel side with no gain to either.

Lincoln received word of the skirmish in the war office, with keen hopes that it might develop into a battle of decisive proportions. But McClellan ordered the reconnaissance withdrawn, and, to the President's bitter disappointment, the old stalemate recommenced.

The morning after the battle, Nicolay brought in a pile of newspapers.

"That may have been only a skirmish at Ball's Bluff, from the military point of view," he remarked to the President, "but politically it was a holocaust."

Lincoln was learning not to read the papers for news. "Do I have to hear that, George?" he asked.

Nicolay nodded. "Greeley demands that this inconsequential waste of blood and treasure cease. Seems that many of the 49 boys who were killed were socially very prominent in Massachusetts and New York. They are frantic over what they term the useless sacrifice of Senator Baker. It's another Bull Run, I guess."

"Baker was one of my dearest friends," said Lincoln, "but I don't think his blood was one ounce more precious than that of one of those poor boys who never put foot in the Senate, or in Massachusetts or New York."

Nicolay nodded. "Of course! But one can't make political capital out of that fact. As it is, our very best families are claiming that this would never have happened were you and General Scott not so hampering McClellan that he cannot make a decisive movement."

"I see!" Lincoln ran his fingers through his hair. "Well, I'm not sorry they're taking it that way. I think this will ease the old gentleman out of his job about as naturally as a fall flood moves one of those old log rafts that gets stranded on a sand bar. We'll see."

Nicolay blinked for a moment then, with a little smile, carried his pile of newspapers back into his own office.

Colonel Baker was given a military funeral in Washington. Willie and Tad, heartbroken over the loss of their friend, insisted that they would march in their uniforms with the soldiers, and not ride in the carriage with their father. And this they did, in spite of their mother's protest that they inevitably would get into trouble. As usual, she was right.

Late in the afternoon, about an hour after the President had returned from the funeral, William Russell appeared at the sitting-room door, a boy holding either hand. Miss Ford and Mary were sitting by the table, embroidering, and awaiting the announcement of supper. Lincoln, passing through on his way to his room, pulled up with a sharp exclamation.

"Trouble, eh?"

Russell advanced into the light with the two boys. His eyes looked angry, yet he was smiling. He was, as usual, well groomed, but the children's uniforms appeared to have been replaced by dirty rags. Tad had been crying but Willie showed no traces of tears. He looked at his father.

"Papa day, I was ashamed of America, this afternoon. I was."

"What did she do?" asked his father, gravely.

"Well, it was like mother said, we couldn't march good with the soldiers. So we ran ahead of the parade to find a good place to watch. And in front of Mr. Russell's windows, Mr. Russell, he was standing with the crowd on the curb. So we pushed in and stood beside him. And when the gun carriage went by, with Uncle Baker in it, why, Mr. Russell took off his hat, and made us take off ours. And nobody else did, and then, when your carriage went by, Mr. Russell took off his hat again, and made us too, but nobody else did."

"We didn't want to, so awful much, just fo' you, Papa day," interjected Tad, wiping his nose on his bloody sleeve.

"Shut up, Tad! I did too, only I always forget. And a big tall man next to Mr. Russell said, 'What in hell you think you are!'"

"That was because Mista 'Ussel said in a loud voice," amended Tad, "that we'd gotta show a gentleman's 'espect fo' the dead, and fo' the head of the United States."

Willie scowled. "If you don't keep quiet, Tad, I'll hit you. And Mr. Russell said to the man, 'I think I'm a man that has better manners than you have.' And some one of the crowd said, 'That's the bloody Britisher that called our soldiers cowards when he wrote to his home paper about Bull Run.' And somebody else yelled, 'Bull Run Russell!—He rotten-egged our soldiers! Tar and feather him!' And some one hit him, and we all began to fight. And us, Taddie and me and Mr. Russell, licked the whole gang. Then he went in and got cleaned up, but we couldn't because we all wanted you to see our honorable scars."

"The blessed babies!" murmured Mary, then aloud, "But what were you ashamed of, Willie, the Americans' bad manners, or the fact that a Britisher and two boys licked them?"

"Of the licking," replied Willie promptly. "Just look at this scratch on my arm, mother."

"My nose has bled all oveh my gullet," observed Tad.

"Gullet! Why gullet?" asked Mary, examining her youngest's tattered shirt, with a sigh.

"A gullet is a kind of coat solda's used to weah, motheh," explained Tad.

"He means a doublet," explained Willie. "There, Mr. Russell, I told you mother wouldn't be mad if you brought us in. Come on, Tad, let's get cleaned up."

"I think Russell is the one that's mad," said Lincoln, giving the war correspondent a keen look.

"It was an humiliating experience." Russell shook his head. "I am convinced that the hue and cry raised against me will end my usefulness to my paper in this country. McClellan dare not give me a correspondent's privileges. And all because I gave what McClellan and McDowell both declare are the plain facts about that wretched rout of your troops at Bull Run. I'm hissed in the streets. My life is threatened daily."

"I don't understand it," exclaimed Miss Ford.

"That's simple." Lincoln sat down by the table and unfolded a crumpled paper which he took from his pocket. "At first our own reporters told the truth too. That made the public so mad that all the papers began to backwater. Pretty soon everybody's vanity about the Army of the Potomac was being bolstered by regular doses of taffy. Then along came a copy of Russell's letter to the London *Times*, once more calling attention to our disgrace. So there's nothing to be done, but call Russell every kind of a liar."

"The newspapers of this country are terrible!" exclaimed Mary.

"M. Mercier remarked to me the other day," said Russell, "that he supposed that I was going to stay in Washington forever, because the New York papers all were announcing that I was leaving immediately for London!"

"I don't think people are so sensitive about what they call your errors in what you wrote." Mary looked at the Englishman, thoughtfully. "It was the tone you used. It didn't sound friendly. You wrote *de haut en bas*. What we need is a breath of strengthening sympathy from old England, not to be looked down on and sneered at by her."

Russell flushed darkly. After a short pause, he said, "Perhaps I deserve that, Mrs. Lincoln, but it's very difficult, really, to write in praise of conditions one knows to be needlessly bad. As for sympathy! The Federal government will get none of that from Great Britain, until it declares this to be a war to end slavery."

"Why do you say that, Mr. Russell?" demanded Miss Ford, "when you know perfectly well that the South and England are inherently sympathetic,—always have been."

Lincoln cleared his throat. He had no desire to listen again to a discussion of slavery. Ever since Frémont's proclamation had been abrogated, he had been hounded by Abolitionists. "Speaking of sympathy," he began, hastily, "I had a very great pleasure to-day. It seems that John Hay isn't the only poetic genius in the Executive Mansion. Willie dropped this into my pocket this noon." He put on his spectacles and with his charming intonation he gave them Willie's first poem:

LINES ON THE DEATH OF COLONEL BAKER

There was no patriot like Baker
So noble and so true;
He fell as a soldier on the field
His face to the sky of blue.
His voice is silent in the hall
Which oft his presence graced;
No more he'll hear the loud acclaim
Which rang from place to place.

No squeamish notions filled his breast
The Union was his theme;
No surrender and no compromise

His day-thought and night's dream.
His country has her part to pay
To'ards those he left behind;
His widow and his children all
She must ever keep in mind.

The tears were running down the President's cheeks as he finished. He smiled however at the little round of applause and at Mary's excited demand to see the paper. He handed it to her with the remark:

"By jings, there's more than uncombed snarls in that boy's head!"

Supper was announced at that moment. Lincoln rescued the paper from Mary, and lagged behind the others to read the verses to Louis, who wiped his eyes and blew his nose.

"Can't say, sir," he said huskily, "whether I'm crying over Colonel Baker or Willie."

"Same here!" agreed Lincoln. "I wish Baker could hear the verses, himself, don't you, Louis?"

"I do, indeed!" agreed the messenger.

GENERAL SCOTT, to Nicolay's complacent amusement, called on the President, a few days after Baker's funeral, and formally tendered his resignation.

"I am tired, sir," said the old soldier. "I am old, and I suffer continuously from an old hurt. Also, I suffer, Mr. President, from the insubordinate spirit shown me by General McClellan. I might almost say that he heaps contumely upon me."

Lincoln was much touched. "When I consider your years, your infirmities, and your well-earned glories, General, my conscience smites me for the heavy burdens I have imposed on you, lately. But, my dear General, where was I to turn? There is no one else in these United States in whose military judgment I have such confidence. I can accept your resignation only on one consideration, that you agree that I may come to you at any time for advice."

Scott's downcast face brightened. "Certainly, sir! You do me honor, Mr. President. It is with deep regret that I withdraw in such momentous times from the orders of a Chief Executive who has treated me with distinguished kindness and courtesy."

"Even at that, I couldn't keep your pace, General!" Lincoln smiled. In a moment, he told himself, he'd be pulling his forelock. "And now, sir, before you leave, I wish to tell you that I've actually sent General Frémont his walking papers. I still think well of Frémont's impulses, I only think he is the prey of wicked and designing men, and I think he has absolutely no military capacity. There'll be another scream from the radicals, I suppose, over the dismissal, but that has to be."

"Your decision is wise, sir. It's a pity you have to make these changes, continually, but it is one of the many prices we pay for maintaining no standing army. I hesitate to say it, sir, and would not, if I were not out of office, that I believe that, while Cameron was a wise political choice, he is not well fitted to be Secretary of War."

Lincoln nodded, a little heavily. Cameron was a charming gentleman, and he liked him. But the public suspected him of being swayed by the money interests, and it was true that he lacked the executive ability needed for the present emergency.

"I'm thinking about putting Edwin M. Stanton in his place," he said, watching Scott's face.

The General blinked and coughed. "An able and irascible man, sir, and your very vociferous enemy."

"Shucks! Mighty few who aren't my enemies, General. His integrity is only equaled by his intelligence. And the public has confidence in him. Folk are uneasy, these days, and they have a right to be. Think him over, and I'll come up to talk to you about him soon." He took the old man's hand. "I'll see that you are kept informed of what goes on down here. I'm sorry not to be able to give you full relief but we still need that wise head-piece of yours. So, while officially, I say, Good-by!—unofficially, what's your New Jersey address?"

General Scott smiled, delightedly. "I'll see that you receive it, Mr. President, as soon as Mrs. Scott and I are settled."

And Lincoln noted, with satisfaction not unmixed with a tender sort of sympathy, that the old soldier's limp was less as he left the office than it had been when he came in.

The pressure brought to bear on Lincoln to place McClellan in Scott's position was almost unbelievable. McClellan was an ardent Democrat. Yet Greeley, the Republican, gave Lincoln no rest in his behalf, and the Northern Democrats, with Raymond of the New York *Times* as their mouthpiece, hounded him editorially, while literally thousands of telegrams demanded McClellan as General-in-Chief.

More than all else, his anxiety to unite the uneasy North in a vigorous war spirit moved Lincoln to make the appointment. A sigh of relief and approval went up from the whole country, when he announced McClellan's promotion; a sigh so deep and full, that even the anger of the Abolition forces over Frémont's dismissal, which Lincoln adroitly permitted to become known at the same time, could not seriously impair the President's momentary popularity with all sides.

Lizzie Keckley, about the first of November, reported to Mary that Miss Ford, who had spent a week-end ostensibly with friends in Baltimore, had actually attended a celebration of some sort, at the tavern at Fairfax Courthouse. The host of this celebration, Jinny had told Lizzie, was a dashing and "powerful smart" Rebel officer, Captain Mosby. The purpose of the celebration was confused in Jinny's mind. She thought that the Battle of Ball's Bluff was the cause. Yet she had heard her mistress propose a toast to General McClellan, the hope of both North and South.

Mary tried to talk this toast over with Lincoln one evening in November, when she caught him alone for a moment at supper. But he was sweating that day under the first news of the intricate problem developing with England, as a result of the Trent affair, and he begged her not to bother him. Mary remarked that she would never mention McClellan's name to him again, but was glad the next moment, as she realized what deep harassment lay in his eyes, that Lincoln probably had not heard her peevish retort.

He had not. Nevertheless, Mary's constant jabbing him with her dislike for McClellan did not leave him unperturbed. Now and again, after she had launched one of her darts at the General, he was conscious of a strange sense of helplessness, a fear that the treachery which lurked in every aspect of the slavery question was too gigantic for his mind to grasp.

McClellan's careless contempt toward himself, his frank scorn of the Cabinet members, which was shown most bitterly toward Cameron, made Lincoln uneasy.

The "Anaconda" plan, backed by Scott, the Cabinet, and himself, McClellan ignored. The plan of movement for the armies in Tennessee and Kentucky, as well as those in the States along the Mississippi, which Lincoln had worked out, and which were later to be proved models of military and political skill, McClellan laughed at. Men of real ability were emerging from the chaos in the middle-west, Sherman, Thomas, Hunter, Halleck. Lincoln desired that their talents be put to work at once. They were not.

Again, and yet again, during the early days of November, the President urged his plans on McClellan, but they were ignored. Nothing happened. A black lethargy seemed to hold the army East and West in a nightmare's spell. At last, Lincoln no longer could endure McClellan's silence. One evening toward the middle of November, he gathered up John Hay, led him across the street to Seward's house, gathered up the Secretary of State, and started for McClellan's house on H Street.

"Of course," remarked Seward, puffing good humoredly on his usual cigar, "I like to be a good fellow, myself, but why, with all you and I have to do, to say nothing of our young poet, should we wait on McClellan? I've got to get that reply to Lord Russell on the Trent affair into Lord Lyon's hands to-night. You've torn it limb from limb, and time will be needed to put the remnants together, Mr. President!"

Lincoln laughed and flung his arm over Seward's shoulders. "We go to McClellan, Governor, because McClellan is too proud to wait on a couple of old cart horses like you and me."

"McClellan is a brilliant soldier, and I love him," commented Seward, "but he's riding a horse several hands too high, I fear."

"If he's as able as a military man as I guess him to be *un*able as a politician, he'll end the war before he ruins the country,—I hope."

Seward gasped. "And what do you mean by that, Lincoln?"

"Just what I said," replied the President.

There was silence, while the three men tramped thoughtfully along the tree shadowed street, so badly lighted that they were obliged to move slowly. John Hay, who felt keenly McClellan's discourtesies toward Lincoln, broke the silence, and changed the subject.

"Mr. Lincoln, may I ask how you got rid of that committee of Senators, this afternoon? They asked for an hour with you, and they came tumbling out in twenty minutes."

"Senator Trumbull and his gang, eh? They didn't want much! Just said they heard I was going to change the Secretary of War, and that, as the entire Cabinet had lost the confidence of the country, they thought it an opportune moment to change all seven of the Cabinet ministers. I couldn't think of a better answer than to tell them a story. I told it and they left."

"What was the story?" asked Seward.

Lincoln chuckled. "Out on the Sangamon, there was a farmer much troubled by skunks, and his wife insisted he try to get rid of them. So, one moonlight night, he loaded his old shotgun and stationed himself in the yard. Waiting in the house, his wife heard the gun go off and in a few minutes, the farmer came in.

" 'What luck did you have?' said she.

" 'I hid behind the woodpile,' said he, 'with the shotgun pointed toward the hen roost, and along came, not one skunk, but seven! I took aim, blazed away, and killed one. But he raised such a fearful stink I concluded it was best to let the other six alone!' "

The trio was still chuckling when McClellan's home was reached. The servant told them that the General was attending a wedding. Lincoln declared in favor of waiting, and led the way into the parlor. An hour later, McClellan appeared in the hall, where the three visitors heard the servant apprise him of Lincoln's presence. McClellan brushed by and ascended the stairs. Another quarter of an hour passed. Then the President sent the servant to remind General McClellan of his presence. Much embarrassed, the man returned almost immediately.

"The General has gone to bed, sir, and sends word that he's too tired to see you to-night."

"Good God!" exclaimed Seward, starting to his feet.

Lincoln laid his hand on the Governor's arm and smiled gravely at John Hay. "Come, boys, we'll go home," he said.

He did not speak during the return to the Executive Mansion.

And he was in no amenable mood when, about eleven o'clock that evening, Miss Ford came into his office. She and Mary had been to the theater, and while Mary went to see that the children were properly in bed, the Virginian embraced the opportunity to drop in on him. She wore an evening gown of green velvet, trimmed with many yards of green beaded fringe. A little green silk hood covered her hair. She removed this, as she sank into a chair by the fire.

Lincoln looked up, pen in hand.

"Mr. President, I've never had a chance to tell you how grieved I was that you and young Gordon, whom I sent to you, didn't seem to agree."

"You put it mildly, Miss Ford!" Lincoln smiled grimly.

She returned the smile. "I reckon that's best, isn't it? Are you still cross at him, Mr. Lincoln?"

"Did he give you an inkling of what happened?" asked the President.

"No, sir, but John Hay did. I'm so sorry. Not only that Gordon annoyed you, but that he's made it difficult for me to ask you a favor for his brother, Nathaniel P. Gordon."

"Don't know the fellow!" declared Lincoln. "What's he done? Run away from sentry duty?"

"No! Nothing so simple as that! He's been convicted as a slave trader by the New York courts, and the fool of a judge has sentenced him to be hanged!"

"Why not?" demanded Lincoln, tangling his legs in the rounds of his chair, and smoothing his hair with an ivory paper knife, while he wondered just what sort of an admission the Virginian was now trying to pry from him.

"It's not fair!" she cried. "Some Abolitionist district attorney has invoked that old law of 1820, prohibiting slave trade. It never has been enforced. Why should those devilish Abolitionists be allowed to make political capital out of this poor fellow? Convict him, and you ought to convict a hundred others."

"Why not?" repeated Lincoln, wearily.

"Because it's an absurd law, absurdly applied. And Gordon has a wife and baby."

Lincoln gave her a long, wistful look. "My dear Miss Ford," he said, sadly, "this is a sorry sort of business for you. You were meant for higher work, surely. You knew before you came in that your request was an improper one, an affront to all I hold sacred. The Attorney General's office is the proper place for you to go, anyhow."

The Virginian flushed deeply, and there was softness in her violet eyes that Lincoln never before had seen there.

"Does it make any real difference to you, Mr. Lincoln?" she asked, clasping her hands.

"Certainly it does," he replied stoutly. "I hate to see a friend go on the wrong track. . . . Now don't waste your time and mine on Gordon. A slave trader just isn't human, according to my notions."

"But you don't understand one angle of this, Mr. Lincoln. You have made a dangerous enemy in the younger Gordon. If you reprieve his brother, he will be your friend. And I tell you, young Gordon is *dangerous*. The story of what you did to him has gotten out, and he is being laughed out of Washington."

"By jings!" exclaimed Lincoln, wonderingly, "I reckon it's foreordained you and I are not to understand each other. Now I don't see how a *lady* of intelligence could say such a thing to me!"

"I understand you, well enough," retorted Miss Ford, half bitterly, and half sadly. The flush slowly lifted from her face, leaving it very pale in the firelight. "I sometimes wonder," she said, with even more than her usual drawl, "if this is not my punishment: to have grown to understand you so well. You are a very fine human being, Abraham Lincoln."

"Well," his eyes twinkling, "I reckon I'm fine enough not to run to cover when Gordon shakes his pen at me. It's getting pretty late, Miss Ford, and I've still a day's work to do."

He nodded at her and turned back to his desk, hoping that she would go without further remarks. If she was now determined to try the personal rôle with him,—well, he'd give her no chance, that was all.

He began to write. He was working on a bill for the Delaware legislature, a bill for the gradual and Compensated Abolishment of the slaves of that State. A Member of Congress from Delaware had given him hope that the bill might go through, for Delaware was really more Northern than Southern. Miss Ford did not move, and finally conscious of that fact, he looked up to say:

"What would you and your friend Jeffie Davis say if I try to get through a bill for Compensated Abolishment in the various State legislatures?"

"I'd say what you said to me, a short time ago, or words to that effect, 'How can a man of your intelligence be such a fool'?" Miss Ford's voice had all its old sardonic flavor.

Lincoln chuckled and returned to his work, forgetting the Virginian again, but with his mind not wholly given over to the abolishment of slavery. One corner of his brain was repeating a warning to him that he knew he ought to heed: that McClellan's last affront was an insult which he could ignore if he wished as far as it was meant personally, but which he had no right to condone, inasmuch as it was an insult to his high office. He ceased to write and stared into space.

He did not see Miss Ford when she trailed from the room. John Hay put his head in the door with a question, and when Lincoln did not answer, said to some one behind him, "The Tycoon must be making war medicine." Old Daniel came in to turn out the light, said "Good evening! Beg pardon," and tiptoed out, and still Lincoln did not rouse from his preoccupation with McClellan. Mary came, about two o'clock, and taking him by the hand, led him to bed.

The following morning shortly after breakfast McClellan's aide appeared with the information that the General-in-Chief would be glad to see the President at his house, where the Secretary of the Navy wished to hold a conference on an expedition against New Orleans.

Lincoln was sitting at his desk, with Willie beside him. He was helping the boy compose a letter to the editor of *The National Republican*, to whom he wanted the youngster to send his poem on Colonel Baker.

When the aide had delivered his message, Lincoln affixed an elaborate title line to Willie's verses before he said shortly:

"Tell McClellan I'm not coming."

The aide raised his eyebrows, saluted, and departed. Willie turned to stare up into his father's face.

"What are you mad at McClellan for, Papa day?"

"What makes you think I'm mad, Willie?" asked Lincoln.

"Ho! I always know. Anybody does. And you'd ought to have been mad at him long ago, I guess." The child, with his moving likeness to his father, nodded his head, deliberately. "I heard Mr. Sumner tell Miss Ford it was nauseating the way you let McClellan sauce you. Papa day," very thoughtfully, "why doesn't Miss Ford want you and Mr. Sumner to be friends?"

Lincoln gave the boy a keen glance. Willie, always old for his age, had matured astoundingly since March.

"I reckon you're biting off more than you can chew on that guess, Willie."

"No, I'm not, Papa day! You see I do sentry duty in uniform every week at mother's tea in the Blue Room. I have to walk up and down the hall, and watch all the folks that go in. And Miss Ford stands by the curtains that hang over the hall door, to meet folks and introduce them to mother. And all I have to do is to stand still on the hall side of the curtain, and I can hear everything she says. And twice I've heard her tell things to Mr. Sumner that would make him think you was his enemy."

"For instance!" Lincoln's thoughts took a leap. He recalled being conscious that the Senator from Massachusetts lately had been harshly critical, less helpful. Better call him in on this Trent affair. Knew more about English thought than Seward,—had the confidence of the English people after his years of residence there. Sumner would be a better man to visit London now than Thurlow Weed, Seward's choice—

Willie was going on. "She said that you didn't 'preciate mother's brain. She said you left mother alone too much. She said she guessed you didn't think much of mother and Mr. Sumner always talking French together. She said she knew from living intimately here, that you never would back up an,—you know,—a law for setting the slaves free. And she said you were the smartest politician in America and would listen to anybody, and use anybody, and then throw them away."

"You have a good memory, boy," said Lincoln.

"She said lots more I don't remember and those ain't the exact words," admitted Willie.

"She's tutoring you boys in what—reading, writing, and 'rithmetic?" asked his father.

"Not arithmetic, Mr. Langley does that. She's giving us elocution lessons, writing, French and German. She does know a lot for a woman, doesn't she, Papa day!"

"She's a queer mixture," mused the President. "Guess maybe she's a trouble maker, and I'd better get your mother to send her home."

"I don't know what mother'd do without her. She keeps company going for mother, and she's awful nice to us boys. I like her, only I wish she didn't talk that way. Now, if mother has anything to say, she speaks right out in meeting. Folks get mad at her, but they always get over it, because she's—she's—"

"Open and above board." Lincoln helped him out. "That's right, we can all trust dear little peppery mother."

Father and son nodded their heads in comfortable unison. "I tell you what, Papa day, mother's awful sharp about finding folks out. If you try to make her get rid of Miss Ford, she'll raise Cain, I suppose. But if you give her time she'll find Miss Ford out and tend to her, herself. Gosh"—with a chuckle—"hope I'm there when things bust!"

Lincoln joined in the chuckle, reminiscently. "All right, Willie, we'll let it stand that way for a while. In the meantime,—yes, what is it, John?" as young Hay came in.

"Brigadier Van Vliet of McClellan's staff, sir, wishes for a few moments' interview."

"It's lesson time for you, Willie, so march," said Lincoln, kissing the child several times, and watching him, with tender, brooding gaze until the door slammed after him. "Show the Brigadier in, John," rising to warm his hands at the fire.

A handsome, upstanding officer clanked into the room and saluted. Lincoln pulled the gray shawl over his shoulders, and deliberately lifted a foot in rumpled wool sock and carpet slipper to the blaze.

"I feel these first fall days more'n I will the real winter, Brigadier," he remarked.

The officer nodded, with a supercilious glance at the shabby legs dangling before the blaze; which glance did not escape the President's eye.

"Mr. President, General McClellan believes that you did not understand the purport of his previous message. This is the conference which you yourself called with regard to the military and naval plan which you, yourself, sponsor."

"I called last night at General McClellan's house to talk that plan over with him, Brigadier."

"Yes, sir?" The officer's voice was tentative.

"That's all, Brigadier. Fine clear weather we're having! Good fighting weather I'd call it. Virginia roads are in prime condition for marching."

Brigadier Van Vliet flushed, saluted, and turned away. There was no smile on Lincoln's face, as he watched that stiff back disappear into the reception room.

He was deep in conference with Seward and Chase over the floating of a new bond issue, not long before the noon hour, when George Nicolay came in.

"General McClellan is in my office, sir, demanding to see you, at once."

"Tell him I'm busy, George," replied Lincoln.

Chase spoke quickly, "I'm sure Governor Seward and I will both gladly withdraw in favor of the General."

"I'm not so sure, Chase, of that fact," said Seward, placidly turning over a pile of notes.

"The subject of this conference is in my province, sir," Chase threw his handsome head up quickly, "and if I am willing to end it you have nothing to say."

"Still strong for McClellan, aren't you, Chase!" interpolated Lincoln a little wearily. The friction between Seward and Chase made a consultation with the two extremely wearing. "It won't hurt him to cool his heels for a while."

"If he cools them!" smiled Seward. Adding as the door burst open, and McClellan strode in, "Which he won't!"

"Mr. Lincoln," demanded the General, "why am I subjected to the sort of treatment you have visited on me this morning?" He stamped up to the table, and paused opposite Lincoln, his gloved hand caught in his yellow sash, the other thrust into the breast of his blue uniform, a picture of the perfect officer.

"You know, McClellan, I didn't have a West Point education," replied the President, "so I'm lacking in a certain polish of manner I could have got there. My wife says she's about given up my manners, in fact, so I'm looking elsewhere for my training. Now you are a West Pointer and a society man, and I've decided to pattern my etiquette after yours for a while."

He paused, watching the young General through half-closed, steel gray eyes. Anger and resentment struggled to free themselves from the tight grip of McClellan's lips. Lincoln brought his bony fist down on the Cabinet table.

"You insulted the high office vested in me, last night, General. Don't repeat the offense, sir." He turned to Nicolay, who had remained standing near the door. "George, send for Welles to come over here. You gentlemen will excuse me, won't you, if I take up another matter now?" looking from Seward to Chase.

Seward, with a twinkle in his fine eyes, replied meekly, "Yes, Mr. President," and rose.

Chase, who was a great admirer of McClellan's, obviously was bursting to speak up for his favorite, but something in Lincoln's eye which he never before had observed there, caused the Secretary of the Treasury to gather up his papers and depart in utter silence.

McClellan walked to a window and stood with his back to the room. Lincoln wrote busily for a little while. Then he said urbanely:

"By the way, General, I see you've refused to make good my appointment of Halleck in Frémont's job. Guess you'd better tend to that, hadn't you?"

Without turning, McClellan replied, "I've got a better man in view. In the meantime, Hunter will do."

"Halleck," said Lincoln, "is a man of more war experience than yourself. He has had long training in organization. He is an authority on military art and science, as his book proves. Some one has got to get those fellows out West to pulling together,—or their armies will eat their own heads off. Scott wanted Halleck to have your job, but I agreed with the public that your youth and general brilliancy were a better bet. The conditions in the West are bad. You need Halleck there."

McClellan whirled round. "You try my patience beyond my strength, Mr. Lincoln."

"Oh, you're a pretty strong fellow, according to my guess!" Lincoln smiled. "Reckon you'd better fix that up with Halleck, George."

McClellan began to walk the floor. "You turn over to me a mob of gutter-snipes and farm boys to make into an army; then you nag me continually, without waiting either for equipment or training, to give battle to the enemy. Next you turn over to me all the armies of the country,— an untrained rabble,—honeycombed by the machinations of politicians, and demand again that I close in on the Rebels, at the same time handicapping me by imposing on me officers in whom I have no confidence.

You, sir, utterly ignorant of the most ordinary military facts are doing this!"

"In a kind of a way what you say is true, George. But the fact remains that I'm the head of this government, and it's also a fact that two men can't drive the same horse at the same time."

John Hay opened the door to admit Welles and Cameron. In a moment, the four men were bending over a map, while Lincoln explained the theory of a joint land and naval operation that should open the Mississippi from Cairo to the Gulf. "Tightening up the Anaconda," he called it.

Cameron and Welles were enthusiastically for it. McClellan, with ill-concealed contempt, declared the plan to be premature, and that he would not detail a single regiment from the eastern forces for such a movement. There was a long argument, interrupted once or twice by different messengers sent by Mary to urge the President to come to dinner. During the last half hour, Lincoln permitted McClellan to do most of the talking, and it was with a sick feeling of anxiety that he listened. And yet, he thought, McClellan *was* brilliant, was not to be beaten in his skill as an organizer, and there was not a soldier in the Army of the Potomac who did not adore "Little Mac." Once let him overcome his strange inertia, and his compact, loyal fighting unit would be unstoppable. But why that strange inertia? Mary said McClellan was a coward, but he was willing to take his oath that McClellan was a brave man.

Suddenly he rose, and ran his fingers through his hair. "I shall issue an order this afternoon," he said, "directing that preparations for the joint movement be begun at once. And now I'm going to my dinner. By the way, George," pausing with his hand on the door knob, "I shall have some special instructions for Halleck as soon as he takes over his job," and he closed the door firmly behind him.

CHAPTER XVI

THE VACANT CHAIR

MARY'S unremitting efforts to care for the President's health were abetted by Miss Ford as winter came on and the strain on him increased. Not that Miss Ford busied herself with the matter of his food and sleep. She kept to her own line, and saw to it that entertainments of a kind attractive to Lincoln were within his reach when he needed them most.

Mary watched her rather grimly, wondering how long her own patience would last. She had agreed with Lizzie Keckley that it would be best for her not to talk to Jinny, but to allow Lizzie to be the repository of all the information the colored girl could gather in.

Certainly Lizzie's gleanings were sufficiently varied to keep one far less vitally interested than Mary Lincoln on the *qui vive*.

Miss Ford wrote long letters to Horace Greeley and to Henry Raymond, purporting to report on the condition of the Slave Unionists in the South. Each letter, Jinny said, spoke a good deal about McClellan, and the growing confidence of the Slave Unionists in his ability as a soldier, and his fair attitude toward slavery.

Miss Ford was seeing a good deal of Senator Sumner at different houses to which they both were invited, and always told him any uncouth anecdotes she could recall or improvise regarding Lincoln's doings.

Mary flew into a fury at this last. Lizzie was washing her hair for her, and Mary jerked from her hands. With dripping head, she started for the door. "I shall attend to that hussy this moment," she cried through set teeth.

Lizzie ran to interpose her strong body between Mary and the scene which Willie had hoped to witness.

"Madam! Madam!" she pleaded. "So much depends on your keeping a still tongue. You *must* wait like the President said until we find out how much of a hold her people can get on General McClellan. If I can't trust you to keep your temper, who can I go to?"

"I'm a fool, Lizzie," replied Mary, shortly. "I'll do all my exploding to you. But," she added, as the dressmaker began to dry her hair, "I don't like her efforts at coddling Mr. Lincoln. That's my job. Isn't that his step now, in his room?"

Her question was answered by Lincoln's opening the door. He came in slowly and dropped down on the sofa.

"My head aches," he said, with a sigh. "Did I eat dinner this noon?"

"Yes, you did, Abra'm. You're worn out, that's what's the matter with you. Lie down and let Lizzie rub your poor head." Mary took the fan with which the colored woman was drying her hair. "Go to him, Lizzie."

Lincoln smiled up at Lizzie. "I haven't time, Lizzie. Senator Sumner is waiting for me now."

"Just let me give you five minutes, Mr. President," pleaded Lizzie. "I know I can help you."

"My tiredness is inside me, where you can't get at it," sighed Lincoln, "but just to prove that I'm taking care of my health!" He smiled again and lay back on the sofa.

Lizzie began to pass her fine hands over his forehead.

"I suppose Sumner is interested in that *Trent* affair," suggested Mary.

"Yes," murmured Lincoln.

"Abra'm, just what is that *Trent* affair? You never tell me anything any more," pleaded Mary.

"The *Trent* affair is my pet bug-a-boo, right now," groaned Lincoln. "It's not easy to explain. Two Americans sent by Jefferson Davis as envoys to England were forcibly taken off the British ship, *Trent*, by an American war steamer. In mistaken enthusiasm, Secretary Welles, the House of Representatives and the Northern press approved most vociferously of the act. England says that unless we return the prisoners within a given time she'll declare war, or words to that effect."

"Shall you do it?" asked Mary, eagerly. "You won't, Abra'm!"

"If I don't, England will fight us. If I do, it'll be the most unpopular thing I can force down the neck of the North. . . . We are wrong in the matter. It's the thing England did to us, and we went to war for it in 1812. . . . Lizzie, I feel as if I were getting nearer heaven every minute."

His eyelids drooped. The two women smiled at each other. Softly and more softly stroked Lizzie. After a moment she nodded. Mary gestured toward the hall door. "Guard it," she breathed, starting for the door into Lincoln's room.

For an hour the two women stood at their respective doors, fending away all comers. At the end of that time, Lincoln came over to kiss Mary, and made his way toward his office.

As he passed through the living room, Miss Ford was pouring tea for Charles Sumner. Otherwise the room was deserted.

"Where's everybody?" asked the President.

"It's too early for most people," replied Miss Ford. "I was trying to pacify the Senator until you woke up. I've got two sleight-of-hand performers who will do some tricks for us at five o'clock. I hope you won't miss them, either of you. They call themselves the Singing Jugglers."

"Oh, I've heard of them!" Lincoln exclaimed, eagerly. "We'll have to attend the show, eh, Charles!"

"I particularly dislike that sort of thing," grumbled Sumner. "It's certainly childish and in bad taste to have such people here, at this time."

"I'm the guilty party," declared Miss Ford. "The President doesn't smoke nor drink. He's got to have something cheering, or I'll not be earning my pay."

"You see, Senator, the women folks have a more kindly feeling for my foibles than my constituents," smiled Lincoln.

"I see!" Sumner was recovering his usual suavity. "William Russell says he's inclined to forgive you anything because you don't chew, Mr. Lincoln. I think the national tobacco-chewing habit has horrified him more than slavery."

"I'm inclined to sympathize with him," said Mary, coming in at the moment, very stately in black silk, and the red India shawl. "The naked beauty of the quid has never appealed to me. After the first levee, in the East Room, I had to have the carpet taken up and burned. It was viscid with tobacco juice. And have any of you visited Mount Vernon? The very walls are coated with brown spit. Faugh!"

"Where is Russell? I haven't seen him for a month and I'd like his comment on this *Trent* business," asked Lincoln, chuckling at Mary's wry face.

"He's hunting prairie chickens in Illinois," replied Miss Ford. "I do like these sporting Britishers. They're like Southern gentlemen."

"Too bad he has to hunt with Northern clodhoppers, isn't it?" snapped Mary. "For a sensible woman, you do say the silliest things, Miss Ford."

"I reckon I do!" agreed the Virginian, good naturedly.

"Charles," said Lincoln abruptly, "a lot of my friends, even Miss Ford here, have been urging me to send you to England on the *Trent* matter. But I'm not going to do it. I need you too much in the White House and the Capitol, to work on Compensated Abolishment."

Sumner, superb in his silver gray broadcloth suit, came to his feet and shook his beautifully kept, white hand in the President's face. "Compensated Abolishment! More quibbling. More quibbling. Destroy it at a single blow! Cease to fear! Emancipate the slaves, and you end the war."

"This is a war to preserve the Union, not to end slavery!" cried Miss Ford, rising behind the tea table, and hurling the words at the Senator as though they were missiles.

"Woman, you lie!" roared Sumner, turning from Lincoln to give her the full force of his passion. His two fists shot toward the ceiling. "Slavery is the ruling idea of the rebellion. It is slavery that inspires every Rebel from general to trumpeter. It is slavery that speaks in the word of command and sounds in the morning drum beat. It is slavery that digs trenches and forts, pitches its wicked tents, and sets the sentries over against the National Capital. Wherever the rebellion shows itself, whatever form it takes, whatever thing it does, whatever it meditates, it is moved by slavery; nay, the rebellion is slavery itself, incarnate, living, acting, raging, robbing, murdering, according to the essential law of its being."

"Oratory!" sneered Miss Ford. "You said the same thing at the Republican State Convention at Worcester in October. But I, and many another, noted that only a few backed you when you urged that emancipation be placed in the party platform. The country is still sound as Mr. Lincoln will find, if he tries to stuff Compensated Abolishment down the throats of the border states. They'll spew it up." She paused, trembling with the force of her vehemence. Then, before Sumner could reply, she turned to the President.

"Where do you hope to get the money to pay owners for their slaves, Mr. Lincoln?"

Lincoln dug in the pocket of his snuff colored, baggy coat, and brought out a memorandum. "I worked this out last night," he said. "One half day's cost of the war would pay for all the slaves in Delaware at $400 a head. Eighty-seven days' cost of this war would free all the slaves in Delaware, Maryland, District of Columbia, Kentucky and Missouri. I wouldn't declare all the slaves free now, but by this plan I'd have each State adopt, now, a method by which the institution absolutely ceased in twenty-five years. See! Isn't that tender handling for you, Miss Ford?"

"No! I warn you, Abraham Lincoln, to keep your hands off our slaves as you would off our cattle or our houses." Her face quivered as she spoke.

Lincoln sighed. "I reckon, that, between you and Charles, I'll be ground to powder!" He returned the slip to his pocket. "Anyhow, Seward shall have his wish and send Thurlow Weed to England and France."

"A politician of his type certainly will make a bad impression abroad," exclaimed Mary.

"You'd say that Adams, our Minister over there, was their kind," agreed Lincoln, "but looks as if he hadn't got very far with Lord Russell. We'll try Weed's self-made manners. Charles, why don't you stay to supper and we'll thresh out this *Trent* affair. And Mary's French is languishing. I like to hear the two of you at it. It's almost as good as a trip to Paris, I reckon, for a backwoodsman like me."

He smiled at Sumner with such honest friendship that the Senator smiled in return, as he said:

"Thank you, sir! Even though I can't approve of your half-hearted approaches to the problem, your attempts at Compensated Abolishment are better than nothing and I'll help you any way I can."

"Good! Thank you, Charles! Ah, Taddie, coming to the show?" as the boy wandered in, followed by Pensacola, harnessed to a small cart. "Where are Willie and Sumter?"

His query was answered almost before it was spoken by the arrival of Sumter at a dead run, barking wildly, and dragging a wagon, in which was tied a much excited, and loudly vocal black cat. In the endeavor of both dogs to attack the cat, several chairs and the tea table were upset. And before the *mêlée* ended, the jugglers arrived, followed by Hay and Nicolay, and a dozen others of the White House family.

Mary scolded, their father laughed immoderately. Miss Ford and John Hay helped to subdue the dogs. The boys indignantly tried to make their mother understand that they had not planned to make trouble, but that they had been staging a parade for the jugglers. Their mother melted at this, and rescinded her peremptory orders that they go to bed at once. Louis and Daniel cleaned up the mess, and the performance began.

Lincoln always was intensely interested in exploits showing physical dexterity because, he said, he possessed so little himself. He beguiled the leading performer into showing him the secret of the rabbit and hat trick, and, after perpetrating the trick successfully with Charles Sumner's respectable beaver, he urged them to continue their song program.

It was a peculiarly interesting scene; the huge oval room, with curtains drawn against the wintry night, the shabby, comfortable chairs, the table on which Mary's books crowded the vases of roses, fuchsias, lilies, she loved; the glowing fire, on one side of which sat Lincoln, with Willie on his knee, on the opposite side, his wife with Tad leaning against the red shawl; seated beside Lincoln, and a little back of him, Sumner tolerantly amused, Seward absent-minded and placid, "Father" Welles impatient, Mrs. Welles lovely and interested, pretty Kate Chase scornful, John Hay with his twinkling black eyes on Miss Chase. Grouped with Mary, Miss Ford, her eyes on Lincoln, Mrs. Seward tired and patiently impatient, George Nicolay interested, Cameron handsome and bland, a notebook on his knee.

Opposite the fireplace worked the jugglers, in black tights, doublets of silver, slashed with red, red velvet caps, each with a long black feather. They sang for Lincoln, in the cheap concert hall manner, several popular songs which did not hold the President's attention. Observing this, one of the singers cut short the rendering of "Seeing Nellie Home," and made an announcement.

"We have the privilege of singing for Your Excellency the new and popular hit, The Vacant Chair, written by a friend to the memory of Willie Grout, killed at the battle of Ball's Bluff."

Even their nasal, mechanical voices could not entirely obliterate the appeal of that tender and sentimental ballad which hundreds were warbling, but which Lincoln had not heard. It was the sort of thing that always tore him:

> "We shall meet but we shall miss him!
> There will be one vacant chair.
> We shall linger to caress him,
> As we breathe our evening prayer."

He listened, with quivering chin. The song made almost unbearably keen his constant grief over the losses the war was bringing to America—this war!—these losses!—how long must they continue, before he dare risk placing in the hands of his countrymen an edict freeing the slaves?

"Makes me think of Uncle Baker!" sniffed Willie, and burst into tears.

Suddenly, the President bowed his great head on the boy's shoulder and wept with him. Mary flew to his side; there was a moment of stunned silence in the room, then, at a gesture from Miss Ford, the company slipped away, leaving the Lincolns alone before the fire.

CHAPTER XVII

THE FIRST WAR ORDER

WHILE moments such as that following the singing of The Vacant Chair added to the sum total of Lincoln's sadness, they at the same time afforded a relief to his tense nerves, that together with the laughter that preceded the tears, made it possible to endure without breaking the burden that daily grew more ghastly.

He found himself, later in the evening, able to discuss the irritating *Trent* affair quite calmly with Seward and Sumner,—that is to keep those two high-strung gentlemen as well as himself to a middle key. The net result of the evening was a letter to England that Sumner prophesied would satisfy John Bull's exacting diplomacy.

The prophecy, in the course of the month, proved itself correct, and, before Christmas, Lincoln had the satisfaction of seeing the two prisoners given up to Great Britain. It was a remarkable diplomatic victory, as none knew better than the President, but he had no time in which to glory in it.

William Russell, at a tea gathering in the sitting room, caught Lincoln, passing through, and congratulated him on what he had accomplished.

The President looked down on the Englishman with a smile. "It was good diplomacy, but bad politics, I reckon. Bigelow hits it off:

> " 'We gave the critters back, John,
> Cos Abra'm thought 'twas right.
> It wa'n't your bullyin' clack, John,
> Provokin' us to fight!' "

He gave the verse with great gusto and strode away, followed by Russell's jovial "Ha! Ha!"

No, even the threatened war with Great Britain had not pressed on him as heavily as his anxiety over McClellan. The young General was carrying things with a high hand, frankly looking on himself as the last military authority in the country. With grim far-sightedness, Lincoln, one by one, cleared away the obstacles about which he felt McClellan could complain legitimately. He seized on Cameron's indiscreet recommendation to arm the slaves, in the War Department's annual report, as a good reason for appointing him Minister to Russia. And one morning, early in January, he sent a communication to Edwin M. Stanton, over which John Hay dared utter a protest.

"Mr. Lincoln, Stanton hates you!" He swallowed hard like a schoolboy, disliking to bear tales, but urged thereto by an overwhelming sense of duty.

The President, observing his embarrassment, helped him out with rather a twisted smile. "Yes, he's the man who christened me the Illinois Gorilla. . . . He's a fellow capable of performing the biggest and the meanest deeds. The country knows him well, and has complete trust in his honesty, as I have, and he can do more to restore confidence in financial circles in the conduct of the war than any one in America. He's a Union Democrat. He's got an exceptionally good head-piece. But, most important of all, he's McClellan's dear friend. . . . As far as I'm concerned, I can hitch along with him, somehow."

John sighed. "Very well, sir! I'm silenced but not convinced." Then he looked up at the President, with his delightful twinkle. "What a wonderful wife you would make, Mr. Lincoln!"

The President doubled up with laughter, and John hurried off with the letter to Stanton.

But for all Lincoln's efforts and personal sacrifices, with the new head of the War Department giving him unprecedented coöperation, with the country clamoring more and more for action on the part of the Army of the Potomac, McClellan did not move. His invariable reply to all urging was that the enemy vastly outnumbered him, and that he still lacked certain essential supplies. Lincoln walked the floor, cajoled, ordered. Still the Army of the Potomac, a wonderful organization now of 150,000 men in the highest state of efficiency, lay quietly in the Virginia hills, "eating its head off."

McClellan began to be inaccessible to the President's messengers, and seldom appeared at the White House. Uneasy, Lincoln decided once more to visit McDowell, himself.

One clear afternoon, late in January, Lincoln, accompanied by William Russell, started ostensibly for a horseback ride, but immediately they were out of the White House grounds, Lincoln said to the war correspondent:

"William, let's go over Long Bridge and visit McDowell. I want to see if he realizes the bottom's going to drop out of everything unless that army moves."

"I'm *persona non grata* with Army Headquarters, you know, Mr. Lincoln, ever since the newspapers dubbed me 'Bull Run Russell.'"

Lincoln grunted. "McDowell himself told me your account was accurate —I suppose I have an occasional privilege of my job. Come along."

"I'd jolly well like to!" exclaimed Russell. "Thank you, sir."

Washington and the Virginia hills were beautiful under a light fall of snow, blue-white in the brilliant sun. Lincoln drew deep breaths of the scintillating air, and felt his spirits rise, as they always did under the open skies.

He was almost cheerful by mid-afternoon, when they reached Arlington Heights, and entered the house. An officer bowed them into one of the parlors, which seemed to Lincoln, blinking with snow dazzle, to be full of women. But, in a moment, he perceived that there were only Mrs.

McDowell, Mrs. McClellan and—Miss Ford. There were highly polished floors, with rugs in soft colors, many spindly gold chairs and sofas—lace curtains, portraits, negro servants coming and going, the smell of coffee and whiskey.

"I say," murmured Russell, as an aide announced them, "headquarters does itself rather well!"

General McClellan, standing before the crackling fire, allowed the President to cross the room to greet him. He shook Lincoln's proffered hand, and bowed stiffly at Russell. As he took in the elegance of the scene, Lincoln deliberately turned backwoodsman.

"I reckon I'm as unexpected to you, George, as you are to me! I thought you were sick," he said, sinking gingerly onto one of the brocaded sofas and crossing his long legs. "What's going on, a church fair?"

McClellan flushed darkly. "May I ask, sir, what brings you here?"

"I thought maybe if I could catch McDowell alone," replied Lincoln, serenely, "I could surprise him into moving such of the army as he could control. And I'll make you a sporting offer right now, George! Since you don't want to use the Army of the Potomac, I'd like to borrow it, and set it to work on some of the plans I've been hatching."

The young general looked over to the tea table where Miss Ford and his wife were sitting. There was an exchange of looks among the three, and an ever-so-slight shrugging of McClellan's shoulders. None of this escaped Lincoln, who put his foot on the rung of a gold chair, took the little ivory paper knife out of his vest pocket and slowly rubbed his black locks with it, smiling inwardly as he thought of what Mary would say if she could see him.

After a long pause, McClellan asked, sardonically, "May I ask, sir, what you would do with the army?"

"I'd make it fight, George. That's what armies are for!" very gently. Then, suddenly, pointing the ivory blade at the general, he asked, harshly, "What's the mystery in your inertia, McClellan? You are not a coward, as far as I can discover! Your constant iteration that the enemy too greatly exceeds you in numbers is too trifling an excuse for a man of your intelligence. You know better. Come, what's the mystery?"

"By God, sir!" shouted McClellan, suddenly. "Don't try my patience too far, or you shall discover my strength. 'Borrow the army!' One of your puerile jokes, of course—but try it! Try it! See if one man would leave me to follow you."

"What General McClellan is boasting of, Mr. Lincoln," Miss Ford cut in a little breathlessly, "is the unparalleled affection his soldiers have for him. It really is remarkable,—unless one knows the general well,—the faith they have in Little Mac, the love they show him."

The President turned deliberately in his chair so that his long body in the gray riding clothes was facing the table. In so doing, he for the first time observed a young man who was standing behind her chair. It was "Obscene" Gordon. "Now where does that get us?" thought Lincoln. Then aloud, with a smile for Miss Ford, very magnificent in her black velvet riding habit, "And what else could I have supposed George meant, Sister Ford? There's nothing better than for a soldier to trust his general, far as I know. . . . By the way, McClellan," his eyes fastened grimly on "Obscene" Gordon, "it is clearly understood that no report of this afternoon's repartee goes to the newspapers. And while I think of it, Miss Ford, if by any chance you discover what reporter is writing to a certain New York paper, claiming that the Administration is considering commuting the sentence of the slave-trader Nathaniel P. Gordon, to satisfy the ardent pleas of Mrs. Lincoln, who, he alleges, is violently pro-slavery in her sympathies—if you discover him, tell him I'll do more than kick him next time I see him opportunely."

Lincoln rose slowly.

"Will you have a cup of coffee, Mr. Lincoln?" It was Mrs. McClellan's sole contribution to the "repartee."

"No, I thank you, Madam." Lincoln made his jerky bow and turned to McClellan, who still stood stiffly at the hearthrug. Something in the sturdy beauty and intelligence of the young general so renewed Lincoln's old yearning toward him that, for a moment, his uneasy suspicions were submerged.

"I hope you feel well enough to attend a war council Stanton is calling for to-night, George. It's his party. I'm just an invited guest."

"I have already written my acceptance, sir, to the Secretary of War," replied the general.

"Good!" commented Lincoln. "Well, Russell, shall we hit the highroad again?"

"Gladly, Mr. President," replied Russell who, throughout the interview, had stood behind Lincoln's chair, an elegant figure in a tweed riding suit, with high boots and spurs of a foreign cut.

The sun was well toward the west as the two mounted their horses and set off for home.

Lincoln reviewed the call, mentally, puzzling not a little over the presence at Arlington of Miss Ford and Gordon. His companion did not intrude on his thoughts, and it was not until they had again clattered on to Long Bridge that Lincoln asked, abruptly, "William, what's the matter with McClellan?"

The war correspondent replied promptly, "Too much adulation, sir, from every one. You, yourself, Mr. President, have contributed not a little to his surfeit of sweets."

"I thought he was too big to spoil," sighed the President. "But he's got a notion, it's obvious, that the Army of the Potomac is his personal bodyguard."

Russell laughed, then said with his usual fairness, "He's a competent engineer. His defense works around Washington are beyond criticism."

"He's only a *stationary* engineer, I'm getting to believe," grunted Lincoln, and changed the subject.

But during the remainder of the ride home, during dinner, with the Welleses and the Sewards as guests, he was pondering on McClellan—McClellan and Miss Ford—Miss Ford, McClellan and Gordon. During the war council, later, he permitted Stanton to take the lead in urging action, while still he studied the General-in-Chief. Stanton had derided Lincoln's assertion that no one could move George McClellan save the Almighty, whom alone McClellan admitted to be his superior. Stanton showed a little impatience toward his favorite, it is true, and was endeavoring, this evening, to move him, himself.

The council dragged through several hours' discussion of plans for an immediate move toward Richmond. For every suggestion, McClellan had the same reply, that the enemy too greatly outnumbered him for such tactics to be successful.

Toward midnight, when McClellan had made this reply for the fifth or sixth time, Stanton's fierce temper rose.

"By the eternal, what hallucination has paralyzed the Federal generals? Read this, sir." He walked over to his desk and, seizing a handful of telegrams, he handed McClellan one from Rosecrans, in West Virginia, asking for more troops.

McClellan read and sniffed disgustedly. "Nonsense, he doesn't need another man!"

"Read this, also, sir!" exclaimed Stanton, tugging with trembling fingers at his beard.

It was a telegram from Sherman insisting that 200,000 more men were needed in the West.

"The man is crazy!" was the General's contemptuous comment.

"I told you, Stanton," said Lincoln, "that George regards every man we sent to any other department as willful robbery of the Army of the Potomac."

"May I ask you, General," demanded Stanton, hoarsely, "what you intend to do with your army, and when?"

A disagreeable silence ensued, with Stanton pulling at his long-suffering beard, McClellan sitting bolt upright, his hand on his sword, with Lincoln looking in a troubled way from one to the other, as he nursed his left knee. He could see Stanton's furious temper rising. The last thing he desired was a quarrel between the two men, each so valuable, each so extraordinarily difficult.

"Have you a date in your own mind for a move, McClellan?" Lincoln urged.

"I have, sir," replied McClellan.

"Then, I shall adjourn this meeting, trusting you to divulge that date to us, in the immediate future," Lincoln said, ignoring the fact that Stanton had called the conference.

McClellan and McDowell left at once. Lincoln pulled his gray shawl over his shoulders, set a dilapidated tweed cap over his nose and faced his new Secretary of War with a brooding eye. Stanton pulled his spectacles off, and polished them with vicious force.

"Why did you interfere, Lincoln? We had got nowhere," he demanded.

"You and Little Mac are good friends, Stanton. I reckon it'll be better for the country if you stay so."

Stanton beat the war map which lay open on his desk with a muscular fist. "I ruined two of my good friends, to-day, whom Cameron had allowed to loot the treasury with fraudulent war contracts. George McClellan will use his great talents to push the war or he'll use them on his old job back with the Illinois Central Railway as a private citizen."

Lincoln sighed and walked into the next room, where the code telegraph operators were at work. He read through a sheaf of dispatches from the West, then sat down at one of the desks and fell into a dark reverie. He was roused when the telegraph instrument before him began to sound, and young Bates reached over his shoulder to reply.

"Young man, I've hunkered you out of your seat, I guess," he remarked, rising.

"Thank you, Mr. President," said the young man. "This is the second time to-day you've given way to some one. I saw you step into the deep snow this morning on F Street to make room for a fat nigger wench."

"Did you?" asked Lincoln. "Maybe I did. I've made it a rule all my life if people wouldn't turn out for me, I'd turn out for them. You avoid collisions that way. Good night, boys!" And again in the dark reverie, he left for the White House.

He went directly to Mary's room.

"That you, Abra'm?" she asked, as he opened the door softly.

"Yes, Mary." There was no light in the room save the warm glow from the fire which lighted his wife's long chestnut braids, and touched her cheeks with delicate rose. He sat down at the side of her bed and took her hand. "Feeling pretty well? Like being here in Washington?"

Mary smiled. "I'm nicely, Abra'm, but I guess I enjoy Washington about the same way you do. How did the conference go, this evening?"

Lincoln shook his head, then asked, abruptly, "Mary, what do you think of Sister Ford now? I'm wondering if she's not brewing more mischief than we ought to stand for."

Mary sat up in bed. "What's she done, now, Abra'm?"

Lincoln told of his suspicions roused at Arlington and added, "Gordon's not her sort, or McClellan's either. They're just using him. But for what?"

"Something connected with keeping the slavery issue holy," retorted Mary, "as Charles Sumner would say. He's having a beautiful time, Abra'm, trying to make an Abolitionist of me."

Lincoln patted her hand. "Is he succeeding, my dear?"

Mary looked thoughtful. "Well, I find his arguments very persuasive. He is really very attractive to a woman who likes to use her brains. You know he corresponds with several highly cultured English and French ladies. His letters from the Duchess of Argyle are fascinating."

"It all helps him in his job," with a twinkle, from Lincoln.

"Aren't you horrible!" Mary laughed softly. "He and Miss Ford have quarreled, I believe. He says he no longer can ignore her attitude on slavery."

"Don't know but what I'm in the same boat," murmured Lincoln. "That new head of the National Detective Police, Colonel Baker, is an intelligent and tactful fellow. I reckon I ought to have a talk with him soon. Though, when you get right down to it, I haven't a great deal to tell."

"Have him talk to Jinny," suggested Mary. "Though I admit that I dread to have him discover anything. She's wonderful with the boys. . . . As to your puzzle about her relation with McClellan, Abra'm, my public teas have shown me one thing. She and her clique, like all the rest of the world, are feeding his vanity until it's inevitable, unless he's terribly defeated on the battlefield, that he'll try to make himself either Dictator or President. And he'll never risk a real battle. I told you he is yellow."

"He's not yellow!" contradicted Lincoln. "He's young—very young—I wonder if he thinks if he dallies long enough the peace parties, North and South, can patch things up, saving both the Union and Slavery— No, he couldn't be such a fool!— What is it, Mary, what is it? Why won't McClellan move on Richmond?"

"He's a coward, and just now cowardice helps on his ambitions," promptly, from Mary.

"No! no, he's no coward! You don't help me by being vindictive in your judgments, Mary." He spoke almost pleadingly.

"My dearest husband, how can I not feel vindictive when I observe his insults to you?" asked Mary, rubbing her cheek affectionately against his arm.

Lincoln kissed her, then rose with a sigh. The puzzle was still unsolved.

He sent for Colonel Baker, the next morning, but the detective was off on a case that would not be finished for several days. Lincoln promptly forgot the matter and turned to putting through the first turn of what he called the thumb-screw method on McClellan. He issued his "War Order No. 1." As Commander-in-Chief of all forces, he ordered a general movement of the military and naval forces against the insurgents. Almost as an after-thought, he called a Cabinet meeting and told the members what he had done. The members, slowly learning that they must bow to Lincoln's solitary rule, did not, for once, resent his autocratic methods, but gave him general approval. Chase, who had begun to hate McClellan quite openly, was especially generous with his approval.

"At last!" he exclaimed. "Finally you've come to realize, Mr. President, that a coward has to be forced to fight."

"McClellan is no coward, sir," snarled Stanton.

"Give me proof of his bravery and I'll apologize, Mr. Secretary Stanton," sneered the Secretary of the Treasury.

Seward interrupted tactfully. "I'm ready to wager with any one that now we may bank on the Mississippi being open by the first of May."

"McClellan won't be ready to move by May," grunted Welles.

Lincoln, employing his usual method of keeping peace, turned to Postmaster General Blair. "I granted a pardon to young Jones but I'm not sure I should have. Of course he is a mere boy. His father put up a good argument for him. For that matter, the man whom I was talking to when you folks came in was a good talker. He, too, wanted to get a relative out of jail." He looked at the grim, impatient faces around the table with an irresistible twinkle in his fine gray eyes. "I tell you, gentlemen, we must abolish these courts! It's bad enough that they put so many good men in penitentiaries to get out, but now they've begun on the boys, that's too bad. And, according to the evidence that comes to me, they pick out the very best men to send to the penitentiary, and this boy Jones is a very good boy, too. The man who was pleading for his relative this morning, made me feel that Massachusetts must be a happy State, if her citizens who are out of jail are as virtuous as this one who is in. Yes, down with the courts, and deliverance to the victims!"

Attorney General Bates, smiling with the others, picked up a great stack of papers. "This seems to be a propitious moment, sir, to speak of Nathaniel P. Gordon, a slave trader. It was your friend Miss Ford who first brought him to my attention. But I've been bombarded since with pleas for and against his pardon. Undoubtedly, the Abolitionists are seeking to make an example of him."

"I know that case," interrupted Lincoln. "The man stinks to heaven with the aroma of his slave ship. This is his fourth offense—I wish such a blow to be struck at slave trading as will stamp it as dangerous and disgusting in the eyes of all seafaring men. Only hanging one of their fraternity will accomplish this."

Lincoln rose and, looking down at Bates, said in a voice husky with emotion, "I will reprieve him until the last day of February, so that he may prepare for the awful change awaiting him. On that day he must hang. Prepare the necessary document for me to sign, Bates, warning Gordon that, relinquishing all expectation of pardon by human authority, he refer himself alone to the mercy of the common God and Father of all men. That will be all for to-day, gentlemen." And he moved out of the room, his head bowed, his hands clasped behind his back.

CHAPTER XVIII

WILLIE

WAR Order No. 1 had no more effect on McClellan than the wind whistling over Arlington Heights. Several of his generals in the West and Southeast made spasmodic advances. Burnside and Goldsborough took Roanoke Island, the key to all the North Carolina coast defenses. Grant sprang into sudden fame by taking Fort Donelson on the Tennessee, a most important step toward the freeing of the lower Mississippi. Had these movements been backed wholeheartedly by McClellan, so that all the coils of the Anaconda tightened, the duration of the war undoubtedly would have been shortened by months if not by years.

But McClellan did not move.

Daily, Lincoln's uneasiness increased. What was McClellan's game? Did any one but McClellan know? Did Mrs. McClellan understand? Did any of their friends—Miss Ford?

He was signing a list of pardons when this thought came to him, one afternoon, in the middle of February. He looked up at John Hay.

"John, how does your 'settin' up' to Miss Ford progress?"

"Not rapidly, sir. The lady, I fear, finds Hay an insipid diet, preferring the roast beef of old England."

Lincoln chuckled. "I advised her once, myself, to take up with Russell. Is Russell really serious about her, John?"

"I believe not, sir. He takes her out a bit but I imagine his heart is on the other side of the water."

"John, I don't like her intimacy with the McClellans, knowing what I know of her beliefs. If I thought she really had an influence on him, on the peace-at-any-price-to-save-slavery side, I'd put her in the Old Capitol prison. As it is— Has Colonel Baker returned?"

"Not yet, sir! I'll see that he comes to you as soon as he gets back. How about some other detective—"

Lincoln shook his head. "There's too much politics in this thing for any but a broad gauge man. I'll wait for Baker. In the meantime, I reckon I'll face her, myself. Send her in here, John, then pray for me."

"You can take care of Miss Ford or any other woman, as far as I can observe," young Hay retorted imperturbably, as he hurried to obey the order.

Miss Ford came in with a look of inquiry in her violet eyes. She took the chair Lincoln placed beside his desk for her, pulling a little green knit cape about her shoulders. The White House was not well heated. Snow tapped steadily against the windows, and a bitter wind swayed the shades.

"Sister Ford," began Lincoln, then paused, wondering what on earth he was to say.

"'Sister' is rather a recent acquisition," the Virginian smiled. "There are arguments both for and against it."

"I'm entirely for it," declared Lincoln. "It has a friendly sound. Sister Ford, what is it you desire most in this world,—to preserve slavery?"

She gave him a little smile. "Do you require a quite literal reply, Mr. Lincoln?"

"Yes!" replied the President, quietly.

"Do you mean what would I desire could I have my wish?"

"Yes. Be frank with me. Would it be McClellan's total quiescence until peace could be declared on a pro-slavery basis?" asked Lincoln, leaning toward her, earnestly.

"You mustn't put words in my mouth, sir! You must permit me to answer your questions freely, and, as I am a woman, that answer must be intensely personal." She drew a breath so tremulous that the buttons on her dress quivered. Her cheeks burned. Suddenly she leaned forward to place her hands on Lincoln's.

"Could I have my heart's desire, dear Mr. Lincoln, it would be that I be beloved by you as you are by me, and that, far from the madding crowd's ignoble fight, we'd be living for each other."

Lincoln gasped, "Good God!" and jumped to his feet. "Are you mad?"

As though stung to the quick by the surprise and disgust in his voice, Miss Ford rose so precipitately that her chair tipped over. Her voice was thick with passion. "Mad? Yes, mad, Abraham Lincoln, when I permit myself to think of you—your magnificent ugliness, your superb intelligence, your utter sweetness and your complete aloofness from all human contacts.—Ah, I have watched you month by month—"

"Stop!" thundered Lincoln. "You are a superb actress, Miss Ford, but you are wasting your talents on me. Take them to James Hackett. He'll be here next week. In the meantime, calm down and consider what you are saying."

"Have I considered anything else for six months?" demanded the Virginian, fiercely.

"Yes, ma'am! You have given deep consideration to George McClellan."

"With the top of my mind, yes. To you, my inmost soul."

Lincoln paused, uncertain whether to laugh or weep. He had no idea as to whether or not Miss Ford had any real feeling for him. It was not impossible. He had known many women. Not a few of them, for some reason endlessly mysterious to him, had made love to him. He believed that the present scene, however, had been carefully rehearsed with an idea of carrying him off his feet. And yet, no anomaly of feeling, he told himself, was impossible to this woman. In no other had he observed such possibilities for a conflict of passions—mental, moral and physical.

Snow tapping on the window panes. Faintly from Pennsylvania Avenue, the sound of a funeral march,—some soldier going to his long rest. An unusual sense of weariness pressed on his heart. He raised a hand to rest on her green, wool-clad shoulder.

"Dear Sister Ford, what a wealth of talent to waste! Ah, my dear, don't waste it! Use it to help save the Union."

"To destroy slavery, you mean!" still fiercely.

"To save the Union, cleansed of slavery. Help me, Miss Ford!"

She looked up at him, nostrils dilating. "That? Never! Never!" She seized his hand, turned it and kissed the calloused palm, then moved away from him. "You are going against tremendous human forces and appetites, Abraham Lincoln."

He clasped his hands behind him and stood staring at her, a slow anger and antagonism mingling with pity in his heart. "Are you warning me or defying me, Miss Ford?" he asked.

"Either or both! The choice is yours, sir!"

Her handsome head in the air, one hand twirling the huge globe beside the table, it sunk in on Lincoln that hers was a terrible power, and that she had no place in the President's household. She had better go and that at once.

As if she sensed what was in his mind, she said in a natural, casual way, "I must get back to the boys. Dr. Stone says he's afraid both of them have a touch of typhoid."

Lincoln started as though she had struck him. Both boys had been in bed for a day or two, with what was supposed to be a bilious attack, following a children's party.

"Typhoid!" he exclaimed. "When did the doctor say that?"

"He had just told Mrs. Lincoln and me when you sent for me," replied the Virginian, her ruffled green skirts sweeping after the President, as he strode from the room.

Tad was drowsy with fever and wished only to drink cold water and to sleep, but Willie's blue eyes were brilliant. He asked his father to sit down and read Scott's Hunting Song to him.

Lizzie Keckley, in a comfortable white apron, was putting a cold towel on the boy's aching head. She smiled up at Lincoln.

"Don't look so upset, Mr. President. A little headache isn't going to worry this boy, is it, Master Willie?"

"Of course not!" exclaimed Willie. "Papa day, I want you to tell John Hay to take care of my pony. He's the only one that knows how a pony feels. And every morning till I get well, I want John to go down and talk to him."

"I'll see that John does it," replied Lincoln, picking up the little leather bound copy of poetry and sitting down beside the bed.

> "Waken, lords and ladies gay,
>   On the mountain dawns the day;
>   All the jolly chase is here
>   With hawk and horse and hunting-spear."

Lincoln read the poem superbly. Willie was stilled as though a healing hand had allayed his misery. In fifteen minutes he was asleep. His father sat for a few minutes longer gazing at him, then he stole away, intending to find Mary and speak a word of comfort to her. She was in Tad's room with Miss Ford. Both women were leaning over the child's bed.

"You let Miss Fo'd hold me, motheh," Tad was saying. "You must be ti'ed and she's so st'ong and comfable and she likes to hold me."

"You're a spoiled baby!" exclaimed Mary, tenderly, moving back with a smile that was utterly without jealousy.

"Anything for her children's comfort, bless her dear heart," thought Lincoln.

Miss Ford lifted the boy easily, Mary wrapped the blanket around him and the Virginian crossed the room to the fire where she seated herself in a mahogany rocking chair and began to croon a darky lullaby. Mary caught sight of Lincoln, and followed him into the hall.

"She's a strange contradiction," he said.

"Yes!" sighed Mary. "The boys are never happier or more docile than when she's with them. Abra'm, do we have to send her away until the boys are well?"

"No! We'll hold off until then. But after that—" He shook his head. "This is hard news Dr. Stone gives us, darling Mary! Can it be real? The boys don't seem much sick."

"They aren't," replied Mary, cheerfully, "but they'll need careful nursing."

"Looks to me like they were getting it!" his anxiety lifting with Mary's manner. "I'll sit up with 'em to-night."

"You won't be needed, dear," replied Mary. "Save yourself for your big tasks. There's Charles Sumner looking for you now!"

The Senator, a great blue cape lined with seal thrown over his shoulders, came up with both arms extended, and stood holding one of Mary's and one of Lincoln's hands.

"Young Stoddard has just told me. What may I do to help? I am an excellent nurse, having had so much illness myself."

Mary smiled at him gratefully. "You and the President have your hands full, nursing a patient that's far sicker than our boys. I refer to your friend 'Compensated Abolishment.'"

Lincoln chuckled. "I reckon he is right sick but we're going to try to pull him out, eh, Charles?"

Sumner smiled. "If you can spare a moment, Mr. Lincoln, that's what I came to consult you about. I have had a letter from John Bright on the British state of mind, which I'd like to read to you. Compensated Abolishment will not bring the British to our side in this war. It would still remain a war of coercion, to their eyes. But come, let's read the letter."

Lincoln proceeded along the hall to his office and seated Sumner in the chair so lately occupied by Miss Ford. Mary was not worried about the boys but, somehow, his own anxiety was only half assuaged.

The next day, Taddie was sharply sick. But after a few days, his fever began to lessen. The onslaught of the disease with Willie was mild, but day after day his fever rose, until one could see it consuming his vitality like an unquenchable fire.

A shadow settled over the White House. The work in the office went on at the same almost unendurable pace, but many times a day Lincoln abruptly left his desk, or excused himself from a conference, or turned away from the unending stream of importuning visitors, to walk hastily over to the children's rooms. There he would question the attending women for a moment, kiss each boy's little burning hand, and hurry back to his work.

People were, of course, astonishingly kind,—astonishing, at least, it seemed to Abraham and Mary Lincoln, who had been the recipients of such virulent unkindnesses during this year in the White House.

On the afternoon of February 20, Lincoln broke away suddenly from Stanton who was berating him, half sneeringly, for not enforcing his full authority on McClellan,—broke away because a sudden prescience of tragedy touched him on the quick. He was gone not more than five minutes. Stanton was sitting by the fire when the President returned. He looked up indignantly, but rose when he observed the expression in Lincoln's eyes.

"My dear Mr. President!" he exclaimed. "Bad news? The boys?"

Lincoln put a great hand against the mantel to support himself. He could see Stanton's bearded face only through a reeling black mist. After a moment he forced himself to say:

"Dr. Stone says there's no hope for Willie. The end may come any moment. I reckon you'll have to excuse me, Stanton!"

"Excuse you! Good God, Lincoln, haven't I buried my own precious child? Don't bother about anything. I'll go out and boot McClellan clear to Richmond. Don't bother!" He gave Lincoln a sudden bear hug, and rushed from the room.

The dreadful minutes marched on. Willie never wakened from his stupor, after rousing feebly toward dusk to ask Miss Ford to hold him. She lifted his head against her shoulder. An hour later he died lying so, with his father's face buried against his feet, with his mother walking the floor, groaning and twisting her hands.

Lizzie Keckley, when the Virginian, with infinite tenderness, had laid her burden down, touched Lincoln on the shoulder.

"Mr. Lincoln, if you will get the Madam into her room, I'll wash him and lay him out."

Lincoln staggered to his feet and going over to Mary, lifted her in his arms and carried her to her room, where he undressed her, and put her to bed. Her self-control was utterly shattered.

Willie's death was, it seemed to Lincoln, the greatest grief of his life. Even the death of Ann Rutledge, that most poignant loss of his youth, had not torn at his very vitals as did this. A ghastly hopelessness, the like of which he never before had felt, day by day increased within him.

Those about him believed that he was bearing up well, far better than poor Mary. Only the President himself knew the deeps that had been probed by Willie's too early withdrawal.

Miss Ford, giving all her time to the convalescent Tad, had perhaps clearer insight than any one, now that Mary's usually alert powers of observation were blunted by grief, into the inroads the tragedy was making on the President's calm common sense.

A week after the death, John Hay tapped on Mrs. Lincoln's door. It was about ten o'clock in the morning. He asked Lizzie Keckley, who answered, if the President were within.

"He must be in his own room," she hazarded. "He locked the door of his room early this morning."

John turned away, and went to Tad's room, where Miss Ford was sitting with her embroidery.

"I guess the Tycoon is locked in his bed chamber," he said. "Ought we to do anything? Do you think he's ill?"

"He's ill," replied the Virginian, "but not in the common parlance. He's keeping vigil, I would suppose. This is Thursday, just a week after Willie's going."

"Poor old fellow!" murmured John. "We must leave him alone, I suppose. But he's badly needed in the office."

All that day, Lincoln sat in his room in a lethargy of despair from which he made no attempt to rouse himself. For hours he thought of the boy, summoned every detail he could recall of the child's picturesque mind, dwelt in exquisite agony on his extraordinary promise,—for he was the cleverest one of the Lincolns' trio,—read again and again the poem to Colonel Baker, and wept because the little hand would write no more. Never again. Gone. Gone forever. But whither? Into nothingness? Lincoln groaned and rocked his long body in anguish.

There was the crux of it. His faith in God was impregnable. In immortality he had little faith. Willie gone, forever, into oblivion! And all those other sons of other fathers that he was sending, had sent, to join Willie,—was the grief of other fathers like his? If so, what was he not answerable for to the Maker of all? Aye, let this Thursday and all his Thursdays be spent on his knees in penance and despair.

He went without food that day, but slept at night, and the next morning appeared in his office, haggard, but calm.

No one questioned him. The struggle to move McClellan, to give vitality to the work for Compensated Abolishment, with the myriad lesser problems that accumulated more thickly every hour, appeared to absorb him utterly. But, on the second Thursday after Willie's death, again Lincoln locked himself in his room, and gave himself over to grief and dreadful hopelessness.

Mary was now recovered from her prostration. She made several attempts to enter her husband's room, but he did not answer when she called him, and, with a little sob of pity and anxiety, she gave over her efforts.

There was perhaps an intellectual as well as an emotional relief in this vigil of Lincoln's, though he was unconscious of either. But his instincts were always basically sane. No man of his powerful affections and emotion could endure fighting them perpetually. Quite unconsciously to him, the idea that if he gave no thought to Willie, to the dead that Grant was strewing in his path in the West,—if he gave no bitter pangs to them to-day, Thursday he could abandon himself to agonizing over them,—it was this idea that made it possible for Lincoln to work, in the days after his little son's death.

On this, his second Thursday of fasting, and prayer, and tears, he found his mind going back frequently to the arguments he had used to himself when he had forced McDowell to undertake the movement that ended in the disaster of Bull Run. He recalled how he had told himself that only blood and tears could unite the North into the demand that emancipation requite the unthinkable sacrifices of the war.

Unthinkable. Much as he had suffered in coming to that decision, it had required Willie's death to make him understand fully what that sacrifice must be. Had God had that purpose in taking the boy from him? Did God wish the war to stop? Had McClellan the truer vision? Was his procrastination an instrument of the Almighty?

A great wave of doubt, more painful than hopelessness, engulfed him. Was McClellan's way God's way? Was McClellan clean of political aspirations? Had he no dreams of being dictator, placed in the White House by the demands of the impatient North, which was growing to believe McClellan's constant assertion that the interference of the Administration held him back? Or, if the answer to this was "no," was Chase correct when he declared that McClellan dreamed of being a Democratic President, elected by Union Democrats, North and South, a soldier President, who had saved the Union, without interfering with slavery?

He groaned deeply, stopped his floor walking to rest his arm on the mantel, his head on his arm.

If McClellan could save the Union, shorn of slavery, if God would give him a sign that such was McClellan's ability, how gladly would he step aside and give McClellan his place!

If God would give him a sign!

Was Willie's death that sign? Did the Almighty wish to show him that what he was forcing on the people was not to be borne? . . . But it was to be borne. People had endured the sacrifice of war ever since history began, and never before with such an opportunity for compensation as lay in the destruction of slavery.

Here memory of Mary's often reiterated comment on his softness, where his affections were concerned, impinged on his brooding. He straightened himself. No one was more conscious than Lincoln of the weaknesses of his character. And now, with a sudden sweat of fear, he asked himself if this weakness was beginning to twist his whole attitude toward the war, —if Willie's death was making him maudlin toward McClellan.

He brought his fist down on the mantel. By the Eternals, this must not be so! He would hunt down McClellan's motives, and act on them without bowels of compassion. It was intolerable that anything connected with Willie should smack of the ignoble. . . . His son! His little son!

He fell to his knees beside the bed, and began once more to fight his way through the morass of loss that engulfed him.

The next morning he came into Mary's room as she was dressing, himself fully dressed, ghastly with weariness and suffering. She ran to him and threw her arms around his neck, looking up into his face with blue eyes, —Willie's eyes, full of love and sympathy.

"Abra'm, *must* you do it? Can't I help you? It would break Willie's heart to see you."

Lincoln's face twisted convulsively, but he replied in a voice of quiet determination, "No one can help me. I shall keep Thursday sacred to Willie, and all the other war dead, as long as I live."

Mary gasped, slowly unclasped her arms and returned to her bureau. She knew better than to attempt to argue or beguile him from this mood. "I'll be ready to go down to breakfast with you in a moment," she said in a practical voice.

That afternoon, an old friend called on Mary Lincoln, the Reverend Francis Vinton of Trinity Church, New York. To his surprise, Mary scarcely gave him time to express his sympathy for her loss, before taking him by the arm, she exclaimed:

"You are a godsend! I want you to talk to my husband. You must do something for him or he will go mad." She told him of the tragic Thursdays.

"But will the President permit me to admonish him?" asked Dr. Vinton. "After all, he is the Chief Executive!"

"He's showing himself the Chief Fanatic, just now," cried Mary. "You must save him for his task, Doctor."

A little connivance with the three secretaries made it possible for the clergyman, somewhat late in the afternoon, to find the President alone in his office. He greeted Vinton without interest, then waited courteously for him to state his errand.

"I have come," said the clergyman, "to protest against your indulging yourself in grief so freely that you are unfitting yourself for your responsibilities. It is not an example of Christian fortitude that you are showing the people, Mr. President."

Lincoln looked at Vinton with lack-luster eyes, wondering dully who would come in to scold him next. In the last two hours, Stanton, Chase, Sumner, and the entire Congressional Committee on the Conduct of the War, had berated him in succession for his mismanagement of various affairs. Suddenly a phrase of Vinton's roused him.

"God is not God of the dead. Your son is alive and with Him."

"Alive!" ejaculated Lincoln. "You believe that?"

"I *know* it, dear Mr. President!" The clergyman's voice shook a little at the simplicity and pain in the question.

"Alive! Alive!" Lincoln buried his face in his hands. Then he looked
at the clergyman. "If I could believe that I'd see Willie again, it would
give me strength to move mountains! I reckon," with a broken, twisted
smile that was partly a contortion of pain, "I reckon it would give me
strength to move McClellan."

Vinton was possessed of the greatest gift of the clergyman. He was convincing. He now fixed Lincoln's gaze with his own, and said in a voice
such as Lincoln thought Christ might have used when he bade the troubled waters be still:

"You must believe that Willie lives. I believe it."

"And you are a man of as good intelligence as my own," murmured
the President. "Why should my mind refuse the faith?"

"Because you shut yourself away with grief for your companion, not
trust and hope. Willie, himself, is troubled by your un-wisdom, as your
wife's dream shows."

"What dream?" demanded Lincoln. "Mary has a kind of second sight!"

"There, you see, dear Mr. President! I told you you were shutting yourself away from hope. You would not permit Mrs. Lincoln to talk to you,
freely. She dared not tell you this. Last night, she dreamed that she heard
Willie laughing. It was so real that it woke her, she thought, and she sat
up in bed, to see Willie reading in the fire glow. She asked him why he
laughed. 'It was a pleasant way to waken you, without frightening you,' he
replied. 'I want to tell you that I'm having a heap of fun.' . . . And that
was all. The next thing she knew it was daylight."

"A dream?" Lincoln smiled wistfully and murmured, "We are such stuff
as dreams are made of . . . I seem to be troubling you all a good deal,
Doctor. . . . You give me a curious comfort—you—and Mary's dream—"

"You lessen the religious faith of thousands of people when you show
yourself so rebellious to the decrees of God," said Vinton.

Lincoln shook his head. "You deceive yourself, Doctor. No one has less
influence than I. I wield authority, not influence."

The clergyman smiled. "Coming down from New York, two colored
men standing near me,—the train was packed,—were discussing you, Mr.
President. I was astounded by their sagacity and understanding. I'll not
try to repeat all they said, but I'll tell you how they ended. One said,
'You hear about Massa Lincum all de time. He's on ebery nigger's lips,
day and night. He walks de earth like de Lord.' And his friend said, 'God
has hewed him out ob rock so's he can stand all de trouble of all de
people.' "

With a great sigh, as he made the renunciation, Lincoln rose and held
out his hand to Dr. Vinton. "There shall be no more mourning Thursdays,
Doctor. If I cannot walk the earth like the Lord, I can walk it like a man,
I reckon. Thank you, sir."

And he turned to greet a committee of Chicago business men, whom
George Nicolay was ushering in.

CHAPTER XIX

"ALL QUIET ALONG THE POTOMAC"

TWO results accruing from Willie's death stood out among many. One was that Lincoln decided that he could not send away, for a time at least, the woman in whose arms his son had died.

The other was that, out of the soul searchings of his dedicated Thursdays, came a hardening of his attitude toward McClellan. On the 8th of March word came that the Confederates, concentrated at Manassas under Johnston, had retreated safely thirty miles to the south, thus denying the Army of the Potomac as cheap a victory as any general could desire. It was after this that Lincoln wrote McClellan, removing him from his position as General-in-Chief of all the Northern forces, leaving him, however, still at the head of the Army of the Potomac.

He ordered General Pope, who had been winning victories in the campaign to clear the Mississippi, to come East and take over the command of three army corps which Lincoln had named The Army of Virginia. He also gave McClellan peremptory orders to divide his army into four corps, and to leave one corps for the proper protection of Washington during the campaign which McClellan now proposed to begin against Richmond.

McClellan's written reply to Lincoln was courteous and manly. But in the call he made on the President later, he was bitter and insolent. Lincoln was sitting at his desk with a supper tray lying on his war maps, and with Mary hovering anxiously near by. She was looking delicate and worn in her deep mourning.

The General made her a sweeping bow, then throwing back his military cloak, he tossed his gauntlets and cap beside the tray, and said in a voice trembling with emotion:

"So you fear me, Mr. Lincoln, to that extent?"

The President returned his look coldly, and took an audible mouthful of soup. "Yes, I fear you, George."

"Only my patriotism keeps me from resigning from the army," cried McClellan.

"I know that," replied Lincoln, taking up a fresh spoonful of soup. "You've got plenty of patriotism, George. What you lack is the kind of gumption Grant seems to have."

"Why not give Grant my place?" sneered McClellan.

"He's doing well where he is," answered Lincoln. "I must have at least 50,000 men to guard Washington, McClellan, and you must clear the rebels out of the river before you take the rest of the army south. I reckon it's not sense to have enemy batteries between you and me."

"I must save the Union!" exclaimed McClellan, "but I must allow myself to be directed by imbeciles! I know your game, Lincoln! You don't want to save the Union, that's why you seek to destroy me."

Mary uttered an angry exclamation, clapped her hand over her mouth and fled from the room. For a long moment, there was silence. Lincoln pushed his tray aside, clasped his knee and stared at the fire, while he sought for words in which to reach the young General.

"My suspicion is this, George. Jeff Davis knows that you are susceptible to flattery. He knows you are politically ambitious. He knows that you are a Democrat, willing to let slavery alone, if only you can save the Union. There's a pretty well-organized gang in this neighborhood seeing to it that you're kept in the frame of mind that you're in now. In fact, that Miss Ford, who's been living with us going on ten months, is an active member of the gang, I suspect."

McClellan stared, incredulity and anger struggling for supremacy in his face. "You needn't drag a woman into this insult."

"She wouldn't consider it an insult," returned Lincoln, coolly.

"I shall tell her your opinion of her!" cried the general. "If such are your suspicions, what right have you to have her here?"

"I have no right," replied Lincoln, catching his breath as the picture he never was to forget flashed before him, of the dying boy in the Virginian's enfolding arms. . . . He gave McClellan a clear glance. "Shall we have her in and talk it over?"

"By all means!" exclaimed the general. "It will give me exquisite pleasure to see this friend of my boyhood accused of treason!"

Lincoln rang the bell and gave James his order. Neither man spoke during the interval before Miss Ford came in. When the froufrou of her skirts announced her approach, Lincoln rose and took his place near the mantel.

She was in full evening dress; a pale green moiré antique with a train two yards long, of green velvet. It was cut so low that no mere man could imagine what kept the bodice in place. The great hoop, the train, the fan of enormous ostrich plumes, the mass of curls in her neck, her unusual height,—she was as impressive, thought the President, as the drum major of a crack regiment.

McClellan bowed over her hand. "Lady Ford, you look fit to devastate hearts, to-night! Even more fit than usual!"

She smiled. "Mr. Russell is taking me to the theater—quite an innocuous evening, I assure you, George."

"Sister Ford," said Lincoln, "the gentleman accuses me of insulting you when I tell him of certain suspicions of mine." He repeated his words of the earlier moment and paused.

The Virginian looked from one man to the other, smiling serenely. "But, George, that's not an insult! Of course, I've done everything I can to bolster up your self-confidence, and, of course, I've done all I can to make Greeley, Raymond, et al., tell the idiotic public that they must support the one military genius the war has so far produced. Is that treasonable?"

McClellan gave the President a triumphant glance. Lincoln's first impulse was to tell all that Mary had repeated to him. His natural caution intervened. But, still, the meeting had performed its purpose. He was convinced that McClellan was entirely unconscious of being regarded as a pawn by whatever clique the Virginian represented.

"The President," exclaimed McClellan, "has accused me, as you know, of possessing a secret,—some secret that keeps me from following his,— pardon me,—his absurd plans for taking Richmond. He wishes me to make a direct attack from Washington. I wish to attack from the lower Chesapeake. Therefore I have a treasonable secret." He shrugged his broad shoulders, then added with a quick change from the sardonic to the condemnatory, "He has not yet replied to my accusation that he does not want to save the Union."

"Give me details, George," urged Lincoln. "How have I given you that impression?"

"By doing all that you can to hamper and ignore the one soldier in the country capable of saving the Union," replied the general promptly.

"No, no, George! You're stupid in that!" protested Miss Ford. "Mr. Lincoln is trying his utmost in his own way to support you. What I accuse him of,—since this seems to be a sort of Truth game,—I accuse him of giving far more attention to his hope of freeing the slaves than he does to putting down the Rebellion. The Union doesn't come first with him."

"By jings," exclaimed the President, "in the game of tag, you're the next 'it,' Sister Ford! You're stupid, now. If the so-called Confederacy is successful, of what avail for me to talk of freeing slaves? The Union *must be saved!* That is the very foundation of every move I make. But"—he paused, then went on with an earnestness that caused both his hearers to change color—"but—the more this war is *prolonged*, the more emancipation will press on me as a military necessity. If time goes on with no marked successful action by our armies, I shall be obliged to cripple the military superiority of the South by freeing the slaves in the rebellious States. If this war is *prolonged*, England and France will find a pretext for interfering, to aid the South. This pretext will be based on the hypocrisy of our Federal Government in countenancing slavery, while attempting to put down a slaveholder's rebellion. Public opinion in England is all for the South. An emancipation proclamation would leave Europe not a leg to stand to justify intervention. Do I make myself clear?"

"Yes!" cried McClellan. "Knowing that I have no desire to interfere with the institution of slavery, you hold emancipation over me as a club to drive me into a campaign with an enemy of double my numbers."

Lincoln groaned, and ran his fingers through his hair till it stood on end. Then he walked back to his desk and began to eat his frugal supper. McClellan bowed to Miss Ford and strode from the room. The Virginian warmed her long fingers thoughtfully at the grate, the fire glow turning her pearls to rubies. Mary, who had observed McClellan's flight, came in through the private door. She gave Miss Ford a not altogether admiring glance.

"Mr. Russell is in the sitting room, Miss Ford," she said.

"Thank you," replied the Virginian, continuing to warm her hands.

"Abra'm, let me send for some warm food for you! You haven't eaten enough to-day to nourish a sparrow." Mary put a pleading hand on her husband's shoulder.

Lincoln shook his head and continued his attack on cold potatoes and gravy. His common sense was urging him to send the Virginian away, now. His intuition was insisting that he hold her at the White House,—his intuition and his love for Willie.

"I would like very much," drawled Miss Ford, "to visit my sister in Baltimore for a week or so. I am a little tired."

Mary's hard glance instantly softened. "You poor soul! You must be, after all these weeks of nursing. Only don't tell Taddie! He'll make such a fuss!"

"No, I'll slip away to-morrow—if Mrs. Lincoln could let me have my month's stipend a little in advance?" raising her eyes with an air of embarrassment that became her well.

"Of course! Whenever you wish it." It embarrassed Mary, in turn, to think of wages in connection with this gorgeous creature.

"Thank you, dear Mrs. Lincoln. I'll go to that blessed Englishman then. He'll be purple with impatience!" and she made a splendid, undulating exit.

Mary turned to the President with a wistful twinkle. "She keeps me in my place just by the way she wears her crinoline!"

"Jinny and Mrs. Keckley will keep us informed about this new move, won't they?" asked Lincoln.

"Yes," replied Mary. "Abra'm, I really am afraid of her. There's something of the tiger in her."

"So am I afraid of her, but only through what she may be able to do to McClellan. . . . What a pity! What a pity! . . . Well, maybe he really intends to move, now!"

"Abra'm, who will be the new General-in-Chief?" asked Mary.

"By jings, the next fellow that gets that job'll earn it by having some real battles behind him!" cried the President. "Ah, Charles," as Senator Sumner came in, "prompt as usual! I wanted to hear of the day's work at your factory up yonder on Compensated Abolishment."

Sumner was holding both of Mary's hands in his. He looked her over, shaking his head, then still holding her hands, he turned to Lincoln. "This dear person needs a change. Send her to New York for a little while."

"No! No!" cried Mary, quick tears springing to her eyes at the touch of sympathy. "I can't leave Mr. Lincoln or Taddie. I'm fatuous enough to believe that neither can do without me."

Lincoln nodded at the tray. "I'm one of her children, you know, Charles."

"Yes, I understand. You are a fortunate man, Mr. President." Sumner's delightful smile gleamed as he bowed to Mary.

"And you are a good friend," declared Mary, picking up the tray and walking out.

Miss Ford, of course, stayed only a few days in Baltimore. She then made a cross-country trip to the Ford plantation, a few miles north of Fairfax Courthouse. Appropriately enough, she reached there late at night in a driving rainstorm. She and Jinny, wrapped in a tarpaulin on the rear seat of the carryall, were wet and cold, when the mud-plastered horse brought up before the portico, the pillars of which were fitfully revealed by a lantern in the hands of old Uncle Bob, who was the only house servant remaining to the Fords.

"Fire in de den, Miss Lady," said the old man, leading the way into the house. "Only jes' enough cheers and sich for dat room left in de whole place. Seems like ebery time Massa Lincum needs a cheer or a table he sent here for it." Something like a chuckle escaped him.

"You dare to laugh, you fool nigger?" exclaimed the Virginian, furiously. "What do you mean by it?" slashing her wet gauntlets across the back of the negro's neck.

He rubbed his neck philosophically. "Like ol' times!" he grunted. "Massa Taylor, he waitin' fo' yo', Miss Lady," pushing open a door.

A small, square room, lined with books and hunting prints. A huge center table, littered with spurs, riding whips, wine glasses. A white marble fireplace—two caryatids supporting the mantel—and Captain Taylor in the uniform of a Federal gunner drying his wet back before the flames. The two greeted each other quietly, as if each was oppressed by responsibility. Jinny took off her mistress's wet green cloak, then went out, closing the door behind her.

Miss Ford sank into the chair Taylor placed for her. "How much time have you, Tom?"

"I dare not risk staying here a moment after you and I have exchanged views. . . . What's Lincoln's state of mind?"

"I can best report that to you by telling you of my conversation with him the day before I left." She repeated the interview with herself and McClellan.

Taylor listened with intense interest. When she had finished he said, abruptly, "That ought to persuade Jeff Davis, finally, that Lincoln is no fool. What's the status of Compensated Abolishment?"

"Sumner in the Senate and Arnold in the House will try to force that through as a recommendation, and Lincoln's going to get through his ancient bill, twenty years or so old, that he tried to get passed when he was a Congressman for freeing the niggers in the District of Columbia. He's arranging to have public schools for nigger brats, in Washington."

"Nothing like fanning the flames to keep the rebellion hot," commented Taylor.

"Compensated Abolishment will never pass with the border States. That's not what worries me," Miss Ford declared. "What I fear is that they will refuse too quickly. As long as we can keep Lincoln hoping for that, he'll let immediate emancipation alone."

"The border States are hard to manage," Taylor shook his head. "The presence of the Yankee troops in them is making the niggers awful impudent and uneasy, and intimidating our loyalists. But we'll do what we can. What's your feeling about McClellan?"

"He'll have to begin his march on Richmond or the country will force Lincoln to remove him. You know his plans, don't you?"

The captain nodded. "Our military spies really are good, you know. What a fool he was not to have taken Lincoln's plan, before Johnston got away from Manassas! . . . Quick action! How can we get quick action with McClellan?"

"By making him believe his patriotic duty is to lead the Army of the Potomac against Washington, and make himself dictator before he starts for Richmond. That done, the next move must come from the Southern Unionists. They must offer to make peace and return to the Union, provided the sanction of slavery is written into the Constitution. Can that be done?"

"I think General Lee would favor it," replied Taylor, carefully. "That dictator idea might work both ways. Lee and McClellan at the head of the armies could control the whole situation, if they were determined to do so."

The two stared at each other, faces pale with the magnitude of the suggestion. After a short silence, Taylor said:

"You're right. We must work rapidly. If worst comes to worst, we'll have to get rid of Sumner, Arnold, even Lincoln—a stray bullet, you know."

"No! Never!" breathed the Virginian, clutching at her heart. "Never assassination, Tom!"

"Names of things don't weigh, in war," said the captain, quietly. "What difference does it make whether a sharp-shooter works on the field and kills a general, or in the city and kills the Commander-in-Chief? When I entered this work I cast behind me all my old ideas of decency and fair play as I've told you. There's no such thing in war,—and I used to pride myself on my delicate sense of honor! As far as that's concerned, you used to be the only woman I ever knew who could be trusted."

A twist of pain contracted Miss Ford's fine lips. "I know, Tom! But not assassination!"

The officer pulled at his mustache and eyed her keenly. "In love with Lincoln, Lady?"

She lifted her head haughtily, caught the keen, yet compassionate look in his blue eyes, hesitated and then with the calm dignity that hushed any comment on Taylor's lips, she said:

"I would cast the whole of my influence and interest in slavery into his lap, if he would give me one half the feeling I have for him."

"Does he know that?"

"Yes."

"And he is impregnable?"

"He is impregnable," said Miss Ford.

Taylor sighed deeply, tested a cigar, drying on the hearth, then laid his hand on the Virginian's knee:

"I'm sorry, Lady. It never occurred to me you were playing with fire and liable to be scorched.—You haven't been South for a year, so you can't understand the degree to which Lincoln is hated,—and Sumner too. If they keep on tampering with slavery, they'll both of them be shot.—Well, it's all a dirty business. I wish to God it was over. I'll report to President Davis within a week."

"Not with regard to Lee and the dictatorship, I should hope!" ejaculated Miss Ford.

"Hardly!" with a cynical laugh. "There are plenty of people dissatisfied with Davis, Lady. Plenty of people who would be glad to end the war and return to the Union, if only they can keep their niggers. My idea is that the thing should be done before summer, before Lincoln's Compensated Abolishment hopes peter out." He rose and began to draw on his sodden blue coat. "You'll hear from me by the usual route."

"Did Uncle Bob feed you, Tom?" reaching out to touch the wet skirts of his coat. "I hope you'll not take cold."

"The old fellow gave me his last plate of 'hog and hominy,' I'd say, from the look of it. No," as she moved to ring the bell, "I have had plenty. As for cold—" Captain Taylor suddenly put his hand under the Virginian's chin and lifted her face—"Lady, do you really care whether I die of cold or a bullet? Before the war, I thought I had a chance with you." His hawk-like face was very appealing.

Miss Ford's eyes filled with tears. "Sometimes I think you're the only real friend I have in the world, Tom."

He stooped and kissed her. "Well, that's something!" he said with a little smile, and gathered up his gloves and cap.

When he had gone, Miss Ford rang for Jinny and told her to serve supper. They had brought a hamper of food in the carryall.

"I'll sleep on the sofa here, before the fire," she added. "We'll start back for Baltimore at dawn."

A week later, the President, ringing for a clean towel, was a bit staggered when Jinny marched into his room. She was a pretty young mulatto, almost as tall as her mistress, but much more slender, with a round saucy face and intelligent brown eyes.

It was barely daylight. Lincoln had had a bad night and was rising early for a walk in the garden to clear his mind. He stood before the washstand in trousers and undershirt, splashing water on his face as Jinny appeared.

"You're the only one up, eh, Jinny?" he asked.

"No, sir, I made James give me the job. Massa Lincum, I ain't goin' to trus' this to no Lizzie Keckley. I'm telling you my own self. I heard ebery word with my own ear at Miss Lady's keyhole." Flourishing one of the towels, she repeated, almost verbatim, the conversation between Miss Ford and Captain Taylor.

The President toweled himself vigorously and brushed his hair while listening to the recital. When she had finished he said:

"Jinny, have you repeated this to any one else?"

"Not a libin' soul, Massa Lincum."

"That's fine. Promise me that you won't repeat it, either!" reaching for his clean shirt.

"I promise, Massa Lincum. You going to scald an' roast 'em, ain't you, sir?"

"God's going to do that, Jinny. All you and I can do is to worry along, day by day. You are a good friend, Jinny. I'm obliged to you."

The door flew open and James appeared. "What you doing here, Jinny? That was my bell!"

"Which bell? The one that rang yesterday?" demanded Jinny. "Come out of here, nigger! Don't you suppose Massa Lincum wants his privacy?"

Lincoln smiled as the door closed abruptly. Smiled and then sighed. How could he work faster and still faster to best the malignancy that Jinny once more brought home to him. And, after all, he had been right in keeping Miss Ford. What simpler way was there for him to keep himself informed regarding McClellan?

LINCOLN entered his office, that morning after the interview with Jinny, fully determined to put Grant in McClellan's place. But, as if McClellan had sensed that he had stretched the President's patience to the limit, the first telegram that met his eyes as he stood over his desk was one from McClellan. He informed Lincoln that that morning the first regiments were embarking on the vessels which were to carry the army down the Chesapeake to Fortress Monroe from which the march on Richmond was to begin.

Lincoln read it and burst into a cheer as he rushed into the secretaries' office to share his relief. He found William Russell there, and brought him back to his office to show him a sample of gunpowder.

"Get your knapsack packed, my boy!" exclaimed Lincoln, as he led the Englishman into the room. "You'll be in Richmond in a month."

Russell shook his head. "Mr. Secretary Stanton will not give me a pass. He too, calls me 'Bull Run Russell.'"

"Shucks! That's too bad," declared Lincoln. "Don't you worry, boy. I'll send you along, William, with a pass that'll carry you plumb to Richmond! Look here! Look at the sample of powder some one's trying to sell Uncle Sam. Any backwoodsman is a judge of powder. I'll wager a first-class carpetbag against that valise you're carrying, William, that there's too much ash left by this stuff."

Lincoln walked over to the grate, sprinkled some of the powder on the hearth and applied the hot poker to it. When the smoke had cleared away he pointed to the ridge of gray ash with an air of mingled triumph and despondency.

"I told you so! I wonder who is honest!"

Russell stood beside the window, silently looking out on the distant river. Lincoln dusted off his hands, removed his spectacles and slowly crossed the room to join him in gazing at the far, magic view.

"Your offer is generous, sir," said the correspondent, finally, "but I've decided to give up and go home. This is a farewell visit to you. There is no getting news for a reporter who is forced down the throats of army headquarters. Not only am I 'Bull Run Russell,' but I am British, and, so, abhorrent to the American people. I cannot recall ever having received such treatment in a civilized, or, for that matter, a barbarous country, in any of my somewhat extensive travels."

"I reckon we lead the world here in America in not being able to see beyond our noses, William," agreed the President, thinking sadly of Willie's exclamation after the funeral of Colonel Baker. "I was ashamed of

America, Papa day." Then he added aloud, "I reckon, too, that the curse, as well as the privilege, of a democracy is self-conceit. Class distinctions keep that down a little, in Europe, I should suppose."

Russell, obviously in no mood for philosophy, smiled ruefully and nodded.

"I'm sorry to have you go, William, and I'm glad too," said Lincoln, "because I've got an errand for you." He turned from the window and paced the length of the room and back, stopping to look long and sadly from the window, his tired eyes deep sunk in his head, lines about his mouth that had not been there six months before. "I want you to take a message for me to Queen Victoria."

"I?" ejaculated Russell.

"Yes, you, because you're British and because you know me and I know you. I want you to talk to the Queen; just sit down and have a good long evening with her. She's full of horse-sense, I believe. You tell her what I'm trying to do and ask her to call off her dogs till I can do it. Tell her her folks are worrying me more than my own, which is saying a good deal. Ask her to play fair and keep out of it. She's a nice sensible woman, and once she learns what my ideas and troubles are, I believe she'll sympathize. Ask her to do this, Russell, in the name of common humanity."

He paused, surveying the war correspondent eagerly and anxiously. He admired Russell. From the very first he had seen him as a distinguished person, whose exceptional qualities were quite lost on the American public.

Russell returned his look, clearly. "You ask me to do that, sir, knowing that I must be bitter against Americans?"

"I don't blame you for being bitter," Lincoln jerked his head in agreement. "Tell her about that too. But what I know is that you're not bitter against the thing this Administration is trying to do—that's the important point. Can't you meet up with the Queen?"

"Yes, Mr. Lincoln, I can arrange that. Look here, sir!" with a little smile. "I'll drive a bargain with you. If I undertake to deliver your message, will you agree to this: When the next crisis arises between this country and England, will you see Lord Lyons, yourself, and give him an opportunity to learn your views, first hand?"

"I'll do that," declared Lincoln.

"The bargain is completed!" Russell held his hand. "Almost, sir, you have reconciled me to going home."

The President held Russell's hand, while he said with the smile that made his face beautiful, "When this war is over, my wife and I are going to pawn the court jewels and take a trip around the world. And we'll look to find you."

"I'll go with you, as your courier, sir!" exclaimed Russell. "God bless you and your great cause, Mr. Lincoln."

"Thank you, William. In the long run, I reckon He's the only one who can bless the cause!"

Russell picked up his dispatch case and went out to say good-by to his other friends in the household.

From that day on, for months, every event in the United States was secondary in Lincoln's mind to what was happening to McClellan and his army. Through the War Office where he spent many hours out of every twenty-four, he watched the progress of that great campaign, on the Peninsula, with breathless, soul-wearing concern. But as day succeeded day, he worked no closer to an understanding of the young General-in-Chief than had Stanton, who in a single day had run the gamut from pronouncing McClellan the greatest strategist that ever lived, to sending him as a criminal fool to perdition.

McClellan, in Lincoln's words, fooled April away in gingerly approaching by siege methods Rebel fortification that could have been taken by assault. But during May, he worked his way to within four miles of Richmond. The North was a tip-toe with hope and enthusiasm. McClellan was a young military god—he was great as Napoleon was great. And then, within sight of his goal, McClellan paused, dallied, called for reënforcements!

His entire campaign on the Peninsula, indeed, was marked by continuous shrill cries for more men. Lincoln and Stanton, walking the floor, in the War Office, strained the resources of the country to the utmost to send him all he demanded. But when, at last, he demanded a hundred thousand reënforcements, Stanton balked.

"If we had a million men, he'd swear the enemy had two millions and then he would sit down in the mud and yell for three. The fool has given the Rebels what they needed, time, and he'll be retreating next, see if he's not."

"Oh, I can't believe that!" protested Lincoln. "Why he's almost on top of Richmond now."

"He'll never get his nerve up to assault the town," growled Stanton.

"Do you mean to tell me that after all this superb fighting by our men, McClellan's not enough of a military man to seize his victory? Come, Stanton, you're not fair to McClellan."

"You'll see!" retorted Stanton, with an oath.

And Lincoln did see. On the last day of June, McClellan sent a dispatch stating that after terrible fighting and losses, he had ordered his army to retreat. His telegram was couched in terms showing such a state of mental panic on the part of the writer, that after his first reaction of anger and dismay, Lincoln decided to ignore the mutinous insolence of its manner.

"Save the army at all events," he replied. "I feel any misfortune to you or the army as keenly as you feel it, yourself."

McClellan's answer to this was a dispatch, a very lengthy one, incoherent and threatening in its tone, from which the startled President deduced that the Army of the Potomac virtually had been wiped out.

"Save what you can of men and supplies, even if you have to retire to Washington," he wired.

Two hours later, Stanton rushed into Lincoln's office with the reply, addressed to the Secretary of War.

"Read this! Read this!" he shouted.

Lincoln read, wincing as he did so, a virulent attack on himself and Stanton for their criminal neglect of the Army of the Potomac, which ended with this astounding accusation!

"If I save this army now, I tell you plainly that I owe no thanks to you or any other person in Washington. You have done your best to sacrifice this army."

Stanton danced about the room, cursing bitterly. "Hold on, Stanton," protested the President. "No use acting like an old horse with a gadfly on his rump. Let's figure this thing out with our heads, not our heels.

"McClellan started on this trip 120,000 strong. We've sent him 40,000 more. What does he do with his soldiers? Are they lost on the way, like a fellow carrying fleas across the barn floor with a shovel?"

Stanton, as he listened to the President's homely phrasing, began to cool down. "It's his cowardly hallucination as to the numbers of the enemy, the damn fool. The Rebels' Peninsula forces all told aren't over 50,000 men. Their losses have been as great as ours which don't total 20,000. I tell you the man is either crooked or a coward."

"If it were not for these good fellows out West and around New Orleans, gnawing at the Rebels' vitals, I'd feel as if the bottom was out of everything," declared Lincoln. "But with folks like Halleck, Hunter, Burnside, Grant, and Farragut upholding each other's fists, I can't quite despair. Reckon I'd better go down to Harrison's Landing and have a talk with McClellan, and see if I can sift out the facts. Will you come with me?"

Stanton shook his head. "Guess I'd better not. Our baby is sick and I must be ready to go into the country to see him, whenever Mrs. Stanton sends for me—to see him die."

"Is it that bad? Stanton, go to your wife now! I'll take your place."

Again the Secretary of War shook his head. The two men gave each other a look of sympathy and understanding, then Stanton said, "Even were I not held by domestic affliction, I'd doubt the wisdom of my going. McClellan claims friendship to my face and applies vile and opprobrious epithets to me behind my back."

"Speaking of epithets," Lincoln's eyes twinkled, "did you hear of my repartee with Lovejoy, the man I sent to you, this morning?"

Stanton, scowling a little, looked at the President over his spectacles with doubt and some irritation in his eyes. "I have no time for repartee, myself," he grumbled.

"Might as well say you have no time to smile!" exclaimed Lincoln. "Lovejoy came back after I'd sent him to you and said that you read my message with the remark that Lincoln was a damn fool. I told him that if you said it was so, it must be so, for you were nearly always right."

Stanton's color rose immediately. "He should not have repeated words spoken in irritation. Your request was unreasonable, sir, and I was obliged to refuse you."

Lincoln pursed his lips speculatively. Stanton was one of the most able men he had ever met, but he was also the most irascible. He was as heady with power as Seward, but lacked Seward's charming sense of humor and his good nature. In spite of the fact that he knew that Stanton, before his induction into the Secretaryship, had tried to incite McClellan to turn dictator, in spite of the vile remarks Stanton had made about his personal appearance, Lincoln's enormous trust in the man's integrity and ability gave him a curious sort of liking for him. He was determined that Stanton should come into line, admit his leadership, and become his friend.

"Stanton," he said, "you fritter away an awful lot of energy on merely getting even. Personal grudges don't pay. Now you do as Lovejoy wants, forgetting that you hate him."

"No!" thundered Stanton.

"I reckon here's where the foot goes down." Lincoln did not lift his voice, but his face was suddenly stone. "You are to do as Lovejoy wishes, Stanton."

Silence. The July heat in the office almost overpowering, sweat running down the faces of both men. Lincoln holding his knee, patiently. Stanton tugging at his beard, then gathering up the papers—

"It shall be done as the Chief Executive commands," he said, hoarsely.

"That's right, Stanton," Lincoln nodded, casually, and turned to a map of Tennessee. "I have written to Halleck to come down here as General-in-Chief. His record would warrant it. Grant can take over the Department of the West."

"You have already written him, and without consulting me?" ejaculated Stanton.

"Without consulting any one," replied the President. "I've studied Halleck more than any of you. His only weakness is lack of decisiveness. Grant supplied that in the West. You'll supply it here. He'll be here the last of July, and we'll sic him onto McClellan. In the meantime, as I've said, I'll go down to Harrison's Landing, where this telegram is from. Hope he stays there long enough for me to catch him! Come to think of it, I needn't wait until to-morrow. I'll borrow John Hay, and we'll go down to-night."

And go he did, reaching McClellan's camp forty-eight hours after leaving Washington.

He made no effort to see McClellan alone, for he was utterly weary of arguing with the general. He hoped only to gather together enough facts to make a final sweeping war policy. He did not permit himself to use any portion of his mind, during his few hours at Harrison's Landing, on any other matter save what he was seeing and hearing.

He viewed the beautifully ordered camp, sweltering in the July moonlight. He slapped mosquitoes and listened to McClellan and his generals discuss the next move of the Army of the Potomac. He issued no orders, though he expressed anxiety as to the health of the soldiers, carrying on a summer campaign in the wretched climate of the Peninsula. The smell of the pines, of the hot, dew-wet sands, of leather accouterments, of horses, of ammunition, depressed him. It had the tang of death in it. The voice of the river sliding between its low banks gave him a vague feeling of homesickness. He had been bred in a land of rivers.

But he learned the facts which he had come to learn. However panic-stricken McClellan was, there was no panic among his officers and men. The majority of his generals believed they were in no danger from the enemy, and were not in favor of a retreat. He learned that the army that remained numbered about 90,000 men, with the astounding number of 40,000 absent with authority. He learned that supplies were adequate, the men as well cared for, as such an arduous campaign could permit.

At midnight he started back for Fortress Monroe and Washington. Just before stepping aboard the gunboat that was to convey him and John Hay down the James, McClellan handed Lincoln a letter. The President read it by the light of a lantern, thanked McClellan for it, casually, and put it in his pocket. Even its contents, he told himself, must not permit him to quarrel with McClellan.

Yet it was as outrageous a document ever a soldier penned to his superior officer.

It presumed to instruct the President as to his duties and power, and warned him against any forcible interference with slavery, declaring that any such attempt on Lincoln's part would rapidly disintegrate the Federal armies.

Its phrases rankled, and after they had left Fortress Monroe and were on the transport for Washington, Lincoln gave the note to John Hay to read. The young man held it close to a ship's lantern and devoured the contents with much muttering and snorting.

"You'll *have* to court-martial him for that!" he declared, hoarse with indignation when he had finished.

"I don't know what I'm going to do," replied Lincoln. "That letter don't amount to so much in itself, except as showing up his dreams. He'd like to have my job, winning back the South by promises about protecting slavery. I suppose I must consider that particular dream, when I make my decisions about what to do with him but it won't influence me greatly. I've got to think of him in his relation to his army, and the war, not to me."

He leaned back in the chair which had been placed for him in the prow of the little vessel, and struggled to clear his mind of all the countless problems that rendered a complete concentration on McClellan nearly impossible. He found this so difficult that finally he had recourse to an old remedy. He turned to poetry.

It was nearing dawn. Dim shore lines and soft salt air were soothing to sight and sense.

"Do you know Browning, John?" asked Lincoln. Then, without waiting for a reply, he repeated in a low monotone:

> ". . . The hills like giants at a hunting lay,
> Chin upon hand, to see the game at bay,—
> 'Now stab and end the creature—to the heft!'
> Not hear? When noise was everywhere! It tolled
> Unceasing like a bell. Names in my ears,
> Of all the lost adventurers, my peers . . .
> There they stood, ranged along the hillside, met
> To view the last of me, a living frame
> For one more picture! In a sheet of flame
> I saw them and I knew them all. And yet
> Dauntless the slung horn to my lips I set,
> And blew.—'*Childe Roland to the Dark Tower Came.*'"

He rose as he finished and stood beside the rail, a giant, John thought, against the pallid sky. After a moment of thought, he went back to the opening lines of the tremendous poem and repeated the whole of it.

John Hay sat in awed silence.

After Lincoln had completed the last verse again, the two remained listening to the chug-chug of the paddle wheel, the rush of wind and water for a long moment.

"But he hasn't the humanness of Shakespeare," said Lincoln. "Take King John, for example." He recited several long excerpts ending with Constance's immortal query,—

> "And, father cardinal, I have heard you say
> That we shall see and know our friends in Heaven.
> If that be true, I shall see my boy again,"—

He caught his head in his hands and pressed it with a deep groan. "If that be true—aye—that's the rub!" Then he laid a gentle hand on young Hay's tired shoulder. "Come, John, let's see if these folks will give us breakfast."

CHAPTER XXI

CHILDE ROLAND TO THE DARK TOWER CAME

THEY reached the White House in the late afternoon. Lincoln asked the doorman, at once, for his wife. He felt a deep need to draw on Mary's affection.

"Well, Mr. President," said the old Irishman, deliberately, "she's having a little trouble with the general public, out by the south portico. You know you said the Wednesday afternoon concerts Mrs. Lincoln called off after Master Willie's death, could begin again. Mrs. Lincoln she's just went out and ordered the Marine Band to go home, and folks are pretty mad about it."

"Where's Taddie, Daniel?" asked Lincoln, wearily.

"Hea' I am, Papa day," shouted Tad, racing up in a linen suit well smeared with chocolate lollypop. "I've been watching fo' you all the time and then you get in without my noticing!"

Lincoln caught him up and kissed him several times. "Let's go find mother, Taddie darling. Where is she?"

"On the south po'tico. Guess she's awful mad. Let's go up stai's and see what you b'ought me. Did you b'ing me something, Papa day?"

"Yes, a rifle one of the soldiers gave me that was through the Seven Days' Battle. It's with my stuff." The President strode through the hall to the south portico.

The leader of the Marine Band was standing before Mary looking down at the little figure in black organdie with anger and embarrassment struggling in his face. Behind Mary were Miss Ford, Charles Sumner and pretty Kate Chase. On the lawns below was a concourse of people gathered in gesticulating groups.

Lincoln bowed to the three behind Mary and, placing his hand on his wife's arm, said:

"I want to borrow my wife for a moment, Scala. Wait here till we come back."

"But, Abra'm," cried Mary excitedly, "you must not—"

Lincoln led her away. "Hush!" he said in a voice so low only Mary and the band leader heard him, so fraught with command that Mary caught her breath as if choked.

He led her to the far end of the portico, moving slowly, for they were watched by a thousand eyes.

"Mary! Mary! Mary! Are you insane? Do you hope to force all the people of Washington to share your grief by antagonizing them?"

She looked up at him, her blue eyes blazing, but he gave her no opportunity to speak.

"What would Willie say if he knew that you were depriving people of music because of him?"

"It's not that!" cried Mary. "You ought to know me better than that. It's just that I can't bear to hear music since he left us. It kills my heart. And the Marine Band is the worst because its music is so exquisite."

"I know!" Quick tears softened Lincoln's eyes.—"But—Stanton's baby is dying. Will Mrs. Stanton make rows for Stanton to clear up, in the name of their dead boy?"

"Abra'm! Abra'm! My cursed tongue!" Mary freed her hand from her husband's and rushed back to the band leader. "Captain Scala, my husband shows me that I've not made myself clear. I'm not expecting others to mourn with me. I've been stupid and selfish. I've not wanted you to play your lovely music because it is so lovely that it makes my heart bleed again. I've been stupid and hysterical. Will you not forgive me and give the people the concert you planned?"

The anger left Scala's flushed face. "Why didn't you say that in the beginning, my dear Mrs. Lincoln?"

"Because I have the awful weakness of speaking with irritation first and thinking with regret afterward!" Mary smiled wistfully up into the band leader's eyes. "I've fought it all my life, but the stress of these days makes it very difficult for me."

She spoke with that endearing childishness so characteristic of her. The little group behind her smiled, sympathetically. Scala bowed over her small, soft hand.

"Takes a good deal of strength, I'd say, Madam President, to 'fess up like that. Thank you!" looking at her with new respect. "These folks have got to thank you, too."

He moved quickly to the edge of the portico and in a few simple words gave them Mary's reason for her unreasonable request. Mary and Lincoln slipped into the house as he began to speak, but the vigorous handclapping that followed Scala's statement reached them as they climbed the stairs and a few minutes later the notes of a waltz floated in at the windows of Mary's bedroom, whither Lincoln had led her.

"Will it be too much for you?" he asked, looking at her flushed cheeks.

"No!" she replied. "That particular foolishness is ended. Sit in that big chair, Abra'm, and let me fan you. We ought to go out to the Soldiers' Home to-night."

"A fan is my idea of nothingness!" ejaculated the President. "Just have Taddie here and let's have a *family* moment, if possible. I must get a little letup."

"And I bring you home to a scene!" Mary gave a heartbroken sigh as she pulled the bell rope.

Taddie flew in, grimy, round cheeks runneled with perspiration, a rifle as tall as himself in his arms. He rested it on the back of a chair, and pointed it at his mother.

"See what Papa day b'ought me!" he shouted.

Lincoln leaped from his place and took the gun. "Don't ever point at anybody, Tad!" he exclaimed with an apologetic glance at his wife, and wondering for the first time if this were the wisest gift for a boy.

Tad shrieked for the return of his gun. Mary sat on the ottoman, a little set smile on her lips.

Suddenly Lincoln laughed. "You're not going to complain, even if your son shoots you, eh, wife? Bless you! Reckon I've made a fool of myself, in my turn. Come here, Taddie darling."

It required some long negotiation but eventually Taddie was the recipient of a silver dollar, and the gun was removed by Louis.

"Now!" the President settled back in his chair, with Tad on his knee and Mary's hand in his, "now, for a little solid comfort! Tad, tell me all the bad things you did while I was away, and all the punishments mother gave you for them."

"She didn't know about most of 'em," retorted Tad. "I did the baddest one to Miss Fo'd and she neve' tells. Will you spank me, mamma, if I tell now?"

"Of course not, goosie," smiled his mother. "Do you think I'd spoil the one precious moment alone with your father in months?"

"Well, I took my goat to bed with me and—you know," looking up into his father's face with eyes of angelic innocence, "it's funny how goat smell makes some folks mad, isn't it? Miss Fo'd acted madda' about the smell than about the things he chewed up. Now I don't notice my goat smell at all. It—"

He paused to listen, half puzzled and half gratified, to his father's shout of laughter.

"Some one is at the do'," he said at last, watching his father mop the tears from his eyes. "So I can't tell you what he chewed."

"Run and open the door, Taddie," sighed his mother. The precious moment evidently was gone.

It was Louis, sent by John Hay to report that the committee of Congressmen from the border States was waiting for the President. Tad took advantage of the interruption to disappear with the silver dollar. As Louis closed the door, Lincoln turned to Mary, the laughter in his eyes replaced by burning sadness.

"I think they've come to make a final refusal of the offer of Compensated Abolishment."

Mary took one of her husband's hands in both of hers. "Abra'm, I hope they will refuse it! Charles Sumner has really made an Abolitionist of me."

"You guess, do you, what I shall do in case they refuse, and what it will cost?" asked Lincoln.

That look of second sight which he so held in awe came into Mary's fine eyes. "I guess and I know. You are predestined, Abra'm. Do what God tells you."

He stooped and kissed her on brow and lips. "You have given me new strength as I knew you would."

What he said, a few minutes later, to the group in his office, belongs to the history of the human struggle for freedom. He stood awkwardly beside the table, his black clothing rumpled and travel-stained, his eyes older than the pyramids.

". . . If you had voted for the resolution in the gradual emancipation message of last March, the war would now be substantially ended. Let the States that are in rebellion see definitely and certainly that in no event will the States you represent ever join their proposed confederacy, and they cannot much longer maintain the control. But you cannot divest them of the hope to ultimately have you with them so long as you show a determination to perpetuate the institution within your own States. . . . How much better for you and your people to take the step which at once shortens the war and secures substantial compensation for that which is sure to be wholly lost in any other event. . . . I pray you to consider this proposition. . . . As you would perpetuate the popular government for the best people in the world, I beseech you that you do in no wise omit this. Our common country is in great peril, demanding the loftiest views and boldest action to bring it speedy relief. Once relieved, its form of government is saved to the world—its happy future assured and rendered inconceivably grand. To you, more than to any other, the privilege is given to assure that happiness and swell that grandeur, and to link your own name therewith forever."

When he had finished his plea, which he gave with a wistful passion indicative of the depth both of his hope and his fear, he stepped into the secretaries' office, to permit the Congressmen to discuss what he had said. Both Hay and Nicolay were absent, and Lincoln was grateful for the moment of solitude. He seated himself on a shabby desk and fastened his eyes unseeingly on a vase of pink phlox—the room was heavy with their scent,—while he concentrated every faculty of his soul on the one hope, that the men whispering in his office would see the light.

Perhaps no one else in the world merely passing the open door could have roused him from his depths of absorption but the one who a few moments later did so. It was Miss Ford. He followed her fine, retreating back with a look of deliberate speculation. It was quite probable that she had looked in on the committee of Congressmen; following up the work already accomplished by Jeff Davis' henchmen! By jings, she was not to beguile them into stalling him off as they had done all spring, and as Jinny's tale would indicate they planned to continue to do all summer! He must have the answer now, so that before he slept that night, his decision on McClellan could be made.

He rose and strode into his office.

Senator Garrett Davis of Kentucky, acting as chairman, spoke quickly when Lincoln entered and took his place at the top of the table.

"Mr. President, we must ask for another month in which to sound out our colleagues."

Lincoln thrust both great arms, palms upward, along the table. For a moment, emotion choked him. His hair lay damp with sweat on his forehead. His lips quivered. Then he spoke, his voice at first only a hoarse whisper.

"I beseech you, make the decision now! You cannot, if you would, be blind to the signs of the time. I beg of you a calm and enlarged consideration of them, ranging, if it may be, far above personal and partisan politics."

Davis tossed his head impatiently. "You belittle us, sir."

The President's voice gathered strength and clarity. "This proposal makes common cause for a common object, casting no reproaches upon any. It acts not the Pharisee, the changes it contemplates would come gently as the dews of heaven—not rending or wrecking anything. Will you not embrace it? So much good has not been done by one effort in all past time, as, in the providence of God, it is now your high privilege to do. May the vast future not have to lament that you have neglected it!"

There was a moment of silence. This group of neutrals was moved by Lincoln's extraordinary eloquence, as were all his contemporaries, always, but the spell was only ephemeral.

Davis cleared his throat. "We must ask you to excuse us for another month, Mr. President."

Lincoln gave him a clear look. "Senator, you must vote *now*." A murmur swept the group. A murmur that was punctuated by angry ejaculations.

"You are unwise to try to force the decision, Mr. Lincoln," declared Davis. "We are agreed that we can do nothing until we know more."

Lincoln looked about the room. Not one of the twenty-seven men present whom he had not labored with, individually! It was his will against the cunning of the Ford and Taylor gang, he told himself. Slowly the muscles on his long jaw showed themselves in knots. Slowly his lips stiffened and hardened. Slowly he clutched both great fists and brought them down on the table. "Take your vote, here and now, Davis!" he shouted in a voice that could have been heard on Pennsylvania Avenue.

A tumult of protest greeted this. Lincoln came to his feet and stood there, long arms dangling, head drooping, great eyes burning, first on one man then on another. He felt as though he were indeed made of rock; that he could outlast any storm precipitated by any man in the room. And he proposed to coerce them by his very immobility.

The storm lasted for perhaps a quarter of an hour. Then men began to glance askance first at Lincoln, then at one another. When he perceived this Lincoln spoke quietly to the Senator from Kentucky.

"I'm waiting for you to take that vote, Davis."

Suddenly the Senator nodded to George Nicolay, who immediately passed slips to the committee members. A little later, Davis gave Lincoln a look, half sneering, half triumphant. The vote stood twenty against, seven for Compensated Abolishment. In other words, only an unimportant minority would recommend the plan to their home States.

When the Committee had gone, Lincoln walked deliberately over to his desk on which the lovely light of summer afterglow was falling and taking up his pen, began to make notes which he headed,

"What I Know."

"McClellan—organizer but no fighter. Bring him back to protect Washington. Send rest of Army of Potomac to Pope.

"Taking of Richmond of prime importance in effect on minds of both sides.

"Must move fast or (1) England will intervene, this year, (2) McClellan will try to make himself dictator. (3) McClellan as dictator would wreck the Union and save slavery.

"If I emancipate the slaves I shall save the Union and probably be shot.

"If I do not emancipate the slaves, I cannot save the Union and shall not be shot.

"If the North does not win this war, democracy will be a failure upon this earth."

Having written thus far, he paused, moved nearer to the window, for the twilight was deepening and with a smile of whimsical sadness he permitted himself to add one bit of sentiment:

"To die; to sleep; no more; and by a sleep, to say we end the heartache, and the thousand natural shocks . . ."

He broke off abruptly, folded the paper and thrust it into his pocket. Still keeping his mind strictly to the work at hand, he pulled a fresh sheet of paper toward him and wrote at the top, "Emancipation Proclamation," following with slowly thought-out sentences, set down in his cramped, uneven hand.

He had not written a half dozen lines when John Hay came to the door, and stared at the bent figure silhouetted against the window. He peered at his watch, hesitated, then walked firmly across the room. Perhaps nonsense would rouse the President when a call to supper would surely fail.

"Mr. Lincoln," he said solemnly, "Richard II is to be played by Hackett, to-night. Unless you at once, eat, ensark and bifurcate dischrysalisize, you will miss the second act, let alone the first."

Lincoln lifted his head with a jerk. "Say it again, slowly, John!" with solemnity equal to the young man's.

John repeated the words and with his inimitable laugh, the President thrust the manuscript into his breast pocket and fled to his room.

In an astoundingly short time he and his two young secretaries were starting for the theater. As they passed through the lower hall, a brawny, long-legged soldier, who had been gaping at the entrance to the East Room came up to Lincoln, hand extended.

"I'm from Indiany!" he announced.

"So am I," replied Lincoln. "I almost wish I was back there again."

"That's just what I was wishin', myself." The big fellow nodded understandingly. "But instead of that I've got to go back to camp. Ain't they aworkin' ye pretty hard, Mr. Lincoln?"

"I reckon they are," answered the President.

"Well, now, some of us boys was saying so. You'd better take right smart good keer of yourself. There ain't anybody else layin' round loose to fit into your boots right now."

"You give the boys my thanks, sir!" Lincoln shook the Hoosier's big hand heartily and hurried into his carriage where he chuckled immoderately all the way to the theater.

CHAPTER XXII

THE RUNAWAYS

O N a burning July afternoon, a day or so later, Secretary Stanton's baby was buried. Mrs. Lincoln had just left for a visit to New York, but Lincoln attended the funeral, taking with him in his carriage, Seward, with Seward's son and daughter-in-law, and the Secretary of the Navy, Gideon Welles.

The occasion was, of course, particularly poignant to Lincoln, but he gave himself no opportunity to indulge in grief. The Stantons were living for the summer in a house several miles northwest of Georgetown. The ride to and from the funeral was long and oppressive. Dust settled heavily on the occupants of the carriage. Young Mrs. Seward's little black sunshade turned a rich tan before the first mile was covered. Welles' white beard took on a youthful brown. The lovely landscape was visible only through a hazel fog. The horses panted, while the harness worked up a muddy lather.

Of the extraordinary physical discomfort of the ride, Lincoln was scarcely conscious. All the way out to the Stantons' he was debating with himself whether or not to sound out the two secretaries on the subject of emancipation. On the way back, he suddenly decided to make the plunge. Welles gave the opening when he said:

"General McClellan's campaign is singularly depressing in its effect on the public. Greeley is again talking peace at any price, I see."

Lincoln nodded. "I reckon we've about reached the end of our rope on the plan of operations we've been pursuing. Things are going from bad to worse. We've played the last card of the original plan, in the campaign against Richmond. Now we've got to change tactics or lose the game."

"What do you propose?" asked Welles.

"I propose," replied the President, looking from Welles to Seward, "to issue a proclamation emancipating the slaves."

"Good God!" ejaculated Seward.

"This is a sudden change on your part, Mr. Lincoln!" exclaimed Welles.

"I'll make any change necessary to save the Union," retorted Lincoln. "This is a military not a political move—a military necessity. What do you think of it, Seward?"

"It's too momentous a question for me to answer off hand. You've taken my breath away," replied the Governor.

"And mine!" Welles shook his head.

Lincoln felt almost a shock of surprise. His own preoccupation with the idea of emancipation had been so constant and deep that he had not realized how little careful thought the members of the Cabinet had given it. Abolition, outside of the small radical group, was still looked upon as fantastic, impossible, by the general public, he knew. But he had thought it was otherwise with his Cabinet. He began to explain, patiently and clearly, his reasons for the move.

Seward, wiping his tired face, constantly, with a large silk handkerchief, shook his head and murmured ejaculations to himself, as he listened. Welles chewed at his beard, blinking like a thoughtful old owl. The two younger Sewards' excitement and apprehension were apparent in the tensity with which they sat erect, staring at the President.

"I see Sumner's hand in this!" exclaimed Seward, when Lincoln had finished.

"Sumner knows nothing about it," declared the President. "You two are the first I've mentioned it to, and I reckon you'd better say nothing until I can bring it up at a Cabinet meeting. What's your idea, Welles?"

"I had supposed your ideas were identical with the Cabinet, sir. We've all felt that this was a local domestic subject, appertaining to the states, respectively, and that they'd never parted with their authority over it," said the Secretary of the Navy, with his usual Yankee caution. "But the reverses before Richmond will change our ideas about many things, undoubtedly."

"Something drastic must be done, of course," said Seward. "I'll have to give my mind to a solution. I'm not at all sure you've found the right one, Mr. Lincoln."

"You'd better give it special and deliberate attention, Governor," Lincoln eyed the Secretary of State with the little sense of amusement Seward's self-assurance always gave him, "because I'm going to put the foot down, very shortly. And while the situation is delicate, the foot is not!" This, with a quiet smile at young Mrs. Seward on whose silk skirt he had trod, earlier in the afternoon. He then began to talk of the hopeful conditions around New Orleans.

He went out to the Soldiers' Home that night, where Tad and Miss Ford were to stay during Mary's absence. When his wife was away the President led a completely erratic existence, eating, dressing, and sleeping as he pleased. When he rode his horse slowly up to the steps of the cottage it was nine o'clock, and he was quite unconscious of the fact that he'd had no supper. He had come out to see Miss Ford, and he had thought of nothing for the past two hours but what he was going to say to her. He had not made up his mind when he came upon her.

She was sitting in a rustic chair on the lawn, a dim, white figure in the starlight. Lincoln crossed the lawn behind her, and dropped into the chair opposite before she was aware of his presence.

She gave a little gasp of surprise, then drawled, easily, "I've found the one cool spot in a burning world. Actually there is a touch of breeze, now and again."

Lincoln unbuttoned his white linen coat and tossed his old hunting cap to the ground. "I hope Mrs. Lincoln is getting a little letup from heat," he sighed. "How's Taddie?"

"Very well indeed, and exceedingly active."

"I don't doubt it," laughed the President. "Anything of a criminal nature, to-day?"

"Can't tattle on my pupil, Mr. President! That's my best hold on him." The Virginian's voice had the tender inflection that always was apparent when she spoke of Tad.

Lincoln, as usual, caught the inflection and sighed. If only she were not so kind to his children! But he must begin somewhere. Without premeditation, he asked:

"Sister Ford, how'd you like another job?"

"I'm perfectly satisfied with this one," she replied, promptly. "There! Feel that little breeze on your cheek? Heavenly!"

"It's what you call a *regular* kind of a job, so I don't suppose you'd enjoy it like this one. I want you to resign from Jeff Davis' pay, and work for me."

A silence broken only by cricket and katydid. Then the Virginian sat forward in her chair. "What are you talking about, Mr. Lincoln?"

The President felt quite calm and clear, now. "I'm talking about your work. You remember that night Mrs. Frémont called on me? You gave yourself away then, and I've been watching you ever since. I had my mind all made up to settle with you, before my darling Willie left us. Then you were such an angel to him, that I couldn't."

"What have I done to merit this?" exclaimed Miss Ford, leaning forward in her chair so that Lincoln could see the dark outline of her perfect features.

"You've helped McClellan make a fool of himself. You're too close to the fountain-head on both sides of the line, Sister Ford. Either you must go down to Richmond and stay there, or you must take a job I can get you in Vice President Hamlin's family in Portland, Maine. Reckon you'd be far enough from McClellan then to dull your claws."

"My dear Mr. Lincoln," with an amused little laugh, "I'm not dependent on a 'job' as you call it, for my daily bread. I've been taking the stipend from Mrs. Lincoln because she wouldn't let me stay, otherwise. And I've wanted to stay—to be near you."

"True enough—I'm the fountain-head!" Lincoln's voice was grim.

"No! You shall not misinterpret me on that point, Abraham Lincoln!" raising one slender hand in dramatic protest. "My love for you is more real to me than the whole slavery cause. You shall not belittle or besmirch that!"

"You go down and love Jeff Davis the same way you have loved me," sardonically, "and my speculation is that Richmond will fall within a month. First time I ever heard treachery called by that name."

The Virginian sprang to her feet, and the President rose to his.

"This is beyond endurance!" she protested.

"Exactly!" agreed Lincoln. "You're like a fellow I knew on the Sangamon who—"

"No!" cried Miss Ford. "Not one of your stories at this moment! I could not bear it!"

"I was merely trying to let you down easy, Sister Ford," said Lincoln, gently. "If you will have it that way,—to-morrow you must start for Richmond."

"Do you mean to tell me that without Mrs. Lincoln's knowledge or sanction,—or does she know you were about to do this, and left for this reason?" demanded Miss Ford.

"She hadn't the least notion of this happening in her absence," replied Lincoln. "Now, dear Sister Ford, what is the use of putting on or carrying on about this? You've been doing what you could for your cause. I've caught you at it."

"Who has maligned me? That brown cat, Jinny? I'll have her whipped. I'll take her myself to Fairfax Courthouse and see it done. The lying Jezebel never has forgiven me about Zeb. I'll teach her!"

Her anger was the more terrible to observe because she did not raise her voice as she raged. Lincoln allowed her to vent her spleen on Jinny for some moments, then he put his hand on her shoulder and said with a patient sort of gentleness:

"My dear, what's the use? I have my work to do, and I must safeguard myself until it's done. After that, no matter. You are a menace to the Union to a degree that perhaps you do not realize, for I truly believe you wish to save the Union. I dare no longer permit my liking for you, my gratitude to you, keep you in my household. To-morrow, you shall start for Richmond."

"I shall not!" for the first time raising her voice.

"It shall be done quietly, with one of Baker's men as escort. I've told Baker nothing so far. How much he learns depends on the degree of your docility."

"You hate me! You speak in a voice of hate! You touch me as you would touch an unruly horse. God! This is my Nemesis and it's more than I can bear. No country, no cause is worth it! God, do you hear me?" raising her face hysterically to the stars. "I repudiate my country and the cause of slavery! I repudiate Jefferson Davis! I am wholly Abraham Lincoln's!" Her voice rose to a scream. "God, do you hear me? Give me a sign! Give me a sign!"

"Hush! Don't tempt Him!" Lincoln shook her gently. "Go in the house, and have Jinny pack you up, for you must return to the White House, to-night, with me."

He could feel her tall body shaking as with a chill.

"I shall not go!" she screamed.

"Come! Lean on my arm!" commanded the President.

Suddenly, she broke down. Weeping heavily, she put her head against his shoulder. "Don't send me away! Don't send me away! Lock me in a room in the White House. Only let me be under the same roof with you."

"Hush! Every window up at the cottage has a listener. Come, let's go find Jinny."

She drew a shuddering breath, then slowly moved away from him. "I will find her without your help," she said, brokenly.

The President stood without moving a muscle until she entered the lighted hallway. Then, with a great sigh, he dropped into his chair.

An hour later, the carriage and his saddle horse, at the President's order, appeared at the door. Lincoln crossed the lawn and sent a servant for Miss Ford. After a considerable delay, the servant returned with the information that neither Miss Ford nor Jinny could be found.

"Go and make a real hunt, of every building," ordered Lincoln. "One of you get ready to ride my horse back to town with a note to Colonel Baker."

He was perfectly sure that the Virginian was not to be found at the Soldiers' Home. He felt decidedly sheepish as he wrote a note to Chief Baker of the Secret Service; sheepish, a little relieved, and somewhat troubled. He had wanted to remove Miss Ford, and to be very sure of her whereabouts before he took further steps in emancipation. He had done only half his job. He remained at the cottage until Baker arrived, then he drove back to Washington.

It was not until morning when he woke with a dizzy headache that he remembered that he'd had no supper!

He sent for Charles Sumner immediately after breakfast. The Senator, immaculate in a cream linen suit, a rose in his buttonhole, appeared while Lincoln was listening to a violent debate between Welles and Stanton. The President lounged in a favorite attitude, deep in a chair, his feet on the mantel. Stanton walked the floor, Welles sat erect and uncompromising at the Cabinet table.

"I hope I don't intrude, sir!" Sumner paused beside Lincoln.

"Not at all, Charles! Welles and Stanton are having a debate on the matter of a bill. You remember last spring when the *Merrimac* sunk the *Cumberland,* and the Congress and we all were scared to death for fear she'd steam up the Potomac to Washington?"

Sumner nodded solemnly, but Lincoln laughed. "Stanton had the shakes a little mite worse than the rest of us. At least he made more noise and confusion. You did, Stanton! Don't glare at me or you'll give me the shakes now!"

"Your levity is ill-timed, sir," said Stanton, savagely.

"Perhaps so! Perhaps so! But I haven't forgotten that you sneered at Welles when he said that the *Monitor* would lick the *Merrimac.* Welles is getting to be a good deal of a navy man. He didn't know the rear from the front of a boat when he began, but he does now."

"Father" Welles smiled dryly. Stanton pulled his beard and waited impatiently for the Chief Executive to give him the floor. But Lincoln was hoping that a little delay would cool Stanton down and he had no objection to trying to puncture some of the Secretary of War's egotism.

"Stanton," he went on, "got me so scared that I consented to his having sixty canal boats loaded with stone ready to sink across the channel at Kettle Bottom Shoals. He went over Welles' head and ordered the navy yard to prepare the boats. Welles was peevish about this, and Stanton, to soothe him, agreed that the War Department should bear the expense. Of course, they were never needed, and are moored by the river bank, now." With a quiet chuckle, "And now Stanton wants Welles to pay for the fleet. Stanton's navy! It's as useless as the pap of a man to a sucking child. There may be some show to amuse the child but they are good for nothing for service."

"My God, but you're disgusting, Lincoln!" shouted Stanton, and he flung himself toward the door. "I'll pay for the boats rather than risk another interview like this."

"Father" Welles suddenly burst into a cackling laugh, gathered up his papers and departed.

Sumner, who had winced at Lincoln's simile, stood eyeing him speculatively. Lincoln smiled serenely.

"Charles, Sister Ford ran away, last night."

"What!" gasped the Senator. "With whom?"

"With Jinny," dryly from Lincoln. "I've been meaning for some time to tell you of what I suspected the lady." He gave the story in detail, adding, "I told her she could have her choice between going to Richmond or to Hamlin's family up in Maine. I implicated no one. Told her she gave herself away during that interview of Mrs. Frémont's."

Sumner groaned. "I've long been uneasy about her. Too bad! Too bad! Did she confess?"

"Not precisely. She did considerable sputtering, but finally seemed to agree that she'd pack and come back to Washington with me, on her way to Richmond. She went into the cottage out at the Soldiers' Home and she and Jinny disappeared while I was waiting. I put Colonel Baker on the case."

Sumner groaned, then said, "You did quite right."

"You feel as I do, Charles—a cross between virtue and remorse. You see, I wanted to make an important move and it seemed best to have her out of the house. Reckon I fumbled badly. Don't know where she'll break out, now."

"Oh, she and all her kind can't stop Destiny's march!" exclaimed Sumner. "What move have you planned, Mr. Lincoln?"

"The inevitable one, I hope, Senator. The present Congress has done almost all it can, unless you have something up your sleeve that I don't know about. Let's see. It's prohibited all persons in the army and navy from hunting or returning fugitive slaves. It has restored the Missouri Compromise. It has abolished slavery in the District of Columbia, and provided for the education of colored children here. It has recognized the independence of Hayti and Liberia. It has passed the Confiscation Act, destroying title in slave property as a punishment for treason or rebellion. It's given me power to use contrabands as soldiers. It seems to me that, if my Cabinet recapitulates the work of the Congress, it can't fail to see that mine is the next step—emancipation."

Sumner had been leaning against the mantel, listening attentively to Lincoln. As the President uttered the last word, the Senator started as if he had been struck. He stared at Lincoln as though he could not believe his ears.

"What!" he said. "Emancipation! At last! Lincoln! Do you truly mean it?" He seized the President's hands. "You will issue a proclamation?— Truly 'mine eyes have seen the glory of the coming of the Lord.'"

His face worked. He dropped Lincoln's hands, turned to rest his head on his arm along the mantel and wept.

The President felt his own eyes sting. He took a turn up and down the room. Then he cleared his throat and said:

"The North is not really ready for it. I'll meet much opposition. It will damn my political future—I'm inclined to be grateful for that.—But it's the next military step in the saving of the Union. With their slaves at home to free the men for service, the Rebels have too great an advantage over us. Whether or not the North has suffered enough to swallow it, I don't pretend to know. When I'll issue it, I don't know. Charles, I want you to go up to Massachusetts and make a close canvass of the situation up there, both military and political, with relation to such a move."

Sumner had fully recovered himself. He smoothed his hair and necktie. "Quite right, sir, and wise, as usual. I'll be going home to-night."

He had reached the hall when the President, recalling certain information, hurried after him and buttonholed him near the stairhead, where the passing visitors stared curiously at the two enormous figures.

"Charles," whispered Lincoln, "it's highly probable that you'll be subject to murderous attack, after this thing is out. Guard yourself all you can."

"How can one guard against a villain?" asked Sumner in a wondering whisper. "Don't be anxious, sir. The Almighty is directing this matter." He squeezed the President's hand and was gone.

CHAPTER XXIII

THE SOLDIERS' HOME CEMETERY

REPEATED thunderstorms toward the last week of July made Washington slightly more endurable. Mrs. Lincoln returned from her visit to the North with wonderful new material for dresses, and established Lizzie Keckley in her bedroom for an orgy of sewing. The trip had done her good. Her nerves were steady. A little of her lovely color showed again in her cheeks. But she looked her husband over with considerable dissatisfaction. He had lost weight, and she saw new lines around his mouth and eyes.

"You look," she said, with a sad little grimace, "as if you've been living on what you picked out of the mousetrap! I thought of you every time I put a taste of food to my lips. You sit down in that chair and I'll send for a glass of milk this minute."

She had been in the house for several hours, but the President had been locked in Stanton's office with General Halleck who had come to take over the General-in-Chiefship. He had hurried to the sitting room the moment he had been released. He held Mary tightly while she chided him, a complacent smile on his lips.

"Jings! It's good to have you spank me again! Don't go away again this summer, wife! Wait till things are more cheerful with the country."

"The war looks bad East and West, doesn't it!" agreed Mary. "I suppose the raising of 300,000 more men has taken what little appetite from you my absence didn't. Do sit down, my dear, and rest, just for a moment, and I'll ring the bell for the milk."

But he would not release her. He clung to her as something warm and intensely human that anchored him once more to the sweet and simple and homely things that were his birthright. He seated himself, holding her on his knees as he did Tad, and looking down into her face with something of the feeling, he was sure, that Taddie experienced when he felt for his mother's hand in the dark.

"Now! Go on and scold me some more, darling Mary," he begged, "while I purr like an old Tom cat!"

She smoothed his hair back from his forehead. He closed his eyes with a sigh. "What shall I scold about, first?" she asked tenderly. "Shall I scold you because I see you are carrying every dead soldier on every battlefield as a notch on your living heart? Shall I scold because you make no reply to the dreadful things the newspapers are saying about your neglect of McClellan?"

Lincoln opened his eyes. "I've asked Dahlgren to make me an invention. Something to use the gas escaping from newspaper offices for war purposes."

Mary laughed, then went on with her inventory. "Or shall I scold you for wearing this heavy coat when your closet is full of linen suits?"

"Whatever interests you most, wife. Only keep on! Might say a few words about my sending Sister Ford off, as I wrote you."

"I think you did exactly right. I'm sorry for poor Jinny, though," declared Mary.

"Jinny can take care of herself and Sister Ford too," relaxing, with a sigh of relief, against the back of the arm chair. "You've seen Taddie, of course."

"Yes, he's been with me all the afternoon. What sort of a boy has he been?" asked Mary, remaking the President's tie.

"He's been the one bright spot in a fog of trouble," replied Lincoln, beginning to chuckle. "Stanton seems to be very fond of him, and he fixed him up a Lieutenant's commission and gave him twenty-five old useless guns. Tad built an arsenal in the basement and drafted every servant and employee on the place for his Company. John Hay and George Nicolay were the only ones who escaped. The first day all went well, but that night your gardener, Halliday, started to go down town. Tad saw him heading for the street and he went out and arrested him as a deserter. He was very earnest about it, and furious that Halliday wouldn't take him seriously. He dragged the fellow up to my office and appealed to me as Commander-in-Chief to force Halliday to submit to arrest."

"What did you do!" exclaimed Mary.

"I stopped Cabinet proceedings while I pardoned Halliday; then I persuaded Tad that he would be doing a real service if he formed a little company of poor boys who couldn't get drill, otherwise. He finally agreed that if I'd let him feed the boys, once a day, he'd disband his present company."

"Good gracious! Is he feeding twenty-five boys here, every day?" cried Mary.

"No, only ten," replied the President soothingly. Then he added, "I knew I'd dig up something you could really scold me about, if I tried long enough."

Mary suddenly kissed him and jumped to her feet. "Speaking of food, shall I send for that milk, or will you promise to come to supper, the moment the bell rings?"

"I promise. Do I have to change my clothes?" looking at her without much hope.

For reply, Mary rang the bell and when James appeared, she said, "James, will you help the President get into a white linen suit? He is very tired, James. Give him an alcohol rubdown, do."

"Yes, Madam. He sure is very tired. I'm glad you're back, Madam, for he sure ain't himself with you away." The colored man offered his hand to Lincoln to pull him to his feet.

The President took the kind brown fingers and said, with a contented sigh, "A good going over by his mother with a fine tooth comb is what every boy needs, at least once a month, James!"

"Yes, sir, Massa Lincum," grinned James.

"I don't like your implications, Abra'm!" Mary's eyes twinkled, but she watched the two depart with an anxious shake of the head. She never had seen her husband look as weary as he did now.

Carl Schurz came in to supper with John Hay. Lincoln was delighted to see him. The young officer always struck fire from the President's brain. But Mary, with John Hay's tactful help, steered the talk away from politics, and kept it on music, about which Schurz could talk so fascinatingly.

"Mr. Lincoln must rest," she whispered in an aside to Schurz as they all mounted the stairs after supper. "He's mulling over some heavy problem—emancipation, I think—and they tell me he's not been to bed for two nights. Will you play for him, General?"

"Ah, poor fellow, yes!" replied Schurz and on reaching the sitting room, he went straight to the piano.

"I'll just stretch out here on the sofa and rest my brittle old bones for a half hour," said Lincoln, sinking among the cushions as he spoke.

Mary and John Hay moved chairs close to him as if to hedge him from intruders.

"What are you going to play, General?" asked Lincoln.

"A little of Beethoven," answered the officer, "a few Volk Lieder, if you will."

"I will!" sighed the President, closing his eyes, and determined to rest his brain during the half hour by not permitting his thoughts to wander from the lovely pattern of sounds Schurz began to weave. For a few moments the desultory conversation between Mary and John impinged on his concentration:

John:—"Dear Mrs. Lincoln, don't urge me to ask favors of Secretary Stanton. I'd rather make the rounds of a smallpox hospital."

Mary, after a silence:—"I had two nights at Long Branch. Heavenly, except for mosquitoes, human and otherwise!"

John: "Washington is a desert. Not a human being here, as far as social intercourse goes. I miss the ladies, I assure you."

Mary: "When do you find time to miss them? You work twenty-six out of the twenty-four, now!"

John: "You're confusing me with the Tycoon, Mrs. Lincoln. I refuse to work more than twenty hours a day. The remaining four hours I devote to regretting lovely women."

Schurz drifted into a lullaby—

When Lincoln opened his eyes, after a long blank period, he was astounded to see that dawn was shining in at the window, through which floated the song of a redbird in the garden. He still was lying on the couch, with Mary's red shawl over his feet. Some one had removed his shoes.

"God bless her!" he thought. "I've had a real sleep and my brain is clear. I can broach emancipation to the Cabinet, to-day. Yesterday, I was too overwrought."

It was the regular Cabinet meeting morning, with steady rain and so of endurable temperature. The members discussed the feasibility of raising negro regiments, for some time, until Lincoln quietly vetoed the immediate carrying out of the idea, and took from his pocket a rather worn sheet of paper.

"I want to read you a memorandum I've been working on relative to the subject of emancipation. I do not ask your advice, but suggestions as to the handling of the subject will be in order after I have finished."

A stunned silence greeted the reading of the document. Chase was the first to speak.

"That's a measure of great danger, Mr. Lincoln, and goes beyond anything I have recommended."

"What have you recommended, Chase?" asked the President, pushing his chair back from the table that he might cross his knees.

The Secretary of the Treasury replied with the rasping note of hostility in his voice that he could not subdue when he spoke to Lincoln. "I should prefer that no new expression on the subject of compensation be made. The measure of emancipation can be much better and more quietly accomplished by allowing generals to organize and arm the slaves."

"Good God, Chase!" cried Seward. "Are you planning to start a servile war?"

"There's no necessity for profanity, Mr. Secretary," retorted Chase, his handsome face pale with emotion. "Arming the slaves would prevent their massacre by the Rebels in case of emancipation."

"You're insane!" roared Stanton. "I'm for the immediate issuing of that proclamation!"

"So am I!" said Attorney General Bates. "And I'm a conservative, from a slave-holding State, too. What about you and your Abolitionist friends, Chase?"

Lincoln smiled at Bates, gratefully.

"Oh, I consider this action better than nothing," hastily declared Chase, "and so shall support it."

"Wait a moment, do, my friends," exclaimed Seward. "Listen to some facts from my department. Foreign nations, on hearing that proclamation, will intervene, immediately, to prevent freeing the labor that they believe produces cotton only so long as the negroes here are in bondage. And they are right. Issue that proclamation, and we break up our relations with foreign nations and the production of cotton for sixty years."

"And you are the man," said Secretary Welles, dryly, "who after your 'irrepressible conflict' speech in 1858, the New York *Herald* called a more dangerous Abolitionist than Beecher, Garrison, or Parker!"

"I wasn't Secretary of State to a nation in the throes of civil war when I made that speech," retorted Seward.

"I'd like to hear your reasons for issuing the proclamation, Mr. President," said Smith, the Secretary of the Interior.

"So would I," echoed Postmaster General Blair. "I only wish to say that if you issue it, it will cost us the fall elections."

Lincoln nodded. "The collapse of McClellan's Richmond campaign may be said to be the immediate reason. The decisive element in the test of military strength between the Union and the Secessionists lies in the slaves. In order to take advantage of that element, we must remove two things: prejudice on the part of the Northern whites; lack of motive on the part of the blacks. The check and embarrassment, at this moment, of all the Union armies are putting our people, even the conservatives, in the frame of mind for reprisals on the Rebels. Here is our reprisal," tapping the document against his knee. "Here, also, is the motive which will inspire the slaves to fight."

"You are mistaken at one point, sir!" exclaimed Seward. "You issue this now, following upon the greatest disasters of the war, and people will misunderstand. They will view it as the last measure of an exhausted government, a cry for help; the government stretching her hands to Ethiopia, instead of Ethiopia stretching forth her hands to the government; the last shriek on our retreat."

This was characteristic reasoning on the part of Seward, thought Lincoln, the ounce of common sense in the pound of sophistry.

"There is rising a sure demand that this war and slavery cease together," said Welles, impatiently.

"I have no patience at all," retorted Seward, "with the irrational clamor for making emancipation, instead of national integrity, the object of the war. I have less patience with paper declarations without the support of armies. It is mournful to see a great nation shrink from a war it has accepted, and adopt proclamations where it has been asked for force."

"Don't purposely and cynically misunderstand me on this, Seward," exclaimed the President. "As I have told you before, I expect to maintain the contest until successful, or till I die, or am conquered, or my term expires, or Congress or the country forsake me. I have felt that only the most horrible suffering could induce this country to include the freeing of the slave in the *casus belli*. I had hoped it now had suffered enough."

Seward leaned forward on the table. "Mr. President, you are, I know, determined to issue the proclamation. You do not desire our advice. Yet I venture to beg this of you. Issue the mandate when you can give it to the country supported by military success, or the whole world will laugh at you."

"Derision cannot seriously affect me." Lincoln smiled a little sadly. "But you have given me a new angle. Perhaps the long suffering had best be capped by hope before we offer this to the people. We'll wait for a victory. In the meantime, I ask you all to preserve the utmost secrecy with regard to this. And pray for a victorious McClellan."

A mirthless laugh from Stanton greeted this, and the meeting broke up. Lincoln followed Stanton to the War Office.

Sumner made only a flying visit to his constituents in Massachusetts. It seemed as if anxiety for the success of the President's "move" made it impossible for him to keep away from Washington. He appeared at the Soldiers' Home, late one sultry Sunday afternoon, to find the President and his wife, with Secretary and Mrs. Welles, drinking lemonade on the lawn, while Tad drove his goat wagon up and down the gravel paths. Lincoln was giving a discourse on trees, taking great delight in tripping Welles as to name and habitat. He greeted Sumner affectionately, and included him in the catechism.

"Come over here by the cemetery," he said, "where the evergreens abound, and I'll show you the difference between spruce, pine, and cedar and a kind of illegitimate cypress I've noticed growing hereabouts. Trees are as interesting to study as men. Each has its own physiognomy."

He rose and strode toward the cemetery, followed unenthusiastically by the company. He looked taller than ever in his white linen suit. The late sun flickering through the trees brought out copper tints in his black hair. Charles Sumner and Mary brought up the rear.

"The President is popularly supposed to have no interest in nature, or particular love for her," said the Senator.

"That's about on par with the usual misconception regarding my blessed husband!" exclaimed Mary. "How could a temperament as intensely poetic as his *not* love beauty in nature as everywhere! Also, how can one with his awful preoccupations take time to enjoy that beauty? I sometimes think that even his religion is only a manifestation of the poet in him."

"That's interesting," mused Sumner. "Ah, he isn't going to let us off reciting! They're waiting by the edge of the clearing."

But, when they reached the President, he had forgotten the recitation. He was standing with the various twigs of evergreen in his hand, gazing at row on row of new-made graves.

"I didn't know they'd opened this to volunteers," he said. "Look! Hundreds of them with not even a name or a number!"

His face worked. Deep within him he felt stirring the mood of despair, which he had been fighting ever since McClellan had begun the retreat from Richmond. Welles looked up at him pityingly. Sumner pressed forward and put his hand on Lincoln's shoulder.

"My dear Mr. Lincoln—" he began, but did not continue.

A shot rang from behind an ancient monument. It grazed the President's forehead, took off a lock of Sumner's hair and severed a branch of the "illegitimate" cypress. Almost at the same moment a colored woman dashed out from the trees to the left and flung herself, screaming, before Lincoln. It was Jinny.

"They shan't git you, Massa Lincum! They'll git me first!"

As she shrieked these words another shot rang out. Jinny whirled and fell. A man, stooping, ran from behind the ancient monument into the grove.

The episode had passed with such lightning rapidity that it was over while one could count thirty. Lincoln stooped to pick up Jinny. Sumner started to run after the assassin, but was stopped by Welles, who pointed to James, who, in his white serving coat, a gun in his hand, was galloping across the cemetery, followed by Tom, the coachman, in a bright pink shirt. Mary clasped Lincoln's arm. She was deathly white, but perfectly calm.

"Come back to the house, quickly, Abra'm, before they shoot again!" she begged.

Welles, supporting his wife, who was half fainting, said quietly, "Sumner, if you are not injured, help me with Mrs. Welles."

Lincoln did not speak. He stood with the mulatto woman in his arms, the blood from her breast running over his coat sleeve. She was staring up into his face, trying to tell him something, and he was listening, moving his lips in sympathy with hers. After a moment of agonizing endeavor, she managed to articulate a name:

"*Gordon! Gordon!*"

Then she died.

"Put her down, Abra'm. We'll send some one to her," urged Mary.

"She saved my life!" said Lincoln, wonderingly, and making no attempt to set his burden down. "She took my bullet. Poor Jinny! Dear, devoted Jinny!"

The tears ran down his cheeks, and thus he bore the slave back through the woods to the cottage, and laid her down on the parlor sofa.

Things moved swiftly, after that. The frightened servants took charge of Jinny's body. Colonel Baker was sent for. Taddie drove his goat into the house, and stabled him in the dining room, which latter fact was not noted for hours. James and Tom returned very shortly. Their man had jumped on a horse, tied a short way into the woods, and had hopelessly out-distanced them, of course, at once. When the two had finished their breathless report to the group assembled in the parlor, the President said to James:

"Boy, how did you happen to be on the job?"

The colored man swallowed a sob. "About ten minutes before that first shot, Massa Lincum, Jinny, she bust into the kitchen, all dust and excitement. We all ain't seen her since Miss Fo'd took her all away. Jinny, she say to me, I'm alone in the kitchen, 'Where's Massa Lincum? Dat man Gordon, he gwine shoot Massa Lincum!'

" 'They jes' went into the woods toward the cemetery,' said I.

" 'You grab a gun and come!' says Jinny.

"She ran out. I took five minutes to load one of Massa Taddie's old guns, and I holler at Tom and run for it after Jinny. We reached the cemetery jes' as that first shot came. . . . Poor Jinny!" His dark face quivered.

"Happy Jinny!" exclaimed Mary, with sudden passion, "whose death saved Mr. Lincoln."

"Don't," protested Lincoln, huskily. "James, is there any chance that the help in the house could be persuaded not to tell this for a while? Supposing you tell them that if this thing is gossiped about it will set me back in my efforts to help the slaves."

"If you call them in here, Massa Lincum," said James, earnestly, "and tell 'em what you want, all the whipping posts in Virginny couldn't drag nothing out of them."

"Call them in, James," said the President. When the man had gone, followed by Tom, Lincoln turned to Sumner:

"Charles, I reckon you'd better go over to the other house and see that the mouths are shut there. As no one has appeared, I suspect the old fellows have observed nothing."

Sumner left immediately and his exit was followed by the entrance of two maids, with James and Tom. The President made his request, and was convinced, as James had been, that these dark lips would be sealed as long as he desired it. He was much moved by the fanatical passion with which they declared their loyalty to him, their faith in him.

When they were gone, he turned to Secretary and Mrs. Welles and Mary. "Somehow I can't seem to stand up under their gratitude. I'm not worth it. Ah, my darling Taddie"—the boy was established on the arm of his mother's chair,—"I should say, Lieutenant Lincoln, you will guard this as a military secret of the Commander-in-Chief, eh?"

"Yes, sa'!" Taddie jumped to his feet and saluted smartly. "And hea' is the a'nica fo' the bump on you' fo'head, Papa day. I was waiting fo' yo' to calm down to give it to yo'!"

Every one smiled and the tension relaxed as the little boy, using his mother's handkerchief, proceeded to sponge the welt that had risen on his father's brow. Lincoln sighed with pleasure under the touch of his small fingers.

"I'm enjoining this secrecy because I want Baker to get this man," he said, as he leaned back with closed eyes, "and because," opening his eyes to look at Welles, "I don't want a lot of reporters ferreting out the relation this may have to the purpose I divulged in the Cabinet meeting. The public must not know that purpose until I am sure they are ready for it."

"Quite right, as usual," agreed "Father" Welles, sitting bolt upright on the long ottoman, and tenderly supporting Mrs. Welles, who leaned against him.

CHAPTER XXIV

CEDAR MOUNTAIN

MARY could not endure the thought of remaining overnight in the vicinity of the tragedy, so, late that evening, when Colonel Baker had finished his long conference with them, the party returned to the city.

Lincoln had lived so close to the thought of assassination, that the fact that it actually had been attempted did not greatly shock him. But he was deeply perturbed at the thought of Jinny's sacrifice. As had Zeb's, her face came frequently between himself and his work on Monday morning, when he settled at his desk.

Taddie and the two dogs were playing "Prisoners" under the Cabinet table when Lincoln came in, and he was glad of the child's society.

In his mail that morning was his first letter from William Russell, and Lincoln read it, eagerly. After a few paragraphs telling of his return to London and of a recurrence of malarial fever, which had laid him low for two months, he said:

"I have only just brought about the interview which I promised to undertake for you. I cannot say whether or not my statements did, or will, have an ameliorating effect on the frame of mind of the person in question. She undoubtedly shares the general English feeling, which is overwhelmingly for the Confederacy and is violently prejudiced against your Administration. The effective blockade of Southern ports by the Federal navy is looked on with great bitterness. You must try to realize how the awful suffering of the cotton operatives in English factory towns has touched her heart. If British recognition of the Confederacy would open her cotton ports, I assure you that recognition would come at once. She believes that freedom for the slaves would starve Europe for cotton for at least a generation. I am, I hope, to have a longer visit at Windsor, this summer, of which I shall write you later.

"The Duke of Argyle and John Bright are the only statesmen for the North. Mr. Gladstone favors the South. Of the London papers only the *Spectator* is for you."

The President finished his letter with a sense of disappointment. He had thought of Her Majesty, Queen Victoria, as a woman of Mary's type, quick to resent, but also quick to understand. However, perhaps the second interview would bear fruit, or at least, show that the first one was not in vain.

Seward entering, at this point in his reverie, Lincoln asked him abruptly:

"Governor, what news from Charles Francis Adams on shipbuilding in England?"

Seward gave an irritated glance in the direction of Pensacola, who did not enjoy the rôle of prisoner, and was voicing his objection. "I've got children, Lincoln," he said, "and I love them, but—"

The President, who, outside the comfortable sense of companionship, had not been conscious of any of the sounds from the prison, now looked over his spectacles at Tad, who peered from under the table with a belligerent expression for the benefit of the Secretary of State.

"I'm not going out, Papa day. I'm in fo' life. I shot my supee-o' offica."

"Not your Commander-in-Chief, I hope, Lieutenant?" asked his father anxiously.

"No, sa'. Only a maja'-gene'al," with a quick look of relief on finding that his father was playing his game.

Lincoln wrote a rapid order on a slip of paper. "Transfer this prisoner to the north portico. Force him to do sentry duty, with cake rations, for two hours." Then he rang the bell for Louis. He read the order aloud when the messenger appeared, adding, "Lieutenant Lincoln admits to shooting a major-general. In some aspects his crime is a public benefit, therefore we exercise leniency. Take him and his two accomplices."

Louis solemnly saluted, took the slip of paper and turned toward the table.

"I'd never move such dangerous persons without shackles," exclaimed Seward. "Here, I'll help! Give us a hand, Mr. Lincoln," and the next five minutes, to Taddie's breathless delight, were spent by the messenger, the Secretary of State and the President in trussing up the prisoners with curtain cords and setting them out in the hall.

Lincoln returned to his desk, wiping his hot face. "Now, as to the building of rebel ships of war in Liverpool, Governor. What's Charles Francis' latest?"

"Mr. Adams is much concerned over a ship, almost completed, known as 290, which certainly is destined for Confederate use," replied Seward. "He can get nothing from Lord Russell, whose complacency is astounding."

"I'd like to see the correspondence in the matter, Seward," said the President, and turned to other business.

Late that afternoon, having read the letters from Adams, Lincoln put on his hat and started out to find Lord Lyons. As he strode rapidly down the north driveway, however, he met the British minister taking the air in his irreproachable landaulet. The President flung up his arm, and the landaulet stopped. The Minister, in spotless black broadcloth, stepped from the carriage.

"I was just going to call on you, my lord," exclaimed Lincoln. "Come over here under the trees a minute, while I tell you what's on my mind."

He led the imperturbable Lyons over to a marble settee, beneath a magnolia.

"Lyons, why don't the English people understand the great principles that underlie this war?" he began abruptly. "Is the fault yours?"

The Englishman gave him a quick look. "No, Your Excellency, the fault lies in the principles, themselves, which any European finds alien to his comprehension."

"Do you?" asked Lincoln, wondering if it were possible to get beneath this gentleman's polished surface.

"I've not looked upon myself as an alien, Mr. President. My sympathies have been quickened for both sides. It is painful to observe cousins in a blood feud. I shall be thankful when peace comes."

"Whichever way it comes?" Lincoln arched his brows. "Are you a perfect neutral?"

"Whichever way it comes," insisted Lord Lyons, fanning himself gently with his tall hat.

"So long as the blockade is broken and cotton starts for England!" exclaimed Lincoln.

For the first time, the Englishman showed fire. "The blockade is a cruel weapon, unwisely used as far as its effect on Europe is concerned."

"If you were in my place," asked Lincoln, "would you fight the war gently? Would you prosecute it, in future, with alder stalk squirts, charged with rose water? Is that the British method of warfare?"

Lord Lyons suddenly laughed. "You have me there, Your Excellency! But truly, sir, I have made no effort to form British opinion. I have tried to meet each emergency as it arrives. Nothing more! Indeed, nothing more!" with a tired sigh.

"I know," nodded Lincoln. "It's tough going—Lyons, as soon as there is a half victory, here in the East, I'm going to issue a proclamation freeing the slaves. I don't want it known in this country, but I want you to prepare the folks in high places in England for it."

The Englishman's ruddy face burned a deeper shade. He stared through the trees at the gray walls of the War and Navy Building, then turned his keen eyes on Lincoln.

"Such an act will have far-reaching results in Europe, sir."

"You mean England and France will be pacified?"

"I hope they will be," very earnestly.

"Well, I've about given up any idea of pacifying 'em, to tell the truth, but," with a whimsical lift to his lips, "I'll leave 'em not a leg to stand on if they wish to intervene. Get my idea, Lyons?"

"I get it, Your Excellency!" The Minister drummed on the curved top of his walking stick in a troubled way.

Lincoln eyed the Englishman. He felt baffled, and told himself that Russell had been wrong in his calculations.

"Too bad I don't speak French," he said grimly.

Lord Lyons looked at him enquiringly.

"They say it's the language of diplomacy. Certainly my kind of English isn't." Lincoln rose as he spoke. "And as for yours—! You might as well be talking Greek to me!"

The Englishman's eyes were puzzled, honestly so, Lincoln thought. The President rubbed his black hair, reflectively, then put out his hand.

"Lyons," he looked down very earnestly, "don't scorn this war as something worthy of contempt, merely because England has never fought a war for such a cause. Believe me when I say that the basic principles over which we are struggling are greater than any for which your country ever has struggled."

The Englishman bowed, and Lincoln, with a sigh, turned back toward his office.

Colonel Baker, a powerfully built man, with a heavy brown beard and a keen gray eye was waiting for the President. Lincoln waved him to a seat, perched himself on the edge of his desk and waited.

"You told me to report all real clews to you, sir. We haven't got on Gordon's trail since leaving the Soldiers' Home, but we've tracked him for the week preceding that time, and, incidentally, that put us in touch with Miss Ford for a moment. He undertook, for McClellan, to get some information about the Rebel forces in Richmond. He was at Harrison's Landing, and claimed that he had means that would take him into Richmond. One of my men had got into Richmond several days before, and he says that, on the night he left that place, he saw Miss Ford, Captain Taylor, and Gordon talking with Jefferson Davis. I might add that my man was perched in a tree, with a good view of Davis' sitting room."

"Do you imply that Jeff Davis is mixed up with any assassination schemes?" exclaimed the President. "Because, I tell you right now, I don't believe it."

"Neither do I," replied Baker. "If Gordon fired that shot, it was a matter of private vengeance on you. But, having fired it, the most sensible thing was to seek safety with Rebels who knew him. I don't doubt Davis will make him useful."

"Well, I hope the three of 'em will stay in Richmond and stop pestering me," declared Lincoln. "That's all I ask of 'em."

"It's not all I ask, by a jugful," grimly, from Baker. "I'm going down to Richmond, myself."

And before the President could finish his protest, the detective had bowed himself out.

It was not the President who suffered from the effects of the attempt upon his life. It was Mary. She endured agonies now, whenever her husband went out of the White House. She was very much alone, during these long summer days. It was extraordinary how much she missed Miss Ford, she told John Hay. If the extremely popular John Hay found Washington hopelessly unsocial that summer, how much more so did Mary Lincoln, all of whose social efforts and successes turned to ashes with the departure of the Virginian! She made no complaints to Lincoln, however, and, absorbed as he was in his work, the President would not have discovered her pitiable state of mind, but for an episode connected with the new campaign in Virginia.

The campaign was forming under Lincoln's urgent touch all the while he was giving earnest thought to the emancipation proclamation.

After reaching the determination to withdraw McClellan from the Army of the Potomac, he did not give a peremptory order to that effect. Instead he told McClellan to bring his forces up to Acquia Creek, a little tributary of the Potomac, about thirty miles south of Washington, and from this spot to send his men to Pope, as Pope might need them. Pope, the first week in August, began to move his army southwest and on August 9th met the superb Rebel fighter, Stonewall Jackson, at Cedar Mountain.

McClellan had received his first order to move to Acquia Creek on August 3rd. It was, of course, a bitter pill for the general to take, for it placed him in the amazing position of having to transfer his troops to Pope, until none were left. On August 9th, he had not reached Acquia Creek.

Late in the afternoon of the 9th, reports of terrible losses at Cedar Mountain, began to reach the War Department. Lincoln, who was in the state of taut nerves usual with him when a battle was in progress, had refused to eat, and was spending the afternoon in Stanton's offices, reading dispatches as they came from the hands of the telegraph operators.

"Supposing this turns into a big engagement, Stanton," he exclaimed a dozen times during the afternoon. "McClellan's in no position to help!"

"He wouldn't help if he were in the right position," grunted Stanton. "But you *would* handle the fellow gently! Why don't you get rid of him now?"

Lincoln sighed. Why didn't he get rid of McClellan? Why not send a telegram now? He was asking himself this question the last of the afternoon, when an unwonted interruption occurred. Mary came in, followed by a little middle-aged woman in black. She wore a very modest crinoline and a serviceable scoop bonnet. There was, even to Lincoln's casual glance, an extraordinary intellectual force in her fine eyes and clean-cut features.

"I know I'm not supposed to enter here, gentlemen," said Mary, smiling, "but I have a legitimate excuse. I claim your ear for this lady, Miss Clara Barton, who came to me because she had been unable to reach the President. Miss Barton has collected a whole warehouse of comforts for our soldiers, and she's been doling them out in the most practical manner. But now she has a new idea."

Mary's eager eyes would have won an audience for Miss Barton, had not the newcomer's own manner vouched for her.

"What may we do for you, Madam?" asked Lincoln.

"I want to go where only evil women go," said Miss Barton. "I want to go to the battlefields. I want to give aid to the wounded there, where it is first needed. If I do and succeed, other women will follow me and some day we shall have nurses at the front where they belong. Mr. President and Mr. Secretary, I want to start for Cedar Mountain, *now*."

"It's a preposterous idea, Madam," declared Stanton. "Preposterous! Why should you think of such a thing?"

Miss Barton clasped her hands. She had beautiful hands.

"When those soldiers I'd taught as children came back from Ball's Bluff, last year, and I saw them suffering from neglect—boys maimed and dying who could have been saved on the battlefield,—I resolved that this was the thing I must do, that other women could follow. I've had months of snubbing and evasion, but at last I have Major Ruckett's passports, but I must have more. I must have President Lincoln's word."

"I have no word to give you, Madam," said Lincoln, sadly. "Your kind heart has made you impractical. Of what avail can any woman be in a sanguinary flood like this?"

"Mr. Lincoln," cried Mrs. Lincoln, "if you don't send Miss Barton off with the word she asks, I swear I'm going with her myself, to show the soldiers how the Lincolns feel! Come to think of it, why can't I go? Why wouldn't it be a singularly appropriate thing for me?" The idea took instant hold of her imagination. She glanced about the dull, heavily furnished room, unseeingly. "I must do something for the war! All of you making such sacrifices, doing such good, and I with my idle, empty hands. . . . The White House is a living tomb to my energies."

Lincoln blinked for a moment, then a flood of self-reproach surged to his lips. "My dear wife," he began.

Mary would not allow him to proceed. "Why not? Miss Barton has only shown me what we all know, that succor on the field is one of the crying needs of war. Let me not go down in history as a social nonentity! Let me give my talents and my energy to this idea of Miss Barton's! Let me too go to Cedar Mountain!"

"No, my dear wife!" said Lincoln, decisively. "You must be content with having won Stanton and me to Miss Barton's cause. Eh, Stanton?"

The Secretary of War was touched by Mary's plea. "We'll give Miss Barton our blessing, of course, if that will make Mrs. Lincoln happy. But it's nonsense, her thinking of such a trip for herself."

"Tell the men I have given you Godspeed and that my every thought and prayer is with them, Miss Barton," said Lincoln.

"Write it on my passport, Mr. President," cried Clara Barton.

"You are a practical soul! I know you'll succeed." Mary smiled in spite of her agitation.

Lincoln wrote, then took Mary's arm. "I reckon I'd better make the acquaintance of my family, again," he said.

They saw Miss Barton on her way, then, at Mary's urgent request, Lincoln took a short turn with her in the garden.

"You've been warning me against strolling for fear of a bullet," he said with a smile, "but I suppose you can protect me, you darling midget."

"Don't joke about it, Abra'm!" protested Mary, then pausing before a magnificent bed of poppies, petunias and coxcomb, she exclaimed: "There! I had to fight for a bed of old-fashioned things that I knew could bloom in this dreadful Washington August. The gardener, in company with the rest of this charming city, thinks I'm very common in my tastes."

"Can't blame 'em, when they see what you've married!" Lincoln chuckled. "But that bed of flowers just suits my liking. Plenty of color, plenty of smell."

He walked slowly around the bed, his hands clasped behind him. He was wearing a much rumpled linen duster over shirt and trousers, just as he had rushed from his bedroom that morning, at the first words from Cedar Mountain. He was a little faint from lack of food and the vivid mass of flowers with its heavy odor in the sultry heat danced before his eyes in utter unreality.

Mary, with her uncanny intuitions, sensed exactly what was passing in his mind.

"You're trying to appear pleased because you think I need calming down, you dear thing!" she exclaimed. "I don't need that, Abra'm, this time! I wouldn't add a straw's weight to your cares. Enjoy the flowers for yourself or not at all."

Lincoln strode quickly back around the bed to her side. "Mary, are you unhappy?"

She took his arm, and they walked slowly into the kitchen garden, between rows of sweet corn with sharp leaves rasping in the burning wind.

"I'm empty!" she said, finally. "No one but myself realizes how much Willie meant to me. He was the child to count on. He was always there. He understood me and forgave me and admired me. He was the son I always felt would take care of me if anything happened to you."

Lincoln pulled off an ear of corn in the milk, and began to nibble on the silk which lay along the grains. The uneasy contrition he always felt when Mary was in one of these moods crowded out, for the moment, his anxiety over Cedar Mountain. He did neglect her. She was bitterly lonely, and through no fault of hers. All the vital, exhilarating emanations of his mind and soul were going to his work, and only his moments of weariness and dullness were left for her. And, lately, he'd shut her out of the future for which she always had been an inspiration. The more his responsibilities increased, he thought, the more he tended to share his real thoughts with no one. In this, he knew he'd been carelessly cruel to her. She was starving for companionship. Small wonder she turned to Charles Sumner, he thought, or now that Charles was immersed in the politics of emancipation, that she had wished to join Miss Clara Barton.

Mary, pulling a weed here, supporting a gourd plant there, did not interrupt his thinking. She loved the garden, and worked in it frequently, in the early mornings. This was the first time the President recalled having entered this spot, and he resolved, after this, to make it a walking place. It was more like home to him than any place he'd found since leaving Springfield.

"Mary," he said, finally, "you know I'm not at all a versatile fellow, and it's taking every ounce I've got in me to husk out this job. I've wondered lately if I'll ever again be able to love any one the way I'd like to, the way a man ought to. I'll tell you, wife, loving takes time and thought!"

"It does, indeed!" agreed Mary, standing quietly by the raspberry bushes, and eyeing a late variety unseeingly.

"I've neglected you!" he exclaimed, abruptly.

"You should have allowed me to join Miss Barton. You should not deny me the chance to use my brain and strength in this war." Mary's voice was not reproachful. She was only stating facts.

"No, by jings!" cried the President, "that's going too far! Do you imagine for a moment I'm going to allow you to go where there's danger of your life? Willie's death was bad enough. I'd never get over yours."

Tears came to Mary's eyes. She looked up into his face. "I know that you depend on me for physical comforts, dear. But you no longer need me on the mental side. That's what's killing me."

"That's where you guess wrong," declared Lincoln. "I need you mentally as much as I ever did but I haven't—or rather I've neglected to come to you. For instance, I've been telling myself for weeks that I was going to talk over emancipation with you and I haven't."

"Have you put it up to the Cabinet, yet?" asked Mary, with quick interest.

Lincoln pulled some raspberries, and began to eat them. "Yes, last month I did so. The reaction was typical of each man." He gave a rapid résumé of the Cabinet meeting, ending with the remark, "I shall have no trouble with any of them. Even Chase will fall into line, nasty as he feels toward me."

"No, they'll make no trouble," agreed Mary. "McClellan, the Unready, will be the one to render your proclamation void after you issue it."

"How can he do that?" asked Lincoln.

"He's now the acknowledged leader of the Democratic Party," answered Mary. "As such, he's bound to oppose emancipation."

"But what do you think his move will be?" urged the President.

"Consider his past record, Abra'm. I remember John Hay's reply to me in April, when I asked him for the latest news from the front. He replied with that grandiloquent air of his, 'Pope is crossing the turbid and broad torrent of the Mississippi in the blaze of the enemy's fire, Grant is fighting the overwhelming legions of Beauregard at Pittsburg Landing, while Mc-Clellan, our Little Napoleon, sits trembling before the handful of men at Yorktown, afraid to fight.' Then he added, like the real human boy he is, 'Stanton feels devilish about it!' . . . Abra'm, can't you feel devilish about McClellan?"

"No! I like him! . . . This isn't telling me what he's going to do."

"He's going to take your place in the White House if he can. And he's going to make this as nearly a bloodless war as far as his share in it goes as he can, in order to entice the Democrats to putting him there. There will be no decisive victories here, in the East, until you break McClellan, Abra'm. He's your evil genius. What does fascinate you so about him?"

"He's a thoroughly likeable fellow, Mary. And, beside that, he has all the qualities that I lack. He's a scholar, a polished gentleman of the world, and a natural born boss. His men worship him. His staff would die for him. Why shouldn't I like such a man?"

Mary's cheeks flushed. "And you think you lack all those qualities, with your splendid mind and your gentleman's soul. You make me indignant! . . ." She paused to eye him reflectively, while he plucked another handful of berries. "Now I understand," she exclaimed. "We've got back to your ultimate weakness. Your affection for McClellan is causing you the whole trouble. *Weakness*, Abra'm. The failing that's been your curse all your life. And now it's proving to be the country's curse. You *must* get rid of McClellan!"

Lincoln ate his berries dejectedly, pondering on the accusation. Was she right? Was this the answer to the question he'd been asking himself all day? Was his affection for this handsome, debonair, brilliant soldier his real reason for keeping him? At any rate, Mary had given him a new angle, perhaps a helpful angle, on the problem.

He suddenly squared his shoulders. "Come! This isn't helping you any, my dear wife! I've a suggestion for you. When, or if, Miss Barton returns from Cedar Mountain, have a talk with her, and organize your own hospital work along the useful lines she'll suggest. Plan to give at least half of every day to that work, and keep me informed of the conditions in the army that one gets only by contact with the men, which I can't get."

Mary brightened. "It will really help? This is not a mere sop to my wailing?"

"It will really help," replied the President, sincerely. "And now I must return to torment!" starting slowly toward his office via the kitchen entrance. Mary followed him, but stopped behind in the sweltering kitchen for a talk with the cook. She knew that if she remained longer with the President she could not keep silence about the linen duster!

THE Northern forces were repulsed at Cedar Mountain, and Pope's Army fell back to the Rappahannock. Still McClellan did not reënforce him. Lee sent a part of his forces to the north to cut off Pope's communications with Washington, and Pope hastily moved back toward Manassas to circumvent him. And still McClellan sent him no men.

These sultry days of August were the most wearying of any Lincoln had experienced. He, himself, had given them a more stupendous significance than they otherwise might have had, by agreeing to postpone the issuing of the proclamation until a great victory would sugar-coat it for public consumption.

Outwardly calm and cheerful, inwardly he was burning with an anxiety that he showed only to his wife, and, occasionally, to young Hay. Nicolay was away a good deal that summer, in the mountains, trying to rid himself of ague, and John Hay was with Lincoln more than ever. The young secretary was conniving with Mrs. Lincoln, constantly, to give the President moments of amusement. Lincoln was conscious of their efforts and grateful for them. But the trip to the Observatory "to take a squint at Arcturus and the moon" which he and John made, was spoiled for him by the fact that the carriage was followed by a lieutenant and eight cavalrymen, the clatter of whose horses he found almost unsupportable.

"Baker and Welles and Sumner are responsible for this!" he groaned to John, on his way back from the Observatory. "It's awful! Let's go to Ford's theater and see what's going on there!"

John, when Mrs. Lincoln greeted them on their late return, insisted that the call at Ford's had been most salutary.

"It was a Sacred Concert of Profane Music," he explained to her, when she half smilingly chided the two whom she found laughing in Hay's room at one o'clock, over a poem of Hood's that Lincoln had clipped. "We had a private box, near the stage, the Tycoon and I, and we carried on a hefty flirtation with the girls in the flies. I will say the Tycoon has a knowing glance."

Mary suddenly pulled the tired young man's face down to hers and kissed him. "I don't know what we'd do without you, John."

Lincoln, sitting with his feet on the window sill, nodded. "I'd kiss him myself, only I'm doubtful about either of us enjoying it."

"You'd better make much of me while you can," declared John, solemnly. "I'm slowly shaking to pieces with the ague. Look!" pointing to the loose buttons on his coat.

"I'll tighten them for you, or get Lizzie Keckley to, if you'll leave the coat with me," said Mary. "Come, Mr. Lincoln, let this boy go to his well-earned rest."

As the President slowly lowered his feet, Mary began to laugh. "Lizzie told me an amusing thing. She was coming up the north driveway behind a couple of soldiers, to-day, and one of them pointed to a second floor window. She says three pairs of feet could be seen on the sill. One of the men said, perfectly seriously, 'The Cabinet is a-setting. Them big feet in the middle is Lincoln's.'"

The President's huge roar drowned John's and tucking Mary under his arm, he ambled off to bed.

But not to sleep. As soon as his head touched the pillow, his mind reverted to McClellan, to Pope, and to his own questionable sanity in keeping faith in the Little Napoleon. Nor was this night an exception to other nights. By the middle of August he was having so few hours of sleep that Mary appealed to Dr. Stone who promptly ordered him out to the Soldiers' Home every night during the remainder of the month. Mary swallowed her prejudice against the place, and moved out for the month and the President, perforce, obeyed, reluctantly riding his horse amidst the attending cavalrymen. The long ride helped him, not so much in sleeping, as in relaxing. At the Soldiers' Home he, as the wise doctor realized, was not within easy access of the telegraph office.

The ride back in the mornings, with Taddie often clattering beside him on his pony, and with Pensacola and Sumter risking their lives among the pounding hoofs, was not so restful. Each rod that they covered brought him an increased sense of burden. The familiar feeling of living in a nightmare would settle on him as he left the shaded country road, and clattered onto the city cobbles, and everything save the impending conflict in Virginia would become unreal to him by the time they reached the White House.

The days crept slowly on, thunderstorms alternating with burning sun. McClellan, moving with unbelievable reluctance and deliberation, did not leave Harrison's Landing until the 17th of August, and did not report himself as available in Alexandria until ten days later.

Pope's campaign had now reached a perilous stage. He and Lee were maneuvering for position. On the 29th of August they met and the second battle of Bull Run was begun.

It lasted for two days.

Lincoln spent practically all of the two days in Halleck's office, observing, in anguished perplexity, the exchange of telegrams between the General-in-Chief and McClellan, watching the fluctuating reports from Pope with growing despondency. Toward mid-afternoon of the 29th, the bickering between Halleck and McClellan got on his nerves; the former giving orders growing more peremptory every hour, the latter giving excuses more or less unsatisfactory for not obeying them. At last Lincoln's patience broke.

"Halleck, in the name of God, doesn't McClellan *want* to reënforce Pope?"

Halleck threw up his hands. Stanton, who had been walking the floor for two hours, without cessation, turned on the President and sneered: "You know he doesn't! I'd call him in and court-martial him for treason, to-night, if you'd keep out of it. Pope says what men he has of the Army of the Potomac are malcontent and insubordinate. McClellan's jealousy and resentment have percolated to the very drummer boys. You'll find that, now McClellan has finally permitted Franklin to start to relieve Pope, he'll arrive there too late."

And Franklin did arrive too late, as did the other army commanders that McClellan finally started toward Bull Run. By Sunday night, August 30th, Lincoln and all the world knew that Pope had been beaten and was again retreating. And not only was he retreating! He telegraphed Halleck that his army was utterly demoralized, and begged to be withdrawn into the defenses of Washington!

Halleck, himself, brought Lincoln this message, before the President was out of bed on Monday morning. Seward, who had come before breakfast for news, and John Hay, both consumed with anxiety, followed the General-in-Chief. Lincoln, having read the message, swung his long legs out of bed, thrust his feet into carpet slippers and began to walk the floor.

"I've sent for McClellan to come to Washington and give us his advice," said Halleck.

Seward uttered an oath, then, with a sudden drawing of his breath that was almost a sob, he said, "Is it true, Mr. Lincoln, that McClellan sent you a letter saying that Pope must get out of his scrape by himself?"

Lincoln did not cease his long, noiseless pacing. "He said we had two courses available! Either to concentrate all available forces to open communications with Pope, or leave Pope to get out of his scrape and use all our means to safeguard the capital."

"What did he mean, sir?" asked John Hay, resplendent in a green and crimson silk bathrobe. "It doesn't seem possible that he could have meant what he wrote."

Seward turned to John. "Hay, what's the use of growing old? You learn something of men and things, but too late to use it. I have only now found out that military jealousy has prevented these generals from acting for the welfare of the country."

"It's something I wouldn't have thought possible!" exclaimed Hay.

"Why should you?" Seward said gloomily. "You aren't old. I should have known it and helped my associates prepare for it."

Lincoln gave no heed to this exchange. His mind was still on Bull Run. "What are our losses, Halleck?"

"Too early for accuracy. Perhaps ten thousand! At least six thousand."

The President wiped his dripping face. "Why did you send for McClellan, Halleck?"

"If he caused this demoralization," replied Halleck, who was trembling with exhaustion, "he'll be the quickest man to end it."

"You go home to bed, Halleck," ordered Lincoln. "See to it that McClellan comes to me, when he arrives."

"Yes, Mr. President." Halleck swayed as he stood. John Hay and Seward ran to his assistance and helped him from the room.

Waiting for McClellan, that day, Lincoln was so uneasy that for once his sense of humor deserted him, and when a deputation of clergymen visited him, the extraordinary character of their demands irritated him. They demanded that the President prohibit Sunday battles. He showed them to the door with the request that they take their complaints to Jefferson Davis and Lee. He still was glowering a half hour after this, when McClellan came in.

He was sunburned but immaculate. At the look of him, Lincoln's irritation found words. "General Pope, I imagine, has had no chance for a shave for a week."

McClellan who had entered with a pleasant smile on his handsome face immediately scowled.

"What am I to understand by that, sir?" he demanded.

"Sit down, General," waving his hand at the chair beside his desk, "and let's see if we can thresh this thing out."

McClellan obeyed, sitting bolt upright, as though his uniform were of steel.

"Pope," said Lincoln, slowly, "is a first rate officer. He proved that out West. His ideas for handling this Virginia campaign were excellent. There is every probability that he'd have whipped, and really hurt, the enemy if you had coöperated with him. You made a mistake in not doing so, General. You have turned popular opinion against you."

"What is popular opinion to a soldier?" demanded McClellan.

"It should be nothing," agreed the President, with alacrity. "But you are playing politics, McClellan, with more eagerness than you're showing in the military game. So public opinion should count with you. Look yonder!" pointing to an enormous heap of letters and telegrams on the Cabinet table. "Those are all requests from people demanding that I remove you. There are several thousand of them now and they're still coming. There's a petition, I understand, circulating among the Cabinet members, urging me to retire you. That's not good hearing, is it, Mac, for a man of your particular ambitions?"

McClellan had grown noticeably pale under his tan. He stared incredulously at the heaped-up contumely on the table. Nothing was more difficult for him to face than adverse criticism.

"It strikes me," Lincoln went on, "that you're acting stupidly. If you want my job, if you carry out the suggestions that are in the very air you breathe, you'll need more than the Army of the Potomac to back you. You'll need Grant and Burnside and Pope. And now, if I read the signs aright, you'll never have them. They'll be like me, hurt in their most tolerant judgment of you. You failed a brother officer in his hour of need."

McClellan jumped to his feet, but the President reached out a long, hard hand and thrust him gently back into his chair.

"George," his voice husky, "this is the crisis of your life. Be frank with me. You may dare to be. I have a great affection for you,—as if you were a gallant younger brother with advantages I'd never had."

The General's face softened. "What do you wish me to say, Mr. Lincoln?"

"Before I answer that," said Lincoln, "let me ask you if you realize what you've done to Pope? He believes that you wished him to fail. He believes that, at the very mildest, you encouraged your officers to enfeeble their movements by vain regrets that they were fighting under Pope and not you. And the disloyalty, the treasonable taint of it, has broken his spirit. You and your henchmen have put Pope through hell in this month of August and he's broken. He's asked me to remove him. And the country can ill afford to lose the officer that Pope was a short four weeks ago. . . . What I want you to tell me, George, is why you did it."

"I was utterly unwilling, sir," said McClellan with convincing earnestness, "to leave Washington unprotected, in order to help Pope. I would not be human and not regret that my place had been taken from me. But that regret in no way influenced my actions in the past month. I could not be a soldier and see you civilian politicians throw Washington into the lap of the Confederacy. Pope's campaign was absurd from the inception. Had you sent him, and all his available forces, to me at Harrison's Landing, we'd have been in Richmond two weeks ago." He leaned forward in his chair and looking into Lincoln's face with his unwavering blue eyes, he said, "No matter what pressure is brought to bear on me, sir, I shall make no military move that I know to be absurd."

Lincoln returned his look thoughtfully. Grant could not be spared from the West. Burnside was, in some ways, a feeble sister. Pope was useless, temporarily, at least. And even as he and McClellan sat talking, there was pouring back upon terrified Washington an army of a hundred thousand men, who had left their morale on the malignant flats of Bull Run. If Lee with his intrepid, fast-moving fighting machine knew this, and could gather himself up after the terrific efforts that had culminated in the victory of two days before, he could scatter the Army of Virginia beyond recall. Superb fighters, these Southerners, he told himself, adding, aloud, to McClellan's surprise, "Why not, they are Americans, too!"

Half despairingly he checked these facts over in his mind, while he returned McClellan's look, feeling meanwhile a resurgence of the half-admiring, half-humorous affection that never wholly disappeared from his attitude toward the general. Talk logically as he would, he could not convince himself that McClellan was not intrinsically honest. What a personality, to have become such an influence with his army! Surely that army could go anywhere, do anything, if McClellan would see the light.

"I particularly wish not to quarrel with you, George," said the President, at last. "But I do think it essential, at this moment, to make you see clearly what I know about you. You have said many times and in many ways, that the Administration was made up of imbeciles. That we wished you to fail. That I am a despicable fool. That Stanton is a bad lot. Believing these things, I suppose they form the mainspring for your actions during the past year. Is this so?"

"I beg of you not to insist upon a reply, if you desire to avoid a quarrel, sir. I will say, however, that you have now shown me the source of your resentment toward me."

"I have no resentment toward you, George. I desire nothing so much on God's footstool as your success. No matter what has been said to me, I've clung to you and my old ideal of you. To prove that to you, I'll make a bargain with you. I will give you Pope's job if you will promise me to give back the army its morale and having done this, to start swiftly after the enemy and *hurt* him. If you win a battle, *follow* him, drive him to Richmond and take Richmond if you can. But whether you can or not, move swiftly, move *swiftly, move swiftly!*"

"There's a reverse side to that offer, Mr. Lincoln?" asked McClellan.

"Yes, I reckon there is. But we won't discuss that."

The general came to his feet smartly. "I accept your offer, Mr. President, in the spirit in which it is given. We'll be on the march within the week."

"Good! Good! You may count on the complete coöperation of Halleck and myself."

The two men shook hands and McClellan clattered out.

Lincoln sat by the window alone for the moment, girding himself for the national uproar of disapproval that would greet the reappointment of McClellan. Had he been weak again? He knew what Mary and Stanton would reply to that query. He was more dissatisfied with himself than he ever remembered having been over a decision. And again his dissatisfaction showed itself in irritation when he was interrupted by the breathless entrance of a bearded man in uniform.

"I'm Colonel Stone, Mr. President," he said. "I was wounded in the Peninsular campaign and my wife came down to nurse me. She was drowned by a steamboat collision in Hampton Roads. I've learned that they've recovered her body and I want a pass to go down and get it."

A deep sense of irritation swept over Lincoln. He looked at the officer coldly. "Am I to have no rest?" he ejaculated. "Is there no hour or spot when or where I may escape this constant call on my feelings? Why do you bother me and not the War Office?"

Colonel Stone looked dazed; as if he could not believe this to be the President. "Mr. Stanton refused me," he said.

"Then probably you ought not to go down the river. Stanton knows. If I override his decision it might work disaster on some important movement. You ought not to come here to appeal to my humanity. Don't you know we are in the midst of war, and that suffering and death press on us all? Works of humanity are trampled on and outlawed by war.—You must not vex me with your family troubles. I have all the burdens I can carry. If the War Office won't help you, then bear your burden as we all must until the war is over. Everything must yield to the paramount duty of finishing the war."

Colonel Stone, looking utterly crushed, withdrew. Lincoln saw, with a sort of pleasure, that he had hurt the man. He'd proved to one person, at least, that he was not always soft!

CHAPTER XXVI

A T first peep of dawn, the next day, after a sleepless night, Lincoln with his yawning escort started for the White House. He reached there before six o'clock, and dismissed the lieutenant. Then he went down through the kitchen and the kitchen garden to elude the guard, and made a successful escape to Pennsylvania Avenue. He strode among the charwomen at Willard's Hotel and asked the astounded desk clerk for Colonel Stone's room. A moment later he was pounding on a door on the second floor.

The Colonel in rumpled uniform admitted him. Lincoln seized his hand. "Colonel Stone," he exclaimed, "I was a brute, yesterday. I have no excuse for my conduct. I was tired, but that's no reason I should be rude to a man who has offered his life for his country, much more, a man who has come to me in great affliction. I've had a regretful night. Will you forgive me?"

"God knows I'd forgive you more than that, Mr. Lincoln!" exclaimed Colonel Stone. "I never realized the stress you were under until yesterday afternoon. Don't give me another thought, sir."

"But you didn't sleep yourself, Colonel, last night, and 'twas my fault," insisted Lincoln, glancing at the untouched bed. "You go to the War Office, this noon. You'll find your passport there. No, don't thank me! I don't deserve it."

And he was gone.

As he passed through the lobby, he came upon Lizzie Keckley. He paused. "Well, Lizzie, what are you doing here at this ungodly hour?"

The mantua maker looked up at him in surprise. "I have just delivered a dress that I finished last night. I'm now on my way to the White House."

"Come along then, we'll both use shank's mare. Getting Mrs. Lincoln all fixed for the winter?"

"No, sir, I'm not sewing for Mrs. Lincoln now, Mr. President. I had news for her. I'd like to repeat it to you, sir, if you're willing."

They were moving along Pennsylvania Avenue, Lizzie at a trot to keep up with Lincoln.

"I'm all ears, Lizzie. You ought to be drawing pay on Baker's staff, I reckon."

"I've discovered Miss Ford. There's a house on F Street, very elegant, that's known to have been disreputable. All the blinds kept down, and all that. Well, one of my girls left me, last spring, and set up for herself. She came to see me, yesterday, and said she'd been sent for by a person living in that house, who signed herself Mrs. Ogden-Ames. And that she was so hard up she'd taken the risk of harming her trade and had gone. She said Mrs. Ogden-Ames was very tall with violet eyes and *black* hair. She asked Anna where she'd learned her trade, and luckily Anna didn't mention me, because she was afraid I'd be cross at that kind of a connection. The lady probably made up her mind that Anna was just a plantation nigger, so she wanted to hire her as a personal maid and seamstress and take her to Europe. Said her own maid had run away."

They were in the White House grounds now, and Lincoln led the way to the kitchen garden.

"Anna was excited over the prospects of going to Paris, so she accepted, and then came to me, last night, to tell me of her good luck. She said the house seemed empty of all inmates, and that only Mrs. Ogden-Ames and an old serving man named Uncle Bob were there."

"What made you suspicious?" asked Lincoln, beginning to eat dew-wet raspberries.

"Well, you see, at first, Mr. President, I didn't suspect anything and I went round with Anna to carry her luggage. Uncle Bob let us in the back way. The whole front was dark, but from the kitchen you could see a light in the dining room. Uncle Bob said he was just serving supper, and that I was to leave before he was called into the dining room. I'd never been inside one of these houses, and I wasn't going without trying to see what I could. I nodded to Uncle Bob and went out into the back yard. I watched through a crack in the shade until Uncle Bob went into the dining room. Then I slipped into the back hall, then into the front hall and peeked through the curtains. Mr. President, Miss Ford, with her hair dyed black, was having supper with a tall, handsome officer, dressed like a Federal, but she called him 'Tom.' It was certainly Captain Tom Taylor. I had a chance to listen to only a few sentences, because they came out into the hall and Captain Taylor left.

"I can't remember whole sentences like Jinny did. But they were talking about when you'd get your nerve up to issuing an emancipation proclamation. They were saying that if General McClellan got control of the army again, it would be best to make him a bold offer from Jefferson Davis. When Captain Taylor said that Miss Ford laughed at him, she said that nothing could change General McClellan's loyalty to the North. She said his honor was perfect. And Captain Taylor asked her if the General's honor was more than the Secessionists had who had deserted the North.

"Miss Ford didn't answer that. But she said she'd seen Mr. Mercy the day before, and he'd told her France was anxious to come in here the minute England would join. He said the sympathy of the French Emperor was all for the South. And she said Horace Greeley had asked the French Minister to get his country to come in to make peace."

"I knew that last," interjected Lincoln. "Greeley's got the shakes."

"Then Miss Ford said she'd go to England the minute Captain Taylor told her to. And that was all."

"You should have gone to Baker at once, Lizzie," said the President, gravely.

"It was past midnight then, sir," said the mantua maker.

"Well, no use criticizing! You go to Baker's office now. Here, take my card," scrawling a line to the Colonel.

"Yes, sir. Will you tell Mrs. Lincoln, sir? She's so anxious and won't be relieved till she knows Miss Ford and her friends are shut up."

"Smart woman, Sister Ford," mused Lincoln. "Yes, I'll tell the Madam. Slip along, now, Lizzie."

He made his way up to his room, musing sadly. Much as he feared her machinations, he still retained a sense of grateful affection for the Virginian. Then he promptly forgot the whole affair, for James met him on the stairs and told him that Sumner was waiting for him in his office.

The Senator from Massachusetts had heard it rumored that McClellan had been reinstated, and he was there to protest with all the eloquence at his command against "once more imperiling the nation and emancipation by this terrible military incubus."

The rest of that day was spent by Lincoln in listening to bitter comments on what he had done. He did not blame even the members of the Cabinet for their outspoken censure. Stanton, in a heartbroken sort of anger, washed his hands of McClellan. Seward remarked that McClellan was the hope of the Confederacy, and the sure forerunner of intervention from England and France. "One more Federal defeat here, and the Confederacy will be recognized," he said. Even "Father" Welles expressed himself as humiliated by the President's weakness.

Lincoln was extraordinarily gentle. "Yes, he's acted badly toward Pope," he admitted when Montgomery Blair exploded on this point. "He really wanted him to fail. But there is no one in the army who can man these fortifications and lick these troops into shape half as well as he can."

"It's humiliating," he agreed with Welles, "in more ways than one. But we must use the tools we have. If he cannot fight himself, he excels in making others ready to fight."

"This will be a body blow at emancipation, if you really wish ever to have opportunity to issue your proclamation," sneered Chase.

"The people are gloomy," said Lincoln, wondering if Chase ever had missed an opportunity to insult him. He had achieved a consistency almost admirable in this! "The Democratic party is uglier in spirit and stronger than it's been since the war began. There's a sullen discontent abroad we dare not ignore. If recruiting is to go on, I dare not offend any large, organized group of people. By his declarations against my policies, McClellan has made himself the leader of the Democratic party. It is common sense to appease that party, at this moment."

A general groan met this statement. Lincoln felt his cheeks burn, but he said nothing, and the Cabinet having talked itself empty on the subject, turned to other matters.

It was Mary, curiously enough, who gave him the one shred of comfort he received. She rode in the carriage with him to the Soldiers' Home, that night. He told her about the Cabinet meeting and she said:

"There are two sides to it, I'll admit, much as I do deplore what you've done. When word of the reappointment reached the hospital, to-day, you'd have thought some one had poured a bottle of wine down the throat of every poor fellow there. They were cured of their wounds, the country was saved, 'God in his heaven, all right with the world!' "

The President pulled her hand within his arm and patted it. They rode in silence for a time then Mary said: "Lizzie Keckley came in this evening and told me the story. Miss Ford and her friends had gone bag and baggage when the detective policemen arrived. But they have some good clews. That's something."

"I hope she does go. It may save some dirty work when the proclamation comes out," said the President.

"Another thing to worry about!" groaned his wife.

And yet, in spite of all the bitterness of the reproaches heaped upon Lincoln and McClellan, before the week had passed, they were forgotten. Between the 4th and 7th of September, General Lee crossed the Potomac, near Leesburg and entered Maryland. The public mind at once focused on this new and terrible menace.

Within a few days, McClellan actually got his army of some 80,000 moving. He began, at once, asking for more men, but on the whole he appeared to be in a complacent frame of mind. He moved only at the rate of six miles a day.

In an agony of apprehension, the nation watched Lee's rapid, McClellan's leisurely, movements. Lee, certain that Maryland would welcome him, paused at Frederick for two days and sent Stonewall Jackson back to take Harper's Ferry. With his usual skill and impetuosity, Jackson accomplished this, and the ragged Confederates helped themselves to the clothing and food with which this Union fort was stored. But the people of Frederick were not hospitable to Lee, and while Jackson was in action at Harper's Ferry, Lee moved on westward to the vicinity of Sharpsburg. Still unhurried, McClellan followed. On the 16th, the two armies, Lee's with less than 40,000, McClellan with more than 87,000 men, drew up in battle line on either side of Antietam Creek, and before dawn of the 17th was begun the bloodiest single day's encounter of the Civil War.

At night it appeared to be a drawn battle, but the next morning, Lee began a retreat with his exhausted forces. He had lost 11,000 men.

Lincoln telegraphed, "Please do not let him get off without being hurt." McClellan's generals begged to be allowed to renew the attack, and drive Lee into the Potomac. But satisfied with having repulsed the invasion of the North, McClellan made camp in Antietam Valley. His losses totalled 13,000 soldiers.

For five days, Lincoln urged McClellan to pursue Lee, insisting that, as a student of war, McClellan must know that to make an actual military success of Antietam, he ought to follow the exhausted enemy. McClellan said that *his* army was exhausted. Lincoln asked if its exhaustion was greater than that of Lee's army. McClellan, hurt, replied by asking for reënforcements. Lincoln gave him every man that could be spared, until the General had 100,000 men with which to pursue the Rebels. On the 22nd the Army of the Potomac still was resting, and the newspapers of the country had begun to question the first wild joy which had called Antietam a glorious victory for the North.

That day, at noon, Lincoln called the Cabinet together. The sullen heat of summer was giving way to the fragrant, delicate air of autumn which is one of Washington's charming apologies for her dreadful climate. Lincoln was glad of this. The ghastly heat was trying to the nerves, and he had a vivid recollection of the physical oppression that had added to the irritability of the first discussion of the proclamation.

He deeply desired that his associates should meet his statements to-day with relaxed minds. For some minutes after the seven men had gathered round the table with him, he refused to be serious. When Secretary Bates asked him how large he believed the Rebel army to be, Lincoln replied, promptly:

"About 1,200,000!"

A gasp went round the table. The President explained. "You see when I ask my generals how great the Rebel forces are, they always guess them to be from three to five times greater than their own. So, at a minimum, if we have 400,000 soldiers, the Rebels must have three times that many."

Everybody but Stanton smiled. The Secretary of War was annoyed by the President's facetiousness. "Mr. Lincoln," he asked, severely, "I sent to you yesterday a delegation of fifty New York millionaires who wouldn't take my 'no' for an answer, though I roared it in their ears. They wished a gunboat stationed in New York harbor for its protection from Rebel rams. I suppose it's too much to hope that you backed my refusal!"

Lincoln chuckled. "They opened up on me wrong! They began by saying that they represented in their own right over $110,000,000. However, I listened with good attention and when they'd presented their plea I said, 'Gentlemen, it's impossible for me, in the present condition of things, to furnish you a gunboat. We are very short of them. The credit of the Government is at a very low ebb; greenbacks are worth not more than forty or fifty cents on the dollar. In this condition of things, if I were worth half of what you are, gentlemen, and were as badly frightened as you seem to be, I'd *build a gunboat and give it to the Government!*' I reckon I never saw $110,000,000 sink out of sight as quick as that did! They disappeared into thin air!"

He took a book from his pocket and put on his spectacles. "This morning, I received a copy from Artemus Ward of his new book. I wish I could write like that fellow! Just listen to this chapter. He calls it a High-handed Outrage at Utica."

Lincoln read with gusto and the secretaries laughed as heartily as he, again with the exception of poor Stanton. But in spite of Stanton's be-

wildered annoyance, there was now an air of cheerful freedom about the
Cabinet table that had been lacking for many weeks, and the President
seized the moment.

"Gentlemen: I have, as you are aware, thought a great deal about the
relation of this war to slavery and you all must remember that several
weeks ago, I read to you an order I had prepared on this subject. I think
the time has now come to act on that order. I wish it was a better time. I
wish that we were in better condition. The action of the army against the
Rebels has not been what I should have best liked. But they have been
driven out of Maryland, and Pennsylvania is no longer in danger of invasion. When the Rebel army was at Frederick, I determined as soon as
it should be driven out of Maryland, to issue a proclamation of emancipation. I said nothing to any one, but I made the promise to myself and—to
my Maker.

"The Rebel army is now driven out, and I am going to fulfill that
promise. I have got you together to hear what I have written down. I do
not wish your advice about the main matter, for that I have determined
for myself. This I say without intending anything but respect for any one
of you. But I already know the views of each on this question. They have
been heretofore expressed, and I have considered them as thoroughly and
carefully as I can. What I have written is that which my reflections have
determined me to say.

"If there is anything in the expressions I use or in any minor matter
which any one of you think had better be changed, I shall be glad to receive the suggestions.

"One other observation I will make. I know that many others might, in
this matter, as in others, do better than I can. And if I were satisfied that
the public confidence was more surely possessed by any one of them than
by me, and knew of any constitutional way he could be put in my place,
he should have it. I would gladly yield it to him.

"But though I believe that I have not so much of the confidence of the
people as I had some time since, I do not know that, all things considered,
any person has more. And, however this may be, there is no way in which
I can have any other man put where I am.

"I am here. I must do the best I can to bear the responsibility of taking
the course which I think I ought to take."

He removed his spectacles, polished them with a red cotton handkerchief, replaced them, and read the manuscript that had become so essential a part of his being that he felt as though he were reading his very heart.

"I, Abraham Lincoln, President of the United States and Commander-
in-Chief of the Army and Navy thereof, do hereby proclaim and declare
that hereafter as heretofore, the war will be prosecuted for the object of
practically restoring the constitutional relations between the United States
and each of the States and the people thereof, in which State that relation
is or may be suspended or disturbed.

"That it is my purpose, upon the next meeting of Congress, to again recommend the adoption of a practical measure, tendering pecuniary aid to the free acceptance or rejection of all the slave States, so called, the people whereof may not then be in rebellion against the United States, and which States may then have voluntarily adopted, or thereafter may voluntarily adopt, the immediate or gradual abolishment of slavery within their respective limits.

"That on the first day of January, in the year of our Lord one thousand eight hundred and sixty-three, all persons held as slaves within States, or designated parts of a State, the people thereof shall thus be in rebellion against the United States, shall be then, thenceforward and forever free. . . ."

He paused for a moment after pronouncing the last two words, thinking as he had thought every time he had written them that no two words in the human tongue ever had been charged with such portentousness, then he went on with the provisions for carrying out the postulates of the proclamation.

There was a silence after the reading was done, broken by a deep sigh that seemed to spring from the heart of every man in the room.

"The die is cast!" exclaimed Seward, with a little smile.

Lincoln nodded. "I can only trust in God I have made no mistake. It is now for the country and the world to pass judgment upon it."

"I'll give it to the newspapers this afternoon," said Seward, briskly. "The storm will break in about twenty-four hours."

And it did!

PERHAPS, as William Stoddard said, the waste paper baskets in the White House, for weeks following the publication of the emancipation proclamation, told best the story of its reception by the public. They could not be emptied rapidly enough to keep poor Stoddard's desk cleared of the thousands of letters and telegrams that poured upon it, daily.

For every word of praise from the Northern radicals, there were ten of censure from the Northern conservatives. The epithets of "unconstitutional tyrant" and "odious dictator" were the mildest applied to Lincoln. The proclamation was a "filthy ukase," a "vicious blow at the sacred liberty of white men," a "vile dead letter, stinking of poison." Lincoln was warned that the Union soldiers would fight no more; that "the Army will disband, rather than be sacrificed on the bloody altar of fanatical Abolition."

Lincoln, as he and his advisers had foreseen, had furnished the Democratic party with invaluable ammunition for its campaign in the fall elections of Governors and Congressmen, now pending. This was to be a source of acute anxiety to the President, for without the backing of Congress the proclamation would be of little worth.

The indignation of the South was volubly expressed in every form by which it was hoped Lincoln could be reached. The mysterious "Grape Vine Telegraph" system, as Lincoln called it, never worked more efficiently than it did in transferring from the South to the North, the wrath and threats of the Southern leaders.

Perhaps nothing more completely epitomized Southern feeling than a letter Stoddard brought to Lincoln about a week after the proclamation was issued.

"Here, sir, is a letter from Miss Ford. Do you care to see it, before I turn it over to Colonel Baker?"

"Jings!" grunted the President, holding out his hand.

The letter, written on Executive Mansion note paper, was undated, and without postmark.

"This is to warn you, Abraham Lincoln, as I have warned you repeatedly, that by this insane proclamation you have not only jeopardized your own life, but you have immensely strengthened the South, and so have wrecked the future of your Government. If the virulent hate you have roused in my soul is a criterion, as I know it to be, of the detestation for you in the heart of every other slaveholder, there is no possibility that you can live after January 1st."

Lincoln returned the letter to Stoddard, with a grunt.

"I'm no braver than any other man, Billy," he said, "but they have threatened me too much! You can get used to anything, even to living in fear of assassination. That's my state of mind. Send that letter to Baker, and say nothing about it to any one."

These things were not easy to bear. Yet there were many demonstrations of approval, from sources of great strength. A conference of Governors, gathered at Altoona to confer on the military situation, was in session at the time of the issuing of the proclamation. Seventeen of these men endorsed the President's act. Only the Governors of the four border States and of New Jersey refused to approve.

The churches, spheres of enormous influence, were unstinting in their enthusiasm. Perhaps the Baptist Convention of New York, as Lincoln said to his wife, "got the point" as well as any one in the world, when it wrote, that, though it saw with agony the slaughter on the battlefield, it could not regard "the sacrifice of life and treasure too much for the object to be procured. Human slavery is the procuring cause of the rebellion . . . the spirit of the age, the safety of the country, the laws of God require its entire removal."

Charles Sumner voiced the solemn joy of the radicals of the North, a day or so after the publication of the proclamation, when he sat at tea with Mary Lincoln. He spoke, of course, as the orator, but with that profound clarity and depth of perception characteristic of him.

"It is a great document. It hasn't, indeed, the sanction of States as a constitutional provision, or of Congress as a statute, or of a high tribunal as a rule of law. It could not, perhaps, be pleaded in any court as securing the liberty of a single slave. But in its significance and effect it stands before any edict, secular or ecclesiastical, since Constantine proclaimed Christianity as the religion of the Roman world."

Mary's cheeks flushed and her eyes kindled. "Yes! Yes!" she exclaimed, ardently. Then her face suddenly blanched. "But, Senator, I live in an agony of apprehension! Assassination!"

Sumner said nothing for a short time. They were sitting by the open window. Mary, in a white silk dress, looked like a Dresden shepherdess against the heavy crimson hangings. The Senator was somewhat haggard, but there was an expression of serenity in his blue eyes.

"Dear Mrs. Lincoln," he said, with a smile that had something of tragedy in it, "the Father of us all will not permit Abraham Lincoln to go until he has done his work!"

Mary set down the teapot to wring her hands. "But that's not enough!" she cried. "Not enough for me!—He plans now to go up to Antietam to see McClellan. If there is disaffection in the army toward Mr. Lincoln because of this proclamation, what can save him? I have pleaded and pleaded with him. But he is obdurate. The only compromise I could effect was to get him to promise to take Taddie with him. I believe that if his son is in his charge, he at least won't go into avoidable danger."

The Senator nodded, then asked anxiously, "You've not been able to influence him with regard to the General?"

"No, he really loves McClellan. I think he looks up to him as the sort of polished gentleman he'd like to be. And that, unconsciously, blinds him. Once he gets past the infatuation, he'll be ruthless."

Still anxiously, Sumner asked, "And you think he'll reach that point?"

Mary again picked up the teapot. She poured a cup and gave it to the Senator before she said, "Only if he is convinced that McClellan is disloyal to the military cause."

"But the fellow is more than disloyal," groaned Sumner. "He's incompetent as a general, and without sentiment for liberty. And, mark me, he's going to do more to block the workings of the proclamation than all other influences combined."

Mary said with sudden intuition, "I wonder where Miss Ford is. If only we could persuade her to come over to our side! They've lost all track of her, but they are convinced she never sailed for England. If once I could talk with her, I *know* I could shame her."

"I think," Sumner scowled, thoughtfully, "that there's more danger of the President being shot by her than by any one else,—all things considered."

"Oh, *don't* say that!" cried Mary. "I shan't sleep a wink to-night!"

"Why not, wife?" asked the President, coming into the room and shaking hands with Sumner.

"I never have got over that shooting scene, at the Soldiers' Home, Mr. Lincoln." Mary tried to smile as she looked up into his careworn face.

He patted her shoulder. "Perhaps they'll get to feel as I do about these fellows who get into trouble in the army. A man woke me up last night. His son was going to be shot at daylight for deserting. He wanted me to do something about it. I decided that shooting wouldn't do the boy any good, so I gave him a reprieve."

"I want you to have more than a reprieve." Mary's voice caught, childishly.

"And so I shall have, my dear! You'll laugh at all this, some day when we're sight-seeing in the Holy Land. I want to see Jacob's well, and Rachel's tomb. Well, Charles, what's the news of intervention?" seating himself on the couch and rubbing his head, which ached.

"It looks very bad, Mr. Lincoln. We can only wait patiently for the response to the proclamation."

The President took his cup of tea, unseeingly, and held it balanced in his great palm, while he eyed Sumner keenly. More and more did he appreciate the Senator's sagacity, where the English government was concerned.

"You believe that she will intervene, Charles?"

"England's permitting the Rebels to build ships in her shipyards with which to fight us," replied Sumner, slowly. "I assume, that unless the proclamation works a miracle, the coöperation between the so-called Confederacy and England will become an alliance. England will acknowledge the slave empire, and thus aid and abet the entrance of this monstrosity into the family of nations."

"The trouble with you is, Charles," protested Lincoln, "that you write only to the upper classes over there. The plain people are sound, in England, as they all are everywhere else. They'll prevent the government from acting either the fool or the villain."

"But it's not the plain people that govern England," exclaimed Mary.

"In the long run they do," Lincoln declared. "We'll hear from them on the proclamation. You'll see."

"I haven't told you of my intense joy in that document, sir," said the Senator. "I waited for it an eternity."

Lincoln nodded. "Of course, issuing the proclamation is only the beginning of the fight. I've got to have the solid backing of the North or the thing is only the Pope's Bull against the comet. If the army will back me, I can almost discount the inevitable increase of Democratic votes this November. If England will hold her hand until the true inwardness of it gets home to every one—well, I'll begin to sleep nights again."

"The army will back you if you can loose McClellan's strangle-hold on the country's freedom of thought," said Sumner. "I suppose the Cabinet is backing you, though Chase told of an ill-timed jest that Seward made, at the moment Lee was in Frederick. He said to Chase that some one had proposed that Lincoln halt the proposed invasions of Pennsylvania by Lee by a proclamation freeing all the apprentices of the State. If that is to be Seward's attitude, the New York Republicans aren't going to be of much service to us."

Lincoln set down the untasted cup of tea, and ran his hands through his hair. He, too, was very uncertain of Seward on this point, but he could see no use in admitting it.

"The Cabinet, at the last scratch, stood behind me splendidly," he said. "I couldn't be sure of counting on Antietam as a victory till Saturday, the 20th. It was too late for a Cabinet meeting, then, so Sunday I fixed it up a little, and Monday I let them have it.—Is Lord Lyons still abroad, Charles?"

"I believe so, sir."

"I must try him again. He's a hard nut to crack.—We must not allow the newspapers to foster this idea of fighting England, Charles. One war at a time, say I!" He rose abruptly. "I'll be getting back to my shop. Here's John Hay to take my place. He's in fine whack."

John came in, languidly, but very elegant in a green suit and puce-colored waistcoat.

"I wish I could continue in as fine whack as the Tycoon does," he exclaimed in an exhausted voice, as the President disappeared. "He's running everything now,—except McClellan. I never knew with what tyrannous authority he rules the Cabinet till I saw him put the proclamation through." Then, as he took his tea from Mary, he said with sudden earnestness, "There's no man in the country so wise, so gentle, and so firm."

"Amen to that!" ejaculated Charles Sumner.

But the President, preparing for his trip to Antietam, was feeling anything but wise. The outcome of the battle of Antietam; McClellan's failure to follow up his advantage, had shaken him in his often expressed conviction that McClellan was no coward. For, he told himself, either it was cowardice that prevented the general from following and destroying Lee's stricken little army, or it was something so wicked that, for the moment, his mind refused to contemplate it.

If, he told himself, as he watched Mary packing up his great black valise, this trip convinced him that McClellan was *not* a coward, then he could have one more chance. Let him back the proclamation, openly and heartily, and he'd retain faith in him. But this, he promised himself, would be the final test.

The party that started for the battlefield was a mixed one. Lincoln was rather appalled when he saw the Chairman of the Committee on the Conduct of the War enter his car, just before the train started. It gave the trip an air of an official investigation. He did not wish McClellan to feel that he was being tried by a jury. He had planned to make only a personal and friendly visit. He decided to insist that the others, Senators and Representatives, fish their own pool, and leave his alone.

Tad was in great fettle. He had been forced by his mother to wear a blue velvet suit, with a wide, white, silk collar, and knit silk stockings of red and black in circular stripes. But by fussing persistently over the loathsome grandeur of his clothes, he had worn her down to permitting him to go "armed." He wore a bowie knife strapped round his waist under his coat, and an army pistol, as yet unloaded, was tucked under his arm, this last conceded because his mother banked on his unfailing facility for losing anything not buttoned or tied to him.

Sure enough, he left the pistol on the seat when his father got out of the train to take a look at Harper's Ferry, and George Nicolay, following, dropped it behind the water cooler.

Holding fast to Taddie's hand, Lincoln stood staring at the spot from which, a fortnight before, Stonewall Jackson had taken 12,000 Union soldiers. The tiny hamlet lay with such apparent unimportance in this beautiful gorge of the Blue Ridge mountains, where the Shenandoah and the Potomac meet! The loveliness of the place depressed him. He was superstitious about Harper's Ferry.

"I suppose it'll have to be captured three times," he said to Taddie, "before we'll be able to keep it."

"Are they any enemies hea' now?" demanded Tad.

"None except the place itself, Taddie," replied his father. "Come, Nicolay, let's get on toward Sharpsburg. How much farther is it?"

"Eighteen miles," replied the secretary. "Hill's Rebel division marched from here in seven hours."

"That's right!" exclaimed Lincoln. "He arrived at Antietam late in the afternoon, just in time to stop the Federal advance on the left. Those Rebels can march McClellan to death! Jings! Wearing our uniforms, our shoes, shooting our very guns, from this very arsenal, they galloped up there and made a snoot at young Napoleon."

Nicolay grunted. "Young Napoleon never recognized it as such, sir, I'll wager."

"I don't suppose he did," agreed Lincoln, turning back to the train.

The major part of the short run to the little town of Sharpsburg was consumed by the search for Taddie's revolver. His father took part in it with great gusto, pressing the dignified Senator Blair into service as a detective, and insisting that each passenger in the private car lay out his "arsenal" for the little boy's anxious inspection. But Nicolay, who had learned, by some nineteen months of experience, Tad's remarkable ability for getting into trouble, kept his secret, and a large portion of the train boy's stock of oranges and lemon drops was able finally to reconcile the little fellow to the loss of half of his equipment!

Sharpsburg lay in a lovely valley between the Potomac to the west, and a spur of the Blue Ridge to the east. To the east of the village was Antietam Creek, a beautiful stream, running north and south through the valley. It was in this valley of meadows and woodlands that McClellan's great army lay recuperating.

There was a carriage at the railroad station, with a smart guard of cavalry to meet the President, and he was driven at once in a wild whirl of dust and a great uproar of trotting horsemen over the rough country roads to McClellan's headquarters.

The camp, as was usual with McClellan, was in the best possible position for the soldiers' comfort, and in the best possible order. The general and his staff welcomed Lincoln with all the dignity and formality that the occasion demanded. Formalities, as Lincoln confided to Tad, take a great deal of time and patience. It was late in the afternoon before Lincoln and McClellan finally sat down before the latter's tent, free to rest and to talk. Tad had long since disappeared with a pink-cheeked young corporal, a Harvard friend of Bob's.

McClellan was in an urbane mood, the mood of a man convinced that, for a second time, he had saved the nation. Lincoln was in no hurry to ruffle that mood. His visit was to be of several days' duration. There had been, he felt, too much tension in the relationship between himself and the young general. For once, he hoped, the contact could have some reality of casualness. So he sat in his camp chair, clasping his left knee, his eyes lifting from the map which lay on the table before him, to the valley, all shimmering gold in the October sun. The battle of Antietam was being explained to him.

"It was the extreme simplicity of my strategy which made the fighting so effective," said McClellan. "Lee held Sharpsburg, about the middle of the map, with the creek before him."

"And a good deal of high ground and woods with him, too," interjected Lincoln, his eyes sweeping up and down the meandering stream that paralleled the camp. "While you folks were down in the bottoms and sloughs Lee had the advantage of position."

"Yes," nodded McClellan, "but it availed him little."

"Your vast superiority of numbers took care of that," commented the President. "Well, get on with it, George, before it's too dusky for me to see the map. Your lines faced each other across the creek parallel for about three miles, eh?"

"Roughly, yes," replied McClellan. "But you are mistaken in regard to the Rebels' inferiority in numbers. They had at least 100,000 men. We were both in position late on the afternoon of the 16th. There was some heavy skirmishing on our right before dark that day, but the actual battle opened at dawn the next morning. There was no ground for maneuvering. My plan simply was this: My right wing was to move forward first. When the battle was well engaged, my left wing was to move across the bridge, you can't see it from here, but it's indicated at the south end of the map, —and thrust back Lee's right until it had retreated through Sharpsburg. And, still speaking the layman's tongue, that's about what happened."

These broad details were, of course, perfectly familiar to Lincoln, who had spent agonized hours on the 17th, transferring the information in telegrams from the front, to his war map. He concealed his impatience.

"Burnside was to move your west wing across the bridge. He never got started until one o'clock. That gave Lee a chance to concentrate on you fellows up at the right. What was the trouble there, George?"

"Pardon me, sir. My order to move reached Burnside at ten o'clock in the morning. He sent Cox to take the bridge, at once, but it was not until we'd spent three hours and five hundred men that we took it. Then I ordered Burnside on up the hill behind the bridge to crowd the Rebels back and take Sharpsburg. He got as far as the Dunker church on the edge of the village when the Rebel, Hill, came up from Harper's Ferry and checked him."

"In the meantime," asked Lincoln, "what was happening in the center?"

"We were gaining ground," replied McClellan, complacently. "All along the line we gained. Nightfall found us here," pointing to the map. "The invasion of the North was ended."

"I see!" murmured Lincoln. "But—" Then he closed his lips firmly. He simply could not talk about that ghastly, that useless slaughter of men, that fruitless heroic endeavor of the magnificent army, without saying something that would irritate McClellan.

He was deeply relieved when a short, thin man with a pointed beard, wearing a dusty, much stained linen duster appeared, hesitating, a short distance from the tent.

"That fellow has a familiar face!" exclaimed Lincoln.

"Yes, that's Brady, the war photographer, a remarkable man," replied

McClellan. "You've heard about what he's done? This will be the first war
in history ever photographed."

"So that's Brady?" exclaimed Lincoln, rising. "I got Allan Pinkerton to
give him the protection of the Secret Service, a year ago. Come over here,
friend Brady!"

The little Irishman hurried forward, carefully set down a black case he
was carrying, and shook hands with Lincoln.

"Well! Well! You're the wild fellow from Cork who almost got captured at the first Bull Run, and that Pinkerton's been wet-nursing on a
dozen battlefields, since!" cried Lincoln. "Come, open up shop and show
us your wares!"

"Just what I wished to be doing, Your Excellency!" grinned Brady.
"With the general's permission, of course!"

"You know you're as popular with me as with my men, Brady," said
McClellan. "We're proud to see the record you make of us. Get yourself
a camp stool."

Brady obeyed with alacrity, lifted the case to the table, opened it and
sat down. It was filled with photographs, from among which he drew an
eight by ten plate.

"I thought Your Excellency would like to have my problem explained
in a general way. My outfit consists of a butcher's wagon, with my living
conveniences in the forward end, and a dark room, where no ray of light
can enter, in the opposite end. Photographs are taken on glass plates, like
this, which have been coated in the dark room with collodion. In it are
dissolved bromide and iodide of potassium. Now, it's impossible to take
pictures on these plates unless they've been freshly coated, within five
minutes of the time the photograph is taken. The least breath of air or
touch of heat or cold, or speck of dust on the plate while it's wet with
collodion will spoil the picture. Perhaps this tells Your Excellency some
of my difficulties in photographing a battle."

"Jings! I reckon it does!" exclaimed the President, keenly interested.
"Let's see the plate," squinting at it, against the sky. "What's it of?"

"That's the beginning of the attack on the bridge, Burnside's bridge,
the soldiers are calling it. Here's the print from that negative."

Lincoln put on his spectacles and gazed at the exquisite reproduction.
A fine stone bridge of arches over a placid stream. A background of
wooded heights. On the bridge a mass of soldiers, half hidden by smoke.
In the foreground a dead soldier in profile, hugging his gun, his face up-
turned to the sky. For a long time the President stared at it.

"Five hundred like that boy," he said, at last, turning to McClellan.

The general's eyes filled with tears. "Don't ask me to look at it, sir.
It wrings my heart."

"I know! You do love the men, as they love you," returned Lincoln,
gently, his impatience wiped away as by magic. "Do something else if
you want to, while Brady has his little show."

McClellan rose. "Thank you, sir," he said, gratefully. "I've a letter to write. There's just time before supper." He strode into his tent.

"He's too tender-hearted for the killing business," said Brady, offering the President another photograph. "It accounts for a lot about him. When he rode over the battlefield on the 18th I saw him crying his heart out."

"Did you?" Lincoln spoke thoughtfully, and a sudden feeling of gratitude rose in him toward the little Irishman. Perhaps this did, indeed, explain away some of his uneasiness regarding the general.

"What's this?" he asked, after a moment.

"The Dunker church to the east of Sharpsburg. The Federals were driven back from there by Hill's men. Seems like a seventeen or eighteen mile walk just whetted the Rebels' appetite for fighting. Of those two men lying in the foreground, one is a Rebel, the other a Federal. You see, sir, the battle began up here," showing another picture. A rail fence with a row of bodies lying beside it,—"Federals—Hooker's men. He flung the first bunch there. When he was used up, Meade and Mansfield brought their men. There was nothing to it but sheer, persistent slaughter. At least, that's how it looked to a picture man. Why the divil didn't all the Federal line start fighting at once, instead of leaving Lee to run his men up and down the line where they were most needed? Looked to an ignorant picture man like there was no plan of concerted action."

"Let's see the next picture, Brady," said Lincoln.

"Well, here's a fine, convincing view of what happened in the center. This is a sunken road. The boys have named it Bloody Lane."

He gave the President the picture of a wide ditch filled with bodies in every contortion of agony, a gray, hideous mass. Lincoln could feel himself turning pale. But he stared steadily at the horror. If the "boys" could go into it, into this hell to which he'd sent them, he, at least, could gaze unflinching on the "counterfeit presentment." The little photographer gave him a keen glance and continued:

"You see, the Rebels had taken all the fight out of our men up at the right. And they were giving Burnside's boys more, entirely, than they could handle easily, on the left. But, in the middle, there were some Irish mixed among the other Federals, and the Rebels were getting what-for. They entrenched themselves in this sunken road. Our men got to the heights to right and left, and poured an enfilading fire into it. And there lie the Rebels, poor boys. Yes, sir, there they do lie!" nodding his shaggy head.

Lincoln dropped the picture and stared off where,—a black gash in the sunset glow on a distant field,—lay the sunken road which McClellan previously had pointed out to him.

Brady pulled forth another photograph, saying, as if to himself, "Corps after corps, division after division into the red whirlpool of hell. Sure, sir," looking up, "one wouldn't grudge it to the divil who runs wars if the result was worth it. We could have pushed those fellows into the Potomac if—"

"Show me the picture in your hand, Brady, then I must go find Tad for his supper."

"Well, you've seen enough carnage. There's only one dead boy in this. It shows you a fine old plantation house the Rebels were burning as our boys came up."

Magnolias, with a two-galleried house in flames behind them. Sitting upright against one of the trunks—a dead Federal cavalryman, staring straight out of the picture, his horse, four legs turned in the air, beside him. Lincoln caught his breath. The sweat started to his forehead.

"I know that man, Brady! His name is Gordon. He's wanted by the detective police!"

"Is it so?" asked the photographer.

"But I reckon the God of Eternal Justice wanted him more," said Lincoln. "Leave me this picture, Brady. No, don't leave it. Send it to Baker in Washington." He continued to hold the photograph in his hand, where the red sunset lighted it. Thoughts too deep for words surged through his mind. He returned the gaze of the dead eyes until they dimmed in the October dusk. Then he murmured: "Hail and farewell to 'Obscene' Gordon," and rose, repeating, "I must find Taddie."

For a great solitude had settled on his heart and he felt the need of his child's love and companionship.

CHAPTER XXVIII

TAD'S KITTEN

GEORGE NICOLAY accompanied Lincoln in his search for Tad. As the two walked along the neat Company streets of the camp, the President said, "George, I want to know this: Does McClellan, in his desire to save his men, actually accomplish the reverse? I'm scared to think of how many men he might now have alive in this camp, if he hadn't held them back when they should have been in. Or am I getting hipped on McClellan's weaknesses?"

"It's a difficult matter to work out, sir," replied Nicolay, chewing savagely on his cigar. "His men think he's infallible. Yet it's a fact that Lee out-generals him, right along. Superb fighters, those Southern leaders."

Lincoln nodded. "Quick on their feet. We have the slows."

"The men do feel that they could have shoved Lee's army into the Potomac if they'd been allowed to follow, next day," Nicolay went on. "They say they weren't as tired as Lee's men. Hadn't been worked so hard."

"There's Corporal Dick!" exclaimed the President. "Well, young man, where's my son?" pausing in the light of a camp fire.

"He started back for you, half an hour ago, Mr. President!" replied the soldier, his eyes a little perturbed.

"Hum! Like looking for a flea on a curly-haired dog!" Lincoln rubbed his chin. "I reckon the best thing to do is to go back and wait for him."

But supper in the officers' mess tent was over, and the President was growing more and more uneasy, before the corporal came up a little breathlessly and saluted.

"I've located him, Mr. President. But he won't budge. He sits down by the bridge, crying. He says he wants you."

McClellan, Hooker, Burnside, sitting around the camp fire that flared outside the President's tent, looked up with amused smiles as Lincoln jumped to his feet.

"Wants his mother, I reckon! Corporal, you just lead me over there and see what I can do."

He strode, bareheaded, past half a hundred camp fires, moving so rapidly that he was gone before the soldiers could more than begin to cheer him. In the starlight, crouching against the stone parapet of the bridge, was Tad's little figure. The corporal fell back as soon as he had pointed the child out to Lincoln.

"Did you get homesick, all of a sudden, darling Taddie?" asked the President, stooping to pick up the boy.

"Don't touch me, Papa day," said the little boy in a voice hoarse from long sobbing. "I'm unda' my own a'west. I sent fo' you to tell you I have to stay hea' all night."

Lincoln sat down on the wall, his solitude yielding at once to the delight Tad's caprices always gave him.

"What bad thing have you done, Taddie?" he asked, solemnly.

"I—I—killed something I loved," suddenly beginning to cry again.

"Hush! Don't cry, or that'll make me cry, and everybody would say the President is a coward. Tell me all about it."

"The co'po'al gave me a little weeny, white kitten. It sang in my neck. I was taking it up to show you. Then I stopped hea' to play with it. It played so cunning, Papa day! Then—then—I played it was Jeff Davis and I was an Indian chief and I tied it to a stake and th'ew my bowie knife at it, like the juggla did, last winte'. I didn't want to hu't it. I wouldn't have fo' anything. But the di'ty skunk of a knife slipped and went into the kitten's little soft belly and all its insidings came out and it mewed and mewed and I couldn't stop it o' help it and it died. I knew you wouldn't punish me so I'm doing it myself."

Lincoln cleared his throat. "Where is the poor little kitten, darling Taddie?"

A little finger pointed in the starlight to a white spot against the gray wall.

"Let's make the wicked bowie knife dig a grave for the kitten. Then let's bury the knife in the same grave," suggested the President.

"No, we'll fling it in the c'eek. It can't lie beside the kitten," cried Taddie.

"Very well! I'll help you dig," agreed Lincoln.

The bowie knife did a neat job, and a few moments later was cast by Taddie, violently, from the bridge into the glimmering black water.

"Now," said his father, gravely, "I'll send the corporal back for my hat, for I promised your mother you'd sleep with me, and I'll have to camp right here, I reckon."

"Motha' wouldn't let you do that," exclaimed Tad. "Pe'haps, seeing it was mostly the bowie knife's fault, I can pa'ole myself to you' tent. And maybe you'd bette' caway me, I'm so sleepy."

"I reckon I had," agreed Lincoln.

He lifted the soft little body across his breast, and the horror of the hour with Brady lessened, as he carried Tad back past the cheering camp fires to his tent.

He gave the days that followed to a personal investigation of the equipment which McClellan declared was inadequate, was preventing him from following Lee. It struck him as very curious that there was no discussion before him, by McClellan's officers, of the emancipation proclamation. He concluded that they were acting under orders from McClellan, and was willing to wait for the general to make the first move.

He mixed freely with the soldiers, joining them about their camp fires or sitting among them as they cleaned their accouterments, groomed their horses, or peeled potatoes for the perpetual stews. At first, they bothered him by cheering him every time he arrived among them, but as soon as they discovered that this was not what he wanted, they took him casually, and talked freely before him.

A great many of them were outspoken in their praise of the proclamation. Some of them shook their heads over it. The vast majority said, quite frankly, that they were waiting to learn what Little Mac thought of it. This depressed him more than he cared to admit, even to himself.

The day before he started back to Washington, McClellan held a grand review for him. There was considerable speculation, Nicolay told him, among the soldiers as to whether or not Old Abe could stick on a horse. And there was obvious interest, among officers as well as men, when a big black gelding, prancing and struggling to rear, was led up to the President's tent. Lincoln, laughing to himself, as he thought of his boyhood hours in the saddle, and of the miles he'd traveled on any sort of nag when, as a country lawyer, he'd "ridden the circuit," took the reins with an expressionless face.

Nicolay wrote Mary about it, that evening. "The officers, and even some of the men, have been a little patronizing to the President up here, taking their cue from the obvious source. It has made me furious. He hasn't seemed to observe it, but I'm sure it cut. You will be glad to learn that he made them smile out of the other side of their mouths, to-day. The moment he vaulted into the saddle, he obviously was at home. It was a very large horse and he looked splendid,—not an awkward line.

"I had a feeling that McClellan was not above making an endurance test of this. He came dashing up with his magnificent looking staff. Mr. Lincoln joined them at a gallop. The band struck up 'Hail to the Chief,' the artillery began to thunder, his horse walked on its hind legs. The President held his tall hat in one hand and received the salute, absolutely unperturbed. It was grand! Afterward came a long dash over very rough ground with ditches and fences to leap. The dear old Tycoon kept right up with McClellan. The soldiers missed none of the significance of it and when, a little later, he rode down the lines, the cheers almost rent the sky. . . . What a man!"

No one had enjoyed the review quite as much as the President. When he sat in McClellan's tent, that evening, with Burnside and Nicolay, he kept bursting into chuckles. McClellan scowled a little, but made no comment until Burnside and Nicolay left, then he asked Lincoln what in the situation amused him.

Lincoln shook his head. He had avoided, thus far, every topic that he thought could irritate McClellan. He had no intention of telling the General he was chuckling because it was McClellan himself who had changed the army's attitude of patronage to admiration. Instead, he paid a compliment.

"I must congratulate you, George, on the morale of your army. It's superb. I don't see how, with the men feeling as they do, anything can stop you now."

"Lack of shoes, for one thing," replied McClellan quickly. "I can't march my men barefoot."

"Lee marches his that way, unless he can shoe them from the enemy's stock!" exclaimed Lincoln. "Come, George, let's not start that old argument again! Quartermaster General Meigs has sent me a full report of the supplies you've had up here. Your men say, themselves, they have everything they want."

"The men's judgment is final, of course," sneered McClellan. "Am I or am I not supposed to be the best judge of what the army needs?"

The old irritation overthrew all the President's resolves. He shoved aside the candle which stood on the table between them. "McClellan," he cried, "when are you going to start?"

"When my army is rested and equipped," replied the general, coolly.

Lincoln tossed his head impatiently. "McClellan, why don't you start to-morrow?"

McClellan did not reply.

The President breathed heavily for a moment, then the "granite look" appeared in his gray eyes.

"Brady was showing me more of his pictures yesterday. He has one set he calls, 'McClellan at the Front.' They're photographs of your different headquarters and of you, during your several battles. George, yours and Brady's ideas of where the Front is don't agree with mine. At your first Peninsula fight at Williamsburg, while Hooker and Kearny and Hancock were out with their men, under fire, you were on the wharf at Yorktown, doing assistant quartermaster's duty. At the battle of Fair Oaks, you were across the river from the fight, and the same at Beaver Dam Creek and Gaines' Mill. Wait a moment! You must hear me out, George, for this thought will poison my affection for you unless you clear it up."

McClellan, who had risen to leave the tent, halted, held by the command in Lincoln's voice. The President went on:

"During the retreat to the James, you were far ahead, locating the spots where Franklin and the rest were to fight their daily battle. At Malvern Hill, a sight that Halleck says a man with true soldier blood would have given his life to see, you were in your camp at Haxall's or down on the river, arranging for the retreat. And here at Antietam, when the sight of you, particularly at your left wing, would have put life into the movements of your men, you were back on the high ground near Pry's house, watching through spy glasses."

Lincoln had risen too. He was trembling with his determination somehow to win into McClellan's soul.

"George, this is an insulting imputation! It is not mine. It is that of the plain people who are carrying this war on their backs. One single move, and you will wipe that imputation from your fame, forever. Get on your horse, lead these boys after Lee, and, when you have found him, show them how to hurt him!"

"Have you finished?" asked McClellan, white to the lips.

"Not quite," replied Lincoln in a voice strident with anger. "I want to add that unless you indicate to me, very shortly, that you are starting at once after the enemy, I shall remove you permanently from the army."

Suddenly McClellan laughed. "*You!* Remove me! You'll have to move more rapidly than your wont, Lincoln! Come! Let's not part in anger! I don't believe you realize the insulting nature of half you've been saying!"

The two men exchanged a long look, then Lincoln, turning on his heel with an abrupt "Good night," left the tent.

CHAPTER XXIX

FERNANDO WOOD

LINCOLN returned to Washington, tanned of skin and clear of eye. It was nearing midnight when he strode into his wife's room, carrying Taddie. He deposited the sleeping child on the bed, and gathered Mary into his arms, kissing her several times. Then he held her from him and looked her over, approvingly. She was wearing a mantle-shaped boudoir gown of white, trimmed with rows of black beads. Her hair hung in a soft braid over either shoulder.

"Somehow, this is pleasanter than McClellan's tent!" he exclaimed. "Jings! I'm glad to have you again! What's the news here? Has Sumner heard from England on the proclamation?"

Mary led him to a chair and pushed him gently into it. Then she placed a bootjack at his feet.

"No business to-night, Abra'm. Take off those riding boots, while I fetch your slippers."

Lincoln sighed with relief as one boot after the other landed with a thud half way across the room.

"That's first rate!" he added as Mary pulled a carpet slipper over each gray wool sock. "Reckon I've been spoiled by you too long, wife, to make a contented soldier."

"How did Taddie behave?" asked Mary, as he put out a great hand to draw her toward him.

"Like an angel," replied his father, promptly.

"Tell me some of the things you both did," perching on the arm of his chair, and leaning against him.

"Well, let's see! The kitten episode was his best achievement, I reckon. I was looking at Brady's photographs. You must see those, Mary. They're wonderful." He described the pictures to her, then told her of Tad and the white kitten.

"The blessed lamb!" murmured Mary.

Lincoln nodded. "I can't explain why the incident meant so much to me. You see, actually being on the battlefield, observing the devastation, seeing Brady's pictures—it smelled so of death—death of my making, Mary." He paused and Mary felt his body quiver with a suppressed sob.

She kissed him. "I know, Abra'm! I know!"

He sat fighting for self-control. He had come back determined that only ruthless decisiveness should govern him until the proclamation was an accepted fact in the country. This, he told himself, was a poor beginning. He cleared his throat and managed to say, casually:

"By the way, one of Brady's photographs showed me 'Obscene' Gordon, as a dead cavalryman."

Mary jumped from her place and stared at him incredulously. Then she laughed, clapped her hands, sobbed and threw herself against him, caressing him wildly. He held her until she was serene again.

"I know," she said, at last, "that it's wicked to feel so about the death of any human being. But half my anxiety about you is lifted. I must tell Mr. and Mrs. Welles, to-morrow, the first thing."

"I ought to go over to the telegraph office and see what Buell is doing in Kentucky." The President looked at his watch. "Folks out West are getting to feel about Buell as the folks here do about McClellan. They both have the slows, that's a fact. I'm going to remove Buell if he doesn't show more desire to pursue the enemy than he has up to date. I won't be gone long," taking up the little gray shawl and the high hat.

Mary followed him to the door. "Now that I know Gordon isn't hiding in a corridor I can let you go. I wonder if Miss Ford knows of his death."

"Lizzie Keckley's friend, Anna, wasn't it, who went as lady's maid,—reports nothing, I suppose?"

"She can neither read nor write," replied Mary and closing the door after her husband, she turned to attend to the sleeping boy.

As a matter of fact, Gordon's fate was of little moment to Miss Ford. She was engrossed in the work that was engrossing every Southern slaveholder,—that of organizing the final fight against emancipation. There had been some thought of sending her to England to see what she could do to hasten the moment of intervention. But the crisis precipitated by the issuing of the proclamation had caused Davis to abandon the idea.

On an evening, shortly before the fall elections took place, several gentlemen met in the parlor of the little house she was occupying on Bleecker Street in New York City. Her disguise was extremely clever. Nothing, of course, could conceal her great height. But she had dyed her hair black, and wore it wrapped in severe bands about her head. She had stained her blond skin to a decided olive tint. She wore, instead of her perpetual green, mourning of a pronounced type.

Captain Taylor, dressed as a policeman, gained admission to the house a few minutes earlier than the other visitors, by seeming to force the lock on the door. The Virginian bolted it after him, and led the way into the rear room where a coal fire burned cheerfully.

"I reckon that's the approved way for a policeman to enter a house of ill fame!" said Taylor. "Unfortunately, the street is so dark that no one observed my histrionics!"

"Don't be too sure, Tom!" exclaimed Miss Ford. "I may be more closely watched than we suspect."

"Did you have trouble getting this place?" asked Taylor, warming his back before the fire.

"None! Mayor Wood had the place raided, one day, and the next day Anna and I moved in."

"Where's Uncle Bob?" asked the Captain.

"He ran away before we left Washington, the devilish old fool!" She spoke with acid bitterness.

Taylor shook his head in sympathy. "Mother writes that not one of ours is left. When news of the proclamation came even Mammy Sophie legged it off to the Union lines. Lady, I wouldn't know you in that make-up if I saw you in your own home.—I loathe your disguise,—and I loathe the type and character you are simulating."

The Virginian shrugged her shoulders and said, "There is some one, now!" rising as voices were heard in the hall, and a man wearing an evening cloak of black broadcloth entered. It was Fernando Wood, Mayor of New York.

The three greeted one another as old friends, and settled before the fire. "Seymour will be along later," said Mayor Wood. He was a good-looking man of middle age, with thick dark hair, fine gray eyes and humorous mouth. He was smooth shaven, and wore a high stock of black satin which added to his look of distinction. "He's very busy and if he doesn't get here, is willing for me to represent him. I prophesy a glorious victory at the polls, on Tuesday. Even Illinois will take a few bites from Abraham's hide. And Governor Seymour has New York State in his pocket."

"You have the emancipation proclamation to thank for all that," said Miss Ford.

"Exactly," agreed Wood. "It is also to be thanked for the fact that enlistments for the past two weeks have been practically nil. Lincoln will have to try the draft, next. Then there'll be revolution in the North."

"Are these your ideas or Mr. Seymour's, Mayor Wood?" asked Captain Taylor.

Wood laughed. "Seymour never had as mild a thought as that about Lincoln! He *says* that the preservation of the Union comes first with him, but I believe he'd turn Secessionist if thereby he could harm the Administration. He'd be better off if he'd calmly admit his sympathy with the Secessionists."

"You don't admit that, as I understand you, Mayor Wood," said Miss Ford, smiling, "except in certain select circles!"

"One has to be careful," admitted Wood. "But I shall never be as discreet as McClellan. I had to declare flat-footed that emancipation was a bitter wrong to the soldiers who were fighting only to save the Union. McClellan issued a statement last week in which he never mentioned the proclamation, or said a word against it. Yet he gave the soldiers as clearly to understand that he disapproved of it as though he'd denounced it in so many words. But, by his subtlety, he's got Old Abe all calmed down, they tell me."

"Don't be so sure of that!" exclaimed Miss Ford. "He's a keen man, Abraham Lincoln. Where the weakness of the plans made by Davis and your group, Mr. Mayor, lies, is that you still refuse to recognize him as being more astute than any of you."

"Let's get on with the evening's business," urged Taylor, impatiently. He sat with his elbows on his knees, pulling at his handkerchief.

"Lincoln is our business, more than anything else," retorted the Virginian. "Davis insists that my main task is to keep Lincoln's character always before all of you. But you insist on treating Lincoln as a Simple Susan. Davis is worse than you are, Tom, and Seymour is a hopeless fanatic in his hatred of the President."

Taylor sat up with a jerk. He had aged ten years in the last ten months. His nerves were uncertain.

"If I'm not to get Wood's report, I might as well go on out to Ohio."

"My report is easy to give, Captain. I have the letter from McClellan," said the Mayor.

"Where is it?" asked Taylor, quickly.

"In a safe place. You shall have it the moment you produce one from Davis, making me Secretary of State in McClellan's Cabinet." Wood's good-looking face was as serene as Captain Taylor's was agitated.

"I have that, also, in a safe place," said the Captain. "What does McClellan say in the letter?"

"Just what your crowd asked for. That he accepts the Democratic nomination for President, that he will carry on the war in a manner to conciliate the South, that he will leave slavery alone."

"Fine!" ejaculated Taylor. "What is the state of affairs between him and Lincoln?"

"Oh, quite as usual," smiled Wood. "Abe pleading with him tearfully to destroy Lee before he can get back to Richmond, and McClellan moving the Army of the Potomac as though he had on hand 100,000 invalids, pausing ever and anon to ask for reënforcements or supplies. He was pleading for horses when I was there. And Jeb Stuart rode completely round his camp! I have my hat off to you Southerners."

"Lincoln's patience is not inexhaustible," said Miss Ford, "and McClellan's ego makes him indiscreet. What do we do if Lincoln actually removes McClellan?"

"He'll never do that!" protested the Mayor. "He's afraid of McClellan's influence with the soldiers. He proved that when he reinstated him, last summer."

"How long are you counting on Lincoln's patience enduring?" insisted the Virginian.

"Until January 1st, when he tries to put in force the threat which he wrote into the proclamation," replied Taylor. "McClellan's letter will then be made public and Lincoln will have either to dismiss him or abdicate, himself. Popular outcry and pressure from England and France will not allow him to throw McClellan out. So Lincoln will abdicate. I'm told he's really only too anxious to do so."

"But if Lincoln loses patience before then?" urged Miss Ford. "You know there's nothing more absurd than the general belief that Lincoln is incapable of losing his temper. I've seen him in a state of terrible indignation."

"I can answer that question," said Wood. "If Lincoln dismisses him, McClellan will march to Washington at the head of his army. So three different officers, very close to him, told me. And the moment he becomes dictator, the war will end.—What am I to do next, Captain?"

"You are to go down to see Lincoln and discover the state of his mind toward McClellan and toward the draft. Urge the draft on him. Nothing can help the peace party more right now than the draft idea." Taylor rose to go.

At the same moment, Anna admitted two more callers. Both were men in evening dress. Miss Ford and Mayor Wood rose.

"Good evening, Mr. Seymour!" exclaimed the Virginian, "and good evening, Lord Lyons! I heard that your packet was in."

The two gentlemen bowed over Miss Ford's hand, and greeted Wood and Taylor.

"I hope that you have recovered from your ill health, my lord," said Wood, as the group remade itself before the fire.

"Ah! Quite so! Quite so! Thank you, Mayor Wood," replied the Englishman, with his usual urbanity of manner.

"And does England still plan to intervene?" cried the Virginian.

Lyons turned on her dark eyes, keen beneath their drooping lids, and stroked his sideburns. "I did not know, my dear Miss Ford, that my government planned intervention."

"Gladstone intimated as much," said Seymour, quickly.

"But Mr. Gladstone is not Her Majesty's Government," replied the Minister. "Her Majesty's Government have declared their neutrality, and is doing their utmost to abide by that declaration."

"Except that they permit the South to build its ships in English shipyards and—" began the Virginian, smiling.

"Come! Come! Miss Ford, you must not embarrass our distinguished guest," protested Seymour. "I invited him here that he might hear from Captain Taylor the latest hopes of the Southern peace party. I beg of you, ask Lord Lyons no more questions."

"I deserve the reprimand, sir!" The Virginian tossed her handsome head, however, as she spoke.

Lord Lyons gave her a friendly smile and turned toward Taylor. There followed a half hour during which the captain, with considerable help from the others, gave to the British Minister a fairly complete picture of the progress made by the peace parties, North and South, during the Minister's three months in England. It was a glowing report, and at its end Taylor asked Lord Lyons if he did not think that the strength of the movement would justify England in intervening, should the northern proslavery, known as the peace party, come into power under McClellan. The British Minister refused to give an opinion, yet as he rose to go, the impression that he left was that he was in sympathy with the South, that he looked on victory for the North as impossible, that the Administration at Washington would, after a moment of bluster, give in if they could be convinced that their opponents were sufficiently in earnest.

"And yet," said Miss Ford, commenting on this impression, after he had gone, "he was as clever as McClellan with the proclamation. He never said a word that could be quoted."

Seymour, pacing with dignified step up and down the little parlor, nodded his head. "He is a clever diplomat. Now, my friends, the moment has come, I think, when we may believe the end is at hand. When I am elected, the tyranny of that murderer in the White House will end, in New York State, at least! I have a curious feeling of elation."

"I wonder!" murmured Miss Ford. "I wonder! I've learned to fear Lincoln. I think, unless President Davis gives me other orders, I'll go back to Washington, where I can watch him. You remember, Tom, you warned me that bullets, carefully distributed, might be the last and best remedy."

"And I remember how horrified you were at the thought," returned Taylor, dryly.

"Humph! I hadn't been tortured enough, then," said the Virginian.

Taylor gave her a look that was tinged with deep concern, then he turned to continue his bargaining with Fernando Wood.

CHAPTER XXX

IT was the evening following the one on which Miss Ford entertained her distinguished guests that Miss Clara Barton sent in her card to Mrs. Lincoln at the White House. Mary was making an heroic endeavor to revive the social activities of the Executive Mansion for the winter, and was working, with William Stoddard and John Hay, on a list of invitations for a "reception with refreshments."

She greeted Miss Barton cordially, then begged her to rest before the fire for a few moments, while she and the two secretaries completed their task.

"Mrs. Lincoln," said Stoddard, completing the protest begun before Miss Barton came in, "you can't pack all the people on this list into LaFayette Square, let alone the reception rooms of the White House."

"If I don't, Mr. Lincoln will be vilified as a snob!" cried Mary.

John Hay laughed. "I think the Tycoon would like that! It's the only thing in the dictionary he hasn't been called. And really, Madam President, this is not a public reception, as your list would indicate. By the way, you mustn't issue personal invitations to reporters. One invitation to each *newspaper!* There's a difference."

Madam President threw up her hands. "But, John and Billy, Mr. Lincoln has promised invitations to half a dozen reporters who've asked for them!"

"It really can't be done!" declared Stoddard, wearily. "Even the members of the Cabinet are invited only by virtue of their office. I'll keep the reporters away from you, Mrs. Lincoln. Better let me manage."

"You can't keep the reporters' tongues and pens from me, though." Mary shook her head ruefully. "However, go ahead, Billy! They can't hate me more than they already do!" She turned to Miss Barton, and the two young men went out.

"You ought to let the newspapers know of your wonderful daily work in the hospitals, Mrs. Lincoln," suggested Miss Barton with a smile.

Mary returned the smile. The two had become fast friends. They talked at some length over a hospital that was being set up in a church at Fairfax Courthouse, then Miss Barton made known the real purpose of her call. General McClellan was pleading for new hospital tents.

"There is another ghastly battle pending, and while the Quartermaster-General insists that McClellan already is oversupplied with hospital tents, and is not sending any, I have the conviction that the Army of the Potomac can't be too well equipped in that line. I can lay hands on tents for five thousand men if you arrange to have them put into McClellan's hands, without offending the Quartermaster-General," said Miss Barton.

Mary pursed her lips, thoughtfully. "Secretary Stanton certainly won't help. He's too angry with McClellan. Halleck is angry, but he does what Mr. Lincoln tells him to do. I suppose, with your usual astuteness, you've discovered that and wish me to overpersuade the President!"

"You can do so, can't you?" smiled Miss Barton.

"Not always, by any means," replied Mary.

The two women sat regarding each other, thoughtfully; Miss Barton in a meager, black merino, with white collar and cuffs, with the smallest possible crinoline, the President's wife in a rich black silk, pleated and ruffled in a hundred pleats and folds over a hoopskirt that dwarfed in diameter the huge center table. Yet, in their earnestness, in the quiet fortitude in their eyes, they were curiously alike.

"I'll try, dear Miss Barton," said Mary, finally. "If I can't win the concession, perhaps Taddie can. You think the tents really will be needed?"

Miss Barton, rising, threw up both her hands. "Can you ask that, after all you've observed in the hospitals here?"

Mary sighed. "I know! And I want to help. Yet I cannot bear to add one dust speck of weight to Mr. Lincoln's burden."

"We are all suffering," said Miss Barton, gently, "but none so much as the common soldiers."

"Don't go!" urged Mary. "I'm expecting Mr. Lincoln any moment. He's having a war council and is two hours late for supper."

"Thank you, Madam President, but I'm leaving to-morrow to join the army. I learned to-day that it has finally crossed the Potomac and is moving down the eastern side of the Blue Ridge. With Lee moving south along the western side, there's bound to be constant clashes. I shall be needed."

Mary sighed. "How I envy you! Miss Barton, may I not ride a few miles with you to-morrow? They say it's such a superb sight, and dramatic, too, that road packed with transports and marching soldiers, all the way between Washington and Army Headquarters."

"Indeed you may! Though—" a mischievous look in her eyes—"I'm afraid the President won't forgive me."

"He'd forgive you anything!" exclaimed Mary. "What time do you leave your house?"

"At ten o'clock," replied Miss Barton.

"I'll be there," declared Mary, accompanying Miss Barton to the door.

She remained standing there after the visitor's departure, looking anxiously toward the stairhead. It was nine o'clock. Tad was with his father, and ought to be in bed. She was debating with herself whether or not to go over to Stanton's office, when Lincoln, Tad on his shoulders, appeared on the stairs. As if by magic, John Hay materialized from the secretaries' room, Seward and Sumner from the President's office. They converged toward the door into the sitting room.

"Please, please!" cried Mary, "allow Mr. Lincoln to eat his supper first!

He's had nothing since noon. All of you come in here, while Tad takes his father to the dining room."

There was half laughing, half impatient agreement on the part of Lincoln, while the others followed Mrs. Lincoln meekly into the sitting room.

"You must not think of me only as a petty tyrant," said Mary, a little sadly, as she seated herself. "Mr. Lincoln looks so old and weary that it frightens me!"

"We think of you as an important part of the President's brains and backbone," retorted Seward.

"For that, you may smoke, sir!" exclaimed Mary. "I told Mrs. Seward the other day that you ought to be taking an iron tonic. You are overworking yourself, Governor."

"Who isn't?" demanded Seward. "I wouldn't be surprised any day to discover a gray hair in John Hay's cherished mustache."

John groaned. "What are gray hairs to me? I'm preoccupied with more serious matters! The price of clothing for example! I can't afford so much as a new waistcoat."

"It's very sad," agreed Seward, puffing vigorously at his cigar and looking up at Sumner, who stood with an elbow on the mantelpiece. "Senator, if I knew as much about the art of dressing as you, Lincoln would never have had a chance at the Presidency."

Sumner glanced down, unsmilingly, at his blue broadcloth trousers. "I see," he said, absent-mindedly. Then, as the others laughed, he added, apologetically, "I was thinking about a favor I must ask of the President. One of my constituents, most important to the proclamation, wants his son to be made a brigadier-general."

"You have no chance whatever, Senator!" exclaimed Seward, briskly. Then he added, with a great laugh, "I know whereof I speak! This morning I urged that very promotion for a constituent of mine, and the President reduced me to pulp."

"What is there humorous about that?" asked Sumner.

"Well, Lincoln told me a story, prefacing it with the remark that we already had more generals than we knew what to do with. 'Look here, Seward,' he said, 'suppose you had a large cattleyard, full of all sorts of cattle—cows, oxen, bulls—and you kept killing, selling and disposing of your cows and oxen in one way and another, taking good care of your bulls. By and by you'd find that you had nothing but a yardful of old bulls, good for nothing under heaven. Now it will be just that way with the army if I don't stop making brigadier-generals!'"

John Hay shouted. Sumner smiled, a little uncomfortably. And in the midst of it Lincoln came in carrying a pitcher of milk and a glass, while Tad followed with a plate of bread.

"Taddie and I decided we didn't like the supper, and we didn't like the dining room," he said, "so we raided the kitchen and here we are," seating himself at the table, while Mary and John Hay jumped to clear a place for him. Taddie, with a glance at the clock, and another at his mother, retired discreetly to a stool behind his father's chair.

"What's the news from England, Sumner?" asked the President.

"A letter from Adams, to-day," said Seward, "says that Gladstone wants the Government to intervene at once. He denounces the proclamation in the most cynical and captious manner."

"I understand the President to be speaking to me, sir." Sumner gave the imperturbable Seward a severe glance. "Cobden is delighted with the proclamation, so is John Bright."

"Yes! Yes!" Lincoln spoke impatiently. "But what of the Government? What of Lord Russell?"

"He is supercilious,—ready to do anything that will make a nation of the South," replied Sumner.

"The same old story!" murmured the President, thrusting aside his scarcely tasted meal, and staring broodingly into the fire. No one intruded on his silence. He thought of William Russell's failure to accomplish what he had asked of him, he thought of Thurlow Weed's last report from France, that only a miracle could keep the Emperor's hand from intervening. When would the common people of England speak? When?

"McClellan is at Rectortown," he said, aloud. "Lee is coming through the Blue Ridge below him, heading for Culpeper, I reckon."

"He's going to get there before McClellan does, too!" exclaimed John Hay. "I wish Grant had his hands on the Army of the Potomac."

"Grant's needed where he is, as I told the Cabinet this morning," replied the President. "You weren't there, Seward. I read them a poem I'd like you to hear,—by that fellow, Edmund Clarence Stedman. The Cabinet was wondering how the Republican North would take it, if the Lord or some other hand removed McClellan. This answers part of the question:

> "Back from the trebly crimsoned field
> Terrible words are thunder-tost!
> Full of wrath that will not yield,
> Full of revenge for battles lost!
> Hark to their echo, as it cross't
> The Capitol, making faces wan!
> End the murderous holocaust!
> Abraham Lincoln, give us a *man!*
>
> Give us a man of God's own mould,
> Born to marshal his fellow men;
> One whose fame is not bought and sold
> At the stroke of a politician's pen;
> Give us the man of thousands ten
> Fit to do as well as to plan.
> Give us a rallying cry, and then,
> Abraham Lincoln, find us a *man! . . ."*

He read through the several remaining verses, then replaced the clipping in his pocket. "Yes, a *man!*" he repeated. "But where?"

"John Hay would be a good gene'al," exclaimed Taddie, unexpectedly. "He's bossy enough, that I know!"

Lincoln gave a sudden shout of laughter and reaching behind his chair, pulled the little boy round to sit on his knee.

Mary seized the moment. "Clara Barton ought to be a general, at the very least. Do you men know that she was with the army, every minute, at the battle of Antietam, that men were shot in her arms, that she brought them bandages, candles, ether, wine, when and where they had nothing? Why, that woman soothed and bandaged Burnside's men as they dropped beside the bridge! She was here, to-night. She fears another engagement. She says McClellan wants more hospital tents and Quartermaster Meigs says 'no!' She has tents for five thousand men in her warehouse. Will you make Meigs send them?"

"No," replied the President, quietly. "I will not."

"Not fo' the sick, wounded men, Papa day?" pleaded Taddie, turning his sleep heavy blue eyes up to his father.

"The men have had everything sent to them that mules and roads can carry!" exclaimed Lincoln. "Clara Barton is a noble woman, but I'd make her General-in-Chief sooner than I'd truckle to another of McClellan's excuses."

"But these are for the men, Mr. Lincoln," cried Mary. "If you could hear the story of their sufferings as I hear them, day after day,—always retreating,—always defeated—nothing to pay for their horrible sufferings—"

Taddie began to cry. "Papa day, please, please—"

Lincoln set the little boy to his feet. "No!" he said, in a voice the child seldom heard. "Go to bed, at once. This I cannot and will not bear."

Taddie, after one glance at his father's face, rushed from the room, colliding at the door with Lord Lyons. The Minister smiled down at him, then crossed the room to bow over Mary Lincoln's hand. The President greeted him with an entire lack of his usual jocularity. The diplomat was equally grave.

"I was requested to deliver a message to Mr. Seward, the moment of my arrival in Washington," he said. "I have only just come from the train."

"We'll step into the President's office, Lord Lyons." Seward spoke with alacrity.

"One moment," interposed Lincoln. "The message would, I presume, interest me, as the head of this Government?"

"Certainly, Your Excellency," replied the Minister.

"Then supposing you deliver it right here." Lincoln folded his arms and leaned against the mantel, opposite Sumner.

Lord Lyons raised his black brows but bowed, courteously. "Lord Russel wishes me to procure your Government's opinion on the following hypothetical query: Has not the time come for offering mediation to the

United States Government, with a view to stopping the useless carnage of this fanatical war?"

Seward cleared his throat excitedly, but Lincoln shook his head at the Secretary. He spoke slowly and thoughtfully.

"Say this to your Government, Lord Lyons: Tell them they will find our opinion if they'll inquire among the cotton operators of England, the people whom the war is starving."

"And what am I to understand by that, Your Excellency?" ejaculated the Englishman.

"You're to understand, sir," replied Lincoln, returning the Englishman's look, keenly, "that a government that does not listen to the voice of the plain people is deaf to its own best interests."

Lord Lyons permitted himself to smile. "That is your theory of successful governing, Your Excellency?"

"It is, sir. Also, I'd urge your common sense to realize that this is a family quarrel. Human nature is such that when the well-intentioned outsider interferes in that kind of a fight, he's apt to find himself embroiled in the mix-up."

"I'm not so sure that England is well-intentioned," said Seward, abruptly. "I'm told that the powers higher up, over there, rejoice every time the North loses a battle. The neutrality is only skin-deep."

Lincoln tossed his head, impatiently. Seward's liking for an argument always annoyed him, but particularly did it annoy him to-night. Sumner started to reply but the President interrupted:

"What I can't seem to impress on you folks is that Lord Russell is no fool, and, whatever his personal feeling is, he's not going to lead his country into a war unpopular with the people."

Seward spoke quickly but with a smile. "If Lord Lyons has been privy to the feeling of New York State he must feel that you, yourself, are heading an unpopular war, Mr. Lincoln."

Lincoln returned the smile. "I'm attorney for the people, and I'm not going to let my client manage the case against my judgment."

The Englishman bowed to the President. "I apprehend that my hypothetical query has been fully answered."

"I aimed to do just that, Lord Lyons," replied Lincoln. "Charles,"—turning to Sumner,—"you go along with Lyons and show him your last letter from the Duchess of Argyle. It might be an eye-opener to him."

"I'd like to hear that too, if I may," Seward said. He bade Mary good night and followed the others from the room.

Mary remarked that Taddie must not take both dogs to bed with him, and hurried out, leaving John Hay and Lincoln alone. The President returned to his neglected supper. He drank two glasses of milk and finished the plate of bread, while John Hay stood silent before the fire. The two were completely companionable.

"John," said Lincoln, suddenly, "do you recall a sort of threat or promise

I made myself in your presence, when I got back from my visit to Antietam?"

"Yes, sir! You said that if McClellan should permit Lee to cross the Blue Ridge and place himself between Richmond and the Army of the Potomac, you would remove him from command."

"And now"—Lincoln rose and took a noiseless stride or two up and down the room—"now Lee has crossed the Blue Ridge and is installed at Culpeper Courthouse, and McClellan is still thirty miles north of him. John," in a voice indescribably mournful, "I've lost my faith in him!" Then, "Come into my room a moment."

Young Hay followed eagerly. Lincoln turned up the light, and strode over to his bedside table, where his Bible lay, with a letter on the open pages. "I was reading this book most of last night, when I wasn't measuring off the distance between my bed and the grate. John, when I get to thinking of the chance George McClellan has thrown away to be the most valuable man, the best-loved man in this country, I could sit down and cry like a girl that's lost her first lover. He should, and could, have been everything to us. Here! Isaiah said it. 'And a man shall be as an hiding place from the wind and a covert from the tempest; as rivers of water in a dry place; as the shadow of a great rock in a weary land—As the shadow of a great rock in a weary land'—but he has chosen otherwise. Here, read what I birthed of my last night's travail."

John took the letter and, with growing pallor, read:

"By direction of the President, it is ordered that Major-General McClellan be relieved from the command of the Army of the Potomac, and that Major-General Burnside take command of that Army. Also, that Major-General Hunter take command of the corps in said Army which is now commanded by General Burnside.

"That Major-General Fitz-John Porter be relieved from the corps he now commands in said Army, and that Major-General Hooker take command of said corps.

"The General-in-Chief is authorized, in his discretion, to issue the order substantially as above, forthwith, or as soon as he may deem proper. A. Lincoln."

John looked up from the letter. "Hurray! Three huzza's and a tiger! The backwoods Jupiter is wielding the bolts of war at last!"

"Shall you still cheer if McClellan leads the army down here and takes my job over?" asked the President, refreshed, as he always was by John's volatility.

"He'll never even try, the coward!" exclaimed young Hay.

"He's drunk with vanity and ambition, and a drunken man is a dangerous man," declared Lincoln. "It's more than likely he'll take a long shot at the White House! John, I'm going to take that order to Stanton, now."

"Want me to go with you, sir?" with a little grin as of understanding.

Lincoln returned the grin. "I reckon I do. He'll still be in his office, awaiting news from Grant."

"Better not venture out until I go into the reception room and engage the attention of the crowd. In two minutes, sir, you hustle down the staircase and I'll join you at the front door."

The little strategy was carried through. "Anybody there I ought to see?" asked the President, as, somewhat breathless, John shot past old Daniel into the shadowy portico.

"No one there, at all, sir, except Fernando Wood. I turned him over to Nicolay."

"I refuse to see Wood again. I don't trust him," said the President, then lapsed into silence, his thoughts on McClellan.

Stanton was standing before his tall desk, signing letters, as the President and his secretary came in.

"Quartermaster-General Meigs proves another lie on McClellan," he rasped, abruptly. "McClellan says he's been waiting for horses, that he's received only 150 horses a week since the first of September. As a matter of fact he's been receiving an average of 1,459 horses a week. I'm ready to court-martial that fellow."

"Is Halleck anywhere 'round?" asked Lincoln.

Stanton glanced at his watch. "He's due here, right now, to get Meigs' report. And here he comes," as Halleck, looking at least ten years older than his forty-seven years, came slowly into the room.

"Come along to the funeral, Halleck!" Lincoln took the soldier's arm, affectionately. "You look all set for it."

The General-in-Chief looked up at the President, his large, fine eyes sunk in his head, as though by a wasting illness. "McClellan has worn me out, Mr. Lincoln."

"We'll fix that up, right now!" Lincoln pushed Halleck into a chair. "Come, Stanton, get off your feet for a while." He shoved Stanton to the sofa beside John Hay, and wrapped his own long legs round the desk stool. Then he read aloud the order dismissing McClellan.

As he pronounced the last word, Stanton jumped to his feet with a roar. "A month late! Six months late!"

Lincoln looked over his spectacles at the Secretary of War. "Do you mean you wouldn't fire him?"

Halleck bit his nails. "Either McClellan or I must go, Mr. Stanton."

Stanton turned on him with a sneer. "What! Has the worm turned?"

"Come! Come, Stanton. Don't visit your impatience with me on poor Halleck. What have you got against my order?" Lincoln's voice was very kindly. He pitied Stanton for his bad nerves.

The Secretary jerked off his spectacles, jerked his head, brought his fist down on the desk where he was again standing, close to the President.

"That it's too late!"

"Then you would keep McClellan? You mean that, Stanton?" urged Lincoln gently. "I really don't think he's to be trusted!"

"Trusted!" shouted Stanton. "Trusted! Why, you simple fool—"

"Mr. Stanton, you forget yourself!" snapped John Hay, springing from the sofa, his black eyes blazing. "No, Mr. President, I will not be silenced," as Lincoln shook his head at him. "I have every respect for the ability and integrity of the Secretary of War. But I take this occasion solemnly to warn him that unless he ceases his attacks on the President, he will be known to history only for the virulent and impertinent epithets he applied to Abraham Lincoln."

Lincoln moved uncomfortably on his stool. Praise always embarrassed him. Hay and Stanton glared at each other, but before Lincoln could discover the tactful word he sought, the Secretary of War put his glasses back on his nose.

"Perhaps I deserve that, Hay," he said, quietly. Then, his voice rising, "But McClellan is a traitorous scoundrel. I hate his very gizzard. If the President had taken my advice six months ago—"

"How dare he take your advice as to persons, Mr. Stanton," asked John Hay, earnestly, "when your counsel is so frequently mixed with insuperable hatreds?"

Stanton sighed and turned to Lincoln. "I really am delighted, sir," he said, with the charm of voice and manner none knew better how to wield. "Tell me your further wishes."

"Better dictate a note to John Hay,—this thing must be kept secret,—to be sent with this order. And you, too, Halleck—" replied the President. "Cheer up, Halleck! You're better at writing than anything else. If I'd written your book on war, I'd have a real claim on fame!"

He spoke with a jocularity he was far from feeling, and paced the floor while the notes were dictated.

"By direction of the President of the United States, it is ordered that Major-General McClellan be relieved from the command of the Army of the Potomac, and that Major-General Burnside take command of that Army.

"By order of the Secretary of War."

Halleck bit his smooth-shaven lips; then, with an unusual note of firmness in his voice, he gave John Hay this dictation:

"General,—on receipt of the order of the President, sent herewith, you will immediately turn your command over to Major-General Burnside, and report to Trenton, New Jersey, reporting on your arrival at that place, by telegraph, for further orders. Halleck."

Stanton stared as he listened, and as the General-in-Chief finished, he shouted, "That's right! Exile him! Make the cut complete and final! That's where your military experience and knowledge come in, General."

"Yes," agreed Lincoln, who was very pale. "And now, whom shall we send with this?"

"General Buckingham," replied Halleck, promptly. "He's an older man, discreet and long-headed and very suave."

"Get him started, at once," directed the President, "and in this manner: He is to go first to Burnside, at Orleans. Burnside is going to be unhappy about this. He's devoted to McClellan and doesn't want this job. I wish myself there was some one better fitted for it. Your messenger must be smart enough to understand this feeling of Burnside's because he's got to persuade Burnside to go with him to McClellan, at Rectortown, or wherever he may be at that hour, and he must see Buckingham deliver the order to McClellan. Tell Buckingham to come to me as soon as he returns."

For the first time Stanton smiled. "I see! Very good! Anything else, Mr. Lincoln?"

"One thing more! How many men have we to-night in the defenses around Washington?"

"About 70,000, Mr. President," replied Halleck.

"Be prepared for McClellan's making a move against them, or for their joining him. He very likely may prepare to become dictator," said Lincoln, gravely.

There was a short silence broken by Halleck's, "Very well, sir."

Lincoln gathered up his gray shawl, took his cap from his pocket and nodded to John.

CHAPTER XXXI

THE KEYSTONE OF PUTTY

MARY was bonneted the next morning, and was wrapping her fur-lined mantua about her, when Lincoln came into the room.

"Tad told me you were going out for the day," he said, explaining his unwonted appearance at that hour, "and I want you not to go, Mary. I had a bad dream, last night. Some one was trying to strangle you. You were alone in a grove of trees, and, try as I would, I couldn't get to you. Mary, you stay right in the house, to-day, where I can get a glimpse of you whenever I want to."

Mary paused in the arrangement of the folds of the mantua over her arms, and stared at her husband. He was looking even more ghastly than usual. His lips trembled nervously.

"Abra'm, has something more than usual happened? Is a battle begun?"

"No! Yes! Mary." He put his hand on hers. "I've removed McClellan permanently."

"Thank God Almighty! Does McClellan know it, yet?" She dropped the cloak, and seized his hand in both of hers.

"He will know this afternoon."

"And you fear almost anything, both military and political! Oh, my dear, I'll not leave you, to-day!" Mary began to pull off her gloves.

"It's not that! I really had an ugly dream. I woke crying." He looked down into her blue eyes, wondering if it would ease the pain in his heart to tell her of all the black forebodings that had made the night horrible. But he dared not, he told himself, permit even a trickle to appear in the levee, lest the whole wall of his control give way. . . . "Mary, I loved McClellan," was what he finally brought forth.

"I know you did,—and so does he know it,—the priceless fool!"

Lincoln stooped and kissed her, then hurried back to his office.

Mary, with a little sigh for the adventure she was giving up, sent off a note to Miss Barton, advising her that she had not yet abandoned hope as regarded the tents, and excusing herself from taking the proposed ride in the ambulance. Then she settled to bandage making.

It was bitter November weather, with heavy clouds and snow flurries. Lincoln looked into the sitting room several times during the day, brightened at the smile Mary gave him and hurried back to his office. The weather, by six o'clock, was very bad, and visitors thinned out, correspondingly. And still no word from General Buckingham. Lincoln spent the evening with the Attorney General, going over soldiers' petitions for pardons and reprieves, as usual reducing poor Bates to despair over his leniency. Shortly before eleven, this task was completed, and Lincoln started for his room. He paused a moment at young Stoddard's desk.

"Working late, aren't you, Billy?"

"I've sworn I'll not leave this desk, sir, until I've finished these letters. They've been accumulating since September, from important people about the emancipation proclamation." The young man smiled and sighed at the same time.

"Better go to bed, my boy! This burning of the midnight oil fits us old fellows, not young ones who should be out courting pretty girls." He patted Stoddard's shoulder, and moved wearily on toward bed.

Gradually the White House settled to quiet, but as the hours wore on, Stoddard became aware that, above the ticking of the clock, there was another steady and monotonous sound, and told himself that the President was walking the floor again. At three o'clock, when Stoddard finished the last letter and started for home, the slow, even sound fell on his ears as he went softly down the staircase.

At five o'clock, there came the tinkling thud of a spurred boot in the hall outside Lincoln's room. He opened the door just as a knock sounded. An officer, wrapped in a snow-covered cape, saluted him.

"General Buckingham, Mr. President. I have just come in from Rectortown."

"Come in, General!" Lincoln closed the door, carefully. "Hang your cloak before the fire. Here, let me help you. You look very tired."

Buckingham, a man with fine, intelligent eyes, and a clean-cut nose above iron-gray whiskers, took the chair Lincoln indicated.

"It was an unsavory job, eh, Buckingham?" asked the President, dreading, yet impatient for what the general had to tell.

"Why, I never had a more difficult one, sir!" exclaimed Buckingham. "I delivered the order to Burnside, first. I never have seen a man so shocked. At first he could say nothing. Then he gathered himself together and said the order was a matter to which he would like to give thought, that he did not want the command. Then he called in two of his staff officers, and showed them the order. They were delighted at his promotion, and so expressed themselves. But for more than two hours he held out against them and me. He insisted that he was not competent to take so large a command; that General McClellan was his intimate friend; that McClellan was better fitted than any one else in the Army of the Potomac to command it. But Burnside's is, essentially, a gentle nature. He yielded, at last, and we set out for Rectortown in a blinding snowstorm."

"You think Burnside weak, General?" asked Lincoln, uneasily.

"He hasn't a big fist," replied Buckingham. "I wouldn't say he was weak. We found McClellan writing letters in his tent, and I gave him the orders. He read them, then he looked at Burnside with a smile and said, 'I congratulate you, General!'

" 'But I don't want the job,' Burnside said, 'I want you to keep it! Call your staff in, General!'

"McClellan kept on smiling and called in his officers. I don't know," hesitating, "whether he thought I was of no significance, or whether he wanted me to get an idea of what he meant to the Army of the Potomac. But, Mr. President, he allowed several of his officers to urge him, in my presence, to march on Washington and take over the Government."

Lincoln leaned forward, tensely.

"There were hours and hours of talk. They forgot their meals. They forgot their military duties. I swear to you, I didn't know what my move was, sir. I finally decided to sit tight, and wait for McClellan to declare himself. He sat hunched up at the table, biting his nails, long after every one had said his say. Finally, he got up and looked at me. 'General,' he said, 'go back and tell Lincoln I'll take his order.'"

"Ah!" breathed Lincoln, almost groaning with relief. "Loyal at the last!"

"Perhaps!" said Buckingham, wearily. "More likely he was afraid. More likely it was just as impossible to his nature to move on Washington as on Richmond. Let history decide that. Certainly his contemporaries can't."

"General," Lincoln put his hand on the older man's knee with a sense of gratitude he found it difficult to express, "how can I repay you for the splendid chore you've done for us?"

"By letting me go home for a bath and sleep, sir!" with a twinkle in his eye that lighted a twinkle in the President's.

"Will you let me find a cup of coffee for you, first?"

Buckingham rose and drew on his cape. "I'd rather go home, thank you, Mr. Lincoln."

"All right, General. But you come back some day, and we'll take time off for a good talk. Come along. I'll let you out, myself." He led the weary general, however, not out to the north portico, but down through the kitchen, where the colored cook was just pouring out her pre-breakfast cup of coffee.

She was not at all confused by the arrival of the President, but grinned at him, affectionately. "Been up all night again, Massa Lincum, I suppose! Sally, bring cups for Massa Lincum and the gemmun."

"Sit down, General!" Lincoln pushed Buckingham into a chair by the fire, and himself passed him the steaming cup before he took his own. "These might seem like funeral baked meats to some," he said to his highly edified guest, "but to me it's a libation to dawn!"

Buckingham looked up with his fine, understanding gaze and lifted his cup toward Lincoln. They drank in silence. Having sped his guest, the President mounted the steps, two at a time, and bursting into Mary's room, roused her from sleep to impart the news to her. She listened, wide-eyed, then said, with extraordinary solemnity:

"Abra'm, the war is won! You are in the saddle, at last!"

"I'm in the saddle and I'm going to ride just as soon as I find the stirrups," Lincoln said, carefully. "This is the crisis. If the peace party accepts McClellan's dismissal, however sullenly, it means that they will also accept the emancipation proclamation. I shall issue the edict of freedom

January first, as I say I will in the proclamation. Then I shall *ride*, spurred boots in the stirrups. I must tell John Hay and George Nicolay."

Word of the dismissal spread over the country like wildfire. By night, the Cabinet table, Lincoln's own desk, Stoddard's desk were covered with messages from the public,—the bitter, vitriolic protests coming first, as usual. Lincoln worked with his secretaries, sorting and reading, struggling to feel the pulse of the country at the earliest possible moment. An unusual crowd of visitors thronged the halls. Mary finally established herself in the Blue Room, and gave tea and guarded information to the motley groups of women, who suddenly claimed acquaintanceship with her. Whether they admired or despised him, certainly McClellan had a greater hold on the imaginations of his fellow countrymen, at that moment, than any other person.

Toward the supper hour, a heavy sleet storm set in, and the women folk fled for their homes or hotels. By seven o'clock, Mary was alone with her empty tea tray. She had risen wearily to go upstairs, when a tall woman in black silk appeared in the doorway of the East Room. She wore a heavy mourning veil which concealed her face but Mary knew her, instantly.

"Good evening, Miss Ford," she said, coolly.

The Virginian flung back her veil, disclosing an olive tinted face distorted with something more than anger. To Mary she looked maniacal. Her eyes were half closed, her lips twisted to one side. She walked slowly across the room toward Mary.

"So," she said, her drawl never more pronounced, "you've had your way about McClellan, at last, you little cat!"

Mary reached toward the bell rope, but with a sudden spring, Miss Ford placed herself before the handle. "I want only a few moments with you." She smiled crookedly. "I have just come from McClellan. I have just seen a man, a great man, contemplating the ruins of his life. I—"

Mary interrupted. She was recovering her poise. Surely, some one would come, at any moment. "No one knows better than you, Miss Ford, that McClellan is not great. Your choice of him was bad. A man small enough to be a tool cannot be big enough for greatness."

"You are learning to be sententious," sneered the Virginian. Then, leaning toward Mary until her twitching face was not two feet away, she said, "My house has been burned down. My niggers are gone. My father was shot as a spy, last week. All thanks to you and your 'intellectual giant.' Look at me, Madam! Half insane, am I not? Fit to destroy anything—hunted—desperate! Multiply me by a million, two million, ten million, and you have the South. Am I a toy? Am I to be ignored? Can you *proclaim* me out of the way? Can you abolish me with words—me and my million fellow devils?"

Mary, very deliberately, sat down and poured herself a cup of tea. She did not believe that the Virginian would lay hands on her, and she felt a sudden conviction that, given free scope, the frantic maker of plots would divulge some important facts.

"A good many people seemed to resent the proclamation," she remarked mildly. "What did you think of it?"

Miss Ford made a gesture of disgust. "Don't try to play with me, Mary Lincoln. You still fail to understand the depth of my desperation. I know Abraham Lincoln better than you do. I recognize the profundity of his political wisdom, as you cannot, because I am among those who have sought to frustrate him. More than that I love him,—yes, scowl with your doll face,—I love him with a passion of which you are incapable. Therefore I read the handwriting on the wall as no other Southerner, and as few Northerners have read it.

"Listen to me and judge, if you can, my despair. When Lincoln removed George McClellan from the control of 300,000 men in the Army of the Potomac, he removed the only practical menace against the carrying out of the threat in the proclamation on January first. If Lincoln is still alive on January first to sign the final paper that frees the slaves, he will have broken the essential fighting superiority of the South, and the end is only a question of time. George McClellan was the keystone of the peace-with-slavery arch. Lincoln has pulled him down."

Mary, her heart beating heavily, sipped her cold tea with a supercilious smile. "He was a pseudo-keystone. He was made of putty. That's where your judgment made its fatal error. Jeff Davis must be grateful to you."

"Yes, he's quite as grateful as you could wish. But I call your attention to the fact that your husband's judgment was almost as weak as mine. It's thanks to you that he came to his senses."

"You flatter me and contradict yourself," rejoined Mary, "having just spoken of his profound wisdom. May I ask why you are displaying the bad taste of telling me you are in love with my husband?"

"Because I know the thought will torment you when you realize how much more suited I am to be his mate than you!" The Virginian loosened the strings of her bonnet as though she found breathing difficult.

Mary laughed. "You poor, crazy thing!"

"Yes, crazy now, thanks to you!" declared Miss Ford, "but at my best, a year ago, the proper mate for him."

"I suppose it's this alleged love of yours that led you to send that fool of a Gordon to shoot the President, last summer!" Mary rose again, moving a little away from the menacing, dark face. "Well, you can't send him again, before January first, because he was killed at Antietam."

Miss Ford looked at her wonderingly. "Did some one shoot at Lincoln?— Gordon?—I warned Lincoln of that possibility. We did not use him for that—" She seemed to fall into a profound reverie.

Mary edged a little further away. "Well, Miss Ford, if I had your conviction of pre-knowledge, I'd go down South and tell my friends they might as well quit now."

"If you had my conviction," returned the Virginian, "you'd do as I do.

Take you with me where neither of us can belong to Lincoln." She attempted to draw a small pistol from the reticule which hung on her left arm, but there was filigree mounting on the barrel which caught in the silk cords of the bag. Mary, who, for an instant, as she saw eternity opening before her, had seemed paralyzed, took advantage of the reprieve. She screamed, and with all her strength, thrust the tea table at the Virginian. It crashed into her, upsetting itself, and throwing Miss Ford backward against the wall. Then Mary fled.

At the door she ran into James and Taddie, followed by half a dozen, then a dozen strangers, part of the President's throng of visitors. She seized Taddie, gasping. "Take her—spy—armed— Don't let her get away!" Then she fled up the stairs, dragging the frightened child with her.

She burst into the President's office. Sumner was with him. "Miss Ford, downstairs, tried to shoot me. Send for Colonel Baker!" she panted, then sank into a chair and began to cry. Taddie, the moment she had freed his hand, ran into the hall. Lincoln and Sumner both hurried to Mary's side, but before they could more than begin to question her, Taddie ran in.

"They a' bwinging Miss Fo'd upstai's!"

A confusion of voices sounded in the hall. Lincoln, with a reassuring pat on his wife's shoulder, went into the reception room. Stoddard was trying to clear the crowd out. Miss Ford, her hands bound together with a handkerchief, stood calmly between James and old Daniel.

"Take her into my office," ordered the President. "Billy, get Baker over here. The rest of you gentlemen will kindly clear the room." He followed the crowd to the door, closed it and locked it after them, handing the key to Stoddard. Then he returned to his office, Taddie still at his side.

Mary was no longer weeping. She was standing before the grate, leaning on Charles Sumner's arm, and glaring at the Virginian, who was leaning against the Cabinet table, her eyes on the blazing fire. Sumner scowled when he observed Taddie who at once slid into an inconspicuous corner behind his father's desk.

Lincoln ran his fingers through his hair, took out the ivory paper knife, and otherwise prepared himself for what he felt would be one of the most distasteful scenes of his life.

"James, you needn't keep hold of Miss Ford's arm, I reckon," he suggested.

"I reckon if he does, there'll be a dead nigger in the White House before another dawn," drawled Miss Ford, without raising her eyes from her contemplation of the blaze.

"'Scuse me, Mr. President." James did not stir. "I saw this lady trying to pull a pistol at the Madam. Guess maybe you didn't understand that."

"Let Senator Sumner take your place, James," ordered Lincoln.

"Senator Sumner must decline, sir." Sumner, very pale, his blue eyes full of pain, patted Mary's hand which quivered on his arm, and resolutely stared at the shadow in which Taddie was shivering.

Lincoln ran the paper knife through his hair. "Just what happened, wife?"

"I was alone in the Blue Room. Miss Ford came in through the East Room door. She seemed demented. She talked wildly for a few moments, then said she was going to shoot me and herself, and tried to draw a pistol from her reticule. It caught, and I pushed the tea table into her and ran. James and a crowd did the rest."

"What did you do, James?" questioned the President.

"I grasped the hand that had the pistol, Massa Lincum, sir, and some more gen'men tied her hands, and Daniel and me led her up here." James spoke firmly, but with an uneasy black eye on the Virginian.

"What on earth could you have against my wife, Miss Ford?" demanded the President, conscious of mounting fury, and determined not to show it.

"Many things, Abraham Lincoln, but chiefly that she is your wife," replied Miss Ford, suddenly lifting her violet eyes to rest on his. "I'd resent any one that has that position."

"Do send Tad out, Mrs. Lincoln," begged Charles Sumner.

Mary started. "Where is the child? Taddie!"

Taddie sidled up to his father. "You want me, don't you, Papa day?"

"Might as well let him stay. He's my shadow, I reckon," said Lincoln, looking at his wife.

"Taddie!" Mary spoke sharply, motioning toward the door.

The child hesitated, then he said, "Yes, I'll go motha'. I know Miss Fo'd's been naughty but don't you fo'get how good she was to Willie and me and how Willie loved he'. I do, too."

He ran across the room, clasped Miss Ford's two imprisoned hands in his, and kissed them. Then, with a child's peculiar dignity, he marched out of the room.

Lincoln looked after him with softened eyes. But his anger was not lessened by the little boy's lovely gesture. Miss Ford had not given Tad a glance.

"If you'd tried to shoot me, I could see your point, you being a Southerner," said Lincoln. "But when you attack my wife—I have no bowels of compassion."

The Virginian had not taken her eyes from his face. "Don't talk nonsense to me," she drawled. "I know how to value what you feel for your wife."

"Miss Ford!" ejaculated Sumner.

Apparently, she did not hear him.

Lincoln eyed her, thoughtfully. Then he looked at Sumner. "I think you'd better take Mrs. Lincoln into the sitting room, Charles. There's nothing for her in this nonsense."

"No, Mr. Lincoln," cried Mary, "I'm not going to move until I am assured that you won't hand this woman a pardon, as you do every one else."

Lincoln could feel himself flushing. Well, perhaps he deserved that. He was pretty soft about the soldiers. But Miss Ford! Her declaration of love made him sick at his stomach. His lower lip pressed firmly over his upper, he made no reply to Mary; only stood looking at her. She gave a little sob, and permitted Sumner to lead her away.

As the door of the private passage closed behind the two, Lincoln turned to Miss Ford. But before he could speak Colonel Baker burst in from the reception room. He was accompanied by a tall bearded sergeant of the detective police.

"My God, Mr. Lincoln!" he exclaimed. "I'm sorry and ashamed about this."

Lincoln nodded. "I want Miss Ford locked up in the Old Capitol Prison, Colonel. And I want her kept there until after January first. I'm going to hold you responsible if, in that time, she communicates with the outside world. After that date, if she has behaved herself, you are to send her down to Richmond with the understanding that, if we catch her about the Northern lines during the rest of the war, she shall have the usual fate of spies. Now, you can go through the motions of whatever you think is necessary to carry out my order. But that's to stand."

"I don't want your leniency, Abraham Lincoln!" cried Miss Ford, suddenly straining to free her hands from her bonds.

Lincoln motioned for Baker and his man to take over James' and Daniel's job.

As Baker deftly slipped handcuffs on her wrists, the Virginian gave a piercing scream that rang through the White House from attic to basement. But she did not resist as the men led her from the room.

Mary Lincoln was in a bad state of nerves. Lincoln went to her room as soon as he had disposed of Miss Ford. He found her in a violent hysterical attack, and sent at once for Dr. Stone and Lizzie Keckley. He held her in his arms until those two experts arrived, but the three were unable to quiet her, and at last the doctor was obliged to give her an opiate. Lizzie and the President sat by her bedside until midnight, then the dressmaker persuaded him to go to bed.

She wakened him at dawn, however. "The Madam's got something on her mind, sir. She's all worked up about it and I think you'd better come in, yourself."

"All right, Lizzie," replied Lincoln, pulling on the faithful and faded dressing gown and slippers.

Mary was sitting up among her pillows, wearily, like a child.

There was a good fire in the grate.

"Pull the big chair up close to the flames, Lizzie," ordered the President, "and we'll see if we can't comfort this girl. Put a shawl round her."

He lifted his wife in his arms, and seated himself in the big chair, while Lizzie wrapped the shawl over them both, then slipped from the room.

"Hush, darling Mary, while I tell you something. I sent Sister Ford off to the Old Capitol. Wasn't that sense enough?"

Mary nodded convulsively.

"You were badly frightened, I know. But can't you think of yourself as one of the soldier boys? What if each of them had hysterics every time a gun was pointed at them? You were brave as a lion, for a while. Can't you keep it up?"

"I'm—not—frightened!" gasped Mary. "It was—what—she said about you—and me!"

"Oh!" He patted her shoulder and stared into the fire. What had the Virginian said? She had insinuated something. A slur on his affection for Mary! Ah, yes! With sudden understanding came sudden sense of contrition. Perhaps there would never be a better time than now for clearing away the fog.

"Did she say more to you, in the Blue Room, than she did to me, in the office, dear Mary?" he asked. "Try as hard as you can, to stop the tears. Before long some one will burst in on us, and I want you to empty your heart to me. Whatever she said was lies, of course. I wanted to throw up my dinner when she spoke about her feeling for me."

A smile crossed poor Mary's swollen face. She was getting herself in hand again. After a moment, she began to speak coherently. And bit by bit, the story of the conversation in the Blue Room came out. Mary had a remarkable memory. The account, Lincoln knew, was complete and accurate. She finished with a sentence that moved her husband more than had her tears.

"Don't waste time trying to comfort me, Abra'm, but tell me the whole truth. Your kindly lies leave me utterly lonely."

The room was lighted only by the candle on the table and the flame from the grate. The uncertain glow was kind to Mary's face, and gave a depth to her eyes that was quite unfathomable. The two stared at each other, struggling, as have so many millions of men and women since humanity was achieved, to pass the impassable barrier of human personality.

"Miss Ford," began Lincoln, thoughtfully, "isn't to blame for all your tears. I reckon she was just the last straw. You've been hearing from all sides devilish things about what you mean to me."

"Taddie came in the other day," said Mary, "and asked me what it was for a lady to be a swear word. It turned out that he had heard some one say that I was a curse to my husband and my family."

Lincoln winced and groaned, then said, "Mary, I don't know what love is, do you? Is it limited to the kind of feeling young folks have when they are sparking? Or has it only to do with begetting? Or is it a never-ending need, one for the other? Isn't it each of these things, not all at once, but in inevitable sequence? Dear wife, can anything shake our knowledge that all these belong to our experience with each other? Mary, how can you let anything any one says enter that holy place of which only husband and wife—you and I—have knowledge?"

Mary drew a long breath. He lifted her hand to his lips, then put it down again.

"Let's lay this ghost, once for all, my darling girl. No one knows as I do how I neglect you and how that neglect feeds malicious tongues. But,

Mary, I'm not big enough to carry the burden of this war, and have left time for the care and attention you ought to have. All that is left is the unending need for you and even for that I have scarcely strength to seek. I feel as a man must feel who is carrying a burden uphill, a burden so great that his knees and his will buckle under him at every step. He yearns for, he needs, he craves, the human tenderness he's entitled to but he cannot indulge and refresh himself in those. The burden requires all of him." He paused and the old Carcassonne of his soul rose again. "Some day, precious Mary, when all of this war is over, you and I will go to the Holy Land and on around the world. And we'll have leisure to give each other."

"Abra'm! Abra'm! Why haven't you said this to me before?" cried Mary.

"I've wanted to," he said, huskily. "But you know me, Mary. I don't do the important things till circumstances force me. I reckon it requires a convulsion of nature to get me going."

Mary smiled a little. "I know. It needed the rebellion to make a real President of you."

"Yes, ma'am," he returned the smile, "and a Miss Ford, with a shooting iron, to make a real husband of me."

Mary laughed outright. "I doubt if even she could do that! But at least she's forced you to lay the ghost."

Lincoln gathered both her hands in his. "Have I done that, most dear wife?"

"Abra'm, I understand, at last. And nothing that any one can say or you can fail to do, will disturb me again." She laid her cheek to his and he held her close.

A rap sounded immediately and Lizzie came in with a breakfast tray.

"Lizzie," asked Mary, "this is so opportune I'm almost suspicious that you were listening at the keyhole!"

Lizzie threw up her brown chin indignantly, but there was a twinkle in her eye as she said, "You do me an injustice, Madam President!"

CHAPTER XXXII

ELECTION day, as Nicolay observed to John Hay, was almost as much of a strain on the President as the day of the battle of Antietam had been.

Lincoln heard the remark and said, with a grim smile, "We're fighting a battle, more important than any in the war so far. If the fellows who say they won't back me in the proclamation and in removing McClellan, are numerous enough to control the State legislatures, Governors and Congressmen, the battle and the proclamation are lost."

And for many days after the returns came in, it did look as if the battle were lost. The number of Democrats in the House of Representatives was increased from forty-five to seventy-five and it looked as though Lincoln had lost the support of that great branch of the government. Huge Democratic gains, indeed, marked the elections in all the Middle West and they were overwhelming in New York State, where Seymour quite literally had fulfilled his prophecy and had placed New York in his pocket.

As soon as the Congress convened on December first, a bitter fight over the proclamation began. This was at its height, when General Burnside, suddenly bolting the plans of campaign which had been agreed upon by McClellan and the War Department, moved the Army of the Potomac against Fredericksburg. A battle was fought on December 13th,—a battle that once more was a ghastly defeat for the ill-starred Union forces. Lee's losses aggregated 4,200, Burnside's over 10,000.

Lincoln passed through the battle-day with his usual travail of spirit. Halleck, as he brought in person to the President the last returns, on the evening of the 14th was in a state of desperation. Lincoln read the figures.

"It looks bad," he said, slowly, "unless we use long-shot arithmetic. Lee had about 75,000 men and lost 4,200. We had about 200,000 men, and lost 10,000. If the same battle were to be fought over again, every day, through a week of days with the same relative results, Lee's army would be wiped out, and Burnside's still be a mighty host. I can't find a general who can face my arithmetic, but the end of the war will be at hand when I do find him. Perhaps Grant will develop that way."

"God forbid the carnage!" ejaculated Halleck.

"The quickest way to end the war, Halleck! Burnside is due to have an awful increase of desertions after this. You'd better go down there yourself, General. Go over the ground with him, and give Burnside some concrete suggestions. He's lost his grip."

"My going would be useless, sir. He disregards me."

"Nonsense!" irritably from the President. "He's the most honest, most reasonable man in the army."

"I know he is, Mr. Lincoln, but he's lost his grip, as you say." Halleck wiped his forehead with a sigh.

"And that's where your skill lies,—in helping him to get it back. Don't fail me, General, in the point precisely where I expect you to be of greatest assistance. Your great military skill is useless to me unless you can do this sort of thing for your generals in the field. Burnside is worth saving. He still, because of his superb character, has the confidence of the country. Now, you go out there in Virginia and save him."

Halleck made a despairing gesture. "I'd rather you'd accept my resignation, Mr. President."

"I don't want it. What would I do with the thing? Frame it? Go out there, Halleck, and uphold Burnside's faltering hands." He gave the discouraged General-in-Chief a smile and turned back to the war map. Halleck mumbled an apology and went out.

When he had gone Lincoln again picked up the figures on Fredericksburg and stared at them broodingly.

"It's what I asked for," he said aloud. "It's what I said was needed to make the North demand a greater reason for fighting. It's the lever needed to make Congress see that we've got to break the fighting superiority of the South by using the slaves, or lose this war— The Almighty must have heard my thoughts—and yet"—wringing his hands and groaning—"it doesn't seem as if I could stand another defeat and live. God will enable—God only can enable, if He will—*if* He will."

He sprang to his feet and rushed into Taddie's room, where he engaged in a game of bear-baiting, until Mary insisted upon putting the excited boy to bed.

She came into his office, afterward, accompanying James and the President's supper tray. She found that often she could snatch a moment with her husband in this manner when there had been no other free moment in the day.

She stood by his desk, watching him as he absently ate his soup. "Abra'm, shall you postpone issuing the edict of freedom on January first, as you announced in the proclamation?"

"Why should I?" asked Lincoln.

"Well," replied Mary, "unless things make a sudden change, it doesn't look as if the edict would have much force."

Lincoln sighed, but declared that nothing could change his purpose. Mary buttered a roll for him, and said, as she placed it in his hand, "Abra'm, Taddie wants to send a present to Miss Ford, for Christmas."

"They may not let her have it." Lincoln's mind reverted, with sudden pity, to the handsome, unhappy creature in a cell. "He'll have to talk it over with Baker."

"You don't object?" asked Mary.

"Of course not! Do you?" smiling at her.

"Yes, I do. But the child needn't be thwarted in a generous impulse for that reason. Anna, that colored maid of hers, is devoted to her, by the way. She told Lizzie Keckley that Miss Ford believes that Jinny made her way to Canada. Seems Miss Ford had sent Jinny to take a message to Gordon and she never came back!"

"Poor Jinny!" murmured Lincoln. "Baker, by the way, tells me some one of his women prisoners in the Old Capitol is keeping Davis informed of my movements. He thinks it's Miss Ford, but he can't make the connection."

"Can't I tell Lizzie Keckley that?" asked Mary. "She might be able to pick something out of Anna where a white man, like Baker, couldn't."

"You're still after poor Sister Ford, eh?" asked Lincoln. "Well, I reckon you ought to help if you can, and Lizzie is mighty discreet."

There was silence again, broken by Mary asking softly, "Are you terribly discouraged, Abra'm, about the proclamation?"

"In a way, yes! I'm very anxious. So far its effect certainly has been bad. Stocks have declined, and troops are coming forward more slowly than ever. The attrition among the old troops is outnumbering the addition by the new. There is a lot of breath from the North about the proclamation, but breath alone kills no Rebels. Since McClellan was removed the morale of his army is very bad. And you know what the Congress is up to!"

"What are you going to do, Abra'm? I worry so!"

"Do? I'm going to bide my time and keep my faith in the goodness and common sense of the average citizen. In the long run, they are bound to support me and their will is what finally rules the world."

And with this statement, Mary was obliged to be satisfied, for Mr. Chase came in, obviously perturbed, and Lincoln set his mind to solving the difficulties that had caused a crisis between the Secretary of State and the Secretary of the Treasury.

Christmas came sorrowfully, for all save the children. Taddie had a glorious time with such an excess of toys that his mother was glad to see him in the basement sharing them with the members of his Company. In the afternoon, the President and Mrs. Lincoln held an informal reception in the Blue Room. There was no crowd, but such a continuous stream of callers that a lengthy talk with any one of them was difficult.

The stream was at its flood when John Hay, his eager face unusually eager, appeared with his arm through that of a bearded, carelessly dressed civilian in his early forties.

"This, Mr. President," cried John triumphantly, "is a friend whom you love but have not met! This is Walt Whitman!"

Lincoln felt his cheeks burn. "The prophet of democracy!" he exclaimed, seizing Whitman's horny palm in both his own, calloused as were the poet's. "How do you do, sir! What brings you to Washington?"

"I have a brother in a hospital here, Mr. President. He was wounded at Fredericksburg and I'm nursing him. I shall stay on and nurse others when he is better. A man is needed there."

"Good! Yes!" Lincoln put his shoulder against the pressing crowd, and clung to Whitman's hand, while he sought for some word that would express his gratitude to him. "Your 'Leaves of Grass,' Whitman,—I know it by heart—it has helped me."

A light as if he had suddenly been glorified leaped to the poet's eyes. "I have known you a long time, my Captain! I have learned the route you take when you get an afternoon drive, and I stand on the corner and watch for you—with your face of the master. The arms of all of us who understand are under you, lifting and sustaining you."

He spoke with such earnestness and simplicity that Lincoln felt a thrill of hope which sent the blood racing through his tired pulses. He leaned toward the poet.

"Are there enough who understand, Whitman, to save the proclamation?" he asked.

"Aye, more than enough! They are modest, slow to speak, but you will hear from all the brotherhood, the indissoluble brotherhood, before the new year comes."

The two men gave each other a long, unsmiling look, then the poet passed on. Lincoln drew a deep, life-giving breath, as though he had for a moment glimpsed final truth.

But even the memory of Whitman could not much lighten the suspense of the following week.

All his pleading, all his threats had so far not moved the slave States one inch toward taking advantage of the opportunity offered in the proclamation. To be sure, Missouri made pleasing gestures, and West Virginia joined the Union, a free State. But gratifying as this was, it could have little effect on the general situation. Since the removal of McClellan, and the consequent collapse of the peace party's hopes, a threatening silence had been the aspect presented by the British. Lincoln found this silence puzzling. Russell, at least, might have written, he thought.

But Russell had not forgotten. On the last day of December, when Lincoln was eagerly surveying the field for every shred of support to be found in every utterance from whatever source, a letter came from the war correspondent.

"I have good news for you," he wrote. "I have just learned that a paper in praise of the emancipation proclamation is being circulated among the cotton workers in factories here, and that already five thousand of these workers have signed it. The signing is continuing. There is no doubt that among the entire working class of England such a current of anti-slavery feeling is rising that Mr. Gladstone and Lord Russell are beginning to soften their cynical hostility to your great principle."

There was more in the letter, but this was the crux of it for Lincoln. He marked the paragraph, and, with a great sigh, handed the letter to Charles Sumner, who had been waiting while he read it.

"You see, Charles," said Lincoln, "while what I said in that proclamation didn't go well at first, it promises to wear well."

Sumner's smile had something of tenderness in it as he read the paragraph. "Yes, dear Mr. Lincoln, it promises to wear well! And I have further good word for you. This afternoon, by a test vote of 78 to 51 the House endorsed the proclamation!"

Lincoln could feel himself grow pale. "By jings, if nothing breaks between now and the first, I'll finish this job!"

"There's nothing left to happen, sir," smiled Sumner, serenely. "And once the edict of freedom is signed, you'll find a fairly solid North behind you. Though the South may hold out for more years than we can foresee, the day you sign the edict will see the turning-point of the war toward the North's inevitable victory."

Lincoln heaved a great sigh. "I haven't been out of the house for a week, Charles! Reckon now I can go get myself a little fresh air. Will you come along?"

"I'm sorry, Mr. President, but I must return to the Capitol. It's a glorious winter afternoon. Shall you take to the saddle?"

"Think I will, if I can duck Baker's cavalry." Lincoln smiled wryly.

A half hour later, Mary burst into the secretaries' room. She was as white as the little lace collar at her neck.

"Where's Mr. Lincoln?" she screamed.

Both young men came to their feet.

"He went for a ride across Long Bridge, I think," replied Nicolay. "What's the trouble, Mrs. Lincoln?"

Mary clutched her throat, and by an obvious physical effort forced herself to speak coherently.

"A plot to kidnap him before he signs the edict! Lizzie Keckley got it from Anna, Miss Ford's maid."

"They can't kidnap him when he's got a company of cavalry at his heels," exclaimed John Hay, ringing the bell violently nevertheless for Louis.

"Did the escort go with him?" cried Mary. "He's always evading them! I'll find out. I'll run to the stables."

Nicolay put his hand on her arm. "We must keep our heads, dear Mrs. Lincoln. The President mustn't come in and find us all drowning in a teapot tempest."

Louis came in at that moment and Hay sent him posthaste for Colonel Baker, then flew to get what information he could regarding Lincoln's movements. As Baker appeared,—Louis had caught him in the White House grounds,—John returned with word that Lincoln had gone out afoot and alone. Old Daniel had supposed that he had stepped over to Stanton's office. But Taddie had seen him heading across LaFayette Square and guessed that he'd be tramping out toward the Soldiers' Home.

Baker nodded coolly. "Why are you so uneasy, Mrs. Lincoln?"

"Lizzie Keckley just came into my room all out of breath," replied Mary, twisting her handkerchief, her eyes burning. "Anna had come to her, crying, as Lizzie sat down in our kitchen, eating her lunch. She'd just got wind of a plot, hatched by Miss Ford, Captain Taylor, and, Anna claimed, 'some big white folks' in Richmond, to kidnap Mr. Lincoln, take him South and hold him till he agrees, she said, not to sign up the niggers' freedom. They've been watching for a chance to get him alone. That's all I know. Quickly, Colonel Baker! Quickly or you'll be too late!"

"I thought I had impressed the President with just this danger!" exclaimed Baker, running from the room.

In the meantime, Lincoln had strolled out into the grounds drawing deep breaths of the brilliant afternoon air. He looked over his shoulders and grinned when he observed that he actually had eluded Baker's shadows.

"Reckon I'll go to a livery stable and hire a horse," he murmured, "and ride out to the Soldiers' Home. Not enough snow to matter out that road, and I'd like to see real country trees for a spell."

A flustered liveryman, half a mile out on F Street, supplied a roan saddle horse and Lincoln, still unshadowed, as far as he knew, started at a rapid trot upon the road which the last eighteen months had made so familiar to him. He was obliged to slow the roan's pace after a half hour's riding as the road, rising gradually above Rock Creek valley, was clogged with drifts. Before one of these Lincoln pulled up his horse, and sat in contented contemplation of the great blue shadows stretching across the snow-filled valley. The sky was flawless. A crow flew over the fields and dropped like a black plummet into the trees that lined the distant stream.

Nothing that had occurred during his administration had gratified Lincoln as had this act of the British workingmen. The warm glow that had filled his heart as he read Russell's letter he still felt and it lightened his burden by many pounds.

A sudden cold wind, rising from the valley, roused him from reverie. It was too late to continue the trip to the Home. He turned the roan's head cityward. As he did so, a man came out of the trees to the east of the road, a young man in fashionable riding clothes. He was limping and snow bedraggled.

Lincoln pulled up the roan. "Well, stranger!" he called, "had a tumble?"

The young man answered breathlessly as if he had been running.

"Yes, sir! My horse bolted into the woods a mile below here, and I only just got free from him. He threw me and now refuses to move. Are you a judge of horses, sir?"

"Roughly speaking, yes," replied Lincoln. "Is the animal down?"

"Not at all, sir! He stands gazing at the trees like an arborealist. I wonder, if you are returning to the city, if you could send another animal to me? I have twisted my ankle." The young man lifted an engaging dark face toward the President.

"He doesn't recognize me," thought Lincoln, enjoying the encounter. Then aloud, "I'll do more than that, mister. I'll go into the woods first and have a look at your balky friend."

"It's wretched going, sir." The stranger hesitated, then, as if his scruples were overcome by the kindliness in Lincoln's smile, he exclaimed, "Well, if you will be so kind! It's not more than five minutes' walk."

Lincoln pushed the reluctant roan after the young stranger.

There was little snow under the spruce and maples, but the ground was boggy and uneven. Lincoln pulled up his mount.

"I don't blame your horse, stranger," he called. "Not safe going in here for any animal. I reckon I won't be as much of a Samaritan as I intended, for I can't risk a fall. I'll go back to the city and send some one to you."

The young man turned and stood in the green dusk of the spruces with, it occurred to Lincoln, something extraordinarily eager and anxious in his gaze.

"It's only a step farther, sir," he urged, "and I'm in such haste to get back to the Capital!"

The President hesitated, his common sense and caution, struggling as usual with his kindness of impulse. And as he hesitated, Colonel Baker, on a dapple gray stallion, hurtled through the trees and brought up beside him.

"Get back into the road, Mr. Lincoln!" he ordered, covering the young man with his pistol as he spoke. "We've got the others, over in the swamp."

The President blinked, grunted and did not move. "What's the excitement about?" he demanded.

"Tell you later! Get back to the road, Mr. Lincoln, and tell Lieutenant Griffith it's all right. I'll follow as soon as I've handcuffed this lad."

"Looks as if I'd stepped into something," murmured Lincoln, obediently turning his horse.

The lieutenant with three other cavalrymen saluted him as the roan leaped the ditch into the road.

"Gave you the slip, didn't I, boys!" laughed the President.

"Only by a half hour, sir," replied the lieutenant.

"What's happened?" asked Lincoln.

"A plot to kidnap you, sir, to keep you from signing the edict of freedom. Mrs. Lincoln heard of it, and got it to Baker. We had no trouble trailing you, but it was pure luck that we pulled up when Colonel Baker saw you through the glasses, negotiating with young Cromwell. We've been watching him for weeks. Think he is a messenger between the Old Capitol Prison and Richmond.

"I need a nurse, all right, Lieutenant," sighed Lincoln. "Here comes the rest of them," as a group of cavalrymen rode out of the roads into the red afterglow. "Who are the prisoners, Baker?" he added, as the Colonel rode up at the head of the troop and he caught a glimpse of several men in civilian clothes in their midst.

"Captain Taylor's one, and young Cromwell another," replied Baker. "I haven't identified the other four."

"Sure one of them isn't Miss Ford in disguise?" added Lincoln, smiling grimly, as he started the roan off beside the detective.

Baker returned the smile. "I'll bet my leg and arm she's inspired every one of these men to this job. If the Rebels hadn't got hold of two of my best women and would make reprisal on them, I'd accidentally hang Miss Ford! She's the most lucid crazy woman I ever knew. Can outwit any three men now. Lots more to be accomplished by kidnaping you, you know, than by assassinating you!"

Lincoln rode heavily beside the colonel, all the glow of the afternoon dead within him. All the superstition in his nature had been roused and he was suddenly filled with a conviction that, somehow, Miss Ford would prevent him from signing the edict. For a moment, he found himself wishing that she could meet the just fate of a spy. But only for a moment. Willie had died in her arms! Was there no appeal he could make to her—? Perhaps, if he could talk to her, once more—

He turned to Baker, dim in the winter starlight. "Colonel, I'd like a word with Miss Ford. Will you take me to her this evening?"

The colonel hesitated. "I hope you won't insist on that, sir. It will excite her terribly and no good can come of it."

The idea that, somehow, he could subdue her had now taken firm hold of Lincoln.

"I reckon you'll have to let me talk to her, Baker," he said.

"Very well, Mr. President," reluctantly, "to-morrow."

"To-morrow!" cried the President, impatiently. "By to-morrow she'll have poisoned me or kidnaped me. She's welcome to me, after I've signed up. But until then, I'm a precious cargo for the ship of State. I'll see her to-night before I go to bed."

Baker half groaned an uneasy, "Yes, Mr. President!" adding, "I'll have to examine these prisoners, then I'll come for you with what information I can of her share in this."

"I don't need the information, Baker. I *know*. The woman is my evil genius. I'm going to make her understand that her desires and those of the Almighty differ radically in this matter."

He felt as if some bitter shadow was engulfing him,—all the vicious forces of anti-slavery focused on him, he thought, through this woman. Every slaveholder in the South thinking of him with hatred, and hoping he would die before the dawn of the next day! He was glad to reach the White House and the sanctuary of the sitting room, glad to have Mary scold him and weep over him, fondle him and tuck him up on the sofa before the fire while she sat beside him, holding his hand and stroking his hair.

"What you ought to do to me is to stand me in the corner for an hour with a dunce-cap on," he said, as the bleak feeling in his heart eased a little.

"Dunce-cap!" exclaimed Mary, scornfully, as she kissed him. "I'd have used that long ago if I'd thought it would affect you!"

He lay for a short time, enjoying her ministrations, then rose and went to his office, where his draft of the edict of freedom awaited his final attention. He worked on this until supper time, and after the meal was finished, went at it again, copying and recopying it, changing a word here, the punctuation there, rearranging sentences, listening as he worked, for Baker's arrival.

At midnight, a messenger came from the colonel, with a laconic note. Miss Ford had escaped from the Old Capitol Prison. Lincoln compressed his lips, and returned to his work on the edict. He made no comment when John Hay, looking in about one o'clock, remarked that there were enough detective police in the White House to fill the vacancies in the Army of the Potomac. About three, he took his Bible to bed with him. He slept uneasily, always with the vague consciousness of evil hopes and plans oppressing him.

The New Year's Day reception was scheduled to begin at eleven o'clock in the morning. Mary tearfully implored him not to attend it, but Lincoln by this time had achieved a fatalistic calm, quite different from his normal half-humorous self-possession, but none the less effective for that. Nothing, he reiterated to Mary, could change God Almighty's plans.

"He's going to let me sign this paper, Mary. What becomes of me after that needn't worry us. I don't imagine it worries Him! Let me see if I can't get the corrections done on it before I have to go down to the Blue Room. It could have a very bad effect on the country if I were to absent myself from an official reception as important as that."

He worked vigorously, revising the engrossed copy of the edict, until Mary, very handsome in a black grosgrain silk trimmed with beaded passementerie, came to fetch him.

For three hours, he shook hands with an unending, never-pausing stream of people. The line was showing no sign of attenuation, when, about two o'clock, Baker came up behind him and whispered in his ear:

"We've got her!"

With one great stride, Lincoln stepped back of the bank of ferns and fuchsias before which he had been established, carrying the detective police with him.

"Where is she, Colonel?"

"In the basement. She got a job as an extra nigger, a man waiter, for to-day. She cut her hair, blacked her face. I didn't recognize her myself till they washed her up." The usually cool and unemotional Baker wiped his dripping forehead. "Never put in such a night in my life! I absolutely knew we'd find her in this building."

"So did I!" nodded Lincoln. "Let me see her now, Baker."

The detective looked up into Lincoln's face. "Not necessary, sir. She's dead!"

"Dead!" gasped the President. "Who slipped on that, Colonel?"

"She did herself," replied Baker, dryly. "Her disguise was so good that one of the nigger wenches in the kitchen tried to kiss her. For the first time, Miss Ford broke through her part. She slapped the wench and there was a mix-up during which Miss Ford received a knife in her back. It wasn't till then my men came to! Sometimes," with bitter sincerity, "I wonder why a detective thinks he has any chance beating fate."

"I want to see her, Baker," insisted Lincoln.

"Very well, sir, that can be managed. We'll work back through the state dining room." He led the way down the servants' staircase crowded with hurrying waiters, through the kitchen where great kettles of coffee steamed to the low ceiling, through the sculleries where half a dozen black wenches slopped cups and spoons about in tubs of water, to the woodshed, where was the clean smell of chips and kindling.

Near the open doors, through which one saw the wintry kitchen garden, the seedling table had been dragged and on it under a red checked kitchen tablecloth lay the unmistakable outline of death. A uniformed guard moved out into the areaway, at a nod from Baker, leaving the President and the Colonel alone. Lincoln turned the covering back.

The dye had disappeared and the short hair that clustered round her face was chestnut again. She was curiously unchanged, her beauty unmarred.

The President, arms folded on his breast, stared down at her. She had been removed, his evil genius! How unutterably just were the methods of Heaven, which had permitted her own desperate antipathies and desires to bring her to her end! And yet, had it not been for the blight of slavery, how lovely, what a supreme work of the Creator, she would have been. Lincoln felt his eyes sting and there were tears on his cheeks when he turned to Baker.

"My children loved her. Willie died in her arms. Baker, I want you to get her a decent coffin at my expense, and see that she gets buried out on her plantation where the rest of her folks lie. Will you do that for me, Colonel?"

"Yes, sir! I'm glad to," replied Baker, promptly. "She was the cleverest spy I ever ran up against and I'd just as soon show my respect for her ability as not."

Lincoln lifted the tablecloth back over the face.

He did not return to the Blue Room but went up to his office. He closed the door behind him and stood looking about him. He had the feeling of one who after a tremendous and dangerous journey, has reached his goal. The details of his office, for so many months unheeded, suddenly appealed to him as curiously pleasant. A rich coal fire crackled in the grate, casting a red glow on the scarred oak Cabinet table and on the two dogs, Sumter and Pensacola, sleeping before it. Snowflakes drifted thickly past the window and their hush was no deeper than the sudden peace that lay on his heart. He was to be permitted to achieve the great beneficence. Now, Lord, let Thy servant depart in peace.

There were a dozen people in the room who had risen at his entrance; members of his Cabinet, his young secretaries, Mary and Taddie. He smiled at them and moved toward the edict, which lay at one end of the Cabinet table. He rubbed his right hand vigorously.

"These fingers are almost useless from handshaking," he said. "Mustn't let my hand seem not to be firm when I do this job."

He sat down slowly and read several paragraphs aloud wondering if they were as nearly perfect as he could make them. He was not completely satisfied but at the moment could think of nothing more to add or subtract:

". . . I do order and declare that all persons held as slaves within said designated States, and parts of States, are, and henceforward shall be free; and that the Executive government of the United States, including the military and naval authorities thereof, will recognize and maintain the freedom of said persons. . . . And upon this act, sincerely believed to be an act of justice, warranted by the Constitution, upon military necessity, I invoke the considerate judgment of mankind, and the gracious favor of Almighty God.

"In witness whereof, I have hereunto set my hand and caused the seal of the United States to be affixed."

He lifted his pen.

"Let me hold the ink bottle, Papa day!" cried Taddie. "Let me!"

The little fellow eagerly lifted the ink from his father's desk and held it while Lincoln dipped in the pen and wrote, firmly,

"Done at the city of Washington, this first day of January, in the year of our Lord one thousand eight hundred and sixty-three, and of the Independence of the United States of America the eighty-seventh.

"ABRAHAM LINCOLN."

With Malice Toward None

CONTENTS

CHAPTER I

A MAN OF INFINITE JEST

SOME ONE shouted, "Fire! Fire! Fire!"

Lincoln, who was standing beside the turnstile in the fence between the grounds of the War Department and the White House, talking to Vice President Hamlin exclaimed, "By Jings!" and pointed to a pink glow above the roof of the Executive Mansion.

Running figures appeared from nowhere, the vanguard of that mysterious crowd which seems to exist only to attend conflagrations. A fire engine belching sparks clanged up Pennsylvania Avenue. The President leaped across the snow-encrusted flower borders of the garden. Hamlin followed. Lincoln's first thought was that here was more of ten-year-old Taddie's mischief. Tad's mother had spanked him that very day when she had found him under her bed smoking one of the cigar ends Seward always was leaving about. It looked to the President as if the east side of the White House were in flames. With Hamlin running easily beside him, he rounded the south portico and immediately exclaimed in relief:

"Oh, the stables! Hope the coachman and the horses are out. There's the coachman, so he's safe!"

In spite of the efforts of mounted guards, people were climbing the iron fence that bounded the grounds. By the time the President and the Vice President had passed the long colonnade that housed the woodsheds and the other kitchen offices, there was a large crowd watching the flames shoot up from the stables, lying beyond the kitchen gardens. People gave back slightly as Lincoln and Hamlin appeared in the brilliant orange light.

The two men were, in this year 1863, the same age, fifty-four. Hamlin, a little over six feet tall, was magnificently proportioned and as lean and powerful as an Indian. In fact, he looked not unlike an Indian with a touch of the Roman in the boldness and regularity of his features.

The crowd was not much impressed by the arrival of the Chief Executive.

"King of America!" some one called in a sneering voice.

Lincoln gave the Vice President a humorous glance. "Must be referring to you, Hamlin! *You* look the part."

Hamlin smiled grimly and with a slight jerk of his head remarked, "Yonder is one who not only looks but feels the part!"

Lincoln's gaze followed the gesture. "Why, it's Charles Sumner! What's he doing here? You're right, Hamlin, he'd be an ornament to my job."

In spite of the excitement of the conflagration, the Senator from Massachusetts was making an impressive approach.

"The man who would be king!" cried the same voice that had been heard before.

Sumner did look the part. He was of equal height with Lincoln, six feet four inches. His whole person breathed elegance and authority. His very gesture as he came to pause, of wrapping his blue broadcloth cape about him, was made with an air of superiority that went well with the dignity of his beautiful face and head. He was clean shaven and his eyes were blue even in the fire glow.

As for Lincoln, although the snuff-colored riding clothes and the high riding boots were of the best mode—his wife saw to that—there was nothing regal in Lincoln's appearance, unless one caught the noble lines of brow and cheek, the depth of the blue gray eye. Nothing of the king, yet Sumner looking at him with a suddenly appraising eye was moved to say:

"King to the commonalty. Whose phrase is that, I wonder?"

Lincoln scarcely heard the query for there was a sudden outcry from the stables.

"They *haven't* got the horses out!" he ejaculated. "They're screeching like women! Burke!" plunging toward the coachman, who was shrieking something incoherent into the ear of the fire chief. "Burke! Tie wet gunny sacks over their heads. I'll show you."

Hamlin caught the snuff-colored sleeve and Sumner put a well-gloved hand on Lincoln's shoulder. He did not struggle against them but he said pleadingly to the fire chief, "My boy's ponies are in there! I'd rather lose the White House than those two little horses, Chief!"

"We'll do all we can, Mr. Lincoln," gasped the fireman whose red shirt was dripping sooty water. "The heat just drove me out. I'm going right back."

Another dreadful outcry and the sound of beating hoofs came from the flaming caldron. Lincoln shuddered. "I can't stand it! Poor beasts!" He turned away. "We're no help here, Hamlin. Were you on the way to my house, Senator?" As he spoke he started along the path, to the east, thinking to swing round the colonnade and gain the north entrance to the mansion.

"Yes, Mr. Lincoln," replied Sumner, following through the snow and slush. "I've been talking with Secretary Seward about that last note from France on intervention. Letting the French minister visit Richmond was a grave mistake. I must have a denial of intent on your and Seward's part to present to the Senate in the morning, if you'll be so— Good God!" as Lincoln clutched his arm and pointed.

They had passed the stables and were moving through the north garden before the colonnade which was brilliantly lighted by the burning buildings beyond. A little figure in red was darting across the end of the colonnade which housed the carriages.

As it dropped from sight, "Tad! come back!" shouted Lincoln.

He leaped forward followed by Sumner and Hamlin. Before they had taken half a dozen strides, the child reappeared swarming up a ladder to the roof of the cow shed, adjacent to the stables. Holding his flannel nightshirt around him, he danced up and down on the icy roof, halted for the moment by his father's cry. His chestnut hair was like a crimson halo round his excited little face.

"I'm going to get Willie's pony, Papa day!" he shrieked, his voice thin and hysterical. "I'm going my sec'et way!" Tad could not pronounce his Rs. He turned and with unbelievable swiftness scrambled up the slippery roof to the air vent in the rear wall of the stable. The three men staring up at him roared in chorus, "Come back!" Taddie gave no heed.

"You see, sir, this is what comes of not teaching children to obey!" exclaimed Hamlin.

Lincoln groaned and leaped to the ladder. Being of Taddie's own manu-facture, it broke with his first step upward. Hamlin darted away, crying, "I'll get a ladder in a moment."

"Give me a back, Charles," said Lincoln.

The Senator stooped and Lincoln swung up on the roof just as the tail of Taddie's shirt fluttered into the vent. Lincoln was about to drop on all fours for the scramble upward when a little voice arrested him.

"Go back, Papa day, go back or you'll slip and bust yo' neck."

Sumner's voice came from below. "Thomas Lincoln, if you lead your father into danger your mother'll punish you as you've never been pun-ished before!"

"But Willie's pony! Willie's pony!" shrieked Tad. "Excepting Pensacola, that's all the flesh and blood we got left of Willie. I'm going, I tell you, I'm going!"

"Don't move, Mr. Lincoln. I've arranged the ladder and I'm coming up," came Sumner's voice urbanely. "I can manage him."

Lincoln hesitated on the brink of the glowing icy sheet that sloped up to his boy, torn between deadly fear for Tad and chagrin over his own predicament. Here, indeed, was one of the critical moments between him and one of his children that Mary was always warning him would come and would find him impotent. The Senator was now beside him, breathing heavily. He had been subject to attacks of angina pectoris ever since Brooks had assaulted him in the Senate seven years before. His great voice now rolled forth as Lincoln had heard it so often in moments of passionate debate:

"Thomas Lincoln, if you don't come down, I'll come up and break my malacca over your nether end!"

Tad's head appeared in the opening, his face distorted by anger and tears. He edged slowly down to the roof. "Willie's pony!" he sobbed.

"Hurry!" roared Sumner.

Tad slid downward to his father's arms.

A moment later, when Hamlin appeared with a ladder and two firemen, the rescue had been completed and Lincoln was leading the way once more toward the north entrance.

"Mr. Sumner performed the miracle," explained the President, "but at cost to his poor heart, I'm afraid. Better come in and lie down, Senator."

"No, thank you, Mr. Lincoln," replied Sumner, "I'm quite able to go home. You'll let me have that denial of intent in the morning!"

"Yes! Yes! And a thousand thanks to you!" exclaimed the President.

Sumner moved slowly but steadily enough toward the gates and Lincoln turned to the Vice President:

"He's as irresistible as the Mississippi in flood, isn't he, Hamlin! Come in for a moment, will you, while I finish the sentence the fire interrupted." He led the way into the vestibule and stood beside the little Baltimore heater used by the doorman, still holding Taddie.

"You were warning me that Charles Sumner was my enemy, Mr. Hamlin, and I was telling you that you were wrong. Sumner thinks I'm slow and he doesn't care about my manners. He doesn't agree with me fully on my reconstruction ideas. He's often annoyed by my lack of knowledge about laces and glass pots and steel engravings. But at bottom, he's my friend. He wouldn't work against me in an underhanded way. I love Charles Sumner. My wife and our two boys are devoted to him. He's always round the house, here."

"That being the case"—Hamlin unbuttoned his overcoat, nervously— "why did Sumner come to me to-day and ask me to run against you for the Presidency next year?"

Lincoln suddenly seated himself on the bench opposite the heater. He felt the need of physical support. Had Hamlin told him that his beloved chief secretary John George Nicolay had turned against him he could not have been more hurt.

"Oh, come, Hamlin! He must have been joking you! I can't swallow that!"

"Then you can't swallow Lyman Trumbull, Ben Wade, Winter Davis, Horace Greeley—" began Hamlin.

Lincoln interrupted. "I know all about those fellows. But not Sumner. No, Mr. Hamlin, not Charles Sumner!"

"Very well, sir!" Hamlin's deep voice was troubled. "I would very much dislike being quoted in the matter, but you'd better tell Sumner what I've said and get the answer from his own lips."

"I don't like to do that!" protested Lincoln. "I don't want to start an issue with Sumner."

The Vice President made an impatient gesture with his mittened hand. "In making no issue, Mr. Lincoln, I beg of you, don't deceive yourself. Sumner would prefer me in the White House, or Chase, or himself, to you. And understand me clearly. I shan't run for the Presidency. I don't want the job. I don't like the one I've got. I'd rather be back in the Senate this minute than anywhere else on earth."

Lincoln loosened his neck scarf with a ruthless forefinger. "This is worse than telling me General Hooker has mired the Army of the Potomac as deep as Burnside did. I need Sumner in Congress. I've hardly a friend up there and I was depending on him."

"Your war with Congress, Mr. Lincoln, is almost as serious in its effect on public morale as the war with the South. You—"

Hamlin was interrupted by the sudden appearance in the inner door of a slender youth in evening clothes.

"Oh, there he is! Father, mother's frantic. She missed Tad only a few moments ago and she's coming right out to look for him. *Nothing* can stop her. I'm sorry, Mr. Hamlin," with an apologetic smile and bow for the Vice President.

"Coming this moment, Bob!" exclaimed Lincoln, rising and smiling down at Tad who during the conversation with Hamlin had been half sniffling, half listening in his father's arms. "Jings, I'd forgotten the child! Good-night, Mr. Hamlin!" He started hastily into the hall, followed by his son Bob.

Half way down the private staircase he met his wife. She was a dignified little person, even in a black padded dressing gown and with great chestnut braids hanging over her shoulders.

"What *does* this mean!" she cried. "Bob, I told you he'd gone to the fire and caught his death's cold, the bad, bad boy."

Tad's snivelling suddenly changed to hysterical shrieking.

"For goodness' sake!" groaned Bob. "Let's move this scene of domestic bliss where it won't bring in the newspaper reporters!"

Lincoln, who had been steadily mounting the stairs, strode down the upper hall to Tad's bedroom. His wife followed. Bob, who was only nineteen, remained rigid with disgust at the head of the stairs.

Lincoln dropped Tad down on the bed. Mary thrust her husband aside, turned Tad's flannel gown up and spanked him heartily. It was exactly the restorative he needed. In a moment, he was sitting up, quietly wiping his face with his father's handkerchief and drinking the milk his mother had set to heat on the hob the moment she had discovered his absence.

Lincoln watched the two, smiling. Tad's escapades and his mother's handling of him were one of his chief amusements. The large square room was shadowy but an enormous hobby horse could be seen in the corner nearest the bed and ranks of toy soldiers marched resolutely across the hearth where the coal fire glowed. Mary's round cheeks were as pink as a girl's. Her beautiful blue eyes in which, as she ministered to her son, her irrepressible sense of humor struggled with a temper of which Taddie's was the replica, were dancing with excitement. Tad, who was like his mother not only in disposition but had also her round face and delicate, sensitive mouth, gulped his sobs with his milk and proclaimed his innocence of any desire to drive his mother to her grave with worry. It was Willie's pony—!

Sudden tears filled his mother's eyes. She stooped and kissed the child's quivering lips. "If the pony's gone up to heaven to join Willie, let's be glad for both their sakes."

"Oh!" gasped Tad. "I hadn't thought of that—" There was a long silence while he absorbed the idea.

His father tiptoed into the hall and across to the sitting room where Pensacola and Sumter, Willie's and Tad's hound dogs, lay as usual asleep on a sofa. He gathered them up in his arms and made his way back to the bedroom.

"There," dropping them on the bed. "All you boys go to sleep!"

A moment of patient waiting on his father's and mother's part—and Tad was in dreamland with a dog on either side of him. Mary turned out the light, Lincoln caught her fingers and they crossed into the President's bedroom which was just opposite. It was lighted only by the crackling fire that brought out highlights on the fine old rosewood and mahogany furniture with which the great room was filled. Husband and wife stood warming their fingers before the blaze.

"Was there anything especially bad at the War Office, Abra'm, that kept you so late?" asked Mary.

"Nothing unusual. Things look as black as they well can. I believe General Hooker can make the Army of the Potomac fight. Whether or not he can keep tavern for a vast army is another matter. Stanton is dissatisfied with him already. I hope Stanton's not going to get one of his hates against Hooker. I don't know where I should turn."

"You'll have to turn to some one soon who'll lead the Army of the Potomac to a real victory or the country will turn completely against your administration," said Mary, succinctly.

"I can't *create* a general, my dear wife!" protested Lincoln. "I remember one of Speed's stories concerned a fellow who advertised that he could make a new man out of an old one and have enough left over to make a little yellow dog. I wish I had the fellow's address. Perhaps if he left in the material for the dog, he could turn me out a general who could stand on his own legs."

Mary laughed. "Goodness knows you've got plenty of old gentlemen in the army to choose from!—but the fruitless slaughter is sapping the country's morale, Abra'm."

Lincoln sighed and said nothing for a moment as he thought of his disappointment in Burnside, whom he had appointed to succeed McClellan in the Army of the Potomac. However, it was a comfort to remember that though he had dallied long in taking off McClellan's head, he had not closed his eyes to Burnside's weaknesses but had given him only a few weeks of trial before replacing him with Hooker. And Hooker was showing little genius, thus far. He shook himself to throw off the familiar miasma and chuckled as he said:

"Hooker's latest remark is that what the country needs is a dictator both for the army and the Government. I told him that only those generals who obtain success could set up dictators; that if he'd give me military successes, I'd risk the dictatorship— He's a handsome fellow."

"So is McClellan," commented Mary, drily. "They're all so childish! As a matter of fact, since you've absorbed what your General-in-Chief knows of the military art, you're the best of them all. Charles Dana told me so."

"Oh, he's just prejudiced by his liking for me." Lincoln shook his head with a sigh. "I think Grant is a coming man in spite of his present unpopularity."

"Grant is a butcher!" exclaimed his wife. "That's why the public is against him."

"Grant *fights!*" insisted the President, but with a sick pang as he thought of the frightful losses that followed in the little General's wake.

"You might feel differently about him if your own kin were in his army," protested Mary.

"Has Bob been talking to you again?" asked Lincoln.

Mary turned a startled face up to him. "No!" she gasped. "Abra'm, don't tell me he's talking enlistment again."

"I haven't had any real talk with him since he appeared on the scene this morning. But I reckon that's what he's come down from Harvard for. There's blood in the boy's eye, if I know the boy. Am I right, Bob?" as their first born put his head in at the door.

"You sometimes are, sir," he replied with his father's own twinkle in his gray eyes. He was of medium height with his mother's elegance of carriage, a curiously quiet face more like his mother's in outline, yet marked by a baffling and inescapable look of his father. He joined his parents before the fire, slipping his arm about his mother.

"What is it you want, Bobbie?" she demanded, suspiciously.

"Can't I hug you without wanting something?" asked Bob with an injured air.

"Never since you were a baby!" retorted his mother.

"Well, then, I do want something. I want to enlist. I want to go just as a private with no preferment because of father. I can't bear to be cloistered up there at Harvard when all my friends are doing their share at the front. I can't stand it and I won't." He tossed his hair back from his forehead with a jerk. His mother turned to face him, her lips quivering. But before she could speak, Bob went on: "And I don't want to wallow round hopelessly in the mud with the Army of the Potomac, either. I want to go out to Grant."

"No!" shrieked his mother.

Lincoln put his hand on her shoulder. "Don't lose your grip on yourself, Mary. The boy's right in his desire. I'm glad he has it. But," smiling down into Bob's belligerent eyes, "you're only nineteen, son. Wait a year for your mother's sake."

"You can't go! It'll kill me!" sobbed Mary. "Baby Eddie and Willie both in their graves. I can't be asked to spare another son."

"They didn't die to save father's Union," protested Bob.

"If they had, I'd have been reconciled," said his mother.

The boy looked up at his father with helpless exasperation in his eyes. Lincoln shook his head. This was an old scene. A year ago Bob had begun his pleading and now his every visit home was marred by this contention with his mother. He was utterly weary of this struggle between the two.

"Mary," he said slowly, gripping both her shoulders and stilling her sobs with what Mary called his "granite" look, "Mary, we'd better let him go. I honor him for feeling as he does."

"Abra'm! Abra'm!" screamed Mary.

"Hush! Oh mother, for pity's sake, the servants will hear you!" Bob ran across the room to close the hall door.

But it was not Bob's expostulation that silenced her. It was the continued look in her husband's eyes. She suddenly put her hands before her trembling lips and waited.

"Bob isn't going without your consent, wife. But you're going to be a woman—certainly not less a woman than these countless other mothers North and South. Bob, you go back to Harvard for another year, then I'll give you a commission and mother'll let you go, eh, mother?"

"I—I'll try!" gasped Mary.

"But I want to go as a private!" Bob flushed.

"Never! Never!" from his mother.

"But, mother, can't you see what a position you put me in? It's bad enough up there in Cambridge to be the President's son, but to be the President's son and a coward—it's Hades, that's what it is!"

Lincoln eyed him a little hopelessly. Bob had all his mother's sensitiveness and all her restless energy.

"I swear," he ejaculated, "you two are worse than a pair of brigadier-generals to manage! Every inch of you covered with corns. You say all your friends are fighting, Bob. Yet your buddy, Edgar Welles, is still in college."

"His father's only Secretary of the Navy. So much isn't expected of him. And besides, he really does some important things for his father and that contents him. Secretary Welles sends him on secret missions that're important." Bob sighed.

"That's true," mused Lincoln, "and Edgar, as near as I can see, isn't one whit steadier than you. It's hard for me to realize you're grown, Bob. You're still the little rare rip whose nose was always running."

Bob managed a feeble grin. His mother eyed the two with unabated anxiety.

Lincoln went on. "I reckon I haven't been taking advantage of the material in my own family! Bob, you go up to Harvard till the Easter holidays. Don't make any plans for visiting during that time because I'll have an errand for you to do."

The grin on Bob's face widened. "Really important, father?"

"Will it be dangerous?" pleaded his mother.

Father and son looked at each other. "It'll be a full-sized man's job," replied Lincoln.

A sob caught in Mary's throat. She started toward the door that led into her room, hesitated, turned and said, "It's just because I love you both so! I'd give *my* life to save the Union, any time, but I can't spare either of you." Then she left them.

Bob held out his hand. "Good-night, father. I'm off early. I'll see you in April."

Lincoln grasped the firm young hand and looked keenly into the clear young eyes. "You go and make it up with your mother, Bob. She carries the dirtiest end of this load in Washington. Don't ever forget that."

Bob nodded and crossed into his mother's room.

Lincoln, undressing slowly, was comfortably aware of their voices but this could not lift his weary depression. Everything he had touched, everything he had planned and prayed for in the past two years, except the Emancipation Proclamation, seemed to have gone awry. He was a potter who could mold only crooked pots, he told himself grimly. And even the Proclamation was heartbreakingly slow in getting military results. The belief he had had that it would bring vast numbers of negroes over to the Union lines had not been fulfilled. Men, colored or white, were needed so badly by the North that the cold sweat started to his forehead as he thought of the imminence of his having to enforce the draft on unwilling Northerners.

But these facts were no sudden burden. They had been accumulating gradually and somehow his shoulders had developed strength sufficient for the load. It had been endurable. But the fact divulged by Hamlin that night, concerning Sumner, he told himself was pretty near a last straw. As he stood by the fire in his dressing gown the significance of it came home to him, making him feel actually ill.

All his plans for saving the Union included Sumner and Sumner was not his friend! Nay, more, Sumner was seeking to undermine him!

He groaned and, laying his arm on the mantel, dropped his head against it.

A clang of a bell and a clatter of hoofs roused him. The fire engine was going home. He looked at the clock. Ten minutes past two. He hoped the sudden clangor had not wakened Tad. But as he raised his hand to turn off the light, there was a sound of whimpering, the hall door opened, and Tad in the red nightshirt appeared.

His face was screwed into a knot as he rushed to his father. "Papa day, I had a bad d'eam. I thought the stables bu'ned up and Willie's and my ponies—"

Once more Lincoln lifted him. "Sh! Sh! You'll wake mother, darling Tad."

"Let me get in bed with you, else I'll d'eam it again!"

"That's a good notion," agreed his father. "I've been having a nightmare myself. We'll protect each other."

He laid Tad on the bed, turned out the light, opened the window and got in beside the child. Tad nestled against him, and as the moon sank slowly below the window ledge father and son fell asleep.

CHAPTER II

HEEL OF ACHILLES

TAD was in good form the next morning. The family dining room was a cheerful spot, full of flowering plants and singing birds. With the birds and Tad competing in eloquence, the whole story of the events of the previous night came out. Horror-stricken though she was, Mary laughed immoderately as the little boy lisped through his tale. She seized on the opportunity to produce one of her inimitable mimicries.

"Thomas Lincoln," she quoted, raising both her plump arms in Sumner's familiar gesture, "Thomas Lincoln, if you ever again make such a little fool of yourself, I shall add your father's malacca to the Senator's."

Even James, the colored factotum, passing buckwheats to the President, grinned while Tad and his father shouted. After a moment Mary suddenly returned to her own character and said, thoughtfully, "Mr. Sumner ought to have a dozen children of his own."

"Can't find a woman good enough for him, I suppose," suggested the President, finishing his coffee.

"He hasn't that attitude at all," contradicted Mary. "Mrs. Seward and I have often wondered if he didn't have an unfortunate affair in his youth."

Lincoln replied, as he rose from the table, that he was not inclined to be sentimental over the Senator's past, and added, "I hope Sumner's future doesn't hold an unfortunate affair for Lincoln!" He left Mary blinking.

As he made his way up the private staircase and along the upper hall to his office, he told himself that he'd enlighten Mary about Sumner when they were alone that night. Then he tried to put the matter out of his mind.

His office, which was also the Cabinet room, was just shabby enough to make Lincoln feel at home in it. It looked south over the marshes to the Potomac. Lincoln liked rivers. They had belonged to his boyhood. His desk stood at right angles to one of the windows. The huge old oak Cabinet table monopolized the center of the room. Mary had tried to hide its scars with a red felt cloth which Tad had promptly spattered with ink. There was a good fire crackling in the grate this morning under the portrait of old General Jackson. A sleet storm was beginning; had already obscured the red Virginia hills. Perhaps the storm would be violent enough to keep people from pestering him, Lincoln thought hopefully as he seated himself at his crowded desk. He picked up a telegram and began to wonder before he read it whether or not Sumner would call in person for the report on the French Minister's indiscretion. Perhaps he'd better ask the Senator, point blank—

He was interrupted by Billy Stoddard, one of his three secretaries. Billy, a tall, slender youth, a good deal worn by the anxieties of his work as mail clerk and first buffer between the President and the public, smiled at Lincoln.

"I know you hoped for a quiet day, sir, but the reception room's jammed already. I was going to hold everybody off for at least an hour but Messrs. Wade, Chandler, and Trumbull have just arrived and are whanging and banging and winding the horn for the drawbridge to be let down."

"I'm sorry my old friend Trumbull's turned on me," sighed Lincoln. "He has too much brain to be taking the course he is with those other two. However, war makes strange bedfellows. If Trumbull ever makes up with me I'll ask him if it's because he's heard it's bad luck to sleep three in a bed. Tell them I'll see them shortly, Billy." He rose, suddenly determined to tell Mary about Sumner now. The thing just wouldn't leave his mind and perhaps she'd have a helpful suggestion. "I'll be back in ten or fifteen minutes," he added, and, rising, made his way into the private passage that led to the family sitting room. This was the President's favorite apartment in the Executive Mansion. Oval in shape, it faced south with a view of the marshes and the Potomac to the hills of Virginia. Its furnishings were old and hybrid. Heavily upholstered couches of President Monroe's régime shouldered the Sheraton chairs of the Adamses' occupancy and the clumsy Empire tables left by the Van Burens. The Brussels carpet in faded reds, greens, pinks, and blues had been laid by the Pierces. It was a rather hopeless mixture from the artistic viewpoint, but it spoke to Lincoln of the domestic life of his predecessors and made them his friends. He was glad that beyond renovating the room, Mary had left it alone. She kept it filled with flowers. Her rare understanding of plants had caused the White House conservatories to bloom as never before.

A bright fire of cannel coal blazed in the grate. Sleet slashed the windows. The odor of a great bowl of white freesias filled the air. Mary was arranging a basket of moss roses on the round table in the middle of the room. She looked up at him with an interrogatory smile.

"I suppose Sumner would know the name of every flower and plant in the house," said Lincoln, pausing before the fire. "Confound the fellow! Lord Lyons told me the other day that when Sumner visits England he tells the natives more about their trees and shrubs than they know themselves. I reckon when you and he run short on French, you talk the 'language of flowers' to each other!"

Mary laughed heartily. "We haven't run short on French yet but that's a valuable suggestion.—What's on your mind about him, Mr. President?"

"I came in to tell you." And in a few crisp words he repeated Hamlin's statements.

Mary dropped her roses and stood staring at her husband, horror, unbelief, and pain following each other across her face.

"Abra'm, there's some mistake! I can't believe it! What motive could he have?"

Lincoln, pulling at his chin, replied dejectedly, "I think, or rather I hope, that mainly he doesn't understand what I'm trying to do."

"Of course he understands!" insisted Mary. "But he's an Abolitionist, and your slow methods exasperate him."

"There's more fire than that behind Hamlin's smoke," shaking his head. "Mary, I just don't see how I can bind the Union together, either now or after the war, without Sumner."

"Do you believe he's strong enough to lose you the renomination?" asked Mary quickly.

"If the Union defeats continue for another year, yes."

"Can't you compromise with him, somehow?" she suggested.

"No!" thinking aloud. "He'll never compromise. If Sumner's my enemy—" He paused, shaking his head.

Mary lifted her chin defiantly. "He's not your enemy! He must have tried to be facetious with Mr. Hamlin. And Charles Sumner trying to be funny is terrible. He says the most insulting and the most insane things, under the impression that he's being playful. You know as well as I do how his lack of humor handicaps him. I don't think he's capable of intriguing, Abra'm. He's as guileless as a child."

"So'm I," declared Lincoln, grimly, "and I'm up to my scruff in intrigue all the time."

"You! Guileless!" Mary sniffed and began to rearrange the roses, but almost immediately dropped them and bit at her fingers, tensely. Then she said, "Is Sumner actually indispensable to you, Abra'm? What worries you most, the fact that he may prevent you having a second term, or that he won't work with you to save the Union?"

"I reckon they both mean the same thing in the long run," replied the President. "You see, I've always counted on him. But particularly since I signed the Emancipation Proclamation last month he's seemed to want to work with me. Mary, I've got to have Sumner."

"Then you shall have him!" Mary squared her small shoulders and brought her small fist down on the marble-topped table. "I don't know how I can help but I will. Incidentally, I've asked him with Alice Hooper and her father-in-law to join us in our box at the theater to-night."

"Do I know Alice Hooper? Any relation to Congressman Hooper from Boston?"

"Only his daughter-in-law!" replied Mary. "Don't you remember her at the Sewards' dinner the other night? She is tall and blonde and young with wonderful yellow hair. Her husband is on General Banks' staff in New Orleans."

"Yes! Yes! Gave me the tips of her fingers and a cold stare! Friend of Sumner's, isn't she? I think I heard some one say so."

"Mr. Sumner almost lives at Congressman Hooper's house. Alice is there with her little daughter during her husband's absence. She's socially very brilliant." Mary tapped her lips softly with a stalk of freesia.

"That lets me out, then," grunted Lincoln. "Perhaps I'd better bring Sumner here after the theater and have Hamlin's rumor out with him."

"No! No! Let him make the first move. Take your own time, my dear!" coming over to pat his arm. "Perhaps when you've had time to think this over it won't seem so nearly fatal."

Lincoln shook his head impatiently and then put his great hand on her shoulder, while he repeated with that enormous earnestness which never failed to convince his hearer,

"Make no mistake about the importance of this, Mary. It was pretty bad when my old friend Lyman Trumbull went back on me and joined up with ultraradicals like Ben Wade and Winter Davis and the rest of those fellows who want to exterminate the Southerners. But I could hitch along without him, as you see. He's no such power in the Senate and the country as Sumner is, though he's a smart man. Sumner, if he wants to, can keep me from saving the Union even though we win the war. Now do you see why I'm so upset?"

"Yes, my dear husband, I see," replied Mary soberly. She reached up to straighten his tie. "I'll do all I can to hold him for you. Perhaps some plan will come to me before a crisis rises between you and him."

"That's what I came in to hear you say, Mary." He smiled down at her, glanced again unseeingly at the telegram in his hand and turned abruptly back to his office.

Nicolay was waiting for him; rather a sallow young man with a little dark goatee and a beautifully modeled forehead and brow. He wore the same anxious, overtired air that had been so marked in young Stoddard but his smile as he spoke to the President was brilliant.

"Trumbull, Wade and Davis wouldn't wait for you, Mr. Lincoln. Senator Sumner and General Butler were here during your absence. Butler wanted Sumner to say a word to you about restoring his command in New Orleans. He was in a terribly excited state; talked so wildly that Sumner dragged him away."

"Afraid he'd kick over a beehive, I suppose," said Lincoln, as he settled to his desk again. "Sumner's always trying to advance Butler; wants the General's political support."

"That's just what Butler did—kicked over a beehive!" exclaimed Nicolay. "I'm wondering if there's anything to what he said. I think I'd better tell you, sir."

"Fire away, George!" Lincoln waited with interest.

Nicolay walked up and down in an excited way as he talked. "Well, after Butler had cussed out you and Secretary Stanton for not restoring him to New Orleans in spite of the French resentment over his Woman Order, to say nothing of the English, Sumner added fuel to the flame by saying that you'd told him you could accomplish more in the way of reconstructing Louisiana through a soft-spoken fellow like General Banks than through the fire-eating General Butler. Butler slammed his kepi on the floor when he heard this. 'God help the Union,' he roared. 'Soft spoken! Why, those fellows down there look on softness as fear. We've got to treat them as the conqueror always has treated the conquered, or there'll never be an end to insurrection. Confiscate their estates and give them to the niggers! Transport the Secessionists and their families to Texas or Mexico!'—and a good deal more along that line."

"What did Sumner say to it?" asked Lincoln eagerly.

"Mr. Lincoln," replied Nicolay, hammering his fist into his palm, "Sumner nodded and said that that was the only way to handle reconstruction of the seceding States; to give the land and the vote to the negro and he'd come to full manhood at a single stride. I couldn't stand that so I remarked that no such double gift would be made to the negro while Abraham Lincoln occupied this room. And Butler came back at me like a charging bull. 'Then we'll put Hannibal Hamlin here as Sumner suggests. Hamlin doesn't see the nigger and the alligator as social equals!' Sumner grabbed him then and rushed him out. Do you believe Sumner has turned on you, sir?"

Lincoln did not answer directly. "I'd say the beehive was turned upside down," was his comment as he turned from Nicolay to stare out the window.

It looked as if he'd have to believe that Sumner was about to head the movement of Lincoln's own party against Lincoln. The party and the country were sick of this war of Union defeats. And every day that Grant dallied before Vicksburg, every hour that Hooker held the Army of the Potomac inactive while he waited for the mud on the Rappahannock to dry, added to the general discontent with Lincoln, the Commander-in-Chief, and strengthened Sumner's hand. It looked as if he must face the idea that he'd have only the two remaining years of his term of office in which to end the war and rebuild the Union, only two years in which to purge and purify the conquered States and weld them into the whole so that never again could secession lift its head; Sumner had well named the process reconstruction.

With all possible speed, he must give the handful of Union men always to be found in each conquered State a chance to restore their State governments. But this was impracticable unless he had immediate victories. If only there were men enough to feed to Grant! Grant who fought and slaughtered and attended to his own business. More men and more men—God help the poor boys! He shivered and suddenly was conscious of Nicolay watching him sadly.

"George, this colored man, Fred Douglass. Have you ever heard him speak?"

"No, sir, but I know he's considered powerful by the Boston Abolitionists. Secretary Chase might be able to tell you about him. He had Douglass at his house for tea not long since. Charles Sumner was there."

"Chase is a great Secretary of the Treasury," commented Lincoln drily.

"I'd place Sumner as one of the greatest Senators we've ever had. But I'd never take the estimate either one of 'em made of another human being. They've got no feelers. George, I wish you'd arrange for Douglass to come to see me as soon as you can."

"Does he come secretly, Mr. Lincoln?"

"Certainly not. Get Sumner or Chase or Hamlin to bring him to my office here and let me have an hour or two alone with him. Who's outside now?"

"A group of men from Boston headed by Wendell Phillips. They want to protest against your dilatory prosecution of the war. There's a woman weeping her heart out. Wants a reprieve for her son. Half a dozen other women not weeping. Ten or fifteen of the generality as you call them. Better let me take care of the lot of them."

"No! No! I'll see what they think about things. Give me the weeping widow first and the Boston set last."

In spite of the weather it was a particularly crowded day. People's deep depression made them restless, made them turn to him as the ultimate authority, with every sort of plea, made them crowd him with impossible suggestions and with preposterous claims and recriminations. He took dinner about three o'clock on a tray in his office, and did not stop for supper till Tad came for him at six.

The storm was over when the Lincolns started for the theater. Their sleigh carried them through a world of icy beauty until it encountered F Street. This unpaved thoroughfare was completely blocked by a train of eight-mule army wagons stalled in the half frozen quagmires left by gun carriages. The moonlight, the flickering lanterns, the kicking mules, the cursing drivers made a more cheering picture than the President had seen that day.

He called to Burke to stop the sleigh. "I can tell those contrabands in a minute how to straighten out their mules," pushing back the buffalo robe.

"Abra'm, don't be a fool," snapped Mary, pulling the robe back vigorously over her husband's knees. "You're in evening clothes and you happen to be Chief Executive, not Chief Mule Driver. Get along, Burke! Turn down to Pennsylvania Avenue."

"Maybe you're right, wife," agreed Lincoln, amicably. "But it wouldn't have taken me half a minute to point out to those drivers that swearing at one another instead of at the mules is plumb foolish."

"Yes, and you'd have provided the newspapers with another priceless bon mot. 'Lincoln finds his level, etc.' Anyhow," snuggling against him, "I want to enjoy this sleigh ride with my beau. Do you remember our first sleigh ride?"

"Yes," replied the President, promptly. "I cut Steve Douglas out and took you home in Steve's own cutter from Edwards' cotillion party. We drove two or three miles out into the prairie just from sheer deviltry."

"You do remember!" Mary gave a contented sigh and for a moment they bumped along Pennsylvania Avenue without speaking. It was picturesque and they both enjoyed it; the cavalryman beside each street lamp, the lines of soldiers entering the gayly lighted oyster bars, the ambulances with mounted drivers, street hawkers, newsboys, galloping aides and the glitter of ice on tree and roof.

Mary gave herself a little shake. "Well, I must come back from Springfield and give you a little gossip I've picked up. Mrs. Seward told me to-day that it's being whispered about that Charles Sumner has a very sentimental attachment for Alice Hooper. I want you to watch them together. If this is true there may be a spot in Achilles' heel by which I can get a real hold on him."

"Now, just why should you want me to bother with a thing like that!" demanded the President. "You know as well as I and all the rest of the world that Sumner is so much above an unwarranted interest in a married woman—"

"Who said there was anything unwarranted in it!" interrupted Mary, indignantly. "But if it gives Alice Hooper an influence on Sumner and I can get her ear—"

"Oh, nonsense!" ejaculated Lincoln.

Mary moved away from him. "Very well, sir! You come to me another time for help!"

The President gave a comfortable, low laugh. "I undoubtedly shall!"

"You'd better not!" snapped Mary, and refused to speak again during the few minutes remaining before they reached the theater. They were a little late though they had tried as usual to be a little early, for it was always something of an ordeal for Lincoln to enter the lighted box and there be greeted by the audience coming to its feet. It was worse than usual to-night, for during the rather perfunctory salutation a man in the dress circle shouted, "Nero fiddles while Rome burns!" There was a spatter of "Bravos" at this, quickly drowned by cries of "Shame! Shame!" A group of soldiers in the front row just beneath the stage rushed up the aisle shouting, "Put him out!" They seized the offending gentleman in the dress circle and hustled him to the door, filing back just as all opera glasses were again trained on the President's box. Charles Sumner was entering with Mrs. Hooper on his arm. Lincoln rose and led her to the chair beside his.

She was a truly beautiful woman of the fine blond type that New England occasionally produces; very tall and slender with thick golden hair worn in curls over her shoulders, with large, light blue eyes heavily shaded, with a faultless skin and delicately perfect features. She wore a low-necked frock of pink satin with an enormous skirt caught up with rosebuds. The Senator arranged her ermine coat carefully over the back of her chair then seated himself between Mrs. Hooper and Mary.

Before any conversation could take place the curtain rose on Maggie Mitchell in "The Cricket on the Hearth." Mary had been reading Dickens aloud to Lincoln that winter as a substitute for Petroleum Nasby in those stark night hours when he sometimes appealed to her for help. Nothing could have suited him better this night than this exquisitely homely play. As the curtain went down on the first act, he turned to Mrs. Hooper.

"How that fellow does understand human nature! My wife's read the 'Cricket' to me and the 'Pickwick Papers.' Dickens has a lot in common with Shakespeare, according to my reading of the two men. Old Weller and Falstaff! Both of 'em tavern clowns of a kind you meet anywhere. Take any character of Dickens or Shakespeare. They're so close to reality you're certain both men picked 'em out of the crowd from actual people. Maggie Mitchell is great. My old, dried, withered eyes are full of tears yet."

"It does seem a pity," said Mrs. Hooper with a sigh, and with one eye on Sumner, "that the British dislike us so when we have such an ardent admiration for their literature."

Sumner cleared his throat but Mary forestalled him.

"One has to distinguish between their literature and their politics!" she exclaimed. "Knowing Lord Lyons has taught me that. Socially, I'm quite in love with him. Politically, I think he's disgusting. When I read British books and plays I admire everything British. When I read their speeches against the Northern cause and see the vile cartoons of the President that *Punch* publishes, I could bite them."

"It's best to base your friendship for men or nations on something that politics can't taint," said Sumner. "Bitterly disappointed as I am in the English attitude toward us, nothing shakes my essential admiration for them. It's their way of thinking that's made England the cradle of the world's liberty. You mustn't let the ebullitions of rather stupid politicians influence you, Madam President!"

"Good heavens, Senator, this from you!" ejaculated Mary. "What of your turning against Mr. Seward and Charles Francis Adams and—"

He interrupted her with a dignified toss of his great head. "Doesn't that prove what I've just said? It's evident I've made no solid basis for my friendship there."

"I shall never dare to differ from you on politics again, Senator!" exclaimed Mrs. Hooper, touching him archly with her pink feather fan.

Lincoln, listening with only half an ear, was brought back by suddenly observing a boyish blush on Sumner's face as he bent toward Mrs. Hooper and said with great tenderness: "You'll make me very unhappy, Alice, unless you convince me that you dare to talk to me about any or everything."

"Jings!" thought the President. "I wonder if Mary's right as usual!" and as Sumner continued to gaze tenderly into the blue eyes turned up to his, "Some one ought to wake him up. Talk about me providing bon mots for the public!" with a glance at the opera glasses leveled toward the box. He looked at Mary. She returned the look with an unmistakable I-told-you-so expression. He smiled at her and her lips twitched. Peace was declared.

Mary touched Sumner on the knee.

"Isn't that Lord Lyons nodding at you from the dress circle, Mr. Sumner?"

Sumner with a sigh followed her gaze. A moment later Lord Lyons entered the box and Mrs. Hooper devoted herself to him during the remaining intermissions. Just as the curtain dropped on the last act, a message came from Secretary Seward to Lincoln. The French had landed an army in Mexico. Lincoln left Mary in the care of Lord Lyons and hurried off to Seward's house. It was long after midnight when he reached home.

He sent for Sumner the next morning and gave him the news.

"I suppose Mr. Seward has already sent off a provocative note to Louis Napoleon?" was Sumner's first remark.

"Seward'll do nothing without my approval," replied Lincoln, a little impatiently. The nearer Sumner came to truth in his comments on the Secretary of State, the more, Lincoln told himself, it irritated him.

Sumner raised his eyebrows and smoothed back his mane of waving chestnut hair with the gesture that was the unfailing joy of sarcastic newspaper men. "This will please the South, inordinately," he said.

"And this will please a lot of fire-eating Northerners," added Lincoln, "that whole set of blind boasters who declare we can lick all of Europe in spite of our difficulty in reducing the rebellion. Mark my word, Senator, some fool will get up in a day or so in Congress and declare war on France. Can you scotch the debate? Better still, can you head it off?"

Sumner spoke quite simply. "I can block the passing of any resolution, of course. Perhaps I can block debate, also, if you think that's advisable."

"With M. Mercier ready to misinterpret and Lyons ready to be grieved—I certainly do think it's advisable!" said Lincoln earnestly. Then he added a little sternly: "Are you whole-hearted about this, Senator? Your sympathy for the cause of liberty in Mexico doesn't give you any desire to help the Mexicans drive the French out?"

"Good heavens, Mr. Lincoln!" Sumner rose from his chair by the President's desk. "I pride myself on being a practical politician.—Good morning, my dear," looking down, with a smile that showed splendid teeth, at Tad who had rushed into the office and seeing his friend had seized his great white hand with both his small grimy ones.

"Senator!" shouted Tad, "the old cat just had fou' kittens in the woodshed and the coachman's dog, Alice, just had nine puppies in the cow shed. Won't you and Papa day—"

Sumner put an arm around the little boy's shoulders. "I don't like Alice for a dog's name, Taddie."

"Don't you?" looking up gravely into the Senator's blue eyes. "He named it after the song, 'Alice, whe' a't thou,' because she is always wunning away. Maybe if I asked him to he'd change the name. What would you like, Senator?"

"I had a very pleasant little dog once named Mischief," suggested Sumner. "She was a brown water spaniel."

"That's a nice name," declared Tad, "I'll go find Pete Kelley and we'll have a cwistening."

Sumner stooped and kissed the eager little fellow. "Thank you, Taddie! And who's Pete Kelley?"

"He's my chum. He lives on 13th Street. His fatha's a wealthy tin man. He twades pots and pans and makes stove pipes and all things like that. I can't say his name well so I call him Pete."

"Perry Kelley," volunteered Lincoln, who sat before his desk watching the little by-play.

"That's Pete!" nodded Tad. "He and I a' going to make a stage in the state bedwoom." He gave his father a violent kiss, rushed across the room and slammed the door after him.

Sumner picked up his tall hat.

"Do you want me to have Seward send you the papers he has on the matter, Senator?" asked Lincoln, following him toward the reception room with a wistful reluctance to let him go.

"I prefer to deal only with you on the subject, Mr. Lincoln," replied Sumner.

"Very well," agreed the President, then he added in a low voice, "Taddie and Bob and Mrs. Lincoln don't complete the list of your lovers in this house, Charles,—without regard to political bias."

Sumner paused and his lips twitched as if with pain. "Thank you, Mr. Lincoln," he muttered, and strode from the room.

That afternoon, Senator McDougall of California offered resolutions in the Senate condemning the French invasion of Mexico and requiring the immediate withdrawal of the French troops. There was an instant eager rousing of the fire eaters. But Sumner with a superb short burst of oratory on the madness of a proposal which would indirectly offer aid and comfort to the Rebels tabled the resolution almost before the Senate as a whole knew what was happening.

Nicolay who had gone up to keep an eye on things for the President described the episode to the anxious Lincoln. "He's the noblest Roman of them all, Mr. Lincoln," he concluded.

"Yes! Yes!" replied the President. "I dread to lock horns with him."

"Humph!" ejaculated the secretary, lifting a huge roll of war maps, "he's the only one worthy of your steel,—just to mix figures of speech a bit!"

CHAPTER III

LINCOLN did not at once go on with his work after Nicolay had left him. He sat thinking over what he confessed was his cowardly attitude in letting slip opportunity after opportunity to bring into the open the issue between him and Sumner. He feebly tried to excuse himself by murmuring that after all he was like Daniel Webster, who had said so often that he fought principles and not men. This being true, why not forget Sumner's charm and look on him as the embodiment of the danger of disunion; call him to the office and bring him to book, by Jings, as an enemy to the Union!

We-e-ll, perhaps not so harshly as that! Why not try a little of this famous diplomacy of which there seemed to be an oversupply in Washington at present. Let some one else draw the truth out of Sumner. Hah! That was the idea! He brought his fist down on his desk and with a grunt of satisfaction wrote a note to Sumner asking him to come to the Executive Mansion the following afternoon for tea. He next made a careful list of names with a memorandum instructing Nicolay to send an invitation to each for tea at the same time. The list included Seward, the Secretary of State, with whom Sumner was quarreling in a dozen matters, "Father" Welles, Secretary of the Navy, who was irritating Sumner by his attitude on privateering, and Lord Lyons, whose relationship with Seward was marked by a courteous endurance that often disturbed even Seward's suavity and caused the latter to make the eagle scream a little more frequently than good taste required. It had the makings, Lincoln thought, of a party wherein several beehives might be kicked over.

But when the President wandered into the sitting room at five o'clock the next afternoon, it was Mrs. Seward and not the Secretary of State who stood before the fire. Lincoln liked and admired Mrs. Seward. She was tall and gracious and a philosopher! One would have to be a philosopher, Mary said, to have such utter patience with the brilliant and facile-minded Secretary as did his wife. She wore black, as usual, over a conservative crinoline. Lincoln hated these abortive petticoats.

"I gave a woman a job for her trifling husband this morning," he remarked, as he ranged himself beside Mrs. Seward, "for no other reason than that she didn't wear hoops."

"The first money her husband earns will certainly go for one," exclaimed Mary, glancing complacently at her own ballooning skirts. "Does Mr. Welles make your life miserable for you about your hoops, Mrs. Welles?" rising to greet this much-loved friend.

Mrs. Welles, whose quiet beauty was Mary's special admiration, smiled as she glanced down at the lavender silk flounces that concealed even the tips of her slippers. "The Secretary of the Navy is a great martinet everywhere but in his own home."

"I don't think Mr. Seward knows the difference between a hoop and a bonnet. You're the crinoline connoisseur of the Administration, Mr. Lincoln!" said Mrs. Seward.

"I've a notion to recommend in my next annual message that they be abolished by act of Congress," declared Lincoln, looking from one attractive woman to another and sipping his tea with great enjoyment. "Not casting any reflections on the delightful nature of this party, as Sumner would say, I'd like to ask what's happened to it? I gave Nicolay a list of men, only, who were to be asked here this afternoon. Who bribed Nicolay?"

"Mr. Welles feared he couldn't get away so I came to bring his probable regrets," said Mrs. Welles. "I always use any excuse to come to one of Mrs. Lincoln's teas. First in the hope that Mrs. Lincoln will be inspired to mimic some one, and second because her cook's a genius at tea cakes."

"Mrs. Welles has spoken for me!" agreed Mrs. Seward. "Ah, here's some one to help balance the crinolines," as Lord Lyons came in.

He was a rather heavy man, smooth shaven, with dark, phlegmatic features, redeemed by very brilliant dark eyes. He wore a black broadcloth coat over silver gray trousers. Lincoln, a little disheveled and in his brown office clothes, shook hands with the Englishman, not entirely unconscious of the contrast between himself and the minister.

"This is good of you, my lord. Was Sumner with you this afternoon, by chance?"

Lyons moved toward Mary and the tea table. "I've just left him, sir. He spoke of coming here, very late. I was to tell Mrs. Lincoln," bowing over her hand, "that he'd promised a little girl, the granddaughter of Representative Hooper, to take her for a ride to Rock Creek. And that promise had to be kept. I hope I've made my answer as meticulous as Mr. Sumner's explanation to me was."

"Isn't that just like Charles Sumner!" exclaimed Mary, as she poured a cup of tea for the minister.

"He's infatuated with the child," said Mrs. Seward. "One can hardly blame him. She's a lovely little thing. She is the image of her mother, so Mr. Sumner, of course—" She paused and a significant smile went around the room.

"Queer he's escaped matrimony so long," said Lincoln. "He's a great hand for the women. I can't reconcile what I see of him round here with what Sam Hooper told me. He said that when Sumner was young he was no ladies' man at all; was just a queer, awkward cockerel, all shank and no crest, like I was."

"But, Mr. President, the ladies always have admired Mr. Sumner, so they must have admired you," said Lyons with a smile. "I hadn't the privilege of knowing you in your youth, but I did know Sumner. I was a mere boy but I remember that on his first visit to us he was the sensation of England. Upon my word, I can't recall a like case. He came to England, a young man in his early twenties, with one or two unimportant letters of introduction. He wished to study international law. Within two months of his arrival he'd become the rage. He must have been overwhelmed with the invitations he received if he hadn't been then, as he is now, of such sound mental integrity. We'd never met an American like him, old or young, so learned, so ardent, so modest, with such a brilliantly acquisitive brain. The men discovered him first and then the ladies! Upon my word, I've heard my mother say he could have had his choice of the best of them. It's a pity that the years have wrapped him in cold dignity."

"He told me once," said Mary, "that his family and most of his friends opposed his taking that trip. I often wonder how our relations with the British would be faring to-day, if the friendships made by that unknown young Charles Sumner weren't alive and vital, a blessed bulwark against complete misunderstanding."

"Hear! Hear!" cried Lyons.

"So I tell my husband," sighed Mrs. Seward, "and he agrees with me and would be so glad to keep friends with dear Charles. But they just can't see eye to eye on our diplomatic relations and I'm always looking out the window to behold the Senator's tall back expressing high dudgeon about something or other!"

"Just now it's privateering!" chuckled Lincoln. "Sumner against and Seward for. They've got the Cabinet taking sides and as usual I've got the thankless job of making a decision."

"I suspect Mr. Sumner of being right," said Mary.

Mrs. Seward sighed again.

"Mr. Seward and he are too funny together," Mary went on. "The other day I watched them debating near the turnstile. Mr. Seward with his necktie under one ear— Ah—" interrupting herself, "here is the Senator to defend himself," as Sumner burst into the room.

"A treasure!" he exclaimed to the company at large. "Here's the first three cantos of Henry Longfellow's translation of Dante's 'Paradiso.' I always thought it dull in the original, but Henry gives it true fire and poetic spirit. Let me read you a little of it." Without throwing off his fur-lined cape, he began:

"Longing already to search in and around the heavenly forest . . ."

But his voice was husky and after a page or two he handed the manuscript to Lincoln. "Go on with it, sir, while I clear my throat with tea. Rock Creek was damp."

Lincoln put on his spectacles and moved nearer the lamp. He read as well as did Sumner although his voice had a less robust quality than the Senator's. Sumner was greatly stirred by the lines, kept murmuring comments to Mary Lincoln, and waved his hands to the cadence of the verse.

"Henry and I always planned to make that translation in friendly competition," he exclaimed as Lincoln came to a pause. "I'm thankful that he, at least, has been able to fulfill the dream."

"I've burst into poetry once or twice myself," admitted the President. "Of the three worst poets in the world I'm at least two, I reckon. It never would have occurred to me, however, that you'd had like aspirations."

"I wished for nothing so much as to devote my life to letters," confessed Sumner, sinking back in his chair with a sigh. "I'm never free of a sense of frustrated hopes."

"And I," exclaimed Mary, "always wanted to be an actress of the Maggie Mitchell type."

"You've real talent for acting, Madam President," Lyons nodded heartily. "As for me, I wished to be a painter, a Landseer, if you please."

"Do you still paint? Have you any of your work in this country?" asked Mrs. Welles.

"Heaven forbid! to both questions, dear Mrs. Welles!" ejaculated the Englishman. "None of my daubs are in existence."

"How do you know your mother hasn't got one tucked away in some obscure bureau drawer?" demanded the President. "Did you ever know a woman not to keep souvenirs of her son's genius? Now, you take Mrs. Lincoln and our Bob— What is it, James?" as the servant hesitated beside him.

"Massa Secretary Welles jus' can't get here, Massa Lincum, sah."

Mrs. Welles rose at once. "He shall not escape the dinner party at our house to-night, if I have to go for him myself!" she exclaimed.

"I think I may as well intrude on the privateering situation," said Mrs. Seward. "The Prussian Minister is dining with us and I must see that Mr. Seward's tie is *not* under one ear!"

Lord Lyons accompanied the two women from the room. As Sumner stood alone on the hearth, Lincoln viewed him with a half sardonic eye. "Lincoln arranges parties," he thought, "and God disarranges them. I feel like a woman who knows her hour has come!" He seated himself beside the tea table and waited for Sumner to speak.

The Senator began the instant James closed the door on Lord Lyons. "Mr. Lincoln, will you allow me to be utterly frank with you?"

The President felt his muscles stiffen. Was Sumner going to confess and as simply as this? Life, after all, allows very few retreats. . . . Well, better get it over with.

"You're all out of patience with me, eh, Mr. Sumner?" he asked.

Sumner looked from Lincoln, disheveled and weary, to Mary, whose eyes glowed with excitement although she sat calmly enough before her teapot. His throat worked in an unwonted manner. There was a wistfulness in Lincoln's blue gray eyes and a sensitiveness about the thin upper lip that may have made him loath to strike.

"My attitude has nothing personal in it, Mr. Lincoln," said Sumner. "Personally, I have a horror of the task I've imposed on myself this afternoon. Only the same overwhelming conviction that swept me into the anti-slavery fight years ago could have whipped me into the position I'm in now with regard to you."

"Get on with it, Sumner! I accept your apology," said Lincoln, drily. He began to run his little ivory paper knife through his black hair; a sure indication of a moment of stress with him. "Let's not have any elocution about it."

"The better element of your own party as well as the same class of the general public are thoroughly dissatisfied with you as our Chief Executive, Mr. Lincoln. You are not enforcing the Emancipation Proclamation as it should and could be enforced. General Banks in New Orleans and Andrew Johnson in Tennessee are playing with that vital promulgation."

"Here it comes!" thought Lincoln.

Sumner swept on. "You're too fearful of offending different factions. The Northern Democrats, the border States, this, that and the other chimerical consideration holds you back. I agree with the general feeling that while we have entire faith in your integrity, you're too slow of action for the present crisis. While you hesitate and your generals procrastinate, the peace party thrives and at any moment the war may end with slavery still on our hands. We have no faith in slavery being forever destroyed under your rule."

He moistened his lips, glanced at Mary, who sat motionless, and went on. "Knowing, as many of us do, Mr. Lincoln, how utterly impersonal and unselfish your attitude toward the nation is, we ask you to show your patriotism to the full by—" He hesitated, then finished firmly "—by resigning from the Presidency."

Mary gave a little scream. Sumner, the great moral leader of the North, the foremost statesman, the most commanding figure in the whole political field, had turned thumbs down on Lincoln, the President. Perhaps some inkling of the enormity of his request touched Sumner for he was as pale as death and breathed heavily.

Long years before, during one of the numerous wrestling matches by which he had achieved young fame, Lincoln had received a terrific knee blow in the groin. It had been a friendly bout. The youth with whom he was contending was a neighbor of whom the young Lincoln had been very fond. Yet the blow had been given deliberately. If he lived to be a thousand, Lincoln never would forget the shock, not only physical but mental, that this foul had given him. Never since had he experienced anything that approximated a like sensation—until this moment.

He felt the room rock about him. He brushed his hand across his eyes. Then he looked up at Sumner and said quietly, "You've upset me." Sumner would have spoken but Lincoln raised his hand for silence and Sumner subsided. "Before I reply to your request, Mr. Sumner, I'd like to ask a question or two. You've picked on Hamlin as my successor. What makes you think Hamlin can handle the South after the war so that Emancipation won't be a dead letter?"

"You've touched on a vital point, Mr. Lincoln," replied Sumner. "In choosing Hamlin, we choose a man who recognizes that reconstruction belongs to the Congress and not to the President."

Mary started to speak but Lincoln laid his hand on hers and she subsided, cheeks scarlet, blue eyes blazing.

"In other words," said the President, "you'd be able to control reconstruction yourself, Senator?"

"I'd be permitted to do my share, which I'm not now nor would be under your régime," very gravely.

"That is to say," Lincoln suddenly leaped to his feet and pointed a long finger at the Senator, "that is to say, you think you're better qualified to handle a bruised and heartbroken South than I . . . you who've just admitted you've no bowels of compassion for those who differ from you! And you actually think that an attempt to thrust civic equality of the negro down those Southern throats already choked with sobs is going to insure civic equality to the negro for the future? Sumner, it's against human nature. I tell you that every gesture that the Congress will make to confiscate the plantations for the negro sets back his enjoyment of equality another ten years."

"Great God!" Sumner's arms shot toward the ceiling. His face was contorted. "Maudlin sympathy with the greatest crime—"

Lincoln interrupted. "Never mind the oratory, Senator."

Sumner, arms still in the air, stared at Lincoln, amazed and indignant.

Lincoln drew himself to his full height, dropped the ivory paper knife into his vest pocket and said very softly and clearly, "I'm not going to resign."

Sumner slowly lowered his arms and groaned, "God help the negro!"

"He will!" Lincoln nodded. "But I intend He shall help him during the next two years by showing Abraham Lincoln how to save the Union."

Sumner picked up the Dante manuscript and thrust it into the pocket of his cape. Mary and Lincoln watched him, motionless. The clock on the mantel chimed six. Sumner bowed.

"Then, Mr. Lincoln, I will wish you good-by. And you, dear Mrs. Lincoln, who have been so kind a friend and hostess, I must say good-by to you also."

Mary made him a sweeping bow and stood with her nose in the air, watching him make his very dignified exit. Then she threw herself into her husband's arms.

"Abra'm! Abra'm! What shall we do to him?"

Lincoln held her close and patted her back. "Mary, we'll make him come back to us if we can. In fact there's no if about it. As I've said before, I've got to have Sumner."

"What will he do next?" asked Mary, moving away from Lincoln to look anxiously up into his face. "Will he try impeachment?"

"Not in the midst of war, I reckon," replied the President. "That would be too much like stopping to set a rat trap while the house was burning up. Even Congress must see that. Well, thank God, that's over. Now I know what I've got to fight."

CHAPTER IV

CREATED EQUAL

SHORTLY after supper that evening, Billy Stoddard came into the office and closed the reception room door behind him to say in a low voice:

"Mr. Hamlin has just come in with Fred Douglass, sir, and the other visitors are making it uncomfortable for Douglass. How about taking him into the secretaries' office?"

"Bring him in here," returned Lincoln.

With a little smile, Stoddard went out. A moment later Hamlin entered, followed by a tall, well-built colored man in the conventional black broadcloth frock suit. Douglass was handsome in a brooding and tragic way. The story of his heroic struggle was written in the distrustful curve of his thin, well-cut mouth and in the unbelief of his dark eyes: eyes set far apart under quizzical brows and a broad forehead. His nose was the Indian's rather than the negro's, well arched, with close nostrils. His high cheek bones and hollow cheeks gave his whole face the look of austerity that marks the thinker rather than the fighter. His chin was concealed by a short black beard and his whole aspect was rendered doubly striking by the mass of black hair that stood up like a great halo round his head.

Lincoln shook hands with him. "I reckon we need no introduction, Mr. Douglass. You were a long time getting here."

"I've been up in Canada, Your Excellency. I was in hopes that some of the fugitive slaves up there would come back and help me preach the gospel of freedom. I was much troubled when I learned I'd been keeping Your Excellency waiting."

"I'd rather be called plain Mr. Lincoln, if you please, Mr. Douglass. Sit down and let's talk. How about the draft bill, Hamlin? Will it go through before the session ends?"

"It'll go through to-morrow," answered the Vice President, sinking into the Cabinet chair next to the one Douglass had taken, while Lincoln took the rocker and slowly elevated his feet to the mantel.

"I sweat when I think what enforcing that measure'll mean," he mused.

"Papa day," called Tad, curled up on a sofa with his kitten, "you wememba what motha said about you' feet?"

"Jings, yes!" exclaimed the President, dropping the offending members. "Will the bill go through as I last saw it, Hamlin?"

"Yes, Mr. Lincoln," replied Hamlin who had twisted about to glare at Tad.

"I've been out of touch with the papers," said Douglass. "Will you tell me if you draw the color line in the bill, Mr. Vice President?"

Hamlin turned back to the fire. "All able-bodied male citizens between eighteen and forty-five are made subject to call after July 1, 1863. Drafted persons can furnish a substitute or pay $300 bounty for exemption!"

"I don't like the bounty idea," commented Lincoln, "but Chase is jubilant over it. Says it will be a full meat course to the Treasury." He turned abruptly to Douglass. "Mr. Douglass, how do you and your colored friends feel about the Emancipation Proclamation?"

"That it's thoughtful, cautious and well guarded," answered Douglass.

"Come now, that's no answer!" cried Lincoln. "The average run of colored man thinks nothing of the kind."

Douglass smiled. "You asked me what I and my friends thought, sir! Most of my people are enthusiastic, if they are anything. I was in Boston on January first with that great mass of people of every color waiting in Tremont Temple to hear by telegraph whether or not you'd signed the Proclamation. It was midnight before word came over the wire, 'It's signed!' People all over the hall began to sob for joy. It looked for a little while as if we could find no other way to express our feelings until a colored preacher with a glorious voice jumped up and began to sing 'Sound the loud trimbel o'er Egypt's dark sea, Jehovah hath triumphed, His people are free—' Everybody joined him. It was superb—this report pleases you more, doesn't it, Mr. Lincoln?"

Lincoln stared at Douglass. This was like no negro he'd ever known. There was no least trace of servility here. Come to think of it, this was the first time he'd ever observed the man beneath the mask of bondage, the first time he'd seen the negro as he showed himself to his own race, never to the white. Douglass actually was sneering at him!

Lincoln found it more stimulating than irritating. He glanced at Hamlin's anxious face and thought with amusement that the Vice President would like to give Douglass an admonitory nudge.

"I'm going to the wrong barrel for soft soap, eh, Mr. Douglass?" he said. "You're not grateful to us for the Proclamation?"

Douglass' tragic face softened. "There's not a colored man who knows of you who wouldn't die for you, Mr. Lincoln, but we wish you weren't so timid. We don't believe you'll really finally end slavery when it comes to reconstructing the Union."

"Et tu, Brute!" grunted Lincoln. "What would you have me do?"

"Organize colored regiments at once on an exactly equal status with white regiments. Let us fight for our freedom ourselves," replied Douglass quickly.

"Colored men have larger motives for being soldiers than white men," declared Lincoln grimly, "and should be grateful for a chance to enlist on any terms."

Douglass leaned forward, his hands on his knees and spoke across Hamlin as though he and the President were alone. "Mr. Lincoln, this war is something the white race has brought on itself by its own hoggishness. So the negro feels. And unless you understand clearly how we feel you will never be able to enforce emancipation or handle reconstruction. It's very hard for us negroes to feel gratitude toward any but God. As a race we have no more inherent loyalty to the whites than they have to us. But we're not fools. We see in this war an opportunity to break our chains and you can't offer us a task too hard for us to tackle. But for God's sake, offer us tasks as you'd give them to men and not to beasts of burden."

James came in to renew the fire just as Douglass finished his plea. His black eyes widened as he saw Douglass, and as he heard his words he dropped the tongs with a clatter that caused the kitten to spit and Tad to giggle.

"Tad," said Lincoln, "you go ask your mother for a plate of those Vermont greenings."

"I'll fetch 'em, Massa Lincum, sah," proffered James with alacrity.

The President nodded and looked broodingly into the flames for a moment before he said, "I've never tried to fool myself about this war, Mr. Douglass. I know we're working out in bitter humiliation the sins of two hundred years. We're drinking the dreadful cup to the dregs. But all this being acknowledged, I still in my humility must face facts as facts. And one fact is that white folks up to now have had an insuperable prejudice against using negroes in the army for anything but servants. I've no such prejudice myself but I've felt I must wait until our need for men was so great that colored soldiers would be welcomed before forming negro regiments."

"Surely that time has come now, Mr. Lincoln!" ejaculated Hamlin. "Our regiments hardly average more than four hundred men. The country's in despair over its losses."

"I can't see why you're so sure colored men would enlist," said Lincoln, looking not at Hamlin but closely at Douglass. "All efforts to organize black troops last year proved, if not actually abortive, at least ineffectual. I'd hoped after the Edict of Freedom was signed that Fortress Monroe and Yorktown might be garrisoned by colored troops to free the whites for weak spots where they're badly needed. But out of all the colored population down there, General Dix found only four or five willing to take up arms. They said they'd work but not fight."

"They're too close to their old masters down there!" exclaimed Douglass. "They fear reprisals. Try Massachusetts negroes."

"Why don't they come North?" insisted Lincoln. "Why has the Proclamation failed to bring them over the line?"

"Most of them have never heard of the Proclamation," answered Douglass. "The South would see to that."

"Ah! now we're getting down to the marrow!" exclaimed the President. "Douglass, how shall we get word to those people that it's time to come over into Canaan?"

"More than a word's needed, sir! There must be a promise that they shall not only be free but shall have equality. If you'll assure me of that, I'll go down into the Richmond country myself, even though I'm liable to be taken as a slave, and spread the tidings. You'll see them swarm across the Red Sea then."

"How can I promise any such thing!" ejaculated Lincoln, his heart sinking at this reiterated shortsightedness with all its implications. "Who can know the Southern attitude on that matter better than you? We can free the slaves by winning this war. We could give them the vote. But you know and I know that we'd have to exterminate the whites in the South before we could give the slave the kind of equality you want. I can't give them that equality. If they are given freedom, and when they've had education, the right to vote, the rest they'll have to earn through the generations to come—and that you and I or our children won't see, Douglass."

The colored man twisted his work-scarred hands together in a gesture of despair. "Oh, that Sumner or Chase were here in your place, sir!"

Lincoln shook his head impatiently. "And you actually believe that a scratch of my pen, or Sumner's or Chase's at my desk there, would change your color to the only shade the white has ever been willing to acknowledge covers his social equal? God knows, I want to see the negro eventually enjoy every civic right and privilege, Douglass, but—"

"'Scuse me, Massa Lincum!" James, almost as black as his clothes, his round face twitching with excitement, appeared before Lincoln with a huge plate of apples which turned to green bronze in the firelight. "'Scuse me but I got to have my say, sah! An' I'm going to say I ain't one of those niggers that's always wanting to set at the white man's table. I got my freedom and Massa Sumner's fixed it so's my chilluns and all colored chilluns is getting a white schooling right hea' in Washington. If you'll fix it so's my chilluns when they's grown kin hev the vote so's to help make the laws they live under, that's all I want. And what's more, Fred Douglass, his own self, knows if he went down below the line and gathered together all the niggers for a thousand miles and tried to lead 'em North, he couldn't lead 'em. Niggers is so jealous among theyselves they don't want to trust or help out a nigger that's gone ahead like Fred Douglass. There's Massa Sumner! What does he know about colored folks? He's too good to 'em. You're the one that knows 'em, Massa Lincum. Not Massa Sumner, or Massa Chase, or, 'scuse me, Massa Hamlin!"

He paused and banged the apples down on the scarred oak Cabinet table, then waved his arm toward the sofa. "You might better give little mischievous Massa Tad over there the vote than the niggers the way they are to-day. Those Southern Massas would make the niggers vote theyselves back into slavery again! I'm telling you truth. Yassa!"

He crossed to the sofa, lifted the sleeping Tad and the purring kitten into his arms and disappeared into the private passage into the living room. No one spoke until Lincoln broke the silence.

"What I wanted to propose to you, Mr. Douglass, is this. Are you willing to organize a group of intelligent colored men into a company of scouts who will scatter themselves through the South and tell the slaves what we're trying to do up here and ask them to come up and help us fight?

I'll guarantee to make them into soldiers, eventually, if I can just get the right men to officer them."

"I'll supply you with one white officer now!" exclaimed Hamlin.

"Who's that, Hamlin?"

"My son, Captain Cyrus Hamlin. He and a group of his friends, such as the sons of James Russell Lowell and Thomas W. Higginson, are tormenting the life out of me to get you to let them raise colored regiments and go under fire."

In Hamlin's face was a touching mixture of pride and sadness.

Lincoln felt quick tears flush his eyes. These New England Abolitionists! Of such stuff were martyrs immemorially made. All his caution was not proof against this.

"I'll give you a letter to Stanton to-night to let Cyrus go ahead. The passing of the draft bill to-morrow is going to put a different face on the negro soldier question, anyhow." He took a huge bite out of an apple.

"Do you mean it?" shouted Hamlin, jumping to his feet. As Lincoln nodded, Hamlin placed pen and paper before the President with one sweep of the hand. "Write that order now, sir, and I'll take it to my boy this minute! How about your boys, Mr. Douglass?"

"My three sons enlisted last year, Mr. Hamlin," replied Douglass.

Lincoln wrote the order and signed his name and smiled up at Hamlin who seized the paper and departed almost at a run.

"You haven't answered my question, Mr. Douglass," Lincoln said, when they were alone.

"I'm afraid our friend James answered for me, sir," replied Douglass. "I would need a white man identified in their minds with you to accompany me South, else the slaves wouldn't believe me."

Lincoln finished his apple and threw the core into the fire. "I think I can help you out there," he said finally. "My oldest son Bob is a level-headed fellow, almost through his law course at Harvard. How would it do for him to go along with you?"

Douglass stared as though he couldn't believe his ears. "Will your son agree to that, Mr. Lincoln?"

"If Cyrus Hamlin can do his job, I reckon my son can do his," answered the President.

"Then, Mr. Lincoln," exclaimed Douglass, "all I can say is that all that I have is at your service." He rose as the President rose and after a moment in which he fought to control his quivering lips he added, "Sir, Mr. Secretary Chase has had me eat at his own table. Senator Sumner, John Brown, Wendell Phillips, have fraternized with me. And yet, in spite of our topic of conversation to-day, you're the only man who's ever made me for a moment forget the curse of my color."

"The thing I don't like to remember is that it's we white men who've made a curse of that color," said Lincoln. "But be patient with us, Mr. Douglass. We're trying to make it right—with our heart's blood." He shook hands and added, "You work out a scheme and come to me when it's finished." He walked with Douglass to the door, came back and looked at his watch. He must see the waiting folk in the reception room before reading the dispatches on his desk and it was now nine o'clock. He rang the bell for Stoddard.

Although the break with Sumner was now the most consuming of Lincoln's anxieties, it was impossible for him to give to it the best of his thought. The public dissatisfaction with himself and with his generals, particularly with Grant, pressed upon him with ever-increasing violence and would not be ignored for a moment, day or night.

A few days after his momentous five-o'clock tea party, he asked Nicolay to bring him the week's vintage of aspersions on Grant's character and ability. Nicolay's solemn face did not change as he with James' help brought in two great baskets heaped with telegrams and letters.

"Here's a part of 'em, sir," he said as they emptied the baskets on the Cabinet table. "I'll bring more when you're finished. We've divided them into States. These are all from Wisconsin, Iowa and Illinois. The newspaper comments aren't filed as yet."

Lincoln grunted, took a turn or two around the table with his hands clasped behind his back, looked out the window, blurred by rain, and shook his head. "Lord, how I dread to wade in! I don't want to see the newspapers, George. These are closer to the people." He seized a handful of letters and began running rapidly through them. "Looks as if Grant were about as popular as I am! 'Can't hope to keep confidence of nation if you permit General Grant to continue his futile butchery before Vicksburg.—Grant, a drunken bum—a common roysterer . . . lazy . . . Rosecrans the real general—'" He dropped the letters. "Oh, take them away again, George! They give me the hiccoughs."

Nicolay carefully began to re-stack the letters. Lincoln watched him, talking half to himself, half to his secretary as had become his custom under the influence of Nicolay's understanding and sympathy. "What's the truth about Grant?—I'm not going to get myself into another blind road like I did with McClellan—I never even saw Grant.—He has no personal hold on me.—But he *fights*, though he mostly loses.—Most of 'em don't fight. They argue. I wish I *knew* about Grant. I have a feeling that he's the general I almost think is a fabled giant. George, I'd like to send you out there to look him over. No, I can't spare you. I'll send Charles Dana. You know, that old newspaper man who did such a fine job investigating cotton speculations in the army last year for Stanton?—I'll make my decision as to Grant on Dana's report on him, plus anything Grant may do in the meantime, plus my own feelings about him—"

He fell into silence, watching Nicolay pile the letters with a growing unease. After all, he ought not to put these messages by with nothing but a grunt.

"The thing I get most strongly from those messages, Nicolay, is that the people are in a dangerous state of gloom. They feel ugly because they feel helpless. They've found their military leaders and they've found me continually failing them. Confidence in man is dead and suspicion reigns. It's a time when every foul bird comes abroad and every dirty reptile rises up. The people need a new sign-post. The only one I can refer them to is the One above—and that's a preacher's job. I'm no preacher, God knows, but perhaps if I tell them how my own mind runs just now it would help. I can put it into the proclamation of the national fast day the Senate has asked for."

He had forgotten Nicolay. He walked to the windows and stood staring out blindly at the dim top of the half-finished Washington monument. Nicolay dropped the packets of letters and listened eagerly to the muttered fragments that reached him. After a moment, he took out his pencil and began to jot them down in his notebook.

"—And insomuch as we know that by his divine law, nations, like individuals, are subjected to punishments and chastisements in this world, may we not justly fear that the awful calamity of civil war which now desolates the land may be but a punishment inflicted on us for our presumptuous sins to the needful end of our national reformation as a whole people? We have been the recipients of the choicest bounties of Heaven. We have been preserved these many years in peace and prosperity. We have grown in numbers, wealth and power as no other nation ever has grown, but we have forgotten God. We have forgotten the gracious hand which preserved us in peace and multiplied and enriched and strengthened us; and we have vainly imagined, in the deceitfulness of our hearts, that all these blessings were produced by some superior wisdom and virtue of our own. Intoxicated with unbroken success, we have become too self-sufficient to feel the necessity of redeeming and preserving grace, too proud to pray to the God that made us:

"It behooves us then to humble ourselves before the offended Power, to confess our national sins and pray for clemency and forgiveness:

"Now, therefore . . . I do by this my proclamation designate and set apart Thursday, the 30th day of April, 1863, as a day of national humiliation, fasting and prayer. And I do hereby request all the people to abstain on that day from all their secular pursuits and to unite at their several places of public worship, and their respective homes to keep the day holy to the Lord and devoted to the humble discharge of the religious duties proper to that solemn occasion.—All this being done in sincerity and truth, let us then rest humbly in the hope authorized by divine teaching that the united cry of the nation will be heard on high and answered with blessings no less than the pardon of our national sins, and the restoration of our now divided and suffering country to its former happy condition of unity and peace—"

He experienced a peculiar relaxation of the nerves as he turned from the window to his desk. In uncovering the sign-post for the people he had once more given to himself the final justification of the dreadful responsibility he had assumed.

CHAPTER V

THE Lincolns missed Charles Sumner. It had been his custom to drop into the White House daily and to stay frequently for a meal; breakfast, dinner or supper. His hours were entirely uncertain. He and Tad were devoted friends and it had not been unusual for Lincoln or Mary to come upon the huge Senator in Tad's bedroom, boy and man on the floor intently reproducing Bull Run with toy soldiers and the contents of the wood and coal baskets. He had discovered that the President's most relaxed moments were during the hour before midnight. He had been apt then to appear at the door of Lincoln's bedroom, a little apologetic but full of some problem of state, usually connected with England. The dearest thing to Sumner, after negro enfranchisement, was the maintaining of peace with this country which he loved so well.

All these delightful moments now ceased.

Lincoln missed him. There was more than deep anxiety in his dismay over Sumner's dereliction. His affections suffered. Mary's sorrow was mixed characteristically with exasperation, but she fully recognized the gravity of the situation and kept her sharp and witty tongue well under control as far as making comments outside the family circle was concerned. She used her husband as usual, as a safety valve.

"How can you delay so long in doing something," she urged at breakfast one morning in April, "about—" a glance at Tad, "you know what?"

"I'm doing something," replied the President. "I've agreed we'll leave on the sixth on the *Carrie Martin*. General Hooker is all ready for us."

"What do you mean, Abra'm?" signaling to James to bring her Lincoln's coffee cup.

"Hoo-way!" shouted Tad, spilling a spoonful of cornmeal mush over his new black Eton coat. "That means we'll see the A'my of the Potomac!"

"You've been hacking at me to get away from Washington for a while, Mary," said the President. "What do you say to four or five days in Virginia with General Hooker?"

"Just the thing for you!" replied his wife with a sniff and a twinkle. "It will be an exquisite rest for you to listen to General Hooker's troubles and quarrels, amidst the dogwood and magnolias of old Virginia, with John Hay at one elbow, introducing the three thousand officers, each with an ax to grind, and Nicolay at—"

"John Hay's gone to do an errand for me in Florida," Lincoln smiled.

"The principle remains the same," replied Mary, airily. "However, I'm grateful even for that much. At least I shall have the ride alone with you to and from the steamer—except for Tad, the coachman, the footman and the cavalry guard.—What I really referred to was Charles Sumner. Why don't you talk to Representative Hooper about him?"

"I don't make a big move there till I see light, Mary. I reckon my cue for a while is to piece along, a little here, a hint there," declared the President. "Isn't that a new flummydiddle you're wearing?" nodding at the little lavender silk shoulder cape of many ruffles.

Mary looked extremely gratified. "Yes, Lizzie Keckley's introducing them over my shoulders as it were! You really are becoming quite extraordinary, Abra'm! You've observed crinolines and capes in a single month. Do you like this?"

"I do!" thinking how pretty she was with her cheeks flushed and pleased with himself for his unwonted gallantry. "I like to see you having what you want after all your years of pinching and going without. You were as good a wife as any poor man ever had, my dear," going round the table to kiss her with the homely sense of comfort that meant Mary to him.

Her suggestion with regard to Sam Hooper remained with him as he ascended the stairs and was still fluttering in the background of his thoughts when General Butler was announced later in the morning. Butler, a small bald-headed man with a large sword ornamenting a magnificent major-general's uniform, entered with his usual pomposity and in a voice that could be heard at the Capitol demanded to be sent back to New Orleans.

"General," said Lincoln, taking off his spectacles and running his fingers through his black hair, "I'd like to send you back there. You're a first-rate executive and you've a big political following. But until the Woman Order's forgotten I don't dast uncover you."

"Seward, again or still, I suppose!" ejaculated Butler. "Why in the name of God don't you get a statesman instead of a peanut politician into his job? Sumner's the proper person to be our Secretary of State. But, of course, you've been so unwise as to break with Sumner." Suddenly he leaned confidentially across Lincoln's desk beside which he was sitting. "Mr. President, I wonder if you realize that there's a particularly nasty kind of gossip going about concerning that?"

Lincoln eyed the General a little wonderingly. Butler was impetuous and said to be none too scrupulous politically. But it didn't seem probable that he was an idle tale bearer.

"I hope you aren't going to make me plug up my ears this very busy morning, General," he suggested.

"It's whispered about," blurted Butler, "that you've forbidden Sumner the house because of his attentions to Mrs. Lincoln."

Lincoln could feel his gorge rise. He came to his feet and glared down at the little military man with extreme distaste. "I've a good notion to show you out the door with my foot, Butler, the way I do Tad's pup when he throws up his bone. Maybe you'd better leave before the notion gets the better of me."

"I know I'm making a disgusting impression," admitted Butler, rising but not moving toward the door. "But in spite of that, sir, I'm a gentle-man, a gentleman driven to use an extreme remedy for an extreme case. Some one has got to be willing to risk his reputation, sir, to save yours. I am that unlucky man, it seems. But I insist that you allow me to say that you ought not to allow the break with Sumner to last another hour. I can mend the breach for you. I have great influence with Sumner. He and I go arm-in-arm on reconstruction. You permit Sumner and me to work out the Louisiana problem together and I'll guarantee that Sumner will appear at the White House as of old."

Lincoln stood motionless, struggling for complete self-control. Political bargaining was common enough and did not offend him. But no one before had dared use in this way the outrageous gossip that was embittering Mary's days in Washington. After a moment he walked slowly to the door, opened it and stood waiting.

Butler measured him with a long glance from head to foot, then moving, Lincoln thought, like a figure on a stage, he stalked out of the room.

Secretary Chase passed Butler on the threshold. The two men bowed but did not speak. Lincoln closed the door, seated himself on the edge of the Cabinet table and waited for the Secretary of the Treasury to make known his errand. Chase stood upright on the hearthrug, his six feet of height as impressive as though he carried Lincoln's extra four inches; a handsome man of fifty-five, of pure Anglo-Saxon type. Lincoln always watched him with a combination of amused tolerance and admiration. Chase with his petty intrigues and his vanity, his dignity and his high ideals—another of his enemies, Lincoln told himself but, Oh, what a superb Secretary of the Treasury!

"General Butler isn't happy away from New Orleans, I fancy," said the Secretary.

"He's as full of poison gas as a dead dog," was Lincoln's deliberate comment.

Chase winced. "He's a very able man. Would do well in Grant's place but of course, as this war is being run, he's too able to be put there." Having delivered this shot he drew a document out of his green bag. "You're not reconciled, I understand, Mr. Lincoln, to the workings of the legal tender act of March third."

"It's too late to be worried about that one. It's the third act you contemplate pushing through Congress, Mr. Chase, that I want to get expert opinion on. I have great confidence in your ability but I think you ought to have an outside expert's report that can be used in the newspapers to make people understand that the acts are a military necessity as well as sound finance."

Chase nodded. "Senator Fessenden or Representative Hooper are the best financial men in Congress. Both have the confidence of the public."

"Excellent!" exclaimed Lincoln. "Let's get Hooper at it. He's a genial fellow, while Fessenden is as bitter as one of his own wild Maine apples. Tell Hooper to come up here for a talk with me. And now, give me some details about the working of the bounty idea. I'll have Nicolay bring in some sample protests that we've had from the West."

The remainder of the morning the two men spent on the bounty and its attendant evils. Lincoln worked with the taste of Butler's nasty proposition still in his mouth. He believed that even Chase, who was devoted to Sumner and to Butler, would have sympathized with his sense of insult. But Chase was the last man in whom he would have cared to confide. He could not, in fact, see how he could speak of the matter to any one.

Late that afternoon, Congressman Hooper called. He was a man of about Lincoln's age, conspicuously well dressed, wearing a high black satin stock which added to his smooth-shaven dignity. He had inherited wealth and was a highly successful importer and banker. The President listened to his dissertation on the green-back with growing satisfaction.

"You put that all into an essay, Mr. Hooper," was his comment, "and we'll get the *Atlantic Monthly* to publish it first, the newspapers later. Do you know anybody else who understands money and has a mellow gift of gab?"

Hooper looked thoughtfully at the open window through which vagrant tidings of young April wandered and after a moment said, "Try Chittenden, the Register of the Treasury. He talks and writes delightfully."

"He's a naturalist, too, of no mean parts!" exclaimed Lincoln. "I met him through Charles Sumner. He helped Sumner on the bill taking the duty off ornamental trees and shrubs. Do you remember that speech of Sumner's ending with 'Encourage them till Burnham woods do come to Dunsinane'?"

"I remember," replied Hooper. "Sumner knows everything."

"The knowledge I most envy his possessing right now is his familiarity with the British," said Lincoln. "My wife calls him England's Lone Lover."

Hooper smiled. "The women all admire him. As for me, he's the best friend I have in the world."

"I wish he were mine!" Lincoln's head drooped wearily.

Hooper walked over to the window and looked at the magnolias flushing below and returned to stand before the empty grate beside which the President sat in his rocker. "I'm in a delicate position, Mr. Lincoln. I'm in Sumner's confidence but I don't think I breach it when I tell you that I warned him that a break between him and yourself on reconstruction policies was a national catastrophe. And for all that I love and admire him as I do no other human being, I cannot go as far or as fast as he does in vindictiveness toward the South. He needs you and you need him. Mr. Lincoln," in a deeply troubled voice, "can't I be of service in bringing you together?"

"I wish you could be," replied Lincoln. "But Sumner wants to get rid of me, not work with me. He asked me to resign. Did he tell you that?"

"Judas Priest, no!" exclaimed Hooper. He did not speak for a moment. Then he said earnestly, "Mr. Lincoln, I hope you didn't take that as representative of any large group."

"Oh, I reckon it's large enough, friend Hooper. You couldn't put it in a pint measure. Would it be in bad taste to ask you what Sumner's doing now?" Lincoln in his turn walked to the window and came back.

"I've heard him say nothing about your resignation, sir. He is, of course, frankly much out of patience with you and is criticizing you freely. That you know." Hooper looked uncomfortable.

"The question *was* in bad taste. Let it go," said the President.

"Did you ever think of Sumner as Secretary of State?" asked Hooper. "His work as Chairman of the Committee on Foreign Affairs has given him such diplomatic prestige that I should think—"

"He'll never bargain with his principles," interrupted Lincoln. "I don't hope for that. What I do hope is to call him off his campaign against me as President.—As to giving him Seward's job, I can't dispense with Seward now, Mr. Hooper. Minister Adams is doing a good chore in England and he and Seward are good friends. A year or so from now, things won't be so critical there. But if Sumner will cease to oppose my Presidency and I'm reëlected, I'll be willing to think of him as Secretary of State then. God knows I'd be glad to loosen his choke on the Senate!"

Both men smiled.

"Are you willing to let me toy with that idea for a little while, Mr. President?" asked the Congressman.

"Yes, I am," replied Lincoln, "and I'll thank you very much for any effort whether it's successful or not." He shook hands with Hooper and went thoughtfully to his room to make ready for a dinner party Mary had arranged for a visiting French prince.

Bob came home the next morning. He had spent a few hours shopping in New York and presented himself to his father clad in the result. Lincoln looked up from his desk to examine him delightedly. Bob wore a short-coated suit of the largest plaids his father ever had seen, purple and green being the dominating tones. A yellow velvet vest. White spats. A broad-brimmed, flat-crowned hat of ivory white felt.

"Bob, whereabouts are you going to exhibit your beauty so it won't cause a riot?" exclaimed his father.

"I'm open to suggestion. Pretty handsome, eh, father?"

"Beats a summer sunset. I suggest Ford's Theater, if you can get there without being arrested. At any rate, keep away from timid horses, young children and ammunition stores.—Sit down, Bob, I've a job for you. Pull your chair up close."

He outlined Fred Douglass' scheme which now was well matured. "You're to go down to Fortress Monroe," he ended, "and strike out from there. You are to promise the negroes but two things, freedom and work. The details are your problem, not mine."

Bob sat on the edge of his chair, blue eyes blazing. He said nothing for a moment, then suddenly gave his father a tremendous bear hug. "When do I start?"

"To-night, with utmost secrecy. Douglass is coming in this afternoon and you must talk with him. You're to be gone not over three weeks. My one insistence is that I hear from you at least twice a week. You know how you neglect your mother on that, Bob!"

"Yes, sir," replied Bob as meekly as he could manage for excited joy. "I guess I'll go out and show these clothes while I can."

He rushed away followed by Lincoln's affectionate smile.

Mary, faced with the ultimatum in regard to Bob's errand was, as usual on such occasions, philosophical. She cried a little, said she didn't want to know details as that would give her the more to worry about, and then called Bob's attention to the fact that a youth old enough to be sent by the President of the United States on an errand of importance was supposedly old enough not to torment his little brother.

"I wasn't tormenting him, mother! I beg your pardon," protested Bob. "I'm trying to give him a little training. He's not only pert and spoiled but he has no manners."

"Is that why he's nearly always shrieking, 'Stop it, Bobbie!' when you're alone with him?" inquired his mother. "Just what were you to stop this time?"

"This time I was to stop covering his mouth with my hand because he was spitting at me!" replied Bob, virtuously.

Mary threw up both her hands. Lincoln gave a shout of laughter.

"Oh, you're all just children!" cried Mary. "No wonder you men can't end the war. I wish we women folks had the chance just—"

Lincoln flew to his office, leaving Bob half laughing and half protesting.

The following day, in a strange April snowstorm, Lincoln, with Mary and Tad, boarded the little steamer *Carrie Martin* to make the promised visit to the Army of the Potomac.

Try as he would Lincoln could not put on a holiday mood. Mary herself was depressed. She said the snowstorm meant bad news.

"Don't say that! The attack on Charleston begins to-day," protested Lincoln.

"Over your opposition?" exclaimed Mary.

He nodded and then yielded to Tad's demands that they go over the boat together. When they came on deck after examining the engine room, the snow was receding among the rose-colored hills and lovely green orchards twinkled in the sunset. Lincoln took the clearing weather as a good omen but Mary shook her head.

"Snow in April means tears," she sighed.

She persuaded him to go to bed soon after supper. But the berth was too short for him and he spent the hours from midnight to dawn on deck, wrapped in a blanket, dozing and worrying.

They reached Acquia Creek soon after breakfast and made a quick landing, with only a glimpse of placid water and rolling hills before they were packed into an army ambulance and whirled toward Army Headquarters at Falmouth.

Virginia in early spring! Poetry incarnate! Lincoln was in the saddle all day long during the short visit, exploring with General Hooker and his aides the terrain over which the next battle with Lee must be fought. Tad, little gray cape flying in the wind, followed his father hour after hour. The child's presence among the grim impedimenta of war seemed as incongruous as the fact that this delicate fairyland of fragrant woods, budding meadows, and red-plowed fields dotted with young plants must be given over to carnage. But war, after all, was incongruous to all that was best and beautiful in life. General Hooker, to whom Lincoln voiced these thoughts, agreed with him.

Hooker's plan of battle seemed excellent to Lincoln. There were but two weak points, one of which he pointed out to the General, the other to Mary. Hooker did not plan to throw all of his 135,000 men into the fight—McClellan's old weakness. Lincoln pointed this out to Hooker and to his officers, not only in conferences but at the dinner party given to the President by Hooker the night before the return to Washington. Lincoln's last word to the assembled company was *"Put all your men in!"*

Of Hooker's other weakness Lincoln said to Mary that night in their tent, "Hooker's too sure of his own powers. It's the worst thing about him and will undo him, I'm afraid. I can't make my orders more positive unless I drive them in with a club. I've said to him twenty times, 'Beware of rashness! Beware of rashness! But use all your resources in one great drive.' I can't say it more clearly, can I?"

"Any one who doesn't understand your English is a fool," replied Mary flatly. "If Hooker fails and puts up the usual excuse that your orders confused him, I'd cut his head off at the waistline, instantly. Don't stand round in your stocking feet, Abra'm. This tent floor's as cold as my heart is said to be. Here are your slippers."

"Is Tad well tucked in?" asked Lincoln, sitting down beside the candle with the Richmond *Examiner,* which had been sent over the river that day by a sardonic Rebel. No news had come through from Washington and he hoped to find some here.

"I wouldn't add Taddie to my burdens, if I were you," said Mary. "You've tucked the Army of the Potomac to bed. Isn't that enough?" She kissed him and began to braid her hair.

Lincoln unfolded the paper and gave a start as the headlines met his eye. He devoured the items that followed and then ejaculated, "The expedition to Charleston failed! They beat off the ironclads!"

"I told you so!" groaned Mary.

Lincoln shook his head. "They would do it! I had no more weight than Taddie." He sat brooding. Queer he couldn't harden himself to taking the Union reverses coolly. Heaven knew there'd been enough of them to inure him. Here was another sleepless night ahead of him unless he put Charleston out of his mind. He dropped the paper and opened the Bible. But he couldn't focus his mind on it and shortly laid it aside.

"What are you thinking of, my dear?" asked Mary.

"Of Charles Sumner! I've tried to forget him, but Jings! I can't. Seems he was down here with the Committee on the Conduct of the War last week and every general in the army seized on the opportunity to tell him how the war could be won were I out of the way." He gave her a rueful smile.

"Who told you that?" Mary's eyes were snapping.

"Hooker, when I pressed him pretty hard to-day on putting all his men in, used it as a sort of hint that I'd better not interfere too much."

"I'd hoped we could forget Charles Sumner for a week," exclaimed Mary, indignantly.

"So had I," agreed Lincoln. "But as a matter of fact he's not been fully out of my thoughts. Hooker's remark didn't startle me into any sudden recollection of him. He was there!"

"Abra'm, why don't you do something about Sumner?" urged Mary.

"I'm doing all that I can see to do," replied Lincoln. "I've got the whip hand at one point. I can appoint military Governors to carry on my kind of reconstruction in the conquered States and he can't. That's one of my duties as Commander-in-Chief. I'm steaming ahead on that as fast as I can as the best way to fight Sumner. I wrote General Banks the day we came down here to begin to enroll the loyalists in Louisiana with the idea of having them hold a fall election. They'll have to form a new constitution and then elect members to Congress. I expect to have things in such shape that in another year I'll have Louisiana, Florida, Tennessee and Missouri functioning again in the Union."

"Don't you think he could be persuaded to keep up even an outward appearance of friendship for the sake of public morale?" asked Mary, wistfully.

"You might try it, through Mrs. Hooper," said Lincoln with a grin. "Here's a chance for you to use your famous plan I miffed you so about."

"I tried it long ago and she found it hopeless," sighed Mary.

The conversation lapsed into a brooding silence on both their parts that lasted until they had gone to bed.

They returned to Washington the next night and Lincoln began at once to work on Stanton to make him send every possible aid to Hooker, and for days the muddy roads of the city were blocked with troops.

On the morning of the 25th of April, Stanton asked the President to review Burnside's 30,000 men who were going down to the Rappahannock from Annapolis. Until noon, Lincoln stood on the east steps of Willard's Hotel, bareheaded, as the troops tramped by him through Fourteenth Street. Many of the soldiers wore sprigs of dogwood which they tossed at his feet and by the end of the review he stood knee deep in blossoms which smelled to him of the fairy woods around Falmouth. The last of the passing soldiers he could not see for tears.

CHAPTER VI

BOB MAKES A CALL

HOOKER'S long fight on the Rappahannock, centering on Chancellorsville, began the last of April, and Lincoln gathered himself together to endure what he called his death sweat. During that week of dark messages he enjoyed but one brief hour of respite. Bob returned, tanned and dirty, one night, just as his father was going to bed. The recital of the boy's experiences Lincoln found as enjoyable as an evening at the theater. He gathered that Douglass had done his part nobly and that during the month over two thousand slaves had seen Bob and spoken with him.

"Not many," said Bob, "when you consider your need for them, but Douglass says that that two thousand will be multiplied by fifty as the word spreads. I'm returning to the job in June. And I'd like to take Edgar Welles along. He'll be useful."

Lincoln smiled and nodded. "The enlistment itch cooled for a while?" he asked, an affectionate arm over the shoulder of his first born.

"I haven't had time to think about it," replied Bob. "This is very important work, father! And it's unique in that only your son will be accepted by the slaves. I wish you could have seen them! I swear I didn't know whether to laugh or cry."

"It has its drawbacks in that the public must still look on you as a coward," said the President, watching Bob's face. The boy had his mother's extreme sensitiveness. "But any one by the name of Lincoln must get used to being misunderstood."

Bob nodded. "I don't mind too much, now that my conscience is clear—" He hesitated and under his tan grew a little pale. "But that isn't saying I don't mind the things they say about you, and as for mother—" He broke away from his father and took a turn up and down the room. "Father, I don't see how I can stand the kind of things they're saying now. If I could get at the originator of this latest lie, I'd kill him as I would a skunk!"

Lincoln paused in drawing on the old red dressing gown and looked at the boy a little anxiously. "I'd have said you were located the past few weeks where you couldn't hear anything, son."

"I was. But on the boat to-day I received an anonymous letter saying you'd booted Charles Sumner out of mother's room." His young voice broke miserably.

Lincoln suddenly hurled the dressing gown to the floor. "Now, by the eternal Heavens!" he shouted—then paused, arrested by the look of agonized shame on his son's face—Mary's face—tormented, quivering. "Jings, Bob! Have I got to explain to *you*—"

"Explain!" interrupted Bob, tensely. "Don't affront mother or me with that word!"

"Right!" agreed Lincoln. "Except as they cause her pain, they're beneath notice."

"You don't mean she's been told?" groaned Bob.

"I don't know. I suppose so. She doesn't tell me these things any more. Thinks she's protecting me, bless her," answered his father. "It's one of the prices we pay for the passions roused by slavery, Bob."

But Bob could not be philosophical. "Does Senator Sumner know what's being said? Is there a break between you and him, father?"

"I don't know: to the first question. To the second: sit down and I'll give an answer in detail," picking up his dressing gown. He began to describe the last interview with Sumner, feeling that it was the best way to calm Bob.

The boy listened with his usual intelligent concentration. "I heard in Boston," he said when his father had finished, "that the Boston set was working to get you out and that Sumner was the leader. But I didn't believe it. Are you doing anything to offset them, father?"

"Only a little, here and there. Looks to me as if winning a few good battles would be the only final quietus I could put on the situation. If Hooker loses this fight—" He sighed and sank into a dreary review of the battlefield and plans. Every outline of both was graved on his heart.

After an uncounted passage of time, he found Bob still pacing the floor. "Go to bed, dear Bob. You'll be returning to college in the morning, I suppose."

"Sometime to-morrow," replied Bob vaguely, as he kissed his father good-night.

Lincoln spent the next morning in the War Office, receiving with Secretary Stanton and General-in-Chief Halleck the telegraphic reports of the fighting around Chancellorsville. Bob bade the family farewell at breakfast and started off, ostensibly to take the train for college. But as a matter of fact, he made a call first which delayed his journey for an hour.

He went to see Charles Sumner.

With or without John Hay, he had called on the Senator many times. Sumner's rooms were filled with choice engravings and *objets d'art* that fascinated this small-town boy who had inherited his mother's taste for fine things. So outwardly there was nothing unusual, save the early hour, about this visit.

Sumner, in a gray velvet dressing gown, was at breakfast trying to eat and at the same time dispose of the enormous pile of mail which heaped the empty spaces on the table, trespassed on the omelette platter, and overflowed to the floor. He jumped to his feet with his usual cordiality as Bob came in.

"Ah, Robert! Not on vacation still? At least, Easter didn't last so long in my day at Harvard. Will you have some breakfast?"

"No, thank you, Senator," replied Bob, then blushing to his own disgust he drew a dirty envelope from his pocket and laid it on the one Sumner had been reading last. "I—I came in to show you this, sir. It's anonymous."

"You've placed it on one from the Duke of Argyll," said Sumner with an amused grimace. But, as he read the missive, his face changed, his jaw worked, his blue eyes darkened so angrily that Bob was surprised when he said with entire urbanity:

"I suppose it's too much to hope that your mother hasn't received one of these—though I know she's protected from any letters that come through the usual channels."

"My father thought it likely that she had received one," replied Bob, irritated by the Senator's calm. "You take it coolly, Mr. Sumner! It seems to me an unendurable insult to all of you; mother, father, yourself."

"It's anonymous, so it must be endured," replied Sumner. "One hardens to this sort of thing, Robert. Ever since I first showed admiration for your wonderful mother, she and I have been made the subject of gossip. It's as well that I've ceased to call at the Executive Mansion. The occasion for any such spasm of venom as this has ceased."

"Senator!" cried Bob. "How can you be so heartless! My father told me all about it. Doesn't friendship with a man like him and a lady like my mother mean anything to you? Oh, I know they're not of the British nobility, but they're the rulers of a great country and young as I am, sir, and clearly as I see their gaucheries, I tell you they're wonderful people, both of them! You'll not find their like in Washington or New York or the whole United States for brain and goodness. It's a pity and a shame for you to try to prevent my father from leading this country as he knows is best!"

Sumner, who had seated himself, listened to Bob's outburst with a certain sad patience. When the boy stopped for breath he gathered the letters out of the omelette dish and said slowly:

"I don't know how to explain to a youth of nineteen. You're very young for your years— What is it you want me to do, Robert?"

"I want you to go on being friends with my parents. To stop trying to oust Abraham Lincoln from the White House."

"I must do whatever seems best to me for the negro cause, Robert," in a troubled voice. "My dear boy, don't look at me as if you hated me!"

"I can't hate you, I wish I could!" groaned Bob. "We all love you at our house. Tad was mourning at breakfast because you've neglected him."

Sumner shook his great head and suddenly walked to the mantel and took down a tiny clock in a crystal globe set on the back of an exquisitely carved ivory camel. "Take this to Taddie. He's often asked me for it. And give him my love."

Bob stood holding the clock, staring at it impatiently. "You just don't understand human love, do you, Mr. Sumner? A clock to solace Taddie's unrequited affection!" he exclaimed wonderingly.

The Senator threw his hands above his head, dropped them, then with a wide gesture of both arms swept the table before him clear of dishes and letters and buried his face in both hands on the table cloth. Bob looked wildly from the leonine head with its mass of chestnut hair to the clock and from the clock to the door. But before he could make an exit, Sumner lifted a tear-stained face and said in a voice of the mellow gentleness that was one of his great gifts:

"That touched me on the quick, Robert. Let me try to tell you something of myself— I had a twin-sister, Matilda, whom I loved to my very soul. I helped my mother to nurse her through a year of consumption. She died in my arms. We were just twenty-one. That was my first lesson in the futility of basing one's happiness on a thing as frail as human life.— Five years later, dear little Jane died of typhoid. She was seventeen—tall, dark, an exquisite musician."

He ruminated for a moment, then went on. "My father was a harsh man. I did my utmost to bring something of gentleness and beauty into our home so that, for a boy, I became peculiarly devoted to my mother, my brothers and sisters.—After Matilda and Jane left me, my dear sister Mary took their place in my heart. She was ten years younger than I. She grew to an extraordinary beauty, tall, stately, with a mind as brilliant and as avid as your mother's, with glorious chestnut hair wrapped round her head. She was a perfect companion, so lovely, so accomplished—"

Bob gently slid the little clock back to the mantel and dropped into the chair beside Sumner. Apparently the Senator did not follow his action, but when the young man laid a sunbrowned hand on the table, Sumner placed his own great white palm over it and clung to it throughout the remainder of his soliloquy.

"Mary too—consumption seized upon her. I remember the day we had to cut her beautiful hair. It hurt me to the soul. She too died in my arms. She was twenty-two. Prescott wrote me to comfort me and said:

> "'Alas! for love if thou wert all
> And nought beyond on earth!—'

"My brother Horace was drowned in 1850 with Margaret Fuller Ossili. My brother Henry died of typhoid in 1852. Brother Albert with his dear wife and child were drowned at sea in 1856.—Only Julia and George and my dear mother are left me of all that fine household.—There's a blight awaiting every affection that grows within me.—I gave my very soul's soul to another when I was in my twenties. She wouldn't be my wife.—Mrs. Longfellow who was as dear as a sister to me was burned to death two years ago.—And as if death couldn't sufficiently blast me, one by one my ideals have destroyed my friendships."

There was a long silence except for the infinitesimal ticking of the little clock. He seemed to be reviewing the sad roster.

"—Charles Francis Adams whom I cared for as a brother, Richard Dana, the Ticknors—for years I was a social outcast in Boston. Men with whom I'd played as a boy, women who had invited me to their homes, who had entrusted their children to me, college mates, old teachers,—all cast me out because I dared to oppose the institution of slavery. I was pariah—unclean—and lonely—dear God, how lonely I have been and am. I am a man acquainted with grief in all its forms, dear Robert.—You tell me I don't understand human love. I answer by repeating to you what William Prescott wrote me of Mary:

> " 'Alas, for love if thou wert all
> And nought beyond on earth!—' "

He crumpled the anonymous letter in one huge white fist and tossed it into the empty grate. Bob did not stir until Sumner, after a time and with a long sigh, freed his hand and smiled at him.

"You'll take the little clock to Taddie, won't you, Robert?"

Bob, with defeat in every line of his face, shook his head and with suddenly quivering lips rushed from the room. He *was* only nineteen.

That evening, as Lincoln worked in his office at his belated correspondence, Taddie, inarticulate with temper, stamped into the room and threw himself on his father with such vehemence that he knocked the President's arm against the ink bottle. He was followed by Pete Kelley, a snub-nosed, freckle-faced boy of ten, in a rusty suit of black. His brother had been killed at Fredericksburg. Lincoln hurriedly scrubbed the superfluous ink off Tad's velvet Eton suit with his handkerchief while above Tad's roaring he shouted to the wealthy tinner's son:

"What's happened, Pete?"

"That there painter that's going to make your picture has taken our theater to work in!" shouted Pete in reply.

"So Tad had to go crazy instead of going to his mother about it?"

"I tried to get him to go to her but he always runs to you when he wants something he shouldn't have," explained Perry.

Lincoln chuckled and placing a hand over Tad's mouth so as to be heard, said to Nicolay who came in at the moment:

"See if you can't get Carpenter to use some other room. I remember Tad's telling me several days ago he and Pete wanted to use this one."

"It's the state bed chamber, Mr. Lincoln," explained Nicolay with what seemed to Lincoln unnecessary vigor, "and the only space available for the artist's purposes. Brady's men are developing photographic plates in there and Tad has locked them in."

"Tad, go unlock that door!" ordered his father.

"I won't!" gasped Tad as soon as he was released.

Lincoln shook his head wearily, "Tad, you do make me a lot of trouble that you don't need to!"

Tad looked up into the worn face and with a renewed burst of tears handed the key to Nicolay.

"Now, let's go to mother." Lincoln rose and with a boy clinging to either hand, started for the sitting room.

"You mustn't say I made you twouble!" sobbed Tad. "It kills me. Pete, give him the clock. Give it to him so he'll fo'get I've been bad."

Very reluctantly, Pete dug into the bulging pocket of his roundabout and brought forth the ivory camel bearing the tiny clock. The children were the recipients of so many extraordinary gifts that the beauty of this particular one could not surprise the President. But its source did.

"Look, Mary!" he exclaimed as they entered the sitting room. "Here's Sumner's clock out of Pete's jacket pocket."

" 'Tisn't Pete's fault," shrilled Tad. "I gave it to him. A man gave it to me just a little bit ago."

Mary took the pretty thing unseeingly. "Tad Lincoln, look at your suit. You'll have a whipping—"

"No! No, Mary!" interposed Lincoln. "I did that with my clumsy elbow."

Mary sniffed skeptically but gave Tad the benefit of the doubt and turned to the clock. "It stood on the mantel under the Dürer's Erasmus. Did a note come with it, Taddie? For goodness' sake, wipe his face, Abra'm."

Before Lincoln could pull out the inky wad in his pocket, Pete thrust a grimy rag into Tad's hand.

"Yes," said Tad, "one came and we tossed it in the waste basket in my woom. Get it, Pete, if the kitten hasn't chewed it. I think the black kitten's motha' plans to have mo' kittens in that basket. She likes it. She goes in it and sings and awanges the scwaps." He blew his nose and stuffed the handkerchief into his breeches pocket. "Does the clock make you feel betta', Papa day?"

"Yes, son, I reckon it helps," replied his father.

"Then come on, Pete, we'll go see what the pitcha' men say to us now," as his friend placed a crumpled note in Mary's hand.

The children departed and Mary and Lincoln deciphered the familiar scrawl. "Dearest Tad: Time heals all things. I shall always love you. Charles Sumner."

Husband and wife gazed at each other. "Shall I acknowledge it?" asked Mary.

Lincoln shook his head. "You might frighten him off. This may mean he's repenting." He placed the clock tenderly on the mantel and stood looking at it. After a moment he turned to say, "Stonewall Jackson was fatally wounded in the fighting yesterday."

"Perhaps since we can't develop good officers of our own, God intends to help us by removing the Rebel geniuses," suggested Mary.

"Hooker is *not* throwing in all his men as I told him to," Lincoln said, laconically.

The two exchanged a long troubled look and left each other, Mary to seek Tad, Lincoln to more torturing hours in Stanton's office.

It was nearing midnight when belated dispatches left him no doubt that Hooker's defeat had been complete. For a moment, as full realization of the extent of the misfortune came home to him, he was panic-stricken. He seized his soft hat, jammed it over his eyes and rushed from the War

Department into Lafayette's Square where, among the trees, he prayed
that he might for a moment be alone. Just to be alone!

He brought up under a magnolia tree, muttering, "What will the country say! What will it say!"

Great magnolia petals showered down on him. He brushed them aside
with a groan. They carried the smell of funeral wreaths. A banging door
roused him. It seemed that solitude for him was an unattainable commodity. His rush across the square had brought him near to Seward's
house. A tall figure strode over the porch, down the step, across the lawn,
and under Lincoln's magnolia. Even in the dim starlight this was unmis-
takably Charles Sumner.

The two men clutched each other to keep from falling. Sumner had
been in mad haste and the impact of his two hundred pounds was tremendous.

"Lincoln!" ejaculated the Senator. "I tell you I must and shall know!
I will not have your various Cabinet members refuse to give me the news
my own high office entitles me to!" His voice was trembling with indignation.

"What news are you after, Senator?" asked Lincoln gently, one arm over
Sumner's shoulders.

Sumner answered with extraordinary vehemence. "What's to be done
about the cursed project of privateering? Will the disgusting Charles Wilson be removed as Secretary of Legation in London? But above all, *what
of Hooker?* For God's sake, what of Hooker, Lincoln?"

"Seward can't answer those questions, Senator, because he doesn't
know," replied the President. "Seward's let too much slip. I have to watch
him. As for war news, Stanton has to censor everything. I get most of my
news through Stanton."

"I've been to Stanton and insisted on getting facts," his voice rising
again, "and he told me to go to the devil."

"And you've run into me!" with a short laugh. "I'll make a bargain with
you, Sumner. You know that's the devil's speciality! Looks like I'm the
only one that has all the information you need. I'll give it to you any time,
day or night, without reserve, that you'll come to the White House and
ask me for it." Lincoln's pulse had quickened. It looked like a heaven-sent
moment. He slid his arm down to link it in Sumner's. He felt the Senator
stiffen.

"You're taking an unfair advantage of me, Mr. Lincoln."

"I reckon I am," agreed Lincoln with a calm he did not feel. "The devil
generally does. Are you really afraid I'll taint you with my doctrines, Sumner, if you call on me occasionally? Doesn't it occur to you that it might
be your duty to try to convert me?"

"It hadn't occurred to me," replied Sumner, slowly, his arm muscles
relaxing.

Lincoln began to lead him toward the lighted north entrance to the

White House grounds, talking as he did so of what seemed to him the least important of Sumner's queries.

"Charlie Wilson's worst failing appears to be that he sits in taverns with his feet on the table, saying hard things about the British and spitting on the floor," he remarked, smiling to himself.

"Isn't that sufficient to damn him?" cried Sumner. "Don't you realize that for every one that judges us Americans by the perfect manners of Charles Adams, there'll be a thousand who say we're all Wilsons?"

"You're absolutely right, of course," agreed Lincoln, lifting his hat as they passed the sentry at the gate. "What do you suggest I do to let Wilson down easy? He's an able newspaper reporter, remember. And whom shall we put in his place?"

"Will suggestions from me be killed by Seward?" asked Sumner.

"No, sir, they'll be used by me," replied Lincoln.

"Let me think it over until to-morrow," Sumner's voice was mollified. "And now, what of Hooker?"

"I mustn't talk of him until we reach my room. Walls have ears. Stanton's determined the worst shall be held back as long as possible." They were mounting the private stairs now and neither spoke again until Lincoln had closed the door behind them in his bedroom. He turned up the gas. The huge room with its heavy red hangings and massive rosewood furniture seemed oppressive. Or perhaps it was not the furnishings. Perhaps the many hours of travail he'd spent there gave it an imaginary dankness to Lincoln. His dressing gown lay across the bed foot, his slippers beneath. The bed was turned back. A volume of Shakespeare and of Petroleum Nasby lay on the bedside table with a plate of cookies and a glass of buttermilk. Mary!—

Sumner had walked directly to the war map fastened between the two south windows. Lincoln followed and began a rapid explanation of the day's movements at Chancellorsville. The Senator listened, breathing hard, but did not speak until Lincoln stopped. Then he sank into a chair and groaned, "All is lost!" in a voice of despair.

"No! No!" Lincoln patted him on the shoulder. "What're those lines from Milton you quoted to me after the second Bull Run?—'What though the field be lost? All is not lost—the unconquerable will—'" Lincoln smiled wistfully.

Sumner shook his head. "You don't give the whole of the thought:

> "'—the unconquerable will,
> And study of revenge, immortal hate,
> And courage never to submit nor yield.'"

"That's a bad line in there," admitted Lincoln. "We'll leave it to Lyman Trumbull and Ben Wade. By the way, I'd like to tell you about an experiment I made lately. Sit down."

He fetched his tooth-brush mug from the stand in the corner into which he poured half the buttermilk, handing the glass to Sumner. The Senator took it with a nod of thanks and helped himself to the cookies. Both men munched with enjoyment while the President told of Bob's recent expedition.

Sumner listened with absorption, nodding and saying, "Good! Good!" And when Lincoln told of one darky who had remarked that Massa Abraham was God and Massa Sumner the Holy Ghost, he laughed but with tears in his eyes.

It was nearing one o'clock when he rose to go, saying with that half-tender care for his friends which they never forgot nor could withstand, "Your face is ravished with weariness, dear Lincoln. Shall I ask James to give you a rubdown as I pass him in the hall?"

Lincoln shook his head with a "Thank you," and murmured to himself as the door closed on Sumner, "I've had something better than a rubdown."

But he sat long by the window wondering how far the news he had given Sumner about the failure of Hooker had gone to seal the Senator's conviction that he was unfitted to be Commander-in-Chief.

CHAPTER VII

OBERON

MARY was very much excited by Lincoln's account of Sumner's visit when he gave it to her the next morning at breakfast, but the President could not share her optimism. A man like Sumner, obsessed by a crusade, was not to be guided or controlled by ordinary sentiments, nor to be estimated by ordinary standards.

"The more I think about him, the less confidence I have in my ever getting what I call true friendship from Sumner," he told his wife. "I tell you honestly that I'm almost as uneasy as ever about him. I wish I knew what he and his gang are up to."

"Don't you expect him to repeat this call?" asked Mary, anxiously.

"I expect nothing but the unexpected from Sumner," replied the President. "However, I'll go so far as to say that I don't think he'll come unless absolutely driven to it for news."

"I'm going to see if I can't supply a different kind of bait," declared Mary.

Several days later, when Lincoln caught a glimpse of young Mrs. Hooper in the garden, he wondered in passing if the lovely lady was not Mary's "bait."

Alice Hooper had come more or less frequently to the White House receptions but this was her first informal call and she brought her small daughter with her. Tea was served in the garden under a young copper beech, the topmost branches of which touched the windows of the President's bedroom. Blooming pink rose beds lay to the south of the beech and green lawn beyond. A slight haze of gold hung in the air, forerunner of the dust in which the marching troops would shortly veil the city. In the pauses of conversation, the women were conscious of a faint sound as of thunder to the southwest. Hooker was trying to head off Lee's cavalry from a charge up the Shenandoah Valley.

Mrs. Hooper, charming in heliotrope silk, explained that she had called to urge Mary to appear at a raffle which the wives of army officers were holding to raise money for Clara Barton's nurses. The two discussed Miss Barton's work in detail. Little Isabella, long yellow curls falling over a little pink dimity frock that rippled in so many ruffles over a tiny crinoline that she looked as if she were wearing a huge hollyhock, ran up and down the garden paths talking to herself in some mysterious game of childhood.

This entirely feminine scene had maintained itself perhaps five minutes when a shout was heard from the President's bedroom window.

"Hey! Sissy! Come up hea'! We want you."

Isabella paused and turned a piquant little face upward.

"I hate to be called Sissy!" she shrilled.

"Tad!" called his mother. "Come down here and be properly introduced." Then, to Mrs. Hooper, "I don't know whether he'll come or not. He dislikes girls."

"No boy of any age really dislikes girls of any age," retorted Alice Hooper. "I speak I assure you from a vast and varied experience."

Both women laughed, but before Alice could continue, an alarming sound of breaking twigs and rending garments came from above and to his mother's consternation, Tad slid rapidly down the trunk of the copper beech. His white linen suit was stained and hopelessly torn. Not at all embarrassed, he placed his dirty little hand on his heart and made a profound bow to the dimpling Isabella who had drawn near.

"We want you for Queen Titania in ou' play," he said. "You a' just a good size and shape."

"Who's the boy in the window?" demanded Isabella.

"My chum Pete. He made the chawiot for the Queen."

"I won't play with him but I will with you," declared the little girl, "because you're pretty."

"I'm not," roared Tad. "I never was. I won't be. You're just a di'ty little—"

Mary clapped her hand over her son's mouth before his favorite epithet emerged. Isabella giggled and danced up and down.

"Pretty boy! Pretty boy!" she squealed.

"Isabella!" said her mother reprovingly.

"Aw, come on, Tad!" came Pete's voice from above. "Bring her along and if she don't stop calling you that, she can't ride in the chariot."

"Will the chariot really go?" inquired Isabella of Tad.

Mary experimentally removed her hand. Tad replied with enthusiasm. "It goes like a gun ca'wage with fifty mules licked by fifty contwabands."

"I'd like to ride in it," exclaimed Isabella.

Tad tossed his head and stood staring at her, obstinately.

"You're as homely as a pig," volunteered Isabella, a little anxiously.

Tad relaxed and taking the little girl's proffered hand, led her away.

"Is it safe?" asked Isabella's mother.

"Not usually," replied Tad's mother, with a sigh and rising. "Especially not now as Tad's tutor is down with typhoid. I really don't have an easy moment while Tad's awake. Shall we follow at a respectful distance?"

Alice gathered up lilac gloves and black lace shawl, touched her plumed Leghorn hat with a delicate hand, and followed up the iron stairs to the south portico, thence to the main hall, where they paused for a few moments' laughing conversation with Lord Lyons. In the midst of this colloquy a frightened shriek floated down from above. Both women gathered up their crinolines and flew up the stairs.

"She isn't killed!" called Tad reassuringly as they burst into the room.

Charles Sumner was standing by the bed, holding Isabella in his great arms. Pete and Tad were restraining Nanny, Tad's beloved goat, who seemed to object seriously to a wreath of artificial flowers tied over her horns.

"Nanny is Bottom and Isabella wouldn't let Bottom kiss he'," shrilled Tad. "If she's going to squawk like that she can't play with me and that's final!"

Isabella from her safe haven spoke quite as firmly as Tad. "If you'll be Bottom, I'll let you kiss me. But I won't not let no goat kiss me ever."

"Pete, you kiss he', just th'ough the wall, you know," urged Tad.

"Not me," declared Pete, his freckled face purpling. "I'd rather kiss Nanny."

"I wouldn't let you touch me!" cried Isabella.

"Then I suppose I'll have to," said Tad, grimly. "Come on! We'll put Nanny back in the stable."

"And about time," said his mother in a voice as grim as her son's.

Alice Hooper, who had been standing with lovely eyes brimming with laughter, now moved toward Sumner. "Put her down, dear Senator! And thank you for rescuing her."

"I was coming up the private staircase in an attempt to see the President alone. Hence my intrusion," explained Sumner, setting Isabella down and bowing.

"But you play with us, Senata'!" cried Tad. "You be Obe'on since I have to be Bottom."

Sumner, with the enchanting smile seldom seen save by children, shook his head. "I can't stay this time, Taddie."

"Oh, stay! Stay just a little while! You've been away so long!" cried the little boy, running to catch Sumner's hand.

Isabella suddenly climbed to the bed and thence to the bureau, from which she could throw her arms about Sumner and kiss him. Pete was handicapped as Nanny's keeper and could only add his plea vocally. Sumner, his serious face transfigured with pleasure, gathered both children in his arms.

"Just fifteen minutes, then."

Mary smiled at Alice Hooper and they withdrew to the sitting room, where they settled themselves on a little sofa from which they could view the hall.

"How children do love him!" exclaimed Alice. "He and Isabella are infatuated with each other. I tell him that if she were fifteen years older and he fifteen years younger, I'd be his mother-in-law."

"I suppose he hates to be teased by you, of all people in the world," mused Mary.

"Why 'of all people in the world'?" demanded Alice with a touch of the hauteur for which she was noted.

"It's perfectly obvious that the blessed goose is infatuated with you, too," smiled her hostess.

"Madam!" the younger woman jumped to her feet. Slender, flushed, beautiful, she swept up and down the room as though fighting to keep down the temper for which she was noted. She and Mary had temperamentally much in common! "Such thoughts should be beneath you. I don't deserve such suspicions."

"Desert has very little to do with what people say of one, I've found," returned Mary, sadly.

Suddenly pale, Alice Hooper came to pause before Mary. The arrogance left her manner and she spoke as simply as a child. "Mrs. Lincoln, is there gossip about Charles Sumner and me?"

"Yes, my dear," replied Mary with equal simplicity, "quite horrid gossip. If it should reach your father-in-law, I fear it might make trouble between him and Sumner. And as for your husband—"

"My husband has perfect faith in me, as well he may have," interrupted Alice vehemently.

Mary nodded. "Of course! Yet he may be convinced that the Senator has been indiscreet in showing his admiration for you so publicly."

"It would break my heart to have Charles Sumner hurt," exclaimed Alice, adding with a little rueful smile, "I want only myself to torment him."

There was a moment's silence during which the children's treble and the Senator's bass floated in at the door.

"Dear Mrs. Hooper," Mary rose to lay a gentle hand on the younger woman's arm, "you're playing with Satan's fires."

Alice gasped as if she had been struck and drew herself up quickly. "I think we'll not discuss the matter further, Madam President! I must fetch Isabella and go home."

But Mary would not allow the conversation to end on this note. "You mustn't be angry with me, my dear. I fear gossip. It has wrecked me socially here in Washington, as you know. Charming and sought for as you are, its clammy hand can beslime you also, make a social outcast of you. Gossip has no respect for place or breeding or wealth. Rather, it prefers them."

Still very pale, Alice had recovered her aplomb. "You are supersensitive for me, dear Mrs. Lincoln. But I'm sure you mean most kindly. I really must beg to be excused now. It's my daughter's supper time."

Mary let her go.

She was standing by the window a little later, thinking over the interview she had forced, when Lincoln came in with Tad, both ready for supper.

"Tad's been describing his afternoon successes to me, Mary," Lincoln said as they started for the dining room.

"Isabella's as much fun to play with as Nanny," declared Tad. "We'll give an honest-to-goodness play soon and he' motha'll let he' come to wehe'sels. The Senata' said he'd come to the play if Isabella's motha' would ask him. She said she wouldn't and the Senata' just picked up his hat and walked out of my room as if she'd kicked him. Can I go to Isabella's house, soon, motha'? She's asked me."

"I'll see," replied his mother. Then to Lincoln, "Did Mr. Sumner have his conference with you, Abra'm?"

The President shook his head. "He must have been too much hurt by the kick! Perhaps he'll come back this evening."

But Sumner did not return and Lincoln spent the evening with Hamlin. Draft enforcement was being met with bitter hostility throughout the North. Lincoln wanted the Vice President to go up to Maine and preach the common sense of this method of raising soldiers. Hamlin, always glad to get home to his constituents, agreed to do so and proceeded to draw on the President's vast fund of information for material to make into "war medicine," as he called it with a dry Yankee grin.

Just before leaving he showed Lincoln a letter from his son Cyrus. Bob had got in touch with the newly made young Colonel and was sending him a group of negroes to be trained as recruiting officers. The two fathers nodded at each other over the letter with mutual pride.

Lincoln told Mary of Bob's prowess, the next evening. They were standing in the window of Mary's bedroom, looking down on the glory of the garden, ablaze now with lemon lilies.

"I didn't know Bob had gone back to Fortress Monroe!" exclaimed Mary. "How did that happen?"

Lincoln cleared his throat. "Well, he wrote me last week that he'd finished his examinations early by special arrangement with his professors and was going down without stopping here."

"Abra'm," ordered Mary, "you let me see that boy's letter!"

Lincoln took it reluctantly from his pocket. Bob had written that he was not coming to the White House, "in order to avoid making Mother go through the ordeal of saying good-by. It breaks my heart and hers too." Lincoln had not wanted Mary to see those last sentences.

But she was very quiet about it. She read the letter and looked up at him with a pathetic smile. "If the Lord had planned for ages, He couldn't have found a more adroit way to punish me for my lack of self-control than in Bob's constant effort to avoid a scene with me. I *must* be cool and calm with that boy!"

Lincoln patted her cheek. "Don't get *too* calm and collected or I won't know you! As it is, you've changed so in the last year that often I wonder who the strange lady is that shares my bed and board."

"Abra'm!" Mary giggled, then gave him a look of affectionate appraisal. He was wearing a new white linen suit with a waistcoat of dull ivory silk. The outfit had cost her many weary hours of conversation and she was proud of it. "You do look nice! You're going to have more widows than ever caressing your left hand while your right signs pardons for their sons!"

"Tut! Tut! Mrs. Lincoln!" He gave a shout of laughter and they descended to supper with Tad sliding down the banisters ahead of them.

"What was General Butler raging about in your office to-day?" asked Mary, midway through the meal.

"He yells louda' than old Stanton but he don't swea' any betta'," volunteered Tad, his mouth full of green peas.

Lincoln winked at his wife and said before she could correct the child, "Butler has changed his mind and wants Grant's job. Guarantees to take Vicksburg in twenty-four hours after his arrival on the spot."

"Ask him how soon he could take Richmond!" suggested Mary. "It looks as if Lee didn't want it. I suppose the way his army is moving up the Shenandoah he'll be establishing the Southern capital at Harrisburg before the 4th of July."

"Don't be sarcastic, my dear," protested Lincoln. "It's too serious a matter."

"And do you think I'm not serious?" cried Mary. "Aside from my own anxiety in the matter, how can I see you agonize so and not be serious? But I can't help wondering with the rest of the public how long you're going to let General Hooker sit in front of Richmond while General Lee escapes him into Pennsylvania."

"Let! Let! Good God, Mary, don't be a fool!"—his taut nerves getting beyond control for an instant. "Do you suppose I'm not doing all I can to get that army out of the mud, onto its legs and moving? You, of all people—"

"Oh, I'm sorry, Abra'm!" contritely from Mary. "Taddie'll think you're really cross at me. I do try to mind my own business."

"As far as that's concerned," Lincoln spoke gently again, "it's as much your business as mine or any one else's. I'm worried, not cross. Don't hold it against me, Taddie," with a smile at the staring child. "Butler is very mad with me. He's staying with Secretary Chase and I suppose the things they're saying about me would turn me against myself!"

"Well, I'm not sure but what Butler ought to have Grant's place," said Mary. "He's a very able man. I suppose you know how he's got the Presidential bee?"

Lincoln looked at her musingly but made no comment on the hero of New Orleans. During the remainder of the meal, he turned over in his mind the probable extent of Butler's enmity to him and the possible use that Chase and Sumner would make of it.

After supper, he strolled into John Hay's room. The secretary was dressing for the evening. The bed, the chairs, the floor were strewn with garments, while the young man in his shirt sleeves stood before the mirror working over an enormous white satin tie. Lincoln sat down on the edge of the bed after sweeping aside a purple lounging robe.

"Where are you going to-night, John?"

"I'm going to call on Miss Montgomery, sir, a beauteous damosel from the fair state of my nativity!"

"Do you mind *what* damosel you call on, John, just so she be beauteous?" asked the President.

"Not at all, dear Tycoon! My affections have been blighted so often that I'm no longer capable of real feeling about any of the sex. Have you a lady in mind?" finishing the tie to his satisfaction and turning to Lincoln with his infectious smile.

The years in the White House had taken some of the red from the young man's cheeks, had hardened a little the full curves of his lips. But he still retained the twinkling brilliancy of the black eyes, with their quizzical lift at the outer corners. He still showed untainted his buoyant young enthusiasm for life. Lincoln was always glad to have him back though he was finding the young man's tact invaluable in performing political errands and John was more and more frequently absent from the White House.

The President returned the smile. "John, how does that flirtation of yours with pretty Kate Chase progress?"

The young man shook his head, sadly. "I have no luck with women! I really produced inspired verses for that flinty-hearted damosel and she read them aloud with derisive giggles to Governor Sprague."

"Somebody said Charles Sumner was trying to cut Sprague out over there," suggested Lincoln. "She's a handsome, ambitious gypsy. Doesn't like me, much."

"She wants your place for her father," John nodded. "Mr. Sumner hasn't a chance there. Gossip says his heart is in another and entirely ineligible quarter. But he and Chase are very intimate, lately—gossip also. If you want me to go round to Chase's, I'm apt to find Sumner, unless he's at the Hoopers."

Lincoln ran his fingers through his hair, clasped his knee and worked his long body back and forth in thought.

"I reckon you'll have to go round to Chase's house to-night and throw a hand-grenade. I want to find out what they're trying to do to me. You give this message to Sumner if he's there or confide it to Kate or her father for him if he's not. Say I'd like to accede to Sumner's request for a negro department for General Frémont but I just haven't got one handy. That ought to start General Butler off his seat. He's been after me for a department for months. He'll sweep over Sumner like a herd of buffalo when he learns Sumner's been trying to help Frémont out. In the exchange of recriminations you may learn where I stand." He returned John's grin.

"Yes! Yes!" the grin spreading. "Do you desire a report to-night, sir? After the flood gates are open—! Well, outside of Seward, if Sumner's there, the three most rapid-fire orators in the western hemisphere'll be gathered at the Chase residence—and I may be late in getting away."

"You come to me to-night, boy. I'm worried. Butler is making bad medicine as sure as Lee is headed for Pennsylvania. Chase is a babe in Butler's hands and so in only slightly less degree is Sumner."

Hay fastened a pink rosebud carefully in his button hole, jerked down his vest, picked up a very tall hat and an enormous cane, bowed formally to the President, shouted suddenly, "Raise the portcullis!" clucked to an imaginary horse and was gone.

"That fellow saves my reason about twice a day," said Lincoln to the empty air and returned to his desk.

Three hours later, John seated himself on the edge of Lincoln's bed. The pink rosebud was wilted. John's lips were drawn but his eyes were vivid. The President pointed to the plate of sandwiches on the bedside table and the two munched while John talked.

He found the party, he said, in the garden, back of the Secretary's house:—Chase, Sumner, Butler and the pretty Kate, sitting close together, clapping mosquitoes, and listening to one another and the whippoorwills. He delivered the message to Sumner immediately on his arrival, confidentially, as among friends.

Butler roared with surprise and indignation, "What, Frémont a department while I stand on the doorstep begging and am denied? What in hell do you mean, Sumner?"

"I mean," replied Sumner, stiffly, "that Frémont is notoriously the negro's friend. If giving him a department will draw out the negro troops rapidly, not only for their own sake but to offset the danger of a draft rebellion—"

Butler interrupted, "That's not the way to do it! Put me aboard a ship with a white regiment. Land me at a Southern port. I'll march North gathering negroes as I come and arming them with their peculiar weapon, as John Brown planned. I'll give them the spear their African fathers used. I'll bring through an army that'll terrorize secession."

"Your plans needn't keep Frémont from having a department," said Chase.

"Frémont with a department means Frémont thrust forward as dictator by the Abolitionists, eh, Sumner?" exclaimed Butler. "I suppose that's the latest hope of the Boston set!"

"Not so," retorted Sumner. "Frémont with a department means Frémont busy and content, leaving you a free field to show your mettle."

"Haven't I shown my mettle?" demanded Butler fiercely, and he embraced the opportunity immediately to utter a long address in which he described at great length his accomplishments at Annapolis, at Fortress Monroe, and at New Orleans.

After what seemed to John an endless period, Butler was interrupted by Secretary Chase who asked point blank if the General were recommending himself for the Presidency, adding that more than military and legal ability were essential in the Executive Mansion in the present crisis— a broad understanding of finance was required. Followed an address by Chase on his accomplishments as Secretary of the Treasury and they were many and impressive.

Sumner listened to his colleagues, a motionless shadow in the heavy scented garden. When they had finished, he said, slowly, "All conversations are idle which do not include the fact that Mr. Lincoln apparently has no idea of withdrawing and that, as he himself says, only those generals that win victories may think of dictatorships."

"In other words," exclaimed Butler, "Lincoln has an object in not giving able soldiers commanding positions. He's afraid of the dictator. Ha! I see it all now!—Hooker won't head Lee off. You'll see. Lee's going to be allowed to win another victory."

Chase took fire at this evidence of Butler's clear vision. "You're right, General! What blind fools we've been! This is dreadful! Preposterous! My friends, if Lee again defeats the Army of the Potomac, I'll publish our discovery to the world and the people will demand an impeachment of Lincoln."

John Hay had dropped into a chair which he had dragged discreetly back of Kate Chase, but he reminded them of his presence at this moment by letting slip an indignant snort.

Kate Chase rose quickly and beckoning to John began to move toward the house. "You may as well know, Mr. Hay, that many people can't endure Mr. Lincoln with your gay insouciance. He's a serious problem to some of us."

John bowed. "That may well be, Miss Chase, I'm sure," he murmured and followed her from the garden.

Lincoln listened to his secretary's lively tale without once interrupting him. When John finished the story and the sandwiches together, the President wiped the sweat from his forehead with the back of his hand and said, with a twisted smile, "Well, it looks as if any fool could now understand what they think of me. Contempt has swamped any idea of secrecy— Seems from most any point of view, John, as if Hooker ought to lick Lee— John, nobody knows the strength of the Presidential itch till he's had it—"

"Interpret for me, sir!" urged John. "The talk of impeachment is idle, of course!"

"I'm not at all sure that it's idle," replied the President slowly. "Any one of those men would like to impeach me. If I could draw Sumner off, though, he could control the others."

John's young face showed a growing astonishment. "Not really, Mr. Lincoln! Why, I was thinking it half a joke! They haven't a leg to stand on."

"What difference does that make?" asked the President. "Sometimes I'm made mighty uneasy with regard to our national future when I realize how frequently a small minority is able to block or wreck the efforts of the majority. And I'm not blinking at the possibility that a majority of the people want to be rid of me.—Sumner may be sitting over there this minute planning to impeach me."

"If I thought that was so I'd go over there and—and—" John looked at Lincoln in perplexity. "What can one do to Sumner, sir?"

"I don't know!" exclaimed Lincoln.

"I do know one thing," said John, "if you'll pardon my saying it, and that is that you are too patient with Sumner. He's the kind of a man that a good swift kick has a salutary effect upon."

Lincoln suddenly laughed. The picture presented was too much for his risibilities, anxious as he was, and John went off to bed, glad to have won the laugh.

The President, after long thought, decided that the most pressing necessity from every point of view was that Hooker should hasten after Lee. Late as it was, he went into his office and sitting in his nightshirt wrote a strong letter to Hooker which he ended with this adjuration:

"Lee's army and not Richmond is your sure objective point. If he comes toward the upper Potomac, follow on his flank and on his inside track, shortening your lines as he lengthens his. Fight him too when opportunity offers. If he stays where he is, fret him and fret him."

He sent this off by messenger before going finally to bed.

Then as the hot June days swung toward July, he awaited the result of his order with increasing anxiety. And it was with a painful sort of relief that before a week had passed he observed the slow line of ambulances beginning to thicken on Pennsylvania Avenue. Hooker for once was obeying Lincoln literally and was fretting Lee.

Lee reached Winchester, Virginia, hungry for the North. Lincoln, as he pushed through his daily tasks, wondered how long human nerves could ache as his did before they were exhausted into numbness. But his taut nerves were revealing to the people something of Lincoln's granite, at which Mary rejoiced. He was nervous and impatient. He touched up Banks again about the fall elections in Louisiana. He wrote to the committee which had protested violently against the arrest in Ohio of a well-known Democrat:

"Must I shoot a simple-minded soldier boy who deserts while I must not touch a hair of the wily agitator who persuades him to desert?"

He wrote to Andrew Johnson in Tennessee hurrying him toward the formation of a loyal State Government. He watched uneasily the taking of Mexico City by the French but forced Seward in no uncertain terms to keep hands off. He sent a bitter admonition to the radical and conservative Unionists who were rending Missouri with their disagreements:

"It is very painful to me that you in Missouri cannot or will not settle your factional quarrels among yourselves. I have been tormented with it beyond endurance for months on both sides. Neither side pays the least respect to my appeals to your reason. I am now compelled to take hold of the case—"

And never for an hour could he forget that narrow gray line marching with such incomparable resolution up the Shenandoah Valley. Again and yet again he urged his generals to make haste.

"General Hooker:—So far as we can make out here the enemy has Milroy surrounded at Winchester and Tyler at Martinsburg. If they could hold out a few days could you help? If the head of Lee's army is at Martinsburg and the tail of it on the plank road between Fredericksburg and Chancellorsville, the animal must be very slim somewhere. Could you not break him?"

On and on—that thin gray line! Could nothing turn it? The people of Pennsylvania were becoming panic-stricken. Lincoln responded to the Governor's plea for help by issuing a call for 100,000 State militia:

"I, Abraham Lincoln, President of the United States and Commander-in-Chief of the Army and Navy thereof—I, Abraham Lincoln, President of the United States—God!—" He dropped his head into his tired hands in pain too deep for tears.

But there was no time for introspection. He could not pause even to agonize over Sumner. Another message must go to the front:

"Major General Schenk:—Get General Milroy from Winchester to Harper's Ferry, if possible. He will be gobbled up if he remains, if he is not already past salvation—"

General-in-Chief Halleck and Hooker quarreled without cessation. Lincoln tried for several days to soothe both men, then he put his foot down and wrote in terms of unmistakable harshness:

"Major General Hooker:—To remove all misunderstanding, I now place you in the strict military relation to General Halleck of a commander of one of the armies to the General-in-Chief of all the armies. I have not intended differently but as it seems to be differently understood, I shall direct him to give you orders and you to obey them—"

Early in the afternoon of June 27th, Lincoln called Halleck to his office. He was utterly disgusted with what seemed to him the puerile and dangerous friction between the two generals.

"Halleck!" he began in a high, strident voice utterly unlike his usual low tones, "I'm ashamed of both you and Hooker. I've reached the limit—"

The office door which he had ordered to be locked, suddenly banged open. Charles Sumner, white linen coat flying, face purple, rushed up to the President's desk.

"Mr. Lincoln, I've just heard that Lee's army has scooped up all the free negroes in southern Pennsylvania and sent them back to Richmond to be sold into slavery. I insist—"

Lincoln jumped up so suddenly that his chair tipped over. He could not see Sumner for the sudden rage that overwhelmed him. "Insist?" he shouted. "Who are you to insist to the President? Insist? I tell you that I'm so full of 'insists' now that another one will make me puke. Sumner, get out of this room and stay out till you can come in with the respect due my office."

Lincoln turned his back on the Senator and completed the interrupted sentence. "—the limit of my patience with you. Undoubtedly Hooker had sent in his resignation only in a fit of petulance over the orders you've given him about keeping his men at Harper's Ferry. But the time's passed for petulance. This thing is too big for petulance. You prepare an order which I'll sign, accepting Hooker's resignation and putting General Meade in his place."

Halleck, with an expression of satisfaction on his pale, harassed face, hurried from the room. Lincoln turned to behold Sumner still standing by the Cabinet table. Sumner cleared his throat but once more the office door was flung wide and a woman burst into the room; a woman whose black bonnet had fallen back from her gray hair, whose black stuff dress was heavy with dust, whose bare feet were bursting from broken gaiters. Stoddard stood hesitating in the doorway.

"She's back again, sir. I've held her away from you two hours."

"It's all right, Billy," said the President. "What is it now, Madam?"

The woman leaned over the edge of the desk, her face working, her eyes half blind with old weeping. "You remember me, last week, Mr. Lincoln?"

"Yes! You said you had three sons and a husband in the army and not a cent from any of their pay. And would I do something about it. And I did. I ordered part of their pay garnisheed for you."

"Yes, sir, you did. And yesterday I learned that my boys are dead. Two of them of wounds at Chancellorsville and one at Winchester. Oh, sir— Oh, sir—will you let me have my man back? He's all that's left and he's too old to fight. Older than you, Mr. Lincoln. Not much good to me but all I have. Save him for me, sir—"

"Don't cry! Don't cry!" urged Lincoln. "Tears make it hard for me to think. I'm learning not to be softened by tears."

He forgot Sumner—and Halleck—and Meade. Here was the bloody sweat of war, indeed! He arose to remove himself from her working, clinging fingers and stared out the window—that ever thickening, never ending line of ambulances—

After a moment he turned to the woman. "I still have two," he said gently, "and you have none. It doesn't seem fair, does it? So I'll give you back your husband." He dropped to his seat again and took up his pen.

The woman crowded close. She made a peculiar sound, thought Lincoln, like an old cow bereft of her calf. He wrote an order to Stanton. The woman looked over his shoulders, her shaking fingers fixed on his arm, then smoothing his black hair; as though they two were alone; as though her trouble was the only trouble; as though the humanness of the thing she sought and Lincoln gave leveled every barrier.

He signed the paper and thrust it into her hand. "There!" he sighed.

The woman's face twisted. "God will—God will—" she could not finish but rushed out of the door which Stoddard still anxiously held open. He closed it after her and Lincoln sank back in his chair.

Sumner cleared his throat. "Such scenes are very painful. You have my deep sympathy, Mr. Lincoln. I—I fear I sometimes forget how driven and overworked you are. I deserved the rebuke. Will you accept my apology, sir?"

Lincoln looked from the proffered hand to the sincere face above it. "I'll take it with one understanding, Mr. Sumner," he said firmly, "that you cease this childish avoidance of me. Dislike me if you will, impeach me if you must, but don't be cowardly. I'm not going to bite you or assault you. Your honor is safe when you're alone with me."

Sumner, still holding out his fine white hand, said seriously, "You really think I'm afraid of that? Well, since you are so frank I'll say that it's not been fear but decency that's kept me away. How can I feel as I do toward your policies—"

"Oh, come, Senator," urged Lincoln, hoping that he was not betraying the astonishment he felt at the effect of the drubbing on Sumner, "what you feel about my policies isn't a patch to what I feel about yours! I sincerely believe that for the good of the state we ought to put up a front of at least casual bearing with each other's infirmities."

"I'm glad to hear you say that," said Sumner. "It is seriously inconvenient, not to feel free to come to you for information. But my conscience—"

Lincoln seized his hand with a short laugh. "The New England conscience is out of place in politics, Mr. Sumner. What do you hear from John Bright?"

Sumner's face lightened. He took a letter from his pocket and the interview ended with the reading of a delightful message from the great Englishman to the American President.

THE next morning at breakfast Lincoln asked Tad for a report on the progress of the play.

"He'd better give it very soon," said his mother, before Tad could reply. "I'm going to keep our family life as near normal as I can between the heat and General Lee, so you can prepare to move out to the Soldiers' Home, next week."

"Then I gotta see Isabella wight away!" exclaimed Tad, throwing down his napkin.

"Finish your breakfast, Taddie," admonished his mother. "I'm not going to move to-day!" Then turning to her husband and looking anxiously at his careworn face, "You'll be glad of the cooler nights out there, Abra'm?"

"Yes, my dear, to say nothing of being free of poor old Stanton!" answered Lincoln, heartily.

He liked the cottage. It was an unpretentious place of the style made popular by Godey's Lady's Book—a peaked little house, set with many dormer windows of the Gothic type, surrounded by trees of enormous beauty. He loved these trees, and the little dwelling with its meager front hall, its tiny parlor and bedrooms, was more homelike to him than all the grandeur of the Executive Mansion.

But he scarcely had uttered his approval when the Secretary of War rushed into the room—"poor old" Stanton who had had no let-up day or night since Lee had started his promenade northward. He was disheveled, had had no breakfast, but would not accept Mary's invitation to sit down. He needed the President, at once.

A stunning collision had taken place the day before between the head of Lee's column and Meade's left wing, near Gettysburg in Pennsylvania. A battle had developed and was continuing with increasing ferocity. Lincoln dropped his fork, seized Stanton's arm and hurried with him back to the War Office. He hardly left there for two days.

It was not a restful spot under the best of circumstances, for Stanton's irascibility kept every one's nerves on edge. With the stress of the great battle added to the usual routine, Stanton was about as easy to get along with, Lincoln thought, as a swarm of yellow jackets. But here was the best place in Washington to feel the pulse of the fight. A fairly accurate detail map of Southern Pennsylvania had been made hastily for Stanton. A procession of messengers gave tardy but roughly accurate information of division movements. Lincoln was now adept in understanding military formation and phraseology. He set the pins and moved them, ejaculated, protested, approved, forgot to eat his meals. It was obvious that one of the great engagements of the war was in progress. The thought of its importance, its implications, its possibilities, were almost beyond calm endurance.

On the afternoon of July third the dispatches, which had been hopeful in tone, ceased to arrive. Stanton lay on the broken springs of the old horsehair sofa, his black beard drenched with sweat, his eyes sunken with exhaustion, but still dictating telegrams. General Halleck, unshaven, blue eyes bloodshot from lack of sleep, paced the floor. Lincoln in his shirt sleeves sat on Stanton's high office stool, his heels caught in one of the rungs. People came and went. Senator Ben Wade, short, sturdy, and very warm in his black alpaca suit, penetrated the fastness to utter a blighting denunciation of Grant and his protracted siege of Vicksburg. With all the vindictiveness at his command he demanded that Grant be dismissed. Lincoln listened with interest. Wade was one of the Jacobins, one of Sumner's allies, but Lincoln wanted no quarrel with him. So when Stanton uttered a preliminary growl, the President said, serenely:

"Senator Wade, you remind me of a story."

Wade whirled on him, his thick pompadour seeming to stiffen like a cock's comb. "Yes, that's the way with you, sir, all story—story! You're the father of every military blunder that's been made during the war. You're on the road to hell, sir, with the Government and you're not a mile off, this minute."

Lincoln grinned. "Senator, that's just about the distance from here to the Capitol, isn't it?"

"My God!" groaned Wade, striding from the room.

Sumner, in lavender silk trousers and a brown alpaca coat, passed him in the doorway, looked after him with arched eyebrows, then entered slowly. "May I know the latest news, Mr. Secretary?"

"No news for hours. Up to noon, looked as if we'd held 'em," replied Stanton from beneath the handkerchief he'd placed over his face. "I'm going to doze for a few moments, gentlemen."

Halleck, oblivious to all about him, continued to walk the floor. He was like a man in a coma.

Lincoln beckoned the Senator to the map on the east wall. The sinking rays of the sun cast a livid, wavering light on it. Lincoln placed his finger on a blue pin.

"Here's the disposition of our lines at six o'clock this morning. Meade's been entirely on the defensive. If he can once turn the enemy and actually take up the offensive, we'll end the war with this battle, yes, sir!"

Long after the President had returned to his stool, Sumner studied the map. Then he took up his station on the window seat, looking down on the White House grounds where Tad drove little Isabella Hooper up and down in Pete's idea of a chariot. Stanton snored but roused at dusk to urge Halleck, still silently pacing the floor, to get some rest. Halleck, with a sigh, went out. James came in with an enormous tray of food from Mrs. Lincoln.

The three men ate without appetite, prowling about the office or strolling into the telegraph operators' room adjacent to listen eagerly to the chittering of the sterile instruments. The breathless moments wore away until midnight. Sumner looked at his watch and had just announced that he was going home when one of the operators rushed into the room with a message addressed to Secretary Welles.

"Six P.M. Have just left the field. All is well. Byington."

"Who's Byington?" demanded Stanton.

No one knew. Lincoln took the message. "I'll just slip over to 'Father' Welles myself and inquire," all weariness suddenly vanishing. "I'll bring the information back to you, Mr. Stanton!"

"I'll come with you!" exclaimed Sumner.

They rushed through the breathless summer darkness to the Welles' house. The Secretary of the Navy came down the stairs in his trousers and shirt, his manner as imperturbable as usual. He paused on the lowest stair to hold the message toward the gas light. Then he smiled at the two faces turned so anxiously toward him.

"Then we can sleep to-night!" he said. "This news is undoubtedly authentic. Byington is editor and owner of a paper in Norwalk, Connecticut. I know and trust him."

Lincoln gave an enormous sigh and suddenly felt drowned in weariness. "I shall sleep for the first time in three days," he said. "You're a very present help in time of trouble, Mr. Welles. Come, Sumner, we must go relieve Stanton's anxiety. We have a reprieve, at least."

But Sumner insisted that Lincoln go home, leaving the errand to him. So the two parted, Lincoln crawling up the stairs to his own room with half-closed eyes and scarcely aware that Mary helped him to take off his boots.

No further news came from Gettysburg during the night nor during the early morning hours. Billy Stoddard and Mary had engineered a Fourth of July entertainment before the White House grounds; had planned it to help offset the dangerous depression that was sure to darken Washington did news of a Union defeat come from Gettysburg. They made use of the tremendous troop movement through the city to stage a spectacular parade with much gay band music. A speaker's stand was set up just outside the north gates and Mary devastated the garden and the greenhouses to decorate it.

At noon, when Lincoln entered the stand to make his speech, there still had come no decisive word from Meade. He was a little aghast at the stupendous size of the audience packed into Lafayette Square. He did not like to address so large a crowd without having written out his speech. But such had been his preoccupation with Gettysburg that he had forgotten completely this morning's engagement until Stoddard had come for him, five minutes before the speech was due.

The sun was brilliant and dust hung motionless and golden over the crowd as he crossed the stand to the speaker's table with its inevitable pitcher of ice water. A band burst into "Hail to the Chief!" at his appearance. He leaned against the table moistening his lips. What to say to that uneasy, unhappy throng!—as he stood hesitating, Billy Stoddard touched his arm. The boy was as white as his linen suit as he handed the President an open telegram.

Lincoln read it, felt the world turn black with the revulsion of his feeling, then turned blindly to the wavering pink sea below. Here in the dispatch was written his speech and he read it aloud:

"Lee began a retreat toward the Potomac at three o'clock this morning. Meade."

A long sigh swept the square. Then a bandsman brought his sticks down on the bass drum and the storm was released. The crowds, the bands, the regiments at rest became an inextricably commingled, shrieking, huzzaing, weeping, embracing riot.

Lincoln, unheeded, slipped back to the War Office. He feared the inertia that would follow the victory and knew that immediate pressure must be brought on Meade to make him follow Lee and give battle. And such was the stimulation of his relief that he really believed that Meade's army might prove to be almost as fluid as Lee's!

After the excitement of this memorable "Fourth" was over, Mary, looking utterly fagged, remarked at the supper table that perhaps now it would be possible to go out to the Soldiers' Home for a decent night's sleep. Before Lincoln could reply Tad exclaimed in protest:

"But to-night we give the play!"

His father and mother looked at him in dismay. A spoonful of ice cream half way to his mouth, Tad returned the stare and tried to make them understand.

"Isabella said she'd come and make he' motha' come. I wanted Pete's fatha' and motha' but they was going to a funewal. All the help in this house said they'd come and so did Lo'd Lyons and Mrs. Welles and a lot of otha' people. I've been asking them all day."

His mother threw up her hands. "Tad, of all the thoughtless—"

"Don't, wife!" interrupted his father. "Taddie, didn't you realize there'd been a terrible battle and people have been under an awful strain and it's no time for a child's play?"

"This isn't a child's play," returned Tad, his lips quivering. "It's Shakespea's. You' own pet, Papa day, and so—"

"Do you know yet whether or not Mrs. Hooper's coming, Taddie?" asked his mother, suddenly.

"That's what Senata' Sumna' asked me," replied Tad. "Yes, she is. Isabella said she'd make he' because Isabella can't come alone."

Mary's mobile lips flexed from annoyance to amusement. Her tired eyes began to snap with excitement.

"Well, Abra'm, since we've a houseful of guests coming, I think you and I had better take a hand. James," turning to the servant, "you and

Ben come up to the sitting room right after supper. Tad, you go see that your theater is all ready for patrons."

Taddie with a whoop of delight ran from the room.

James at that moment laid a note at Mary's plate. She read it with a smile. "Alice Hooper wants to know if the children's invitation is authentic. I'll send a line to her at once, if you'll loan me Louis."

Lincoln nodded.

The guests arrived, most of them in an obviously tentative frame of mind. Baron Gerolt, the Prussian Minister with the Baroness; Dr. Stone, the family physician; three of the President's cavalry guard; Pete's little sister Martha in wonderful pantalettes; Lord Lyons, amused and affable; Job Cotter, who ran the gingerpop stand near the White House; lovely Mrs. Welles and a dozen others were seated in the state guest chamber when Lincoln and Sumner entered the room. As he identified the silhouettes of most of the guests, against Tad's candle footlights, the President whispered to Sumner:

"We ought to send Tad as minister to England. He can handle any combination!"

Sumner, catching sight of Alice Hooper's exquisite profile in the front row, agreed with an enthusiastic, "Yes! Yes!" and picking up a chair carried it to an empty space beside her. Lincoln laughed to himself and slumped into a seat by the door where a messenger could find him easily.

If Tad had his father's genius for friendship, he also had his mother's executive ability. The bedroom furniture had all been removed except the enormous four-poster bed. From this, Tad had stripped the bedding and covered the frame with boards to form a solid platform. The bed curtains enclosed all save the front where he had hung one of his mother's gorgeous red Persian shawls. Exits were provided by using the closet to the right and the door of the one bathroom the house contained to the left.

The entertainment was a Shakespeare potpourri;—bits chosen here and there as Tad's understanding and liking might dictate. As James drew back the shawl for the first scene, Lincoln heard his wife gasp with surprise and amusement. Taddie wore one of his mother's basques of white velvet which came half way to his knees, a pair of her white knit silk stockings which more than met the basque, his own toy sword and belt. He was ridiculously like Booth's Hamlet which Mary had taken him to see. Ridiculous, yet his boyish prettiness never was more pronounced than when he stalked across the stage toward a flag-draped packing case. Here stood Isabella in one of her mother's night dresses, caught up by a great blue sash, her hair falling in molten beauty around her lovely, excited little face.

"He jests at sca's that neva' felt a wound! But soft, what light th'ough yonda' window bweaks—" began Tad, in his clear treble.

"Oh, Romeo! Romeo!—" interrupted Isabella.

"Shut up, can't you, till I finish?" demanded Tad.

"If I wait, I'll forget, so I won't not wait," replied Isabella, emphatically and with a resolution that reduced Tad to silence while she finished the four lines.

"You've spoiled it now. It won't make sense," declared Tad, folding his arms mournfully over the white velvet tunic.

"Taddie, don't not be cross with me!" pleaded Isabella. Then with happy intuition she added, "I'll sing my song while you remember," and in a voice like a tiny silver thread she began, "Hark! Hark the lark at heaven's gate sings—"

Tad, still with arms folded à la Booth, recovered himself under the spell of the song and as the little voice died away he exclaimed:

> "Thine eyes a' lodesta's and thy tongue's sweet a'
> Mo' tuneable than la'k's to shephe'ds ea'
> When wheat is gween and hawtho'ne buds appea'."

Some one touched Lincoln on the arm and he followed Stoddard into the hall. "Secretary Welles is in your office, sir, and says he must see you." Lincoln hurried into the Cabinet room.

"Father" Welles was standing before the war map and as the President joined him, he ostentatiously moved below Vicksburg the line of blue-headed pins that crossed the Mississippi.

"What!" gasped Lincoln.

"Yes, Mr. Lincoln! I've just received a dispatch from Admiral Porter. Vicksburg fell on the Fourth of July." Welles gave his rare dry laugh and for a moment Lincoln thought he was going to try a hornpipe!

"No!" shouted Lincoln. Then words failed him. He stood staring at the Secretary's smiling face while he let the good news sink into his blood. "I swear, Mr. Welles," he brought out at last, "I don't know what we'd do without Uncle Sam's web feet. I don't believe you've ever brought me any but good tidings.—And so the Father of Waters goes again unvexed to the sea!" He suddenly enveloped Welles in a bear hug. "This is great! Great! I'll telegraph the news to Meade, myself," releasing Welles to pick up his hat.

As the two men crossed the lawn, another angle of the glorious news struck Lincoln. "What a relief to General Banks, down there in New Orleans! What a help toward renovating Louisiana and bringing her home to the family!"

Welles gave an enigmatic grunt. "Our friend Sumner won't find that angle of the event happy."

"I shan't remind him of it," said Lincoln.

"Sumner's no fool, sir," retorted Welles.

The theatrical performance was over by the time the President returned to the White House. He caught the first group of departing guests at the stair head and holding out his arms to halt them, shouted, "Vicksburg has fallen!" then hurried through the chorus of rejoicing to his office. Sumner was there, staring grimly at the gloomy portrait of General Jackson over the fireplace.

Lincoln cried his news.

"Yes! Yes!" said Sumner, sadly, "I heard you, a moment ago."

Lincoln wondered if the implications of the victory were responsible for this unwonted apathy. He clapped Sumner on the shoulder. "Whoever controls the Mississippi, controls the Union! This makes a young man of me. Come, Senator, the children didn't produce tragedy, did they? I hated to leave, I'd rather have missed a performance by Booth than Tad as Oberon. I'm glad you gave up the rôle."

But Sumner only jerked his head impatiently. "I'm glad of the victory. None rejoices more than I do in it. But taken in connection with your known attitude on reconstruction, I could have wished it delayed until you had reached a better attitude. Come, Mr. Lincoln, do this for me. Agree that you'll make no move on reconstructing Louisiana until—"

The President interrupted—no use fencing longer. "I've already ordered Shepley and Banks to get moving on fall elections down there!" He parted the tails of his evening broadcloth and sat down on the edge of the table.

Sumner, still standing under General Jackson, turned on Lincoln furiously. "You have no authority for any such action, sir! When Louisiana seceded, she committed State suicide. She became a Territory. All local institutions ceased and Congress automatically assumed jurisdiction over the vacated territory and only Congress can make a new State there and admit it to the Union."

"My idea is," Lincoln said gently, "that if the majority of the people in Louisiana transferred their obedience to a foreign power, the loyal minority constitutes the State and should govern it. I'm merely giving the loyal people a chance to exercise a function they've never lost."

"And do you think the vote can change treason to devotion?" demanded Sumner, excitedly. "Can the wedding veil make a virgin of a harlot?"

"No, but one harlot in a convent doesn't make common women of the whole lot," retorted Lincoln. "There are a good many loyal folks down there."

"Are you looking on the blacks as loyal folks?" asked Sumner, quickly.

"My feeling toward the blacks," replied Lincoln carefully, for here was Sumner's tenderest point, "is that the very intelligent ones and those that have fought as soldiers should be given a chance to prove themselves. These should be given the vote, but by the Southerners, themselves."

"Impossible! Hopeless!" groaned Sumner.

"Not so," contradicted Lincoln, but still gently. "If the loyal people of Louisiana, for example, will make a new constitution, recognizing the Emancipation Proclamation and while they're at it adopt some practical system by which the two races can gradually live themselves out of the old relation into the new it would be entirely feasible. After all, the power or element of contract may be sufficient for this probationary period by its very simplicity and flexibility."

Sumner stared at the President as though he thought him insane. "You don't know what you're saying, Mr. Lincoln!"

Lincoln glanced through the door into the reception room where several people were waiting to see him.

"Let's go where we can have privacy, Senator," he suggested and led the way into the sitting room.

Mary was standing by the table with a book in her hand. She looked up and said as casually as though their entrance were expected, "Carlyle's, 'French Revolution,' in French, than which there could be nothing more amusing."

Sumner's face softened. "Yes, even in July!" He gave no heed to the chair Lincoln pushed toward him but stood staring wistfully at Mary. "Your husband and I are arguing and I'm in no mood to argue. I feel more like—what is it you ladies say?—having a good cry."

"Don't let me interfere!" said Lincoln, glad of this sudden shift in the Senator's part.

"Why tears? Because you've neglected our friendship so cruelly?" asked Mary, quickly.

Sumner did not answer this directly. He looked down at the determined little person in the rose point evening dress and said, "I've missed you."

"Well, whose fault is it?" asked Mary in much the same tone she would have used to Taddie. She seated herself and the lamplight deepened the tender beauty of her blue eyes. "I'm not worrying too much. You'll be back, asking a favor of me. I know men. Helpless creatures!"

Lincoln rubbed his chin reflectively. Sumner, he reminded himself, or any other man, was helpless when Mary was in this archly maternal mood. One felt like melting into tears and telling more than the facts warranted. She could woo a catamount to the confessional. The Senator was no exception. Ignoring the President, he pushed a great stool to a place directly in front of Mary and seated himself on it. Mary folded her hands sedately.

"The Hoopers," began Sumner, opening and closing the feathered fan he took from Mary, "are very old friends of mine. I've known the family all my life. Alice was a Mason. Her mother and my dear twin sister were devoted to each other.—I have almost no intimates left save the Hoopers and not even them now, for some time ago Alice sent me to Coventry. I couldn't learn why. To-night, when I seated myself by her, she made an excuse and joined Mrs. Welles. When I asked to see her home, she frigidly said, 'No!' and when I pressed her for a reason she replied only, 'Ask Mrs. Lincoln.'"

"Reckon he's forgotten me and secession," thought the President with a sigh of relief. "I don't envy Mary her job," and he made his way back to his work.

But he gathered that Mary, from her story of the interview at bedtime that night, was well pleased with her rôle.

"Alice shouldn't have left such a thankless task to me," she told Sumner when he made his plaint. "It wasn't kind of her. But after all, it's not kindliness in Alice Hooper that fascinates one."

"Kindliness?" repeated Sumner. "I suppose she has the normal amount of that commodity. I've evidently offended her seriously. What have I done, Mrs. Lincoln? Do you know?"

"Yes, dear Charles Sumner," very gently. "I know. You've shown the fashionable world of Washington too clearly that its most fashionable belle fascinates you. After all, she *is* married and so there's been horrid gossip about you both."

Sumner sat perfectly still, his blue eyes fastened on Mary in growing consternation. "I've caused people to gossip about Alice Mason? I, who would not let a harsh breeze stir a hair of her head?"

Mary smiled. "You know as well as I that there's been a horrid mess of talk about you and me, Senator. Rightly enough, you've been philosophical about it. Where's your philosophy regarding Mrs. Hooper in like case?"

"But Alice is—" protested Sumner and paused.

"Alice is—" mimicked Mary, then went on earnestly. "Wait a moment, I'll read you what Alice *is* from the *Intelligence* of yesterday. It gives an account of Mrs. Eames' benefit for the Sanitary Commission." She turned the pages of the sheet, Sumner watching her somberly. " 'Mrs. Sturgis Hooper was there with her beauty, grace, slender and stately form, her high bred manners and her aristocratic reserve.'—The aristocratic reserve," commented Mary, laying down the paper, "is a little gratuitous. I've seen her when she showed the bad temper of a spoiled child."

But Sumner was not to be drawn into a discussion of Alice Hooper's character.

"But, Mrs. Lincoln," he asked, "why didn't Alice tell me this herself?"

"Because I think she couldn't bear to hurt you. I think she cares too much for you."

Sumner's great head sank to his breast and when after a pause he looked up, his face was drawn as though by a long illness. "There's a curse on my affection for women," he said. "Well—that's ended! You've been a good friend to me in this, as in many other ways, dear Mrs. Lincoln." He rose. "I'm—I'm not quite myself. This has been a greater blow than you know. Ah," clenching a great white fist and allowing it to fall upon the table, "she is lovely—lovely—"

"Memories are one of life's great compensations," said Mary. "Memories particularly of what never was and could not be. All our poets know that—'Heard melodies are sweet, but those unheard are sweeter'—'The spirit ditties of no tune'—'She cannot fade, though thou hast not thy bliss'—" she paused and sat with brooding eyes on the empty fireplace.

"You have a great gift for sympathy!" ejaculated Sumner. "I shall come back to you often, often.—I haven't the resiliency of twenty-five years ago—" He bowed over Mary's hand and went out.

Lincoln, listening to Mary's account of this, made as she brushed her gorgeous chestnut hair before his mirror, bit his thumb and sighed, "Poor fellow! Poor Charles!—Mary, you really feel sympathy for him? Your little intrigue isn't all intrigue?"

Mary paused with the brush posed. "I'm devoted to Charles Sumner.

Even were nothing else involved, I'd have wanted to give him this warning. But"—shaking the brush at him earnestly—"I'd stoop to *any* intrigue known or unknown to help you. And there's no use in your looking sanctimonious, young man!"

As there seemed nothing to be said in response to this, Lincoln suddenly kissed her and turned to another subject.

"I have a feeling that Meade is going to sit down and nurse his wounds in spite of all my urging. Lord, send me a general with legs!"

CHAPTER IX

POOR NANNY

AFTER all, Lincoln went out to the Soldiers' Home alone. Taddie had a sharp attack of ague late in July and little Isabella Hooper wilted in the terrific heat of Washington. Dr. Stone ordered both children away. The Hoopers departed for their summer place on the Massachusetts shore and Mary left her husband reluctantly and took Tad to the White Mountains. Sumner started on a lecture trip without appearing again at the White House. Lincoln was glad to see him go.

There was no wooing Sumner by any method he had thus far discovered. One might as well, thought Lincoln, coo to Bunker Hill monument! He was pleased to be left with a few months before him clear of Sumner and Congress in which to speed forward reconstruction in Louisiana and Tennessee. If he was to have only the one term in office, it behooved him not to waste an hour, a moment, in doing all that he could to commit the Government to his own peculiar plans. The need for haste became an obsession with him; an unceasing urge that chafed him day and night. He began a campaign of letter and dispatch writing, in an attempt to inspire Governor Shepley and General Banks in Louisiana and Governor Johnson and General Rosecrans in Tennessee with his own conception of speedy action.

The month of August remained long in his memory as a not unhumorous combination of chills and fever which afflicted his own body and mental chills and fevers which affected the mental processes of the men whom he sought to use for the great cause. Recrimination and indifference, feverish preparations and tardy performances. Rosecrans, slow and querulous. Burnside tardy in crossing from Ohio to Rosecrans' aid and between them the battle of Chickamauga lost. Banks and Shepley snarling over the question of authority—only Andrew Johnson, among them all, showing marked ability. And most heart-twisting of all, Meade losing Lee and settling down, apparently for life, on the Rapidan.

After a few weeks of this Lincoln wrote to Mary and asked how soon she thought it would be safe to bring Tad back to Washington. He was homesick for them. With this same letter he wrote one to Tad telling him news calculated to revive the boy's interest in home affairs. Poor Nanny goat had disappeared. She had been found by the gardener chewing up his pet flower bed and had been dealt with so harshly by him that she had retired to Tad's bedroom. The chamber-maid had found her lying on Tad's bed, chewing her little cud. The chamber-maid, too, had been harsh and Nanny had run away. Perhaps her wounded feelings had driven her to extreme ends such as joining the Army of the Potomac. Perhaps she would return when Taddie did.

The letters had the desired effect. Within a week after they were written Mary and Tad appeared at the White House with many trunks, with a cage containing a skunk, a turtle and a hoot owl, and with the flurry of domestic excitement that Lincoln loved because it meant Mary and Tad.

An hour after her arrival, Mary had completed an examination into the President's ways of eating and sleeping during her absence and repaired to his office with her report. He was a disgrace, she declared, to any wife.

"No! No! Don't break my old heart like that!" he protested with a grin.

"But you are! Even your giant strength can't stand up under Washington, the war and politics, plus your idiotic habits. James says you have attacks of heartburn. I'm going to put a box of saleratus and a teaspoon here on your desk. See that you use it. You haven't been eating enough and you're as thin as a bodkin. Oh, my dear, my dear, you do upset me so! Now, drink this glass of buttermilk and come with me for a ride."

"Where's Tad?" asked Lincoln after he had drained the glass with relish.

"He and Pete have organized a hunt for Nanny. I'm going to order the carriage right now. The horses are positively dying for exercise. Put that letter down and come, my dear husband," laying a tender hand on his.

He rose with alacrity and offered her his arm which Mary took with a sweeping curtsy and a little giggle.

Physically the ride was not particularly pleasant. September was very hot and very dry and Washington was playing host to a pest of flies unprecedented in any one's experience. People said that the proximity of many battlefields and the great number of hospitals in and around the city were the cause. However that might be, no means availed against the dreadful, buzzing, biting swarms that made waking hours a burden and sleeping almost impossible. They settled by the hundreds on the carriage. Mary's veil was a partial protection to her. But Lincoln, the coachman, and the footman were in misery while the horses almost kicked out of the traces in their irritation. In spite of this, Lincoln was glad to get away from his work; glad to see something beyond Lafayette Square; glad to be with his wife again.

"Tell me about the skunk," asked Lincoln after they were well started. "Is he to be a bedroom pet, also?"

"Good heavens, no! Tad promises to keep him in the stable. For a long time I held out against bringing him home but Tad was so heartbroken about Nanny that I gave in. He bought the beast from a farmer boy up in Vermont, or rather traded for it."

"What did he swap?" asked Lincoln.

Mary's eyes twinkled. "That I didn't discover till we reached here. He gave the boy a photograph of yourself."

"No! Jings! Oh! Oh! Couldn't be better!" Lincoln's laughter caused a cow grazing pensively by the roadside to break her tether rope.

"What's he named it?" he gasped when he could.

"Louis Napoleon! The turtle is McClellan and the hoot owl is General Halleck."

"Better not let M. Mercier hear the first," laughed the President. "Tad's the joy of my heart. We must get him another goat."

"He says he doesn't want it. Nanny was his only love. He's written to all his friends telling of his loss. To Stanton, among others, who curiously enough sent him a wonderful formal letter of sympathy, and to Charles Sumner, from whom he has not heard. But that's not strange. Sumner wrote me from Boston that his brother George is dying in a hospital there. Poor Charles! He'll be the last brother left out of five!"

"That's hard news!" exclaimed Lincoln. "I'd like to write him a letter of sympathy. But if I do, he'll think I'm soft-soaping him."

Mary considered this for a few moments. "Perhaps you're right about it. You usually are in such things. Have you heard that he's joined in a quiet boom of Chase for the Presidency?" Lincoln nodded and she went on, "And have you heard that Butler is talked of as the Democratic nominee? You ought to get rid of Butler by putting him in your Cabinet."

Lincoln smiled. "What a crazy quilt you'd make of my poor Cabinet if I gave you your way! Who next?"

"Sumner next as Secretary of State," replied Mary promptly.

"Sam Hooper's idea, too," said Lincoln. "Another one of those blind boils you can neither cure nor bring to a head. I'm going to use Butler's executive ability by putting him in charge of the Department of Virginia and North Carolina and then pray to God he won't hamstring Meade. Now let me tell you about the good work Bob is doing in bringing his dark children up out of Egypt."

Somehow, in spite of dust and flies, it was a most refreshing drive. Yes, it was good to have Mary back.

With his wife's return and the arrival of cooler weather, Lincoln's wonted intellectual energy revived. This was well, for the annual message must be prepared and he must bring to this work a brain that functioned freed of the fog of weariness, for in it he proposed to take his stand, foursquare, on his own method of reconstruction. And he proposed in it also to hush for all time the complaint of Sumner and his radical followers that the President was only half-hearted in his efforts to enforce the Emancipation Proclamation; that he did not strenuously desire to free the slaves; that he was willing to make a peace with the South on slavery terms. It was a difficult paper to prepare not only as a state document but as a matter of literary composition—to make it lucid, to make it final, to make it beautiful.

The varying fortunes of Grant's campaign in the West with the thousand pressing details of his position as Chief Executive kept his office in a turmoil and he found it impossible to write there. He formed the habit of stealing away to his bedroom just before supper. Here he would seat himself before a window, feet on the sill, rest his long telescope on his toes and gaze at the Virginia hills. Something in this mild occupation released his mind from other perplexities and allowed it to clamp completely on the problem at hand.

Frequently he sat with meditative eye at the end of the telescope long after dusk had settled, blotting out first the red hills, then, in sequence, Long Bridge, the unfinished shaft of Washington Monument, the marshes, the Mall, his own garden. His mind was refined to an etcher's point as he traced the delicate subtleties of his task.

Tad, the free lance, alone had power to rouse him from his absorption in this work and Mary used the little boy as messenger to summon his father to the evening meal. Tad was still mourning for poor Nanny. He came in one evening at dusk and taking the telescope from his father's unresisting hands applied his own eye to it.

"Maybe Nanny did join the A'my of the Potomac," he murmured.

Immediately Lincoln roused himself. "Poor Nanny! You won't let me buy you another nice she goat, Tad?"

"No!" from lips that quivered. "Nanny was *hand*-twained. She wasn't just a plain she goat, Papa day. She was educated as much mo' than wegular goats as a West Pointa' is than a wegular pwivate. I'm getting so old now I don't feel like I could begin educating anotha' goat."

Lincoln kissed him. "What can I do to ease your heartache, darling Tad?"

"Take me to supper!" Tad wheedled and hand in hand the two descended to the dining room.

"Somebody's got to do something," Lincoln declared to his wife that evening. "Tad's mourning for poor Nanny would draw tears from an army sutler. What do you say we try to locate a she goat that will look like Nanny and, we'll hope, will have better manners? And just thrust it on him?"

"It might work," agreed Mary. "I'll see what James can do."

But James' efforts were forestalled. A day or so after Lincoln had made his suggestion, Tad rushed into his father's office.

"Come quick and see what Senata' Sumna' has given me!" he shouted, ignoring Halleck and Stanton who were seated with the President.

"Is Mr. Sumner here?" asked Lincoln.

"Yes! In my woom! Come on! All of you come," Tad added hospitably.

Stanton shook his head irritably. Halleck did not trouble to answer. Lincoln rose. He always felt a little offended when Tad was slighted. "If you gentlemen will excuse me, I'll report on that matter in person at the War Office a little later." And he allowed Tad to lead him out.

Lincoln paused in the door of the child's bedroom. Two baby she goats, each a tiny replica of poor dear Nanny, were horning each other vigorously on the hearth rug. Senator Sumner, in deep black, held their lead ropes.

"They a' Boston goats!" cried Tad. "I'm going to name one Beans and the otha'—" He hesitated.

"Cod," suggested his father, crossing the room with hand extended to

Sumner. "This is like your kindness, Senator! How can we help loving you?"

"Don't try!" heartily from Sumner.

He looked worn and very sad, Lincoln thought. "What's the news from our Boston friends," he asked, aloud. "How is Sam Hooper and Mrs. Hooper—" He paused, conscious that he had been tactless.

But Sumner was cool enough. "I saw Sam, yesterday, but I've not seen Mrs. Hooper or little Isabella since July."

"I heard from General Banks not an hour ago that there was a great deal of sickness on his staff and that Captain Hooper was among those afflicted," said the President. No use trying to be tactful. Sam Hooper was his own friend as well as Sumner's. Not but what it was a queer situation. Perhaps he'd better try to make it sound a little less pointed. "I've got a couple of neighbor boys down there in New Orleans and their folks got me to ask particularly for them. That's how the matter came up. I wonder if Sam Hooper knows?"

"He didn't mention it to me," replied Sumner, slowly. "Is Captain Hooper very ill?"

"Stanton is getting me a report on him, with the other boys," replied Lincoln. "Will you go over to the War Office with me while I get it? If things go wrong, you'd be the one to break the news to Sam. I'll try to head off the regular death notice going to him. Would you prefer to have me bring word back here?"

"I'll wait here with Taddie, if you don't mind, Mr. Lincoln," replied Sumner.

The President nodded and went out. His feelings, as he made his way to the War Office, were difficult to analyze. There was typhoid down there on Banks' staff. Sturgis Hooper and the neighbors' sons had little chance of recovery. If young Hooper died—well, it was like the most of life. One man's loss was another man's gain. Sort of indecent, his own hasty exit to get news for Sumner. When he reached the War Office, he found that Stanton had received the delayed telegram from New Orleans. Sturgis Hooper was dead and so were the two other young officers. Lincoln took the yellow slip from the operator and without waiting to check over the entire list with Stanton, he hurried back to the White House. What a situation! Shakespeare should have had it to play with or Charles Dickens! Sumner still stood quietly on the hearth rug watching Tad with his new pets. Without a word Lincoln handed the Senator the death list. Sumner read it slowly, then looked up at the President.

"I know several of these boys," he said, quietly. But he was white to the very lips. "If you wish, I'll write to their families."

"Check them off and I'll delay the army notices," agreed Lincoln, purposely businesslike and crisp but watching Sumner closely. The Senator looked as if he were about to faint.

But Sumner was steady enough. He folded the tragic slip and put it in his pocketbook. "I'll send this back to you in an hour or so, Mr. Lincoln," he said. His voice was husky. His eyes suffused.

"Thank you again for Tad, Senator," said the President.

"I love Tad," murmured Sumner and he went slowly out into the hall.

On his way back to his desk, Lincoln met Mary and told her the news. She gasped, blinked and exclaimed, "Isn't it ghastly how one man's grief may mean another man's solace!"

"I'd say Sumner had a long hard row to hoe before he found his solace," Lincoln nodded grimly.

"Poor fellow! I'm afraid he has!" agreed Mary.

CHAPTER X

LINCOLN finished the annual message about the middle of November. His preoccupation with this had caused him to leave until the last moment the setting down of a speech he had been asked to make at the dedication of the Gettysburg cemetery on November 19th. He left for Gettysburg on the 18th with John Hay, Seward, Nicolay, Stanton and others, both reluctant and eager to go. Tad was ill, not seriously, but he disliked leaving him. He and Mary since Willie's death could scarcely contain themselves for anxiety if either Tad or Bob so much as sneezed. Lincoln was feeling ill, himself. He was feverish and his head ached and buzzed.

His back ached too. But he was eager to get away from Washington for a few hours. Eager, too, to see the battlefield, every rod of which he knew vicariously as he had known Antietam and Chancellorsville. He was afraid Mary would discover his condition and sic Dr. Stone on him. Then his holiday would be nil.

But he got away without trouble and finished writing the little speech on the train. He delivered it the next day. It sounded flat, it seemed to Lincoln, after Edward Everett's long hour of superb oratory. The people seemed unimpressed and he supposed they looked on his effort as a sort of benediction following Everett's great sermon. He hoped it was not an entire failure, he told Everett, who praised it.

Not that it mattered. Nor did the view of the battlefield later matter much. He felt ill and wanted to get home. He got there late in the evening of the 19th. Mary gave him one look, then made him lie down on the sofa in the sitting room. Then she sent for Dr. Stone.

The doctor examined the President carefully. When he had finished he said gravely, "I'm afraid we've got a case of varioloid here, Mr. Lincoln."

Mary gave a little scream. "Smallpox, doctor! My poor husband!"

"Mild smallpox," agreed Dr. Stone. "You must get to bed, sir, and we must put the White House under quarantine."

"Has Taddie got this, too? Are you deceiving me about him?" gasped Mary.

"No! No! Tad only has malaria and is doing well." The doctor smiled at her. "Keep him away from his father. Take off your shawl, Mrs. Lincoln, I'm going to vaccinate every one in the house beginning with you. We doctors all go armed these days for just this."

"But it took with me, last summer," protested Mary, nevertheless baring her plump white arm, her voice steadying as she did so.

Dr. Stone grunted and rubbed the firm flesh with alcohol. He talked as he worked. "You must get to bed and stay there, Mr. Lincoln. Varioloid can be dangerous. I don't want to frighten you. But you're a very sick man and must take care of yourself."

Lincoln glanced up at the doctor who looked curiously unreal. In fact he seemed to waver back and forth like a ghost disturbed by wind. "I can't go to bed," he said hoarsely. "I've got to finish my annual message and discuss it with the Cabinet. And those poor fellows out at Chattanooga are beginning a fearful fight. I'm needed at the end of a telegraph wire. I'm not catching, am I, till I begin to erupt?"

"Not necessarily. But you must stay in bed, Mr. Lincoln, or you'll endanger your life. Can't you control him, Mrs. Lincoln?" He looked at Mary. He knew she would rise wonderfully to the emergency, though she might have hysterics afterward.

She gave the doctor a little nod and taking both Lincoln's hands, she gave him a gentle tug. "Come, my dear! You've no excuse for not spending this night at least in bed. You've got a new kind of patronage to distribute now, eh?"

Lincoln staggered to his feet, blind with pain. "Yes," he mumbled, "it's the only time I've had something to give away that nobody wanted."

He passed a wretched night, his fever giving him horrid, inchoate fantasies. But he woke in the morning with brain clear enough to realize that he was going to be very ill and that unless he discussed the annual message with his Cabinet, at once, he might not be able to do so at all.

When Nicolay came in to say that the Cabinet members had convened and wished to know what of the President's work they could perform, he sat up in bed and told the secretary to help him on with his dressing robe. This done, he said:

"Now you go out and ask them if they're afraid to come in here for a little while. I'm not catching yet. And I want to read them the message. Then I can go ahead and be sick right comfortably."

All the seven followed Nicolay back into the bedroom. The sight of them steadied the President to a supreme effort. His brain cleared marvelously. He was even able, he told himself with a grin, to observe a certain hopeful aspect in Chase's concern for him, as if the Secretary of the Treasury were wondering how often varioloid proved fatal or if it ever ripened into black smallpox or if black smallpox in a President were grounds for impeachment. When they were seated around the room, he took the message from Nicolay and read it aloud.

It was a remarkable state document, more remarkable than Lincoln at all realized until he saw its effect on this particularly astute audience. As an annual message must, it contained the usual report on the condition of the country, but it contained three other clauses all of which Lincoln considered exceedingly and equally important. First it contained a proclamation of amnesty for repentant rebels with the oath of allegiance they must sign. Second, a succinct statement to the effect that when ten per cent of the pre-war voters in any rebelling State should take this oath of allegiance, they could form a State government which would be recognized by the Chief Executive as the authentic voice of that State. Third, he magnificently reassured Congress and the country of his abhorrence of slavery and of his unbreakable determination to end the "execrable institution."

When he had finished, he dropped the manuscript a little feebly and took off his spectacles that he might perceive clearly the effect his explosives had had on his associates.

Seward smiled. "In other words, Mr. Lincoln, you've forever put to rest the howl of the radicals that you won't permanently end slavery."

"Yes! Yes!" exclaimed "Father" Welles. "You've closed Sumner's mouth for good!"

The other members joined in with enthusiastic congratulations on his restatement of his attitude toward the slaves. Lincoln waited with growing surprise for their comments on his reconstruction program. To his utter astonishment none came. Gradually, it dawned on him that these men, too, had been skeptical as to his determination to down the "slave empire"—these men who, one might have thought, must understand clearly his every political purpose. And in the intensity of their relief and joy, they were ignoring the importance of the methods by which he proposed to carry out his promise to end slavery. It was a staggering thought to Lincoln. If the message had this effect on his official intimates, why might it not have the same effect on Congress? Wasn't it possible that in swallowing his declarations on Emancipation, Congress would swallow his plans for reconstruction? If this were possible, then the message would go farther than his wildest dreams of its purpose had carried him.

He listened to the ejaculations of the Secretaries—even Chase piped up feebly, although the clause on slavery robbed him of his choicest criticism against Lincoln—tried to thank them and suddenly realized that he had gone beyond his strength. The faces about his bed faded away and when he came to himself, the room was empty and Mary was holding smelling salts to his nose the while she chided him.

He was very ill for a few days; so ill that he found himself during lucid intervals earnestly tabulating Hamlin's weaknesses and strength and wishing that he'd been able to make the man from Maine more fully his partner in his plans for reconstruction; so ill that, as he learned later, the whole country was speculating on Hamlin's known and unknown biases. The fever, the pain, the almost intolerable itching finally engrossed him and he was obliged, as he told Mary, to leave the country for a while to stew in its own juices.

But he was splendidly strong and by the first week in December he was mentally himself and able to rejoice mightily in the great news of Grant's victory at Chattanooga. There was no such dearth of information concerning this battle as had been the case with Gettysburg. Charles Dana was with Grant and he kept Stanton informed.

"Dana's reports for six months have been giving us fair warning that

Grant's the man," said Lincoln, as he read Dana's vivid story of the battle to Mary. "I reckon that what with Dana's opinion and Grant's vindication of it, the little General's in line for that dictatorship. And what will Butler and his friends say then?"

Mary shook her head. "Butler'll say *he* never had a real chance."

"Then he'll say a lie," returned the President, flatly.

He was chafing now over the quarantine restrictions. He wanted to get up to the Capitol and read the annual message himself to a joint session of the Houses. The more he thought of the reception the Cabinet had given his paper the more excited and sanguine he became about its possible effect on the Congress, the more he grew to believe it might be possible to sweep some of his own reconstruction legislation through on the wave of enthusiasm he was sure now the message would engender.

But when he told Dr. Stone his plan, the physician vetoed it with all the large vehemence at his command. He tried to win Mary, but she became half hysterical at the mere mention of such a strain on his weakened nerves. Still, not till the day the message was due did Lincoln really give up the struggle. Then, while eating his breakfast in bed, he sent for John Hay and dispatched him to the Capitol with the manuscript.

John was gone for hours and Lincoln worked himself into a fever before the young man appeared. He had waited until Congress had exhausted its first comments. The story of the day lost nothing, of course, in John's telling. However, Lincoln was convinced that there could be no question but that Congress had received the message with wild enthusiasm.

Charles Sumner had gone about, saying, "The slaves are free! The slaves are free!" Boutell, the extreme radical, had kept shouting, "It is right at last! The free are forever free!" Owen Lovejoy, the Western Abolitionist, had sobbed, "I shall live to see slavery ended in America!" And Greeley, on the floor for the day, had cried that it was devilish good!

Not a single question had been raised about his reconstruction clauses. Every thought had been focused on the slavery issue. It was astounding! Lincoln felt his physical weakness drop from him like a discarded garment.

"Why, John, the millennium's arrived! The radicals are praising Lincoln!" he cried. "Here, give me a shoulder. I'm going into the office and do an hour's work instead of sitting here like an old lady tatting. Even Lyman Trumbull and Henry Winter Davis approved me, eh?"

"Trumbull did. Davis asked that the reconstruction portion of the message be referred to a special committee and that was done," replied John, as he offered the President his hand.

"Who is chairman of that committee?" asked Lincoln, sharply.

"Winter Davis himself," replied John.

Lincoln sank back on the sofa. "My mortal enemy!" he groaned. "Still, you say he didn't talk against the message?" hopefully.

"Not at all, sir," replied John. "I'm sure you can rest easy. There's a real feeling of loyalty to you to-night in Congress. Davis or Sumner either won't be able to get any dirty legislation through."

"Loyalty!" ejaculated Lincoln. "You poor puling babe! Haven't you learned yet, dear John, that there's no such word in the lexicon of politics? Even Sumner, the finest Roman of them all, can't be loyal. Human nature's a pretty weak thing, I reckon. The world is full of Judases. Come to think of it, the Saviour of the world chose twelve disciples and even out of that small number, selected by superhuman wisdom, one turned out a traitor!" Then with a twinkle, he added, "Maybe it's not improper to say that Judas carried the bag, was treasurer to Jesus and his disciples!"

John laughed ruefully, then asked, "Is that why you have no real intimates among the politicians, Mr. Lincoln?"

"I reckon that's part of the reason," agreed the President, a little sadly. He sighed, then looked over the young man appraisingly as he lingered before the fire. "You look as if you needed to get out to grass, John. Being tied to an office job is hard on a young fellow like you. You've got some so-called political friends among the Unionists in Florida, haven't you?"

The young man grinned. "Had a letter from one of them last week. They want me to run as their Representative in Congress."

Lincoln returned the grin, then said seriously, "We'd better work while Congress debates. General Gillmore plans to try to take over the north of Florida, soon. How'd you like to go down there and try out this oath of allegiance of mine? Fix up some blank books and so on and see how it works."

John's black eyes blazed. "I'd like it above all things, sir! You aren't going to lose any time, eh? When do you want me to go?"

"As soon as you can get ready. I'm going to have one or two tight jobs finished before Winter Davis can get his committee to agree on a hostile program. They won't have the heart to *de*struct a state after I've made it, I'm sure."

"Oh! even Congress isn't that idiotic!" agreed John Hay, as they moved slowly toward the office.

CHAPTER XI

HOPE

SUMNER came up to call as soon as the quarantine was lifted, perhaps a week after the reading of the annual message. He congratulated Lincoln heartily on the stand he had taken with regard to slaves, but made no mention of reconstruction.

Lincoln, who wished to let sleeping dogs lie until Winter Davis reported his program, was glad to have it so. Sumner was looking extraordinarily young. Hope, Lincoln thought, is a great rejuvenator. It was curious finally to have achieved the friendliest of outward relations with Sumner when he never could forget for a moment that Sumner was really his deadly adversary, was at the moment of uttering his perfectly sincere congratulations undoubtedly planning to put Chase or himself in the White House, was figuring how to force Lincoln's resignation, was scheming to block his every effort at rehabilitating the South on lines of mercy! Yet there was nothing dishonorable in Sumner's attitude. All these strange complications belonged to the political game. "No, not game!" Lincoln corrected himself grimly. With Sumner politics was not a game but his very life. Perhaps, he thought more grimly, this was true of Lincoln too!

Not the members of Congress alone reacted happily to the annual message. His stock rose with the whole country. And though the facile pendulum of public approbation began to swing back after a week or so, Lincoln believed that his ideas had made real progress with the nation at large. The belief became a certainty when, soon after the holidays, Arkansas loyalists began to take the Oath of December 8, as that portion of Lincoln's amnesty clause was called. Andrew Johnson began administering the oath in Tennessee. Louisiana was at work on her new constitution along the line of Lincoln's plan. John Hay left for Florida in January, full of a great faith. The President was pleased and sanguine.

He said to Mary one night not long after John Hay's departure, "Well, three of my baby States are well on their way to birth and both parents doing well;—myself and the ten per cent loyalists claiming that proud title. I don't believe Congress will have the heart to drown 'em, like blind kittens."

Mary, who was hearing Tad's French lesson at the library table, looked up to say, "You're misjudging the cleverness and the vindictiveness of those men, Abra'm. You're judging them by yourself. I believe Charles Sumner and Lyman Trumbull and Winter Davis are just hoping you'll take enough rope to hang yourself."

"Nonsense!" replied Lincoln. "Sumner's so sure he's going to get me out of here by the time the war is over that he isn't going to trouble too much about what I do in the interim." He seated himself before the fire and Tad at once embraced the opportunity to drop his lessons and crowd onto his father's knees. He was small for his ten years but still was growing a little large for this old posture. His mother reminded him of this and ordered him back to his lessons but his father gathered him close and Tad prepared for a nap.

" 'Father' Welles told me to-day," Lincoln went on, "that Sumner lately admitted to him that he had vague dreams of himself for my job but was willing to relinquish them in favor of Chase."

"Abra'm," Mary suddenly leaned toward him, "why wouldn't it be a great move, if you're renominated, to have Sumner run for Vice President instead of Hamlin? You know as well as I do that nice as he is, Hamlin's not a bit of good to you. He's a radical and works with Trumbull and Davis and Wade."

"Sumner would scorn the suggestion," replied Lincoln. "Not but what you're right about Hamlin. I've been feeling round on the subject. Even tried out General Butler for the job, to oblige the anti-slavery Democrats. He thanked us kindly and told us he had a *real* job, now. I've a good mind to try Andrew Johnson in the place."

Mary gave a little scream. "Oh, you great fool! Why, he's nothing but white trash! A narrow, ignorant, hidebound Democrat who gets drunk in public. Now don't do this thing! Don't!"

"He's a true and valuable man," declared Lincoln. "The work he's done has been simply indispensable. His suppressing disorder in Tennessee would be enough to immortalize him. But on top of being Governor and General, he's been a Quartermaster, relieving want and sheltering the homeless. He's re-made that old State and done it intelligently, too. And I tell you, Mary, I'll have to have the help of the Democrats if I'm to have any chance at all of being reëlected. Johnson can swing the border States for me."

"Oh! Oh! Oh!" Mary wrung her hands. "You're wrong in this, Abra'm, indeed you are!"

"I reckon you haven't watched his work in Tennessee," said Lincoln. He was a little uneasy, as he always was when Mary opposed his judgment of men. Mary suddenly burst into tears. "Surely, my dear," he protested, "you don't feel that strongly against him!"

"I feel as if you'd dug your own grave," she sobbed.

He tried to take a light tone. "Come, now! You mean I've nipped some scheme you and Mrs. Hooper had hatched."

Mary, biting her lips, dried her eyes and as she saw Tad stirring, tried to play up to her husband's lead. "Alice Hooper is back looking very handsome in mourning."

"Isabella and me," remarked Tad, suddenly opening his eyes, "a' going to be mawied as soon as I get a new pony instead of a goat I can't get he' to like Beans and Cod. If poo' Nanny hadn't got lost, she might have liked he'. When I was playing with Isabella yeste'day, Mista' Sumna' said he'd give Isabella a pony but she said to give it to me. But I told him I couldn't take anything from an enemy of my fatha's."

The yawning little boy sat erect, his face rosy with sleep and firelight. His mother crossed the room to sit on the arm of Lincoln's chair. Lincoln rested his hand on hers.

"And what did the Senator say to that, son?" he asked.

"He didn't say anything," replied Tad. "Anyhow, motha', can I have a pop stand down in the hall to sell to the folks that come to fuss at Papa day? I want to make money for the hospitals. I told Isabella she could wash glasses. She said she wouldn't. She'll be a lazy wife but I'll be wealthy so I don't mind. Can I, motha'?"

"I'll see," replied his mother.

"Isabella's mamma," Tad went on, "is the only one I know who don't like Mista' Sumna'! She's always saying teasy things to him."

"I reckon it would be a wise thing if some one of your parents had the common sense and courage to send you to boarding school, son," groaned Lincoln, gathering the little figure in the black velvet suit close to him.

"I'm not going away from you and motha', one inch," replied Tad with the complacency of sure knowledge. "I don't see why she don't like him. He's stylish and famous and she likes people like that. I asked he' and she only laughed and pulled my ea'. She's so tall and pink and white—" He gave a wide yawn and Lincoln rose, still holding him.

"Well, Taddie darling, seems to me you've given your mother and me enough thoughts to make into cuds for a while. You, to bed!"

Tad spoke sleepily over his father's shoulder. "Motha', will you give me fifty cents to start my pop stand with?"

"If you'll get your French lesson first thing in the morning," replied his mother.

"Ho! Easy!" Tad threw her a kiss which she returned with a smile.

It was the day after this conversation that Henry Winter Davis introduced his reconstruction bill in Congress. Lincoln studied a copy of the bill. It ignored the President's plans and declared that as the Rebel States were out of the Union, Congress was the only agency by which they could be readmitted. It then gave a tight formula for reconstruction that Lincoln knew would enrage the South. For a moment his heart sank, then, as he thought further, he said with sudden relief to Nicolay, who had brought him the bill:

"Sumner won't back this. It doesn't include negro suffrage in its plans. The Senator will inevitably line up against it. I'm not going to worry. Sumner will kill it."

"Perhaps—!" said Nicolay with a doubtful smile.

Tad came in on this conversation demanding to know where his mother was.

"In the garden, most likely. She always tells James where she's going," replied his father. "If you've looked in the garden and she's not there, ask James."

"I have, Papa day," said Tad. "James said he saw her talking in the ga'den to a lady in a black veil and he thinks she walked out the back gate with the lady. He thought it was one of her poo' folks she was going to visit. But Pete Kelley says he saw motha' going into a house way out on Seventh Stweet whe' he was c'lecting old wags. I to'd him he was a big lia'. But he says he isn't."

Lincoln glanced at Nicolay. The threat to kidnap different members of the Lincoln family and hold them until the President made peace had been made so frequently that no one paid much attention to the letters containing the threats. Yet the fear that some one might attempt to do this dastardly thing to his wife or children never was very far from the President's thoughts. So now he said to Nicolay, casually, for Tad's benefit, "This reminds me that I had arranged to go to the hospitals with Mrs. Lincoln this afternoon. Will you tell James to tell her I'm ready?"

Nicolay went out followed by Tad. Half an hour later, he returned without Tad but with Pete Kelley's hand in his. "This small boy insists on his story, sir," said Nicolay. "We can't seem to locate Mrs. Lincoln, nor to extend the facts beyond Tad's account. I've sent him around to visit with Isabella."

"How do you know it was Mrs. Lincoln, Pete?" asked Lincoln, his heart sinking with premonition of evil.

"Because it was, sir," insisted Pete, his freckled face pale with earnestness. "She had on that spotted purple dress she wears in the garden and that big floppy hat with the purple veil. I'd know it in—in—in heaven."

"I think Pete and you and I had better make a quiet trip out to that house," said Lincoln to Nicolay, rising.

"Let Pete and me go alone, sir. I'm sure it would be wiser," begged Nicolay.

"No, sir," replied the President, picking up his hat, "if my wife is in a tight fix, nothing can stop my going to find her. Not Grant nor Meade nor Sumner is big enough for that."

He started for the door, filled with a nameless terror.

Nicolay suggested the carriage.

"And have a cavalry guard follow me and a string of reporters later?" cried Lincoln, leading the way rapidly down the servants' path to the rear gate. "No! How far is the house from here, Pete?" he asked, taking the child's hand.

"Just out the Seventh Street pike a little way, that old farmhouse where they raise pigs," replied Pete, at a jog trot to keep up with the President's stride.

"Can you show me a short cut?" asked Lincoln.

"Yes, sir," suddenly turning to a path that led through the pasture lot beyond Lafayette Square.

It was not difficult to avoid passers-by in this direction. Washington was a sprawling wilderness here with no sidewalks and the right of way along the road when they reached it was disputed only by pigs and cows.

Fifteen minutes' walk plastered them to their knees with red mud and brought them to a lane at the end of which stood an old red brick house. Its white-pillared portico was falling down. Its front garden was a pigsty and duck pond.

"Here it is, sir!" Pete wiped his nose on his sleeve and pointed. "I saw Mrs. Lincoln walking up the steps into that house with a lady in black."

Lincoln groaned and Pete suddenly began to cry.

"Hush! I'm not cross. I'm obliged to you, dear Pete. Nicolay, you and the boy stay here."

Nicolay ventured to protest, but Lincoln, still driven by a mysterious certainty that Mary had called him, silenced him sternly.

"I always know when my wife needs me. Let me do this my way, George."

He splashed through the pigsty as certain that Mary was in this ruined farm as he was that the afternoon sky was blue overhead and that blackbirds called from a marsh beside the lane. He banged on the door. There was no response. He thrust it open with his foot.

Mary lay on the floor of the deserted hall. Lincoln leaped to her side. She was unconscious but breathing heavily. He lifted her and rushed from the house.

Nicolay, as he saw the President emerge, sent Pete running like a rabbit with a note to Billy Stoddard. Lincoln did not speak and did not answer Nicolay's questions as he started on a mighty pace along the muddy road. But when the President paused for breath at the edge of Lafayette Square, the secretary produced a little silver brandy flask.

"Try it," ordered Lincoln briefly.

But Mary could not swallow. While they were working with her, the White House carriage galloped up with Pete beside the coachman and in a few moments they whirled through the White House gates.

Dr. Stone was in attendance almost as soon as Lincoln had laid Mary on her bed. To the President's unutterable relief, he announced after a few moments that she was not poisoned but was suffering from a heavy dose of morphine. He began at once to work on her, but it was midnight before Mary recognized her husband's anxious face beside her pillow.

"Where's Taddie?" was her first question.

"Over on your sofa, asleep," replied the President, laying her hand against his cheek. "He wouldn't go to his own bed until you could kiss him good-night."

Mary raised herself on one elbow and after a glance at Tad lay down again with a sigh of relief. "I had a feeling that something had been done to him." She stared at her husband. "Just what has happened?"

"That's just what we want to know," replied Lincoln. "I'll tell you what occurred here."

Mary listened intently. When he had finished his account, she said, "I did call you. I knew you'd hear."

They gazed into each other's eyes for a moment, then Mary said, "That

Rachel Atkins who's been helping me with my hospital sewing came to me this morning while I was at work in the greenhouse and told me with great secrecy that brother John was in hiding in her house out on Seventh Street. She said he'd recently been brought as a prisoner to Point Lookout, that he had escaped with the help of her husband, who I knew was a guard over there, and wanted to see me before he died of a bad wound he'd gotten last fall at Chattanooga.

"Of course I got excited as usual. The one thought I had was that such news about my half brother would start the gossip about my being a Southern sympathizer all over again. But I just had to go to John in his need. So I told no one and started off with Rachel. Well, she had a wounded Rebel there, all right, but it wasn't John or anything like him. I was suspicious at once and accused Rachel of deceiving me. While we were arguing I began to feel faint, the way I do so often and Rachel got me a glass of water. I remember later trying to get out of the house and that's all."

"About enough, I should think!" exclaimed Lincoln, heatedly.

"Don't scold me, dear! I know I was a fool."

"Scold you!" ejaculated the President. "I feel more like weeping over you."

And he did weep, with his head beside hers on the pillow.

The Detective Police unraveled the story easily enough. The woman Rachel Atkins and her accomplices were Northerners, who had planned to hold the President's wife subject to orders from a group of influential Rebels in Richmond. It was extraordinary how near their scheme came to working. A depot hack had been at the back door ready to convey Mary to parts unknown when Lincoln thundered at the front door. The plotters' escape into the woods had been easy and they were not found until the following day.

Mary was a long time recovering from the morphine poisoning and the shock. It was given out that the President's wife was suffering from an attack of malaria and no one questioned this or asked why the ague should be accompanied by the profound nervous symptoms that accompanied the attack.

CHAPTER XII

A LOVER AT FIFTY

IN one way, Mary's prolonged illness was a good thing for her husband. He alone had power to soothe her restlessness and he snatched many moments from his busy day to go to her and sit beside her sofa talking or reading. These moments, though brief, gave him intermittent respites that helped him a great deal in enduring the frenzied business of the spring.

To every one's astonishment, Charles Sumner came out late in March in favor of the Davis bill. At first, the news staggered Lincoln. He and Sumner had a short passage at arms over it when they met in Stanton's office one day.

"Changed your notion about negro suffrage, eh, Senator?" Lincoln asked, looking up from the telegraph operator's seat he was occupying.

"What do you mean, Mr. Lincoln?" demanded Sumner.

"I mean that I can't understand why you support the Davis bill," replied the President.

"Because it does insure the negroes freedom and I believe that I can amend it to include suffrage." Sumner spoke in a voice that silenced the whole room.

Stanton irascibly asked if it was necessary to bring Senate debates into the War Office and Lincoln at once turned back to the message he had been reading, while Sumner, affronted, stalked out.

Lincoln watched the progress of the bill with anxiety but, as the days wore on, with a certain amount of philosophy too. The lengthy debate gave him what he needed most—time. Moreover, with the newspapers giving a great deal of space to the speeches, the country at large must inevitably become more or less educated as to this difficult problem of statecraft. He thought that when people understood the matter their common sense would put them on his side. Perhaps this would help him at the polls. And as spring came on his thought as to this appeared to be justified. An astonishingly large number of States were instructing their delegates to the pending Republican convention to vote for the renomination of Abraham Lincoln.

Gradually he became conscious of a thrilling fact; that beyond the yammering, noisy throngs who wrote to him and talked to him and scolded and hampered him with their hates, there was a great, voiceless multitude which believed as he believed. Sumner's phrase, "King of the Commonalty," occurred to him many times that spring as he compared the vicious statements made about him in Congress with the silent comment of the common people sending their delegates to the convention. Perhaps if Sumner did get around to starting that impeachment, the plain folks wouldn't stand for it!

Even when his own plans on reconstruction miscarried, he did not falter as he might have without this consciousness of the backing of the commonalty. John Hay returned from Florida early in April, the picture of despair. Both his mission and that of General Gillmore had failed.

"Pshaw, John!" exclaimed Lincoln. "Don't go round with your tail between your legs! We were merely premature. I'll send you down there later and you'll put it through—after the convention."

As warm weather advanced and roads dried, active military campaigns pressed upon his attention. He had to be the main guiding hand of the general scheme, for Halleck was breaking under the strain—poor Halleck—and becoming each day more helpless to make decisions, more sullen and recalcitrant under Stanton's battering and the contempt of his commanding generals.

It was evident that a firmer hand than Halleck's was needed at the head of all the fighting forces, but Lincoln did not want to oust him and hung on to him, trying to bolster Halleck's weaknesses with his own strength. However, it was a decided relief to Lincoln when, the tide of public opinion about Grant having caught up with the President's, Congress requested Lincoln to elevate Grant to the grade of Lieutenant General. This was the highest rank ever held by any American officer save Washington. Halleck was thus automatically subordinated to Grant, although he retained his position in Washington.

Grant at once assumed personal command over the Army of the Potomac and went to Headquarters on the Rapidan. Lincoln, with a feeling that it was now or never, girded himself up to watch for signs that Grant would not be smitten with the lethargy that had overtaken all his predecessors.

It became obvious in April that the Sumner group was concentrating its efforts on putting Chase into the running for the radical nomination. Lincoln hoped that this meant that they were done, for the moment at least, with the impeachment idea. The fact that he was flagrantly disloyal to his chief did not prevent the Secretary of the Treasury from clinging with all his brilliant and vindictive strength to the prerogatives of his office. Indeed, he so frequently overstepped his prerogatives this spring of 1864 that Lincoln's patience broke.

He refused to ratify a highly improper appointment made by Chase. Chase immediately sent in one of his periodic resignations.

Lincoln accepted it!

It was not an easy thing to do from any point of view. Chase was superb in his official capacity, but as Lincoln told Mary, after he had made his decision, the Secretary had become so increasingly irritable and uncomfortable that he was making the whole Cabinet irritable and uncomfortable with him. People at large would be bound to misinterpret the act, would be bound to construe it as revenge on Lincoln's part because of those Presidential aspirations. But hardest of all to bear must be the effect it could have on Charles Sumner.

As Lincoln had foreseen, immediately after word had gone out that Senator Fessenden of Maine had accepted Chase's portfolio, Sumner descended on the White House.

It was a lovely May morning, and Lincoln was walking with Mary in the kitchen garden looking for the first signs of fruit in the strawberry beds when the Senator found them. The President almost groaned aloud. His failure to get on with Sumner was becoming a nightmare.

"Shall I stay or disappear?" asked Mary, as they saw the gigantic figure in the checked suit striding over the asparagus beds.

"Better stay. I need support. My moral knees click together like the ague whenever he gets after me, now.—Well, Senator, loaded for b'ar this morning, I see!"

Sumner bowed to Mary, the early sun bringing red lights to his bared chestnut head which was as yet untouched with gray. But his face was lined. He looked as if he had slept little.

Lincoln gave him no chance to speak. "I thought you wanted Fessenden out of the Senate. You hate him and are always fighting with him."

"No one can take Mr. Chase's place!" exclaimed Sumner. "Least of all a sick man like Mr. Fessenden."

"If Chase is going to run for the Republican nomination, his resignation is only decent, Mr. Sumner." Lincoln's voice was carefully patient. "I want him to take a full sporting chance in the race."

"You're playing with me, Mr. Lincoln!" protested Sumner. "What's back of this? Revenge for Chase's Presidential aspirations?"

"The study of revenge—immortal hate again, eh? You don't know me yet, do you, Senator!" Lincoln stood biting the edge of his forefinger. How to make Sumner understand! It was the most difficult human problem with which he'd ever wrestled.

Red birds whistled in the copper beech below his window. An oriole flickered among the roses. Mary, moving a little from them, stooped near the strawberry plants, a dainty figure in her lavender print. Beyond the iron fence a line of army ambulances was moving. One heard groans and inarticulate cries as they turned the deep rutted corners. Lincoln wiped the sweat from his forehead with the back of his hand. Sumner stood waiting. The fellow was as unavoidable and as inexorable as fate. He would try the effect of the simple truth on him.

"It was this way, Senator. When Chase again tendered me his resignation I felt bitter chagrin. It meant that he wanted me once more to go to him and urge him to remain and that I had accepted what he meant as disciplining me. It meant that the Secretary of the Treasury and not the President is top dog, that Chase is no longer subordinate to Lincoln, that the President abdicates his constitutional powers. I have mighty little personal pride, Senator, as I think you've found, but the longer I hold this office, the more sensitive I grow as to its dignity and sacredness. You know as well as I that Chase has crossed the line with me as deliberately and grossly as ever McClellan did. I'm through."

Sumner, cane planted in the garden loam, listened with an unusual expression dawning in his eyes. Unless, Lincoln told himself, he was foolishly vain, that look was one of respect. He was sure of it when Sumner said with his captivating simplicity and earnestness, "I beg your pardon, Mr. Lincoln. I'm afraid we've all been a little intrusive at times. I withdraw my protest."

"Jings," thought Lincoln, "John Hay is right! What the fellow needs is just a good licking every once in a while!" Aloud he said, "Granted, Mr. Sumner! And let me add that no one in these United States has as much admiration for Chase's ability as I have. No one has put up with him as much as I have for the sake of keeping that ability harnessed to the nation's needs. And I'm not going to give up hope of using it again, but in another direction. In case old Chief Justice Taney peters out while I'm still in office, what do you say to Chase on the Supreme Bench?"

Sumner's whole expression changed. His eyes glowed with pleasure. "Is that a promise, Mr. Lincoln?"

"No, it's not a promise—but to this extent—if I can make myself believe that Chase's unfortunate judgments and personal ambition won't sway him in such a position."

This did not dampen Sumner's enthusiasm. "Oh, fine! Oh, splendid! How you relieve me, Mr. Lincoln!" He held out his hand to the President.

Lincoln took it, thinking in astonishment as he did so that Chase might have been instead of an asset, something of a white elephant on the Senator's overburdened back.

"Come in and have breakfast with us, won't you, Mr. Sumner?" asked Mary.

"Yes, I will, thank you, Mrs. Lincoln," following her along the path. "I wonder if you know the French method of raising asparagus? I have a friend near Albany who uses it with marvelous results."

"I've heard of it," replied Mary. "Do tell me about it."

Lincoln smiled to himself.

The dining room was cool and dim and scented with syringa blooms. Tad, beginning the day in angelic white, threw himself into Sumner's arms with a shout and moved his chair close to his friend's. Mary and the Senator plunged at once into the subject of gardening for which Sumner, who owned no garden, had such a passion.

In the midst of this, as usual, a messenger came from Stanton. Lee had entangled Grant's troops in the wooded swamps of the Wilderness as he had entangled Hooker's a year before. Lincoln hastily finished his meal and left Mary and Sumner debating over the best site for the new asparagus bed. In the War Office, the ghastly details of the unspeakable slaughter in the Wilderness engulfed him and he forgot his mild elation over Sumner.

Mary herself fetched her husband that night from the War Office, a place she rarely visited, though oddly enough with two such explosive natures, she and Stanton got on well together. But James and Tad both failed to bring the President back to supper, and Dr. Stone had warned Mary early in the spring that Lincoln was becoming exhausted. About ten o'clock she appeared carrying a small embroidered pillow and a gray afghan and wearing on her delicate features an expression of indomitable purpose.

Stanton jumped from the sofa and Lincoln turned from the war map.

"Just pull that old armchair to the window, Mr. Secretary," said Mary, briskly. "I've come to keep watch with you and Mr. Lincoln. I can't sleep till he gets home and I'll worry less if I can actually see him."

Stanton gave Lincoln a helpless and humorous glance. Lincoln buttoned his vest and took the pillow and afghan from his wife. One might as well give in gracefully.

"Very well, my dear," he said meekly, "I'm coming."

He followed her down the hall, through the turnstile and into the garden again. Immersed as he had been all day in the reports of the destruction of the flower of the Potomac Army, he felt as if a century had ground by since he had talked with Sumner. The walks were vague and sweet. They paced slowly, arm in arm. Lincoln began to speak of the horrible losses of the day.

"No, let's not talk about the war," interrupted Mary, flatly. "I want you to sleep to-night. Let's talk about Sumner. Poor fellow! I hope he'll have a garden of his own some day. He was so eager and so pathetic about that foolish asparagus bed. Never has a man needed a home and family more than he."

"How do he and Mrs. Hooper make it?" asked Lincoln, rubbing his head wearily, yet knowing that unless he followed Mary's lead and thrust the war out of his mind, he'd get no sleep that night.

"Oh, he's in a terrible state of mind! Bob couldn't be more bowled over than the Senator is.—I wish Bob would write me. Have you heard from him lately?"

"No, but no news is good news. Go on about Sumner. Did he reveal details of his state of mind to you? Sumner in love rather appeals to my sense of humor."

"Well, if that's the effect it has on you"—indignantly—"I'll not open my mouth and you can just stay awake all night."

"Sumner in love is a perfect sleeping potion," he cried hastily and with a little laugh. "And you know I wouldn't miss one of your stories of an interview for six bits, Mary."

She squeezed his arm. "Sit down here under this magnolia and I'll tell you. No one can find you for a moment. Put your arm about me and they'll think we're two of the servants!"

He drew her close against him and she felt his body relax.

Sumner, she said, selected a spot for the asparagus trench to the south of the greenhouse, and then gave Mary the name of an ornamental evergreen shrub whose identity had puzzled both Mary and the gardener. Tad, who had tagged after them, announced at this point that he was going to give the evergreen to Isabella for a Christmas tree. Then he suddenly added that he was going to play with Isabella and darted away. Sumner looked after the little boy, flying along the paths, and said with a great sigh:

"Oh, for his spontaneity, there! Oh, for his sureness of a welcome!" Then as if he could not control himself, he added in an anguished voice, "This is killing me!"

Mary did not pretend to misunderstand him but she spoke with her usual briskness. "You're so silly in your attitude toward her. You're much too deferential. Her attitude toward you is just her way of teasing. As a matter of fact, she's deeply interested in you. She talks to me a great deal about your work and has ambitions for you. She's really very clever. Go ask her advice on politics and if she's saucy, squelch her the way Mr. Lincoln does me. You mustn't expect a woman of her social prestige to be overwhelmed by the fact that you're a United States Senator. Let her feel that she could help you to be anything."

Mary paused in her recital and Lincoln gave a sudden loud shout of laughter. "What did he say then?"

"He said good-by and went straight to call on Alice Hooper. Taddie saw him there. I'm dying to know what happened. I'm afraid he was late getting to the Senate."

Lincoln laughed again. "Poor Sumner! Come, darling Mary, you've done your job. I can sleep now!" He took her hand and led her toward the dimly lighted basement entrance.

HE did sleep for a few hours that night, but was roused by the wakening birds to lie and struggle for a long time with what he called his battle horrors. He assured himself that this battle of Grant's in Virginia was actually the beginning of the end if only Grant had the grit to continue until Lee's Army was destroyed. Grant's blood-proof will was what he had been seeking since that April night, three years before, when he had sent the telegram for the relief of Fort Sumter. He must set himself to endure with greater equanimity the sight and sound of those dripping ambulances that filed continuously by the White House.—But Grant's losses were nearing the fifty-thousand mark.—He must gird himself to a new endurance.—God send that the people's nerve stand up under the slaughter! He'd send John Hay at once to the Middle West to see how deep was the despondency there. Mary had said that Grant was a butcher. Well, after all, war was a butcher's job.

The next thing, undoubtedly, would be Greeley yelling for peace. Queer that Greeley couldn't get it through his head that North and South must drink to its dregs the bitter cup. Halleck was claiming that in some of the battles down there Grant's losses were unnecessary and fruitless. Perhaps Grant really was— Well, let that go now. Halleck naturally was disgruntled at being subordinated in rank to the little General. After the Republican convention was over, he'd get down to see Grant for himself and give him a word of warning.

He rose with a sigh and dressed.

Fred Douglass met Lincoln after breakfast as he was making his way to Stanton's office. The colored man was standing by the turnstile, his soft black hat in his hand, the blazing sun turning his black hair to bronze. The President shook hands with him.

"Well, Mr. Douglass, what are you and Bob hatching now?"

Douglass smiled. "Will you allow Mr. Robert to go with me again this summer, Mr. Lincoln?"

"Let's sit down," suggested Lincoln, leading the way to the bench he and Mary had occupied the night before. "Do you and Bob want to carry out the same program again?"

"No, sir, the colored people are coming over well enough now. I want you to let Mr. Robert lead up a regiment of negroes I'll pick myself. Sir, we'll sweep from Fortress Monroe to the end of Florida with it."

"But, Mr. Douglass," protested Lincoln, "he's only an untrained boy! Does he know of this?"

"No, sir. But he's your son. That's all that my people care about. And he's very able. Oh, Mr. Lincoln, don't veto this without long consideration. I want to hush forever the plea of the whites that negroes can't stand the gaff of battle. Jefferson Davis says that if negroes will make good soldiers, their whole theory of slavery is wrong. Give us a chance to show our mettle, Mr. Lincoln." Douglass clasped his hands as if in prayer.

Lincoln stirred uneasily. "But, Mr. Douglass, your people have already proved themselves nobly. Their performance with Colonel Shaw alone was enough for that. My dear friend, you can have no idea of the difficulties your plea presents. It's almost impossible. I can't undertake it."

Douglass got the note of finality in his voice. "There's no use in pleading!" he said, heartbrokenly.

"I'm afraid not, Mr. Douglass. Come! Come!" laying his hand on Douglass' arm. "Don't make me feel like a criminal. Ask me something that I can grant."

"Give our soldiers equal pay and equal promotion with the whites," returned Douglass, instantly.

"You've earned it," said Lincoln, "but only Congress can remove those disabilities."

"If such an amendment is added to the Davis bill will it stand a chance with you to become a law?" asked the colored man.

"What, are you so blind as to favor that bill?" Lincoln's voice was astonished. "That bill doesn't grant you even civic equality."

"But it's at least a guarantee of our freedom!" Douglass' black eyes glowed.

"A constitutional amendment would be a surer way to get that. The States themselves have to ratify an amendment," said Lincoln. "I don't mind confiding to you that I'm insisting that a pledge to pass such an amendment be written into the Republican platform."

"Ah! Glorious! You make me glad!" The colored man gave a great sigh, then said, abruptly, "But that means you may veto the Davis bill if it is sent you to sign? Oh, sir, I beg of you, do sign it."

Lincoln turned in his seat to face Douglass. "I'm not saying as to that. But ponder this well, Douglass. We'll certainly assure freedom to your people. But having done so, I'm not going to try to legislate the former slave holders into carrying the slaves to the voting booth or sitting down to a meal of victuals with them."

"Then you're going to veto the Davis bill, sir?" insisted Douglass. Lincoln saw suddenly that his sensitive mouth was trembling and that his eyes were suffused with tears.

He slid his hand to Douglass' broad shoulder. "Now, I've hurt you! I'm sorry about that. But I'm getting too old to lie or to give false hopes."

"General Butler said you'd say no to everything," said Douglass with a mournful smile.

"You've been down there, eh? How does the exchange of colored prisoners go on?"

"It doesn't go, of course, Mr. Lincoln," replied Douglass, "and it won't,

General Butler assures me, as long as General Grant is in full command."

"Didn't Butler give you Grant's reason?" asked Lincoln, sharply.

"Oh, yes, Mr. President!" replied Douglass wearily, as though, Lincoln thought, the weaknesses of the whites were utterly childish in his eyes. "He says that General Grant's been drinking hard ever since things have gone so badly and he leaves his decision to his subordinates, who are nigger haters."

"And Butler's the man," ejaculated Lincoln, "that they say would be superior to Andy Johnson as Vice President! It's an ornery lie, in plain words, that Butler's given you, Mr. Douglass. General Grant, whether his personal habits are or are not perfect, is a superb military man, and he knows we need all the fighters we can get, without regard to color. He sent me a copy of his letter to Butler. Grant said to stop all exchanges until the South agreed to swap even-steven as to numbers and *without regard to color*. Understand?"

Douglass jerked suddenly to his feet. "But why should General Butler tell me a lie?"

"Oh, that's simple!" The President spoke wearily in his turn. "Butler fancies himself as a military genius when he's really a military fool. He wants to run the Army of the Potomac. But his genius is as a civil executive."

Douglass stared at Lincoln and slowly the expression of alienation softened. "You're the only person of authority in the country who tells me the truth! Mr. Lincoln, do you think Mr. Sumner reads General Butler correctly? They're very intimate. General Butler's planning to swing all his political weight in New England to help Sumner defeat you if you're nominated."

"Did Butler tell you that?" asked Lincoln.

"Yes, sir," replied the colored man. "I like Mr. Sumner and I think I'll warn him as to Butler's character. And I want to say this: If colored men had the vote, nothing could stop your reëlection, sir."

"In spite of my views on reconstruction?" Lincoln smiled as he rose.

Douglass returned the smile. "They only know and care that you've struck the chains from their ankles.—Mr. President"—clasping his hands and speaking with deep earnestness—"isn't there something I can do or say that will persuade you to turn reconstruction over to Mr. Sumner?"

"No!" Lincoln put into the negation all the weight of his months of anxious pondering.

The look of despondency with which the colored man bowed and turned away hurt the President. He didn't want the interview to end in despondency. He had too many such endings lately. He called Douglass back.

"Mr. Douglass," he said, "will you do some recruiting of your people under General Thomas? I'll try my best to get you a captain's commission. We need soldiers, Mr. Douglass. Terribly we need soldiers. When General Grant once gets possession of a place he hangs onto it as if he'd inherited it. But he pays a price for his nighness!"

"I'd be proud and happy to serve under General Thomas," replied Douglass.

Lincoln nodded. "I'll see Stanton as soon as his mind's free." He shook hands and hurried to the War Office more than ever determined to get down and visit Grant.

But he would not leave until the matter of the renomination was settled. He was keeping in touch in every way possible with the intricate political intrigues that prefaced the convention and brought to bear all his hard-won political wisdom on details of the preparations for the struggle. Once the convention was set at Baltimore, however, he sent John Hay and George Nicolay to keep him informed of the proceedings and wiped his mind of active concern for it.

He received the news of his nomination with mingled gratification and apprehension. The next few months would make him more than ever the center of unprecedentedly bitter political fighting. It was not a pleasant prospect.

A day or so after the convention was over, the nominating committee waited on him in the East Parlor.—That little parlor in Springfield where he'd received the committee of 1861 seemed poignantly remote.

He sent Mary to Vermont shortly after this to finish her convalescence, and then gathered up Taddie and went down to visit Grant. Charles Dana had told Stanton that the morale of the Army of the Potomac was very low. The long-drawn-out failure of the siege of Petersburg, the frightful losses, and the low type of men now recruited made it a vastly inferior army to that with which McClellan and Meade had been blessed. It was evident too that Lee had not too much respect for Grant's forces, for just before Lincoln's visit he detached 20,000 men from the Richmond defenses and sent them up the Shenandoah Valley under General Early to destroy whom and what they might. Stanton was worried about this destroying horde. But Grant refused to share the Secretary's anxiety. One of the many errands Stanton urged Lincoln to do on this visit was to rouse Grant's interest in Early. But the President, after thinking it over, told Stanton he didn't feel competent to argue with Grant over military tactics. He found Grant as usual, clean-cut as a hound's tooth, not in the least boastful—sanguine—a very great soldier. The other officers drank freely at meals. Grant and he turned down their glasses. The atmosphere was different from any he'd ever found enveloping the Headquarters of the Army of the Potomac. Cold efficiency was the watchword, and although he rejoiced in it, it depressed him. He made no suggestions to Grant save that he hoped he'd accomplish his task with as little bloodshed as possible.

The one warm memory which he carried back to Washington was of the negro troops.

Some one at officers' mess remarked the night before Lincoln left that the colored soldiers were strangely silent. There was a division of them camped by the river. Colonel Thomas, who had a colored regiment, nodded.

"Yes, they learned to-day that they were to lead the assault on the fortifications east of Petersburg."

"Are they frightened—deserting?" asked Lincoln, quickly.

"So far, we've never had a negro deserter," answered Thomas, "and they certainly aren't frightened. But where with white troops important military news is received with cheers followed by great argumentation among themselves as to its value, the colored men sit down and 'study.' They're 'studying' now. Later on, they'll sing. That is, some fellow, like a Quaker moved to prayer, will be moved to improvise a chant that expresses the philosophy of the occasion. If the others agree, they'll join him. If they don't, he'll have to try again. No! No! Those men aren't frightened. They're profoundly stirred by this honor of making the initial dash."

When Lincoln left the mess tent, he slipped away toward the section of the camp where the four thousand colored soldiers were living. He made his way well into their midst without being discovered, coming to pause in the shade of a giant sycamore.

There were many campfires gleaming, throwing dusky faces, liquid eyes, white teeth against the spangled sky. And silence. It was profoundly moving. Lincoln wondered what would be the effect if he discovered himself to these men so lost in contemplation. Just as he had concluded to try the experiment, a heavy bass voice at a little distance from his tree began to chant.

"We-e looks like me-en a-a-marchin' on.
We looks li-ike men-er-war—"

No one joined him. He changed the melody slightly. In the faces of the groups nearest Lincoln there was no slightest shift of expression, no gleam of interest. The singer changed to a minor key and lifted an octave. A remote tenor now joined him. A baritone came in, then a weird falsetto. As if this last were a signal, there now rose a deep wave of song that increased in volume with each note until with "men-er-war," Lincoln was sure that the whole four thousand had joined.

They chanted the lines again and yet again and again until the President could feel the gooseflesh rise on the back of his neck. He stood with his hands clasped behind him, his heart swelling and suddenly—just for one ineffable moment—he was engulfed with gladness, such gladness, he thought, as Moses had felt when he had led the way across the Red Sea. This, this that he had brought about surely was reparation for the two hundred years of wickedness—

He turned slowly and keeping to the shadows, returned to his tent and went to sleep with that soul-stirring chorus still in his ear, "We looks like men-er-war."

CHAPTER XIV

LINCOLN returned to Washington the next day still a little uneasy about Grant. It was Grant's stolid countenance perhaps that troubled the President. He did not believe that the little General was as sure of himself as his poker face might indicate. A man sure of himself doesn't bother, Lincoln thought, to build up such a wall of indifference. Grant was a hard man to get at. No commander of the Army of the Potomac ever had treated Lincoln with the cordial respect accorded him by Grant. Lincoln appreciated this deeply. Yet Grant baffled him, held him off.

Thinking his visit over, Lincoln was glad that he'd offered Grant no advice. He had come near to breaking his self-imposed silence only once. He was sure that Grant was underestimating the potentialities for serious trouble in Early's little trip up the Shenandoah. But when he had felt round about it Grant had assured him that Hunter coming in from the West with 10,000 men could control Early's 20,000 and he was glad to have Lee weakened by that many troops. Lincoln had opened his lips to protest but had closed them without speaking.

Lincoln had a feeling that Early was going to knock loudly on Washington's back door before many weeks, and as Grant had all the city's trained forces with him in Virginia, Washington lay naked for the taking. Well, he concluded his thinking, perhaps now was as good a time as any for Grant to learn Lee's possibilities in foot work.

Stanton alternately cursed and expressed satisfaction over Lincoln's story of his visit. Both men agreed that news of Early must be kept as much as possible out of the local papers while as quietly as possible home guards should be organized to man the forts that ringed the city. It was not easy to carry out these plans. Halleck refused to originate anything; would do only the specific things that the President ordered him to do. Stanton was not a soldier. Neither was Lincoln. And a soldier with ideas was very much needed in Washington.

Lincoln worried about this when he was not sweating over the Davis bill which Congress still debated. Soon after the President's return from Grant's Headquarters, Bob came home for the summer vacation, and in the absence of his mother at once constituted himself Tad's mentor. Tad had not the least intention of permitting any one on earth to act as his mentor. Nicolay who usually played peacemaker was off to Arkansas to inspect the progress of reconstruction in that State and John Hay ardently encouraged Bob in his rôle of disciplinarian. So, as Lincoln wrote Mary, the siege of Richmond was a quiet affair compared with what was taking place in the upper and lower reaches of the White House.

"Bob," he wrote, "is sure enough man's size in his understanding of many of my problems. He's taking a great interest in the Davis bill, goes up to the Senate and listens to the debates and comes back, his eyes crackling like yours, and tells me about them as intelligently as Nicolay could. And two minutes later he's fussing with poor little Taddie as if they both were ten years old.—Outside of their abortive attempt to reform my darling Tad, he and John are making an heroic effort at filling Nicolay's job, but no one can push through the day's run like John George. I reckon you'll have a warm welcome when you get back—"

On July 3, the day before Congress was to adjourn, Lincoln was sitting in his own room just before supper with a heavy heart, thinking over Bob's report on the speeches made that day, when the loud outcry across the hall caused by Tad's refusal to wash his ears at Bob's behest ceased so suddenly that he came startled to his feet and made for the door. It opened before he reached it to admit his wife, in lilac bonnet, sunshade in hand.

"Thank God, Mary!" he ejaculated, gathering her in his arms. A moment later, he said, "You squelched the boys, of course."

"I certainly did—" smoothing his hair with the old loved gesture. "Bob looked so disgusted with me.—That boy grows handsomer every day, Abra'm."

"He looks exactly like you, my dear," smiled Lincoln.

"You are positively wilted!" said Mary. "I shall move you straight out to the Soldiers' Home the minute Congress adjourns. Have they sent you the Davis bill to sign?"

"Not yet," replied Lincoln. He looked down into her face as she stood leaning against him. "Mary, if I veto that bill, I knock my chances of reëlection sky high. The people can't be expected to understand my reason. They'd have to have been here day by day to see it."

"But I thought you felt the debate helped you with the voters," protested Mary.

"It did, for a while. But they've been at it longer than I anticipated. And constant dripping wears away a stone."

"Are you going to veto it? Does Sumner know?" asked Mary.

"I haven't said I'm going to, have I? I'm thinking aloud to you, that's all. Sumner's pretty mad at me again. He knows I've sent Nicolay out to Arkansas to tell General Steele to give the new State Government the same support and protection that he would have if Congress had seated the new members from Arkansas."

"But that's openly defying Congress!" she ejaculated.

"Only incidentally. Primarily, it's helping Steele do the best he can toward suppressing rebellion. In no event and in no view of the case can it do any harm."

"Except to you, with Congress," sighed his wife. "You poor dear!—I wish Senator Sumner had more common sense. No wonder Alice Hooper—"

"He's in father's office now," said Bob laconically, coming in on his mother's remarks. "He wants to see you right away, sir," turning to his father.

Lincoln threw up both his hands. "Oh, I don't want an argument with Sumner to-night!"

"Then you shan't have it!" and Mary rushed from the room.

As Lincoln would have followed, Bob put his hand out to detain him. "Let her go, father! He was just telling me how much he admired mother's brain. She may make him mad but—"

Lincoln laughed. "But he'll come back asking for more just like the rest of us do." He walked over to the washstand, slipping off his cuffs.

Mary was in her room finishing her supper toilet when Lincoln put his head in a little later.

"Well, you made short work of the Senator. What did he want?"

"I suppose something about the Davis bill. But he put me off with small stuff. Talked about General Banks speculating in cotton and the chance of Banks getting into the Cabinet." She watched Lincoln as she said this, but he made no sign. "I told him he and I agreed about Banks, so that was all right. Then it seems that Stanton doesn't give Fred Douglass his commission and Sumner fears Douglass may make trouble with the Abolitionists for you. I remarked that Mr. Sumner was probably pleased at that prospect and he looked pained. Then before he could start arguing, I asked him how Alice Hooper was. He said they left to-day and asked me at once if I agreed with her that the office of Senator was too small for his powers. I said that I did and he groaned that he was surprised at the lack of vision in women of our intelligence. Good for Alice, thought I. But aloud I bade him good-night.—He's tired, poor fellow. Well, you're rid of him, to-night, anyhow."

But as it turned out, Lincoln was not rid of him. Seward, his pale face beaded with heat, his necktie as usual under one ear, rushed in as they were at dessert. Maximilian, Napoleon's man, had reached Mexico City, and MacDougall of California was clamoring for passage of a bill declaring war on France.

"Bob," said Lincoln, "you go fetch Senator Sumner. He'll have to bury MacDougall again. Seward, you go home to bed. You look like Hamlet's ghost."

"Bed! You make me laugh for the first time in a week, Lincoln! Give me something to eat, there's a dear, won't you, Taddie? We don't want bed on an empty stomach, do we?"

They fed him. He talked constantly as he ate but consented to go home and let the President deal with Sumner. The Senator was in a committee conference and came late. He made short work of promising to silence MacDougall, then he asked Lincoln what he proposed to do with the Davis bill. Lincoln refused to be drawn. Sumner, nervously overwrought, walked the floor and harangued. Lincoln, leaning back against the window frame where a rose-scented breeze touched him now and again, heard the Senator's voice more and more remotely. Gradually the tall form in black dinner clothes seemed to merge into the black and white of the slave map behind him. He closed his eyes for a moment.—When he opened them, an hour later, Sumner was gone.

Lincoln rose the next morning with the Davis bill taking precedence over every other anxiety. Congress was to adjourn that day. They were leaving him scant time to study it in its final form. As soon as possible after examining his morning mail, he went up to the Capitol as was customary for the President on the last day of the Session. Bob and John Hay accompanied him in the barouche. It was a heavy sultry day. Small boys added firecrackers to the confusion of the streets. People had hung out flags on Pennsylvania Avenue but in general there was little heart for celebrating the Fourth of July.

Lincoln took a peep at the Senate Chamber before going to the President's office in the same wing. Chaos reigned among the Senators. Several important new bills had been thrust before the body this last morning. Old bills of equal importance still were under debate. Sweating pages rushed up and down. Anxious-eyed engrossing clerks ran about carrying long sheets of parchment for which they were demanding the signature of the Speaker, the Vice President, the Clerk.

No one gave special heed to the President and he was grateful. After one look at the Senate he was glad to withdraw to his own quarters. He seated himself at the handsome rosewood desk beside an open window that gave a wide view of sprawling, half-finished Washington—an ugly town, he thought, conceived as a city and born as a village without the compactness that gave a village character. Little trees with whitewashed trunks, pigs rooting about them. Pasture lots deep with weeds masquerading as suburban plots. There was something shabby and full of sham about the place. Springfield was much prettier.

John divided himself between the House and the Senate. Bob arranged the bills on the desk and slid them one by one under his father's hand. Lincoln was familiar with most of them and after an identifying glance wrote his signature firmly. It was about 11 o'clock when, after a whispered conference with John Hay, Bob laid the Davis bill before him.

Lincoln stared down at it.

Weeks before he had decided to give it a pocket veto. Yet, in spite of long hours of preparation for it, he found that the act took a supreme effort of will. After all, he told himself, it was bitter hard for a man of his friendly nature to be obliged to do continually these things which roused a frenzy of hatred in men of a fine and ardent patriotism. He knew that under all the confusion, the members of Congress and the visitors in the gallery were concentrating their desires, their prayers, on his signing this bill. He knew that a group of pages just without his door were poised like carrier pigeons, ready to wing with news of his decision to the Senate and the House. Ben Wade's page was there and Lyman Trumbull's and Sumner's and Davis' and the faithful Arnold's messenger.

He laid the bill gently to one side and went on with others. Bob bit his lip and John Hay gave a satisfied grunt. Several members of the Cabinet drifted into the room and seated themselves, waiting. Sumner entered and stood by the window, pale with anxiety. But no one ventured to question the President until Zachariah Chandler came in. This gentleman, who respected nobody's dignity of office, bluntly demanded of the President:

"Mr. Lincoln, are you going to sign the Davis bill?"

Lincoln took off his spectacles and looked mildly up into Chandler's belligerent eyes as he replied:

"This bill has been placed before me only a few moments before Congress adjourns. It's a matter of too much importance to be swallowed that way."

"If it's vetoed," cried Chandler, "the Republican party'll be fearfully damaged! Especially as to the point prohibiting slavery in the reconstructed States."

Lincoln shook his head. "That's the point on which I doubt the authority of Congress to act."

"It's no more than you've done yourself," exclaimed Chandler indignantly.

Lincoln answered with great care. "I conceive that I may in an emergency do things on military grounds which can't be done constitutionally by Congress."

"This is a fearful calamity," ejaculated Chandler. "Your attitude is fatal! Fatal!" He rushed from the room.

Sumner, with a look of unutterable reproach at Lincoln, strode after Chandler. The President turned to Seward and Fessenden.

"I don't see how any of us now," he remarked, "can contradict what we've always said, that Congress has no constitutional power over slavery in the States."

To Lincoln's surprise, "sour old Fessenden" exclaimed, "You're absolutely right, Mr. President! I've even had doubts of the constitutional efficacy of your own decree of emancipation where it hasn't been carried into effect by the actual advance of the army."

The room was full now and Lincoln observed that most of the faces crowded behind the Cabinet chairs were flushed with anger. He tried to marshal his thoughts of the past three months and reduce them to the simplest English at his command. He was determined not to be misunderstood.

"The bill and the position of these gentlemen in asserting that the insurrectionary States are no longer in the Union seem to me to make the fatal admission that States, whenever they please, may of their own motion dissolve their connection with the Union. Now, we cannot survive that admission, I am convinced. If that be true, I am not President, you gentlemen are not Congress. I have laboriously endeavored to avoid that question ever since it first began to be mooted and thus to avoid confusion and disturbance in our own councils. It was to obviate this question that I earnestly favored the movement for an amendment to the Constitution abolishing slavery which passed the Senate last year and failed in the House. I thought it much better if it were possible to restore the Union without the necessity of a violent quarrel among its friends as to whether certain States have been in or out of the Union during the War,—a merely metaphysical question and one unnecessary to be forced into the discussion."

He rose as he finished and bowing, left the office. John Hay followed. When they reached the carriage, Lincoln missed Bob. John explained that the young man was making a hurried tour of the two Houses.

"Looking for trouble," commented Lincoln with a little shake of his head.

"They're all so shortsighted," said John Hay, pulling at his tiny mustache in a knowing manner! "People at large aren't interested in the abstruse questions involved."

"If the Radicals try, I don't doubt they can do me harm with the veto," replied Lincoln. "But at all events, I must keep some consciousness of being somewhere near right. I must keep some standard or principle fixed within myself. Here comes Bob, mad clean through! Jings, he looks like his mother! Well, boy, had a good time?"

Bob sank into the seat opposite his father, his lips actually trembling with anger. "Davis is making a speech about you, waving his arms like a crazy man and talking like one, too. He ought to be sued for slander for the things he said."

"What did you listen for, Bobbie?" asked Lincoln, patting the checked linen knee that touched his own.

"I just wanted to measure the depth of his hatred," replied Bob. "And I'd heard him through if Senator Sumner hadn't come up and taken me away. He wanted my opinion on a letter he'd had speaking of the negro's opinion of emancipation—or he said he did. Maybe he was just trying to save me further humiliation. And do you know," with a sudden smile, "he said that if he had your political gifts he'd be Emperor of the world. It was the nearest to a joke I've ever heard from him."

"He wasn't joking! You flatter him!" declared John Hay. "Did you see the pantaloons he was wearing this morning, Bob? They were silk, by Jove, like the lilac checked stuff your mother wears. I dare you to ask him if he has his clothes made by Lizzie Keckley."

Both young men roared with laughter and Lincoln joined them. After all it was a relief to have committed the murder since it had to be done.

But there was no use pretending to himself that he could bring any philosophy to bear on the look with which Sumner had left him. He could not endure with any sort of equanimity the thought of the Senator leaving for the summer with bitterness in his heart against him. He seldom acted on impulse, but now as they plowed through the dusty road before Congressman Hooper's house, he called suddenly to the coachman:

"Burke, leave me here and take the two boys home."

"No! No!" protested John Hay. "We'll walk and leave the carriage for you."

"I don't want my rig recognized in front of here," said Lincoln decidedly. "I'll walk back, myself," and he strode up to the door.

The servant showed him into the long drawing room, draped for the summer closing, but cool and dim and smelling of rose jars newly filled. Alice Hooper, in a ruffled white dimity, her golden hair caught back in a black net, came in at once. She moved down the room like a naval sloop with all sails set, to greet the President standing in the window.

"Mr. Lincoln, this is very kind of you! We have only just finished dinner. May I not—"

Lincoln bowed over her hand and interrupted with his fine smile. "No, dear Mrs. Hooper! Mrs. Lincoln will expect me and my business won't take long. I've come to ask a favor of you."

He seated her close to the shuttered window. Through the open slats came little hot drafts from the garden and he placed himself opposite her where he might share the breeze, for he felt suddenly oppressed.

"I've just come from the Capitol, Mrs. Hooper. I have given the Davis bill a pocket veto and thereby finally cooked my goose with the Radicals. I *say* finally, but I still have hopes of mollifying Charles Sumner."

"Through me?" asked Alice, her blue eyes twinkling. "But, Mr. President, I'm busy quarreling with him myself! He's due here any time to finish a debate we began yesterday."

"Seriously?" asked Lincoln, his own eyes twinkling.

"Well, the Senator takes it seriously. And I'm certain he'd take any championing of you in regard to this pocket veto as a personal affront. He might even wish to fight a duel about it!" She laughed, softly.

"Of course, I don't want to injure the Senator's chances," began the President jocosely, "but—"

"But," Alice took him up, soberly, "as a matter of fact both father and I would be glad to help you, Mr. Lincoln. What may I try to do as to the Senator?"

"Do you allow him to talk politics to you now?" asked Lincoln, running his fingers violently through his hair, then clasping his knee tensely.

"Mrs. Lincoln persuaded me to be less adamant there," laughing again and again sobering quickly to add, "I enjoy politics, as a matter of fact."

"Do you think you could persuade Mr. Sumner to take no active part in calling another convention and nominating another Republican candidate until after the Democratic convention next month? Mrs. Hooper, if the Democrats nominate McClellan on a peace platform, if our military outlook continues black, if the Republican party is split by internal dissensions, McClellan will go into the White House next year and all will be lost." He paused to see if she had taken in his statement.

"Yes! Yes! I see," she said, shaking her pretty head anxiously.

Lincoln thought he could begin to understand Sumner's fascination. "I know what Sumner will say. He'll say that if I'd withdraw the Republican party could unite on some one. When he says that, you tell him that if, after the Democrats have nominated McClellan on a peace platform, the leaders of the Republican party can agree on any one man who can be surer of beating McClellan at the polls next November than I, I'll withdraw."

The effect of this last sentence on his hearer was astonishing.

She leaned forward and with great deliberation placed a slender hand over Lincoln's clasped knuckles. "No," she said, quietly, "I'll deliver no such message to Charles Sumner! I haven't enough confidence in his common sense. I'm not going to be the one to jeopardize your tenure of office that way. Why, Mr. Lincoln," rising suddenly, "I'm surprised at you! Lack of vanity may be as serious a fault as arrogance. Don't you know that? And you are *the* friend to the Union in these United States. I'm descended from men who died in creating that Union . . . I'll deliver no such message."

Lincoln was singularly touched. Here was the woman whom he had always found cold and snobbish speaking with an understanding loyalty that was all the more remarkable in a woman when one realized that her loyalty was impersonal. For he knew as well as though she had said it that his kind of man had no appeal for her. It was a real triumph of mind over matter! And it healed some of the hurts he'd felt that day.

He rose with her and walked over to the mantel, looked into the Chinese dragon jar and with his paper knife stirred up the rose leaves with which it was filled, then turned back to the slender white figure still standing by the window.

"You have confidence in *my* political common sense, have you, Mrs. Hooper?" he asked.

She tapped her lips thoughtfully with the little silk fan that dangled from her wrist, then a smile broke through her anxiety.

"Even Charles Sumner has that! He often sighs in envy of your riches in that direction."

"Then," very earnestly and walking toward her again, "trust that possession of mine enough to go ahead and do what I ask you."

She was really troubled, but Lincoln held her gaze and would not let it go and after a moment of staring at his sunken, weary, and very tender blue gray eyes, she sighed and capitulated.

"I'll do what I can, Mr. Lincoln. The Senator's not a simple person, you know—and apropos of this conversation in general, I have a great and affectionate respect for him."

"So have I," agreed Lincoln. "And I thank you for—well, for this conversation, Mrs. Hooper. You've cheered me on my way. And now I've got to make tracks for home." He bowed again over her hand and without waiting for the servant to show him to the door, he hurried out into the burning heat. Charles Sumner was just turning in from the sidewalk. The two men lifted their hats and bowed without a word. Then Lincoln made his way to his belated dinner and the Senator went on into the house.

Alice met him in the hall. "Ah, Senator, you met the President!" giving him her hand.

He clasped it in both his, released it and said, "I did not speak to him. I dared not let myself. He turned chaos loose on the Republican party to-day."

"Come in and tell me about it, Senator!" leading the way into the drawing room. "You can't have dined. Let me send for some sandwiches and a glass of wine."

His sober face lightened at this touch of kindliness. "Thank you, Alice! I was afraid you'd be leaving for Boston on the early boat so I came here direct from the Senate chamber. Lincoln has ditched the Davis bill."

She rang for a tray to be brought, then gave her attention to Sumner's account of the pocket veto. When he had finished, she toyed with her fan for a moment, then told him what she knew he was eager to know,—the reason for the President's call.

He was much agitated by the recital. "Do you mean, Alice, do you actually mean that you're giving me that message with any desire of your own that I'll agree?"

"I told Mr. Lincoln I didn't want to deliver it," said Alice.

"Ah!" in a tone of relief, "then you don't wish me to agree!"

"But why don't you want to do what he says, dear Senator?" She patted the sofa beside her. "Now you've finished your lunch, come here and we won't have to shout."

He obeyed with alacrity. "I don't agree because he's so diabolically clever. I haven't the remotest idea of what he's trying to do."

"He's trying to save the Union," said Alice, "first, last and always. He's as utterly beyond selfish motives as you are. You're the two biggest men I shall ever know, even if I were to be fortunate enough to live in the diplomatic circle of England. It's too bad that Mr. Lincoln can't compete with you in those little elegancies of manner and speech that every woman delights in."

Sumner smiled down at her, the irritated and anxious lines smoothed from his face as if she actually had laid her delicate hand on them. "And why don't you want to deliver the message to me, dear Alice?"

"The saddest thing in our history to-day," she said in a low voice, "is that Charles Sumner and Abraham Lincoln are not in agreement. I am very jealous of your future! I feared that you'd misunderstand the message and that it would serve only to drive you two farther apart."

He scowled a little and folding his arms on his breast sat in heavy thought. Little Isabella's voice floated down from upstairs. There was a sound of heavy objects being moved. Alice sat in unusual patience. Finally Sumner said:

"If we have a bad war summer, it will be difficult to find any one to beat McClellan, if he's nominated."

"Could you beat him?" asked Alice.

"I? No, Alice, I've too many political enemies in my own camp."

"Who could beat McClellan?" she urged.

"Only some man that the entire Republican party could agree on," he replied, dejectedly.

"Senator, I've hurt you often when I've teased you over your absorption in politics. And I'm sorry about that because I'm really trying to learn not so much politics as statesmanship. Do forgive me enough to explain what would be the result if you agree with Mr. Lincoln's proposal. Wouldn't there be a chance that you'd have him on the hip and be rid of him?"

"Yes, certainly," answered Sumner.

"Then he's willing to take a bigger risk than you are? Oh, don't let him do that! I don't want you to lag one microscopic dot behind him!" She looked up into his face pleadingly.

"Are you trying to influence me, Alice?" he demanded, sternly.

"Yes, I am, Senator! I am sincere and I'm in earnest. I want you to accede to the President's request because I think it's the most statesman-like thing for you to do."

Sumner moved uneasily and again sat pondering. Then he said, "Never in my life have I been bribed. Any request of this sort from you to me is a sort of bribe because I care so much about your good opinion. Even at that, if this were a question of principle with me, I could hold out against you. But I'm honestly puzzled which way to go, and so for a few weeks I'll agree to go as you suggest. I'll wait to see just how farsighted the President is."

"Now, that is my idea of wisdom and fairness!" exclaimed Alice. "And since you've been such a good little boy, I'm not going to leave until the night boat and you are going to forget all the world of politics and war and play with Isabella and me. We'll go for a picnic supper out to Rock Creek Grove!"

"The world forgetting and by the world forgot!" ejaculated Sumner, rising and offering Alice both his hands.

She accepted them and rose with a smile of such sweetness that his pale, tired face flushed like a youth's.

CHAPTER XV

THE REBEL HAVERSACK

LINCOLN did not hear from Alice Hooper again nor did he see Sumner before he left for Boston. He had not expected either event. He could only wait for results. The newspaper reports on his reasons for the pocket veto, in spite of his efforts at clarity, were not satisfactory. He was resolved that this should not be so and on the 8th of July he issued a short proclamation giving a copy of the Davis bill and reiterating his stand upon the method of reconstruction it contained. That done, he felt satisfied to leave the matter to the common understanding.

The family migrated to the Soldiers' Home the morning after the Fourth. On the 6th, Stanton hurried into Lincoln's office and peremptorily ordered him to bring his family back to town.

"Early crossed the Potomac at Shepherdstown yesterday and levied $20,000 on Hagerstown," said the Secretary in reply to Lincoln's protest. "He'll be in front of Washington this week if General Wallace can't hold him. Hunter's asleep somewhere west of Winchester. Can't possibly help. I'm going to put a lookout station at the top of your house at the Soldiers' Home. It commands the best view to the north. By God, you shall not stay out there under Early's guns, Mr. Lincoln!" Stanton wiped the sweat from his spectacles with an enormous silk handkerchief.

"Tut! Tut! Keep your shirt tucked in, Mr. Stanton! We'll come back! What does Grant say?" Lincoln spoke anxiously but without Stanton's excitement.

"Grant thinks I'm a panicky old woman. You'll have to work on him yourself. Tell him he's got to get some fighting men up here. I've telegraphed the Governors of six States to send us militia, but Early'll be here before the militia arrives, mark my words! If Early frees the 20,000 Rebel prisoners at Point Lookout, hell will be popping here in forty-eight hours."

"I'll wire Grant, Mr. Stanton." Lincoln rose to follow the Secretary to the War Office. "Keep the news as quiet as you can. Panic won't help the city."

"Panic might help Grant," growled Stanton. "He's started one division of the Sixth Corps to Baltimore by boat. That's 5,000 men, and 3,000 cavalry of which 2,500 are sick. Early has 30,000 men. Grant's drunk or crazy."

"He's neither!" snapped Lincoln. "He's a man harassed even as you and I. I'll wire him something that'll get him going."

His protest to Stanton was stout enough yet not wholly stout! Lincoln had more faith in Grant than in any military leader the war had developed, but the past three years had deprived him of the power to feel full confidence in any man. Moreover he had a theory that there was no drinking man who under a heavy strain was not liable to get drunk at a crucial moment.

He sent the little General a strong dispatch and made Stanton and Halleck wire to him also. Then he sent a summons out to the Home for Mary to come back to the White House. Mary, somewhat more irritated than alarmed, did not alleviate his general uneasiness by a conversation she held with him that evening. They sat in the kitchen garden. It was Lincoln's idea that they would here be free of callers. The night was steaming hot with a thunder storm threatening.

"Fred Douglass came to see me to-day. He's a smart nigger," began Mary.

"How did he happen to visit you?" asked Lincoln, with the old wish that Mary would keep out of this kind of politics.

"Senator Sumner sent him to see if I could hurry up the commission you said you'd try to get him. Are you going to give it to him, Abra'm?"

The President chewed meditatively on a stalk of pie plant. "I've had to put it up to Stanton. If Douglass comes to you again, bring him to me. While he's waiting for Stanton, I'll get him to go down to Fortress Monroe and set his scouts at work again. We are in awful straits for soldiers. I've got to issue a call for 500,000 more men. Seems as though I couldn't stand it."

"He's in no mood toward the Administration now to be sent on any such errand," protested Mary. "And he's very cross with General Butler. Did you know Butler is really blackmailing Grant? Grant wants to get rid of Butler and doesn't dare."

"I don't believe it!" shouted Lincoln angrily. Then he added apologetically, "Not but what Ben Butler is capable of trying it."

But Mary gave no sign of offense. She was worried and merely said, "Well, you'll see!" in the tone that always irritated her husband; it so frequently accompanied a true prophecy!

"I'll see what, my dear?" he asked.

"Well," veering as she so often did when crowded to another topic, "you'll see that Grant won't come up here and take personal command of this chance to destroy 30,000 Rebels."

"Good Lord! How'd you learn about that?" He jerked around on the bench to stare at the diminutive figure beside him.

"I went over to see Secretary Stanton about Douglass to-day and he boiled over to me. Why don't you put your foot down with Grant, Abra'm?" She sounded a little excited.

"I wrote Grant to provide to retain his hold where he is, then bring the rest of his forces personally and make a vigorous effort to destroy the Rebel forces around here. But I also told him it was a suggestion, not an order. I'm not smart enough to give orders to Grant."

"But you are!" Mary almost screamed at him.

Lincoln gave a low laugh. "You do have a tough row to hoe in running this war, don't you, darling Mary?"

She giggled. "It would be simple enough if I could control you! . . . The gnats are eating me up."

"I knew callers of some kind would drive us out of here!" said Lincoln, rising and pulling Mary to her feet. "Though the gnats are better than the Temperance women I had with me to-day."

"I suppose the Rebels think they'll get you, if they get Washington," said Mary, uneasily, as they started for the house.

"Maybe they'll be satisfied just to steal Halleck," remarked Lincoln.

"Oh, my dear, nothing so unimportant! Taking Halleck couldn't be considered, even by the North, more than petty larceny," and she laughed at her own tart wit.

Mary's inexplicable intuition proved correct. Grant did not come to Washington. On the 8th, frightened folk began to pour into the town from the north. The Rebels were approaching Rockville and Silver Springs. With their arrival the carefully guarded news broke and Washington went panic. Every one that could fled to Baltimore, but in a few hours this route was closed by the Rebels. The male population of the city was hurriedly armed and sent to reinforce the scant number of soldiers holding the surrounding forts. Bob, without saying a word to his mother, joined the defense of Fort Stevens just north of the Soldiers' Home. Tad, however, boasting of Bob's bravery, gave the boy away and every one was surprised but Lincoln when Mary tossed her head and said:

"Of course he's gone! The Todds were all military men."

"And Bob's father killed mosquitoes in the Black Hawk War," added the President.

Early was putting the torch to the farms and crops of Maryland. He had laid Frederick under requisition for $200,000. He had defeated General Wallace and was within a day's march of Washington. Still no help came from Grant, although he wired that the remainder of the Sixth Corps had left for Washington on the 9th.

On the evening of the 10th, Early's guns fired on the northern defenses of the city.

"It's no credit to Grant that Richmond's safe while Washington's in danger," remarked Mary on the afternoon of the 11th as she came into Lincoln's office with a glass of buttermilk.

Lincoln turned on her sternly. "Mary, if you think this continual jabbing at Grant helps me or the Union cause, you're mistaken. If you can tell me something good to do, tell me. If not, stop this impotent slashing."

"I'm sorry, Abra'm," said Mary, meekly.

Lincoln set down the glass of milk and stared at her. "Are you sick?"

Mary began to laugh. "Both of us are out of character, you, cross, and I, humble! Have you heard from the Sixth Corps?"

As if in answer to her query, Tad, who had been standing at the window with the telescope, suddenly dropped the instrument with a shout. "Pete's given me the signal. The vetewans have come!"

Lincoln seized his straw hat and followed Tad.

The city was strangely silent. The streets were half deserted. Store windows along Pennsylvania Avenue were boarded up. A great barricade of cord wood cut off Twelfth Street on the north side. At the intersection of Seventh Street and the Avenue, a crowd had gathered. Lincoln did not try to pierce it. He lifted Tad to his shoulder and together they looked over the heads of the people.

Up Seventh Street from the wharf was marching a line of soldiers with a single drummer at its head. As the tanned and seasoned veterans of many battles appeared, the crowd broke into cheers. "The Sixth! The Sixth! Go get 'em boys!" Lincoln stayed to watch several regiments pass, his heart growing lighter with every sturdy boot thud. Good old Grant! He'd sent his best!—Then, although Tad protested at his haste he returned to relieve Mary's anxiety.

The proximity of battle he found curiously exhilarating. It gratified him to discover that he was not frightened. On the contrary, the next day he tried to slip away for a visit to Fort Stevens, but Mary caught him just as he was seating himself in the carriage. She sat down resolutely beside him.

"Mary, this is absurd!" he exclaimed.

Mary unfurled her little lilac carriage shade and cocked it over her bonnet. "If you and Bob get shot, Tad and I want to be also."

"But where is Tad?" exclaimed Lincoln.

Mary's lips quivered and Lincoln now observed that she was pale and that her eyes were dilated. "I've just learned that he left in his goat cart for Fort Stevens, several hours ago. I thought he was at Pete Kelley's house, but Pete went along as Taddie's aide. I don't mind telling you," her voice breaking, "that Tad's going to get a spanking."

"Nobody's going to let harm come to the little fellow, Mary," said Lincoln, more stoutly than he felt, however. And he made no further protests against her accompanying him.

They reached the Fort two hours later, having had to drive round the trenches dug across the various roads from the north. They found Stanton's carriage drawn up before the Fort and Secretary Stanton arguing with a man in colonel's uniform as to the propriety of a civilian visiting the Fort at that moment. When Mary and the President descended from the phaëton and joined Stanton the officer threw up his hands in horror.

"But Colonel," cried Mary, "I came for my little boy, Taddie!"

"We sent him back to the White House an hour ago with a guard, Madam President," the Colonel told her. "One of his hounds got killed by a stray bullet from a Rebel sharpshooter. He insisted on taking the little brute back in his cart. He and his freckled friend and the goats and six privates with a sergeant made quite a funeral cortege."

"Jings!" ejaculated Lincoln. "What'll he do next? My son Robert here?"

"We sent the Home Guards back for city duty as soon as the regulars got here, Mr. Lincoln," replied the officer, moving uneasily. "And now, Mrs. Lincoln, allow me to show you back to your carriage. This is only a little lull in hostilities. We've been under fire all the morning."

"But I want to see the Fort under fire," protested Mary. "Look, you've got some more visitors," as a handsome span of horses appeared drawing a surrey.

"My God!" groaned the Colonel.

Lincoln slipped away and entered the inner works. Shortly he reached the gun emplacements where, unheeded in the confusion, he mounted a parapet. The Fort lay on the crest of a low range of hills. In the valley below, a line of blue coats advanced toward smoking hills opposite. Minié balls began to sing over the Fort. A Sergeant standing near Lincoln grunted and sank to his knees. The President hardly heeded him. He was watching the line of soldiers. It was like sitting at a play.

Suddenly a great mass of Rebels rushed from behind bushes into the road to the north. The Fort guns opened fire on them at once. Empty spaces appeared in the Rebel ranks. Perhaps ten minutes of this and the Rebel line had been wiped out. Silence reigned except for distant rifle fire. Some one grasped the President firmly by the ankle. A young Lieutenant was looking up into his face.

"Sir!" he cried, his very lips blanched, "unless you come down at once, I shall be obliged to bring a file of soldiers to remove you, though you are my superior officer! I've just forced Mrs. Lincoln to retire from bullet range."

"Jings!" exclaimed Lincoln, "I thought she was back there with Secretary Stanton and the Colonel— I reckon the kindest thing I can do for you fellows is to take myself and my family, official and otherwise, out of here! How does the attack go?"

"They're in full retreat. This is only the Rebel rear guard protecting the movement," replied the young officer. "You will go back now, Mr. Lincoln?"

"Yes, of course, my boy! What State do you hail from?"

"I'm from Pennsylvania. Drop your head below the range of those Minié balls, sir," as Lincoln started to cross the open parade.

Lincoln ducked his head obediently. "All right!" he laughed. "I'm leaving!"

He found his wife and the Secretary in a place of comparative safety under a south abatis. "They're falling back!" he told them.

"Thank the kind Father!" ejaculated Stanton. "I'm going home to get some sleep. Mrs. Lincoln, don't be cross with me," leading the way to a point where they could beckon for the carriages which were sheltered in a little wood.

"But I am cross," returned Mary. "If you continue to be obdurate about giving Douglass that appointment I shall turn as ferocious as you at your worst."

Stanton laughed and Mary exclaimed, "Oh, you men! I'd like to run this government for ten minutes."

"You're not the only one who wants to run things not in your own department," exclaimed Stanton, pulling his black beard with sudden grimness. "Postmaster General Blair is all out of patience with us too."

"What have we done now?" asked the President, his eyes on the efforts of Burke to bring the horses out from the shelter of the wood. The heavy blanket of smoke that lay over trees and buildings was as frightening to the poor beasts as the crack of the Parrotts.

Stanton replied with his familiar note of irritation.

"It's a damnable shame the way Postmaster General Blair is permitted to talk about the army. He's going about now telling everybody that the officers in Washington are poltroons. He means Halleck and me, the coward! He's been my consistent enemy ever since I entered the Cabinet, as you well know, Lincoln. You've simply got to dismiss him."

"*Mr.* Lincoln!" said Mary quietly. Stanton ignored her.

Lincoln took off his soft gray hat and fanned himself with it. He was very tired of the bickering of Stanton and Blair and their unceasing efforts to oust each other from the Cabinet. "On that kind of an order I'm like a woman Speed told me about years ago," he began.

Stanton muttered impatiently, but the President went on, while Burke, who had now driven up, held the prancing horses with difficulty.

"A little lady was sitting in a train when a man with a wooden leg took the empty seat beside her and started to talk. He informed her that at one time he had been the proud possessor of a mechanical leg. All he had to do was to wind it up and set the size of step and she'd carry him round all day. One day not long before, he happened in his travels to come to a fine clear pool of water in a creek and he took off his clothes, unbuckled his wooden leg, and went in swimming."

"Good God, Lincoln!" ejaculated Stanton as the rumble of battle began again in the northern hills. "Let's get home!"

The President went on solemnly and without moving while Mary gazed stoically on the rearing horses, though her eyes twinkled.

"It happened that a raccoon came down to drink while he was in the water. Now a raccoon is a very curious animal. He got interested at once in the wooden leg and what with his sniffing and poking he set the mechanism off and the leg got up and began to run across the prairies. The man yelled and started hopping on his single leg after it. But he'd hardly gone a mile when his single poor old leg got caught in a prairie dog hole and broke. There he was helpless till a tin peddler with a cart came along and rescued him. He never did hear of his mechanical leg again. Now all the while the man was telling this story, the lady kept smiling, so he felt encouraged to add at the end that he was taking up a collection to buy him a new patented leg and would the lady give him a dollar toward it. The lady, still smiling, opened her pocketbook and took out a card which she handed to the man. The card read, 'I am deaf and dumb and would be glad for a contribution toward an ear trumpet!' "

With a great laugh, Lincoln offered his arm to Mary and started toward the carriage. But Stanton was outraged.

"What sort of an answer is that, on an occasion like this! Do you call it dignified, Mr. Lincoln?"

The President paused. "I can be harsh if you prefer it, Mr. Stanton," he said tersely. "Blair's house was burned by the Rebels the other day because we had no help to send him. I don't know whether he said those things or not but it's improbable. If they were said, I don't approve of them, but under the circumstances, I wouldn't dismiss a member of the Cabinet for them. Besides this, I propose continuing to be myself a judge as to when a member of the Cabinet shall be dismissed."

Stanton bit his lip, bowed, and entered his own carriage. The President chuckled at intervals all the way home.

Pete Kelley, with a black rag round his hat, met them at the gates of the White House. He was dust from head to foot. His blue eyes were dark with weariness and excitement. He stood on the step of the carriage and delivered his message.

"Lieutenant Lincoln says you're to come straight up to his room. Pensacola's got shot, but Tad ain't cried a tear. Tad and I washed him clean in the bathroom."

When they reached the house, they both obediently followed the child up the stairs. Taddie's sorrows were not to be treated lightly. The late afternoon sun filled Tad's bedroom with rose color. Taddie, his linen suit incredibly soiled, his chestnut hair in moist ringlets, his cheeks flushed under the crust of sweated dust, stood beside the bed leaning dejectedly on a rifle. On the bed lay the little hound dog, unwontedly white as to hair, a bandage round his chest. His head was pillowed on a wreath of Mary's choicest roses. Sumter sat beside Tad dejectedly scratching fleas.

As his father dropped his hand on his shoulder, Tad looked up. "Ev'ything of Willie's is dead now," he said, his cheeks quivering.

"Except mother and Bob and you and me," said his father. "Well, I reckon he's wagging his little tail off in heaven now."

Tad looked up into his face. "Do you suppose he's found Willie, already?"

"Sure he has!" exclaimed Pete Kelley. "He'd find Willie, if't he was in hell."

"Well, he isn't in hell, you di'ty skunk!" shouted Tad, "not eitha' of them!"

Lincoln looked helplessly at his wife who had been eyeing the scene through tear dimmed eyes. She spoke in a carefully practical voice.

"Have you arranged for his casket, boys? You'd better go down to the steward and ask him for an empty box. I'll give you a piece of my old white velvet cape to line it with and you'd better work quickly so we can have the funeral right after supper."

"Come on, Pete!" exclaimed Tad. He placed his gun in a corner and ran from the room.

That evening, after little Pensacola had been laid to his long rest, Tad came into his father's office and placed a battered haversack on a letter the President had been reading.

"This is something to wememba' the wa' by, Papa day," he said. "The sa'gent got it off a webel that was shooting at Fo't Stevens. It's fo' you. Open it up."

Lincoln obeyed and emptied on the desk a jackknife, a plug of twisted tobacco, a tin cup, and about two quarts of coarsely cracked corn with a little salt tied in a rag. The corn had been ground up with the cob.

"The sa'geant said that's all the di'ty webels had to eat now and a good thing too—"

Lincoln sifted the meal slowly through his fingers. "He was a human being, Tad, exactly like you and me. Don't speak of him so. And he had wonderful spunk to march all the way from Richmond and fight on this horse fodder— You'd better go to bed now, my boy."

"Do you like the gift?" Tad asked, anxiously.

"Liking doesn't express it," replied his father with a twisted smile. "Give me a kiss, dear Tad and go, won't you?"

"I'll miss Pensacola!" said Tad, turning abruptly from the room.

CHAPTER XVI

THE TANGLED BURDEN

LINCOLN, after a moment, lifted the haversack gently from the letter he had been reading and finished its excited phrases. It was from Greeley. "I venture to remind you that our bleeding, bankrupt, almost dying country longs for peace; shudders at the prospect of fresh conscriptions, of further wholesale devastations and new rivers of blood. And a widespread conviction that the Government and its prominent supporters are not anxious for peace and do not improve proffered opportunities to achieve it is doing great harm now and is morally certain unless removed to do far greater in the approaching elections. . . . I fear you do not realize how intently the people desire any peace consistent with the National integrity and honor. . . . I have information on which I can rely that two persons duly commissioned and empowered to negotiate for peace are at this moment not far from Niagara Falls and are desirous of conferring with yourself or such persons as you may appoint. . . ."

Lincoln rang the bell for John Hay. "John," he said, when the young man appeared, "you remember I wrote Greeley that if he had any peace envoys from Jeff Davis to bring them here to see me—that is if they had a proposition in writing from Davis asking for peace on terms embracing the restoration of the Union and abandonment of slavery. He's ignored that reply of mine and has sent me another screed. I want you to go to New York and see Mr. Greeley and make him go with you to meet his commissioners. Tell him that if they're qualified, I intend not only a sincere effort for peace but I intend that he shall be a personal witness that it's made."

"But Greeley has nothing bona fide, Mr. Lincoln! He's just a timid little editor!" exclaimed John.

Lincoln nodded. "But he thinks he has something and we'll make him do the investigating himself, which is exactly what he won't want to do. You've a nice job there, John! Get out to-night, if you can. I think the road is clear up to Baltimore. Early is retreating. The Sixth certainly got here just by the skin of its teeth!"

He shook hands with the young man and turned back to his desk to finish a message to General Grant. "In your dispatch of yesterday to General Sherman, I find the following, to wit: 'I shall make a desperate effort to get a position here which will hold the enemy without the necessity of so many men.'—Pressed as we are by the lapse of time, I am glad to hear you say this and yet I do hope you may find a way that the effort shall not be desperate in the sense of a loss of life."

He dropped his pen and stared at the haversack. Tad's memento moved him unaccountably— If only the dreadful trouble would end! If only he could be sure he wouldn't break before the finish! He jumped up and went over to the war map to move a little to the southeast a pin which represented Sherman headed for the Atlantic,—that wild adventure! As for the menace to Washington, *that* was over, but Grant must somehow be made to send up a man right away who would drive Early out of Maryland before his depredations there equaled those of Sherman in Georgia. Stanton had suggested Sheridan. The thought of Stanton made him frown. He went back to his desk and wrote a memorandum for his Cabinet.

"I must myself be the judge how long to retain in and when to remove any one of you from his position. It would greatly pain me to discover any of you endeavoring to procure another's removal or in any way to prejudice him before the public. Such endeavor would be a wrong to me and much worse, a wrong to the country. My wish is that on this subject no remark be made nor question asked by any one of you here or elsewhere, now or hereafter."

Mary came in as he finished this. He showed it to her with the remark that it was a further moral from the tale he had told Stanton that afternoon.

Mary read the statement and smiled complacently. "You really are becoming a tyrant, Abra'm!" Then she haled him off to bed.

It was a relief to have Congress not in session. Before it convened again, he hoped to have Louisiana well on her legs. Banks wrote that there never had been a better constitution than the loyalists had just completed. It embraced all the best points of the old one, and in addition it abolished slavery, making negro suffrage optional with the State legislature. It provided for an election of members to Congress, early in September.

It looked at first as though Lincoln's proclamation on the Davis bill had served its purpose, at least as far as popular acquiescence was concerned. He was relaxing his watchfulness on the matter when he received a terrific jolt. Ben Wade and Winter Davis published in the New York *Tribune* a bitter manifesto concerning the pocket veto and the President.

Lincoln brought the newspaper to Mary's room before breakfast.

"Look at this!" he exclaimed. "Just as I was loosening my galluses a little bit, along comes this! Nothing's hurt me so much since I came to Washington."

Mary read the screed, then tossed it scornfully out the window.

"Well, I don't see why it should hurt you most of anything," she remarked. "It's a horrid document, but it doesn't say things that haven't been said hundreds of times before. It says your attitude on reconstruction is based on your desire to be elected, that it gives you a chance to hold the electoral votes of the Rebel States at the dictation of your personal ambition. They say your motives are sinister and that you want to defeat the will of the people by perverting the Constitution—sickening balderdash! Why let it sting, as you say to me?"

"Because it does, Mary! I've done everything I can to make Winter Davis my friend. I like the boy and I love his father. And he's a Republican. This thing comes, remember, from representatives of my own party. To be wounded in the house of your friends is a grievous hurt, Mary."

She came over to put her arm about him and rub her face against his coat sleeve. "You're tired, Abra'm, or this wouldn't rub you on the raw. I wish you could go away for a few days."

"I hope Charles Sumner didn't back it," said the President.

"He'll live to regret it, if he did," Mary proclaimed, stoutly. "Can this do any real harm?"

"I fear so," replied Lincoln. "It gives a head and a mouth to the impatience of the Radicals with me. But I can do nothing more to counteract that."

For days the sense of hurt clung to him, but his preoccupation with the war gradually overset the pain. It seemed to him during the next few weeks that he and Stanton and Grant were the only people in the world who could see an end to the war. The depression of the people shown by their bitter criticism of himself and Grant hung about him like an evil-smelling fog. He thought that Grant was affected badly by the hostility, for the General seemed to lack his usual eagerness and activity. He was the soldier of Shiloh, not of Chattanooga. This was alarming. And when Lincoln received a request from General Grant asking that General Butler be demoted, he made a quiet trip to Fortress Monroe and sent for Butler.

Butler came in from camp, sunburned and, for once, shabby. He seemed honestly glad to see the President, and after supper they settled down for a talk. Butler had finished the story of his terrible failure to take Petersburg and the two men had sat in silence for some time watching the moon rise over the black walls of the Fort before Lincoln asked the question he had come down to ask.

"Butler, why do you work against Grant?"

The General's camp chair creaked as he turned on Lincoln. But the President put out a protesting hand.

"For God's sake, General, let's talk without elocution! I like you. I'm not down here to spy. I've come down to see if I can't beguile you into upholding Grant's hands. You know as well as I do you've no business to say Grant's a drunkard."

"I never said so," declared Butler. "I never saw General Grant take a glass of spirituous liquor in my life. I've seen him drink wine at the dinner table but nowhere else. The shoe's on the other foot, Mr. Lincoln. Grant's trying to get rid of me. I tell you, this army needs me. And I tell you, both you and Grant need the support I can give you from Massachusetts and the other New England States."

"The *war* needs the support you can give it," replied Lincoln. "The peace party is almost out of hand. You know you don't want Grant's job. You want to be free to return to politics on short notice."

"What do you mean?" asked Butler, lighting a cigar with a steady hand and showing his aquiline face in startlingly clear profile.

Lincoln was prepared for the question. "It's no secret, is it, that a call has gone out for a new Presidential convention next month. The feeling is that I can't be elected and the Radical Republicans must have another ticket to save it from complete overthrow. They say for the ticket, you and Sumner or Sumner and Farragut. The men back of the call are Chase, Davis, John Jay, Whitelaw Reid, Greeley, Bryant, Sumner. You and Sumner ought to make a very strong run together. . . . Well, you're all within your rights, I reckon. But such being the case, why in the name of common sense and General Jackson, don't you get off Grant's neck?"

"Your political intelligence bureau is good but not infallible, Mr. Lincoln," said Butler, puffing calmly. "I think you're doing Sumner an injustice. I had a letter from him yesterday. I'll just read you a paragraph." He drew a letter from within the breast of his tunic and leaning forward so that the light through the doorway fell on the sheet he read: " 'I do not see how anything can be done except through Mr. Lincoln and with his good will. If he could see that patriotism required his withdrawal, and could sincerely give his countenance and support to a new candidate, I am sure that the candidate of that convention, whoever he might be, could be chosen. But any adverse proceeding would disaffect him and his friends so as to destroy the unity of the party. This unity must be had at all hazards and at every sacrifice. If Mr. Lincoln does not withdraw, then all who now disincline to him must come in to his support. I have declined to sign any paper or take any part in any action because I am satisfied nothing can be done except through Mr. Lincoln and with his good will.' "

Butler finished his reading and returned to his previous position in the shadow. Lincoln listened with mingled feelings of gratification and chagrin. Sumner's attitude toward him hurt in spite of all the philosophy he could bring to bear. He did not propose, however, for Butler to know this.

"He told me some of that months ago, but in what *The Baltimore Sun* calls the scathing and withering style. When he finished with me that time, I was struck blind and found myself feeling with my fingers for my continued existence. A little of the bone was left and I gradually revived. And here I am."

Butler stirred impatiently in his chair. "I was merely trying to do Sumner justice with you, Mr. Lincoln," he said stiffly.

"Oh, you've done that!" The President's voice was bland. "Even at the price of having to wade through the Senator's cursed, unreadable, and ungodly handwriting!"

Butler suddenly laughed and relighted his cigar.

Lincoln laughed too, then asked, quietly, "Cæsar having done all these things, as I've heard Bob translate his Latin to his mother, why can't you leave Grant alone, General?"

"Hah! Let Grant leave *me* alone!" ejaculated Butler.

"General, go to him! Tell him all that's penned up inside your heart and lock arms with him for the remainder of the time you're in the Army. If you'll do this, I promise you, I'll not lift a finger against your nomination and if you do win it, I'll do everything in my power to help you."

"I'll go see General Grant to-morrow," declared Butler.

"Then I reckon I can go back to Washington to-night with an easier mind." Lincoln rose and put on the deerstalker's cap he wore aboard the boat.

He reached the White House late the next morning and the following day received a dispatch from General Grant, containing a withdrawal of the request for Butler's demotion.

Bob, who had returned to his secretarial duties, brought the dispatch to his father and said, "I didn't think Grant mixed in politics."

"He doesn't. Has too much sense and too hard a job. This is some of Butler's back-alley calling," replied Lincoln, reading the message with a sigh of relief. "I made Butler straighten it out. Wish I could do the same thing by Winter Davis and Lyman Trumbull."

"Well, no one could call their methods of the back-alley variety." Bob's voice was rueful. "What are you going to do to counteract their thunder, father?"

"Bob, I'm not going to do anything. My stock is so low over the country that even a Papal Bull couldn't lower me, let alone one from Davis. I was badly upset at first but I've reached the point now where I feel like the man did whose son had a scientific turn of mind. He bought the boy a microscope. The youngster went round experimenting with his glass on everything that came his way. One day, at dinner table, his father took a piece of cheese. 'Don't eat that, father,' said the boy, 'it's full of wigglers.' 'My son,' said the old gentleman, taking a large bite, 'let 'em wiggle: I can stand it if they can!' "

Bob joined in his father's laughter, then said, seriously, "But are you really discouraged about your reëlection, father?"

Lincoln nodded his head. "The only thing that can reëlect me would be a 'return to slavery' plank in the Democratic platform. Even Sumner would stand by me to defeat that— Are you glad to be through soldiering?"

"Oh, of course, being a Home Guard isn't real soldiering! But even at that I can go back to Harvard next month with a fair amount of swagger." Bob smiled.

"I may try to arrange with Grant to take you on when you finish. Your mother's more reconciled than she was, I think," taking up a handful of letters Stoddard laid on his desk.

"Mother's pretty philosophical about anything she sees is inevitable," said Bob with a boyish grin, and picking up a tray of telegrams he went out.

Secretary Stanton entered shortly after. His dark eyes behind his spectacles were red-rimmed for lack of sleep but were full of their usual fiery earnestness.

Lincoln rose to meet him. "Well, old friend, we've weathered through another night, eh? I always tell myself that when I waken.—Anything of the nature of a catastrophe for me this morning?"

Stanton's eyes softened. "You look as if you'd barely scraped through, though, Mr. Lincoln! God Almighty, but you look tired!"

"Same to you!" The President threw a long arm across Stanton's shoulders and the two men stood silent for a moment.

Finally Stanton said, "I've got another letter from Grant to the effect that Phil Sheridan is expected to do real damage to Early. He gives details as to how the various forces will move. Sensible enough but for one thing. You know as well as I do, Mr. Lincoln, that unless Grant gets up to Maryland to see the ground himself we're in for another damn fool fiasco. The officers will do nothing but quarrel and fight for prestige. They need a head on the spot. And for some reason, Grant won't go. Here, read it yourself."

Lincoln read the message and looked up. "You're right, Stanton. It's good but not good enough. Here, let me see if I can't start him." He seated himself at the desk and wrote, "I have seen your dispatch in which you say, 'I want Sheridan put in command of all the troops in the field with instructions to put himself south of the enemy and follow him to the death. Wherever the enemy goes let our troops go also—' This I think is exactly right as to how our forces should move but please look over the dispatches you may have received from here ever since you made that order and discover, if you can, that there is any idea in the head of any one here of putting our army south of the enemy or of following him to the death in any direction. I repeat to you, it will neither be done nor attempted unless you watch it every hour of every day and force it."

Stanton read the message, nodded delightedly and said, "This is splendid! Of course it's in violation of all official etiquette and propriety."

"I reckon it is," replied Lincoln serenely. "I'm proud of the solid reputation I'm building for just that thing. Get it off, Stanton."

Grant's reply came at noon. He said, laconically, that he was leaving at noon for the Maryland front.

Lincoln heaved an enormous sigh of relief and announced to Nicolay and Bob that he was giving himself a treat on the strength of Grant's decision. The boys received his announcement with cheers and forthwith he went over to Chittenden's office and induced the Register of the Treasury to go with him to visit Professor Henry, head of the Smithsonian Institution. "I want to get you two fellows stirred up to talk. I want to travel far from war and politics."

Luck was peculiarly with him, he thought, when they found in Henry's office the explorer Kennicott, who had just returned from three years' exploration of the Yukon. The room was overflowing with pelts, heads, eggs and other fruits of the trip. Kennicott was only too glad to tell his story, and Lincoln put his feet on the mantel and settled down for a real feast.

It was seven o'clock when the President looked at his watch and ejaculated, "Jings, I've been in Alaska four solid hours! I'm a new man, gentlemen!" And with a regretful farewell glance at Kennicott's loot, he rushed back to his office to make up for his holiday.

It was well past ten o'clock that evening when he decided to go out to the Soldiers' Home to spend the night with the family, again sojourning there. He had told the servants and his guards that he would remain in the city, but when he passed through the empty sitting room on his way to bed, he realized that he was lonely. It would be good fun to slip out and tell Mary about Kennicott while the story was fresh in his mind. He evaded his guard, saddled his own horse, led it out the servant's gate and was off.

It was over a year since he'd ridden alone. A thrilling sense of freedom swept over him. There was a brilliant moon. His horse was fresh and lively and inclined to shy at shadows. No chance to worry or think, with this beast to control, he thought contentedly. He allowed the animal to gallop the length of the turnpike, only slowing him down when he reached the turn into the Home. The August night was lovely—burning stars above and heavy scent of harvest fields on either side the road with locusts droning placidly.

He brought the horse to a full halt as he entered the gates and sat looking at the beautiful view to the north. Suddenly a rifle shot rang out and a bullet whined by the President's ear. The horse bolted, then another shot came.

Lincoln felt as if some one had hit his hat a violent blow. The frightened horse could not be brought up again until his forehoofs struck the porch of the cottage. Mary screamed from above and as Lincoln stood soothing the horse, she appeared on the porch with a candle.

"Abra'm, are you hurt?"

"Not at all," answered the President, still struggling with the plunging horse. "Hold the candle here, will you, Mary? Let's see if this fellow got scratched."

"Who cares about the horse? It's you! Abra'm, what was it? What brings you here?" Her voice rose hysterically.

A yawning colored boy came round the corner and took the reins.

Lincoln lifted the candle from Mary's shaking hand. "You brought me here, dearest wife!" He took her hand and led her up the stairs to their little bedroom, talking quietly as he moved. "I had a glorious afternoon in Alaska with Judge Chittenden and Doc Henry. I came out to tell you about it. A fine fellow named Kennicott—"

As they entered the room, Mary interrupted him. "It's all right now, Abra'm. I'm not going into hysterics. I've learned more self-control in the past three years than in the forty years before. Who shot at you?"

"I don't know that any one did," setting the candle down on the bureau. "There was a shot as I turned from the turnpike that scared my horse. He bolted and jerked off my hat and here I am."

Mary stared up at him. She looked very young with her long braids hanging over her night dress. "Abra'm, how are we going to endure the strain to the end! And you want four years more!"

"It's queer what a man's conscience and vanity working together will bring him to, eh," chuckled Lincoln, sitting down on a stool covered with a cross-stitched tidy and beginning to pull off his boots.

"We'll have a lot of bad news. I broke a mirror to-day!" She stooped to help him with his boots and he saw that her teeth were chattering and her hands shaking. The superb fight she had waged for self-control ever since Willie's death was a constant source of admiration to him. He helped when he could.

"Let's go down to the kitchen and get something to eat, Mary. I'd give five dollars for a cup of your tea. You haven't made me one since we left Springfield."

"Haven't you had supper?" she demanded, straightening up and looking at him disgustedly.

"I forgot to," he replied meekly.

She pulled on a dressing gown, the color coming back to her face. "You are the greatest fool about your stomach that ever lived. I should think you'd learn sense, sometime. I let all the servants go to town except that cotton-headed Jake. You come straight down to the kitchen with me. No, don't start without your slippers. These floors are full of slivers."

She continued scolding as he followed her to the kitchen. She ordered him to sit down at the clean-scrubbed pine table. He did so, watching her contentedly as she manipulated the fire which still glowed. He finally lifted both feet to the opposite chair and interrupted the steady flow of her admonitions with a groan of satisfaction.

"Lord, isn't this fine! Mary, see if those darkies haven't hid some of their own ash-cakes round somewhere. A stone jar they would be in—then some New Orleans molasses, and your tea!—Ah," as she returned from the pantry with corn bread and the molasses jug, "Mary, I wouldn't swap you for Queen Victoria."

Mary dimpled and suddenly laid her cheek to his. "I worship you!" she whispered. Then she poured him his tea.

The next morning he rode back to town accompanied by James and the cotton-headed Jake. When they reached the turnpike, Lincoln dismounted and picked up his felt hat which lay in a clump of goldenrod. There was a bullet hole through the crown. He crushed the hat into the pocket of his coat. He would give it to Colonel Baker of the Detective Police and then forget the matter.

And Mary's prophecy of evil didn't come true that day, for Stoddard met him at the door of the White House with the news that Admiral Farragut had defeated the Rebel fleet and taken Mobile Bay!

CHAPTER XVII

JEANIE DEANS

JOHN HAY, who had returned from Greeley's futile peace mission more than ever discontented with what he called mere clerical work, was eager to attend the pending Democratic convention in Chicago, but Nicolay was better at that sort of thing, so it was he who went. It was John Hay, however, who brought the first news of the Chicago "surrender." He burst into Lincoln's bedroom, showing for the first time since Lincoln had known him, a real despair. Standing by the bed, wrapped in a purple and yellow smoking robe that was much coveted by Bob, his black hair rumpled, his black eyes deep sunk and his lips quivering, the young man read the news aloud to the President.

The Democrats had nominated McClellan on a platform the basic premise of which was that the war was a failure and peace with Unionism the only feasible aim—with no conditions attached to the restoration as regarded upholding the Emancipation Act.

John dashed the paper to the floor and kicked it under the bed. "I warned everybody last spring when I came back from the middle West that there was almost revolutionary feeling against continuing the war and a growing enthusiasm for McClellan."

"I know you did, John!" agreed Lincoln. "But I didn't exactly nominate the man!"

John's lips quivered. "I don't know whether the nation's worthy of you for another term, sir. But if the dumb cattle aren't worthy of another term of Lincoln, then let the will of God be done and the murrain of McClellan fall on them!"

He jerked the cord of his robe viciously and banged out of the room. Lincoln lay for a moment staring blankly at the ceiling. Then the door again flew open and John, one broad grin, appeared, followed by Bob and Taddie. John waved a slip of yellow paper.

"The war a failure, eh! Allow me to read you the answer General Sherman makes to that! 'September 3. Atlanta is ours and fairly taken!'—How's that for a plank for the Republican platform?"

"By Jings!" shouted Lincoln. "What news for a fellow to receive in his nightshirt! How can I do a hornpipe? Hand me my breeches, Tad."

But instead of dressing himself, he sat on the edge of the bed, holding the yellow slip and smiling at it. Finally he said:

"I reckon that this is the moment to call the folks' attention in no uncertain terms to the fact that this war is not a failure. They've been ignoring what Farragut's done. And they've got to take notice that Sherman's army is now substantially the same as it was when it left Chattanooga.

After all the bloodshed—what a relief!—what a relief! 'A victory is twice itself when the achiever brings home full numbers.'"

Mary came in on the last of his soliloquy and shooed the boys out after she had heard the glorious news. But Lincoln would not allow her to lead him to breakfast until he had written a proclamation in which he adjured the people to give thanks to the Supreme Being for these victories and ordered a hundred-gun salute to be fired at each arsenal and navy yard of the United States.

Then he ate an unusually hearty breakfast.

"You'd lay on some flesh and be a credit to your clothes if you could get a telegram from Sherman every morning," said Mary as she refilled his coffee cup.

"Or just one from Sheridan! I'm getting discouraged about him," said the President.

For Sheridan still maneuvered for position against Early while Early continued to choke the railroads into Baltimore and Washington. There was now grave danger from a food-and-fuel famine in both cities. Grant had felt that the consequences of a defeat at the moment of the nation's terrible depression would be so grave that he was hesitating to have Sheridan take the initiative. Lincoln had felt the reasonableness of this but now, backed by the news from Sherman and Farragut, he began to urge Grant to take the gamble. In spite of his efforts, however, two weeks went by without apparent results. But on the 20th of September, Stoddard ran all the way from Stanton's office to Lincoln's with Sheridan's reply to the Chicago convention.

"We have just sent them whirling through Winchester and we are after them to-morrow."

Lincoln read the telegram, then looked over his spectacles to exclaim, "Boys, I reckon this will do! We'll shut up shop for the rest of the day."

He spent the afternoon visiting hospitals with Mary.

He awaited, eagerly now, the effect of the Chicago surrender on his own party. The answer came again through the newspapers. On the 29th of September they reported a long speech by Charles Sumner in Cooper Institute, New York, *ardently supporting Lincoln for President!*

From the moment that he read this speech, Lincoln began to cherish a real hope that he might be reëlected.

Sumner first, then Chase!

The former member of his Cabinet dropped into the President's office on the last day of September. He never had seen Chase looking so well, though he was handsome at all times; a big man physically with almost perfect features. What impressed Lincoln most at the moment was the fact that the familiar look of irritation had left Chase's lip and eye. He appeared as urbane as a sleeping child.

"The White Mountains have done you good, Governor," said Lincoln, shaking hands.

"What a pity you couldn't have been up there, too, Mr. Lincoln," re-

plied Chase as he looked from Lincoln's weary face to the shabby, overloaded desk. "We've thought of you and Mrs. Lincoln often, suffering here
in this dreadful town."

"I suppose it isn't a dreadful town, really," returned Lincoln, thoughtfully. "In fact, I recall having a sort of affection for the place when I was
in Congress. But after this four years' siege— Well, when I leave it, I
hope never to see it again.—Sit down and swap a few lies with me. What
are you going to do with yourself now, Governor?"

"I'm going to devote myself to your reëlection, Mr. Lincoln," sinking
into his old place at the Cabinet table.

Lincoln kept his countenance with difficulty, eased himself onto the
edge of the table and clasped his left knee with both hands as he asked:

"You've changed your mind about me, eh?"

Chase looked up at the President and replied slowly, "I don't feel that
I really know you and so I can't found my actions on what you say or do.
But I've never desired anything but your complete success and I've never
indulged in a personal feeling incompatible with absolute fidelity to your
administration."

Lincoln bit his lip and told himself that Chase had taken his swapping
invitation literally. Aloud he said:

"I reckon it's not in the books for you and me to understand each other,
Governor! Won't your friends be grieved at losing their pet candidate?"

"I never really desired to be President, Mr. Lincoln," Chase leaned forward earnestly, his eyes as clear and candid as Tad's. "It's my conviction
that the cause I love and the general interests of the country will be best
promoted by your reëlection and I've made up my mind to join my efforts
to those of almost the whole body of my friends in securing it."

"This is very pleasing to me! Very!" Lincoln suddenly choked, and it
was not with laughter. He jumped from the table and walked hastily to
the window. Chase really meant what he said. What a strange mind! He
stared at the distant Potomac—hopefully—almost cheerfully. The sails
were pretty in the September sun. He couldn't recall when he had noticed them before. He went back to the table and looked down at Chase,
suppressing a desire to laugh or to weep, he couldn't tell which. "I'm
glad to hear this news, Governor."

Obviously moved by the President's emotion, Chase rose and held out
his hand. The two men shook hands and Lincoln uttered a silent prayer
that the act prove symbolical of a real loyalty from the former secretary.

"My first move will be in my home State," said Chase. "In Ohio I
ought to have weight, though I'm ashamed to say that McClellan's strong
there."

"But not as strong as Salmon P. Chase," cried Lincoln joyfully. Then
with a little hesitation, "Have you seen Charles Sumner lately?"

"I last saw dear Charles at Longfellow's house in Nahant on my way
to the mountains," replied Chase, a reminiscent smile lighting his face.
"The three of us spent the day on the piazza reading aloud Tennyson's

388 WITH MALICE TOWARD NONE

last poem, 'Enoch Arden.' Longfellow's small daughter nestled in Sumner's lap much of the time. I must remember to tell little Isabella Hooper that. We avoided politics. Of course the Chicago treason hadn't occurred then."

"But he's come out for me!" ejaculated Lincoln. "Now with Phil Sheridan galloping up the Shenandoah Valley— Did you ever see him, Governor? He's not much more to look at than I am, a little chap with a round head, red face, legs longer than his body and not enough neck to hang him by. But he will actually chase Rebels! He and Sherman—after all these years—! Whew! Well, you've brought a fine grade of corn to the mill this morning, Governor," as Chase picked up his hat.

"Perhaps it was time, Mr. Lincoln," said Chase enigmatically.

Lincoln looked at his broad back almost with affection. "Patience is a tired nag," he murmured, "yet will she jog."

Mary was inclined to be scornful of Lincoln's hopes of Chase's personal loyalty.

"It suits him just now to make up to you because Chief Justice Taney is dying. Let's see what he does after the old man is gone."

But though poor Taney obligingly died in late October, Chase made no direct move in relation to the event. However, even before the funeral, a letter came from Sumner reminding Lincoln of their conversation the previous spring. He added his usual few words of admonition.

"I insist that from this time forward, the Constitution must be interpreted for liberty as it has been thus far for slavery. I remind you also that our war measures must be sustained. A Chief Justice is needed whose position on the slavery question is already fixed and will not need argument of counsel to convert him. Chase's appointment should come hard on the heels of Taney's funeral."

Nicolay gave this letter to the President with a questioning lift of the eyebrows. Lincoln read it, and said, "We'll be swamped with petitions. Every jerkwater lawyer in the country is going to ask for the job. Give them all the same answer: that the President's going to be very shut pan about this matter."

"There's a letter in this mail from Governor Chase. He's still in Ohio," Nicolay grinned.

"What's it about?" asked Lincoln.

"Simply a kind and friendly letter."

"File it with his other recommendations," said Lincoln with his shrewd smile.

Lincoln had no intention of appointing Chase immediately. After pondering on the matter for some time, he came to the conclusion that it would be salutary for this man with his uneasy ambitions, his incapacity for reading men, his unkind tongue, to spend a few weeks in uncertainty. In seeking the reason for the delay it was possible that the Governor might bring his brilliant brain to bear on his own weaknesses of character. Only when he understood these would he be fit for the high office.

So under all the enormous pressure, pressure so widespread that one might have thought that even the war and the pending election were less important to folk than their winning of the vacant place on the bench for themselves or their friends, Lincoln was silent.

He watched the work of his party on his reëlection with deepest concern, gave advice, kept Nicolay on the go. But he made no election speeches himself. When election day came, to his own surprise, he found himself quite calm and going about his routine business with a clear mind. Mary was tense and irritable with anxiety. She finally lost patience with Lincoln's apparent indifference and went off with Taddie to take supper with Mrs. Welles.

A heavy rain came on late in the afternoon. The wind rose almost to a hurricane. It was Cabinet day, but only Bates and Welles were there, for Stanton was down with malaria and the others had gone home to vote. Lincoln dismissed the meeting shortly and as the twilight came on, suddenly realized that he was alone and that he was lonely and uneasy. He prowled about from room to room. The sitting room with a single light burning low and the little dog Sumter asleep on a sofa, Martin Van Buren smirking above him. Mary's room with the faint odor of attar of roses—the toilet things in perfect alignment on the bureau—dear Mary! she'd find Springfield dull, but heavenly dull, after all this. His own room. No, that enshrined too many agonies. He wouldn't go in there. Across the hall to Tad's room. Tad had been playing with his toy soldiers. A pistol, present from some officer, lay on the bed. Lincoln purloined it. He'd had an ugly dream about Tad and his pistol, the night before.

From Tad's room into Willie's. It had been kept without change, though Mary never had entered it from the day of the boy's death. Lincoln lighted the gas and stood looking about. Willie had been Lincoln over again with all Lincoln's boyhood yearnings. Thank God, Willie's father'd been able to satisfy some of them. He smoothed the bed and patted a copy of Scott's poems, still open, face down on the table. Then seated himself on the bed. . . . If it was the will of the people to refuse him this day at the polls—what a relief, what a tragic relief! . . . Life could compensate him best by bringing him this refusal. . . . Life, what was it? God functioning? or man? And who was he, Abraham Lincoln? Who—? President of the United States of America! God! God! . . . He twisted his hands together and groaned, then sat motionless.

John Hay came upon him, a little breathless from his search. One never knew when the kidnapers would be given their opportunity by Lincoln's carelessness of self. The young man gave a sweeping glance round the room and his face was very tender but his voice casual as he said:

"So many wires are down owing to the storm, sir, that the only news will be in the War Office. Let's go over there and see what's happening."

Lincoln rose, blinked, and with one hand on John's shoulder turned out the gas with the other. He twisted a blue army cape round him and followed the young man toward the War Office. It was difficult to negotiate the turnstile, so fierce was the buffeting of the wind.

There was a crowd in the War Office, Welles, Bates, Nicolay, Stoddard, and several newspaper men. Somebody had treated to an oyster supper on trays. It was good to be back in the world of men.

By midnight, it was certain that he had been elected.

About two o'clock Mary sent word that in spite of the rain that still fell, a huge crowd was serenading his empty bed chamber. He hurried home through the kitchen premises, made a little speech from the window of his room and went to sleep a little later, almost unbearably convinced that the Supreme Being was setting the seal of approval on the thing he was trying to do.

But even now, he did not give Chase the reward every one said Chase expected. He was waiting to see Sumner. He would not send for Sumner. But, as he expected, the Senator appeared just before the opening of Congress.

It was a cold, sleety day with Tad lying on the office hearthrug reading aloud from a book of fairy tales while his father worked on his message to Congress. Tad was wild with joy at seeing his friend. Before his father and the Senator could shake hands the boy was embracing him while his shouts of welcome brought James to the door. Sumner hugged and kissed him and exclaimed over his summer's growth. But when Tad had subsided, the two men clasped hands in silence: Lincoln deeply glad to see this man he loved, deeply apprehensive of what this greatest of his adversaries might have in store for him.

Sumner broke the silence, his voice tender and deep. "My dear Mr. Lincoln, you make us all feel selfish, always here, day after difficult day," he glanced around the office as Chase had done, "and the rest of us—"

"And the rest of you," smiled Lincoln, "riveting the chains for another four years. I'm mighty grateful to you for your efforts and your self-sacrifice, Senator. I've followed things with fair accuracy, this summer."

Sumner chose to ignore the implications. "We're all happy over the results, Mr. Lincoln."

"Even Chase?" asked the President, deliberately.

"You must try to overlook the indecorous things Mr. Chase once said about you," said Sumner, drawing Tad down beside him on a sofa and patting the small grimy hand that lay on his great knee.

"Oh! I bear no grudge," answered Lincoln. "They sting but they concern Chase more than they do me. Would he as Chief Justice say indecorous things about the persons and cases connected with the Supreme Court? You perceive that here's where his hens come home to roost."

"I'm sure he won't," answered Sumner earnestly. "It's only where his ambition's concerned that he's unwise."

Lincoln rubbed his head. "Of Mr. Chase's ability and of his soundness on the interpretations of the Emancipation there can be no doubt. But— he's a man of unbounded ambition and he's been working all his life to become President. I'm afraid if I make him Chief Justice, he'll simply become more restless and uneasy and neglect the place in his strife and intrigue to get this job. If I were sure he'd go on the bench and give up his aspirations and do nothing but make himself a great judge, I'd not hesitate a moment. What do you say to this idea, Senator? What if I'd send for Mr. Chase and tell him frankly that the way was open to him to become the greatest Chief Justice the Supreme Court ever had if he'll dismiss at once and forever the subject of the Presidency?"

Sumner raised both white hands in horror. "No! A thousand times, no! Can't you see the construction Mr. Chase and all his friends would put on such a proposition coming from you?"

Lincoln answered thoughtfully, "If he were more my friend, I'd risk it. . . . I'm convinced of his great powers. I hope rather against hope that once upon the bench he'll see in what direction his best prospects of usefulness and fame rest. . . ." He ran his paper knife through his hair several times, Sumner watching him anxiously, then slipping it back into his vest pocket, he said, "Well, Senator, I'll risk it!"

"Thank God!" ejaculated Sumner. "I'm sure you'll not regret your decision, Mr. Lincoln."

"I hope not." The President spoke soberly. "Of course, he'll keep on bringing me up by hand but I'm almost hardened to that."

"Mr. Lincoln," Sumner's deep voice was very soft, "I want to say that I think you're showing fine magnanimity in this. Chase should be most grateful to you. . . . Between you and me, I think this act of yours may save him from political indiscretions that would blast his fame. I wish your treatment of him could be written into history."

"Tut! Tut!" Lincoln shook his head but he felt warmed in spite of his protest. "I don't want praise. I'll tell you a story that will explain why. Do you remember what Jeanie Deans said to Queen Caroline when the Duke of Argyll procured her an opportunity to beg for her sister's life?"

Sumner shook his head and frowned a little. Lincoln went on, serenely:

"I remember it. She said: 'It's not when we sleep soft and wake merrily oursel's that we think on other people's sufferings. Our hearts are waxed light within us then and we are for righting our ain wrongs and fighting our ain battles. But when the hour of trouble comes to the mind or the body and when the hour of death comes that comes to high or low,— oh, then it isna what we hae dune for oursel's but what we hae dune for others that we think on maist pleasantly.'"

There was a short pause during which Sumner patted Tad's hand gently. The little boy broke the silence by asking the Senator if he'd not like to borrow the book of fairy tales.

Sumner accepted the offer, gravely. Lincoln wondered if this were the moment for a few cautious advances on Louisiana but Mary came in with a glass of buttermilk, and a moment later, Sumner, with the fairy tales under his arm and Tad clinging to his hand, followed Mary on a visit to a century plant in bloom in the greenhouse. Lincoln saw him go with a sigh of relief.

CHAPTER XVIII

THE GREAT ISSUE

THE storm for a while after Sumner's departure shut off the stream of callers. Lincoln was glad of the opportunity thus offered for work on the annual message, but he found it difficult to take it up again. Instead his mind ran on Sumner. The thought of the struggle that could no longer be postponed came between him and all his other problems. And suddenly he asked himself why, if he ended slavery and successfully ended the war, he should so seriously concern himself with reconstruction. He would have done his share and he was unutterably weary of strife and contention. Why not let Sumner have his way? Why not?

He tilted his chair back against the wall, put his feet on his desk and abandoned himself to marshaling the thoughts of the past four years. Cleared of the débris of half thoughts, they presented themselves about like this:— The issue embraced more than the fate of these United States. It presented to the whole family of men the question whether a constitutional republic, a government of the people, by the same people, could or could not maintain its territorial integrity against its own domestic foes. It presented the question whether discontented individuals could break up their government and thus practically put an end to free government upon the earth.

Was there in all republics this inherent and fatal weakness? Must a government of necessity be too strong for the liberties of its own people or too weak to maintain its own existence?

There had been many hours when he would have said "Yes!" to this query, but now it looked as if so far as physical force was concerned the answer was "No!"— But "No" only as to physical force. It looked as if the Rebels were not the only enemies to the conception of the Union as the beginning and the end of the nation. Sumner with his contention that State suicide was a possible and an accomplished fact nullified the basic conception of the Union. Once let Sumner put through his idea of reconstruction, based on the admission that the States had left the Union, and the whole Secession contention on State sovereignty was ratified.

The nation had purchased with money the land out of which several of the seceding States had been formed. The nation even now was in debt for money applied to these purchases. It was paying the old debts of Texas. If one State could secede, so could another, and when all were gone who would be left to pay the debts? Then how about the creditor? He must ask Sumner that.

No, he wouldn't ask him that, either! It would get them nowhere. There was no blinking the fact that after nearly two years of effort, he and the Senator from Massachusetts were no closer to seeing eye to eye. Any advantages the President had won had been through luck, the gratuitous gift of the march of events. If he was to go on, he must now make a supreme effort.

Was it worth the struggle?

He recalled his state of mind in '61. He reviewed what the years in Washington had done to his high faith in his fellow man. A throng, more wretched in spirit than those poor fellows he'd seen freed from Libby prison had been in body, filed past his mind's eye; a throng of unequaled sleekness and prosperity of aspect. But in its pettiness, its self-seeking, its dishonorableness, its cruelty and stupidity, this unending file of self-seeking men and women who had passed through his office was leprous.

He wondered if, to the President of a republic, humanity could remain beautiful—or to any ruler of any country. God, how pitiful the human animal was! A bleakness like death-horror descended on him. Should he struggle against Sumner to maintain a nation whose citizens had not been made better than those of other nations by its beneficent institutions? Men should become better citizens here than in England or France or Russia. Our initial object was clear on that.

Ah, wasn't that just the point? After all, wasn't the struggle to maintain the Union a plain people's contest to perpetuate that form and substance of government whose leading object was to elevate the condition of men? To lift artificial weights from all shoulders, to clear the paths of laudable pursuits for all, to afford all an unfettered start and a fair chance in the race of life?

From the bird's-eye view, it really mattered little that in the paltry three-quarters of a century of the nation's life, so little had been accomplished spiritually. The experiment had only begun. It was an experiment which if successful would have a supremely important effect on civilization. Didn't one then have an unshiftable obligation to carry it on? Didn't the issue have a breadth of aspect that made slavery seem only a local and temporary portion of it? Sumner was near-sighted.

He began to wonder, at this point, just why this vast, impersonal problem of the philosophy of government had taken so vital a hold on him. At what point in his career had its import moved beyond the slavery issue to include the whole theory of human liberty? Slowly he reviewed his boyhood, his memories of his father, his mother. Much that would make a man ambitious there, but nothing to give a man this overweening interest in the great political experiment. His young manhood in Springfield? Mary and Herndon had helped stock his mind with facts, Mary had urged him on—but not from these the vital interest. Washington, the war—Lord, what a long, dusty road!

How unbelievable that he, he of all people in the world, should be the ruler of a great nation! a man of such poverty of opportunity—

Hah! He gasped aloud as understanding swept over him.

In these United States there was no such thing as poverty of oppor-

tunity! His own career was proof of that. And in his own career lay the cause of his vital interest in the experiment of government!

He was a living witness that any man's child could look to come to the White House as his own father's child had come. Here at last was the answer to his first query. His absorption in the saving of the Union was based on the desire that any one else might have through this free government an open field and a fair chance for his industry, enterprise and intelligence; that he might have equal privileges in the race of life with all its desirable human aspirations. To save the Union was to secure this inestimable jewel to mankind.

As he reached this conclusion, the sense of depression, of seeing through a glass darkly, that had haunted him so long, melted into thin air. He felt a sudden influx of mental vigor and sureness unprecedented in his experience. The office slowly impinged on his consciousness. The desk took shape before him—the papers—the first sentence of the annual message. He dropped his chair back into position and took up his pen.

He had decided long since to repeat the amnesty offer and to urge again the passing of a constitutional amendment freeing the slaves, thus giving the States a chance to ratify what already had been done as a military necessity. He dipped his pen in the ink but before he had put down a word, Mary spoke from the doorway in a voice of unutterable weariness:

"At last! Do you know that it's midnight, Abra'm, and that you've not been out of that chair for eight mortal hours? Do come to bed! I've a cold supper waiting for you in your room."

"I did take a long trip this time, I reckon," he said apologetically.

Congress made no bones about its intention to fight Lincoln on reconstruction. Just where it would strike the first blow he couldn't be sure, but he took it for granted that the effort would be via Sumner and Louisiana. Sumner went back and forth between the Capitol and the Executive Mansion with great frequency but always on anything rather than reconstruction. Then the newly-elected members arrived from Louisiana and presented their credentials and Sumner showed his hand. He rose in the Senate and served notice that he would in a short time outline his suggestions on handling Louisiana.

Thus the storm broke on Lincoln. And he was still without a program!

On the day of Sumner's pronouncement, Alice Hooper gave a tea which Mary attended. Sumner, of course, was there, and Senator Trumbull dropped in. Alice Hooper deliberately precipitated a discussion by saying that she had met the wife of one of the Louisiana Senators-elect and hoped that Congress would admit the new members if all the wives were as charming as this one.

Trumbull said with a grin, "Ask Senator Sumner! I hear he and the President compromised the matter."

"I wouldn't think of suggesting compromise to the President," Sumner shook his head sadly.

Mary spoke quickly, "I would, for you, Senator, if you really have a possible one in mind."

Sumner looked at her thoughtfully. "Perhaps you could get his ear, Mrs. Lincoln. Certainly I've failed for weeks. There's nothing more necessary before the country to-day than that there be no break between Mr. Lincoln and Congress on reconstruction. Much as I am against the premature recognition of Louisiana, I'll hold my peace if I can secure a rule of equality for the negroes of other States."

"Why don't you tell Mr. Lincoln that yourself, Senator?" asked Mary.

"He has made it clear that he won't discuss compromise with me," replied Sumner. "Therefore we can't admit the persons from Louisiana."

"Oh, there are worse things done every day in the Senate than admitting those men would be," smiled Trumbull.

"What's that?" demanded Sumner, soberly.

"Letting fanatics like Ben Wade and Winter Davis get a strangle grip on reconstruction," replied Senator Trumbull, coolly.

A gasp went round the tea table. "What!" shouted Sumner. "After your intimacy there! What do you mean?"

"I mean," retorted Trumbull, flushing but without fumbling his words, "I mean that along with other Northerners with open minds I've been seeing these past months that Lincoln is farther sighted than the rest of us."

"By the living God!" shouted Sumner. "You! You, the Jacobin who scourged Lincoln, the tyrant! You would now join with him to keep the negro in outer darkness?"

"Senator! Senator!" protested Alice Hooper, wiping up the tea he had spilled on the lace cloth.

"I'm sorry, very, very sorry, Alice!" Sumner lowered his voice at once and helped her to repair the damage. Then he turned to Trumbull with his charming, apologetic smile. "Fanatics have no place at a lady's tea table, eh, Senator?"

"Seems to me the ladies put up with a good deal from you, Senator," replied Trumbull. "I suppose it's because you're so ornamental."

"Handsome is as handsome does!" exclaimed Alice. "I've a notion to send you up to the nursery to have tea with Isabella."

"Don't suggest it or we'll lose him, Mrs. Hooper," protested Mary in mock alarm.

Trumbull turned to her immediately and asked her if she had had recent news from her brother-in-law in Springfield, Ninian Edwards. Mary followed his lead and they renewed their old acquaintanceship elaborately while Alice Hooper and Sumner murmured over the tea table. Mary rushed home immediately after Trumbull left, impatient to tell her story to Lincoln. Rarely enough she and the President had the supper table to themselves and she was able to finish without interruption.

Lincoln listened with increasing surprise and pleasure. "Well! Well!" he exclaimed when she was done, "that's a sort of left-handed atonement on Trumbull's part but, to mix figures, I won't look a gift horse in the mouth!"

"Isn't it wonderful? How do you account for the change?" cried Mary.

"I think he accounted for it," said Lincoln. "Trumbull is honest. Mary, I've got my program! I'll execute a flank movement on Sumner. I'll send for Trumbull to-night and get him to head it."

"I don't see," insisted Mary, "why on earth you don't make Mr. Sumner Secretary of State, then he'd be out of your way."

"Because I won't give him the satisfaction of refusing the offer," replied Lincoln. "And anyhow, he'd never bow to the yoke of a Secretaryship!"

"No man can be one of your Cabinet officers and not learn to mind you, Abra'm, I've learned that," agreed Mary.

"Chase never learned to mind," Lincoln pointed out.

"So Chase resigned!" She smiled impishly at him. "But jokes aside, my dear, I'm dreadfully concerned about the men you plan to invite into your new Cabinet. How can you consider General Banks when you might have Sumner?"

"In the first place, Sumner would scorn such an invitation," said Lincoln with dawning irritation, "and in the second place, what makes you think I'm considering Banks?"

"Everybody's saying so, and all sorts of people have been to me with protests," answered Mary, using her finger bowl vigorously.

"I've never thought of him in that connection," said Lincoln shortly. "Nor has any one mentioned him to me. He's gone back to New Orleans."

Mary dropped her napkin. "Good heavens! Then I've put my foot in it again! Has Charles Sumner said anything to you about Banks lately?"

"I said no one had!" looking at Mary with the old uneasiness. "You ought not meddle where you've no authority, wife. You can make me an infinite amount of trouble. Where does Sumner come in on this? What have you been doing?"

"Well, you're so absurdly patient and Banks is such a—"

"Never mind that, Mary!" pushing away his tea cup untasted, "just where does Sumner come in?"

"Well," defiantly, "I wrote him last week asking him to use his influence with you to keep Banks out of the Cabinet."

Lincoln could feel his cheeks burn. "Don't you see that you've put me in a humiliating position before him, Mary? I thought there was one person on earth who wouldn't try to intrigue against me!"

"Nothing of the sort!" Mary's voice was furious. "I'm trying to help you. That letter—I've kept a copy. You shall see it."

"Very well, I'll come with you now." Lincoln rose, more hurt than he could readily explain to himself.

He stood under the chandelier in Mary's room and read the letter. "Hon. Charles Sumner, My dear sir: Our best Republican friends, those who have been the most ardent supporters of the administration through the last trying conflict, are very much exercised over the attempt which

General Banks, *himself*, is making most *strenuously* for *imaginary* services;
also the leading conservatives who would like to use Banks are urging him
for the Cabinet. Our true friends write me frequently and deplore such a
prospect. I am sure *such* an appointment would not meet with your approbation. Will you not exercise your great influence with the friends who
have a *right* to demand something at the hands of a Government they
have rescued from tyranny? I feel assured *now*, whilst this subject is agitated, your voice and your pen will not be silent. General Banks is considered a *weak failure*, overrated, a speculator and an associate of Secession
agents. I believe General Banks would bow submissively to General
McClellan if he were in power as to Mr. L. himself. Perhaps you will
consider it unbecoming in me to write you thus. But the whole country
is anxious about this and it is very natural that discriminations should be
made between true, loyal men and those whom the country considers *time
servers*. The services of such certainly are not required at a momentous
time like this! I can scarcely believe that this news will not meet with
your own ideas on the subject. If I have erred, pray excuse me.

"General Banks has been in W—— ten days past, unremitting in his
attentions to the President. *You* can do much in this case. Any communication on this subject will be considered private. Your friend, Mary
Lincoln."

The President's indignation mounted as he read. When he had finished
he dashed the letter to the floor.

"This! From my wife! I thought you had more intelligence!"

"I don't think the letter lacks intelligence," protested Mary, with spirit.

"It's the rambling screed of a woman who'd like to be queen consort
but hasn't the requisite training. Now, Mary, I won't have this kind of
thing going on. You go over to your desk and write a letter to Sumner,
cleaning this up, and let me see it before you send it." He did not raise
his voice but he was the more emphatic for that.

Mary stood before him, sparkling with anger. Her little figure in the
purple velvet trembled. Her fine eyes flashed unutterable things.

"Don't speak to me as if I were a Cabinet member, Mr. Lincoln."

"I speak to you as to a woman who's interfered foolishly in her husband's business," he said sadly.

"I thought ours was a partnership," her voice shaking.

"So did I, but it looks as if you didn't understand the word. I'm waiting
for the letter, Mary!"

She flung herself down before the rosewood desk, lifted the lid, jerked
out a sheet of paper, slammed the lid down, wrote. Lincoln paced the
floor. If Mary, who for four years had withstood the wooings and the
bribes to which any ordinary woman would have succumbed in a week—if
Mary now went to pieces, the one comfort of his life was gone, the one
steady solace, the one source from which he never failed to draw sanity,
the final support he counted on for enduring this thing to its bloody end.
He had used to have, in addition to Mary, laughter. But of late laughter

had frequently failed to come when he beckoned. He was tired—strained. God! a man must have peace in his bedroom. It must be his ultimate, never-failing retreat. Otherwise he'd break and the cause was lost.

He took with a stern look the note Mary handed him with her finger tips.

"Dear Mr. Sumner: I take this opportunity of offering an apology for having written you so candid, and as it *now* appears, so unnecessary a letter as I did a few days since. Mr. L. now says that no one ever has mentioned the subject to him, he had no idea of it himself and General Banks has returned to his command at New Orleans. And now that I have made the amende honorable for my *sympathetic interest* in General Banks, and with apologies for having trespassed on your valuable time, I remain, respectfully yours, Mary Lincoln."

"That will answer," said Lincoln, dropping the letter into his pocket. "I realize that I've brought a part of this on myself by asking your help with Sumner. Now remember, Mary, you're to promise me to keep out of politics from now on."

"I'll do nothing of the sort!" exclaimed Mary, rushing into her own room and slamming the door.

Lincoln groaned and went into his office to meet a committee from Chicago come to protest against their draft quotas. He gave the note to Bob, who had finished his law course and was awaiting an army appointment. Bob was instructed to find Sumner and to deliver the note into his hands.

Bob traced the Senator to the Hooper mansion and delivered the note to Sumner as he emerged from the door. It was not a fortunate moment.

Immediately after the departure of the President's wife, Alice Hooper had said petulantly to Sumner, "You think more of the darkies, Senator, than you do of your friends."

"You mean that I think more of human liberty than I do of my friends," returned Sumner, gently.

"It amounts to the same thing, my good man," declared Alice. "Will you kindly ring the bell?" She directed a servant to remove the tea tray, then crossed the room to stand with one fine foot on the hearth rail.

Sumner leaned an elbow on the mantel and divided his gaze between the fire and the beautiful woman on whom his heart was set. She was the type for whom men of Sumner's kind are doomed to care. In appearance she was elegant, with an indescribable graciousness and suavity of movement that never deserted her even when as now she was in a captious mood. She had a genius for fashionable living that made her, as the newspapers said, preëminent among all the fashionable women in Washington. Nor did this preoccupation with society completely obscure the fact that she had a good mind: not as keen nor as avid as Mary Lincoln's, but a good mind nevertheless. Her interest in large political problems was real and highly intelligent and she had an independence of opinion that led back to her Puritan ancestry.

Sumner admired her much for her intellectual qualities, but her social cleverness attracted him as strongly. His life as scholar and politician left him little time for the life of fashion, but ever since his sojourn among the great families of England in his youth he had yearned for it. He once told Mary Lincoln that Alice was the beau ideal of the lady of some fine old English manor. That she was like the President's wife in some points of temperament he had observed. But he had so little understanding of women that he did not see that she lacked the quality that made the Lincolns' marriage sound. She lacked Mary's understanding of and repentant acknowledgment of her weaknesses. Mary's final charm was her quick and fiery grief over her quick and fiery temper.

As she stood now with the fire glow in her delicate face, it seemed to Sumner that Alice embodied all the beauty, mental, spiritual, physical, that a man could desire in his life. It was over a year now since Sturgis Hooper's death. She was no longer in mourning; was leading a gay life. He would wait no more.

He drew himself up, a superb figure of a man, flushing, his moving, tender voice low, a little broken.

"Alice, will you be my wife?"

She looked at him gravely, without surprise. "Senator, I could give no one what I gave Sturgis. I gave him all. Yet I made him none too happy. You and I would both be unhappy together."

"But why, my dear Alice?" asked Sumner, staring at her with painful anxiety. "Why? Is it the disparity in our ages that frets you?"

"That's one consideration, certainly," she said. "After all, you were past your first youth and known to fame when I was in the cradle."

"There's no denying that. But, Alice, a young man couldn't give you the prestige that perhaps I may say without too much vanity will go with my name." He took a step toward her.

Alice did not move but she gave a little laugh that halted him. "Without belittling your achievements, Senator, I'll have to admit that a seat in the United States Senate doesn't seem to me to compass the final glory of what the country has to offer."

He turned to stone. "You're laughing at me!"

She nodded, her lovely eyes melting in blue fire. "After all, we're not children, my good man! Even at that, in some ways, I'm more experienced than you. For example, I know what marriage is. I know that it requires a deep and common interest to carry it through. Love is the best interest. If not love, ambition. I'll admit that I've wondered at times, if you asked me to marry you, what I'd say. And so wondering I've studied you more closely than you've known. And I've come to the conclusion that you're wasting your great powers. You should be Secretary of State, then Minister to England, then President."

"What!" ejaculated Sumner. "Are you asking me to bribe you to marry me? And at the price of all I hold most sacred!" He stared at her incredulously. "Do you know me so little?" He brought his fist against the mantel with a thud that shook the clock. "This hurts most damnably. I bring to you my love. Yes—my love,—all the pent-up emotions and devotions, adorations and yearnings, loneliness and soul hunger of a man who has been denied love all during the years natural to its fulfillment. I tremble like an untried boy at the touch of your finger tips. I flush at the sound of your voice, your very name rings in my ear with all the poetry, music, and beauty that artists have made for us in all the years, and you toss all this aside with a laugh and say, bring me a Secretaryship! It's unbelievable!" His face twitched.

Alice watched him with interest, a little pale, for Sumner deeply stirred was as impressive as a forest in a storm. But there was a curious sort of determination in the set of her lips as if she were forcing herself not to be too much impressed. After a moment she said with her own air of graciousness, touched now with regret.

"I've been archaic and after all, romantic. You must forgive me, Senator. I suppose I had a vague picture in my mind of the knight going out at his lady's behest to bring home the impossible for her, in order to win her hand. And I'd thought of you as romantic—sentimental as a boy. I'm sorry. Let it pass. Will you take supper with us, Mr. Sumner?"

Sumner was breathing heavily. "Thank you, no. I'll wish you goodnight, Alice." He bowed and went out.

Bob Lincoln with his note met him as he hurried down the steps to the street. There was only a feeble light from a street lamp near by. Bob could not see the Senator's face.

"I don't want to delay you, sir," the young man fell into step with the older, "but here's a letter my father asked me to put into your hands. It needs no answer."

Sumner looked down at him. "Ah, Robert!" he said gently, putting out a shaking hand for the letter.

"You aren't feeling well, Senator!" exclaimed Bob, perceiving the unsteadiness of the hand. "Can I call a carriage for you? Your heart?"

"Yes, my heart!" grimly. "But I'm only a block from home. If you'll give me your arm—I ought to have a son about your age, Robert. I wish I had one. And like you too, a gentle fellow with a peppery temper." He leaned heavily on the strong young shoulder.

"You've been overdoing," said Bob.

"No! Yes!—I've had a blow, Robert. I've had a blow."

"That's hard! Can I help?"

"Only by getting me to my house, dear boy, and calling my secretary."

He was better by the time the house was reached and able to mount the steps and the stairs without much difficulty. But when Bob saw his face clearly in the light of his bedroom he went off on his own responsibility to find Dr. Stone.

Then he sought his father, but the President, having given the Chicago committee short shrift, was closeted with Lord Lyons. The Englishman looked ill, and in reply to Lincoln's inquiry if this were not true, he answered:

"I fear so, Mr. President. Between its malaria and its typhoid Washington has been a little rough with me." He warmed thin hands at the fire. "I've called for an informal good-by."

"Seward told me to expect you," said Lincoln. "Well, my lord," moving over to stand beside the Minister and warming his own hands, white enough now themselves to bear the contrast with the visitor's, "well, my lord, you and I haven't been precisely intimate! But we've managed to hitch along, somehow, together, eh? I don't like to see you leave us. I don't see how any one short of one of the twelve disciples could have filled the bill better than you. And come to think of it, they hadn't a cupful of tact among the lot, while your well of it is bottomless. Sit down and let's have a talk. You said this was informal, you know!"

Lyons pulled his chair close to the fire. His tired face was curiously softened. Even his impeccable evening clothes had a relaxed air, Lincoln thought, or perhaps his loss of weight made them sit more easily on his big frame.

"It looks, Mr. President, as if the end were in sight! I say, thank God for that!"

"It may be a few months off but not longer," replied Lincoln cautiously. "It's been a great comfort to me, my lord, that your country and mine haven't become embroiled. It was hard sledding for a while, but all's well that ends well. Seems to me nobody could have done a better job than Charles Francis Adams has done over there. Unless Charles Sumner. What do you think, now that you can speak like a person and not as the British Empire?"

"I think Mr. Sumner would have been a better initial choice, Mr. Lincoln, because he was already known and loved there," replied Lyons. "But I doubt if his tact would have been as unassailable as Mr. Adams' has proved to be.—Sumner's greatly admired in high places in my country though, where Adams is unknown. You've asked me a difficult question, sir," with a smile.

"I've found it so, myself," admitted Lincoln. "How would Seward have done over there?"

"Oh, not at all!" ejaculated Lyons. "His attitude on political morals, on statecraft, is utterly cynical. And I'm never sure from one day to the next where I'll find him. I transact all my business with him in writing. This quite aside from the fact that I like him tremendously."

"You've found him to be what our negro James calls sometimey, eh? Well, would you have liked it better if Sumner had had *that* job?"

"Infinitely! There's one appointment that would have been quite perfect! If I may ask, Mr. Lincoln, why did you need Seward's following more than you did Sumner's?"

"Seward's following has much more power within the Republican party than Sumner's. Sumner's gathered about him too many radicals from all parties. What would you think of Sumner in Seward's place next year?"

"Very favorably. Especially if you wish to take advantage of the prestige Mr. Adams has given your diplomacy."

"That's the devil of it!" sighed Lincoln. "Sumner and Adams are at outs with each other."

"Nevertheless, they're both sincere, both brilliantly well-trained men, Mr. Lincoln. *Sincere*, sir!" Lyons repeated emphatically. "With the war over, I should suppose the cause for contention between them would be removed. I would earnestly recommend that you make the appointment."

Lincoln gave a low laugh, and in reply to Lyons' surprised look, he explained:

"It's the first time in four years I've ever heard you express a personal opinion. I like it! I'm going to get over to England one of these days myself. I shall do myself the honor of looking you up."

"The honor will be mine, Mr. Lincoln," said Lyons with unmistakable sincerity. "And as you say I'm being frank for once, will you permit me to add that four years ago I'd not have believed it possible for a man to grow to the terrible task as you've grown. You've reached a point where your imperturbable sagacity astounds me. I only wish my fellow countrymen could see you as I do!"

Lincoln reddened with pleasure. "What! that green fellow from the Sangamon?"

"I'm not at all sure but what much of the greenness was assumed," said Lyons. "At any rate, it's mellowed now into something so rich and original that any Anglo-Saxon may be proud of his kinsman."

"I—I—you mustn't praise me, Lord Lyons," stammered the President, rising and crossing the room to hide his embarrassment before the war map. "I'm not hardened to it, like Sumner."

"You've had all too little of it from your compatriots as well as from others, sir," with a charming air of apology as he rose. "Some day there'll be few, I fancy, self-deprecatory enough to admit that!"

"Oh, come! Come! You'll have me asking for a chance to kiss you, in a moment," protested Lincoln, turning round. "Good-by, my lord, and thank you."

"Good-by, Mr. Lincoln. God bless you, sir." He wrung Lincoln's hand and was gone.

Lincoln stood before the fire reviewing the interview with considerable amazement. He was glad to know the Englishman's opinion of Sumner and he determined that, if Seward would agree, he'd offer the secretaryship to Sumner, when and if the emergency required it. It was very cheering, he thought, to have seen, if only for a moment, the hearty man behind the diplomat. The praise was good, by Jings!

He had a feeling that Lyons' going rang down the curtain on one of the last acts of the drama.

Bob slipped in now and told of his encounter with Sumner.

"Did you tell your mother?" asked Lincoln.

"I tried to. But she's upset over something"—ruefully—"and I can't be sure she listened to me. She's even so unlike herself that she never said a word when I told her that you were going to make a formal request to General Grant to give me a job. I'm sorry now I didn't say I was going to enlist."

Lincoln put his arm around the boy's neck. "To tell the truth, son, your mother and I are at loggerheads over a matter and she was probably planning what she'd do to me next."

Bob made a wry face. "What's the matter with everybody? Sumner, mother, Tad—"

"What's the matter with Tad now?" smiled the President.

"Oh, he got mad at his tutor to-day and fired him. Fractions, I believe, caused the crisis. Or perhaps it was the sugar scattered in the tutor's sheets, or the pet turkey under Tad's desk. At any rate, the tutor took his discharge seriously this time, and he's gone."

"When did all this happen?" asked Lincoln with huge enjoyment. Tutors came and went as frequently as cooks in this household.

"Well, Tad came in and told mother, just now. But it seems the tutor went at noon and without risking an interview with mother. Of course, he knew she'd entice him back to the hateful job."

"What did mother say to Tad?"

"Turned him over her knee and spanked him and sent him to bed."

"Taking one thing with another," said Lincoln, thoughtfully, "I reckon I'd better go quietly off to bed, myself. I'm tired."

"'Fraid cat!" grinned Bob. "John Hay and I are going out to see the town."

"If I were twenty years younger, I'd go with you," said the President.

CHAPTER XIX

BUT although he fumbled noisily about his room for an hour, Mary did not, as he hoped she would, burst repentant through his door. It was always harder for him to bear her aloofness than a scolding from her. When he woke the next morning, his first thought was not of Trumbull nor of Sumner nor of Grant, but of Mary. He dressed with great care, put on the gray suit she liked best, and went into her room.

But Bob was there before him, sitting on the edge of his mother's bed, talking rapidly and earnestly. She had been reading "Enoch Arden"—the book lay face down on her knees. She was staring at Bob with tragic intentness. To Lincoln's cheerful "Good morning, mother!" she replied with an icy nod, keeping her eyes fixed on her son. Lincoln stood at the foot of the bed, biding his time.

Bob was pleading, "But to shoulder a gun and face danger, that's the major part of it, mother!—Last summer when I was a Home Guard you said of course the Todds all were soldiers."

"So I did," retorted Mary. "You proved your steel then. That was enough. I thought you and your father had settled that you were to go to Grant. Why open up the old subject of being a private?"

"Because I just can't be reconciled to sheltering myself behind father's Presidential coattails! Billy Stoddard's leaving next month. He's going into the ranks and no favors asked," blurted Bob.

His mother threw up her hands. "Oh, do as you please! You're of age, anyhow!"

"I know that, mother, but— Oh, pshaw, why can't you send me off freely like other mothers do? We ought to be willing to contribute one man to the Union cause."

His mother sat as erect as a small soldier. "And you think we haven't contributed one man? Would the lives of twenty men be equal to—"

Bob groaned.

His mother stopped short, stared at his angry, mortified young face, then tossed her hands apart and said with a little sob, "Do as you wish, Bobbie! I'm ashamed of myself, as usual."

Bob gave a whoop of joy, threw his arms around his mother and kissed her several times, started for the door, then rushed back to say with Mary's own impetuosity, "I'll go to Grant, mother, for your sake!"

"I'll tell you, Bob," said Lincoln, "let's compromise. I'll ask Grant to take you, and when you get down there with him if you find you aren't really useful, you go into the ranks."

"Fine!" cried Bob. "I'll have to go and gloat over John Hay!" This time the hall door slammed behind him.

Lincoln seated himself in Bob's place on the edge of the bed. Mary eyed him with a cold and appraising air.

"I've shaved," he said meekly.

She picked up "Enoch Arden." He deliberately put out a great hand and took it from her.

"Let's have it out, Mary, without any grand flourishes. I'm sorry I hurt your feelings but I've got to have that promise from you!"

She gave him one of her direct looks. "I can't promise unless you give me a substitute. You admit I've got a brain. You know that all my life I've lived in an atmosphere of politics. I watched my father and mother help Henry Clay in his career. I worked from the time I met you to help you get here. Yet now you tell me to fold my hands and devote myself to my clothes and to spanking Tad. I can't do it, Abra'm. I know my limitations. The very first time something came up, I'd break that promise, unless, as I say, you give me other work. Three years ago you headed me into hospital relief. But the Sanitary Commission has taken over all that."

Lincoln pondered. All that she said was true. This was the energetic little engine that, for better or for worse, had puffed and pushed and with much shrieking of escaping surplus steam had landed him in the White House. It was too much to ask her to sit idle on a side track, accumulating more steam. It was dangerous too, because, smiling inwardly at the figure of speech, her little boiler was sure to burst, sooner or later.

"Will you promise me this, then, that whatever you do, you'll do only with my knowledge and consent. That's true partnership, Mary."

"But that's only getting at me from an indirect angle," she protested. "You've only to veto everything I suggest and there you have me!"

"Just to prove that I'm *really* compromising," retorted Lincoln, "I've something to suggest, right now. I want to have a resolution introduced immediately in the Senate as well as the House recognizing the so-called ten per cent government of Louisiana. I want to act before Sumner does. The House, I think, is safe, but the Senate—!" He shook his head. "If Trumbull can be got to introduce the bill, it would work miracles."

Mary's sober face quickened. "I thought of that last evening. It would be wonderful!"

"Your news was what made me dare think of it, of course," said Lincoln. "I want you to land Trumbull for me, Mary. You can do it better than I."

She looked at him suspiciously. "You're just soft-soaping me, Abra'm!"

"I couldn't afford to soft-soap you in this issue, Mary, because I've got to make you see I mean business. I've got to have that promise!"

They gazed at each other implacably. The household had roused. Tad and Bob were in altercation in the hall. A broom was thumping intermittently against the sitting room wall. At any moment they might be broken in upon, but the issue must be settled now. Both of them knew that the situation was fraught with more perils than any save themselves could appreciate. Mary sat stiffly erect, cheeks and eyes blazing. Lincoln drooped on the bedside. His face settled into its lines of weary melancholy, but his blue gray eyes bore a granite gleam in their depths. Yet there was more than granite; there was yearning unutterable. Suddenly Mary threw herself forward and he caught her in his arms.

"Oh, my dear! My dear!" she cried. "Truly I was only trying to save you from an insincere man! But you're right! I should have talked it over first with you. If only I could learn to curb my impulsiveness! It's a curse! I promise! Of course, I promise, if you'll forgive me."

He pressed her close, burying his tired eyes in her hair. "I've nothing to forgive, my darling wife. I reckon we need your impulsiveness in the family to balance my slowness. Only—Mary—if you want my old brain to reel, just let me find that you're really planning to be underhanded with me. Chittenden makes a good retreat for me—so does Dr. Henry—but here—here is my perfect retreat. Keep it for me, dear wife! Keep it for me!"

Her reply was to press her lips to his with a little sob.

A moment later he went back to his room, his heart at rest.

He wrote Bob's letter to Grant, that morning.

"Lieutenant-General Grant: Please read and answer this letter as though I was not President, but only a friend. My son, now in his twenty-second year, having graduated at Harvard, wishes to see something of the war before it ends. I do not wish to put him in the ranks nor yet to give him a commission to which those who have already served long are better entitled and better qualified to hold. Could he without embarrassment to you or detriment to the service go into your military family with some nominal rank, I, and not the public, furnishing his necessary means? If no, say so without the least hesitation, because I am as anxious and as deeply interested that you shall not be encumbered as you can be."

About five o'clock that afternoon Stanton came in to see the President. "I want to make some final disposal of Ben Butler, Mr. Lincoln," he said, dropping into the chair by the desk. "He's made life miserable for Grant and Grant's finally screwed himself up to ask for Butler's removal. Are you willing to consent to it and do you think, if we do, that Grant'll be forced to change his notion within twenty-four hours? My idea is that we ought to back Grant up and send Butler to hell where he belongs."

"Butler should be in town to-day," remarked Lincoln. "He telegraphed me a few days ago, asking permission to come and testify before the Committee on the Conduct of the War."

"He's down in your parlor at this moment," growled Stanton, "having a dish of tea with Mrs. Lincoln. I put my head in the door and backed out. The Committee on the Conduct of the War has my sympathy! Butler'll stand them on their heads. He's clever as Satan. How much money do you think he's made out of the high offices he's held during this war?"

"I don't *know* that he's made a penny," replied Lincoln with a troubled air.

"I do!" exclaimed Stanton. "I have positive proof that when he went to New Orleans he was worth about $150,000. To-day, he's worth $1,000,000."

Stanton's word on such a matter was not to be doubted. Lincoln's lips tightened. He knotted his black tie which hung loose, smoothed his hair and rose. "I reckon old Ben has outlived his usefulness to this administration. You O.K. Grant's request and I'll go down and break the news to the General before he comes up here and camps. I've learned that it's easier to move myself out of the parlor than it is to move some folks out of my office."

Stanton smiled and patted the President's arm affectionately. "Need any help, sir?" he asked, following him to the door.

"Thank you for nothing!" grunted Lincoln.

Stanton laughed.

He accompanied Lincoln to the very door of the red parlor and left him with a snort compounded of sympathy, approval, and amusement. With a little sense of dread Lincoln entered the softly lighted room. One never knew just how yellow Butler might turn.

Mary with the tea equipment sat before the fire talking to General Butler, who stood in full dress parade on the hearth; sword, yellow sash, epaulettes, gold oak leaves, velvet cuffs, buff gloves, a contrast to Lincoln's memory of Grant's shabby uniform.

"Well, General," said Lincoln, quietly.

"Not well, at all, Mr. President." Butler shook hands. "Grant and I are at serious outs."

Lincoln slumped into a rocking chair opposite Mary and shook his head at her gesture toward the teapot. Butler resumed his place on the hearth.

"I thought you and General Grant had patched up a water-tight peace," said the President.

"So did I. Come, Mr. Lincoln, tell me why Grant has asked for my resignation?"

The President gave him a keen look. "You shouldn't come to me with questions of that sort, General. Let your own conscience answer."

"Oh, Mr. Lincoln!" protested Mary. "To a man who's done such splendid work as General Butler?"

"Conscience?" ejaculated Butler. "Then you too have a grievance against me?"

"General Grant's grievances are bound to be mine," Lincoln spoke coolly. "The only complaint he's made to me is that you've been letting too much food be traded into Richmond. He says you and your brother-in-law are getting rich off it. But if you hadn't failed him in a military way, he could get around the other, I reckon. Has he gone after you on this matter?"

"I've learned that he's written to Stanton asking him to retire me. I know I can get nothing from Stanton so I've come to you. This can't be, Mr. Lincoln. I'll make it so hot for Grant—"

"Tut! Tut, General! That's childish. Grant is winning the war for us. If he says you must go, you must go." Lincoln clasped his left knee and looked at Butler with a slight scowl.

"Don't you think General Butler should be told why?" asked Mary.

"Butler knows why," replied the President, quietly.

"The tune is changed, I see, since you won your reëlection, sir," sneered the General.

"Yes, the tune has changed. But it needn't have. You've slipped on the banana peel of your own avarice, General. Come now, you've done a great work for your country. Be content to leave the military clean-up to Grant. There'll be plenty of administrative work later that will demand your peculiar genius."

"One needs to be in Congress for that," said Butler sourly. Then he gave the President a wary glance. "Though I have my influences up at the Capitol right now that're not precisely despicable."

"I know you have, General," agreed Lincoln heartily. "I wish I had 'em myself."

"They're at your disposal, Mr. Lincoln," said Butler, "if—"

Lincoln shook his head. "No, thanks, General. One simply can't handle Sumner that way."

"Sumner? Sumner has his price, like any other man!" cried Butler.

"No, he hasn't! Indeed not, General!" Mary leaned earnestly across the table.

"Oh, well, I'm not going to debate with one of his lady friends as to that!" The little officer's voice was mocking.

Lincoln suddenly rose. Butler was going to be nasty. "If you'll come over to Stanton's office, right now, we'll see if he's holding anything up from Grant," he said.

"Oh, but wait a moment!" protested Mary. "Ah, there he is now!"

Senator Trumbull was emerging from behind the red velvet door hangings. Butler's jaw dropped. Lincoln walked slowly to meet his old friend. The two paused under the gilt chandelier. Trumbull was a thin man with sharp features and keen blue eyes behind spectacles. He looked like a village schoolmaster but his air was that of a man of the world.

He looked up quizzically at the President and held out his hand. His voice was preternaturally grave and dry as he said, "Mother, I've come home to die! But I want your forgiveness first."

Lincoln let out a roar of laughter such as the White House had not heard from him in many months.

"Your figure's a little mixed, Senator! What you want is the fatted calf. How about it, Mrs. Lincoln? And here's General Butler! You know the author of the Woman Order?"

Butler shook hands, remarking with a curious smile, "I can fully understand why my poor offer of a few moments ago was refused so lightly." Senator Trumbull gave him a puzzled glance but did not rise to the insinuation. Instead he asked Mary if she was attending the Italian Opera that night. Butler listened for a moment, then bowed and went out. Lincoln wondered a little uneasily what sort of pressure Butler would next exert, then he forgot him.

Trumbull was seated near the tea table and the President joined him. Mary covered what might have been an awkward moment by asking the Senator if he thought this Congress would pass the Thirteenth Amendment.

"We're still doubtful," replied Trumbull. "I don't quite understand Sumner in this, unless he hopes that if it fails he can get an amendment phrased in his own way. He has that kind of vanity, I'm afraid."

"I think you're mistaken there," protested the President. "What does he do or say? Is he actually blocking it?"

"Well, no! He merely refused to help." Trumbull accepted a cup of tea from Mary. "He says he'll *permit* it to pass if it has the strength! But he prophesies that there'll not be enough States to ratify it, even if it passes Congress. If he kills the admission of Louisiana, of course, he may be right."

"No, he isn't!" said Lincoln grimly. "When I fixed it up last year to get Nevada in and on the right side I settled that point. It cost me two internal revenue collectorships and one customs' house appointment to get the requisite votes from certain members of Congress, and was an altogether unmoral proceeding. Sumner twitted me with it at the time, so he's talking nonsense. How much depends on him?"

"The Camden and Amboy Railroad interests," replied the Senator, "promise that if Congress will postpone the Raritan Railroad bill over this session they'll make the New Jersey Democrats help about the Amendment. Sumner's in charge of the Raritan bill in the Senate. His theory is that the bill, in crushing the railroad monopoly, will crush out the last of the States' rights dogma. The Camden and Amboy exacts toll from everything passing through the State, you know, Mrs. Lincoln."

Mary nodded. "Sounds as if Mr. Sumner had right on his side."

"He has," agreed Trumbull, frankly, "but in this instance he ought to let the lesser evil help to wipe out the greater. The monopolies will be crushed in good time. Mr. Lincoln, we'd like to have you send for Sumner and urge him to be practical."

Lincoln looked doubtful. "I'm willing but useless, Senator. I can do nothing with Mr. Sumner in these matters. While he's very cordial to me, he's making his history in an issue with me on this very point. He hopes to succeed in beating the President so as to change this Government from its original form and make it a strongly centralized power. I think he'd be all the more resolute in his persistence if he supposed I were at all watching his course in this matter. I think the Amendment'll go through, Trumbull. I'm not worrying about it. What I'm lying awake nights over is the recognition of Louisiana."

Trumbull leaned forward to poke the fire. Lincoln and Mary exchanged glances, then Lincoln cleared his throat and plunged.

"Are you still hostile to my ten per cent governments, Senator?"

Trumbull set the poker carefully in the rack and leaning back in his chair placed his finger tips together and said thoughtfully, "What has come to me as I've watched the quarreling of my own committee, the indecision and vacillation of any committee that has tried to draw up a hard-cast rule for all the seceded States, is that it's impossible to reconstruct on any rigid theory of coercion. It has thus gradually dawned on me that your idea of encouraging the loyalists to keep alive a form of State government that shall allow the people to make their own laws is the only feasible plan."

"Yes! Yes!" exclaimed Lincoln eagerly. "Now here's the nub of it! You are chairman of the judiciary committee. Your committee must pass on the eligibility of the Senators-elect from Louisiana. Can Louisiana be brought into proper practical relation with the Union sooner by admitting or by rejecting the proposed Senators?"

"I believe in admitting the Senators," replied Trumbull cautiously.

"How does your committee stand?" asked Lincoln, his pulse quickening.

"They're doubtful. They're afraid Banks has misrepresented facts. They feel the matter's been too much a personal arrangement between you and Banks."

"That's easy to disprove!" Lincoln rose. "Mrs. Lincoln will excuse us while I take you up to see the correspondence between Banks and me." He led the way out. "I'll show you all of Banks' letters with those of the rest of the Louisiana crowd."

They mounted the stairs rapidly, both men moved by this revival of their old friendship and anxious to avoid showing their emotion. In the office Lincoln placed his files before the Senator. Banks' letters proved him to be a man of parts and Lincoln was glad to have one of his critics read them.

After a few moments, "This is exactly what I need," gloated Trumbull. "Now, to quote yourself, I can ride!"

"How far?" asked Lincoln tensely, his throat suddenly constricting.

"Well," Trumbull was pale, "give me a little time and I'll introduce from my committee a joint resolution, recognizing the Government of Louisiana."

"Ah!" breathed the President, his lips twitching.

Trumbull looked at him. "Of course, you realize, Mr. Lincoln," smiling sadly, "that I'm turning traitor to my old running mates and that they'll fight me to the death, with Charles Sumner leading them."

Lincoln jumped to his feet and put his hand on Trumbull's shoulder. "I know! I know! But you have the strategic advantage of your position.— This—this," he put a hand on Trumbull's other shoulder, "this is a great evening for me, Senator. 'For this my brother was lost and is found—' You know, Trumbull!"

"Yes, I know, Lincoln— I'll just take these along and have copies made."

When Lincoln went into his wife's room later, she was lifting a great sheaf of roses from a florist's box.

"Mr. Sumner's reply to my apology," she said, with a little unhappy smile.

"I told you you'd both resort eventually to the language of flowers!" Lincoln laughed heartily and after a moment Mary joined him.

CHAPTER XX

SUMNER received the news of Trumbull's treason in the cloak room of the Senate. Ben Wade told him. Senator Sumner stared at him, listened with scorn to the oaths that adorned Wade's tale, then stalked out into the Capitol rotunda where he stood wrapped in his blue fur-lined mantle, head bowed over his folded arms—the conventional picture of outraged despair. To do him justice, he was quite unconscious of posing. He had been so long in the public eye that it had become second nature to the Senator to live up to people's favorite conception of him. Men passing to and fro looked at him with interest but no one spoke to him and he was not disturbed until, following an altercation, a man in a wide-brimmed felt hat struck a man in a sealskin cap standing at the Senator's elbow.

Sumner roused and stepped between them, recognizing at once one of the Congressmen-elect from Louisiana and a radical member of the House.

"Come, gentlemen, this won't do!" protested Sumner firmly. "Blows will never settle this bitter problem. Think! Think!"

"Think hell!" shouted the Louisianian. "What we should have brought up here is one good nigger overseer. He'd have handled a few of you spouting Yankees so that you'd have known that Louisiana was something more than a State of mind."

The crowd, that had gathered quickly, laughed. Sumner turned away with disgust. As he did so, he caught sight of Representative Hooper peering over the heads of the crowd.

"I was looking for you, Charles," said Hooper, as Sumner came up to him. "You've neglected us lately. Come home to dinner with me now. Yes," as the Senator began to shake his head, "I know you breakfast late, but we don't dine until two. I want to hear about Lyman Trumbull and what your plans are. Nothing has occurred, I hope," looking up into Sumner's face a little anxiously, "to anger you with us? I've always been frank with you about my sympathies with Lincoln."

Sumner jerked his great head impatiently. "No! No! Don't make me appear too infantile, Sam. I've not been to see you lately because Alice and I—"

Hooper interrupted. "Alice told me. But Alice's vagaries have nothing to do with the relations between you and me. Alice is a law unto herself."

"Do you think she'd object to my coming?" asked Sumner. "I—I long to accept your invitation, Sam!"

Hooper thrust his arm firmly under the Senator's. "You come along with me, Charles," and he did not loosen his hold until he had established the Senator in a nest of fur robes in his sleigh.

It was a glorious winter noon and Washington was out enjoying it. Sleighs and the jingle of sleigh bells mingled with drum rolls and bugle calls. Even the mud of Pennsylvania Avenue could not tarnish all the bright beauty of the great snowfall of the previous night. Hooper could not resist the temptation to prolong the short drive between the Capitol and his house. They drove along New Jersey Avenue until they met Alice and Isabella prancing homeward in a gay red sleigh that flaunted a dozen plumes from dashboard and horse collars. Alice, palely magnificent in seal-skin, bowed, while Isabella, in white rabbit, screamed:

"Oh, Senator! Senator! Take me in with you!"

"He's coming home to dinner, so calm your ardor, Isabella!" called her grandfather, turning his Morgans cleverly to follow his daughter-in-law's equipage.

Alice met them, later, in the dining room, her manner cool and a little watchful. Hooper kept the conversation in his own hands, made Sumner tell him about Trumbull and allowed the Senator to give vent to his excited irritation only when he told of the fight he proposed to organize against the renegade Jacobin. Alice did not contribute anything but polite necessities to the conversation until Sumner had finished his outburst. Then she said, as she used her finger bowl daintily:

"If I were you, Senator, I'd have a talk with the President before actually going on the warpath. I do still think, as I've said repeatedly, that the most regrettable thing in public life to-day is that Abraham Lincoln and Charles Sumner aren't working in harmony."

"By Judas, you're right, Alice!" exclaimed Hooper. "Charles, do be persuaded! Give yourself and the President another chance. Don't let your personal—"

"Please!" Sumner stretched out a long arm in protest. "I beg of you, Sam, don't insist again on my petulance. No one appreciates Lincoln more than I. I outgrew my prejudices against him long ago. I recognize his essential integrity of purpose. I know he's utterly free of malice and un-worthy ambition. I've even come to enjoy his speech. It's logical and spirited and full of quaint humor. His mind works with a sinewy senten-tiousness that sometimes captivates me. He's an utter original. In fact, he's instituted a new and superb order of state papers that Seward's quite in-capable of appreciating. I've learned to love him. But with all that, I can-not and will not agree with him on his way of reconstruction. I must not!"

Alice rose from the table. "Won't you both have tea or coffee with me in the little parlor, rather than wine together here?"

Both men rose, Sumner with alacrity. But Hooper said with an in-quiring glance at the other two that he was due at a committee meeting at three.

"Then the Senator must let me continue my pleas alone," said Alice, graciously.

Sumner blinked but opened the door for her with a distinct look of pleasure. He seated Alice before the fire in the cozy little parlor off the formal drawing room, gave her a fire screen, then in the armchair opposite warmed his hands.

"So I'm forgiven, dear Alice?" he said.

She arranged the folds of her dark velvet skirts for a moment before she looked up at him to say, "I thought that I was the one that gave offense!" Her face was sober. "I was sorry that you misunderstood me, dear Senator. I've missed you and your approval."

He leaned forward, studying her face. Then he said earnestly, "Don't play with me, Alice. I shall need all my forces the next few weeks. Even a tragic certainty will scatter them less than an uncertainty with regard to you. And yet," laying his hand for a fleeting moment over hers, "I would to God that I was uncertain!"

She smiled. "Let's leave it that you may be uncertain and go on to consider my request that you go for a final talk with Mr. Lincoln."

"Alice, he and I have talked until neither of us dares say more for fear of an utter break." He leaned back in his chair, his eyes on her delicate loveliness.

"You must promise me not to break with him!" cried Alice, her cheeks flushing. "Senator, a break with him must mean a break with me."

"No!" he winced. "*Don't* say that, I implore you, for I can't promise, Alice. This is a brutal game I'm playing. Don't weaken me."

She tried to press her advantage. "I must say that."

He moved his head uneasily as though in pain. "But must it always be so?" he mourned. "Can't I keep my dearest associations in life untainted by battle? Why must you thrust Lincoln between us?"

"Why did you break with the Adams, the Sewards, the—"

He sighed. "I can't stand this. Will you allow me to go up to see Isabella?"

Alice pulled the bellrope beside the mantel. "I'll have her brought down here. But"—leaning forward in her turn and for a fleeting moment laying her hand over his—"love is a force greater than patriotism and eventually, if you truly care, you're going to give in to me, *Charles*," accenting his name which she used for the first time in all their long friendship.

His whole face lighted. It was as if his youth had miraculously returned. But as they sat waiting in silence for the child and he turned over in his mind the full significance of her words, the light behind his eyes burned lower and lower, until, as Isabella danced into the room, it flickered out to be replaced by a quiet tenderness for the little girl.

When Sumner started back to the Capitol a half hour later, Fred Douglass, who had been waiting outside the gate, fell into step with him. He, too, had heard of Trumbull's about face and wanted information. When Sumner had told him, he exclaimed:

"Mr. Sumner! I'm more discouraged than ever. If Mr. Lincoln's actually going to back such a bill, we're lost. He's a terrible fighter. The patient, good-humored kind sometimes are. What shall we do!"

"Fight harder than he does," replied Sumner. "I'm sure we'll win in the end because we're right."

The colored man shook his head. "I've learned to know him well and from a side no white man could get. I wonder—his heart is so large—do you suppose if I went to him and pleaded I could get him to give up this bill?"

Sumner, striding over the snowy paths at a terrific rate, gave the matter thought. At first he shook his head, then as if to prove how desperate he actually felt his need to be in the impending struggle, he said, "Well, a good general misses no chances. It can do no harm for you to talk with the President and it might accomplish something. God bless you. Let me know what comes of it."

A little later in the afternoon, Lincoln looked up from his desk to greet the colored leader.

"Ah, Douglass!" he exclaimed, rising to shake hands, then drawing Douglass down into the chair by his desk. "How are you getting on? Tired like the rest of us, I can see. Well, it can't be long, now. Are you moderately well satisfied with the course of events? Are you worried sick like the rest of us for fear General Lee'll escape to the mountains? Guerilla war prolonged for years, that would mean."

"General Grant will take care of that, sir," replied Douglass, twisting his soft hat in his powerful, gnarled hands. "As far as guerilla warfare goes, colored people properly armed have a gift for it greater even than the slave holders have."

"Well," Lincoln rubbed the back of his aching head, "I hope you're right. Did you come with something special on your mind to-day, friend Douglass?"

"Yes, Mr. President, I'm breaking my heart over your pending bill for Louisiana. It leaves negro suffrage out. I can't understand your attitude in spite of all you've said to me."

"Can you understand Mr. Sumner's attitude toward the Thirteenth Amendment?" asked Lincoln slyly.

"No, sir, but I can explain him, in general, better than I can you."

Lincoln laid down his pen and settled himself with his feet on the rim of the waste paper basket. Douglass always succeeded in rousing his interest.

"Come now, what's the difference between the Senator and my humble self, if the comparison isn't odious?" he asked, with a smile.

There was something dogged about Douglass' manner in replying, as though he was determined to humor the President but equally determined not to be drawn too far from his purpose.

"Mr. Sumner's a lawmaker for all men, white or black. You, sir, are preëminently the white man's President. Mr. Sumner's willing to sacrifice even the Union to free the slaves. You, sir, are ready to deny or postpone or sacrifice the human rights of the colored people to promote the welfare of the whites. You were ready to execute all the supposed constitutional guarantees in favor of the slave system anywhere in the slave States. You were ready to suppress a slave rising for liberty, although his guilty master was already in arms against the Government."

Douglass paused and his piercing dark eyes fastened on the distant half shaft of the Washington Monument, softened and dulled until it seemed to Lincoln that the man was in a trance. To rouse him, the President said:

"I had thought the negro looked on me as his friend. Is this name, Father Abraham, mere flattery?"

After a moment, Douglass replied slowly. "They don't know as I do that we're not the special objects of your consideration. Your own race has your deepest solicitude. They're your children. We're only your step-children, children by adoption, children by force of circumstance and necessity."

"The man thinks in straight lines, straighter than most of my associates," thought Lincoln. Aloud, he sought to prick Douglass on by saying, "And with Mr. Sumner it's different, eh?"

"Yes, sir, we come first with Senator Sumner. And yet, it's not strange that it's Abraham Lincoln who set us free."

Lincoln shook his head at Nicolay who appeared with a tray of papers. The sweat was standing on Douglass' forehead.

"The reason for that is that yours is the bigger mind and you have better self-direction. And the very fact that you share the prejudice of your countrymen toward us has made it possible for you to organize them for this war. If you'd been like Mr. Sumner, without prejudice, and had put abolition before the salvation of the Union, your people never would have resisted the Rebellion. The Abolitionists think you're tardy, dull, cold. But for the average slow-thinking white, you're swift, zealous, determined. Your statesmanship, not Mr. Sumner's, has made abolition possible."

Lincoln spoke firmly. "You mustn't speak as if I approved of slavery! I despise it. If slavery's not wrong, nothing's wrong."

Douglass nodded vigorously. "We know that and on that we've pinned our faith. And, sir, I wonder if you realize what a lot of faith we've needed at times. You tarried long in the mountains. You advised us to migrate from our native land. You refused to use us as soldiers. You said you'd save the Union, with slavery, if necessary. You revoked General Frémont's proclamation of emancipation. You clung to General McClellan, who was more zealous to save slavery than the Union. And yet," turning suddenly, his beautiful eyes now burning with intensity, "our hearts believed while they ached and bled that the hour and the man had somehow met in the person of Abraham Lincoln."

"Don't you understand why I did those things, Douglass?" exclaimed Lincoln.

"Yes, Mr. President, to save the Union."

Lincoln jerked his head impatiently and would have spoken but Douglass was before him.

"Aye, sir, you have strained our faith but though the Union is more to you than our freedom or our future, we bow before you when we count the blessings that have come to us under your reign. Hayti's independence recognized, slave trade abolished, and the Proclamation of Emancipation. Sir, having given us all this, why do you continue to deny us the franchise?"

"Still harping on my daughter!" groaned Lincoln. "I've no new reasons, Mr. Douglass. You know them all. I'll add though that I'm very certain that, in the next four years, every slave-holding State will pass laws themselves giving suffrage to the negroes who can read and write; certain if we don't now, by national legislation, try to cram it down their throats. I fear a reign of horror after the war in which your colored folks'll get the worst of it, unless we conciliate where we can conciliate. I'm immovable on this, Mr. Douglass. The part of wisdom for you is to make both your white and your black friends understand this. That is if you've fully grasped my reasons yourself. I sometimes doubt it, because I seem to make no impression on you."

"I understand," still pulling and twisting the soft hat. "But again you're arguing the white cause, Mr. Lincoln, and I'm the negro."

After a thoughtful moment Lincoln rose and held out his hand. "Well, thank you for coming to see me. Good afternoon, Mr. Douglass."

Douglass took the extended hand and stared up at the President, his eyes slowly filling with tears.

CHAPTER XXI

ALICE HOOPER told Mary that she was doing her utmost to get Senator Sumner to compromise with the President but when his wife reported this to Lincoln, he laughed. "Sumner's less apt to compromise now than ever. He's too mad with Trumbull and he's pretty sure we've got him licked. We've got the majority of the Senate with us and the House is going to pass the bill after it finishes with the oratory. Mrs. Hooper has no chance at all to drive Sumner in this."

"But you wouldn't prevent his talking to you, would you?" asked Mary, anxiously.

"Certainly not. He's in and out of the office every day or so on other matters. I'm giving him every opportunity either you or Mrs. Hooper could demand. But," with a cheerful laugh, "I've finally taught him how to take a licking!"

But even this optimistic mood could not do much to mitigate the strain that the march of events was bringing upon him. As Grant slowly but surely closed the terrible jaws of war on Richmond, the President was besieged more and more by excited Northerners demanding that he make peace at once. People were frantic to stop the bloodshed. Lincoln felt the pressure of their outcries more than had been his wont. Dr. Stone warned him again that his nerves were nearing exhaustion. Lincoln, apropos of this, told Mary that he supposed he was like one of the ancient Marathon runners, who, as he neared the goal, eyes popping, tongue hanging out, moved his legs on hope and nothing else.

Lincoln did not believe that Jeff Davis had been licked enough, yet. But, not unwilling to learn the views of the Rebel President, he allowed the elder Blair, who had been a close friend of Davis before the war, to go down to Richmond to feel out conditions there. But he still thought so little of peace probabilities that when, as a result of Blair's gesture, three commissioners from Richmond asked for a hearing on peace proposals, he did not go down to the meeting place off Fortress Monroe himself, but sent Seward. These men were not coming, his intuitions told him, in an attitude of mind that could bear fruit. And anyhow, he could not bear to desert Trumbull in the preparations for the impending struggle in the Senate. Every moment he could spare was given to what he told Nicolay was the conversion of souls.

"Even the war mustn't come between me and Trumbull," with a twinkle of tired eyes. "I often wonder how it'll seem to handle reconstruction without Stanton and Grant on my back: and with Andy Johnson actually helping instead of hindering like dear old Hamlin. I've an idea that any

difficulties I'll have with Johnson will be with his disposition. They say
he's very irritable. Maybe he does drink too much. I hope the time'll
come when there won't be a slave or a drunkard on earth!"

The Thirteenth Amendment passed on the last day of January and
this gave the final touch to his optimism. Sumner, after all, was not in-
vincible!

But Seward, somehow, didn't bring events on as Lincoln had hoped he
would at Fortress Monroe. Grant, watchful and uneasy and with a growing
appreciation of Lincoln's diplomatic powers, urged the President to join
the Secretary of State. With the arrival of the General's message, Lincoln
roused from his immense preoccupation with reconstruction. Perhaps
Grant saw a chance for making an advantageous peace now! He slipped
quietly from Washington and on the army steamer, *River Queen*, went
down to Fortress Monroe.

The three commissioners came aboard early in the morning of February
third, and the conference lasted four hours. The Southerners, haggard,
hungry, their eyes ravaged by old ferocities, made an enormous appeal
to his sympathies. This then was the look of the champions of a lost
cause! But their requests touched him not at all. He listened for a time in
silence. Seward liked to lallygag, to talk back and forth, to give here and
take there, quite unconscious of the fact that this verbal bargain hunting
invariably convinced people that he was insincere.

Lincoln took a grim pleasure in cutting across these vast vagaries with
the blunt remark that he couldn't treat with parties in arms against the
Government. Hunter, who had aged twenty years in the past four, reminded him that Charles I had done so when at war with the Parliament
and Lincoln said, "I don't profess to be posted in history. On all such
matters I'll turn you over to Seward. All I distinctly remember about
Charles I is that he lost his head in the end."

Seward laughed and urged the commissioners to partake of the excellent
whiskey he'd brought with him. They thanked him and absorbed the
mellow fire with pleasure. Lincoln sat watching for his chance to strike a
blow for reconstruction. There was more conversation. Stephens was eager
to know how Washington had changed and was the Capitol finished?

Lincoln finally interrupted. "Stephens, if I resided in Georgia with my
present sentiments, I'll tell you what I'd do if I were in your place. I'd go
home and get the Governor of the State to call the Legislature together
and get them to recall all the State troops from this war: elect Senators
and members to Congress and ratify the Thirteenth Amendment, pros-
pectively, so as to take effect, say, in five years. Such a ratification would be
valid, in my opinion. Whatever may have been the opinion of your people
before the war, they must be convinced now that slavery is doomed. It
can't last long in any event and the best course, it seems to me, for your
public men to pursue would be to adopt such a policy as will avoid as far
as possible the evils of immediate emancipation. This would be my course
were I in your place."

Stephens shook his head, but thoughtfully. It appeared to Lincoln that the seed was going to root and he went on.

"It seems to me that when the war ceases, members of Congress will be received from the Rebel States. Some of your States are now so functioning that when war stops they'll be at once restored to their practical relations to the Union."

"And you think," cried Hunter, "with the temper of Sumner, Wade, Stevens, Trumbull, such things are possible? They'll grind our faces with their heels. They plan to confiscate—"

Lincoln interrupted. "The enforcement of the confiscation and penal laws is in my hands, gentlemen. I shall be liberal. The people of the North are no less responsible for slavery than those of the South. If the war shall cease with the voluntary abolition by the States of slavery, I would favor payment by the Government of a fair indemnity to the owners."

Hunter bit at his nails. There was no sound for the moment but the rush of water past the *River Queen*. Suddenly the scene seemed utterly unreal to Lincoln; the flickering lamplight in the little salon, with its white painted walls, the red cloth on the round table, the ravaged faces of the Southerners—Stephens, old, old, with a feverish color in his sunken cheeks —Seward with his cigar and with his tie riding over his collar—this was he, Abraham Lincoln, actually preparing the way for peace! The end was in sight, the runner nearing the goal. He must not quicken his pace or all would be lost—

Stephens broke the silence. "We'd like an armistice while we consider these matters!"

An armistice! To end the bloodshed now! God, how he wished he could grant one! For a moment, the desire to do so was almost irresistible. Such a gush of pity and love rose in his heart that he dared not speak lest he show it. He closed his eyes and sat breathing heavily then opened them to say in a voice spent with emotion:

"I'll grant an armistice only to consider the restoration of the national authority. And it is to be clearly understood that any proposals must be made on the basis of the position on slavery assumed in my last message to Congress."

"Nothing for us, in other words," exclaimed Hunter, bitterly, "but unconditional surrender to the mercy of the conqueror."

Lincoln stared at him. The man was dense! Had he not been licked enough? Or was it possible to frame a proposal that would not be a compromise, yet that would entice him out of his battered stronghold. He must have time to consider this possibility. There was no use prolonging the fruitless talking. He rose abruptly and held out his hand to each of the Southerners in turn. As far as Seward and the commissioners were concerned, the conference had failed. Of course, Seward was sanguine. Good old Seward would have been sanguine if Noah had refused him sanctuary in the ark.

But Lincoln was not sure that, for himself, the meeting was a failure. It had served to convince him that it was possible now as it had not been before, to buy peace—peace and a certain amount of good will. With a sudden rush of hope and exhilaration he sat up in his berth that night and, by the light of a wretched lamp, wrote out again an offer of compensation. He phrased it as a message to Congress, asking Congress to make a joint resolution empowering the President to pay four hundred million dollars, about what it would cost to prolong the war two months, to the slave holders of the seceding States if they would cease resisting the national authority on or before April first. If this were done, "war will cease and armies be reduced to a basis of peace, all property except slaves liable to confiscation or forfeiture will be released."

He reached Washington obsessed with the idea that he had found the answer to all the intricate problems that blackened the sky. He locked himself in his room and perfected the message, then called the Cabinet together and submitted it to them. He was keyed to so high a pitch of hope, he saw the feasibility of his plan so clearly, that he could not believe when he looked up from his reading that he was interpreting the expression of their faces correctly. But when they began to put their indignant negation into words, he understood that he'd been living for twenty-four hours in a fool's paradise. His high hopes collapsed with a roar about his ears. He did not listen long to the members but dismissed them wearily. If his own Cabinet reacted thus, it was worse than foolish to present the idea to the hostile Congress. He made a memorandum on the back of the document:

"Feb. 6, 1865. Draft of message to Congress not signed or sent. To-day these papers which explain themselves were drawn up and submitted to the Cabinet and unanimously disapproved by them."

He was still staring sadly at the papers when Nicolay came in. "George," Lincoln said in a voice scarcely articulate, "they wouldn't listen to me!"

Nicolay returned through teeth set with disgust, "My dear Mr. Lincoln, you didn't expect them, did you, to recognize pure charity or true wisdom? If I were you, sir—"

He was interrupted by the Attorney General, who rushed in with violent disapproval in every line of his face.

"Mr. Lincoln, I cannot let all these pardons for deserters go through! Indeed I can't! Stanton—"

Lincoln looked up at him and shouted, "If you think that I, of my own free will, will shed another drop of blood—"

He paused, for the Attorney General's face grew suddenly distorted before his eyes. The walls of the room closed in on the very desk. Lincoln put out an uncertain, appealing hand—and fainted.

A little later he became aware of excited voices and of being carried to his room. When he came completely to himself he was in bed. The fire burned brightly. Winter twilight framed in the windows with the curtains stirring slightly from the draughty cracks. Some one sitting by his bed

holding his hand—Mary. Dr. Stone's beard at the bed foot. Lincoln smiled
at him.

"Back again, eh!" said the doctor, drily. "Now, I tell you once more,
Mr. Lincoln, that unless you have shorter work hours, Andrew Johnson'll
be the occupant of the White House before another year's out. You
fainted from exhaustion. I'm leaving no medicines, but I'm holding Mrs.
Lincoln responsible for the amount of rest you take in the next twenty-
four hours."

"How much do I have to take?" asked Lincoln in alarm.

"Twenty-four hours of it. After that, a ten-hour day of work only,"
ferociously from Dr. Stone. "I'll be back in the morning. Nothing but
food and a sniff of your smelling salts, Madam President, remember," and
he stalked out.

It was peaceful—peaceful—*had* to stay in bed. . . . After a time, Mary's
tender voice, "How do you feel now, my dear one?"

"Well, just about like I've felt every day lately. As if every one of the
grist grinding through the office, from Senator MacDougall demanding
war with France down to some poor woman after a job, had darted at me.
As if they'd taken their thumb and finger, picked out their special piece
of my vitality, and carried it off. I feel flabby. Mary, I was in the midst of a
talk with the Attorney General. I reckon I can have him in here, eh?"

"I'd shut the door in the face of one of the British Royalty if he tried to
come in here to talk to you," declared Mary. "Your next interview's going
to be with Mr. Pickwick."

She read Pickwick to him until laughter made him hungry, when she
gave him food. Then "Midsummer Night's Dream" until he fell asleep. It
was late the next morning when he awoke. After breakfast she sent Tad in
with his game of lotto and the two worked happily at this until Lincoln fell
into another deep slumber. When he roused from this she was ready with a
bowl of broth and a recent volume of Whitman which she had borrowed
from John Hay.

"I've found a new way for you to get out of Washington," she said,
opening the book and beginning to read to him "Starting from Paumonok."

He lay entranced until she had finished the last fine line. Then he
begged for the book and his spectacles and, during the remainder of his
second evening in bed, he memorized passages that had caught his fancy
particularly. His mind was packed with poetry he had been treasuring
since childhood. He told himself he could well move out some of the old
lumber to make room for this pure treasure.

CHAPTER XXII

THE BLIND VICTOR

TRUMBULL'S idea was that the chief thing he had to fear for the Louisiana resolution was prolonged debate. This would give Sumner, the arch debater, a chance to delay the voting until the end of the session, March 3. So it was not until the last week in February, when numerous important financial bills were still before the Senate, that he introduced what was called the President's bill. Lincoln agreed that if the bill would go through at all, it would go in one day's time, perhaps two. He and Trumbull had an easy majority, once a vote was forced.

On the morning of the twenty-third, he sent Nicolay up to the Capitol to follow the course of the battle. Then he set himself grimly to work at his inaugural address. Nicolay came in just before supper. Lincoln looked up at the saturnine young face and dropped his pencil.

"Let's have it, George," he said quietly.

Sumner, Nicolay said, as soon as the resolution had been read in full, rose and stated his position.

"I have joined other Senators who resisted the recognition of the Government of Louisiana because it was initiated by executive and military orders and an insufficient voting population. I insist on these objections in association with these aforementioned Senators. But I stand alone inexorable in the demand that all men, irrespective of color, shall be equal as citizens in the reorganized States. In this stand, I will yield to no asserted urgency, no supposed adverse public opinion, no technical point of constitutional disability, no vote of caucus, no defeats in either House, not even up to the pressure and prestige of the President himself. I have made up my mind to stop the admission of rebellious States to the Union without absolute guarantees of freedom and equality, including suffrage, for negroes upon precisely the same terms as applied to white men. I propose to avail myself of all the resources of parliamentary law to defeat this measure even if, its promoters refusing to yield, the revenue and appropriations bills shall be lost."

As Sumner paused, a stir swept over the Senate Chamber. Senator Trumbull came to his feet but before he could get Hamlin's attention, Sumner, great head stretched forward like a charging stallion, roared:

"You, sir, are keeping strange company and talking a strange language. Why this sudden change of front? By whom or what have you been seduced?" Laughter came at this point from the Democratic Senators, who were delighted beyond measure by this split among the Republicans. Whirling from Trumbull to Hamlin in the chair, Sumner continued, "I move an immediate consideration of the interstate commerce bill, which is a practical measure, while the Louisiana measure will prove a mere dance of debate."

Trumbull's voice, low but peculiarly clear, cut across Sumner's roar: "Mr. President, if a single negro is expelled from the street cars in the District of Columbia, the voice of the Senator from Massachusetts is raised in protest. He will take up the time of Congress about the rights of the negroes, but he will not give a hearing to the 10,000 loyal whites of Louisiana. Let us not waste time, Mr. President. Let us take a vote. There is no need to debate this matter. Every Senator present knows every detail of this bill and already has expressed an opinion on it. The majority here are in favor of it. Let us not permit an infinitesimal minority to block its passage. I assure you, Mr. President, that I shall not speak at length, shall not attempt debate. If the other members will act in harmony with me, it will be a simple matter to pass this bill and return to the financial measures. Let us take a vote now."

Sumner spoke calmly. "I assure the Senator it is utterly impossible."

Senator Wade jumped to his feet. "I refuse to be drawn into debate, but I wish to ask the Senator from Illinois whence comes this new-born zeal for Louisiana? How long is it since he believed it should not be recognized? How long? It is the most miraculous conversion since St. Paul's. You and I didn't differ formerly on this, sir."

Trumbull stood with lips firmly compressed, eyes blazing behind his spectacles. "I am not to be drawn off. I move a vote."

"I move a substitute!" exclaimed Sumner, and began to read aloud a bill forbidding elections in any State until the President had proclaimed that all hostility had ceased within the State and Congress had declared it entitled to representation.

Trumbull was able to cut discussion of the substitute short, bring it to a vote and defeat it. Sumner then proposed an amendment. Senator Howard of Michigan immediately plunged into an elaborate speech, backing Sumner, and for two hours would not yield the floor. When he finished, Ben Wade got through a motion to adjourn, which Trumbull defeated. Johnson of Maryland now made an hour's talk for the bill. The dance of debate was on and was still on when Nicolay left.

Lincoln listened to Nicolay in silence till the young secretary had read the last of his notes, then he asked, "Is Trumbull discouraged?"

"No, sir. Only seven men voted for Sumner's substitute. He thinks you can handle most of them and hamstring Sumner so."

"None of them can beat Sumner in longwindedness," mused Lincoln. "I'm disappointed, but we've still got a fifty per cent chance of winning."

The several recalcitrant Senators called on the President the next morning. He was able to win Howard but not the others. The debate began again that afternoon. Sumner attempted again and again to introduce other business but each time was voted down. The temper of the members grew bitter toward him. Shouts rose, "Don't waste our time, Sumner!" "Give it up!" "Give it up!"

"That's not my habit," answered Sumner and he introduced another substitute, which was voted down. Then he proposed an amendment.

Men went round to his seat and pleaded with him, confidentially, to let the vote on the President's bill be taken.

"But that would be to pass it," smiled Sumner. "And the passage of that bill would prove to be the political Bull Run of this Administration."

He rose to propose a fourth amendment. People in the gallery hissed. Representatives who had strolled over from the House, which had passed the bill, groaned. After this amendment had been voted down, and the early winter twilight proclaimed that the day was done, Trumbull moved an evening session "to give the Senator from Massachusetts an opportunity to say all he has to say." Amidst sardonic laughter, the motion passed and at seven o'clock the Senate again convened.

The galleries were packed. The moment the session opened, Sumner moved to adjourn. He lost. Ben Wade then repeated the motion and was voted down. Zachary Chandler moved to adjourn. He lost amidst hoots and groans. It was now nine o'clock. Trumbull deliberately rose and accused Sumner of "keeping up a factious resistance in order to feel a spurious authority over the eighteen Senators who desired to pass the bill."

Sumner laughed, sardonically.

Senator Doolittle rose to his feet and called on the American people to witness this scene in the Senate, "particularly the arrogance of the Senator from Massachusetts, who is attempting single-handed to break down the right of every State to judge its own suffrage."

Wade remarked that if the Chief Executive had to depend on poor things like Doolittle to press his measures, the Chief Executive was in a bad way. Doolittle retorted and many precious minutes were consumed before Trumbull could silence the Senator from Wisconsin and plead with Sumner to say his say on the bill.

Sumner rose. It was some time before silence could be obtained from the exasperated members, but when he had done so, Sumner said, "I counsel the Senator from Illinois to look at the clock and to note that it's now twenty-five minutes to eleven with Sunday morning near. An effort to force a vote will be as fruitless as sowing salt in the sand by the seashore. The Senator's attempt to cram this resolution down the throats of the Senate is comparable only to an attempt once made by Senator Stephen Douglas, also from Illinois, who brought in the Kansas-Nebraska bill so proudly, confidently, almost menacingly, with the same declaration that it was to pass in twenty-four hours. I beg of the Senate to devote the remnant of the session to tried measures instead of consuming it with a bantling not a week old."

"Why don't you favor the President's bill, Mr. Sumner?" shouted a man in the gallery. "Because you despise Abe Lincoln, eh!"

"No!" shouted Sumner in reply. And he launched into an explanation of his position that continued until the galleries were nearly empty.

When he at last sat down, Trumbull said, "It's half after eleven. We cannot reach a vote to-night."

"I told you so some hours ago," said Sumner.

And the weary Senate adjourned.

Sunday was spent by Lincoln and Trumbull in anxious consultation, both of them hoping against hope. Trumbull went to see Sumner to urge him to come up to the White House for a conference. But the Senator from Massachusetts was ill in bed.

He was in his accustomed seat, however, on Monday and listened with inscrutable face to Senator Wade's fierce denunciation of the President's work in Louisiana. Wade spoke at enormous length and with the extraordinary vehemence which always was so exhausting on his hearers. Before he had done, men were leaning wearily on their desks. Some of them left the Chamber.

Senator Sherman of Ohio, as the afternoon waned, tried to obtain consideration of a revenue measure, but this only served to change the tenor of Wade's remarks. He began a bitter personal attack on Trumbull who flushed, but sat as grim as any schoolmaster watching the antics of an incorrigible boy. Winter twilight again darkened the chamber.

Sherman appealed to Sumner and Sumner, silencing Wade by a gesture, rose and in a voice of indescribable weariness once more stated his position, ending with a comment which Nicolay took down verbatim for Lincoln's benefit.

"The pretended State Government in Louisiana is utterly indefensible whether you look at its origin or its character. To describe it, I must use plain language. It is a mere seven months' abortion, begotten by the bayonet in criminal conjunction with the spirit of caste and born before its time, rickety, unformed, unfinished, whose continued existence will be a burden, a reproach, and a wrong. That is the whole case."

There was a dead silence after this. Sumner stood immovable, a shadowy giant, and the men staring at him recognized the fact that he could not be defeated. He was arrogant, insolent and implacable. He was as terrible and as splendid as Vesuvius.

Trumbull turned to Nicolay and whispered, "We've lost!" Then he walked dejectedly from the room. His fellows gave the President's lost bill the tribute of a sigh, half of regret, half of relief that the battle was over, and turned to Sherman's bill.

Nicolay dragged unwilling feet back to the White House. As he sadly climbed the stairs to the President's office, he met Mary on her way to serve tea in the Red Room. In response to her eager questioning, he showed her Sumner's final comment.

She read it and looked up at Nicolay, her face slowly losing color. "This will come very hard on Mr. Lincoln, George, in his depleted state. I don't see how he's going to stand it. I've never seen him so wrapped up in anything else but the Emancipation Proclamation. Perhaps I'd better go with you. No"—tapping her lips—"he'll need me more, later."

Nicolay nodded and continued heavily on his way.

Lincoln, who even yet had not permitted himself to give up hope, turned from his heavily littered desk. "News so soon? . . . Ah, George, my boy, don't say we're finally licked!"

"But we are, Mr. Lincoln," said Nicolay, huskily. He gave his account of the afternoon, ending by laying on a sheaf of naval reports the slip of paper containing Sumner's final words.

Lincoln read them. "A seven months' abortion." He covered his eyes. After a moment, he groaned, "Sumner! Sumner! Why, with your other incomparable gifts, weren't you given the prophet's vision! Well—I must think this out again, George. Keep people away for a while, will you?"

Nicolay went out. Lincoln felt a little dizzy, and crossing the room to a sofa stretched himself out on it. Thinking—thinking—he and his soul together again viewing the problem; moving through endless space and gazing down in cold agony on the bloody struggle which it seemed he would not be permitted to shorten or alleviate. Why was this so? Of what use his seeing eye if he could not convince others of the actuality of what he saw. Where was his weak point and what, if any, was the remedy? Hour after hour, he pondered on the panorama of the future which was as vivid and as real to him as the Army of the Potomac on parade.

CHAPTER XXIII

MARY sat beside the President all night. She tried, while she knew their futility, all the devices she could invent to rouse him to something more than his gentle "Let me think it out, my dear." But at the breakfast hour, fate took a hand. James rushed in, his black eyes rolling.

"Madam, Massa Taddie ain't been in his room, all night! We've done searched every inch of this house and grounds, and just now Congressman Hooper's drove up all in a lather to say little Miss Bella's gone too and was she here?"

"Kidnaped!" screamed Mary, leaping to her feet.

"Look for them at Senator Sumner's," cried Lincoln, his eyes opening with a jerk.

"Mr. Hooper did, sah. The Senata's in bed with a heart attack and can't be disturbed. His man says they ain't been there."

"When was Tad last seen?" asked the President.

"He said good-night at eight o'clock," replied Mary, adding regretfully, "I didn't leave you to tuck him in. Send some one round to Pete Kelley's to make inquiries, James. And you, Abra'm, had better get in touch with the Detective Police right away. While we're waiting for Colonel Baker to get here, we'll have breakfast."

"Yes, Mary," replied Lincoln, nodding to James, who flew.

A hurried toilet and a more hurried breakfast on trays in the sitting room were followed by the entry of John Hay, carrying a bit of greasy writing paper.

"I found this under the blotter on my desk," he explained. "I'm sorry to intrude, Mrs. Lincoln."

"Don't be foolish!" protested Mary, seizing the paper and reading it aloud. " 'Don't serch. Gone to Urup!' "

It was badly printed and signed with the bloody cross that adorned many of the anonymous threats which Lincoln and his family received so constantly. As the President studied the message over Mary's shoulder, Hay said, "Baker is here. I'll fetch him, if you wish."

Colonel Baker scrutinized the note and put it into his pocketbook. Then, after asking Mary and the President numerous questions, he called in the household, questioned every one, and enjoined absolute secrecy on each for twenty-four hours until, he said, he could get his men planted. He begged Lincoln "to try to continue his day's routine and Mrs. Lincoln to go to bed with an opiate." They both stared at him, Mary with contempt, Lincoln with astonishment.

"There's a gang of kidnapers bent on getting your whole family," explained Baker, rubbing his beard and shaking his head at once. "You must allow me to protect you."

"I'm going to the home of every child Tad knows in Washington," declared Mary. "Any one of them may have a valuable clew."

Baker nodded. "That's good! I'll send a man if you'll give me a list. But I must ask you not to go out of these rooms to-day, Mrs. Lincoln, and you too, Mr. President."

"Oh, come!" protested Lincoln. "I can't stand inactive while my young son is at the mercy of God knows what villains."

"Where would you go? What would you do?" asked Baker.

"He's right, Mr. Lincoln. Do both of you be advised by the Colonel," urged John Hay anxiously.

"I'll stay in only if my wife promises to do so, also," declared Lincoln, seeing an opportunity for controlling Mary's rashness.

Mary stamped her foot. "Oh, I'll agree! Only don't stop here arguing. Every moment is precious."

Colonel Baker seized his hat and a moment later the search had begun.

The hours moved with agonizing deliberation, second merging into slow second. It was a horrible day outside, with gray lines of sleet cutting through gray fog. Visitors arrived with faces raw from the slash of the storm. At intervals Lincoln tried to finish his second inaugural address, but finally gave it up. He could think of nothing but Tad and Isabella. His imagination ran riot. Were they sheltered from the storm or had the brutes destined them to die of exposure? Was there information they wanted from the children and would they torture them to get it? Wasn't there an accomplice in the house who had sneaked Tad out of his room? Where was Sam Hooper? What was he doing? He rang for James. The man came in with a swollen eye and cut lips.

"What's the trouble, James?" asked Lincoln.

"Massa Lincum, sah, one of the police that Colonel Baker's got posted downstairs 'lowed I knew something more than I was telling about little Massa Tad. I give him a bust upside of his head. Did you ring for me, sah?"

"Yes, I did. James, my boy, you look up Congressman Hooper and see how he feels and if there's anything I can do. Ask him if it would buoy him and Mrs. Hooper up any to come over here where we get reports every few minutes of what's being done. . . . James, you know Taddie well. Did he have any enemies? He's been mischievous, you know. I've sometimes wondered if it didn't bother some people."

"Enemies! That little fellow! Taddie! I'm surprised at you, Massa Lincum. 'Deed I am, sah!"

James gave a great blubber, seized Lincoln's hand, pressed his bruised lips on it, and rushed away.

At noon, Lincoln joined Mary at lunch in the sitting room. Her face was swollen from prolonged weeping, but she was now outwardly calm.

As she poured her husband's tea she said, "Abra'm, what puzzles me is why they took Isabella, too. If this is a political kidnaping to bring you to terms, why bother with Alice Hooper's child?"

Lincoln shook his head and stared at his steaming bowl of soup. "I've sent them an invitation to come over here."

"That's a good idea. Eat your soup, Abra'm," setting him an example by forcing down a mouthful.

He obeyed her and a moment later urged her to eat the fish she was eyeing with somber distaste. They finished the meal somehow, and then stood together in the window, clinging to each other's fingers and looking at the storm.

"I've got a part of the inaugural address done," said Lincoln, trying to ease the tension. "Do you think you can look it over?"

"I'll try," biting her lips. "Ah!" whirling as James made an announcement. "Mr. Hooper, what news?"

Hooper looked old and drawn. He dropped his sable-lined cloak and took Mary's hand. "No news. No trace. It's the strangest thing. Isabella was put to bed as usual at seven o'clock. Her nurse had an evening out. She went philandering and never got in till near dawn, when she went directly to bed on the third floor. Alice and I had been at the opera and afterward at supper with Mr. and Mrs. Eames. For once Alice went directly to bed without looking in on Isabella. The poor girl is bearing up, which it's not her nature to do. Did you know that Mr. Sumner has gone to seek them on some private line of his own?"

Lincoln scowled. "I thought that Sumner's recent victory had put him to bed."

"But he did have one of his heart attacks!" protested Hooper. "So it's all the more remarkable. He sent over just before noon to borrow a closed carriage from me."

He rubbed his chin and looked up at the President, who leaned dejectedly on the mantel. No one spoke. The cannel coal made tiny explosions. The sleet beat at the window. Tears ran down Mary's cheeks as she huddled on an ottoman but she did not wipe them away.

"Mrs. Hooper, Madam President," said James at the door.

Mary rose to meet the tall figure in sealskin and the two mothers clung to each other for a moment. Then James took Alice's wraps and moved toward the door. As he did so, Sumner's unmistakable tones were heard in the hall, above a sudden confusion of voices.

"Pray don't crowd us. I must immediately find—"

James opened the door. Mary screamed. Standing in the hall was Sumner, Tad clinging to one hand, Isabella to the other.

Lincoln was the first to realize that Sumner was still by the door, unheeded during all the prolonged greetings. He put Tad into his mother's lap and crossed over to place his hand on Sumner's shoulder.

"Tell us about it, Senator," he said, drawing the tall figure toward the fire.

"My share won't take long." Sumner wiped his eyes. "I didn't hear of the matter until late this morning. When my secretary finally told me I began turning all Taddie's recent pranks over in my mind. Knowing the young gentleman intimately as I do, I didn't believe Baker's theory was essential. I recalled among many things the fact that Taddie had made a great fuss because Isabella's mother forbade the two children to skate on the pool in the garden. He said that when he and Isabella were married they were going to live at the Soldiers' Home where they could skate every day. Isabella suggested that they get married right away. This was followed by a great whispering and giggling."

The two children now devouring the bread and milk James had brought stared at the Senator in wonder. He smiled and added:

"Having reached this point in my deductions, the next step was obvious. I borrowed my friend Sam's horses and set forth for the Home."

"And there we were in the hay loft!" exclaimed Isabella. She was dirty and disheveled but still lovely.

"Why the hay loft?" asked her mother.

"Our cottage was all locked up and we didn't dast go to the house the old soldiers live in," replied Tad, his mouth full. "We was just going to hitch up and come home, because Isabella had boo-hooed he' eyes out."

"Hitch up what?" demanded Tad's mother.

"Pete Kelley's hoss," replied Tad. "He got his dad's old tin pan hoss fo' me, the one he peddles pans with in the spwing. In winta it just stands in the ya'd and Pete has to feed him so no one knew when he loaned the hoss to me. Papa day, I have to pay Pete a dolla' fo' that."

Lincoln slipped his hand into his pocket.

"Mr. Lincoln!" shrieked Mary. "Don't you dare!"

"You're right!" The President hastily withdrew his hand. "Tell us how you managed to get away so quietly, Isabella."

"I did just what Taddie told me to," replied Isabella with a toss of her yellow curls. "I just got out of bed and dressed myself the minute Nurse left me so's I wouldn't go to sleep, you know. Then I went down to the coat closet under the back stairs and rolled up in one of grandpa's buffalo robes there and went to sleep and by and by Tad came and got me."

"Aw, it was easy," boasted Tad. "I just slipped in the back hall and woke he' up and we sneaked out the back alley and Pete was waiting fo' us. We cova'd Isabella up in the bottom of the sleigh and she went to sleep and I hustled that old hoss out to the Home, I tell you. We took about a ton of cookies. They lasted till this noon."

Quite beyond comment for the moment, the dumfounded grown folk listened to this naïve recital. But as Tad gulped the last of his milk, his mother set him off her knee and said, "You go to your room, Tad."

Tad wiped his mouth on his sleeve and looked appealingly at his father. His father returned the look yearningly, but Mary forestalled any appeals for mercy by saying, firmly:

"I hope you feel as I do, Mr. Lincoln, that Tad has got to be taught that he can't cause such agony as he did to-day and not get punished for it. He's too big a boy to do a thing like this and go scot free."

"Exactly!" ejaculated Sumner.

"Amen to that!" cried Hooper.

Tad gave a loud howl and rushed from the room. His mother followed.

Alice Hooper looked from her small daughter, who had assumed an expression of injured innocence, to her father-in-law. "You'd better go up to the Capitol, my dear father," she said, "because I'm in complete accord with Mrs. Lincoln on this and it's not going to be pleasant at our house for the next hour."

Small Isabella flung herself from her mother's lap and rushed toward Sumner, screaming hysterically, "I'm going with you, Senator!"

Congressman Hooper seized his sable-lined cape and he and Lincoln fled while Sumner gathered Isabella in his great arms. He stood, the little girl's face hidden in his neck, looking at Alice pleadingly.

"If I've earned any thanks, Alice," he said, his deep voice tender and a little amused, "pay them by letting off this small sinner. After all, Tad was most to blame."

"Isabella knew she was being naughty. The elaborate secretiveness proves that. I can't risk such a thing happening again."

Isabella turned to show one deep blue eye. "I wouldn't not run away again for a million, million dollars and kisses. It was hoddible. I feel that way now. But if you whip me, you'll make me want to run away all over again."

Sumner and the child gazed at the beautiful woman, anxiously. If Alice was amused, she did not show it. She had suffered a thousand deaths that day. It was not easy to have Sumner plead the naughty little girl's cause.

After a moment, she said, "I recall with vividness the fact that my last very earnest pleading with you for a favor, you refused with implacable firmness."

"But my principles—" exclaimed the Senator.

"To train Isabella properly is my greatest principle," declared Alice. "But I'm going to set you an example of magnanimity."

"You mean you won't whip her!" cried Sumner. "Oh, thank you, thank you, Alice!"

"What a great child you are!" groaned Alice. Then she began to laugh, though with a hint of tears in her eyes. "Yes, I'll let her off, this time."

The child suddenly patted Sumner's cheek and relaxing in his arms began to weep in long hard sobs.

"Give her to me!" demanded her mother, fiercely. And as Sumner obeyed, she clasped the little golden head passionately to her heart.

Sumner eyed them with a soft smile and stooping, kissed one of the lovely hands that supported Isabella. Then he murmured that he'd call the carriage and take them both home.

CHAPTER XXIV

ANDREW JOHNSON

LINCOLN returned to his desk and fell to work on an accumulation of letters. It was routine work and he could think steadily of other matters while performing it.

It was hard to realize that only twenty-four hours had passed since final news of his defeat at Sumner's hands had reached him. Hard, because he now found himself viewing his own downfall not without a certain philosophical amusement. He had been licked in a fair fight and if the cause had not been so serious he could have shaken hands with Sumner, have acknowledged that the best man won, and have set himself to forgetting the battle.

But this he could not do. The battle must be fought again and won. Trumbull, poor fellow, must have more help from the Democrats. Andrew Johnson must be beguiled into putting his own great resources among the Democrats at Trumbull's disposal. Until Congress convened again next December, the new Government in Louisiana must struggle to function without Federal support except such as the President could give. Thanks to Sumner. It was outrageously stupid. And in spite of the Senator's charming and characteristic gesture of the afternoon, a renewed wave of anger against him flooded Lincoln's heart.

He signed papers, rapidly, mechanically, as John Hay and Nicolay thrust them under his hand. He would have Andrew Johnson up for a talk as soon as the Vice President had gotten his bearings in Washington. As long as he was in his present mood, he'd better not see Sumner, though he supposed he ought to thank the Senator more adequately for what he had done for Tad.

As the two secretaries moved out with overflowing mail baskets, Mary entered in evening dress.

"Supper's been waiting a half hour, Mr. Lincoln," she said.

"My dear," he pleaded, "I've only got this supper hour in which to finish a dozen important matters. Won't you let me have it on a tray up here?" He rose and looked down at her contritely. It had been a dreadful day for her. She deserved and needed the sort of quiet hour they might have together if—

She smiled up at him. "Don't make me out such a tyrant, Abra'm," she protested. "Let me have a tray in here with you. I won't interrupt."

"Fine!" settling back at his desk again. "Some day I'll build you a castle on the edge of the Golden Gate, after you've finished buzzing around Europe and California has woven its spell over us."

Mary rang the bell and gave the requisite orders, then seated herself before the fire and did not speak until supper was spread on a little table beside her. When the President had fallen to with a good appetite, she asked if he had seen Sumner again in order to thank him.

"I suppose you'll have to forgive him now," she added.

"I'm angrier at his stupidity than I ever was at anything before in my life, if that answers you," he said. "How's our poor little Romeo?"

"Sound asleep," she replied, complacently. "Sumner certainly loves him."

"So he does and I'm obliged for what he did," agreed Lincoln, "but" —determined to nip Mary's campaign in the bud—"but he's done the Union a fearful disservice in defeating my resolution."

"Everybody's talking about the break that's inevitable between you and Mr. Sumner. You're immensely strengthening the Democrats by this party split."

"Andy Johnson'll take up that slack," the President assured her.

"I don't suppose you can feel friendly toward Mr. Sumner," agreed Mary. "But I think you're making a mistake in not making some sort of a move that will stop the gloating. Why not ask him to go to the Inaugural ball with us? We'll only be there a half hour but all the world will see and know he's our guest."

Lincoln buttered a roll, thinking this over. It was hard common sense, of course. But it was curious how hard it was to swallow his anger. Not but what somewhere inside him was an unquenchable flame of affection for Sumner!

"Well," he admitted, grudgingly, "I suppose you're right about it. I'll get the note off after supper. I hope," grimly, "that he'll accept it in the spirit in which it's written!"

"Oh! he's not cross at you!" laughed Mary. "He thoroughly beat *you!* Do it as soon as you finish your pudding, my dear. I'm afraid you'll weaken if I leave before it's done. . . . Am I acting the good partner, Abra'm?"

He smiled at her tenderly. "You're my mainstay, as usual."

The next morning, inaugural day, dawned with a heavy downpour of rain that, as the hours wore on toward noon, showed no signs of letting up. Lincoln dressed himself on rising in the same frock suit that he had worn at his first inauguration. It was well made, but he had lost weight and it hung a little loosely on him. Still, Mary looked him over carefully and said that he'd pass muster, so he promptly forgot his appearance.

His office was packed with a portion of the office seekers who were blanketing Washington again like a pest of locusts, but at eleven John Hay moved them all out and the start was made for the Capitol. The mud was so heavy that going would be tedious. Mary had gone still earlier, to sit in the diplomatic gallery of the Senate where Johnson would first be inaugurated. Some one told him that the Vice President was only scarcely recovered from a fearful attack of typhoid. Poor fellow! . . . He must get in touch with him immediately and outline that new battle.

Johnson's glorious record in Tennessee proved him Sumner's equal if not his superior in fighting prowess.

Lincoln entered the Senate Chamber at the head of his Cabinet. The dim mahogany dignity of the room had been turned to a mass of brilliant color by many flags, by the gay spring clothes of the women who crowded the galleries, by the splendors of the diplomatic corps in court dress and by the uniforms of naval and army officers with their gold lace and epaulettes and wonderful sashes. The chatter of women filled the great room despite the embarrassed pounding of the gavel by Senator Foote in the chair.

What would Johnson think of it, the poor tailor from Tennessee? The shrill chorus in the gallery rose high, then fell again. The justices of the Supreme Court were entering in their long black silk robes. Chase looked extraordinarily handsome. Then the members of the House. Buzz, buzz! the chatter rose again, then a sudden silence. It was twelve o'clock and Andrew Johnson on Hannibal Hamlin's arm was making his way to the dais.

Lincoln scrutinized his new partner closely; a tall man with fine strong shoulders, black hair, swarthy skin, smooth shaven; remarkable eyes,—not large but piercingly keen and set under a splendid brow. It was evident that he had been ill, for he was furrowed and worn far beyond what even the war strain could have done to him. He was deeply flushed;—embarrassed and excited probably.

Johnson began his speech. It was broken and incoherent. "I am a plebeian and glory in it." He paused, swayed a moment, went on. "Tennessee never went out of the Union. I am going to talk two and a half minutes on that point and want you to hear me. Tennessee always was loyal. We derive all our powers from the people.—I want you to hear me two and a half minutes on that."

Lincoln stirred uneasily. Johnson was always excitable and in the heat of speech-making was said sometimes to be carried away by his feelings. But this! The man's voice was thick, his eyes suffused. Hamlin leaned forward and nudged Johnson but the rambling words poured out in ever-increasing volume. Lincoln half turned in his seat. Charles Sumner covered his face with his hands and bowed his head on his desk. Seward as usual looked bland but Stanton might have been gazing at a specter. Welles, above his whiskers, was blushing. Chase looked like outraged marble. His confrere, Judge Nelson, stared at Johnson with his jaw apparently falling from his face until Chase tapped him on the shoulder, when he closed his lips with a snap.

Drink! Good God! Drink! This was the man he'd insisted on for a running mate, the man who was to defeat Sumner!

Hamlin rose and deliberately interrupted Johnson, requesting him in a half whisper to take the oath of office before he became too ill. Johnson gasped, blinked, then in a low voice repeated the fine words and kissed the Bible, then stumbled to his seat.

Lincoln moved from the Chamber in a daze. What treachery had fate played on him now? No, not fate, drink—

Outside, in the east face of the Capitol where the platform stood, the rain had ceased. Below the platform faces, faces, faces, that familiar pink-tinted sea which had grown so familiar to him in the past ten years. The pink tint reached back and back among the trees. The roar that rose as Lincoln appeared continued until the Sergeant-at-Arms had waved his high black hat and in pantomime bade it be still, and it was still.

Lincoln put on his spectacles, took his little speech from his breast pocket and stepped up to the table.

"Fellow countrymen: . . . On the occasion corresponding to this four years ago, all thoughts were anxiously directed to an impending civil war. All dreaded it. All sought to avert it. . . . Both parties deprecated war; but one of them would make war rather than let the Nation survive and the other would accept war rather than let it perish. And the war came.

"One-eighth of the whole population were colored slaves, not distributed generally over the Union, but localized in the Southern part of it. These slaves constituted a peculiar and powerful interest. All knew that this interest was somehow the cause of the war; to strengthen, perpetuate and extend this interest was the object for which the insurgents would rend the Union even by war; while the government claimed no right to do more than to restrict the territorial enlargement of it.

"Neither party expected for the war the magnitude or the duration which it has already attained. Neither anticipated that the cause of the conflict might cease with, or even before, the conflict itself should cease. Each looked for an easier triumph, and a result less fundamental and astounding. Both read the same Bible, and pray to the same God; and each invokes his aid against the other. It may seem strange that any man should have to ask a just God's assistance in wringing his bread from the sweat of other men's faces; but let us judge not that we be not judged. The prayers of both could not be answered—that of neither has been answered fully.

"The Almighty has his own purposes. Woe unto the world because of offenses! For it must needs be that offenses come; but woe to any men by whom the offense cometh. If we shall suppose that American slavery is one of those offenses which, in the providence of God, must needs come, but which, having continued through his appointed time, he now wills to remove, and that he gives to both North and South this terrible war as the woe due to those by whom the offense came, shall we discern therein any departure from those divine attributes which the believers in a living God always ascribe to him? Fondly do we hope—fervently do we pray—that this mighty scourge of war may speedily pass away. Yet, if God wills that it continue until all the wealth piled by the bondman's two hundred and fifty years of unrequited toil shall be sunk, and until every drop of blood drawn with the lash shall be paid by another drawn with the sword, as was said three thousand years ago, so still it must be said, 'The judgments of the Lord are true and righteous altogether.'

"With malice toward none: with charity for all: with firmness in the right, as God gives us to see the right, let us strive to finish the work we are in: to bind up the nation's wounds: to care for him who shall have borne the battle, and for his widow, and his orphan—to do all which may achieve a just and lasting peace among ourselves and with all nations."

He stood only half listening to the applause. Sumner! Johnson! Would God they could hear his words as he had meant them!

He turned toward Chief Justice Chase and the applause was stilled. The clerk of the Supreme Court, on whose cheeks were undried tears, brought forward the Bible. Lincoln laid a steady hand gently on an open page. The sun gushed forth and for a moment blinded him. Then Chase, yes, Chase (humor in this to be savored later), Chase administered the oath of office which he answered clearly, "So help me God," and kissed the Book.

He asked for Johnson immediately after the ceremony but was told that Preston King had taken him home for a visit.

"He acted as if deranged," said "Father" Welles, whom he had questioned.

"Oh, no!" protested Seward. "He's sick, and emotion on revisiting the Senate overcame him. I can appreciate Johnson's feelings, myself."

"God Almighty!" grunted Stanton.

The afternoon and evening, a blur of people; an endlessly twisting, turning kaleidoscope of faces—faces, some of them quivering as his speech was mentioned. Mary said that she had seen many people weeping during the last half of the address. They did not meet alone until after two o'clock that night, when they smiled wearily at each other before the fire in the President's bedroom. Mary had with her the inauguration Bible in which Chase had marked the verses that the President had kissed. Lincoln read them.

"None shall be weary nor stumble among them: none shall slumber nor sleep: neither shall the girdle of their loins be loosened nor the latchet of their shoes be broken."

CHAPTER XXV

THE QUALITY OF MERCY

LINCOLN did not sleep that night, he was too weary. He went to his office after an hour or so and brought back to his bed an envelope of Petroleum Nasby clippings. The man's rough, satirical remarks on politics were the essence of wisdom. Still he couldn't sleep. In the morning exhaustion made him giddy and he was glad to have Mary forbid his rising.

She was not too strict for his peace of mind, however. She permitted the Cabinet to meet in his bedroom. It was pleasant except for the discussion about Johnson, who was reported ill in bed. Sumner had been to Welles and kicked up a great row. Said Johnson must be forced to resign. Hamlin had told Stanton that Johnson was ill in the Vice President's room before the ceremonies.

"Asked Hamlin for a drink of whiskey," said Stanton. "Hamlin told him that one of his first acts as Vice President had been to have drink forbidden in the Senate restaurant and that Sumner had gotten the buffets moved out of the committee rooms. So Johnson sent across the street to a saloon and got a quart of whiskey, of which he drank three tumblers."

"Even at that," said Welles, stroking his beard wisely, "he may not be an habitual drunkard. Did any one ever hear that he was?"

It was agreed that no one had. Lincoln said that he'd had General Sickles investigate Johnson's personal career before his nomination and that it had seemed to be without blemish.

Seward closed the discussion by saying in his usual cheerful, good-humored way, "It will pass! He's a valuable man. Let's forgive and forget."

Lincoln nodded and changed the subject.

The ball was postponed till the night of the sixth. Lincoln felt in fair trim by that time, though a bit unsteady as to leg muscles. After he had gotten himself into his evening clothes, Mary wouldn't let him return to his office; so he lay on the sofa with Tad beside him, reading aloud to his father.

> "When all the world is young, lad,
> And all the grass is green,
> And every goose a swan, lad,
> And every lass a queen,—
> Then hey for boot and saddle—"

Taddie, in his flannel nightgown, ready to go to bed when his parents should leave, little round face unblemished by life—Lincoln watched him and through half-closed lids listened to the verses—

Mary came in. She was lovely; lovelier, he thought, even than on the night of the first inaugural ball. The lines that the four years had etched in her fine skin softened her firmness with a look of sadness. All true loveliness, he told himself, was sad. She wore velvet, of a lavender so delicate that at some angles it was only shadowed white. Her chestnut braids were twined round her head with pansies. Her eyes looked larger and bluer than ever.

She smiled at the two on the sofa. "How do I look, boys?"

Taddie clapped his hands. "You look like Queen Titania. I love you to death!"

"So do I!" with a low laugh from Lincoln. "How anything as pretty as you could have chosen me—eh, Tad?"

"You're kind of beautiful," declared Tad, stoutly.

The father and mother exchanged an amused glance.

Sumner came in now, carrying a great bunch of orchids for Mary and a new book for Tad. Lincoln had not spoken to him since what he called the Senate murder, excepting on the afternoon when he had rescued the children. Sumner, he told himself, as he rose from the sofa, was a long way from returning to his bed and board. He bowed and shook hands coolly with the Senator, then turned to his wife.

"If you're ready, Mrs. Lincoln, we'll proceed at once. I've an hour's work in the office after we're finished with this affair."

Mary gave him an appealing look. She didn't want him to don his rarely used cloak of dignity with Sumner. But he chose not to see the message in her glance. Mary sighed and called Tad to help her with her wraps. For a moment, the two men stood rigid by the fire. Then Sumner said in a low voice:

"I dread to mention Vice President Johnson's dreadful lapse, but I must. Mr. Lincoln, won't you force him to resign? He's a public calamity."

Lincoln raised his eyebrows. "You seem to be 'resigning' for every one but yourself, Senator! That's a matter you'd better discuss with Andy Johnson, not me."

"I beg your pardon." Sumner spoke stiffly, his face flushing.

Mary came in and with a glance from the President to the Senator, hurriedly announced that the carriage was waiting.

It was a dreadful party. The crush was so tremendous that neither detectives nor police could control it. So many people rushed into the supper room, soon after the Presidential party arrived, that the tables were wrecked and the food trampled on the floor. The confusion was so great that after a short half hour Lincoln insisted on going home. Sumner spent that half hour standing at a little distance from the President, a picture of patient suffering. Acted as if he were enduring a bad smell, thought Lincoln, glancing at him occasionally over the heads of the milling crowd. It was good to get back to the quiet of the White House.

The memory of the evening and of Sumner's attitude was still in Lincoln's mind when he woke the next morning. It had left a bad taste in his mouth. He told himself that the unwonted rôle of being mad at some one he loved was hard on his digestion.

For over a week now, he saw nothing of Sumner, and Johnson also was invisible, taking a rest out at Silver Springs with the Blairs. Lincoln ground the grist of office seekers, keeping the best of his pondering for his relation to Sumner and for the war. The roads were drying up in Virginia now and soon Grant's army must move from its winter quiet. Stanton and Lincoln were beginning to sweat lest Lee should slip away into the mountains before Sherman, coming like inexorable fate from the South, Sheridan coming down the Shenandoah, and Schofield coming from the West had closed every exit and forced Lee to fight Grant.

About the middle of March, Grant invited the President and Mrs. Lincoln to Army Headquarters at City Point, Virginia.—"I would like very much to see you and I think the rest would do you good."

Mary was delighted at the thought of seeing Bob. The boy was, as usual, careless about writing. "But," she added, "I do think you ought to make it up with Charles Sumner before you go away," reaching up to straighten his tie as they started down to breakfast.

"But how can I, my dear wife?" he asked impatiently.

She looked at him uneasily. "This is so unlike you! I've never known you to hold a grudge before."

"This isn't a grudge! Sumner's hurt the Union. It's not mine to forgive."

"Yet you offer amnesty to Rebels!" she cried.

"After they've taken the oath of allegiance," was his retort. "Mary, there's no use in my going after Sumner until I know what I want to do. Just as soon as Johnson gets well I shall have him get to work among the Democrats and see if Sumner can't be snowed under. He'll never compromise, any more than I will."

"It's no longer a question of compromise with him, Abra'm," said Mary. "He thinks he's finished the job. He told Alice Hooper that after peace is declared the States themselves will prevent you from carrying out your theories."

"Ah!" exclaimed Lincoln thoughtfully as he followed her into the dining room. "That's news! . . . Has Mrs. Hooper given up hope of making him Secretary of State?"

"She said she couldn't do much as long as you didn't seem to support the idea," replied Mary. "My dear, I could go away with a much freer mind if you'd invite Sumner up for a political conference before we go."

"Didn't the wonderful one-scene act at the Inaugural ball satisfy your greed?" asked Lincoln.

"Oh, you know what I mean!" She poured cream over Tad's oatmeal with an impatient jerk. "Let me ask him to go to the Italian Opera with us as soon as we return from City Point. I'll send the invitation before we go and let it leak out. I can't bear to see the Democratic newspapers saying the horrible things they do."

"Are they including you again?" asked Lincoln, quickly.

She nodded. "But that isn't my reason, Abra'm. I'm used to that. It's the political side."

"I'm not used to it for you!" His voice was grim. "You send your invitation. He's been trying to see me on some sort of business for a week and I've avoided him. I'll arrange to see him soon and conspicuously. But I warn you now there's going to be no kissing and holding of hands between Sumner and me."

Mary heaved a sigh of relief and devoted the rest of the meal to Tad's outrageous table manners.

Lincoln had no opportunity that day to find the conspicuous moment for seeing Senator Sumner. But on the next, chance arranged the matter with signal success. Early in the afternoon, Lincoln entered the carriage with Mary for a last round of the hospitals before leaving for City Point. Two reporters dogged Lincoln down the steps with questions about Grant and just as the coachman lifted the reins, Sumner rushed up and laid a detaining hand on the carriage door.

"Mr. President, I *must* see you on the matter of that naval court decision. I can get no satisfaction out of Mr. Welles." He turned to the reporters. "May I ask you two gentlemen to step out of earshot? I have a matter of great urgency and privacy to talk over with the President."

The two reporters fell back but watched the group with rapacious interest.

"You mean you want me to set aside the sentence of those two Boston acquaintances of yours who've been convicted of defrauding the Government?" asked Lincoln, casually. "Well, drop in on me at lunch, tomorrow."

Sumner, flushed and impatient, shook his head. "In my opinion, Mr. President, you ought not to sleep on the case. If Abraham Lincoln had suffered unjust imprisonment as a criminal, degradation before his neighbors, an immense bill of expense, trial by court-martial and an unjust condemnation, he would cry out against any postponement of justice for a single day."

Lincoln sighed. "It's evident that in order not to be a miracle of meanness in your eyes, Mr. Sumner, I must take a great deal of trouble. Very well. If you'll come around at eleven to-night, I'll see you. I'd like you to write out your legal opinion on the case before then to take as little time as possible."

Sumner, with raised eyebrows, bowed, and the carriage moved on. Lincoln turned to Mary, winked at her solemnly and lapsed into his perpetual study of Sumner's character.

There was a frightful thunderstorm that night, but in the midst of it Sumner kept his appointment with the President. It was significant of the intense anxiety and preoccupation of the two men that neither mentioned the dreadful turmoil that beat at the windows. Sumner began at once to read a superbly prepared brief. It was half an hour after midnight when he finished.

"It looks to me as if you were right," was Lincoln's comment. "Leave the brief with me, Mr. Sumner. I'll write my conclusion before I sleep and you can have it as soon as I open shop in the morning."

"And when will you open shop?" asked the Senator.

"At nine o'clock."

"Thank you, Mr. President." Sumner rose and went out into the storm.

At three o'clock, Lincoln finished his reply. Promptly at nine o'clock Sumner appeared. He stood beside the President's desk and read what Lincoln had written, then with a softened face and a voice that broke with gratitude he exclaimed:

"Thank you! Thank you! A wonderful résumé indeed! May I send a telegram from your office here, saying the men are to be discharged?"

"Do so and I'll have Hay attend to it," replied Lincoln, reaching into his desk as he spoke for the envelope of Petroleum Nasby clippings. He wanted Sumner to go without any attempts at personalities. When he was ready to move on the Senator, he'd do so with one big jump. Until then—

"Let me read you something funny, Mr. Sumner," and he began to read aloud with great gusto. He had only started the second clipping when Sumner gave vent to an enormous sigh and departed. Lincoln grinned at John Hay and turned to the war dispatches. Lee had not yet made a move.

The visit to Grant was begun very quietly. The country, in its long-drawn-out agony over the siege of Richmond, must not be roused to undue optimism by news of the President's departure for the front. The party was small: Mary, Tad, the President, Crook, the bodyguard Stanton had bullied Lincoln into enduring. Also on the morning of the departure, March 23rd, there arrived at the White House a tall, fair-haired, handsome young officer, Captain Penrose, detailed by Grant to act as aide to the President.

The party of five drove to the wharf at one o'clock in a closed carriage. But alas for secrecy! A crowd had collected and there were anxious shouts as Lincoln walked up the gangplank of the *River Queen*. "Where are you going, Mr. President? . . . Is it peace this time? . . . Has Lee skinned out?"

Lincoln could only smile and wave his hand. He went at once to his little stateroom and did not emerge until they were well out into the river with the tugboat, *Bat*, snorting along behind and making a tremendous impression on Tad. Then, in a deerstalker cap, his old gray lounge suit and a blue cape, he joined Mary on deck. They watched the receding city till they could see it no more.

Toward night a cold wind rose, with rain, and they went into the little salon where the boat's captain hovered over them, anxious about their comfort. He'd had a partition torn out, he told them, and a berth of adequate length built for the President.

"I noticed it first thing, Captain." Lincoln stretched his long legs out with a sigh of comfort on the padded lockers that ran the length of the cabin. "You were mighty clever to remember my extra inches so kindly."

"I'm going to enjoy your housekeeping instead of my own, I know, Captain," added Mary, dropping into a rocker near the President. "Taddie's gone to the engine room. Will you tell the engineer and the sailors to send him to me if he's a nuisance?"

"Oh, any one can get along with young Tad!" said the Captain. "Will you give the Steward your order for supper, Madam President?"

"Indeed I won't," exclaimed Mary with a laugh. "Didn't I tell you that's just what I want to avoid? We'll take what you're going to take, Captain, and you're to eat with us."

"Right!" agreed Lincoln. "And, Captain, I want you to be prepared to repeat to Mrs. Lincoln and my two guardian angels here some of those adventures with blockade runners you told me about last February."

The Captain looked pleased. "I don't need to repeat, Mr. Lincoln. I've had a whole new set of experiences since then."

"Good! I'm determined not to think of the war to-night. So hurry up the supper, Captain, and get my mind out of Washington and onto the sea in ships. I've all an inlander's love of sea tales."

The Captain of the *River Queen* was a really fine story teller. They kept him talking until midnight. Then Lincoln slept without dreams, ate a good breakfast, and slept again until noon. He was preparing himself for the final stupendous act of the drama. He would know in the next few days whether he was to witness the death struggle of the Rebellion or one of those tremendous coups of Lee's that would prolong the agony for another year.

CHAPTER XXVI

THE James and the Appomattox come together at City Point. The little town was perched high on a bluff that overlooked the harbor thus formed. All the afternoon of the second day, the *River Queen* made its way up the beautiful James, which was crowded by the shipping that ministered to the Army of the Potomac. It was after dark when the boat made fast to its wharf. All that could be seen of the town were lights straggling upward, with a long row of them bordering the sky line.

Lincoln, lying in a deck chair which he had occupied most of the afternoon, saw Captain Penrose leap to the pier, heard a sentry challenge him and a low-voiced colloquy follow. A moment later, Penrose came up to him and reported that General Grant wished to come aboard.

"Good!" Lincoln rose, his muscles stiffening to the load, and went into the salon where he stood by the red-covered center table waiting. Little Grant came in followed by a group of officers, Bob among them. The cabin was filled with the glitter of accouterments and the smell of leather and horses and tobacco. First a confusion of greetings; then Grant began his report. The Lieutenant-General seemed to Lincoln to be in better trim than he'd ever seen him before. He was very thin, but hard and brown and quick. The discipline of the many adversities of the past year had been good for him. He was optimistic and had every thread of the gigantic pending operations gathered into a steady hand. He was not underestimating the enemy, neither was he overestimating him. He said that Sheridan was coming in for a conference the next day and so was Sherman on a flying visit from Goldsboro, North Carolina. And he said casually that there'd been no fighting worthy of mention, lately.

But Bob told his father in their one moment alone that what looked to his green eyes like battles were going on all the time and he'd had the satisfaction of carrying messages under fire, several times. So he'd not have to go into the ranks, after all.

Grant ended the interview by giving Mary an invitation from Mrs. Grant, now at City Point, to "visit about in the handsome new ambulance that was to be devoted to the ladies." Grant's horse, Cincinnati, was again at the President's service. Young Beckwith, his own telegraph operator, was to report from now on to Lincoln. Beckwith's tent as well as Grant's office tent were now Lincoln's. Grant was a gentleman. He did these things with a quiet *savoir-faire* that Mary said made her disbelieve half the stuff she'd heard about him.

Lincoln went up to Beckwith's tent the next morning. From its opening he could see the long curved lines of the Rebel entrenchments which stretched between Petersburg across the river and Richmond, thirty miles north. After an exchange of telegrams with Stanton, he visited General Meade's headquarters. Here for two hours, from a little hilltop, he watched what Meade called a light skirmish—shells bursting, thin lines retreating and melting away.

The war council was held on the *River Queen* that evening. Sheridan and Sherman both were there. Lincoln was deeply stirred at seeing these two again. He thought they looked more gaunt and weatherworn than any of the other generals. They were more nervous, like racers held in unwilling check. He liked Grant's manner with them. To these men, he was no autocrat but a brother-in-arms.

Rain and wind were having their way with the *River Queen*. The light on the war maps was uneasy. The grizzled heads bent over the table on which the maps were spread were now in shadow, now in full yellow glow. Lincoln walked the floor a good deal, though with difficulty, as his imagination took hold of the details the soldiers discussed so dispassionately.

Once he interrupted to say, "I hope this will all be accomplished with as little bloodshed as possible."

The stern faces were lifted to his, somewhat confused and blinking.

Grant answered after a moment. "You tell me the country's in a mood where anything less than entire success will be interpreted as disastrous defeat. That kind of success will cost a good deal of blood, I'm afraid, Mr. Lincoln." Then laying a broad finger on the outworks of Petersburg, he continued the sentence the President had interrupted.

All in all, he felt strengthened by the conference. He knew everything now. Stanton had had no chance to censor this. His last remark to Grant that night was:

"Keep me informed. Don't let me be in suspense and I'll come through as well as the rest of you."

"That's why you have Beckwith," replied Grant crisply.

Sherman was returning to Goldsboro that night. He went out before the rest, saying with his face shining, "This will end it!"

End it—and the heartache and the thousand shocks! But Hamlet did not express the war mood. It took Macbeth for that. Lincoln read himself to sleep with Macbeth that night.

Nature herself provided a terrible backdrop for the first movement of Grant's advance. A thunderstorm of unprecedented severity swept down the James on the night of March 29th and the Lieutenant-General took advantage of its confusion and fury to start the great advance. Lightning fought with bursting shells. Thunder contended with the roar of artillery. The *River Queen* strained and groaned at her moorings. Tad refused to go to bed but cried himself to sleep on the sofa in the salon. Mary, wrapped in a shawl, her face blanched, sat beside him all night. Bob was out there with Grant! Lincoln knew that the strain was too much for her and wanted her to go to bed, but she couldn't.

Wrapped in his cape, he paced the deck all night, going inside only occasionally to look after Mary. The tumult without suited his mood. Nothing could so nearly express the four years' accumulation of agony and of unalterable purpose as this night. He shook with exaltation, muttered broken prayers and expletives.—"Blow wind! and crack your cheeks!"—"Oh, ye lightnings and clouds, bless ye the Lord!"—"And thou, all shaking thunder, strike flat the thick rotundity o' the world."—"Lay on, Mac-Duff—! . . ."

But as the hours wore on, the clamor became torture. Death, out there! Death and suffering.—For a long time he wept silently and as a dawn of battleshot gray lifted the river and the hills from fitful eclipse to steady, dull visibility, he pulled off his cap and lifting his face to the shell-ravaged heavens, pleaded that this be the final eruption of blood and fire.

That day and the next, as the rains forced the army to construct corduroy roads as it moved, the firing slowed down. Lincoln began to urge Mary to go back to Washington, taking Tad. She would not hear of this. She proposed to remain in order to prevent the President from going to the front and to be near Bob if he were wounded. Lincoln did not argue the matter at any length. He was too deeply immersed in following Grant's movements as Beckwith reported them. However, after a third sleepless night, Mary was so exhausted in mind and body that her own good sense told her to give in to her husband's advice. But with a pathetic heroism she insisted that Tad stay and never leave his father for an instant.

"But it's no place for Tad," protested Lincoln, uneasily. "He'll see sights and sounds that'll give him nightmares for the next year. This is no place for a child."

"No, it isn't," agreed Mary. "And war's no work for human beings. But since we're all in it, Tad must pay with the rest of us. I admit I'm no good here but I think if Tad's with you, you won't run as many risks as if he weren't."

With a shake of the head and a sigh, Lincoln gave in.

Mary left on April first and on that day he moved up to a tent next to Beckwith's on the bluff. Tad had a cot beside his father's, but Lincoln was grateful to note that the child did not take his mother's orders too literally. He spent the afternoon with the Grant children, while Lincoln on Cincinnati rode slowly over the deserted battle lines, viewing the still unburied dead, blue and gray. After all, Grant did not keep him fully in touch now with his movements. Perhaps it was impossible. Yet suspense here was less difficult to bear than in Washington.

The bombarding of Petersburg continued without cessation. He grew so habituated to the uproar that when it suddenly ceased on the night of the second he woke from a light sleep and went into Beckwith's tent. The young operator, wrapped in an army blanket, sat beside his candle and chuttering instrument. Lincoln in trousers and cape stood over him waiting. It seemed an hour before Beckwith looked up to say in an uneven voice:

"Petersburg has fallen, Mr. President!"

"Almighty God, I thank thee!" murmured Lincoln and returned to his cot. The ring of fire around Richmond was complete.

He really fell asleep now and did not rouse till Crook came in long after sunup to tell him that Captain Penrose was waiting to take him to visit Grant in Petersburg.

He told himself as he rode the fifteen miles to Petersburg that it ought to be utterly impossible for him to realize that this nightmare city actually had given up the ghost. So long had it held out against all attacks, so often had it proved the Waterloo of officers on whom he had built great hopes, that this success ought to seem like a dream. But not so. His brain never had been clearer or his nerves steadier, his imagination quicker. He was not weary—this for the first time in many, many months.

Petersburg was utterly silent and utterly deserted. Not a living creature in street or window, not even birds in the ragged trees or flies on dead things in the gutters. The National Army had gone on in pursuit of the retreating Rebels. Grant with a few members of his staff awaited the President on the piazza of an empty house. He said that as he had come into the town that morning the Appomattox bottom at the north end of the city had been packed with the Confederate army.

"But I hadn't the heart to turn the artillery upon such a mass of defeated and fleeing men. I hope to capture them, shortly."

"That's right! That's the spirit!" ejaculated Lincoln. He stood with one arm around Bob's neck. "I thought you'd forgotten me, General."

"No! You couldn't have thought that!" Grant smiled. "But you've had so many disappointments and I couldn't be sure this was coming so quickly."

He spoke then of his desire that the Army of the Potomac should have the reward of its four years' struggles and actually take Richmond, rather than the Western armies. He was quiet and businesslike, utterly unlike a conquering hero. He was impatient to be off after his army, now several miles in advance, and Lincoln let him go. With Crook and Penrose he rode slowly back the fifteen miles, across the trenches that had protected the city. They were full of dead. Poor fellows!

He had reached City Point and was slowly pushing his horse up the long road to the bluff-top when a messenger came at a gallop to meet him. He thrust a telegram into Lincoln's hand. The President halted his panting horse and tore open the message. It was from Grant.

Richmond had fallen.

He wiped his spectacles, put them in his pocket, and looked up and down the river.

Peace!

He had a physical sense that a load was being lifted from his shoulders. A dogwood tree in early bloom by the roadside suddenly impinged on his consciousness. Dogwood no longer need break his heart. He'd stand no more knee-deep in its blooms plucked from soldiers' kepis—

Crook touched his arm. "There's Vice President Johnson riding up ahead of us, sir."

A door in Lincoln's mind opened and reconstruction crowded in. He felt irritated. Could he not be allowed to savor this moment to the full? "Johnson?" he asked. "What's he doing here?"

"He came down yesterday, Mr. Lincoln. There are a number of parties here from Washington. I've heard that Representative Hooper is in a tug below with the Secretary of the Treasury."

"I don't want to see them, not Mr. Johnson or any of the rest, Crook. I came down here for a rest and a change. And Grant's seen that I've had it, God bless him!"

He pushed on up the hill, to the telegraph tent. There was a telegram from Stanton, dear old granny. "Ought you to expose yourself to the consequences of any disaster to yourself in the presence of a treacherous and dangerous enemy like the Rebel army?"

He laughed aloud as he wrote his reply. "Thanks for your caution, but I have already been to Petersburg, stayed with Grant an hour and a half, and have returned here. It is certain now that Richmond is in our hands and I think I will go there to-morrow. I will take care of myself."

Ship bells were ringing now. The river was pandemonium with the shrill of whistles and shouts of soldiers and sailors. Tad came tearing up shooting a pistol into the air.

"Wichmond's fallen, fallen, fallen!" he chanted.

His father hastened out of the tent. Tad with a pistol always made him uneasy.

"How much money do you want for that cannon, Taddie?" he asked.

"You went off to Pete'sburg without me!" cried Tad reproachfully, firing another shot.

"Give me the pistol, Tad," insisted Lincoln.

"Will you take me with you if you visit Wichmond?" bargained Tad, dancing about with the smoking weapon dangling from his hand.

"Yes! Yes! Anything!" exclaimed his father.

"And a dolla'," added Tad.

His father gave him the money and told Crook to lose the pistol. Then he seized Tad's dirty hand firmly in his own and took him down to the *River Queen* for supper. He decided to send Tad back to Washington with Hooper, if the Representative was returning soon.

But the next morning, before he could get in touch with Hooper, the *River Queen* had joined Admiral Porter's fleet and the visit to Richmond was in process. The fleet steamed up the river to Drury's Bluff. Here a wreck had blocked the narrow channel. Lincoln and Tad were transshipped to the Captain's gig, manned by twelve sailors. They were very close now to the death that made the James horrible, bodies of men and horses—Tad clung to his father's fingers but made no comment.

The trip was almost too much to bear. The shore, for a quarter of a mile before they reached their landing place beside Libby Prison, was packed with negroes. They were not noisy. But a continuous, rich murmur rose from the dusky lines, broken occasionally by soft cries:

"Massa Lincum, the sabior of the land! Mass' Lincum—Lincum—Lincum—"

Too much for a man's heart, this. He felt half suffocated.—The wharf was packed with soldiers and marines, with Admiral Farragut hovering about, smiling tensely. Six marines armed with carbines, then the President with Admiral Porter and Captain Penrose on his right and Crook clinging to Tad's other hand on his left. Behind, six more marines. Absurd precaution, when any window might hold a gun. He felt like an intruder —an unwelcome, hated alien in a foreign country. He was sorry he had come.

They began a march up the middle of a street. It was thick-bordered with spectators, that pinkish border so familiar. People clung to the telegraph poles like ants to grass stalks. The sun was hot and almost obscured by smoke. The Richmondites had tried to burn their own city. There was an appalling, a sickening silence, an utter stillness, through which the tramp, tramp of their own feet sounded loudly. It was a march through borderlines of hate. He wished he hadn't come.—This view of the wreck of Jeff Davis' dream was a hurting thing. Suddenly he felt unutterably weary.

CHAPTER XXVII

"god's in his heaven"

THERE was a group of people standing on the wharf when the *River Queen* made her moorings at City Point the next day. Tad recognized its members with a shout that roused the waterside: "Motha'! Senata' Sumna'! Goody! Goody!"

A moment later, Lincoln was greeting Mary's party: Sumner, the Harlans, Marquis de Chambrun. He was so tired! Why had Mary done this? She told him why under her breath. Stanton had complained to her that the President was jeopardizing his life daily, but he wouldn't make arrangements for her to come back. So she had organized this party and Stanton had been obliged to move. They were going to visit Richmond and then bring the President back with them to Washington.

"I don't suppose you had any idea of Sumner and me working each other over a little, crowded together on the *River Queen?*" Lincoln whispered, half amused, half irritated.

Mary looked up at him pleadingly. "Abra'm, promise me that you'll be nice to the Senator!"

He looked down at her and said, half wonderingly, "Mary, it comes to me for the first time what Grant has given *me*. Do you know there isn't a resentment in my heart toward any one in the world? The same God that brought peace to this distracted country isn't going to let Sumner's crazy notions rend it. God is going to let me bind the nation's wounds in my own way. You needn't worry. It's going to be easy for me to be nice to Sumner."

Mary stared up to him and suddenly blinked back tears. She patted his arm and turned to her guests.

Lincoln was upset by the news the party brought of a bad accident to Secretary Seward. His jaw had been broken in a runaway. It was time for him to get back to Washington. He did not care to accompany the group to Richmond; to hear Sumner and the Marquis and Mary chattering in French while death muttered all around them.

Sam Hooper and Alice called on him soon after the others departed. Nice fellow, Hooper, with no fanatical notions about anything. Mrs. Hooper had mellowed too. He invited them to come to supper to meet Mary's guests on their return. Sumner's face when he beheld Alice Hooper ought to be worth any price paid for the experiment!

But as it happened, the President did not behold the meeting between the two. The party returned from Richmond in mid-afternoon and Sumner arranged for a visit to the army hospitals. Crossing the wharf, he met Alice. She was followed by a maid, carrying a great basket of the sour pickles so passionately craved by the wounded. They had just landed from the skiff that had brought them from Hooper's boat.

"Alice!" ejaculated the Senator, standing for a moment as if frozen.

"Senator!" she returned, looking extremely handsome in the dark blue silk cloak and tiny white bonnet she was wearing. Simple clothing merely enhanced her beauty.

Sumner rushed forward and took her hand. "You're not surprised to see me?"

"No!" shaking her head, "Mr. Lincoln apprised us of the tremendous fact of your presence when he invited us to supper to-night."

"Don't laugh at me!" he begged. "I can't bear it. May I go with you, wherever you may be going?"

"If you wish—I'm on my way to one of the hospitals where they say there's a large number of our Boston boys. If you'll take the basket, Becky can return to the boat," smiling up into his face. "It's a long time since we've had a tête-à-tête."

"I've a vehicle of sorts out on the road, driven by a colored Jehu," said Sumner, taking the basket with alacrity and piloting her carefully among bales and crates to a decrepit victoria drawn by a mule scarcely more un-kempt than the old negro on the seat. "This is hardly up to your father's Morgans, but it's the best I could lay hands on," he continued. He handed her gravely to her place and ordered the colored man to find a route to the hospital unknown to ambulances. Then he stepped into the carriage. "So I'm to have the pleasure of being with you at supper to-night? Strange the President didn't mention it."

"He said that if we surprised you, the look on your countenance would be worth any price the experiment might cost." Alice looked up at him, eyes twinkling.

"And what did he mean by that?" with a puzzled scowl on his pale face. He was looking very much worn.

"He didn't explain himself," replied Alice. "He can't know how we last parted, so he couldn't have been anticipating a public reconciliation. In fact, I'm not sure that there will be or has been a reconciliation. Let's see! Our last quarrel had to do with my telling you what I thought of your defeat of the President's bill! I still am unchanged as to that, Senator."

"Don't! I beg of you, Alice. Let's not mention politics. Let's sing a Te Deum together that Richmond has fallen and then let's talk only of our two selves."

Alice looked from the disreputable mule to the disreputable darky and from the darky to Sumner in his blue broadcloth coat and fawn-colored pantaloons. The thought of herself and the immaculate Senator chanting together under such chaperonage was too much for her risibilities and she bubbled over with laughter. The old darky looked round sympathetically.

"That's right, Miss!" he said, "you-all be joyful in de Lawd dis ebening! You'se a-riding with the Holy Ghostes self that helped the Sabior of the niggers to dis day of Jubilee. Yaas'm." He turned back to the mule which had come to a halt during this apostrophe. "Git up, Judas," he urged.

But Judas was aweary. He had halted under a budding tulip tree in a quiet lane where the westering sun could not strike him and where there was a matchless view of the harbor with the long half-moon of war vessels sheltering the wharves. He slumped well down between the shafts and went to sleep.

Sumner leaned forward impatiently but Alice touched his arm. "This is the South. There's no hurry. Let's see what happens."

The Senator looked down at the little hand and leaned back with a sigh of deep content.

The darky did not move for a full minute. Then he turned round with a rueful twist of the lips under the grizzled white beard. "I reckon I might just as well tell you-all lady and genmun that I cayn't get Judas goin' lessen I build a fire under him or lessen I go get old Peter to hitch to his forelock and drag on him. Peter bein' my brudder's mule."

"How long will it take you to fetch Peter?" asked Sumner.

"Not mor'n half a hour, Mass' Sumner. I'd be obleeged if I could work it that way, cuz burning his old hide do make him kick." The old man's voice was very pleading.

"Very well! But you must move rapidly," agreed the Senator.

"Yassir! Faster'n Uncle Robert Lee's hoofin' it from Gineral Grant!" clambering down and making off over a fresh-plowed field.

"What a glorious mischance!" exclaimed Sumner, tossing his felt hat to the seat opposite. "Dear Alice!"

"I deserve no credit for it, Senator!" protested Alice. "But I'll admit I'm very well content. Do you think there's any chance that Judas will come out of his coma and start? Our Jehu has left his reins dragging."

Sumner rescued the knotted ropes that answered for reins and hung them within easy reach over the whip. "I shall be grievously disappointed if he starts before Jehu's return.—Alice, coming down on the boat from Washington I spent much of the night on deck thinking of you. Somehow, under the stars, it was impossible to concentrate on affairs of state. My mind was filled with your lovely self. And thinking so, free of all the irritations inseparable from Washington, I realized that I'd played a petty part with you."

She looked up at him, her face a little sad. "Dear Senator, you're never petty. You were merely true to yourself. It was I with my ambitions that was petty. You and I both have our arrogances and our egotisms, Senator, but I see some things clearer than you do. I shouldn't have criticized your splendid career. It was putting my own little dreams ahead of your big ones."

"No! No! You shall not say that!" cried Sumner. "Let's not talk of it. Let me tell you of my love for you and how it's filling me more and more with an unrest that will not be stilled. Let me ask you again to be my wife! Give me yourself to cherish and adore and take me as I imperfectly am. Alice! Alice!"

She sat quite still, her head in the little white bonnet bowed. Faint bugle calls came from the ships below. There was a smell of new earth. Robins and red birds called.

Then Alice said in a low voice, "I shall not be a perfect wife, Charles, but I love you dearly, dearly and admire you extravagantly."

Tears filled Sumner's eyes. He slipped his arm around her waist and drew her gently against him. And then he kissed her; at first softly but in a moment with the passion that told of the breakdown of the dam of loneliness and frustration built by the years. For a moment she was only tender with him and then, as the years passed from him and she saw the youthful beauty that age had only covered in his face and not destroyed, she kindled to his fire.

The sun had set when the colored Jehu appeared, dejected and empty handed.

"Pete, he done balked too," he reported. "Reckon I'd better get that fire started."

"Mercy, no!" cried Alice. "How far is it back to the wharf?"

"About fifteen minutes' walk, Miss," replied Jehu, hopefully.

"Then, Charles, let's walk," suggested Alice. "I feel the need of expansion, as you would say. The man can bring the basket back to me, when Judas permits."

Sumner tossed a bill to the smiling darky and gave Alice his hand from the carriage. He did not release it when she was beside him and with the grinning Jehu watching they strolled off into the dusk.

Sumner began to press Alice to agree to an early marriage. From his point of view there could be no reason for more than a few months' engagement. But here the amenability that had marked Alice during their two hours together showed signs of hardening. The Hoopers, she protested, would feel badly if she were to marry so soon after the death of Sturgis.

"In fact," she went on, "they're going to oppose any marriage at all. They're quite content with the present arrangement. So we mustn't think of the wedding before another year. And you're so tied here that after we're married, I shall expect never to get abroad again. Mr. Hooper plans to take us all over to London this summer and leave us for six months."

Sumner groaned. "Alice! You almost make me want to be Minister to England."

"Well, why don't you be? No! Don't be cross, dear!" as she felt his fingers stiffen. "You shall be and do whatever you wish. Keep right on fighting the darkies' fight for them. Kill yourself in another struggle in the Senate, if it'll make you happy! I warn you now, though, that I'll not invite Fred Douglass to eat at our table."

"There'll not be another Senatorial struggle," declared Sumner firmly, "unless Mr. Lincoln precipitates it. And after he ceases to be Commander-in-Chief, he'll have no authority whatever. No, that fight is finished."

"And do you think he'll try to precipitate another struggle?" asked Alice, casually.

"No, I don't. I never saw a man more thoroughly whipped than he was, last month. They tell me he was actually despondent. And I know he's made no move since. In fact, he can't move now, without Congress. He can't appoint military Governors and cause them to call elections. No, thanks to killing that iniquitous bill of his, Congress is now in the saddle."

"You mean you're in the saddle with Congress riding postillion fashion," laughed Alice. "Do you see the rim of the moon behind the masts of those ships, Charles? It looks like Holland. I'm afraid we're going to be very late for the President's supper. We must not delay to dress."

They boarded the *River Queen* just as the party was sitting down at the table. Lincoln, eyeing them keenly as they stood together in the doorway, wondered just why Alice had wished to rob him of his surprise. He was half minded to joke her about it. But although Sumner was extraordinarily whimsical and cordial at the supper table and Alice so gentle that her father-in-law eyed her wonderingly, no mention of the obvious situation between the two was invited by either Alice or Sumner.

When supper was over, Lincoln went out on the deck. He wished very much to go up to Beckwith's tent but wasn't sure that Mary wouldn't feel he was neglecting the guests. There was a full moon on the river. Its enchantment softened the brutal paraphernalia of war to delicate beauty. Even the distant sounds of Grant's pursuit of Lee lost some of their suggestiveness in competition with this enthrallment of the eye. As Lincoln stood by the rail in contemplation, Sumner joined him.

"Mr. Lincoln," he said in a low voice, "Mrs. Hooper and I wish that you and Mrs. Lincoln shall be among the first to know of our great happiness."

The President took the proffered hand in a mighty grip. "I saw it on your faces when you arrived! All the good things in the world be showered on you, Senator! Your wife will be a beautiful and gifted lady."

In the moonlight, he saw that Sumner's face was indescribably softened and moved. "I can't believe that after all these years, I'm to know the bliss of marriage," he murmured.

Lincoln dropped his hand on the Senator's shoulder. "You'll be the handsomest couple in Washington, by Jings, and I shall certainly dance at your wedding. When will it be, Senator?"

"That's the one fly in the ointment," replied Sumner with a sigh. "Mrs. Hooper wishes to postpone it for a year." He gave the President Alice's reasons.

Lincoln shook his head. "Too bad! But I reckon she'll give in if you let her see how you feel about it."

"I don't want to be selfish in my demands," said the Senator. "She has been so generous with me."

"Didn't insist that you lay your future career in her pretty little hands, eh?" asked Lincoln, with a smile.

"No! No!" protested Sumner. "Strange as it may seem to you, Mr. Lincoln, she cares for me without reference to my career."

"Now, why should it seem strange to me?" asked Lincoln.

Sumner leaned against the rail, facing the President. "To tell you the truth, sir, I've felt that since February you've hated me."

"Oh, come now, Senator! Allow me a little slack! You knocked my dearest hopes higher than a kite. Trumbull and I felt as if a cyclone had been playing tag with us. It's a wonder I didn't return the ring and all your letters! Instead of that I got your friends out of jail for you!"

Sumner smiled slowly. "It was a fair fight, Mr. Lincoln."

"Absolutely! And the best man won. Trumbull says he's through," with a chuckle.

"And you?" asked Sumner.

"I'm telling you frankly, Senator," sighed the President, "that I never felt so beaten in my life. I have no more ideas than an egg. I'm certain of just one thing. I'm going to keep your friendship. I've gotten very little to take away with me out of Washington, Senator. But I'm doing my best to take that. Friendship isn't as precious to you as it is to me."

Sumner's face contracted with pain. "Don't say that! I don't deserve it, truly. Friendship means much to me. It's all I've had."

"I think you've been careless with a good many of your friendships," insisted Lincoln. "With mine, for instance. But I won't let you go. Sometimes I'm surprised when I examine my feeling for you, Charles, because I reckon I've never had before or will have again just that kind of a liking for any one. I suppose a lean, sallow, cadaverous fellow like me is bound to be attracted by your handsome looks. I couldn't have the same liking for you if you were a little, slim, consumptive man like Stephens of Georgia. I like your prideful way of comporting yourself.—'Why, man, he doth bestride the narrow world like a Colossus and we petty men walk under his huge legs and prowl about to find ourselves dishonorable graves.' —And there's your glorious voice. Makes mine sound like a rabbit's squeak."

"No! No! You embarrass me, dear Mr. Lincoln!" Sumner's eyes were full of tears.

Lincoln, watching him, felt his whole heart go out to the Senator. There was something pathetic, something that tugged at all his sympathies about Sumner. He felt that same almost overwhelming gush of pity and love rising within him against which he had fought at Hampton Roads. But he didn't strive against this.

"Charles! Charles! You're a very noble figure of a man! I wish I were one of the monarchs of old who could tap a loved favorite on the shoulder and make him a knight! *Sans peur et sans reproche*. I know a little French, myself. That's it! It's your integrity, Charles! That's the core of your charm for us. I'd rather my boys had it than any other single quality. We all rest on your integrity, Charles, as on the Everlasting Arms."

"Don't! Ah, don't, Mr. Lincoln!" Sumner's face worked. "You overwhelm me with your generosity. Me, who have worked against you, thwarted you, beaten you." He took a step across the deck and turned back holding out both his hands. The tears were running down his cheeks. "Mr. Lincoln, I will be Secretary of State for you!"

Lincoln could feel himself grow faint. He clung speechlessly to Sumner's hands. The leap of relief in his breast was physically painful. *Sumner out of Congress giving Lincoln a free hand with reconstruction!* "Is that a promise, Charles?" he finally gasped.

"Yes! You must give me a few months to arrange my affairs."

"Take all the time you want!" Lincoln paused, still holding the firm fingers in his own. "You and Grant between you to-day have given me perfect happiness. I've had only one other hour as great. That was when I signed the Emancipation Proclamation. Go down to your Alice now, Senator, before I weep!"

Sumner gripped Lincoln's hands and obediently turned away.

Shortly after this the Hoopers left, and the *River Queen* started back to Washington.

Lincoln's mood of exaltation demanded expression. He went to his cabin and procured the beautiful quarto volume of Shakespeare that Mary had given him on his last birthday. Then he joined the group in the cabin. Mary looked up with a smile.

"We're debating Jeff Davis' fate," she said.

"Judge not, that ye be not judged," he replied, soberly. Then he seated himself under a lamp and opened his book. "If you all are in my frame of mind, Shakespeare alone can satisfy you. And of Shakespeare, only Macbeth."

"Oh, not Macbeth!" cried Mary, shuddering. "Give us something gentle and tender, Mr. Lincoln, like Tennyson or Longfellow."

"Like 'Resignation,' I suppose—" smiled Lincoln and he repeated aloud:—

> " 'There is no flock, however watched and tended,
>   But one dead lamb is there!
>   There is no fireside, howsoe'er defended
>   But has one vacant chair—'

No! No! That's too tame! Give me Macbeth. . . .

> " 'Duncan is in his grave;
>   After life's fitful fever he sleeps well.
>   Treason has done its worst; nor steel nor poison,
>   Malice domestic, foreign levy,
>   Nothing can touch him further. . . .' "

He adjusted his spectacles. "That has teeth! Let's have the witches next.

You should have seen them at work on the night of March 29 over Petersburg."

He read for an hour in his dramatic fashion, then closed the book. After all, Macbeth was a tragedy and his was no tragic mood. He went on deck for one last look at the serene beauty of the night. Mary followed him and they stood together by the rail in silent communion.

After a moment, Lincoln said, "Mary, Sumner has filled my cup to overflowing."

"You've made up?" cried Mary.

"Well," smiled the President, "you might call it so. You know that a hundred times the last two years I've tried to woo Sumner and I couldn't. But to-night, without thinking of a thing except my honest love for him, I wooed and won him." He told her of their conversation and of its extraordinary climax, ending with the remark, "I don't yet see why he came to my arms!"

"Oh, but I do, Abra'm! He thinks, as I've told you before, that you're finished. He thinks you're powerless now to hurt his cause."

Lincoln laughed softly. "Then I wooed him under false colors because I am certain that as soon as Andy Johnson and I get our heads together we can pull the teeth of the Vindictives.—No, not false colors either. I love Sumner and he knows it."

"Yes," murmured Mary, "at last, thank God, he knows it."

She leaned against him. Lincoln put his arm about her, pressing her warm body against his side, and in deep happiness they watched the sliding Virginia shore.

The Last Full Measure

CONTENTS

CHAPTER I

I T was a lovely day, though cool for September in Baltimore. It was a day on which one might well grudge a moment spent indoors. Yet three young men remained crouched over a table in the all but deserted bar-room of Barnum's Hotel for a long two hours of that ambrosial afternoon, talking in low voices and drinking rum. They drank a considerable amount in the course of the conversation but this did not account fully for the excitement shining in their eyes.

They were old schoolmates. Yet save for the liquor they were consuming their meeting had no aspect of a class reunion.

The delicate-looking one of the trio was Sam Arnold. He had served in the Confederate army but had spent a long time in hospital, had grown weary of the war and was living with his parents in Baltimore. His face was intelligent with steady black eyes, full, well-shaped lips and thick black hair. A dark mustache and close-trimmed beard made him look older than his twenty-eight years.

The smallest of the three men was Mike O'Laughlin. He too had served in the Confederate army but the year before he had taken the oath of allegiance to the Union. He now worked in his brother's feed store in Baltimore. Mike was dark, with irregular features, large brown eyes that did not hold one's gaze and lips inclined to twitch behind the small mustache and fashionable imperial. He also was twenty-eight.

The most talkative of the group was the man who drank the most. He sat taller in his chair than Arnold and where both the others were of an ordinary comeliness, he was extraordinarily and luminously handsome. His face, smooth shaven save for a black mustache, was perfect in its contours. His great black eyes were of a haunting beauty and as he talked, a thousand varied expressions flashed in these and in his voice and on his lips. He was twenty-six years old. His name was John Wilkes Booth.

It had been noon when they had seated themselves in the deserted bar-room, and conversation had been difficult for the town was rocking with the salute of a hundred guns President Lincoln had ordered in honor of General Sherman's march through Georgia. Sherman had just taken Atlanta. The three young men had accompanied the booming of the cannon with curses for Lincoln and his generals—large and not unobscene oaths which left no doubt of their political convictions. When the salute was over however they brought their respective histories up to date.

Sam Arnold couldn't get a job and was keeping soul and body together by working on his brother's farm. Michael O'Laughlin was discontented. There was no future for him in his brother's store. Mike needed capital.

But Wilkes Booth was already famous in the acting profession. Women mobbed him at the stage door and young college men kept the programs of his plays tacked to the walls of their rooms and, he said, tried to imitate the inimitable toss of his head, his graceful gasconading stride, his delightful smile. Wilkes' mother had extracted a promise from him which he explained to his two friends.

"No, I haven't been able to shoulder a gun for Maryland, poor dishonored beauty! All my people are staunch supporters of the Union, I'm sorry to say. And my mother made me promise—when I thought it was only a matter of sixty days before Secession won—made me promise not to fight against the Union. God, how I've regretted that promise! But, out of that sacrifice has come a great good, dear old friends! Sweating to find how I could do my share has led me to the discovery of how to end this war at once, with victory for the Confederacy."

Sam Arnold stared.

Mike O'Laughlin laughed. "You still do fancy yourself, Booth!"

Wilkes flushed and his eyes flashed. "I'll thank you both to listen to me with civility! You're dull if you don't realize that if the South's beaten, it means either extermination or exile for every Southern gentleman. That shall not be while I live!" He sprang to his feet and took a stride or two up and down the room, dodging chairs and now and then making an imaginary sword thrust, left palm in the air.

The others exchanged amused glances! The same old Wilkes, living in bravado! But he was always interesting and they waited, with outward respect at least, for him to explain himself. He returned presently, dropping into his chair with graceful abandon. He took a stout drink of rum and then leaned toward them and began a tirade that wiped all interest from the two faces opposite.

"Four years ago I'd have given my life to keep the Union as I'd always known her. If one could just wake up as from an unspeakable nightmare and know that the fearful scenes never had been enacted! How we'd bless God! That's true, isn't it, old schoolmates?" He leaned toward them with a smile of infinite sweetness.

His listeners nodded languidly.

"I've studied hard," he went on, "to find on what grounds the right of a State to secede can be denied. But I can find none. The North is wrong, wrong, wrong! And I love justice and right more than I love a country that disavows both."

"Oh, come, Wilkes," protested Sam Arnold, "we've heard this sort of gab a hundred times a week since we could remember anything. Save it for Richmond. You say you're going down there."

Wilkes bit his lip but controlled his quick resentment to urge, "Please don't interrupt! What I've got to say is important. Heaven knows, no one is more willing to help the negroes than I am. But Lincoln's policy is only preparing the way for their total annihilation. And if Lincoln wins in the November election, Southern chivalry will be annihilated too. He's a curse to the world!—And yet, how I've loved that old Union flag will never be known! A few years ago, no country in the world could boast one so spotless and pure. Oh, how I've longed to see her break from the mist of blood and death that circles round her folds, spoiling her beauty and tarnishing—"

O'Laughlin slumped dramatically in his chair and Arnold groaned.

"I will be heard!" shouted Wilkes Booth, bringing a surprisingly large fist down on the table. Then his voice softened. "Old friends, I've found a way, a simple, bloodless way to end this anarchy of death."

"So you say!" grinned O'Laughlin. "The insane asylums are full of fellows who think they're God."

Booth set his teeth and taking out his pocketbook, laid a twenty-dollar gold piece on the red enameled tray which held the bottles. "I remember your characteristics, Mike," he snarled. "Let me purchase your attention."

"Good boy! I'm all ears," chuckled O'Laughlin, but he did not pick up the gold piece, though he drew the tray to his side of the table. Arnold made a playful grab at the coin. O'Laughlin ostentatiously imprisoned his hand.

Wilkes began again, with increased earnestness. "To show you how serious I am let me say that in order to carry out this plan I shall have to give up my profession which earns me twenty thousand dollars a year. I must give up my mother and my brothers and sisters, all very dear to me though they differ so widely from me politically. I must give them all up, though to do so seems insane. But God is my judge."

He had caught their attention at last. He gazed from one to the other for a long moment, took another drink and then whispered, slowly, "Sam and Mike, I am going to kidnap old Lincoln and carry him to Richmond. There I shall turn him over to the Confederate authorities to hold till the North lays down its arms."

"Great God!" gasped Sam Arnold, half in fear and half in admiration.

"I've heard that dream from many another fool," grunted O'Laughlin. "Take back your gold, friend Wilkes!"

"You sneering jackass!" furiously from Booth.

Sam rose, pulling down his purple vest and picking up his little round felt hat.

"Don't go, Sam!" pleaded Wilkes, instantly. "It's really a great scheme."

"And the drinks are free!" exclaimed Mike O'Laughlin, refilling his glass.

"Such being the case—!" Sam dropped into his chair. "But you really have no outer skin, Wilkes. You must be the devil to act with."

"On the contrary, every one loves me," returned Booth, coolly. "But I'll admit that I've brooded over this idea until my nerves are set on hair triggers. I've just completed the details and you are the first human beings to whom I've breathed a syllable. You see how I trust you! I need help. Loyal help. And I'm going to begin by sharing more than my secrets with you." He placed another twenty-dollar gold piece on the tray.

Arnold did not touch the coins but O'Laughlin dropped one in his vest pocket.

"What are the details, Wilkes?" he asked.

"Some evening when I'm playing on the stage and old Abe's alone with a single companion in the President's box, you two will be hidden in the passage behind the box. At a cue agreed upon, the lights will be turned out, and you two will enter the box and knock out Abe and his companion with a blow from a black-jack. Then like lightning I will clamber into the box from the stage. We will tie up both men and leaving the companion to his fate, we will lower Abe to the stage and rush him to the rear of the theater. In the alley I'll have a suitable carriage and horses. We'll drive through Washington, across the unguarded bridge over the Eastern Branch and down lower Maryland to Port Tobacco. There a boat will be in waiting and we'll ferry him over the Potomac. After that it will be simple enough to get him into Richmond." He paused to observe the effect of this statement on his friends.

Sam was motionless. But Mike smoothed his little imperial, took the gold piece from his pocket, kissed it and shoved it toward Booth. The actor scowled.

"Be patient, Mike," he urged. "There is more to this than a personal whim. Last April President Davis appointed four commissioners to live in Canada for the purpose of coöperating with the Northern peace party. Nobody on either side can deny that that is a laudable purpose, eh? They have quite a perfect system of communication between Montreal and Richmond, sending a messenger back and forth through the lines and using the personal columns of the New York *News*, which reaches Richmond regularly."

"They're the men that worked on Horace Greeley and would have got somewhere if old Abe hadn't played the tyrant. We know all about them," said Arnold, impatiently.

"Well, did you know this?" demanded Wilkes. "That through Vallandigham of Ohio and other northern friends of Secession, they've got innumerable groups within the secret organizations of the Knights of the Golden Circle and the Sons of Liberty, armed and officered to oppose army drafts and otherwise harass the Federal authorities, so that the morale of the people at home will be broken?"

"Yes, the 'Copperheads,'" grunted Mike. "Tell us something new."

Wilkes moved his shoulders exasperatedly. "I'm merely trying to prove to you that I'm not on a wild-goose chase. Jacob Thompson, one of the commissioners, told me, himself, that there are in New York City alone, 20,000 Copperheads in well-disciplined organizations. He estimates that he has at least 60,000 men scattered over the North who'll go any length for the Confederacy. Thompson was distinguished enough to be Secretary of the Interior under President Buchanan. You certainly ought to believe *him*. If you're not members of some such organization, you ought to be. I mustn't reveal any more to you but I'll add that I'm in possession of the cipher code used by Jacob Thompson in his letters to the Secretary of the Confederate Treasury and by Mr. Davis, too. I've recently had a long interview with Thompson and with C. C. Clay, Jr., another of the commissioners. I dare say no more at the moment. Now, will you two young nonentities condescend to trust me and listen to my plans about old Abe?"

He had caught their interest at last. Sam Arnold now spoke in his gentle way. "Everybody knows old Abe could be abducted. I've often heard talk of how he could be carried down to Richmond by the route the Confederate Secret Service uses. It could be done, I reckon, if any one wanted to take the risk. The absurd part of your scheme, Wilkes, is the beginning of it. That theater business—gosh!" He shook his head.

"I agree with Sam!" exclaimed Mike, for once making a direct statement. "That theatrical background is just a method for you to show off, Wilkes. You always were a good fellow as a kid until your love of showing off got the best of you. That characteristic, I suppose, makes a first-class actor of you, but a poor conspirator. I'm all for doing anything to get rid of old Lincoln, short of killing him. He *can* be kidnaped. But you've got to catch the old flea when he's hopping from the White House over to the War Building at midnight. That would be a cinch. Then find an empty house in the neighborhood and carry him there while another group carries an imitation Lincoln off, lickety-cut, in a buggy. At a suitable moment, the old fellow himself could be smuggled across the Potomac. Plenty of loyal Southerners over there to pass him along."

"Yes, that could be done," mused Sam Arnold, twirling his glass with none-too-clean fingers. "Or you could grab him and his wife some day when they're driving out to the Soldiers' Home. But the theater notion's no good. Even at that, I'm not inclined to go in with you. The risk is too great. I'd rather go down and join Uncle Bob Lee's army again."

"Me too," agreed Mike, lighting one of Booth's cigars.

"What if I told you that there was big money in it," whispered Booth, eyes half closed as again he leaned across the table. "Millions of dollars, to be shared by us three and any others whom we may take in. The Confederate government will pay that gladly."

"Prove it," said Mike, laconically.

"I can prove it only if you'll believe what I say," said Wilkes. "Jacob Thompson has deposited in his name in a bank in Montreal, 65 million dollars with a commission from Jefferson Davis to devote that money to furthering the interests of the Confederacy in the North. Thompson told me himself that if he could rid the world of the tyrant Lincoln, he'd consider all his work had been done. Do you need to be taught to put two and two together?"

"Christ!" ejaculated Mike. His flippant manner left him. "Count me in, Wilkes, if you'll give up the theater as the starting point."

"Look here," urged Wilkes, "if we're going to father the stupendous event that ends the war, are we going to do it like thieves? No! Let it be openly, showing the world there's more than one kind of a general."

"There's something in that," said Sam, slowly.

"There is not!" grunted Mike O'Laughlin. "Come, Wilkes, agree you'll try the Soldiers' Home scheme first, the path to the War Office next and the theater only as a last resort and I'll agree."

Wilkes bit his lip and sighed, helplessly. "Well, I'm willing to subordinate my original plan in order to bring in people I know and trust as I do you two. But it's against my better judgment."

"I'll go in with you," drawled Arnold. "I'm dead busted and that gold piece looks good to me."

"I'm with you," said O'Laughlin, "partly because of the money but still more," his face suddenly twisting, "still more because I'm willing to risk my life to get my hands on the bastard who's made it possible for a nigger to marry my sister."

The three exchanged looks, then Wilkes Booth rose and led the way out to the steps of the hotel. The sun was sinking and there was a locust shrilling in the tulip-tree above their heads. The air was full of the smell of drying foliage.

"I must leave for Montreal, to-night," said Wilkes. "I have a perfectly open reason for going as I'm hoping to play stock up there. I'll see Jacob Thompson and Clay. As soon as I get back, I'll get in touch with you. In the meantime, I'll send you money." He waved a gloved hand toward the southwest. "Well, confusion and damnation to old Abe! I don't think God can be cruel enough to the South to let him be elected for another four years. But we'll get either him or his successor to America's new throne. Fare-thee-well, friends!"

They shook hands and left him.

CHAPTER II

ESCAPE

CONFUSION and damnation!

Abraham Lincoln at the moment Wilkes Booth was bidding his friends good-by, on that exquisite September afternoon, was talking to a committee of Baltimore colored people who had presented him with a Bible. The little group had waited a long time for him and very timidly, in the reception room on the second floor of the White House. They took it for granted that he had put them off because they were negroes and were astounded when he apologized to them.

John Hay, one of the President's secretaries, came for them just as twilight touched the reception room which received none of the afterglow. He was an elegantly habited young man with black eyes, a round face on which three dreadful war years had etched premature lines, though they had left intact the humor on the lips above his dimpled chin.

"The President will receive you now," said John Hay with a casual nod.

They trooped after him in silence.

The President's office was on the south side of the White House, a room perhaps twenty by thirty feet. Its windows looked out across the lawns and shrubbery, across the marshes, across the Potomac to Alexandria and Arlington Heights, crimson now in the dying light. The long Cabinet table covered with a red cloth ran down the center of the room. Between the windows was a bureau for state papers. There was a sofa on either side of the room and on the west side a marble fireplace over which was an engraving of General Jackson. On the mantel was a fine photograph of John Bright which the great Englishman himself had sent to Lincoln. There were several war maps on the east wall. A tall standing desk stood in the southwest corner. On it lay the Bible, Shakespeare's Works, the Statutes of the United States and Whiting's "War Powers."

A long table desk was placed at right angles to the southwest window with a chair before it so situated that its occupant could swing round and easily reach the books lying on the standing desk behind. As the colored men came in, Lincoln rose from this chair and came toward them.

He had grown thin to emaciation in the three and three-quarter years of war, this man who was six feet, four inches tall but in his thinness looked taller. Still, he gave the effect of wiry muscularity, not of attenuation. His loss of flesh became his plain face better than had its former meager fullness. Or was it a plain face? Certainly the bony structure of the head was superb, as were the deep, huge eye-sockets, the wonderful thrust of jaw and chin, so adamantine yet so finely cut. Could a face be plain that carried between and around the eyes and from nostrils to mouth corners those profound grooves which spiritual agony alone could have cut?

"I'm sorry you had such a long wait," he said as he shook hands with his visitors. "If it's any comfort to you, I'll confide to you that the three Senators, two Brigadier-Generals and the Secretary of the Interior who preceded you, had a longer wait! And I've not had my noon meal yet! This, for me?" as the chairman, a very dark man with Caucasian features, placed the huge red plush Bible in his hands.

"Yes, Mr. Lincoln, sir," replied the man. "We couldn't think of any other present good enough for you-all," and he launched into a little speech of praise and gratitude.

Lincoln laid the book on the Cabinet table and, keeping one hand upon it, took a small paper knife from his pocket and ran it through his hair. The thanks of colored people always moved and embarrassed him more than any other. It was hard when human beings had to thank other human beings for the right to draw a free breath! He was glad when the halting little address ended.

"The occasion is fitting for a lengthy response to you, my friends," said Lincoln, "but I'm not prepared to make one. I would promise to respond in writing had not experience taught me that business will not allow me to do so. I can only say now as I've often before said that it always has been a sentiment with me that mankind should be free. In letters and documents sent from this office, I have expressed myself better than I now can. In regard to this great book I have but to say, it is the best gift God has given to man. All the good Saviour gave to the world was communicated through this book. All things most desirable for man's welfare here and hereafter, are to be found portrayed in it. To you, I return my most sincere thanks for the very elegant copy of the great book of God which you present."

He bowed gravely and stood with his hand still on the red plush cover while the negroes filed out of the room.

"The carriage is waiting to take you out to the Soldiers' Home, sir," said John Hay.

"I can't leave before midnight, John," protested Lincoln. "Tell those fellows to go get their suppers and not pester me."

"Meaning the cavalry escort, I suppose," grinned John. "I wish Mrs. Lincoln were here at this moment."

"So do I! So do I," murmured the President, turning back to his desk, over which the doorman was lighting a lamp. "Any news from General Sheridan, John?"

"He's still chasing Rebels in the Shenandoah Valley, Mr. President," replied John, cheerfully, as he sorted a new batch of letters at the standing desk.

"Thank you for nothing," grunted Lincoln. "Run over to Stanton before he leaves the War Office and get the last word, like a good fellow! John!" Young Hay paused by the fireplace. "John, I think this was the worst of our four summers here, don't you? That newfangled device the

Rebels have of wire entanglements before their trenches is hellish. Yet Grant throws his men against them as calmly as a woman shakes crumbs into a fireplace. Somehow, those wires haunt me every waking moment. His losses are crucifying. The only bright and cheering note in this week of bad news was brought me to-day by Colonel Baker. I mean the detective, Baker. He swears he's unearthed a plot of Jacob Thompson and his gang in Canada to kidnap Stanton and Seward and me."

John looked steadily at the President. "What's so cheering in the idea of kidnaping you, sir?" he demanded.

"Think of any one's wanting me that much!" chuckled Lincoln. "Anyhow, I don't believe it. But we keep a pretty close eye on those fellows up there."

"It's not a bit funny to the rest of us, Mr. Lincoln!" protested John. "Not to those of us who love you and who know that the fate of the Union rests with you and who know how easily you could be abducted!" He strode angrily out of the room.

"Well," said Lincoln to General Jackson scowling over the mantel, "there wasn't much comfort in John that time, was there!"

He returned to his chair and drew from a drawer a little pile of bristol-board squares. He had found that he could rest these on his crossed knee and write on them with less strain than in the usual posture at his desk. He was preparing a letter of thanks to the hundred-day troops of Ohio. It took him a moment or two to collect his thoughts.

The noise of Pennsylvania Avenue drifted through the window. The remnant of cobblestones on that popular thoroughfare added an irregular cannonading to the rumble of heavy traffic that was not unlike the sound of battle skirmishing. Dust settled on the cardboard. Mosquitoes buzzed—

The prospect of his re-election seemed practically nil. It looked as if the North might turn heavily against him—No use brooding about that—He wrote a sentence, paused and threw down his pencil. Tired—tired—tired! What would he not give to be, say, on a raft on the Sangamon, floating with the current, the smell of ripening paw-paws and of fresh water and of goldenrod making heaven of the soft damp air—

Suddenly he rose and, with an air of combined guilt and cunning decidedly reminiscent of his eleven-year-old son, Taddie, tiptoed across the private passage to the family sitting room. He crossed this and the adjacent guest-room to Mary's room, and across this to his own chamber. Here he changed to comfortable walking shoes, found his cane and then boldly walked down the private stairs and to the front door. He paused a moment on the steps and wondered if he ought not to change his contemplated run-away into a call on the Secretary of State. Seward was an excellent fellow but still too wordy. That next dispatch to Minister Dayton in Paris about the Mexican situation must be cut to the bone. "Least said soonest mended" was the best rule on earth for the conduct of foreign relations. Seward was always skating on the thin ice of conversation. Only the most careful watching thus far had kept him from putting his foot through.

Lincoln wiped his forehead and replaced his soft hat. No, he'd let Seward go, this evening. He started along the bricked path which led west from the portico to the turnstile letting into the War Department grounds. To the south, this walk was bordered by a red brick wall which shut the vegetable garden from view. To the northwest was a grove of black walnuts and cork oaks planted by John Quincy Adams fifty years before. It was a solitary, sheltered little journey to the War Office and for that reason, Lincoln was fond of it.

As he moved deliberately along the path, he became vaguely conscious that he had passed some one. He turned. In the dim portico light, one of the two infantry sentinels was standing at present arms and would be obliged to stand there until the President returned his salute. This was one of Lincoln's many reasons for disliking the guardianship Stanton recently had forced on him. He sighed, then smiled and taking off his hat bowed to the soldier. The soldier returned the smile and Lincoln continued his journey.

The sentinels by Lincoln's orders were not permitted to patrol beyond the actual line of the White House structure. So it was simple for him to elude detection, to slip into Adams' Grove, to cross the grove, leap the fence and skirt Lafayette Square without any one's taking alarm. Not that his desire was to do anything less innocuous than to cover alone the three miles that led to his summer residence in the grounds of the Soldiers' Home. He sometimes thought that being buried alive could be no worse than to live as he did, forever under view. Frequently, he felt suffocated by it, half maddened.

He covered the three miles rapidly and when he reached the cottage where Mrs. Lincoln and Tad were waiting for him, he silenced his wife's reproaches for coming alone by remarking that he'd eaten nothing since breakfast. While Mary was giving rapid orders for a tray supper, he sat on the little front porch, rocking gently and smiling to himself. He felt better.

He insisted on having the tray on his knees with only the light from the parlor window to see by and was eating blackberries and cream when the Presidential carriage, with its cavalry escort, swept furiously up the driveway.

A man with a black chin beard and silver-rimmed spectacles sprang out of the barouche and rushed up the steps. The light turned the white streak in his whiskers to a golden ribbon.

"Hello, Mr. Stanton! Has Sheridan caught Early?" Lincoln grinned at his caller.

The Secretary of War stood speechless, for a moment. He was hatless and wore a black alpaca office coat. His eyes behind his glasses were furious.

"By God, Lincoln! Is it nothing to you that you've taken ten years from my life? How did you get here?"

Mary Lincoln, who had been walking through the garden, gathered up her billowing black muslin skirts and scurried up the steps. She was very pretty. Her great blue eyes with lashes that an actress might have envied would have given her beauty even had she not been possessed of a fine blonde skin and of dimples that flashed in her round cheeks when she spoke.

She interrupted her husband's apology. "You really mustn't speak so to Mr. Lincoln!" she protested. "You turn your care of him into mere vindictiveness, Mr. Stanton."

"I'm sorry you don't like my manners, madam," roared Stanton, "but I know no other way to affect him. The times never were so malignant for your husband! There are thousands of people North and South who would rather see him murdered than re-elected."

Mary, suddenly white, turned on the President. "He's right! How could you do this, Mr. Lincoln? Was it fair to me or our children since you won't recognize what you owe to the country?"

Lincoln looked at the Secretary of War reproachfully. "See what you've done, Mr. Stanton?—brought war into my peaceful home." He showed his fine white teeth in a grin.

Stanton tugged at his beard and his lips twitched. "If your wife will agree to discipline you, I can retire with a relieved mind!" he exclaimed. "I always have said I wish Mrs. Lincoln were one of my generals. The war would have ended in six weeks if I'd had a few fighters like her."

Mary raised her eyebrows. "If that's your idea of a compliment, Mr. Secretary—"

"Help!" ejaculated Stanton, backing down the steps. "I've got to get back at once, Mr. Lincoln. I'll borrow this vehicle, if you don't mind. I leave him to you for correction, Mrs. Lincoln. Don't spare him!"

He jumped into the barouche and was instantly whirled down the avenue in a cloud of dust. The cavalry escort withdrew to its position for the night.

Mary Lincoln watched the men maneuver and said in a satisfied voice, "At least you're safe for twelve hours."

"You're getting a mania on the subject, Mary," said Lincoln, pulling her little hand within his arm. "Let's take a walk in the garden."

"We're going to stay right on this porch," she exclaimed, freeing her hand to draw an envelope from her skirt pocket. "Look at that!"

The President looked. Within the envelope was a card on which a picture of Lincoln had been pasted. Some one had drawn a rope around his neck and a few clever touches had put into the face the agony of strangulation. Crimson ink made a horrible and suggestive splotch on the breast.

Mary gave a long-drawn sob. "That was on my desk, this morning! Abra'm, it *kills* me to see these things. And on the top of this you run away from protection just as Bob used to when he was a baby! Just that childishly! The anxiety is turning my brain!"

For a moment Lincoln saw red. "Good God!" he shouted. "What's that mail clerk doing to let such a thing get by him! Why should *you* receive that thing?"

"It's better for me than for you!" Mary laid her head wearily against his arm.

"Nothing of the sort! Nothing of the sort! They don't bother me in the least! But why any one should want to torture *you*—that mail clerk will have to go! He's a fool!" dashing the picture to the floor.

Mary was quick to follow her advantage. "Promise me never to come out here alone again!"

He looked down at her and his charming smile replaced the indignation on his lips. "I'll promise, if you'll agree not to let these maunderings of diseased minds upset you."

"I promise," she whispered with quivering chin.

Then they went into the house together.

The following morning Lincoln took the offensive photograph with him to the War Office, and while waiting for Stanton to come in, he showed it to Major Eckert, the Superintendent of the military telegraph. Eckert winced as he gazed at the horror. He was a powerfully built man of about forty, with a handsome smooth-shaven face of extraordinary intelligence. He was directly responsible to the Secretary of War who had made himself absolute czar of all military telegraphic communications. Even the President received no messages that did not pass through Stanton's hands. It was at times a most exasperating arrangement but on the whole a wise one, Lincoln felt, and so he acquiesced to it. Major Eckert, as Superintendent, had in many aspects the most confidential position in the entire war-service. It was no less difficult because of Stanton's unequable temper. But the Secretary had as much confidence in his Superintendent as he had in any human being and Lincoln trusted Eckert, completely, and liked him.

"Major," he said, "I don't see how any human being could be vile enough to send such a thing to a man's wife, do you?"

Eckert's clean-cut jaw set stiffly. "Yes, sir, I do. This war has produced unsounded depths of villainy on both sides. I'm ashamed of my kind." They were standing in the cipher-room and the Major added as he walked toward David Bates' desk, "That fellow whom Chief-of-Detectives Baker planted for Mr. Stanton as confidential messenger between Jacob Thompson in Montreal and the powers-that-be in Richmond has already justified our confidence. He notified us day before yesterday that Thompson was going to send some of his henchmen to take our lone-lorn war boat out there on the Great Lakes."

"The steamer *Michigan!*" exclaimed Lincoln.

"Yes, sir," nodded Eckert. "But we telegraphed at once to Detroit headquarters and told them to warn the *Michigan*. A fellow named John Beall had the job in charge for Thompson. He gathered up about a score of trusty souls and they boarded the merchant-steamer *Philo Parsons* as passengers, yesterday. It plies between Detroit and Sandusky. They easily took the old tub from the crew, then in true pirate fashion they sailed up to another merchant boat, took off her passengers and sunk her. Next they headed for the steamer *Michigan* in Sandusky Bay but when they saw the *Michigan* was cleared for action, they turned tail and paddled for Canada and actually got there safely. There was no one killed."

Lincoln laughed heartily. "Well, I suppose that was a defensible expedition under the rules of warfare! You must thank our detective friend for me. Do you know him?"

"Not personally but we shall, later. He will pass through here with his letters and we may copy them if we wish. They'll be in code but we've yet to meet a cipher our chaps have been floored by." He waved a proud hand at the young cipher-men, hard at work at their desks.

Lincoln followed Eckert's glance admiringly as he remarked, "Mr. Stanton says he wouldn't exchange his cipher-men for the whole of the Union army and I don't know but what he's right. I want to see that messenger, Major, first time he turns up. What's his name?"

Eckert whispered, "He has only a number here, Number Seven. But his name is Richard Montgomery. He's highly intelligent and adroit and certainly as brave as they make 'em."

"Must be," agreed the President, going on into Stanton's room.

It was not many days after this conversation that the towns along the Canadian border were thrown into panic by an attack on St. Albans, Vermont, a village about fifteen miles from the frontier. On October 19th Confederate Lieutenant Young and twenty-five other Confederate soldiers, not in uniform, rode upon the town and attempted to burn it. They used a chemical preparation, however, which failed of its purpose in any wholesale way. Shouting that they were Confederate soldiers getting even for Sheridan's campaign in the Shenandoah Valley, the party turned the peaceful town into a riot. They robbed the three banks of some $200,000 and seized all the horses to be found. They killed one citizen and wounded another and then galloped off. A posse started in pursuit and with the help of the Canadian police arrested Young and twelve others. They were thrust into a Canadian jail.

The telegraphic news of the arrest of the raiders had scarcely reached the War Office and Lincoln and Stanton were holding council on it when Major Eckert broke in on them with word that Number Seven had come in. Stanton ordered him to appear at once.

There sauntered into the room a short, slender man of indeterminate age and of most ordinary type; brownish whiskers, a brownish sack suit and cloak. Only his eyes, which were deep gray or black, Lincoln could not be sure which color predominated, told of a personality that must have been anything but ordinary.

The spy bowed and said, quietly, "I tried to get word to you about St. Albans, Mr. Stanton, but I learned of it too late."

"More of Jacob Thompson, eh?" ejaculated Stanton. He suddenly lifted a tiny bottle from his desk and shook a few drops of its contents on his beard. The odor of eau-de-cologne filled the room.

Lincoln, repressing a smile, watched the effect of this familiar rite on

Number Seven. Not a muscle of the man's face changed. Poor old Stanton must be much perturbed. He only resorted to eau-de-cologne when his nerve was shaken.

"Not Jacob Thompson directly, sir," answered Montgomery. "At least, one of the other commissioners, Clement C. Clay told me that the scheme was all Young's own. He had authorization from the Confederate Secretary of War to organize a small company in Canada for special service. Mr. Clay says he, himself, gave Young $400 for this particular expedition and added his personal authorization for the attack."

"Now laugh at that, Mr. Lincoln!" snarled Stanton.

But the President only sighed. "What can those fellows at Richmond think to gain by such foolishness!"

"Foolishness!" Stanton stared hopelessly at the President and turned to Number Seven. "Do you know of further plans of this dastardly nature?"

"Yes, sir, Rochester and Buffalo are to be raided, though perhaps the jailing of Young may head that off."

"I'll head it off, Young in jail or out," ejaculated Stanton. He called in his secretary and dictated several telegrams, while Lincoln sat on the old sofa ruminating on the general cussedness of human nature but not deeply disturbed by either Clay's or Thompson's efforts, which he was convinced could do no real harm. Number Seven standing at the end of Stanton's tall desk made entries in a notebook.

Major Eckert came in as Stanton's secretary went out. "We've deciphered this letter, Mr. Lincoln."

"Read it to us," said the President.

It was a letter from Clement C. Clay to Judah P. Benjamin giving a detailed account of the circumstances of the St. Albans raid. He said that Lieutenant Young was well known to him, that Young's heart was in the Southern cause and that in burning and robbing St. Albans, he had acted in accordance with Clay's instructions. But for the aid of Young and his associates in their pending trial, he begged for additional documents showing that they acted under the authority of the Confederate States government. He had, of course, he said, such authority, "but it should be more explicit as regards the particular acts complained of. When Young proposed passing through New England burning some towns and robbing them of whatever he could convert to the use of the Confederate government, I approved as justifiable retaliation—. All that a large portion of the Northern people especially in the Northwest want to resist the oppressions of the despotism at Washington is a leader. They are ripe for resistance and it may come soon after the Presidential election. No people of Anglo-Saxon blood can long endure the usurpations and tyrannies of Lincoln."

"We ought to be able to keep the original of that letter," said Lincoln. "If Canada is going to permit armed forces to be raised on her soil and these forces to invade our territory, it can be taken as a gross example of non-neutrality. This letter, if endorsed by Davis, will be first-class evidence."

Stanton nodded. "But we mustn't give Montgomery away. He's too valuable a man."

"Why don't you catch me, and put me in prison, sir?" suggested Number Seven, coolly, "and after you've robbed me of my papers, let me escape."

"It must be done very carefully." Stanton grasped at the suggestion eagerly. "We'll set Baker after you but not even your jailors must know. How you'll manage the escape, I can't see."

"You could—" began Eckert.

"Better leave the escape end to me," suggested Number Seven, "the more sincere it is, the better."

"Return the papers, Major," ordered Stanton.

The spy glanced at the clock. "I'll be at Surrattsville, Maryland, in the tavern, this morning." He buttoned his cloak.

Lincoln shook hands with him. "My hat is off to you, sir."

"Thank you, Mr. President," said the man, simply, and he followed Eckert from the room.

CHAPTER III

MUDDLEHEAD

THE next day but one, Mary called her husband's attention to an item in a Washington paper. A suspected spy, it said, had escaped early in the night from the Old Capitol Prison. He had knocked down a guard, gagged and bound him and had used the guard's keys. The alarm had been given almost instantly and the spy had been shot at as he ran across the yard into the tree-grown street. He had been wounded as a splotch of blood showed where he had fallen. But even at that the man had escaped in some one's carriage.

Lincoln gave a chuckle. "By jings, what a man!"

Mary looked at him disgustedly. "Sometimes, Abra'm, I actually wonder whether you know there's a war going on in this country or not. That man was a *spy*."

"A *suspected* spy, my dear," said Lincoln, apologetically. Then he laughed, delightedly, and left the breakfast table before Mary could call him further to account.

He did not see Number Seven on his return trip from Richmond. Charles Dana, Assistant Secretary of War, however, told him that the spy had been wounded in the arm. It was a most realistic escape! Dana also showed Lincoln the de-coded copy of a letter from Jefferson Davis to Jacob Thompson. "—there is yet time to colonize many voters before Nov. 8. A blow will shortly be stricken here. It is not quite time. General Longstreet is to attack Sheridan without delay and then move north as far as practicable toward unprotected points.—He will endeavor to assist the Republicans in collecting their ballots. Be watchful and assist him."

The President gave the letter back to Dana. "Looks as if Jeff was as worried about my election as I am!"

"Mr. Stanton's comment was that Davis is an unmitigated scoundrel!" smiled the Assistant Secretary of War. "One can't imagine you stooping to such tricks as Davis has, Mr. Lincoln."

"Well," replied Lincoln, mildly, "I'm not as desperate about Jeff as he is about me!"

"You mustn't ignore the menace in this, sir," protested Dana. "Remember there are 100,000 Sons of Liberty in Indiana alone bent on defeating you by any method and the North by any treachery."

"Nothing could make me believe that 100,000 Democrats were disloyal to the North, no matter how they hate me," was Lincoln's reply vehemently given.

He could not bring himself to take the Rebels' war behind the Union lines too bitterly, however technically outlawed were their methods; not when their abortive efforts were consonant with Sheridan's dreadful march through Virginia. That Jacob Thompson and Company were not discouraged by the failure of their efforts to date was proved a day or so after the President's conversation with Dana when Seward showed him two letters he had received. One was from the Federal consul at Halifax, Nova Scotia, stating that Secessionists in that city were asserting secretly that plans had been completed for setting fire to the chief cities of the North on election day. The letter had been turned over to Stanton and he at once had set his telegraph operators at work sending warnings to the civil and military authorities from the Atlantic to the Pacific.

The other letter concerned the routine business of the Adjutant-General of New York. The only bite in its otherwise dull contents was in the post-script. "There is reason to believe that Lincoln will be assassinated soon."

Stanton was present when Lincoln read the missives. Under the Secretary's stern eye, the President admitted that the communications were disturbing. But, he insisted, the country's and his own welfare were in the best human hands obtainable, namely those of Edwin M. Stanton. He therefore refused to worry. Stanton actually blushed, forgot his proposed threats and the session ended in his listening with patience not untinged by enjoyment to a long reading from Orpheus Kerr.

Just before election day, Number Seven slipped into Washington and told Eckert and Stanton that the commissioners were having trouble with the chemical formula for setting the fires and that the incendiary attack had been put off until Thanksgiving week.

Extraordinary precautions were taken to prevent violence on election day, November 8, and it passed with, all things considered, astounding orderliness.

After all, God was, as Lincoln believed, on the side of the Union and he was re-elected.

On November 9, John Wilkes Booth registered at the National Hotel on Pennsylvania Avenue and was as usual, given the best room in the house. He had no engagement to play in Washington, Wilkes told the clerk who knew him well and was one of his ardent admirers. He was, said the actor, planning a little vacation trip across the Eastern Branch of the Potomac in lower Maryland. The young actor was very restless. He took a drink or two and played a few frames of pool, then sauntered out onto the Avenue.

The November night was raw but the street was crowded. Ambulances and army transport teams rattled and banged over the muddy, rutted paving. Officers, whether on business or not, galloped at breakneck speed. Wounded soldiers moved up and down the sidewalks, loitering in the bright lights of saloons and oyster houses. Women of the streets plied their trade brazenly.

Immorality and brutality were at flood height in Washington. One of the bureaus of the Treasury Department had just been cleared of the harlots whom the bureau chief had been employing as clerks. On election day, a well-known Senator had been knocked down not far from where Booth was standing by a woman he had outraged. Drunkenness in Congress was a common occurrence. Cheating the Government was so prevalent that Lincoln despaired of preventing it and Secretary Stanton's gallant fight against army corruption far outweighed in the President's mind any smallnesses of the War Secretary's character.

Wilkes Booth strolled or stopped to gaze as the whim took him. He wore a soft white hat set rakishly on the side of his handsome head, a black cape was flung Spanish fashion across his chest and over his shoulder. He was the target not only of the invitations of prostitutes and of the jibes of the drunk, but of the delighted attentions of admirers, men and women who shook his hand eagerly and asked him when he was to play and what.

To all the latter he made the same graceful bow and the same reply in a carefully modulated voice: "I'm in quest of relaxation now. A little later, Hamlet and Mark Antony. The date—not yet!"

Toward the White House end of the Avenue a marching brass band and a long procession of citizens carrying kerosene torches and transparencies shoved all other pedestrians to the walls or the gutter. Wilkes Booth joined the tail of the parade. Constantly growing, the line was over a thousand strong by the time the north gates of the White House were reached. The Cavalry Guards stationed at either post made no effort to question or control the procession. Indeed, it was well known that Lincoln would not suffer them to challenge any peaceable persons who sought to enter the grounds. The beautiful pile of the Executive Mansion was dim against the sky. Some of the upper windows were lighted but the lower floor was in darkness save for the gas lamp which threw up in glowing relief the chaste loveliness of the columns upholding the roof of the front portico. The crowd packed itself on the lawn before this colonnade and began to shout, "Lincoln! We want you, Lincoln!"

Wilkes Booth, silent but very observant, worked his way to the inner pillars of the entrance. Here stood two sentries and a doorman. Several persons ran up the steps and entered the hall but a sudden cry, "There he is! There's Father Abraham!" brought them back. Booth returned with them to the outer columns and followed the upward gaze of the crowd. At the second story window above the main door appeared the tall, familiar figure, the quiet face lighted by a candle in the hands of eleven-year-old Tad Lincoln.

Booth decidedly did not wish to hear the President's speech. And anyhow, he had other business. He bit his nails and started on a quiet prowl. The sentry walking slowly in the shadow of the west wing did not challenge the actor, though he saw him leave the brick path and cross the lawn in the direction of Adams' Grove of walnuts. He was facing the portico when Wilkes emerged from the wood, and rounded the brick wall near the turnstile and so Booth investigated the vegetable garden, unmolested, though he flashed a dark lantern from parsnip and turnip heap to grape and peach growing thick against the wall.

It was quite feasible, the actor decided, to hoist a man over this wall from the path and to carry him thence across the grounds southwest to 17th Street. A house must be found in the lonely marsh-reaches of 17th Street with proper access to the Potomac. Thinking deeply, Wilkes returned to the front lawn and as he worked his way back through the crowd he listened reluctantly to that deliberate voice which in accent still was haunted by its Kentucky beginnings.

"—While deeply grateful for this mark of their confidence in me, if I know my heart, my gratitude is free from any trace of personal triumph. It is no pleasure to me to triumph over any one. But I give thanks to the Almighty for this evidence of the people's resolution to stand by free government and the rights of humanity."

Lincoln bowed and Tad, with a grin, blew out the candle. The band struck up "The Star-Spangled Banner" and the crowd, cheering and huzzaing, dispersed.

Back in his room at the hotel, Wilkes lighted an excellent cigar and poured out a stiff drink of brandy. Then he began to study a map of Washington and of that portion of Maryland which lay south of the city, separated from it by the Eastern Branch. After an hour at this he rose and walking slowly up and down the room began to declaim with faultless elocution:

> "Why, man, he doth bestride the narrow world
> Like a Colossus, and we petty men
> Walk under his huge legs and peep about
> To find ourselves dishonorable graves."

Then he stood for a long time before the mirror staring at his own beautiful reflection.

The next morning after a late breakfast, he strolled over to a livery stable on 6th Street and had a talk with the owner. He wanted to buy a couple of horses, he explained, which he could use either for driving or riding.

"Then you won't get nothin' much of neither," was the liveryman's comment. He was a red-headed man with a snaggle tooth which wiggled as he chewed and spat. "I keep my horses to one job or the other. If you want a family horse of that kind you'd get it over in Maryland. I hear there's a lot of Secesh folks hiding good horseflesh. They might part to you."

"What makes you say that, Pete?" demanded Wilkes, quickly.

"I reckon I've heard you often enough to realize you'd wheedle a dog to give up his tail if you wanted it."

Booth laughed. "You flatter me, Pete! Where shall I go in Maryland?"

"Oh, cross the Eastern Branch and work south! I don't know a living soul there myself, officially, so that's the best I can do for you."

"I'll try my luck!" Wilkes nodded. "But not to-day. Instead I'll try one of these highly specialized nags of yours and view the dirty city of Washington from its back."

He was a good judge of horseflesh and after going over the stable he rode forth on a gay little bay mare who was all muscle and good will.

Late in the afternoon he located just the dwelling for his needs. It was known as the Van Ness house, built in 1820 and now deserted. It stood on 17th Street, alone, and was accessible to a lonely part of the Potomac. A story and a half brick house, it had one marked peculiarity. The partition walls were of brick and those of the first floor were continued in the cellar, dividing the under portion of the dwelling into several unlighted cells. Nothing could have suited Wilkes more completely. He rode back to the livery stable, humming in the twilight, and gave orders for a horse on which to ride into lower Maryland the next day.

That night he again followed a rejoicing mob to the White House and continued his investigations of the west end of the twenty acres that comprised the grounds. And again he heard that thoughtful slow voice from the upper window giving to the milling crowd portions of the philosophy wrought in his soul by the exquisite pains of his experiences.

"The strife of the election is but human nature applied to the facts of the case. What has occurred in this case must ever occur in similar cases. Human nature will not change. In any great national trial we shall have as weak and as strong, as silly and as wise, as bad and as good! Let us then study these as incidents to learn wisdom from and none of them as wrongs to be revenged—"

Booth grinned sardonically. "The man's uneasy," he said aloud.

He went directly to bed from the White House for he planned an early start next day.

He had not needed Pete's suggestions as regarded lower Maryland. He had come down from Canada armed with a letter from Thompson to a certain Dr. Queen near Bryantown, about thirty miles south of Washington.

He reached Queen's place late in the afternoon. The doctor and his family looked the actor over and rose at once to his charm. They asked him to stay over Sunday while he searched for the horses and the farm he proposed to buy. Wilkes was known even in this quiet back-country. That evening he intrigued the Queens still further with sleight-of-hand tricks and recitations from Shakespeare. And on Sunday he went to church with them.

After service, at the church gate, where the neighborhood congregated for the week's gossip, Wilkes was introduced to Dr. Samuel Mudd. Mudd was a tall, slender man of thirty-five with fine ascetic features, keen blue eyes and sandy hair. He greeted Booth with grave courtesy and when Queen observed that the actor had brought a letter from Canada, Mudd asked,

"How can I serve you, sir?"

"By telling me where I can buy a horse broken both to saddle and harness, yet retains its spirit," replied Wilkes instantly.

Dr. Mudd pulled thoughtfully at his reddish mustache. "I think my neighbor, Mr. Gardiner, has such an animal," he said at last. "If you'd care to ride to my place this evening, I'll take you to him."

Wilkes bowed and replaced his soft black hat. Dr. Mudd returned the bow and replaced a shining stove pipe.

That evening, Wilkes rode through the gray, crisp twilight along the red clay roads to Mudd's house. It was a comfortable white frame farm dwelling, set in brown fields and surrounded by a split rail fence. Mrs. Mudd had cleared up the supper when he arrived but in spite of his protest she prepared a fresh meal. After supper, he sat with the family talking brilliantly of his acting career. It was not until all the others had gone to bed that he drew his chair close to the doctor's and began really to tell his tale.

He felt that he was not at his most debonair with Mudd. The sensitiveness to opinion begot by his extreme egotism, told him that the doctor did not like him. Why, Wilkes couldn't imagine. He set to work to win this quiet, keen gentleman.

First, he gave the preamble which he had used with Sam Arnold and Mike O'Laughlin. Leaning forward with the wood fire lighting his beautiful, expressive face or pacing the floor, big white fingers running through his hair, he made his declaration of faith in the Confederate cause.

When he paused, Dr. Mudd threw another stick of wood on the coals. "Very pretty, my boy!" he remarked, dryly. "Now to get down to cases, what do you want of me?"

Wilkes bit his lip and had more than half a thought of walking out of the house. But he needed Mudd, so he sat down again and stretched his booted legs to the fire, saying coldly, "I suppose you are at one with all of us in seeing that Abe Lincoln is the backbone of Union solidarity?"

"Of what solidarity there is, yes," eyeing the actor keenly.

"I propose to kidnap Abe Lincoln, take him to Richmond and turn him over to President Davis as the perfect means of giving us the victory."

"Will Davis accept him?" demanded Mudd, bluntly.

"Will he *not*? Certainly, he will accept him. If he has any qualms, Secretary Benjamin will quiet them. I'm going on Jacob Thompson's authority."

Dr. Mudd, with nervous fingers on the arms of his chair, frowned into the fire. After a long moment he said, "Kidnaping is a dirty, dishonorable business."

Wilkes' face went purple. "Is it as dishonorable as the acts which brought this war on our beloved country?" he shouted. "Could any act known to history outside of the crucifixion be as filthy as Abe Lincoln's Emancipation Proclamation? Come, doctor, let's be frank. My honor's as dear to me as any other Southerner's. But what does personal honor weigh against the ending of this war? That's what I shall do, sir, make an end of bloodshed in our lovely land.

> "No more shall trenching warfare channel her fields
>   Nor bruise her flowerets with the armed hoofs
>   Of hostile paces,—"

The doctor jerked his shoulders impatiently. "Oh, I'll grant your intimacy with Henry IV as well as an honorable purpose! Go on and give me details."

Wilkes outlined the three plans clearly and succinctly. Mudd, when he had finished, made a grimace of distaste. "Because the North is bestial is no reason we should be. But—"

"What is there bestial in my plan?" cried Booth. "I shall give old Abe every care. Not a hair of his gorilla head shall be harmed, I'll make his way sweet with myrrh and anoint him with attar of roses if it'll ease your scruples, sir."

"Don't be more melodramatic than you can help. Keep cool, Booth," warned Mudd, "or you'll defeat yourself. A conspirator must be ice. I suppose your two problems in lower Maryland are to find the route and the proper people. I will take you to Gardiner to-morrow. You can get a horse from him. Tell him you wish to look at farms further south. While you've been talking, I've been thinking of a family at Surrattsville. The father was a stout Unionist but he died a year or so ago and Mrs. Surratt and her son have dared avow to those of us in the know, their equally stout Southern loyalty. They own the tavern and are a headquarters for Confederate loyalists hereabouts. John Surratt, the son, is a messenger for the Richmond government and must have a wonderful knowledge of the country-side between Washington and Richmond. I don't know whether he's at home or not but I'll make inquiries."

He sat staring at the fire, thinking, Wilkes supposed, of ways and means of helping him. But not so. Mudd suddenly looked up to say, "It's an extremely risky and unsavory business and I don't like it. Let's go to bed."

Booth stared at him in silence and in silence followed him upstairs to the guest-room.

He bought a bay horse with one eye from Gardiner, the next day, and went to Surrattsville which is about thirty miles south of Washington. It was a rough, desolate hamlet but the tavern was a comfortable-looking place and Booth riding up to the door decided to spend several days there. But the decision was immediately modified for the man at the bar told him that Mrs. Surratt had just leased the place to him and had gone to Washington to live. Wilkes sat down thoughtfully with a bottle of brandy. The last three days had taught him that it was going to take a great deal more time than he had realized to mature his plans and, even were they complete, the frightful condition of the roads must prohibit any immediate attempts at abduction. Granted that through young Surratt he'd be able to place relays of fast horses along a carefully selected route, the mud would practically prohibit their use for weeks to come. He had believed that by the middle of November, he would have Lincoln imprisoned in Richmond. He now saw that this was hopeless. He decided to spend only the night here, then return to Washington and try to locate the Surratts. Mudd must be beguiled into giving him the right kind of an introduction. Patience! Patience! Abe Lincoln's sort of patience. And on this thought he slept. Nor was he troubled by evil dreams.

CHAPTER IV

W HEN Booth, however, reached the National Hotel late the next night, he found a letter which, once more, unsettled his mind. The letter was from his brother, Edwin. Edwin was going to give a benefit performance of "Julius Cæsar" to help raise money to erect a statue of Shakespeare in Central Park, New York. The three Booth brothers, he wrote, were to take part. Edwin would play Cæsar, Junius would play Cassius and Wilkes would play Mark Antony. Their mother would be in the audience. What a moment for a mother! thought Wilkes. The play was to be given on November 25. So on November 15, Wilkes went up to New York.

Major-General Dix, commanding the department of the East, had been incredulous from the first about Thompson's incendiary plot and so had the city's mayor. Both had tried and failed to track the conspirators and both finally laughed at Stanton's fears and warnings. After two weeks of excited orderings and warnings by mail and telegraph, the Secretary, thoroughly exasperated, sent Major Eckert to New York with orders to "throw the fear of God into the damn' fools."

Eckert reached New York late Thanksgiving evening and the next morning set about his difficult task. But General Dix and the Mayor were overworked and overstrained and utterly fed up on false alarms. They declared that they could handle any average riot but that vague notices hinting of fires yet to be set must be ignored. How could the city be better guarded than it already was against fires? If Stanton had told them *where* the fires were to be started, they would guarantee to put out the flames. Eckert understood their position and was not unsympathetic. But he knew Richard Montgomery, therefore he was in an advantageous position. One who had heard Number Seven's colorless recital must believe it. He told the two officials so.

"Yes! Yes! No doubt!" shouted the much-hectored Dix. "But where, where in this city of half-a-million-or-I-don't-know-how-many-buildings are these devilish fires to be set?"

Utterly baffled, Eckert left the City Hall where the conference had taken place. It was drawing toward twilight. His first impulse was to return to Washington to learn if by any chance Number Seven had turned up with further details. Then with a contraction of his heart, he realized that Thanksgiving week was half spent and that he dare not take time for the trip to the capital. He decided to return to his room at the St. Nicholas Hotel and make Secretary Stanton a full report in cipher, asking for further orders. He boarded a Broadway bus and sat with folded arms, oblivious to his surroundings, a black cloud of dread befogging his keen mind. Sherman's march was no such horror as this threatened to be, he told himself. Sherman was not putting the torch to dwellings filled with unsuspecting men, women and children.

He moistened his lips and suddenly becoming conscious of some one's gaze, looked up. Opposite him sat a clean-shaven, shabby man, who seemed to be actually ill, he was so pale, so haggard. At first glance he seemed to be an utter stranger to Major Eckert, then something familiar about the fine, dark eyes pierced through the fog of apprehension. He returned the man's anguished stare and then recognized him. It was Number Seven!

Neither man made the slightest gesture of recognition. But when, a moment later, Eckert left the bus, Montgomery followed him. They entered the hotel, the spy following the Major to his room. Here Eckert locked the door, closed the window curtains and lighted a lamp, while Montgomery sank exhausted into a chair and began to speak.

"I only found it out last night and dared not wire. There was no time to use the newspaper columns. I was in despair until I saw you—To-night at ten o'clock the fires will be started. The hotels are—get paper, Eckert, —there are twelve of them." In a weak voice he recited the names of the city's best known hotels, adding Barnum's Museum, and several theaters and other places of amusement with a long list of public buildings. "They're to use Greek fire. In the hotels they will take rooms, pile up the furniture and at exactly ten, squirt on the sulphur and phosphorus, lock the doors and disappear. In the theaters they'll work beneath the stage. In the public buildings, clockwork. In the—" He toppled over in a faint.

Eckert sprang to his aid with his brandy flask and in a moment Montgomery sat up to say, apologetically, "I've neither eaten nor slept for forty-eight hours. All I need is a little food."

The Major rang the bell and holding the door so that the spy could not be seen, he ordered a bountiful meal. While he waited for its arrival, he finished setting down Montgomery's facts and when he had received the tray at the door, he left the spy to his food and rushed out into the night. There were four hours in which to prepare for the flames.

With the list flung at them by Eckert, General Dix and the Mayor rose magnificently to the emergency and when, an hour later, the Major returned to his hotel, the buildings threatened were already policed and fire apparatus in experienced hands was waiting for the clock to strike ten. Richard Montgomery had disappeared.

The play of "Julius Cæsar" had progressed to Cæsar's death when a shrill cry of "Fire!" broke in on Mark Antony's oration. Instantly the audience was in an uproar. A sudden burst of smoke swept through the windows. Edwin Booth lying in Cæsar's last poignant sleep, sprang to his feet and striding to the footlights, sent his magnificent, magic voice to the outermost doors of the theater, hushing the outcries, stilling the panic. As the people paused to listen, a policeman walked up the aisle, toward the orchestra-pit, proclaiming that the fire was in the adjacent building, that it was under control and that there was no danger to the theater. And so the threatened catastrophe was checked.

Throughout the city, the story of the incendiary attack was much the same. Soldiers, police and firemen by the hundreds met flame and fear as they were born and although in spite of their efforts considerable dollar damage was done, no human life was lost. The net effect of the attempt was to turn many erstwhile friends of the Confederacy to contemptuous enemies.

Major Eckert, feeling a decade or two younger, set out for Washington on the following afternoon. He was on a Cortlandt steam ferry, crossing to his train in New Jersey when he picked up an envelope, unsealed, soiled and unaddressed. Moving to the prow of the boat where he could find solitude, Eckert examined the contents of the envelope. He was dumb-founded to discover first a photograph of Lincoln, with a noose around his neck, a distorted face and red inkspots on the breast. It was a precise duplicate of the card which Mrs. Lincoln had received. As if this strange coincidence were not enough, there accompanied the picture a letter con-taining minute directions for the bearer's part in the burning of New York, also referring to a plot to kidnap the President. There was no name used.

Eckert hid his find in his pocket and sauntered through the boat. It was fairly well filled but he could see no evidence that any of the pas-sengers was conscious of having lost something. The discovery was so im-portant that instead of taking his train, he returned with the boat to New York. He at once sought the headquarters of the military detective police and left the envelope with them after exacting a promise that they would within the week, send it to Secretary Stanton. Eckert had great faith in Stanton's fertility of suggestion in the delicate art of sleuthing!

Wilkes Booth had heard in Montreal of the schemes to fire New York but absorbed in his own schemes he had failed to think of the plan as a source of danger to those he loved. He was horrified at the thought of his mother sitting proudly and placidly in the Winter Garden while fire swept against the very walls. It was, he told himself, another example of what such despotism as Lincoln's could bring a desperate people. More than ever he felt his duty to be manifest.

There was only one man in New York to whom Wilkes hinted of his secret. This was his friend Samuel Chester, an actor in Edwin's company. Wilkes told Chester that he was not going to act in the North any more.

"I've taken my wardrobe to Canada and from there, I'll take ship and run the blockade into Charleston. I've got a big speculation with a lot of risk but a lot of money in it. Don't you want to come in?"

"If it requires money," replied Chester, "I don't. And I've got a family so don't expect me to take risks."

"I'll supply the money!" Wilkes took out his bill case.

"Don't show off, Johnny Wilkes," grinned Chester. "I won't be pa-tronized."

"Oh, go to the devil!" grunted Wilkes and turned on his heel. After all, he'd take no one else on until he'd met the Surratts.

He found himself feeling a little sentimental about his old New York friends as the Christmas season approached. They all loved him so! They were so proud of him! It was a pity to think that shortly they'd all be hating him. The thought of this hurt his vanity. If only they could be made to understand, surely they'd not judge him harshly. He could say nothing now, of course. But he could write, afterward. Or he could write now and leave the letter with some one to be opened when old Abe should be safely deposited in Richmond.

He settled down in Edwin's beautiful library one morning about a week after Thanksgiving and wrote a letter embodying all the reasons which had proved efficacious with Arnold, O'Laughlin and Mudd. It required hours of writing and re-writing before he had completed the task to his own satisfaction. Then he deposited the letter with his brother-in-law, to be opened only when Wilkes gave him permission to do so. This task completed, he began his preparations for returning to Washington although he promised his mother to be back in New York for Christmas.

The attempted burning of New York appealed to the President only as another example of what war can do to human decency. War was the breakdown of moral law and if General Sherman, that upright, kindly father of a family, could put the torch to Georgia, driving whole towns into the swamps, one couldn't be too nice in judging Jacob Thompson. He was quite willing to admit that this war behind the lines was illegal according to the laws of civilized nations, that the citizens of the North had not turned traitor and were not in the same class as the Secessionists and yet he was not willing to agree that, if they identified the men who had done the dirty work, they should be hanged. He voiced this unwillingness to Stanton on the evening of the day on which Wilkes Booth had turned his mad letter over to his brother-in-law.

"If—*if* we can identify!" grunted Stanton. "You forget Number Seven, sir!"

Lincoln who was drooping over the end of the Secretary's desk straightened up with interest. "So he's turned up again! Where is he?"

"Came and went while you were visiting hospitals this afternoon," replied Stanton. "Here's the trophy of his most recent hunt."

Lincoln put on his spectacles and took the de-coded letter. It was from Jacob Thompson to Judah P. Benjamin, the Confederate Secretary of State, dated December 3, 1864.

". . . I have relaxed no efforts to carry out the objects which the Government had in sending me here. Money has been advanced to Mr. Churchill of Cincinnati to arrange a corps for the purposes of incendiarism in that city. I advanced money to a Mr. Minor Major, $2,000 in Federal currency and soon after several boats were burned in St. Louis, involving an immense loss of property to the enemy. Having nothing else on hand, Col. Martin expressed a desire to burn New York City. He was allowed to do so, and a most daring attempt has been made to fire that city but this reliance on Greek fire proved a misfortune. It cannot be relied on as an agent in such work. I have no faith in it and no attempt shall be made hereafter under my direction with any such material. During my stay in Canada a great amount of property has been destroyed by fire. . . . Should claims be passed at the War Office for this kind of work not one dollar should be advanced until parties concerned present proofs. Several parties claim to have done the work at St. Louis, New Orleans, Louisville, Brooklyn, Philadelphia and Cairo . . .

"The nomination of McClellan, followed as it was by divers disclosures, arrests of persons, prominent members, totally demoralized the Sons of Liberty. . . . The vigilance of the Administration, (Federal), its large detective force, the large bounties paid for treachery and the respectable men who have yielded to the temptation, added to the large military force stationed in these States makes organization and preparation almost an impossibility. A large sum of money has been expended in fostering and furthering these operations and now it seems to be of little profit. . . . I infer from your personal in the N. Y. *News* that you wish me to remain here for some time and I obey you. Indeed I have so many papers in my possession which in the hands of the enemy would utterly ruin and destroy very many of the prominent men in the North that a due sense of my obligations to them will force on me the extremest caution in my movements . . . the attempt on New York has produced a great panic which will not subside at their bidding—"

Lincoln laid the shabby missive down and put his glasses back in his vest pocket. "Small potatoes, and few in a hill," was his comment.

"If I can lay hands on Jacob Thompson," said Stanton, "I'll put him in a hell that will roast more than potatoes!"

"I hope this war isn't going to blow out *all* the moral lights in these United and dis-United States," murmured Lincoln. Then he added clearly, "Don't let a desire for retaliation taint your sense of justice, Mr. Stanton—. By the way," with a sly grin, "what are you going to do to the people who planned to kidnap *you*, Brother Stanton?"

Stanton sat down suddenly on the sofa. "Who's blabbed now?" he groaned.

"Hill Lamon told me," replied the President. "Since Hill's come back from the front, he's done nothing but turn up abduction schemes. That pursuit has taken the place of music, the drama, politics, practical jokes and every other side line with which he used to pass the time. What about this young woman who was spying on *you*, Mr. Secretary?"

"Nothing at all! Nothing at all," fumed Stanton. "Still they might have got me, if you hadn't telegraphed me to come back to Washington. You didn't realize you were playing Providence to me! There is a Secession group with headquarters across the Ohio from Steubenville. They've kept a very pretty girl running back and forth with an unsuspecting neighbor of mine in Steubenville, to keep them informed when I made an anonymous visit back home. Neighbor Burgoyne has regular business in West Virginia and supposed the girl was teaching in Ohio. She crossed on the ferry often with him. When I was out there last month I was going to Wheeling with Dr. William Stanton and they were all set for me, thanks to their young lady spy. But you wired for me the day before I made the trip. Detective Baker unearthed the plot two weeks later."

"Why didn't you tell me so's I could return a few of the compliments you've been paying me for alleged carelessness?" grinned Lincoln.

Stanton did not reply for a moment, then he smiled in his turn. "Here's something else I wasn't going to tell you but it's too good to keep—as showing how different things look from one's own side of the fence. A couple of weeks ago a group of preachers, headed by the Rev. Byron Sunderland called on me and suggested that if Jefferson Davis were captured and brought here to the Old Capitol Prison, the war would end. They offered their services personally for the abduction. They were so insistent that I finally sent Colonel W. P. Wood to Richmond to see if the project were feasible. He came back last week and reported that the idea was entirely impracticable. Davis is too well guarded. So we heard no more from—"

It was the President's turn to interrupt. "Good God, Mr. Stanton, don't tell me you countenanced such a plan for an instant!" He brought his fist down on his knee. "You astound me! You shock me, Stanton! You should have thrown those fellows out at the first breath of their suggestion." He rose and stood looking down upon the for-once-abashed Secretary of War. "Nothing that's happened since I've been here has impressed me more painfully than this. Is there no one whom war can't contaminate?"

He banged his tall hat on his head, twisted the gray shawl round his shoulders and walked out.

The following afternoon, Charles Dana, Assistant Secretary of War called on the President. He was a heavy-bearded, serious-looking man whom Lincoln never wearied of reminding that he had been an associate of Horace Greeley, the pacifist.

Dana's eyes were twinkling as he laid some papers on the President's desk. "Mr. Stanton says he's afraid to deliver those in person, sir."

"Don't praise me too highly, Mr. Dana! I've never succeeded in suppressing Stanton for more than five minutes! What are these? Must I read them?"

"General Dix thought they were important enough to rush them down from New York by special messenger. A woman picked up these two letters from the floor of a Third Avenue street car. They were dropped by a very handsome young man, dark and well dressed. The woman reported that as he talked with his companion, he gestured with memorably beautiful white hands. I know you get many threatening letters but one of these is so succinct we hoped it might lead to your being willing to take on a personal bodyguard."

Lincoln sighed and opened the letter and read:

"Dear Louis. The time has come at last that we have all so wished for and upon you everything depends. As it was decided before you left, we were to cast lots. Accordingly we did so and you are to be the Charlotte Corday of the 19th Century . . . Abe must die and now. You can choose your weapons, the cup, the knife, the bullet. The cup failed us once and might again. . . . You know where to find your friends. Your disguises are so perfect and complete that without one knew your face no police telegraphic dispatch could catch you. . . . Remember, he has ten days. . . . Get introduced, congratulate him, listen to his stories. Not many more will the brute tell to earthly friends. Do anything but fail and meet us at the appointed place within the fortnight. . . . (signed) Charles Selby."

Lincoln removed his spectacles and looked from Dana's deeply concerned eyes out the window. He tried to analyze his own feelings. There was no use telling himself that this note didn't twist him a bit. It hurt to know a man could feel thus about him. Must he for the next week or so look on every stranger as a possible assassin? If he must, his usefulness would cease.

"Has this any connection with the photograph and so forth Eckert found?" he asked, after a moment.

"We don't know," replied Dana. Then he added very earnestly, "Mr. Lincoln, won't you take these clews more seriously?"

"No! No, Mr. Dana!" exclaimed the President, "I dare not take this sort of thing seriously. Here, leave it with me, I'll attend to it!"

"And the private guard, Mr. Lincoln?" urged Dana.

"Hill Lamon, since Congress took all the job out of the marshalship of Washington, has nothing on earth to do but to nurse me. He's equal to seven guards. Don't worry, Mr. Dana. And tell dear old Stanton not to worry."

Dana went out with a dissatisfied expression on his face. The President picked up the letter to give it to the flames as he had all other threats. But something unaccountable stayed his hand. He folded the document gingerly and placed it in an envelope on which he wrote one word, *Assassination*. Then he filed it in the bureau which stood between the windows.

It seemed to Lincoln an inscrutable coincidence that as he turned from the bureau, John Hay admitted Benjamin Wade, a bitter radical Congressman, who had been trying for months to oust Lamon from his job as Marshal.

"Mr. President," began Wade, abruptly, "I have come to insist that Ward Hill Lamon must go."

"You *insist?*" asked Lincoln, mildly, eyeing Wade's smooth-shaven, tragic face with interest.

"I *insist*. He's an enemy to the black man and you know it. He—"

Lincoln let his anger take command for a moment. "That'll do, Mr. Wade. Don't come to me with any more knocks at Lamon. I backed him in his enforcing of the fugitive slave law here in Washington. It was the

only way I knew to show you fellows what that law meant, under your
very noses and force you to repeal the iniquitous legislation. This is nothing
but malicious persecution of him by the Abolitionists. You should have
learned a lesson from Greeley. He learned his when the Grand Jury found
a bill of indictment against him for malicious libel of Lamon."

"Are you threatening me, Mr. Lincoln?" demanded Wade.

"Take it as you please," replied the President, sternly. "I understand you,
fully. You fellows at the other end of the Avenue seem determined to
deprive me of every friend I have who's near me and whom I trust. Now
let me tell you, sir, that Hill Lamon has been my friend since he came from
Virginia to Illinois as a lad of nineteen. He was my law partner and rode
the circuit with me. I *know* him, I trust him and I love him. He's the most
unselfish man I know. He's discreet and he's the most desperate man in a
fight I ever saw. He's my friend and I'm his, and as long as I have these
great responsibilities on me, I intend to insist on his being with me. I'll
stick by him at all hazards. You can say to your friends in the Congress
and elsewhere that they'll have to bring stronger proof than I've seen yet
to make me think Hill Lamon's not the best man I have around me."

He paused. Wade's face was still implacable. Lincoln debated for a moment whether to dismiss him or to attempt further to reach his understanding. He decided on the latter and reaching out a long arm, pulled the
bell rope by his desk.

"See if Mr. Lamon's around and send him here," he told the doorman.
Then, before Wade could voice his protest, "You never met Lamon, did
you?"

"I've never wished to meet the pompous fool," declared Wade.

Lincoln bit his lip but before he could remonstrate with Wade the door
opened and Lamon came in.

He was at this time about thirty-five years old. He was six feet two
inches tall, broad of shoulder and slim of waist, with regular features and a
peculiarly noble cast of countenance. The lips under the drooping mustache were clean cut and very firm. He paused just within the threshold.

"Mr. Lamon," said Lincoln, "this is Senator Wade. I want you two
gentlemen to meet each other. One time Charles Lamb pointed to a man
and said, 'I hate that fellow.' Lamb's companion said, 'I thought he was
a stranger to you.' 'He is,' Lamb retorted. 'That's why I can hate him.'"

Senator Wade and Marshal Lamon bowed to each other, but did not
speak. The President, feeling like a schoolmaster, went on:

"What strikes me as queer, Senator, is that you whose whole life is a
sacrifice to what you consider your duty should seem incapable of making
allowance for the other man doing his duty with just as much of a feeling
of sacrifice. Lamon is a first-class lawyer and a man of education. He didn't
want to take the job of Marshal but back in 1860, my Illinois friends were
convinced I'd need a true friend, close to me, one who'd guard me with
his life, and cheer me and support me when I flagged. And they worked on

Lamon to take the job and, thank God, he took it. What he's paid for it, nobody knows better than you, Senator."

Lamon moved uneasily. "Don't—" he began.

"I shall," interrupted the President, "do my best to make Mr. Wade see you through my eyes. If he could have had one day with us on the circuit!— I told him you were the best man I ever saw at catch-as-catch-can. Only once did you ever show scars of battle!" He laughed with remembered gayety, his face, so changed since the days of which he spoke, lighting marvelously. "One day, Senator, during the sitting of the Circuit Court in Bloomington, Lamon wrestled at noon intermission with some fellow and got the seat of his pantaloons split. Court was called before he had time to change and he trusted that his coat was long enough to cover the accident. He had to begin a plea, immediately, and when he rose—well, the coat *wasn't* long enough. All of the lawyers were sitting round a table beneath the judge and one of them quietly started a subscription paper to buy Lamon a new pair of pants. It was passed from one lawyer to another, each putting his name down for some absurd sum—excepting myself. I wrote that I could contribute nothing to the end in view!"

He finished the story with a delighted shout in which Hill Lamon joined. Senator Wade looked from the President to his friend. "A very pleasing sample of Western wit," he murmured. "I wish you good day, *gentlemen!*" He bowed and jerked open the door into the reception room.

Lincoln wiped his spectacles and put them in his pocket. "Well, Hill, when did you return? And how is General Grant feeling?"

"I got back about an hour ago," replied Lamon, unfastening the long blue broadcloth cape he wore and dropping into a chair near the President's desk. "Grant is his usual quiet, sober self."

"Is he whipping General Thomas on to pursue Hood instead of settling in Nashville for the winter?"

"Yes, sir, he's giving Thomas no peace. I'd say he was really nagging the poor fellow. General Sherman's living high down near Savannah. They haven't got any clothes through to his troops yet but they're as fat as butter, and in spite of their rags, they're the finest, toughest, sauciest lot of fighting men I've ever seen. Sherman's as proud of them as though he gave birth to every man Jack of 'em!"

"Good! Good! But what of the country down there, Hill? What of the plain people?"

"Well, Sherman says his soldiers live on turkey, chickens and sweet potatoes but that the poor women and children are hungry. He tells them that if Jeff Davis expects to found an empire on the ruins of the South, he ought to afford to feed the people. He tells them that it's time they realized war is cruelty and that you can't refine it."

Lincoln groaned. "Will it never end?"

Lamon shook his head. "Not till Sherman and Grant do their awful work. And the weather's so bad Grant can only strengthen his lines and make an occasional demonstration against Lee."

"Another sweat of waiting!" muttered Lincoln. "I wonder if the country can endure it? I wonder if I've got enough muscle left in my soul to back every one up."

Lamon's clear eyes met his friend's. He did not reply to Lincoln's wonderment but he said, with a little smile, "I heard of a nice thing that occurred at Grant's headquarters, last July. He saw bonfires blazing one hot night along the Rebel lines and told some one to 'holler' over and learn the reason for the celebration. It seemed that General Pickett,—you remember Pickett's charge at Gettysburg,—had just received word of the birth of his first child, a son."

"George Pickett! I know him well. I got him the appointment to West Point, the rascal, and he turned Secesh! A delightful fellow! Well! Well!"

"He was Grant's friend too, it seems, and also well liked by some of Grant's staff. When they learned the reason for the celebration they had some bonfires started on our side and sent a note through to the Confederate lines. I made a copy for you."

With a very gentle smile he handed the President a bit of yellow copy tissue and Lincoln read, "To George Pickett! We are sending congratulations to you, to the young mother and the young recruit. Grant, Ingalls, Suckley. July 18, 1864."

"By jings!" ejaculated Lincoln.

"And to do the matter up in style," grinned Lamon, "a few days later, under a flag of truce they sent through the lines a baby's silver service, engraved, 'To George S. Pickett, Jr., from his father's friends: U. S. Grant, Rufus Ingalls, George Suckley.'"

"And those two armies locked in a death struggle!" exclaimed Lincoln. "What a war! What a war!—Young George Pickett with a son!—What a war!—Thank you for telling me, Hill. It takes some of the bitter taste out of my mouth."

"General Grant wants you to get down to City Point when you can. Also he urged on me the necessity of your being extremely careful of yourself. He says the end of the war is now only a matter of weeks and that bitterness against you, personally, is going to rise like a tide. He says you must cease to send me on these errands which keep me away for months or you must consent to a personal guard at your elbow."

Lincoln tapped the desk thoughtfully. The idea of a man dogging him was almost intolerable. But so was the constant nagging of Mary, Stanton, Lamon and now of Grant. After all, the war was nearly over and he'd be a free man again!

"Arrange what will relieve your mind, Hill," he sighed. "Only I won't have men in uniform and won't have them insult people by carrying arms openly."

"Thank God! *Thank God!* Mr. Stanton and I've had picked men waiting months for this. I'll have one on duty in half an hour. I'm grateful to you, Mr. Lincoln."

"You dear damn' fool!" was the President's response as he threw a long arm for a moment over his friend's shoulder.

Lamon's smile was uncertain and so was his voice as he placed his dispatch box on the desk. "General Grant wishes you to read and return these, by me. I'm willing to go, *now*."

CHAPTER V

JOHN SURRATT

NOT all the men connected with the firing of New York escaped. During the weeks before Christmas several of them were arrested. While they were awaiting trial, three Sons of Liberty in Indiana were found guilty of conspiracy, insurrection and violation of the laws of war and sentenced to death. The judgment of the military tribunal which tried them could not be executed unless signed by the President. When the papers reached his desk Lincoln found himself the recipient of violent protests and pleas from relatives and friends of the men under sentence and he referred both the protests and the papers to Judge-Advocate-General Holt, who recommended death.

Death! The President, in the midst of a crowded morning, glanced at Judge Holt's close-written conclusion only long enough to absorb its purport. Legally sound, perhaps. But Abraham Lincoln, the fixed center in a whirlpool of destruction, felt his gorge rise at the thought of the power his position gave him. Why should he deal death to these men who, whatever may have been their designs, had failed to kill? If he ordered them to be hanged, then inevitably he must order Jefferson Davis and his Cabinet hanged, when the end came, as it must come.

He placed the papers in his bureau and returned to a report from the Secretary of the Treasury on a proposed bond issue.

"What," asked John Hay, a few hours later, "shall we do with these petitions about the Indiana conspirators?"

"File them," replied the President. "They can't hang them until I confirm the judgment."

John Hay grinned and obeyed. "They've caught John Beall," he said as he returned to the President's desk. "That's the fellow who tried to capture the steamer *Michigan*. He was trying to derail an east-bound express train near the Suspension Bridge at Niagara. He *is* a dirty dog. He'd have killed any number of women and children."

He looked at the President keenly, but Lincoln would not commit himself beyond admitting with a nod, "Yes, he is a low-down skunk!"

"I wonder how much Jeff Davis actually knows about these filthy little contrivings?" said John.

"Mighty little, I reckon," replied Lincoln. "Of course, he appointed Jacob Thompson and the rest of the gang but—" he paused uneasily.

"And authorized the expenditure of moneys to destroy the Northern morale. Well, what more do you want to incriminate him?"

"I'd want absolute and final proof," declared Lincoln, crossly, "which we probably never will have." Then he went on casually, "I'd like to have seen those three Booth boys playing 'Julius Cæsar' that night in New York. Edwin tops the world I think. I like his voice. The other two are only middling."

"John Wilkes Booth is in Washington now," said John as he laid the final sheet of a document under Lincoln's waiting pen. "I saw him drinking at the Herndon bar, yesterday."

"I hope that means we'll have Shakespeare here too," inscribing his name with his usual unhurried care. "By the way, what were *you* doing at the Herndon bar?"

Young Hay returned the President's sly smile impudently. "Sir, I was distributing temperance tracts!"

Lincoln's hearty laugh dismissed the subject of conspiracy for the day.

Wilkes Booth, coming out of the National Hotel that morning ran upon Dr. Mudd who was hurrying along Pennsylvania Avenue.

"My dear doctor!" he cried. "You're the one man on earth for the moment! I want you to introduce me to the Surratts. You must have forgotten that you were going to put me in touch with them."

"How can I do that, at this time?" asked Mudd, coldly. He was in riding clothes, his boots clay-spattered. "I want to go change my clothes, Booth. Don't hold me, please."

"Only to make an appointment, doctor. I have Mrs. Surratt's address. They're on H Street, near 7th."

"You mean they're in Washington? I didn't know that! But at any rate, Booth, I can't accommodate you. My brother and I are here meeting friends who are going home with us for Christmas. I've no time to spare." He turned to go but came to an abrupt halt. "Ha! Luck's with you, Booth! Here comes young Surratt, now! Surratt! Come here a moment!"

A tall young man of twenty-two with a cadaverous face ornamented by a little black mustache waved his hand. "All hail, Dr. Mudd! And Christmas gift!" He shook hands and then introduced his companion, a stout youth named Louis Weichmann. "Louis went to college with me and now boards with us."

Dr. Mudd, after salutations, introduced Wilkes Booth.

"I've seen you act many times, sir," exclaimed Weichmann, "and I've always dreamed of meeting you in flesh and blood!"

"You must have seen me as Banquo's ghost!" laughed Wilkes. "Come in here where I'm stopping and join the ghost in drinks and cigars."

"Just so the drinks are spiritual but not unreal!" volunteered John Surratt. "Louis and I are on our way to buy a Christmas present for my sister but I suppose this delay will only increase our generosity! Come along, doctor."

They followed Booth to his room where he ordered milk punches and cigars, stirred the fire to a splendid blaze and moved chairs around the hearth. The talk was general for a moment, then Dr. Mudd rose and called Booth into the hall with him. For ten minutes, the sound of their whispers reached Surratt and Weichmann. Then Mudd called Surratt out, leaving Weichmann to listen indignantly to the low murmur of a still longer conference. Finally the doctor came in briskly but apologetically.

"Too bad to leave you alone so long! Very ungentlemanly! But Mr. Booth had some private business with me. The fact is, he wants to buy my farm but doesn't want to give me enough for it."

Booth and Surratt now returned, full of apologies. Nevertheless the three continued to carry on a conversation in whispers, leaving Louis Weichmann to stare uneasily. When the discourtesy became too much to bear he rose. Dr. Mudd then ended the conference by saying:

"Come over to the Pennsylvania with me, all of you. I must attend to my guests but I want to talk to Mr. Weichmann."

Wilkes put his hand on Weichmann's arm. "Walk with me, my dear fellow, and tell me just how rude we are."

The stout young man melted and the party reached the Pennsylvania in great harmony of mind.

Dr. Mudd's room was not so comfortable as Booth's. It lacked the red window curtains and the armchairs. But there was a good fire. Neither Mudd's guests nor his brother put in an appearance. The doctor made no comment on this fact. Perhaps he forgot it in the interest of his examination into Weichmann's politics. The young man was working in the War Department. He was a gentle-spoken fellow, of the student type, preparing to enter the priesthood, when the war should end.

He said that he wished he could get a job in Richmond for he was a Southern sympathizer. But that, of course, as long as he took Union money, he was bound to play straight with them.

"What are you referring to?" asked the doctor, abruptly.

"You asked me just what my work was in the War Department. Well, all I really know is something of the military census."

"In which I'm not interested," returned Mudd, promptly. A moment later he murmured something to Booth about "a weakling" and again the embryo priest was left to himself. After a quarter of an hour of this, Weichmann again rose. Surratt imitated him, remarking as he did so to Booth that he'd be glad to go into the cotton speculation the actor had described.

Wilkes went to bed that night highly pleased with his luck. Young Surratt had agreed to act as his agent in lower Maryland, and would begin at once to investigate the best routes for the kidnapers. Weichmann was an effeminate impossibility. Surratt, when Wilkes spoke of needing at least two more men, spoke of one David Herold, an old schoolmate living in Washington. But Wilkes clung to the idea of having an actor in the scheme, some one who would have a legitimate excuse for being on the stage, if the theater abduction came about. His mind returned to Samuel Chester and he resolved to talk to him further as he was going to New York for the holidays.

Shortly after Christmas, therefore, he called on Chester and invited him out for some drinks. They fortified themselves well in a saloon, while Booth talked of his mysterious speculation and the enormous wealth it was going to bring.

Chester, a sad-eyed man of a cynical cast of countenance spoke but once. "What are the details?" he asked after Wilkes had held forth for a half hour.

But for some time, Wilkes held back. Conglomerate as New York was of loyalty and disloyalty to the Union cause and to Abraham Lincoln, still it was more difficult to reveal his plot in this Northern atmosphere than it had been in the Southern air of Baltimore. He continued to absorb brandy, however, and in the course of a second half hour, had gathered sufficient determination to lead Chester out of the saloon and after looking up and down the street, to whisper:

"I'm in a large conspiracy of fifty to a hundred men to capture the heads of the Federal Government, including the President and to take them to Richmond. There's literally millions in it! I hope the abduction of old Abe will take place at Ford's Theater, early in January. I'll be playing there then and I want somebody to be playing with me who'll help me. See?"

"For God's sake!" exclaimed Chester, "I always feared you'd go mad, like your father! What are you trying to do? Ruin me and my family?"

"How dare you say such a thing to *me?*" shouted Wilkes, fiercely.

"I've a notion to turn you over to the authorities," retorted Chester.

Wilkes seized Chester by the coat lapels. "If you breathe it, I'll swear you *fathered* the scheme!" he said hoarsely.

Chester turned pale. Then he shook himself free. "Don't ever mention this to me again, then," and he strode away.

Wilkes stared after him in the wintry sun which shone brilliantly on the drifted snow of 4th Street and cursed him loudly and bitterly. But Sam Chester was quickly beyond earshot. It was evident that Wilkes' method had been wrong with his fellow actor. Well, there might be some one playing in Ford's in January who would not be as stupidly difficult as Chester.

Restless and distrait during the next few days, he annoyed and worried his family, particularly his mother. She tried to beguile him into staying in New York but he insisted that his opportunities were greater in Washington and early in the New Year, he once more left his brother's house. But he did not go at once to the capital. He stopped over in Baltimore for a talk with Sam Arnold and Mike O'Laughlin. They were very impatient and faintly derisive. He met their complaints by turning over to them a trunk. It contained guns, pistols, cartridges, bowie knives, a pair of handcuffs and several false beards. The two men were to drive down to Washington bringing the trunk in a buggy Booth had purchased as well as a horse. Wilkes promised to meet them there.

BOB LINCOLN had come home from Harvard for the holidays and his mother insisted that he take part in the New Year's reception, which was always a great strain on everybody in the White House, with the exception of Tad.

"But, mother, I wouldn't lessen the strain for you and father," Bob protested at breakfast the morning of the reception.

"Perhaps not but it'll help you to overcome your shyness and also it will feed my vanity," replied his mother. "You've grown very handsome, my son."

Lincoln gave a delighted laugh and looked from Mary to her boy. He thought Bob was the image of his mother although Mary insisted that in the last year the young man had taken on a more pronounced look of his father. The President was sincerely thankful that in all four of their sons, Mary's pretty contours had softened and beautified his own physical contributions. In Bob, the combination of Lincoln and Todd was singularly felicitous. The length of Lincoln's jaw and the hollows in his cheeks were reduced by a fining of the firm chin, a lessening of the high cheek bones, with a closer chiseling of the wide mouth. It was a charming boy's face with enough of the father's melancholy cast to give it strength.

"The fact is, mother," muttered Bob, staring at the bowl of blue hyacinths which graced the breakfast table, "I'm helping Mrs. Harlan with her reception."

His mother and father exchanged glances.

"Hum!" murmured Lincoln. "I always did dote on the name Mary. Prettiest name in the world for a woman."

Bob blushed and when Tad giggled he said fiercely, "You have the manners of a chimpanzee, Tad!"

"Now don't start a quarrel, boys!" protested their mother. "Well," thoughtfully, "I'll be satisfied with an hour of your valuable time, then."

"Thank you, mother!" Bob sighed with relief.

"He's in a soft mood and actually overcome with gratitude and surprise at your leniency, Mary!" smiled Lincoln. "You could have got two hours out of him just as easy."

Bob grinned. "Quit kicking the table-leg, Tad."

Tad raised a round face from his bowl of mush, his blue eyes indignant. "You 'tend to you' gels and I'll 'tend to my legs, Bob. Ma'y Ha'lan has got a lot of beaux besides you."

"Don't repeat gossip, Tad," his mother admonished him sharply as she rose from the table. "I do wish you'd make a real effort to pronounce your R's, my dear. You'll be twelve in April."

"Oh, let him alone, mother!" protested the President, rising also. "Come on, Tad, before they begin to abuse you."

"I don't mind a fight with Bob," returned the little boy, taking a second helping of mush.

Lincoln warmed his hands at the blazing fire for a moment, then went upstairs to his office. He was smiling not only at Tad's retort but at the thought of Bob and dear little Mary Harlan. Nothing would please him more than Bob's marrying young and marrying this daughter of Senator Harlan.

The President had a great admiration for James Harlan of Iowa who had been a teacher, a lawyer and a college president and possessed all the educational qualifications of which Lincoln never ceased to mourn the lack. As a member of Congress, Harlan had been harshly critical of the President many times but Lincoln was convinced that the Iowa man liked him. This was so rare a conviction for the President with regard to the feeling of any Congressman toward him that it was a very precious possession, although he had not the affection for Harlan that he had for Sumner nor could he be the friend of his heart as was Hill Lamon. Harlan had agreed that later in the spring he would take office in the Cabinet as Secretary of the Interior.

At noon, the White House was thrown open to the public and all day long, Lincoln greeted people, now with his right, now with his left hand. Different shifts of friends and officials stood in the reception line with the President and his wife during the long hours. Senator Harlan and Mrs. Harlan alternated with Secretary Welles and Mrs. Welles. Mr. Frederick Seward relieved Speaker Colfax. Any and every friend whom Lincoln could persuade to help, literally lent a hand.

Something over five thousand citizens greeted the President during the levee. People in general paid more attention to Mary than to her husband. She was very handsomely dressed in a deep purple brocade with an exquisite black lace shawl over her shoulders. She was vivacious and eager while he in very weariness could only permit his helpless fingers to be crushed by hand after hand. He insisted that Mary should not suffer this imposition but only bow her greetings.

As the day wore on the throng grew rough and it required all of Marshal Lamon's skill and strength, with the help of both the infantry and unmounted cavalry guards to steer the lines past the hosts and out at the great window from which a gang plank led to the lawns. Late in the afternoon when the crowding was at its height and Lincoln was ready to drop with exhaustion, a voice reached him out of the medley of sounds.

"Did you bring any mail out to-day, Abe?"

He focused his gaze on the face below him—wrinkled, strangely changed and yet, he knew it. He put a hand on the old man's bent shoulder.

"Zack Simpson, by jings!"

The farmer grinned delightedly. "Yes, Mr. Lincoln and here's Allie!" pulling forward a tiny old lady whose black bonnet had been knocked askew.

Lincoln deliberately turned his back on the milling crowd, drawing the old couple around with him, while he smiled into their delighted faces.— A little field bordered by walnut trees and paw-paw thickets suddenly shut out the East Room. "Zack," said Lincoln, "is the old farm the same?"

"Just the same, sir." The watering faded eyes twinkled. "And now I'll ask you the question that's been bothering me for over thirty years. What did you do with the whetstone you took out of the shed when you mowed the ten-acre lot for me?"

Lincoln closed his eyes. That ten-acre lot which edged the creek! He spoke after a moment. "Zack, if you'll cross that field to the north-east corner you'll find the whetstone just where I left it in a crotch of one of the posts."

"I'll go home and look for it and if I find it, shall I let you know, sir?"

"Do! Do!" exclaimed Lincoln. "Thank you!" He stooped and kissed Allie's cheek and turned back to the impatient line with a smile that did not fade for a long time.

There was one other iridescent moment in the day. This was long after when the crowd had all but disappeared and Bob, in irreproachable broadcloth, gravely approached with a slip of a girl in white silk ruffles hanging on his arm.

"Well, Mary! Sweet Mary of Argyle! Did you ever hear Lamon sing that ballad?" asked the President, bowing over the little white-gloved hand.

"Not yet, Mr. Lincoln," replied Mary Harlan, sweeping a perfect curtsey, her flounces billowing like a wind-blown daisy field.

It was curious, thought Lincoln, that her delicate features could be so reminiscent of her father's heroic mold. The same large clear eyes, the same broad brow, at least what one could see of it beneath the hair parted thick over the temples. He told himself he never had seen so sweet an expression on a woman's face.

"I've found the source of that quotation I made to you, sir, the other day," said Mary.

"The one about lilacs?" asked the President.

She nodded her head and said softly while Bob watched her, his heart in his eyes, and Lincoln listened, his face infinitely wistful:

" 'There was a child went forth every day
And the first object he looked upon, that object he became—
The early lilacs became part of this child,
And the grass and white and red morning glories—
And white and red clover and the song of the phœbe-bird.'

It's Walt Whitman's—from 'Leaves of Grass.' "

"Good heavens!" exclaimed Bob, "does your father know there's a copy of that book in his house!"

"My mother does," replied Mary demurely. "It's a great poem, Mr. Lincoln. I'll recite more of it to you on a better occasion."

The President smiled his thanks and the two having done their duty departed.

As Lincoln, several hours later, crossed the East Room to make his way toward the family staircase, he observed two of the guards and Hill Lamon in acrimonious conversation with an elegantly dressed young man whom Lincoln thought he'd seen somewhere. He was too tired to investigate at the moment but when Hill came to his office shortly Lincoln said, "Who was the fellow you were arguing with, down below? I had half a notion to tell you I'd say Howdy to him and save you trouble."

"It was one of the Booth brothers, John Wilkes," replied Lamon. "He'd been drinking heavily. I didn't want the ladies to see him. A nice fellow but he's been hanging around Washington off and on for months in idleness."

"I hear Edwin Forrest is going to play 'Richelieu,'" said Lincoln. "Booth will probably act in his company. I want to see 'Richelieu.'"

"When you go, Mr. Lincoln, don't let the date be known ahead of time. My detectives have just discovered that the organization which came into being five years ago to kidnap President Buchanan is still in existence as an apparently harmless drinking club."

Lincoln ran his fingers through his hair impatiently. "I've given Blair his permit to go down to Richmond and satisfy himself as to what kind of a peace Jeff Davis thinks he can get."

Lamon sighed. "But you will not let the date of your theater visit be known, will you, sir?"

The President shook his head. His mind had left "Richelieu" and it was less on Blair than it was on the Thirteenth Amendment which was to come before the Senate again on January 6th. He was worried lest Charles Sumner delay again its long-delayed passage by being too finicky over the wording.

"As a matter of fact," he said aloud, "it couldn't be phrased better."

"Eh?" ejaculated Lamon. "What's that?"

Lincoln said slowly,

"*Neither slavery nor involuntary servitude except as a punishment for crime whereof they shall have been duly convicted shall exist within the United States or any place subject to their jurisdiction.* Nothing could bite closer than that. Sumner must stand aside. The old juggernaut of anti-slavery is on the final lap of its fearful journey. I advise Sumner to get aboard or to stand away from the wheels. But moving him is like trying to move an elephant by the laying on of hands."

He picked up his pen to write a note of condolence to Chief Justice Chase who had lost his sister but his mind was still ruminating with pleasure on the Amendment. "A question might be raised whether or not the Emancipation Proclamation was legally valid. But this Amendment is a king's cure-all for all the evils. It winds the whole thing up.—Well, Hill, to-morrow's Cabinet day and I've got to work till midnight going over some decisions on cotton cases Father Welles is pressing me for. Even the navy is entangled in that devilish fluff. What do you want, Hill?"

"In other words, will I nimbly remove myself," said the younger man, rising wearily from his place before the fire.

"Not till you tell me what brought you here. I can see there's something bothering you, my boy."

"There is, but you're too tired to take it up, to-night." Lamon began to move toward the door.

"Wait, Hill! You know I never have a free moment and this is as good a time as another. Out with your trouble." Lincoln laid down his pen and smiled at his friend.

Lamon bit his lip, folded his blue broadcloth arms for a moment in thought, kicked the fire with an elegantly polished boot and said in his low-pitched Virginian voice, "Well, the New York *World* is still harping on the alleged Antietam episode. It's repeated the dirty lie daily for three months and other papers are almost as bad. For heaven's sake, for your family's sake, let me deny it."

"Let's see," mused Lincoln, doing his best to clear his mind of the heavier problems, for he knew this matter concerned Lamon's reputation as well as his own. "Let's see, the theme of that particular lie is to the effect that when I was visiting the battlefield of Antietam, we made a special trip in an ambulance to see the carnage, accompanied by McClellan. That as we passed the heaps of unburied dead, I slapped you on the knee and asked you to sing 'Picayune Butler' and it was only McClellan's decency that headed you off."

"That's the original lie, but it's grown in two years." Lamon's face was flushed, painfully. "I don't care so much about myself but how can any one knowing what you endure—" He gulped and went on more calmly. "The latest addition is this bit of doggerel—

> "Abe may crack his jolly jokes
> O'er bloody fields of stricken battle
> While yet the ebbing life-tide smokes
> From men that died like butchered cattle.
> He e'er yet the guns grow cold,
> To pimps and pets may crack his stories—"

Lincoln raised a thin, protesting hand. "That's enough, Hill!" He felt nauseated, but after a moment he said, quietly, "Write down the plain facts, Hill. It was sixteen days after the battle. The dead were all buried. . . . No, there'll be too much vinegar and gall in your wording of it. I'll write it for you . . . let's see. On that drive over to review General Porter's troops, I did ask you to sing me my sad little song. And you did sing it, but we were not on the battlefield, of course."

He pulled a sheet of paper toward him and slowly and carefully wrote the statement of facts.

Lamon read it and nodded. "They ought to be drawn and quartered. I'll mail it to the *World*, to-night."

The President took out his paper knife and rubbed his cheek, thoughtfully. "Don't do it, Hill. You and I know that this is the truth and the whole truth about that affair but I dislike to appear as an apologist for an act of mine which I know was right. Keep this paper and we'll see about it, later."

Lamon ground his teeth but Lincoln smiled at him and suddenly the Virginian's face melted.

"You promise to be sketchy about any theater date, don't you, Mr. Lincoln," he urged, again.

"Yes! Yes!" returned the President, turning to Chase's letter and glancing with a sigh at the "cotton" papers he had promised Welles for the morrow.

"You'll not go alone," insisted Lamon.

"No! No!" a little impatiently.

"Remember that we have new evidence of plots."

"Oh, that's enough!" snapped Lincoln. Then he laughed. "I'll have to use on you the story I used the other day on a man who came to get a job from me. He was armed with vouchers as to his character and I told him to read one or two to me. He started off and by jings, he'd read twenty before I could get my breath. 'Stop!' I told him finally. 'You're like the man who killed the dog. The dog was vicious and he knocked out its brains with a club. But then he continued striking the dog till a friend stayed his hand. "You needn't keep on," said the friend. "The dog was dead at the first blow." "Oh, yes, I knew that," said the dog-killer, "but I believe in punishment after death!" ' "

Hill grinned. "Did you give him the job?"

"I did, sir!"

"By the same analogy will you give me the promise?"

"I will, sir, if you'll just get out and let me set up some socks for the Cabinet to knit on."

Lamon went out, still grinning.

But Lincoln did not get on with the knitting.

He looked at his watch. It was eleven o'clock and he was tired. He finished the note to Chase, then walked over to the fire and pulled up his trouser legs in the vain endeavor to warm his shins. His vitality was not what it had been. And instantly the memory of the dream returned to him as it had for days, whenever he ceased for a moment to occupy his mind with work.

It was not, he told himself, as he eyed the fire, that he believed in dreams as such. He did not consider himself superstitious in the ordinary meaning of the word. He always had had a sense of predestination and the years at the White House had increased his conviction that he was not altogether master of his own decisions. And he had come to believe completely that the Almighty was very close to the North these days, very close to Washington, but closest of all to Abraham Lincoln who was doing his utmost to lead the righteous cause.

He did not think that ordinary dreams were of any particular significance. But, he told himself, there must be out there, beyond time and space, a reservoir of Universal Knowledge and at times of dire need surely it must be given to man to tap that reservoir. How else could the miracles of Christ be explained? And since this war was one of the great, significant events of all times, might it not be that the soul of the man who carried its overwhelming burden could in dreams slip its leash and plumb the vasty depths of pre-knowledge—of prophecy?

Was this dream that haunted him such a one? He walked uneasily to the window by his desk. Snow was whirling down on Mary's pretty garden —God, how lonely it was. How lonely life was!—He was glad to realize that Mary would be waiting for him as usual in the sitting room. Suddenly, he plunged across the private passageway to find her.

The room was full of the fragrance of forced white lilacs from the greenhouse. A warm light from a leaping cannel coal fire gave the octagonal room with its heavy stuffed, half shabby furniture a homelike look. This was the only room in the White House of which Lincoln really was fond. Mary was not alone. She and Hill Lamon were sitting at the center table, checking over dinner lists.

"This is a nice job for a man of brawn if not of brain," remarked Lamon, making a grimace of distaste.

The President did not reply. He stood on the hearthrug in a profound melancholy.

"What is it, Mr. Lincoln?" asked Mary, eyeing him soberly.

"Did you ever notice how much there is in the Bible about dreams?" he asked, rousing himself. "I've counted some sixteen chapters in the Old Testament and four or five in the New in which dreams are mentioned. And there are many passages scattered through the book referring to visions. If we believe in the Bible we have to believe that in the old days God and His angels made themselves known to men in dreams."

"Is it a dream that's depressing you?" asked Mary, quickly, while Lamon looked on, pen poised.

"I'm not saying I believe in the Biblical sort of dream," replied Lincoln. "But I've been having one that haunts me as if it were about as important as one of those."

Mary's blue eyes darkened with anxiety. "You frighten me when you speak so solemnly, Abra'm. What was the dream?"

"I oughtn't to have mentioned it," he said contritely. "But somehow the thing's got possession of me and like Banquo's ghost, won't down."

"I refuse to be superstitious!" declared Mary, slapping a plump hand on the table to emphasize her independence. "But you'd better tell us the dream, my dear. A dream shared will never repeat itself."

Lincoln smiled at her.

"Tell us about it, Mr. Lincoln," urged Lamon, strolling from the table to join the President on the hearthrug.

Mary looked up at the two gigantic forms and thought of how much more of real beauty there was in her husband's expression than in the handsome Hill Lamon's.

"About ten days ago," said Lincoln, slowly, "I was so late going to bed that I fell asleep immediately and instantly, as near as I can calculate, I began to dream. First there was stillness. Then I heard subdued sobs, as if many people were crying. I thought I left my bed and wandered downstairs. There the silence was broken by the same pitiful sobbing but the mourners were invisible. I went from room to room. No living person was in sight but the mournful sounds met me wherever I went. It was light in every room and all the furniture was familiar to me. But I couldn't find the people and I was puzzled and worried. The last room I entered was the East Room. And there I found the root of the trouble. Before me was a catafalque on which rested a corpse, the face covered. Soldiers guarded it and there was a throng of people, some gazing mournfully and some weeping.

" 'Who is dead in the White House?' I asked one of the soldiers.

" 'The President,' he said. 'He was killed by an assassin.'

"Then such a loud burst of grief came from the crowd that it woke me up and I couldn't get to sleep again."

"I shouldn't think you could have!" gasped Mary, white to the lips.

Lincoln, who had been oblivious to his actual surroundings while he lived the dream again, came back to reality with a start. He looked at his wife, contritely.

"O my dear girl, I shouldn't have told you!" he exclaimed.

Mary rallied at once. "Whom should you tell if not me? And after all it's a cheering dream for it couldn't have been you on the catafalque. You were a bystander."

"So I was! So I was!" agreed the President, without conviction. "Well, let it go. The Lord in His own good way and time will work this out. I must get back to my work."

"Not to-night," protested Mary. "You need sleep, fearfully, my dear."

Lamon, always sensitive to Lincoln's mood, quoted softly,

> "Sleep hath its own world—"

The President took up the quotation eagerly and went on for several lines:

> "—A boundary between the things misnamed
>   Death and existence. Sleep hath its own world
>   And a wide realm of reality—"

Mary shook her head vigorously. "I don't call that a tactful illustration for the case in point," she protested.

"Anyhow, I feel better," insisted Lincoln. "You were right when you said a dream shared loses its horror, Mary."

"I didn't quite say that, but I'm glad it's the way you feel," said his wife, with a cheerful smile.

CHAPTER VII

SPREAD OUT!

LINCOLN kept his own counsel as to when he would make the proposed visit to the theater to see "Richelieu." But he promised himself when he awoke on the Saturday following New Year's that he'd hustle through enough work during the next ten hours to justify him in indulging himself to that extent.

He worked without pause until an hour before sunset. There never had been a busier day. It was as if every one who had the remotest interest in the war took this particular day to urge his or her cause. Petitions for pardons, for passes, for special trade dispensations, flowed in an ever-increasing flood. Members of Congress stood in his outer office in serried ranks seething with unconcealed impatience while various Cabinet members took precedence in making their demands. The tremendous crisis on the Thirteenth Amendment was pending. The Committee on the Conduct of the War was seriously displeased with Lincoln, with Stanton, with Grant and with the unregenerate Benjamin Butler. Its members consumed an hour, stinging the President like angry wasps. These were succeeded by the elder Blair, urging greater concessions for a possible peace. Stanton came in on Blair and the two became abusive of each other. This was the last straw. Lincoln suddenly threw down his pen and bolted.

He eluded his new guard who as yet was no match for the President's guile and slipped out the back way for a walk in the grounds. A heavy snowfall gave him the perfect privacy he craved. He made his way to Adams' Grove, which was a world apart, that afternoon; so silently remote that he might have been a boy again, wandering in the woods with his young mother. This idea pleased Lincoln and for an hour he tramped among the trees, thinking of his youth, of his mother and sister, of his early earnest absurdities, some of which made him laugh aloud and some of which brought a grunt of reminiscent mortification.

He thought more about his mother than any one else. His stepmother was dear to him but he had observed that the older he grew, the clearer and more frequent grew his memories of his own mother. With the years, her image became more vivid. And during the past year, at night, little episodes that had rested untouched by memory for nearly half a century returned to quicken his heart. Reaching the fifties, he decided, brought its own rich virtue.

The gentle though heavy fall of the snow was very soothing. He felt his nerves relax and when dusk recalled him to his whereabouts, he emerged from the trees in cheerful mood. He returned the salute of a guard at the north portico and would have passed into the house immediately had not the man broken through formalities to exclaim:

"Secretary Stanton's gone out in a carriage looking for you, Mr. Lincoln, and Marshal Lamon followed him. Everybody's been upset, sir."

"When they come back, send them to my office," said the President.

He strode into the hall where the doorman took his snow-covered coat and climbed the stairs, smiling. "This'll teach 'em not to distrust me," he told himself. "Mary won't be back for another hour so she hasn't been bothered." He laughed aloud as he settled to the gigantic pile of documents John Hay brought him. He confided the joke to John who did not find it humorous and said so frankly.

"I was just going to start out myself. Mr. Stanton fired your guard, out of hand. I thought he was going to kick the poor devil downstairs."

"Oh, I'll reinstate Smith," chuckled the President. "The joke is that for once, I'm guiltless, by jings!"

John Hay gave up and with compressed lips laid a letter from one of Grant's generals before him. Lincoln continued to smile as he adjusted his spectacles and read the few lines. "Hah! do you know, John, this fellow's a philosopher and a truly great man. He's grappled with the problem, *know thyself*, and he's solved it. He's a remarkable man. The war hasn't produced another like him!"

"Mr. Lincoln, he's been a complete failure!" protested Hay.

"And he's discovered it and admits it and greatly to my relief and that of the country, he resigns! He's a great philosopher. I wish he could teach the rest of the dress parade commanders to follow his example."

They both were laughing at this sally when Secretary Stanton and Marshal Lamon burst into the office.

"Do you know I nearly shot Lamon, sir, thinking he was an assassin!" roared Stanton.

"How come?" asked the President blandly.

"How come? I was returning madly after failing to find you at the Soldiers' Home and he loomed up on horseback in the dark and commanded me to halt." Stanton glared from Lincoln to Lamon.

Lamon, pale, the snow melting from his riding cape, stood panting and speechless.

"Assassins don't work that way, Mr. Stanton," persisted Lincoln. And then he exploded in the heartiest laugh in which he had indulged for weeks. "I was in President Adams' little grove all the time, by jings, harmless as a woodchuck!"

Hill Lamon threw up his great arms and collapsed on a sofa. "I resign!" he groaned.

"So do I!" snarled Stanton.

"I wish I could!" Lincoln gasped.

"I already have!" contributed John Hay.

Stanton hesitated for a moment, then his face relaxed and he joined the others in swelling the President's delighted Ha! Ha!

That evening, Lincoln and Hill Lamon slipped out to hear Edwin Forrest as Richelieu. They took rear seats in the gallery. Wilkes Booth, prowling about during the play saw the two tall backs silhouetted against the footlights, and leaning against the exit door watched the President's great head bent forward in charmed concentration. If Lincoln was going to do this sort of thing, the theater abduction was not to be considered further!

The attempt to kidnap the President from the White House grounds waited only on the discovery of a further accomplice, some one physically capable of actually knocking Lincoln down and out at one blow from a black-jack. Wilkes was an expert fencer but he reluctantly recognized that this skill would not serve him in a black-jack attack on a man nearly eight inches taller than himself. A cell in the Van Ness house was ready for Lincoln. A boat was moored at a lonely spot beyond the marshes on the edge of the Potomac and young Surratt had arranged to have the party taken aboard by a blockade runner used by the Confederate Secret Service. The snowfall which had followed the New Year had turned the roads south of Washington to rivers of mud, making the flight through lower Maryland temporarily impossible.

The greatest gamble in the plan, as Booth saw it, was whether or not the President visited the War Office on the night chosen. Lincoln had been ill once or twice during the winter and it was conceivable that he might be again, to the temporary frustration of the schemers.

The actor spent Tuesday completing details. Sam Arnold and Mike O'Laughlin arrived in the morning with the trunk. He met them at the National and after giving them drinks at the hotel bar, Booth joined them in the buggy and they drove to the stable he had rented behind Ford's Theater.

"The theater notion sticks, eh?" asked Mike O'Laughlin as he walked round the shed which Spangler the stage carpenter had converted into a make-shift barn.

"We can't have too many plans," replied Wilkes, driving carefully under the low roof and leaping out to eye the roan horse with pride. "I'm an efficient campaigner. If my family had only permitted me to join General Lee, I'd have been his chief of staff by now."

"And not have been obliged to go into the kidnaping business to make your reputation," jibed O'Laughlin.

"My reputation is already established, sir," said Booth haughtily.

"Don't try to be funny at Wilkes' expense, Mike," said Arnold quietly. "What's the use. Hit me! I'm bullet proof." He shivered. His delicate face was drawn. "Let's find a fire."

"Haven't you been well, Sam?" asked Wilkes, solicitously. "Jove, old man, you look like a plucked chicken! Come back to the hotel and get warm!"

"Oh, I'm very well," replied Sam, "thank you, Wilkes. But this whole business works on my nerves. I'll be glad when it's over. And this weather puts on the last touch of gloom." He shivered again.

Wilkes put his arm affectionately through Arnold's. "Come and have a drink. That's the answer."

"It is!" exclaimed Mike, enthusiastic for once.

They sat for two hours in the bar of the National, during which time John consumed a quart of brandy. He became deeply excited and very irritable but he did not raise his voice and his hand remained steady. The others, drinking very much less, watched him with admiration not untinged with uneasiness.

They went over details, studying the careful map Wilkes had made of the west half of the White House grounds and repeating his instructions for their individual jobs until they were letter perfect. Toward the end of the two hours, Wilkes began to feel sure that they could do without an additional accomplice. But Mike, in no-wise brandy-inflamed as to his own or any one else's physical prowess derided the thought. Arnold told Wilkes frankly that he was talking like a whiskey hero.

Booth cursed them both, softly, but did not urge the point further. He dismissed the two with a lordly wave of the hand to the boarding house he had found for them.

He sat in thought for a while after they had left, muttering to himself and opening and closing his big white fingers. The bar-keeper watched him with the respect due a man who could carry liquor as Booth did and was a little disappointed on approaching Booth to have the young man look up at him and say in a full rich voice:

"The ambitious youth who fired the Ephesian dome
Outlives in fame the pious fool who reared it!"

However, Wilkes was not drunk. He rose, pulled on his gloves and walked steadily out to the front entrance where he stood wondering if Mrs. Surratt could help him find his man, if he gave up the condition he himself had imposed that the man be one of Booth's own acquaintances. As he hesitated a youth shambled by staring at him. Wilkes was accustomed to the gaping admiration of strangers but this fellow was so intent that the actor returned his look.

He was only a youngster, but huge. He seemed as tall as Lincoln to Booth but built like a bull with a curiously steadfast gaze from deep-set gray eyes. His face was beardless, white and haggard.

Booth ran down the steps. "Halloo, young Powell! What are you doing here?"

The boy's face lighted extraordinarily. "I'm called Payne now, Mr. Booth, I—I—"

"Come in and have a drink and some supper! Jove, you look perished with cold and hunger, my boy," taking him by the arm and leading him up the steps. "We'll go to my room. You're the very man I want to see!"

The young man looked utterly dazed but followed willingly. Safe in Booth's room he made for the fire.

"Take off your coat, you'll warm quicker. Never mind what you have on beneath." Wilkes firmly unbuttoned the other's threadbare overcoat.

Beneath was a soiled red flannel undershirt and blue jean pantaloons. Booth handed him a purple silk dressing gown and while the boy forced his great body into this, he ordered a substantial meal. Then he poured out a small drink of whiskey which he handed his guest saying:

"More, when your stomach's full. And while you sip it, tell me about yourself."

"I can't get over your remembering me, sir! I saw you in Ford's Theater in Richmond in the spring of '61. It was the first time I'd ever been in a theater, my father being a preacher. I never dreamed a man could be like you and I made up my mind to meet you if you were to be met. I got round to the stage door, remember, sir?"

"Haven't I just proved I remember?" Booth's fine face glowed. "Such admiration as you expressed that night is unforgettable. You told me you were only sixteen but had been in the Confederate service several months. What's happened since?"

"I was in constant fighting until after Gettysburg. I got a bad wound there and was put into the prison hospital in Baltimore. I acted as an orderly in the hospital there for a while after I got well. I—I got to care about a young lady who was working as volunteer nurse and after she left the hospital, I left too and got through the Yankee lines to ours again. But last summer I got a chance to come North with some letters for Jacob Thompson in Montreal and I took it. In fact I made several trips, via Baltimore—" He paused with a bashful grin.

"And was she kind?" asked Wilkes, smiling in return.

"She's a fine girl," was Payne's reply, given stiffly. Then he went on, "I saw you in Montreal in October, sir, talking with Mr. Clay and Mr. Thompson, and I saw you again at the Winter Garden on November 26, when you played in 'Julius Cæsar.'"

"What were you doing in New York then?" demanded Wilkes with sudden interest.

"Well, I had undertaken to help burn New York. But I lost the directions Col. Martin had given me and I got scared to think I'd handed a rope to hang me on to any one who picked them up, though they were not addressed. So I went back to Baltimore and stayed at the boarding house my girl's folks keep and took the oath of allegiance."

"But was that wise?" exclaimed Booth.

"I don't know," with sudden sullenness, "I'm always in trouble. While I was waiting for further orders, and mighty sick of hanging round in my room, a sassy nigger wench refused to sweep my floor and I handed her the knock over the head she deserved. But instead of taking it as she would have before the old bastard Lincoln got busy, she set up a howl, rushed out of the house and got me hauled before the Provost-Marshal.

He ordered me to leave Baltimore. So here I am. I reckon the best thing for me to do is to get back to Richmond."

"And leave your girl? There's no necessity for that, my boy!" exclaimed Booth. "I remember all about you now. You told me, in Richmond, that your name is Lewis Payne Powell and that your father is a minister in Florida. You had two older brothers in the army."

"They've both been killed!" with quick ferocity. "By God, I hate war! Seems as if there never had been anything but stinking battlefields in my life! And now the South's licked, what's going to become of us all? When Grant's and Sherman's armies meet, there won't be a white man left living that's ever owned a slave or fought against freeing 'em."

The supper came in now and Wilkes tactfully went to his desk and wrote a letter or two while his guest devoured oysters and a beefsteak. He did not speak until Payne pushed himself away from the table and said:

"Well, Mr. Booth, I reckon you saved my life and I wish I could do something in return."

Wilkes turned quickly in his chair. "Sit down, Lewis, and hear my tale."

Payne dropped into a chair before the fire and the actor walked over to stand with an elbow on the mantel. The firelight lighted his face into angelic beauty. Twilight was closing in. A servant drew the red curtains over the windows and removed the supper tray.

"Lewis," said Wilkes softly, "I am a man ordained! A man consecrated to a supreme act that will save the Confederacy! When you passed the hotel, I was racking my brains to find a man to help me. And you—you came! Like an answer to prayer, Lewis!"

The quick blood mounted to young Payne's forehead. "I'll help you, sir, though I don't see what anybody can do now for the Confederacy!"

"I'll tell you what's going to save her. I propose to kidnap Abe Lincoln and hold him in prison in Richmond until first, all our men are freed from the hell holes known as Northern prisons and second, until peace is made on President Davis' terms. Then we'll return the old gorilla to the White House."

Payne scowled thoughtfully into the fire. "It's a good idea," he said slowly. "I've heard a lot of folks scheme about it. Of course, if we fail, they'll shoot us, some fine sunrise, and from their point of view, we'll deserve to be shot."

"From their point of view, yes. But the Ruler of all nations won't condemn us nor will history. Ours will be as great a blow for freedom as the Magna Charta. Of course, I realize we must face the dangers. They are stupendous just in the degree that the game we play is stupendous."

"Well," mused the boy. "I've been through three years of war so I can't say that the dangers in this rock my foundations. The point for me, sir," he looked up at Wilkes shyly, "the point for me is that you ask my help. I'm with you, whatever you want."

Booth held out his hand, his eyes soft with sudden tears. "You unman me, Lewis!—Is your strength much depleted?"

Payne grinned boyishly. He jerked off the lounging robe and rolled up a flannel shirt sleeve, displaying an arm muscled, Booth delightedly exclaimed, like a strong man's in a side show.

"All I need," declared Payne, "is twenty-four hours of rest and food."

"That you shall have, and some clothing," nodded Wilkes. "I'll find you a room in a boarding house where you can pose as a sick man, and two days from now, we'll tackle the job. I'm afraid after the loss of Col. Martin's memoranda to you, you may be a marked man, so you must be reconciled to remaining more or less hidden."

Within an hour, Lewis Payne Powell was asleep in a comfortable room, a short distance from Booth's hotel.

When he left his new recruit, Booth strolled up to the White House grounds for a last rehearsal of his plans.

Stanton had done what he could to safeguard the President. A company of Pennsylvania infantrymen camped to the south of the White House. From this company were drawn the two guards who paced innocently the length of the front of the building. In a barracks located on 15th Street, south of the Treasury grounds, were the barracks of the Union Light Guard, which company furnished the cavalrymen at the north gates. If he timed the abduction to elude notice by the infantryman on the west side of the front portico, Booth did not believe there would be the least danger from the two companies south of the White House.

He passed the cavalryman at the gate, walking briskly and slipped quickly to the right, toward Adams' Grove, meeting no one. Half way between the turnstile which let into the War Office yard and the west end of the White House a large clump of laurels grew against the garden wall. The bricked path made a slight curve around the clump. Here Booth planned to hide, with Lewis Payne. On the other side of the wall, O'Laughlin and Arnold would crouch. The moment they heard Booth's signal they would climb to the top of the wall, help hoist over the President, senseless, roped and gagged and the four would then carry him across the vegetable garden to 17th Street where Surratt with the buggy would be waiting to bear him to the Van Ness house. Booth, groping in the black shadows, went through the abduction in pantomime. It was perfectly feasible, he was sure—if old Abe went to the War Department.

It rained for the next two days but the weather changed during the second afternoon and by dark, it was freezing. The White House lawns were first spongy, then hard to the foot. When the conspirators crept to their places at eleven o'clock it was starlight and very cold and it seemed a very long hour of waiting before the turnstile creaked and footsteps sounded. In a moment, Booth and Payne saw the tall, shadowy form, but accompanied by a lesser figure. Well, thought Booth, they were prepared for that. Lewis would knock out old Abe while he would use his lead pipe on the stranger.

"By jings, it's freezing harder than ever," came the President's slow, soft voice. "Look, Major, this brick path acts like a dug canal. There were three inches of water in it, last night, and now there must be a quarter of an inch of ice. But it's a Tad-size crick, not ours, Eckert. Spread out! Spread out! It's deeper there by the bushes and we'll go through!" He laughed and with mock heroism in his voice and gesture, pulled the Major quickly clear of the laurel shrub and rushed him rapidly out into the open lawn, in clear view of the sentry now standing watchfully at the west end of his beat.

"Spread out!" Lincoln laughed and his words came clearly to Booth and Payne on the still air. "When I was a boy, Eckert, in Indiana, we had to go seven miles to the grist mill, carrying the bag of corn on the horse's back along with the boy of the family. I remember joining up with a group of neighbors in just such weather as this and coming to the crick that ran the mill, we all crowded out on the ice. It began to crack and some fellow yelled, 'Spread out or we'll all go through!' We scattered like dried leaves and sure enough the ice held. I've thought of that a good many times in this war. You know that man—" He lifted his hat to the sentry's salute and lowered his voice confidentially as he passed on.

An hour later, the conspirators gathered in Booth's room at the National and attacked an oyster supper. Wilkes walked the floor, cursing his luck. O'Laughlin watched him sardonically; Arnold, anxiously; Lewis Payne, with sympathy, his eyes those of a faithful setter. John Surratt made a great show of consulting a road map.

"I told you fellows the theater idea was the only one," Booth declared, finally, tossing his pistol to the bed and pouring a drink of brandy. His eyes were bloodshot, his hair disordered. "Boldness and openness are the only keys to success in this venture. I hate this skulking behind bushes."

"Booth, it's the one feasible method," contradicted Arnold who had taken enough liquor to ruffle his usual serenity. "We'll give the old brick wall another trial."

"No, we sure Gawd won't," drawled Lewis Payne. "I know my luck and my luck'll never be good against Abe Lincoln's when his is like what it was to-night." He sipped at rum and water, shaking his head knowingly. The new blue coat and fawn-colored trousers with which Wilkes had outfitted him made a different being of him, showed to the full what a splendid young animal he was.

"So I say, Lewis!" cried Booth. "If ever a man had a charmed circle drawn round him, it was old Abe, this evening."

"It sure was a warning," agreed Payne. "If you-all want my help, it'll have to be on a new deal."

"Well, something's got to be done soon or I can be counted out," declared Sam Arnold. "My folks are fussing because I don't get a job."

"Come now, boys, I've tried out your plan," pleaded Wilkes in his most winning manner. "Give mine a try. Lincoln doesn't live at the Soldiers' Home in winter as you very well know. Let's snatch him out of Ford's while Forrest's playing."

"How can you carry out that scheme until the roads in Maryland are good?" demanded young Surratt who had continued to study his map during the entire conversation. "And I haven't found a satisfactory way of crossing at Port Tobacco yet. It'll take money."

"I'll give you the money! How much?" exclaimed Wilkes, drawing out his pocketbook.

"I'll want at least a hundred to stir some one's imagination," replied Surratt.

Wilkes peeled off several bills and threw them on the map. O'Laughlin made a gesture toward the money and when Surratt laughingly pushed him back, he closed his eyes and began to snore. No one troubled to find out whether he was clowning or in a drunken coma.

"Now then," said Wilkes, "you take a few days off your job, Surratt, go down to Port Tobacco and fix things there." He then gave Arnold a fifty-dollar bill and thrust one into O'Laughlin's coat pocket. "Will you all agree to give either the Ford or the Soldiers' Home plan next chance, depending on whichever place Abe first favors with his presence?"

Surratt, Arnold and Payne nodded.

"All right. I'll keep you informed," said Booth. "Lewis, you help Sam to take O'Laughlin home."

"Don't need any help," mumbled Mike and he walked out of the room. And thus the conference ended.

Four days later, John Surratt, mud-spattered from head to foot, rode at a quick trot up to the door of his mother's house on H Street and within found Wilkes Booth and his mother awaiting him. He reported that two members of the Confederate Secret Service, a man and later a woman, would stop at the house on their way to Canada. He also reported that he had found not only a boat for Booth but an enthusiastic assistant.

At Port Tobacco, he had been directed to a coach painter named George Atzerodt, as a man through whom a skiff could be found. Atzerodt was a blockade runner of the row-boat status. Surratt described him as about thirty-three, a short, thick, stooping man, with a receding chin, partially covered by a curly light beard. He was a good-natured country lout with a reputation as a clown, very ardent in the Southern cause and still more ardent when he received fifty dollars over and above the price of the boat. He had agreed to come up to Washington to meet Booth at Surratt's house. Surratt also had arranged for relays of horses and said that if the weather held good, roads would be passable in two days' time.

The plan now waited entirely on Lincoln's movements. It was announced that he would attend a play at Ford's on the 18th of January.

CHAPTER VIII

ON the morning of the 18th of January, Lincoln yielded, after deliberation, to the importunings of the elder Blair to be permitted to go to Richmond to see how Jefferson Davis was feeling about peace. The President had no intention of agreeing to peace except on his own terms but the pressure on him by the war-weary North was all but intolerable. It would be a relief to make a gesture toward peace even though he was sure it would be futile. He was very cautious, however, admonishing Blair over and over not to raise false hopes in Davis' breast. He made Blair take with him a letter, which he wrote while the veteran newspaper man waited.

"F. P. Blair, Esq.   Sir: You having shown me Mr. Davis' letter to you of the 12th instant, you may say to him that I have constantly been, am now and shall continue ready to receive any agent whom he or any other influential person now resisting the national authority may informally send to me with the view of securing peace to our common country."

He took an hour to the writing of this note. When he had made a fair copy and passed it to Blair, the old man rubbed his bearded chin. "That's so diplomatic it says nothing at all!" he exclaimed angrily. "You mustn't be—"

Lincoln interrupted gently as he took off his spectacles, "I know you're dissatisfied, old friend, which pains me very much. But I wish not to be argued with further."

Blair rose, thrust the letter into his breast pocket, bowed and went out.

Bob's sleek dark head instantly obtruded itself through the door to the secretary's office. He had finished his course at Harvard and was awaiting his mother's approval of his joining Grant's army.

"Father," he said, hurriedly, "mother's going to a tea fight, this afternoon. Mary Harlan and I want to know if we may ride with you in mother's place."

Lincoln smiled delightedly. "Any particular spot she wants to take us, Bob?"

"I didn't ask her, sir!" admitted the boy, blushing.

"So tickled at the idea, forgot everything else, eh? All right, my son, I accept with pleasure. Perhaps she'll want to go to the theater with us this evening?"

"I'll ask. Thanks, father!" The sleek head disappeared and Lincoln turned back to his desk, still smiling.

The day's rush engulfed him then and he did not think again of his unusual invitation until Bob appeared at four o'clock clad in his new fawn-colored broadcloth overcoat, with a gardenia in the buttonhole. He came in, adroitly, just as a committee of Quakers departed, rushed over to his father and seizing the President's hand dragged him at top speed into the sitting room.

"I told your doorman to give me one minute and I'd capture you, father! I also told Nurse-maid Crook that you'd emerge from this room and not the office. Mary is sitting in the carriage and the cavalry guard paws the driveway!"

"Everything's at the church, in other words, except the bridegroom," exclaimed Lincoln, allowing Bob to tool him rapidly through the rooms that separated the sitting room from his own quarters. "I put on my best overcoat, I suppose, sacred to funerals and parades, but I draw the line at a gardenia."

"That's all right! Yours is a camellia, sir." Bob grinned and held up his father's overcoat, the flower already in the buttonhole.

Lincoln laughed and pulling on his gloves followed Bob into the hall where William Crook, one of the bodyguards selected by Lamon, awaited them. "Coming to the wedding, Crook?" asked the President as they hurried down the private stairway, after Bob.

The young guard nodded. "I guess I'll have to, Mr. Lincoln, or never face Marshal Lamon again!"

When they reached the carriage, Crook mounted beside the coachman. The President seated himself beside Mary Harlan, with Bob opposite, but as the carriage started he insisted on changing places with his son. He enjoyed looking at the two young faces.

"Where are we going, Mary Harlan?" asked Lincoln. "That's another new bonnet, isn't it? The last one I saw you in was purple."

"Not purple, lavender, sir," replied Mary Harlan. "What color would you call this one?"

Lincoln considered gravely not only the little velvet head-covering but the charming, delicate face beneath it. Then he said, "I'd say the color was pink and white."

"Wrong!" cried Bob. "It's buttercup yellow."

"Some one told you!" protested Lincoln. "And a woman at that! No regular man ever thought of such a name. Where are we headed, my dear?"

"Well, Mr. Lincoln, some of my friends are preparing a benefit entertainment for the Soldiers' Home Hospital. They have a dress rehearsal this afternoon at one of the houses and I thought you'd like to see it because you probably couldn't officially attend the actual performance. I won't tell you the name of the family to whose house we're going so you won't be embarrassed by introductions. You shall just slip in and out as informally as if you were back in Springfield."

"What is the performance?" asked the President, a little uneasily.

"The singing of Scotch, English and Irish ballads in costume."

"Oh, bless you!" exclaimed Lincoln with delight. "How did you know those were my favorites of all forms of music?"

"We all know it," replied the young girl demurely. "Any one who's watched your face when Marshal Lamon sings 'Sweet Alice, Ben Bolt' couldn't avoid knowing it."

"My sad little song! Yes! Yes!" He leaned back and let his long body relax.

The young people, content only to be together and with precocious sympathy for his weariness, did not speak until the carriage halted before a snowy lawn beyond which stood a white frame house with porch of Georgian pillars. It was a small house and unpretentious.

Lincoln, on emerging from the carriage, said to the coachman and the captain of the cavalry guard, "You fellows disappear for one hour, I don't want to notify Washington that I'm here. Crook, I reckon you'll have to come along."

Mary Harlan gathered up her ruffles and led the way up the path and into a little cold hall that smelled of baked apples. "Hang up your coats, here," she ordered. When they had obeyed, she opened the door into a parlor, which was so like the parlor of the Lincolns' house in Springfield that the President gasped; the same, long, low room, with rosewood and horsehair furniture, and the same indefinable air of homely elegance that Mary Lincoln had achieved in her own house.

A dozen young men and women were variously occupied in the room. A gray-haired lady sewed at a window. All rose as Lincoln entered but sat down immediately at Mary Harlan's gesture.

"Well, here we are!" she said gayly. "I hope we're not late."

"They are just having the preliminary skirmish over what number shall be first," said the gray-haired woman, her cheeks flushing as she looked at the President. "Will you sit here by the window, sir, or by the fire?"

"By the fire, madam, if you don't mind," replied Lincoln, sinking into a familiar-looking rocking chair.

"Bob, you come over here to the piano and turn music," ordered a red-haired girl in a Scotch costume.

Bob fell over a footstool in his haste to obey. Some one struck preliminary chords and the red-haired girl in a soft contralto began to sing,

> "I heard them lilting at our ewe-milking,
> Lasses a-lilting before dawn o' day;—"

For an hour, no one gave heed to Lincoln save to glance with young awe, not untouched by pity, at the tragic head resting against the cross-stitched antimacassar. It was an hour of unalloyed pleasure for Lincoln. The simple homeliness and pathos of the ballads precisely suited him. He did not permit himself to think but gave his mind utterly to the music and to watching the young people and their charming dresses. A young shepherd sang in a sweet, high tenor, "O come with me and be my love!" A Highland chief lamented "I wish I were where Helen lies!" and a youngster whose voice had not yet changed warbled from beneath a white wig, "I remember, I remember, the house where I was born," bringing a smile to accompany the tears in Lincoln's eyes. Many of the songs he never had heard before. Of these he particularly enjoyed Shelley's perfect "Invocation to Night." He asked that this be repeated and wrote down the title. At the end of the program he wondered, he said, why no one had sung "Sweet Alice, Ben Bolt," and his gray-haired hostess, with a smile, displaced the young man at the piano, then to her own accompaniment and in a soft rich soprano, she gave him the "sad little song."

Perhaps, when the rehearsal was over, they would have gathered around him had Mary Harlan not led him instantly into the hall, permitting him to call only a general Good-by!

"They aren't going to be allowed to trouble you," she said stoutly, as Bob helped her with her cloak. "That was the bargain they made with me, that you'd be merely a neighbor dropping in."

"Well," sighed Lincoln, "I can only pay you the highest tribute in my power. You're rightly named Mary."

He drew her hand through his arm and led her down the steps, Bob following.

It was dark when they reached the White House. Bob retained the carriage to take Mary Harlan home. Lincoln stood for a moment with the carriage door open looking at the two. "Thank you both," he said. "And it just occurs to me that I've missed the farewell visit of the British Minister."

Hill Lamon came bareheaded into the portico. "Mr. Lincoln," he said in a low voice, "I hope the rumor isn't true that you're going to Ford's Theater to-night. You've forgotten your promise to me."

"Jings, so I did!" exclaimed the President. "But anyhow—"

"Anyhow, sir," said Lamon, firmly, "Lord Lyons called to say farewell to you and is returning this evening informally, if you are willing. John Hay made the engagement positive."

"But, anyhow," Lincoln repeated, "I wouldn't want Forrest after my hour this afternoon. You children go in my place with some of your friends."

"No, we'll wait until you are able to go!" exclaimed Mary Harlan.

"Look here," protested Bob, energetically, "I thought it was I who is said by the papers to be paying you marked attentions, Mary Harlan."

"The next item will be a true one," laughed the girl, "to the effect that two Marys are paying marked attentions to your father!"

Lincoln laughed heartily, closed the carriage door and went arm in arm up the stairs with Hill Lamon.

At seven o'clock that evening Wilkes Booth placed each member of his gang in a rehearsed position at Ford's Theater. The horses were hitched to the buggy and held ready in the alleyway by Spangler.

At ten o'clock, Booth rushed out of the theater and took a train for New York, where he remained for a month. The flame of his hate was fanned while there by the trial of John Y. Beall. Wilkes knew the unsuccessful hero of the steamer *Michigan* fiasco and was full of a furious sympathy for him in his misfortune.

Lincoln also was seriously perturbed over Beall but from a different angle. The whole country watched the trial. There could be no doubt that Beall was a spy and for that cause alone merited the fate of the spy, just as Richard Montgomery would deserve hanging by the Rebels if they caught him. But Montgomery was a spy, only. Beall, on the other hand, had been carrying on a guerilla warfare such as was "condemned by the common judgment and the common conscience of all civilized states except when done in open warfare by avowed enemies" as General Dix said in his report.

Notwithstanding that Beall's guilt was beyond doubt, a tremendous effort, North and South was made to save him. A manifesto from Jefferson Davis was produced assuming responsibility for Beall's acts and declaring that they were done by his authority. But as the trial proceeded it was obvious that the manifesto did not help Beall. For as again Dix pointed out, even if Davis had been at the head of an independent government, recognized as such by other nations, he would have no power to sanction what the usage of civilized states had condemned.

As it became obvious that Beall would be condemned to death, pressure was brought to bear on Lincoln to show executive clemency. He was visited by a large delegation of influential New Yorkers. Orville O. Browning of Illinois was retained by Beall's friends and he prepared a petition begging for a reprieve, which was signed by ninety-seven Congressmen. Lincoln placed the imposing document on his desk and made no comment for several days. James A. Garfield called and spoke of Beall's distinguished family and of the fine effect the President's reprieve would have on the South. The librarian of Congress, the president of the Baltimore and Ohio Railway, Thaddeus Stevens, Governor Andrews of Massachusetts, the older and the younger Blair, were among the many who made Lincoln's hours wretched as the date of Beall's hanging approached. Finally, when Beall's counsel, James T. Brady, who had served without compensation called, Lincoln sent word to him that the case was closed and that he would not see the lawyer.

The night before the execution, John W. Forney and Washington McLean, two distinguished newspaper editors, called. They were accompanied by Confederate Major-General Pryor who was a prisoner and for whom they wanted a parole. The President was cordial and granted the parole but scarcely had he done so when Forney asked leniency for Beall.

Lincoln grunted but said nothing until Pryor had finished enlarging on the grandeurs of Beall's social standing. Then he said his last word on the case.

"Here is a telegram from General Dix. I procured six days' reprieve but no more for Beall. Dix says that Beall's execution is necessary for the safety of the community. That is true. I can and frequently do save the man who sleeps at sentry post, or the deserter, but the man who tries to murder women and children, the derailer of trains, the pirate, the robber with intent to kill who when caught tries to excuse himself because he says he is a gentleman, whatever that means, no! Nor do I intend to permit Jefferson Davis to give his bastard government a name and place in society, by this method. The case for John Y. Beall is closed, my friends, and may God have mercy on his soul."

He looked like a block of granite and he felt like one. There was, after all, a foundation of rock on which his tenderness toward his fellows was built. Beall had touched that foundation.

He went to bed that night exhausted, body and soul.

CHAPTER IX

EVIL FANTASIES

ON the 31st of January, Lincoln sent William Seward to Fortress Monroe. He was to meet there a Confederate commission in a conference which was an outgrowth of Blair's visit to Richmond. He had little faith in any vital movement toward peace developing from the meeting and, after he had sped Seward, he turned his attention to the titanic struggle which that day was taking place in the House of Representatives. The final vote on the Thirteenth Amendment was imminent.

The galleries of the House were crowded with women as well as men. The streets were full of people. A restless multitude moved about the capitol grounds. Telegraph lines were cleared of war news, in readiness to speed the stupendous Yea or Nay across the continent. In every town and village in the North folk waited for the word.

All during the morning debate, it looked as if the pro-slavery party would succeed again in blocking the measure. There were the usual pleas for postponement, for amendments and for substitutes. But finally a vote was forced by the Republicans and the roll call began. The clerk read each name clearly and impressively. Members and visitors on the floor and in the galleries kept tally on old envelopes or in notebooks. As each member voted, word was passed by those crowding the doors to those less fortunate in the halls, and those in the halls called the votes to the eager throng outside. Even the Radicals had little hope for a majority for the measure. And so when, one by one, Democrats who for years had fought the Amendment, sadly recognized the handwriting on the wall and voted Aye, applause swept the floor and the gallery and ran like an ever-spreading ripple out of the capitol and into the streets and up the streets to the White House, where Lincoln sat waiting.

When all other names had been called, the Speaker, Schuyler Colfax, asked the clerk to call his. There was a breathless hush as he stood up, his blond face working and answered, Aye!

The Thirteenth Amendment had passed.

The crowded room went mad. Men wept and hugged each other. Women clapped and cried and swept unhindered onto the floor to embrace the men who had pushed the great resolution through. The pandemonium spread to the streets. A salute of guns shook the city. A huzzaing mob surged into the White House grounds and Lincoln spoke to them from the familiar window.

". . . The occasion is one of congratulation to the country and to the whole world. But there is a task yet before us—to go forward and have consummated by the votes of the States that which Congress has begun so nobly. I have the honor to inform you that Illinois has today done the work. Maryland is about half way through but I feel proud that Illinois is a little ahead. I wish the reunion of all the States perfected and so effected as to remove all causes of disturbance in the future. To attain this end it was necessary that the original disturbing cause should be if possible rooted out. This amendment is a king's cure-all. It winds the whole thing up. I repeat, it is the fitting if not the indispensable adjunct to the consummation of the great game we are playing. I can but congratulate all who are present—myself, the country, the whole world—upon this great moral victory."

John Surratt was in the crowd on the White House lawn. He wrote Booth that night and described the rejoicing in Washington. "Old Abe gloated like a monkey over a stick of candy that at last he'd ruined the Confederacy. I'm coming up to New York to see you." He followed close on the heels of his letter.

Wilkes, unable to settle to his work, restless, unhappy, suffering with the South as she watched Sherman dismember the eastern Confederacy, tear out her very heart with fire and sword, needed only Surratt's letter and visit to rouse his dormant purpose. He returned to Washington.

O'Laughlin and Arnold were working at odd jobs in Baltimore. George Atzerodt had come up from Port Tobacco and had established himself on the friendliest social relations with the Surratts. Lewis Payne was keeping to himself in his boarding house, living on the money with which Booth had supplied him. He called occasionally on Mrs. Surratt. And Wilkes too looked up this passionate friend of the South as soon as he was established at the National.

His first move was to make another effort to find an actor to aid him on the stage. He learned that an old friend, John Matthews, was playing with the Ford Theater Stock Company. Wilkes went to call on him. Matthews was living in the Peterson house across the street from Ford's. His was the hall bedroom on the first floor. He greeted Wilkes pleasantly enough but his caller scarcely had divulged the first words of his plot when Matthews cursed him, adding:

"And get out of here and stay out!"

Wilkes looked at him contemptuously. "You're a damned coward and not fit to live!" he growled and stalked from the room.

The next day, Booth invited David Herold to come into the conspiracy. David was a Washington boy whose father, recently dead, had been chief clerk of the Navy Yard stores and a staunch Union man. His son, at nineteen was an idle, amiable lad, spoiled by his mother and sisters. He was charmed beyond expression by Booth's personality and flattered by his attention. He accepted the invitation without question.

Before the North at large got the news, Wilkes learned through the Surratts that Lincoln's and Seward's visit to Hampton Roads had failed to bring even an armistice. He was more convinced than ever that the salvation of the Confederacy lay in his hands.

He was unwearying in his efforts to get a part in a play at Ford's, but it was not until the 1st of March that he received the promise of one. And that was for the 18th, when a benefit performance was to be given for John McCullough. There was nothing to do but wait for a chance to apprise him of some prospective move of Lincoln of which he could take advantage. Wilkes was untiring in his watchfulness of the President. He encouraged Payne to prowl at night in the White House grounds. On the day of the Inauguration, he went with Dr. Mudd to witness the ceremonies.

"I'll bet I can get within ten feet of the old dog!" boasted Booth as they stood in the rain before the platform. "Close enough to kill him."

"If you try anything here, Mr. Booth," whispered the doctor, "this crowd will tear you to pieces with bare hands."

"I don't know what fear is!" declared Wilkes.

He slipped away from Mudd and made his way into the rotunda of the capitol building. There he began to worm his way to the entrance which gave onto the platform. He actually reached the door and could see Lincoln's bare head. Then a guard seized him. Maddened by what he characterized as an affront, Wilkes struck the man. Another guard appeared. The people gathered about bade the disturber be silent. The guards dragged Wilkes away, threatening him with arrest.

"Aw, he's only drunk, the bum!" exclaimed one of the guards.

"I don't like his kind of drunk. It's fed on brandy," grunted the other, sniffing insolently at Booth.

But he contented himself with pushing Wilkes violently from the basement entrance. By the time the actor had joined Mudd again, the brief ceremonies were ended.

He attended the reception at the White House that evening but could not bring himself to greet the President. He stood with folded arms at the north end of the East Room observing with malicious disgust the vandalism of memento-seekers. He saw them cut pieces from the couches and chairs and even from the carpet and wondered if such a people were worth the sacrifice he was about to make!

He attended the ball on March 6th with no clean-cut purpose save that of adding to his hate by another glimpse of the President. He saw Bob Lincoln, resplendent in a captain's uniform, with lovely little Mary Harlan on his arm. But to his chagrin he learned that Lincoln had stayed but a short time, leaving before Booth's arrival.

Handsome young John McCullough now arrived in Washington and claimed some of Wilkes' restless attentions. Wilkes wondered if McCullough might not be worked into the scheme and tested him out accordingly. He insisted that McCullough view the sights of Washington on horseback with him.

"I'm no horseback rider, old man!" protested McCullough.

But Wilkes was insistent and McCullough, who was familiar with Booth's uneasy habit of mind and his love of physical excitement, at last humored him. However, Wilkes did not take him around Washington. He led him instead on a long and tedious trip over the various by-roads along the Eastern Branch that could be reached via the Navy Yard Bridge.

"For heaven's sake! What is there to these mud traps?" protested Mc-Cullough.

"Well, you see, Johnny," replied Booth, "if a fellow was in a tight fix, he could slip out of Washington this way."

"When I leave Washington," cried McCullough, "I shall leave on the cars. I'm all raw now with riding this old horse. For God's sake, take me back to the hotel! And don't talk nonsense to me. I'm not expecting a Booth to have to leave Washington by stealth."

His tone discouraged Wilkes and he went no further toward taking his fellow actor into his confidence. A few days later when McCullough, as was his wont, walked without knocking into Wilkes' room he found him seated at a table on which were a map, a knife and pistols. He had gauntlet gloves on his hands, spurs on his boots and a military slouch hat on his head. As McCullough stepped in, Booth seized the knife and sprang at him.

"What in the name of sense is the matter with you, Booth?" demanded McCullough. "Are you crazy?"

Wilkes rubbed his eyes and laughed sheepishly and the matter passed as a joke. McCullough saw that he'd been drinking.

Not until the 15th of March, did any definite word of Lincoln's movements reach Wilkes. Very late that evening, he read in the newspapers that a play, "Still Waters Run Deep" was to be given at the Soldiers' Home on the 16th and that in the afternoon, the President would attend. He at once sent Atzerodt who had become a sort of valet to him to round up all the conspirators and fetch them to the National.

By midnight all were in Booth's room, including Arnold and O'Laughlin who had come to Washington several days before to be drilled for the possible great *dénouement* on the 18th. Wilkes had provided their favorite oyster supper. There was a box of cigars as well as brandy and whiskey. On a side table were laid carbines, bowie knives, false beards, handcuffs and pistols.

Wilkes welcomed them all with warm hospitality. "Fall to, gentlemen, fall to!" he cried as the last man entered. He began at once to ladle out oysters in generous portions and insisted that they eat and drink well before getting down to serious business.

It was well on toward one o'clock when he rose in his place and rapped on the table.

"A new opportunity has come to hand, friends," he said. "But first, I shall review the plan for the 18th just to be sure there is no fundamental change necessary." He read from a slip of paper. "John Wilkes Booth playing Piscara in the Apostate. Atzerodt and Herold will turn off the gas all over the theater. Payne and Arnold will enter the President's box and knock him senseless, then throw him down to me on the stage where O'Laughlin will join me in dragging him out to the alley. Here Surratt will be waiting with the buggy, in which we will throw old Abe, I gagging and tying him while Surratt drives like lightning over the bridge to Maryland. The rest of you will follow, discreetly but rapidly, on horseback. So much for that. Are there any suggestions?"

"Good God, Wilkes!" grunted O'Laughlin. "When you read it out like that it sounds like a crazy nightmare."

"I don't want to throw cold water," said John Surratt, sipping whiskey and water to cover a real anxiety, "but I learned this evening through a friend in the War Department that our plot is suspected up there."

"Nonsense!" cried Wilkes. "Of course, there's danger to all of us. We face that and glory in it. What are you, cowards?"

"Don't call names, Booth!" sneered O'Laughlin. "You're in no position to do so. You've been all promise and no performance so far and the thing's dragged on, a muddleheaded farce, for months. As near as I can see, the Richmond authorities will have no further use for old Abe after another month."

"Ah, won't they? Won't they?" Booth set down his empty glass. "They'll thank us on their bended knees for giving them means for dictating the terms of peace."

"I'm out of it," said Arnold, rising suddenly, his face flushed.

"Sit down! You ought to be shot!" snarled Booth.

Arnold gave him a cold, fearless stare. "Two can play at that game, sir!"

"Don't quarrel, don't!" drawled young Payne.

Sam Arnold swallowed, then said carefully, "Well, let's take a vacation. Suspicion rests on me, I tell you. Not only from my family but the neighbors. I've got to leave home and this part of the country."

"You don't want the money?" demanded Booth, excitedly.

"Money! Money! Why, I'm as you might say in rags. You've never fulfilled your promise about the cash and I'm sick of depending on you. You're really most inconsiderate as a boss, Wilkes. I'm not trying to insult you. I was one with you at first, but nothing happens and I can't live this way."

"Just what do you mean?" asked Atzerodt who had sat silently staring from Booth to Arnold, an unchanging grin on his bearded lips.

"It means Sam Arnold is a traitor!" cried Wilkes. "Wait!" as Sam raised his fist. "Wait! Let me explain again what the facts are that make me undertake to capture Abe Lincoln."

O'Laughlin shouted suddenly, "If you lecture, I lecture, brother Piscara."

"Hell, let's play poker while everybody cools down!" suggested Atzerodt.

"I've got a deck of cards," said David Herold, eagerly.

"Cards! Listen to me!" shouted Wilkes. "You've given me no opportunity to tell you of the new turn of events." He then told them of Lincoln's prospective visit to the Soldiers' Home.

But Arnold, O'Laughlin and Surratt were out of hand now and although they listened to the latest scheme, they would agree to nothing and left the room. It was five o'clock before the others departed.

The details of that conference were clear in nobody's mind the next day for every one had drunk heavily. But late in the morning Wilkes called on Arnold and O'Laughlin and apologized for anything he may have said, begging them to agree to join him that afternoon in the abduction near the Soldiers' Home. Surratt, he said, had yielded to his pleas and was heartily with him again. O'Laughlin shrugged his shoulders.

"I don't mind one more fumble at the old man," he said.

"I'll do whatever you wish, this week," was Arnold's unwilling concession. "But after this week, I'm absolutely through."

"Meet me at the café I told you of last night, then, going at once, but singly," ordered Booth and he rushed out to his horse, mounted and galloped off through the mud.

They gathered, one at a time, in the restaurant at the foot of the hill below the Home. By two o'clock all were present and after several rounds of drinks, Booth whispered their final orders.

They all would hide in a clump of trees a quarter of a mile below the restaurant. While the others attacked the cavalry guard, Booth and Payne would attack the occupants of the carriage, shooting the coachman whose place Surratt would take and drive them across country while Booth and Payne secured the President.

Just before the time set for his start to the Soldiers' Home, Chief Justice Chase called on the President at the White House. Lincoln had been ill, had in fact been holding his Cabinet meetings in his bedroom but he had insisted in the face of his wife's protest that he felt well enough for the drive that afternoon.

Chase, his usual condescending, handsome self, greeted Lincoln as if there never had been a difference of opinion between them and asked for a Presidential permit for a friend of his to trade in tobacco with the South.

The President hesitated. "Mr. Welles says I'm a fool to issue any more of those. Hold on! Welles is outside. We'll have him in." He pulled the bell rope and the Secretary of the Navy entered before Chase could voice his displeasure.

"Mr. Welles has decided views on the matter of trade permits, haven't you, Mr. Secretary!" said Lincoln. "I'm rather inclined to agree with them. Just repeat what you said at the last Cabinet meeting, will you?"

"With pleasure," replied Father Welles, smoothing his white beard and looking benevolently at Chase whom he disliked. "I've had a great deal of annoyance with those Presidential permits. Several of the holders have called on me for permission to pass the blockade, even demanding a gunboat to convey them! Colonel Segar, the last of them, was very importunate. I told him, as I've told all the others, that I won't yield in this matter;

that I've been opposed on principle to the whole scheme of special permits to trade ever since the time you, Mr. Chase, commenced it. I am no believer in the policy of trading with public enemies, carrying on peace and war at the same time. I have no doubt you merely expected to make political capital out of this corrupting and demoralizing scheme, sir, but it has impaired my confidence in you."

Chase, who was sitting across the Cabinet table from Welles, while Lincoln watched him from his desk, grew purple. His smooth-shaven face stiffened.

"I've heard a great many rallying cries in the political world, Mr. Welles," he said angrily, "but none so absurd as one that would link Chase and corruption."

Lincoln cleared his throat. He had desired Welles to deliver his blast but he wanted no quarreling between the two men. He said, quickly:

"There are no rallying cries any more! Petroleum V. Nasby ridiculed them out of existence." And he quoted with great enjoyment. "'Arouse to wunst. Rally agin Conway! Rally agin Hegler! Rally agin Hegler's family! Rally agin the porter at the Reed House! Rally agin the cook at the Crook House! Rally agin the nigger widder in Vance's addishun! Rally agin Missis Umsted! Rally agin Missis Umsted's childern by her first husband. Rally agin Missis Umsted's childern by her sekkand husband. Rally agin all the rest of Missis Umsted's childern. Rally agin the nigger that kum yesterday. Rally agin the saddle kulured gal that yust to be here. Ameriky fer white men!'"

Welles smiled dryly. But Chase, who had little sense of humor in general and none at all where Lincoln's pet stories were concerned, rose with dignity.

Lincoln came to his feet. "There'll be no rallying cries against you, Mr. Chase, but in spite of Nasby's efforts, our friend Mr. Welles has created such a strong one against me and my cotton-tobacco permits that I can't permit *him* to make political capital of it. Come with me to the Soldiers' Home play and I'll tell you what I can do for you. Though you observe, I have very little influence with this Administration! You come too, Mr. Welles. I know you both are going anyhow and you may as well fill up my carriage."

His tone made it impossible not to accept the invitation and a few moments later the three descended to the front entrance. But as the President put his foot on the carriage step, Dr. Stone hurried up and caught his arm.

"Mr. Lincoln, I can't answer for the consequences if you go out this afternoon! Lung fever may be the least of it. Gentlemen, add your pleas to mine! You know how exhausted the President is and now with this heavy cold—"

The President stared down at the doctor's anxious face. Come to think of it, he did feel ill. And more than that, there never could be a better opportunity for Salmon P. Chase to be alone with the one man who dared and cared to warn him off the political quicksands near which no Chief Justice of the United States ought to tread. He drew back:

"You two take my place," he said and slammed the carriage door. To his surprise, they drove off without protest.

Lincoln went upstairs to bed.

Dr. Stone promised that he would be well enough to attend the benefit performance to John McCullough. But late in the afternoon of the 18th, Mary asked him if he didn't think it would be tactful to accept an invitation from Charles Sumner.

"He has a box at Grover's Theater for 'Faust,'" she said, "and he's asked us to go."

Hill Lamon, who was present—Lincoln was resting on a sofa in the sitting room—exclaimed quickly, "The very thing! It's leaked out somehow that you are expected at Ford's to-night and I don't want that. I was relieved you kept your agreement about going to plays when your purpose had been made public, and didn't go to the Soldiers' Home performance."

Lincoln smiled guiltily but made no confession. "I'd like to hear 'Faust,'" he murmured. "Well, let it be so." He closed his eyes, opening them shortly to say, "You can stop worrying about me, next week, Hill. I'm going down to visit Grant for two weeks, if nothing interferes."

"Thank heaven!" groaned Lamon.

Nothing did interfere and Lincoln with Mary and Tad left Washington on the *River Queen* on March 23rd.

On March 27th, John Surratt went to Richmond, returning on April 3rd, and leaving the same night for Canada. Before leaving, he told Weichmann that when in Richmond he'd had a conversation with Jefferson Davis and Judah P. Benjamin and that they had given him two hundred dollars in gold. He showed Louis several gold pieces in earnest of this.

Wilkes Booth was dicomfited but not entirely discouraged. The failure of the latest scheme did, however, increase his conviction that Lincoln was under Satanic protection. If he could not be abducted, then other and more drastic means must be used to remove him from office. He talked with Lewis Payne about this. Payne, after all, was the only altruistic person in the conspiracy, excepting himself, Booth thought. Yet even Payne was not, at first, prepared to go farther than abduction. Even when on April 3rd news reached Washington of the fall of Richmond, Payne was not sure that anything like shooting old Abe would save the South. Still, he remained in his boarding place, playing sick and sneaking out only when Booth urged him to attend the sessions held by a group of Sons of Liberty in a room rented from a colored woman on D Street.

Sam Arnold went down to Fortress Monroe and got a job. Mike O'Laughlin returned to Baltimore. Atzerodt and Herold continued to hang around at Wilkes Booth's heels like unthinking hounds waiting to be loosed on their prey.

Shortly after the fall of Richmond, Wilkes told Atzerodt to sell his buggy, told Payne to remain in hiding and he himself went to New York to see Samuel Chester.

Chester, in spite of his obvious distaste for the scheme and in spite of his previous apparent firm refusal, permitted Wilkes to talk to him again in their favorite saloon, the House of Parliament. The dialogue was much the same as before.

"But it would ruin my family if anything went wrong and I have no money to leave them," muttered Chester.

"I have three thousand dollars I can put at the disposal of your family," pleaded Wilkes. "There is real money in this thing, Chester. I haven't any myself. I or some of the party must go to Richmond to get money. I've already spent five thousand dollars."

"Supposing I came in," Chester looked uneasily around the crowded room, "what would I have to do?"

"Merely open the back door of the theater for me," replied Wilkes.

Chester stared at him suspiciously. "I do believe you're crazy, Booth," he exclaimed. "Now, once for all, don't mention this matter to me again."

Booth brought both great fists down on the table. "My God, why didn't I settle this myself when I had such an excellent chance to shoot him on Inauguration Day. I was as near to him as I am to you."

Chester grunted and Wilkes, giving him an uncertain glance, subsided to silent drinking of his usual astounding amount of brandy.

CHAPTER X

IT was misty April dusk when the *River Queen* made her moorings in Washington again. It was Sunday, the 9th, Palm Sunday, and the Seventh Street wharf was deserted save for the cavalry guard and the carriages of the President and his party. Lincoln felt Washington close in on him like a familiar miasma as he crossed the quay. But nothing could change the fact, he assured himself, that Richmond had fallen, though he still had not assimilated that glorious truth. Now, if only Lee's army would surrender, the end of the dreadful conflict would come. He had had no word from Grant for twenty-four hours, of course. Perhaps the much-prayed-for *finis* had been written while the *River Queen* had been paddling up the Potomac.

As the carriage turned into the mud of Pennsylvania Avenue, he saw that the street was ablaze with bonfires. He spoke to William Crook, his bodyguard who sat with Tad, opposite Mr. and Mrs. Lincoln.

"What are they halloo-ing about, Crook? Not still for Richmond? Here, stop the carriage a moment!" The coachman pulled up. Lincoln leaned out of the carriage window and beckoned to a lad who was breaking up a barrel. "What are you celebrating, my boy?" he asked.

"Why, where you been that you don't know that, Mr. Lincoln?" grinned the youngster. "Richmond's fallen and Grant's chasing Lee across Virginia!"

Lincoln smiled and ordered Burke to drive on.

Pandemonium reigned on the Avenue. Bands marched up and down the sidewalks. Near Fourteenth Street was a special stand with an illuminated sign, "Jeff Davis' Band!" The musicians wore Confederate gray. Again Lincoln ordered the carriage to halt and made inquiries of a bystander.

"Why, Mr. Lincoln," said the man, "those fellows marched into Washington last week, playing 'The Star-Spangled Banner.' They claim they were with Early and got away just before Sheridan captured them. They scuttled in here with their tails between their legs and asked the Marshal or anybody else to take 'em back into the Union. Marshal Lamon gave 'em this job."

The President laughed heartily and once more the carriage drove on.

A huge illumination over the White House gates said, "The Union! It must and shall be preserved!"

"Stanton did that!" exclaimed Lincoln. "He's been planning it for four years!"

"Now the wa' is ova', Papa day," said Tad, "Mr. Stanton can't be Secretawy of Wa', can he? You'll have to find him a new job."

"Stanton can be anything he wants to be," declared the President. "Only he and I know what his work has been worth. I'll give him my place if he wants it."

"Mercy!" smiled Mary. "And just as your place has become humanly endurable! Well, I'm more than willing, my dear! Let's be off to Europe."

"No! No!" shouted Tad. "Califo'nia o' bust!"

His father and mother smiled but Lincoln, as the carriage drew up under the portico, said soberly, "Mary, I reckon I'll drive right over to Seward's house. We don't know much of anything except that he was badly hurt in the run-away and I'm worried about him."

"You won't be late?" asked Mary. "Crook, don't let him out of your sight."

"I won't, Mrs. Lincoln," replied the young man, reassuringly.

"Mary, the war's over," protested Lincoln, as he lifted her from the carriage.

"And the bitterness of defeat will treble the desire of Southern cranks to attack you, dearest," returned Mary, smoothing down her crinoline. Her husband always would swing her out of a vehicle as if she were a little girl but she'd given up protesting.

"You have a low opinion of human nature, madam!" jibed the President, as he returned to his seat.

There was straw before the Sewards' steps and the door-bell was muffled. Fred Seward, the Secretary's son and the Assistant Secretary of State, opened at the President's knock and would have led the way into the drawing-room but that Lincoln stood fast in the dimly lighted hall.

"Fred, I want to see your father."

"He's very ill, Mr. Lincoln. His jaw was broken in two places and is in an iron frame. His right shoulder was dislocated and his whole body is frightfully bruised. He's been delirious until to-day and he can't talk at all."

"Poor fellow! Poor fellow!" ejaculated Lincoln. "It was just an accident? You don't suspect foul play?"

The young man smiled grimly. "Of course, we suspect anything! He'd only just received word of a devilish plot against him via Canada and France. But at least, he will live and for all his agony, he's where assassins can't touch him for a while. My poor mother says that's one crumb of comfort in a terrible meal!"

"Let me see him, Fred," urged Lincoln, "even if I can't talk with him. We've been through several cyclones together, your father and I, and we mean something to each other."

The young man's bearded face softened. "I'll go up and see, sir."

But Lincoln would not wait. He followed up the stairs and in at the door of the chamber where his friend lay. A man nurse rose hurriedly from the bedside and bowed.

"I'm going to sit with Mr. Seward for an hour," said the President urbanely. "You may leave us for that time. You, too, Fred!" and he seated himself on the edge of the bed.

Only Seward's fine blue eyes were visible above heavy bandages. Lincoln picked up the hand which lay on the coverlid and the blue eyes smiled. The President said nothing for a moment. He liked Seward heartily. The liking did not occasionally flare into affection as did his feeling toward Stanton, and this, he thought, was curious because he had more confidence in Seward's loyalty to himself than in Stanton's. Ever since 1861 when he had forced William Seward to perceive that the President of the United States was Lincoln and not Seward, the Secretary of State had been his faithful adherent. He was in many ways more congenial to Lincoln than any other member of the Cabinet. He liked the New York man's vivacity and his genial ways. He ignored his illusions of greatness as well as his loquacity and he deeply admired his gifts as a politician and lawyer.

As he sat looking at the injured man, he thought most of all of how uncritical Seward had been when every one else in the world save Mary had been harshly critical. Even Hill Lamon had reproved him for his manners! And yet, in those early days, when Seward had held Abraham Lincoln in contempt, he had withheld harsh comment. The President felt emotion rising in his throat and with a mental shake he said softly:

"No one can tell you your necktie's riding over your collar, right now, Mr. Secretary, eh?"

The blue eyes twinkled and much encouraged, Lincoln went on. "If you want some details about the late War of the Rebellion, squeeze my hand! Hah! You'll be demanding a cigar, next. . . . Seward, I went into Richmond—not to crow over them, you know. Grant wanted me to take possession, as it were. I never felt sadder in my life than when I walked through those streets and thought of what their desolation signified. General Lee had ordered the tobacco warehouses and the ammunition and other stores destroyed before he evacuated the town. The fire spread and the business section was pretty well burned out along with some of the residences—and pillaged by the city riff-raff before our boys got there under General Weitzel. It was still on fire when I arrived the next day and our troops were working hard to put out the flames. Those Richmond folks were starving and Weitzel fed them. I'm taking for granted this interests you, Mr. Seward?"

His fingers were pressed quickly and he continued. "Weitzel had made his headquarters in Jeff Davis' house, about two miles from where we landed. A nice place with a big pillared porch. By jings, it was well furnished and plenty of food! Jeff didn't live as hard as the rest of Richmond, I can tell you. Weitzel was out when I got there, but he soon came rushing in all out of breath to tell me that Judge Campbell and some other Rebels wanted to see me. Campbell is just as full of tricks now as he was at the conference on the *River Queen*, in February. He almost had you once or twice, then, Mr. Secretary."

Again the blue eyes smiled and the hot fingers said *"Touché."* Lincoln chuckled and went on.

"While we were waiting for Campbell, Weitzel told me that the day before when the fire was at its worst, a darky had run out of a house and told Weitzel's orderly his mistress wanted him. The orderly went in and was met by a lady who told him her mother was ill and she needed assistance and protection for moving her out of the zone of danger. The orderly sent for an ambulance and a guard and then he discovered that the invalid was Mrs. Robert E. Lee and the younger lady was her daughter! They took mighty good care of them. I was glad to hear of it. What Sherman's had to do in Georgia sticks in my throat. I told Weitzel to let all the Richmond folks off easy."

He sighed.

"Well, Campbell came along and informed me that the war was over and how about peace. I didn't let him tie me up—just let him talk and then promised him a written memorandum next day. He looks as bad as if he'd fought the war single-handed.—The memorandum simply reiterated the terms we'd given 'em at Hampton Roads. Before I left, I gave Weitzel a letter to the effect that the gentlemen who'd been acting as the Legislature of Virginia in support of the Rebellion might now desire to assemble in Richmond and withdraw their Virginia troops from resistance to the General Government. On the face of it, it's a military measure, so nobody up here can misinterpret it as a sinister move on my part to organize a permanent State Government. Isn't that so?"

Seward's eyes looked heavy.

"I mustn't bore you!" ejaculated Lincoln. "I'll tell you a little story and then leave you in peace. Peace, literally, eh?—Well, one of my excursions down there was in an ambulance drawn by six mules. The roads were frightful and the driver certainly cursed those mules as fully and completely as I've ever heard it accomplished. Finally I leaned forward and touched the man on the shoulder. 'Excuse me, my friend,' I asked, 'but are you an Episcopalian?' The man looked scared. 'No, Mr. President,' he said, 'I'm a Methodist!' 'That's queer,' I told him. 'You swear just like Governor Seward and he's a church warden!' There was no more cussing!"

He laughed heartily and was glad to see the amusement in Seward's eyes. "That's about all the news," he said as he rose, "except we brought home a yellow kitten we found prowling in the Petersburg trenches."

He moved softly from the room. Fred Seward and the nurse, standing uneasily in the hall, looked relieved. The doctor had forbidden visitors. But when they examined the Secretary they found him in his first normal sleep.

Mary was waiting for him as usual in the sitting room. He slumped with a sigh into a chair before the fire.

"Change your boots for your slippers, do!" pleaded Mary.

"No, I've got to go over to see Stanton before I settle down."

His wife sighed. "You are going to have a vacation this summer if I have to get Congress to pass a law about it. In fact there's nothing I'd like better than to appear in the Senate and compare the amount of rest you get per year with the amount they get, the lazy things."

Lincoln's white teeth flashed. "Go ahead, Mary! I'd like to hear you, myself."

She joined in his laughter as she pushed a glass of milk within reach of his hand. He began to drink it slowly as he told her about his call on Seward. In the midst of the account, the yellow kitten pattered briskly up to the hearth. Lincoln lifted her to his knee and watched her with interest while she washed her face on this precarious perch.

"A kitten is a comfortable kind of creature," he murmured. "Well, poor old Seward!" He finished the account.

They sat in a silence that lasted until Lamon came in, eager for news.

"Now, Hill," protested Mary, "don't get Mr. Lincoln to talking to-night! He's extraordinarily tired. I don't want him even to see Mr. Stanton."

Lamon leaned a powerful elbow on the mantel and looked keenly at the President. "You're right, as usual, Mrs. Lincoln. And Stanton's not in his office, so far as I know."

"There!" triumphantly from Mary.

"Hill, you must remind me to tell General Grant," said Lincoln, "that I went round and called on George Pickett's wife while I was in Richmond."

"I will, sir," replied Lamon with a little smile. "How did Crook behave himself, Mr. Lincoln?"

"Admirably! I'm here, am I not?" laughing softly.

Mary spoke quickly. "What's your next most pressing problem, Mr. Lincoln?"

"In general, to get the Southern States to functioning while Congress is not in session. In particular to try to get Andy Johnson to understand what I'm trying to do."

"A Vice-President's understanding isn't important, my dear," was Mary's comment. "I don't like that man. He's a drunkard." She began to fold up the tidy she was knitting.

"I know that was a bad slip he made at the Inaugural," admitted Lincoln. "I had my fears at the time. But I'm over those. I've known Andy for many years. He's not a drunkard."

Mary compressed her lips.

Lamon nodded and asked, "Do you think he can lift part of your burdens, sir?"

The President nodded. "If he can't skin the animal, he must be ready to hold a leg."

Mary elevated her firm little chin. "I don't want that man at my table!"

"Well, you'll have to have him as need arises, my dear," returned Lincoln mildly. He smoothed the kitten with a long gentle hand. "Has Tad named the kitten, yet?"

"Anna Dickinson!" answered Mary.

Lincoln laughed. "Trust Tad's genius for a smart christening!"

He stifled a yawn and rose. "I'm going to bed, by jings, and let the rest of you put the lights out and wind the clock for the nation. I dare to realize now how much I need sleep." He strolled off to his room, the kitten on his shoulder.

That familiar refuge was particularly welcome, to-night. The huge mahogany bed would be grateful after the cramped affairs he'd occupied for ten days. The only light in the room was from the lamp on the round table by the pillow. A Bible lay here and a copy of "Macbeth." He thrust aside the heavy red window curtains and stood looking out into the night as he wound his watch. The dull sky reflected distant bonfires. He had stood there a long time, the kitten purring against his ear when the hall door opened and Stanton, in evening dress, rushed in.

"*Lee's surrendered!*" he gasped.

He darted across the room, seized the President round the waist, gave him a mighty hug and started to sing:

> "Praise God from whom all blessings flow!
> Praise him all creatures—"

He stopped, pulled Lincoln's great head down and kissed the President's hollow cheek.

"It's over!" whispered Stanton.

Then he burst into hard sobs and rushed from the room.

Lincoln stood rigid. The relief was too great. The chairs and tables did a fandango for a moment before his eyes. After a deep breath or two, he took up his night lamp and opened the door into Mary's room. She was asleep, her great braids drooping in the familiar way over the edge of the bed. Since the fall of Richmond, she'd been sleeping well. He returned soundlessly to his own quarters.

Now he lighted the gas and looked about him. There by the fireplace hung the map with its great black blotches—the slave map, he had worked out four years before. He deliberately unhooked it and with his jackknife cut it to pieces and began slowly feeding it to the fire.

They must head off Sherman. . . .

There would be no more death. . . .

God!

He stretched out his long legs and leaned back in the rosewood rocking chair. The kitten clambered over the back and leaped to the night table which held his little milk pitcher.

Perhaps, after prolonged labor in childbirth, a woman felt like this. Just about like this, utterly worn out, but happy, knowing all was well with the child— He closed his eyes for a moment and thought he was back on the *River Queen*, listening to the bombardment of Petersburg. No, it was a knocking on the door. Elphonso Dunn, one of the bodyguards, put his head in.

"Lee has surrendered, Mr. Lincoln," he whispered, loudly.

"I know, my boy, I know!" whispered Lincoln. "I'm trying my best to soak it in."

"It's midnight. Won't you go to bed, sir?" The young man came in and with a persuasive air handed the President his old dressing gown.

Lincoln heaved himself to his feet. "Not a bad notion, I reckon. Jings, look at Anna Dickinson! Young woman, you're under arrest!" .

Dunn laughed and, seizing the little thief, dropped her into his coat pocket. She immediately thrust forth a small face which she began to wash sedulously.

Lincoln said good night to the guard and turned off the lights. He would undress after a moment and dropping to the bed, he fell instantly asleep.

CHAPTER XI

CHARITY FOR ALL

AT dawn, the thunder of guns—Antietam!—Gettysburg?—Heaps of unburied dead whom he, Abraham Lincoln, had sent to the trenches— What was the use of firing on dead men? It must be stopped! He jerked himself up indignantly and sat blinking. Boom! Boom! The window glass in his room tinkled to the floor. The White House trembled to its roots. Suddenly, Lincoln laughed aloud. As he did so both doors of his room opened. Mary came through one. Through the other, John Hay appeared, followed by Taddie, both solemnly walking on their hands. They paraded around the room and out again, uttering raucous sounds.

Husband and wife smiled, first at the young people, next at each other. But the smile slowly faded as gray eyes gazed deep into violet and then Mary cast herself into his arms. They clung to each other in silence.

Mary saved them both from breaking down by freeing herself and saying, severely, "Abraham Lincoln, you slept in your clothes last night!"

"Yes, ma'am," he replied meekly, and went about making his toilet, grateful for the steadying force of simple duties.

As soon as he was dressed, he joined Tad and John Hay on the south steps of the Treasury Building which commanded a view of Pennsylvania Avenue. The sun was only just rising but the familiar street was packed with an embracing, singing, laughing, weeping crowd. The horse-cars could not move. Racing from side streets came several steam fire-engines which planted themselves in a group, nose to nose and proceeded to bellow hoarsely. Stanton's salute of five hundred guns was augmented by the firing of the cannon in Lafayette Square. The red glow of the sunrise over the capitol was shortly obscured by rain but nothing reduced the ardor of the people. A small boy perched on the iron fence near the President's group flung a bunch of unlighted firecrackers at Tad and screamed, "There's the Lincolns." A man caught sight of the President and beckoning to the crowd, scrambled over the fence, shouting, "Speech! Speech!"

Lincoln was in no mood for speaking. He fled into the Treasury Building. Early as it was, the employees had assembled and were now gathered in the great main corridor, singing:

> "—Praise Him all creatures here below!
> Praise Him above, ye heavenly hosts—"

The President drew his sleeve across his eyes and covering his lips with a cold, shaking hand, slipped unobserved through a side door into the White House grounds. He made his way past the lilac hedge by the stables toward the kitchen entrance, pausing once as a familiar scent broke in on his pre-occupation. On this sheltered south slope, the flowers were opening precociously. He broke off an exquisite, half-blown spray and buried his face in its indescribable fragrance. The little round purple buds were wet with April rain.

Mary, waiting for him at the breakfast table, pinned the spray on her India muslin breakfast-sacque.

"Your favorites always come early there by the stables!" she exclaimed.

"It's a homely blossom and as sweet as home is," he replied, accepting his cup of coffee from the butler. His hand was still shaking and he smiled at it ruefully. "Those Treasury fellows, Mary—"

Just outside the windows which gave on the north lawn with a view of Adams' Grove, there arose a mighty chorus:

"O say can you see, by the dawn's early light—"

"Let's have that window closed!" urged the President. "I can't stand any more."

As the butler hastened to obey, Tom Pendel, the door-keeper came in. "They want you to speak, sir."

"I *can't*, my boy!" looking at Pendel beseechingly.

"I'll stave 'em off!" exclaimed the man stoutly, closing the door.

"Now here's where I put my foot down," said Mary, who had been watching her husband's twitching face with anxiety. "You eat those eggs and three slices of toast. Here it is, hot and crisp. James, you go lock that door into the hall."

Her cheeks were pink with vehemence. Lincoln obeyed her literally and afterward climbed the private staircase with Mary holding firmly to his elbow. She deposited him in his office and spoke to William Crook standing slim and alert at the door.

"Listen to me, William Crook," lifting a small plump forefinger, "only the usual visitors! No strangers, I don't care how they come recommended by themselves!"

"Nonsense, Mary!" protested Lincoln, half irritated. Then he smiled and hastened across the room. Andrew Johnson was standing at the window. The two men shook hands cordially. Mary bowed and went out with her nose in the air.

Johnson was fifty-seven years old but looked ten years younger, in spite of his embattled history. He was nearly six feet tall and strongly built. His hair, as thick and as black as the President's, fairly crackled with vitality. His clean-shaven face with its long nose, too sensitive of nostril, the lips, too much compressed and drooping, told little of the dreadful years in Tennessee. His eyes were as magnificent as Hannibal Hamlin's, his predecessor's, black, deep-set, intelligent, and in Johnson's case, unfathomable.

When he spoke it was in a soft drawl. "I hope I'm not intruding, Mr.

Lincoln. I came early to avoid the crush. I want to offer my congratulations and to present a petition!" He smiled whimsically.

"You too, Brutus!" exclaimed Lincoln. "Well, if no one had pestered me more with petitions than you, Mr. Johnson, this would be an easy job. What can I do for you?"

"I want to protest earnestly against Grant's terms of surrender to Lee. He shouldn't have been allowed to surrender as a soldier of honor. Grant should have retained the entire command as prisoners of war and held Lee in confinement until instructions could be received from this Administration." His voice grew tense. "Do you know, Mr. Lincoln, Grant's sent that whole army off home, on parole, taking their horses with them?"

"I would expect General Grant to do about that," replied the President, looking at Johnson with a peculiar sinking of the heart. "Sit down, and let's talk it over."

The Vice-President dropped into the chair beside Lincoln's desk, crossed his knees and sat motionless.

Lincoln pulled out his paper knife. "What do you think we'll gain at this point, Mr. Johnson, by increasing General Lee's agony of mind?"

"General Lee is a traitor, sir, and should be treated as such. I'm entirely indifferent to his state of mind." Johnson's voice was cool.

"You have nothing personal against Lee?" asked Lincoln.

"Nothing. I'm doing my utmost to see this whole tragedy only in terms of the Union although they did their best to crucify me body and soul, in Tennessee. They dragged my sick wife from bed and imprisoned her. The exposure killed my son. They pulled me from a train and manhandled me with every physical insolence they could devise. My life has been in hourly jeopardy. Yet I know that Lee had nothing direct to do with all this. No, he only upheld the whole traitorous gang from which this poisonous vapor escaped, upheld them with his army. How long would the rebellion have lasted without Lee? I tell you, Mr. Lincoln, treason is a crime, the very highest crime known to the law and these are men who ought to suffer the penalty of their treason."

Lincoln moved uneasily but Johnson's even voice, an exceptionally pleasant voice, floated on.

"To the unconscious, the deceived, the conscripted, to the great mass of the misled, I would say, mercy, clemency, reconciliation and the restoration of their government. But on those who deceived, on the conscious, intelligent, influential traitor, I would inflict the severest penalty of their crime."

The President told himself that he ought not to be impatient. After all this was the man who alone of all the Southern Senators in 1861 had remained true to the Union and in the Senate Chamber yonder had stood up and defied Secession to seduce Tennessee from her loyalty. This was the man who as military Governor of Tennessee had held the old State to the Union, attainted though she was. The North owed an enormous debt to Johnson.

He put a firm though gentle hand on the Vice-President's knee. "I tell you, my friend, if you think you can restore this nation on the Mosaic law, an eye for an eye and a tooth for a tooth, you lack understanding of human nature. The wisest measure Grant could take was to send all those men home."

"And what will happen when they get there?" demanded Johnson. "What will human nature lead them to do? They'll attack and rob the folks who've been loyal. And all your work of reconstruction will go for naught. You'll see anarchy in Tennessee, in Louisiana, in Missouri and—"

"You don't know the people," interrupted Lincoln. "It couldn't but be that every man not naturally a robber or a cutthroat would gladly put an end to such a state of things. Neither non-Union nor Union men want their homes destroyed or want to continue the war. They need only to reach an understanding with each other. I propose to have neighborhood meetings called everywhere, all entertaining a sincere purpose for mutual security in the future whatever they may before have thought, said or done about the war or about anything else. Let all such meet and waiving all else, pledge each other to make common cause against whoever persists in making or aiding further disturbance. The practical means they will best know how to adopt and apply. At such meetings, old friendships will cross the memory and honor and Christian charity will come in to help these afflicted people."

"You really believe that, sir?" demanded Johnson. "Is that as far as your disciplining of these traitors will go?"

Lincoln brought his fist down on his desk and shouted, "It was hate that made this war! The war is over. Let no man come to me asking me to express his revenge or his hate for him. By the cross of the Saviour, I'll not do it!"

Johnson bit his lip and for a moment there was only the sound of Washington's celebration to be heard in the room. Then the Vice-President said, huskily, "I suppose I'm naturally a violent man, Mr. Lincoln. If it hadn't been for my wife, I'd have been dead in some political feud, long before the war. She's been the restraining force that's helped me to get this grip on myself. And I can keep it except when I think of what Southern chivalry did to her. Perhaps I do permit something personal to come into my attitude but—" He scowled thoughtfully and sighed, "No! No! I cannot see it as you do."

"Then you must let me do the seeing," said Lincoln, gently. There was no mistaking the authority in his voice, however, as he went on. "You must stand foot to foot with me against those men in the Capitol whose nostrils belch revenge. *There shall be no revenge, Johnson.*"

"What'll you do with Jeff Davis, sir?"

"Give him a chance to run away, clear to Mexico or Europe. I propose to keep my eyes strictly at home while the leaders of the rebellion skip abroad—if only they have the sense to do so. Do you see, my friend?"

"I see," replied Johnson, "but how are you going to carry it out?"

His skeptical voice disappointed the President. He leaned back in his chair and let his vision wander far beyond the man facing him, over a panorama of battlefields where lay thousands of still gray and blue forms which had paid the last full measure of devotion. Their wounds like those of the dead Cæsar were poor, dumb mouths that bade him speak for them. But not to counsel murder! Nay, it was not revengeful demands from soldiers living or dead that troubled him. It was the demands from civilians who never had smelled blood that would keep mutiny smoldering in the broken hearts of the South. And as revengeful as any were the men nearest him, members of the Cabinet as well as the Vice-President. He must make his own stand known immediately. And yet, he had a curious conviction that this would be another losing fight for him as had been his struggle to direct the reconstruction of the seceded States. Charles Sumner had absolutely blocked the Presidential plan there. This matter of handling the Confederate leaders was closely bound up with the policy for reconstruction. It was going to be difficult—very difficult. Well, thank God, he still held the whip-hand. He'd remind people of that. He rose, and in a decisive manner said, "You'll greatly oblige me, Mr. Johnson, if you'll refrain from talking revenge from this time forward."

Johnson rising also, looked distinctly affronted. "I have never acknowledged the right of any man to muzzle me, Mr. Lincoln."

Lincoln's eyes suddenly twinkled. "Then I'll have to ask Mrs. Johnson to take a hand. I believe in petticoat government. Look where it's put me!"

The Vice-President smiled coldly and went out.

Secretary Stanton passed him in the doorway. "Look here, Mr. Lincoln," he demanded, "do you know the terms that fool of a Grant has given Lee? I tell you, sir—"

"Sit down, Mr. Stanton." Lincoln had always observed that men raved less when sitting than when standing. "Now then, I've had no official word as to what General Grant has done, but I know what his purpose was when I left him. He's done the right thing— You go to the window, Stanton and bow. It'll calm those fellows outside, perhaps."

The Secretary of War jumped impatiently to his feet and stalked over to the open window. The crowd by now had packed the south as well as the north side of the house. Cheers greeted Stanton's appearance.

"Speak to 'em, Mr. Secretary!" urged Lincoln. Grinning to himself he turned to his desk and began to sign documents.

Stanton leaned out into the softly falling rain obediently and began to talk. He was an excellent impromptu orator and Lincoln, signing mechanically, listened with pleasure. But at the closing sentence the President's eyebrows began to go up.

"Let us ask Divine Providence to teach us how to be humble in the midst of triumph, how to be just in the hour of victory and how to so secure the foundations of this republic, soaked as they are in blood, that they will last forever and ever."

A mighty roar came from below. Stanton bowed and came back to his chair.

Lincoln laid down his pen. "I take it from your speech, then, that you're going to let Jeff Davis go."

"Go! Do you call that justice?" demanded Stanton. "No, sir, we're hard after Jeff Davis. Grant's got to keep Lee. I want him and Davis in the same basket. We must let them see what they've been doing. I'll hang them and a half a dozen of the chief traitors in each state. That'll teach 'em."

"Mr. Stanton," said Lincoln, slowly, "we'll do nothing of the sort!" He steeled himself for an argument but the mercurial Stanton laughed.

"Well, cut off their heads, then!" he said. "But not to-day!"

"I accept the armistice! What do you hear from Sherman?"

"Nothing," answered the Secretary. "I don't even know whether he's heard of Lee's surrender or not."

"I hope the fighting's stopped, down there. I want General Grant to come up here for a talk and I'll send for Governor Pierpont, too. He's been carrying the government of Virginia around in his breeches pocket for so long I'm doubtful whether or not it'll function. But he's the spokesman for the Virginia loyalists. By the way, I told General Weitzel to let the Virginia Confederate legislature get together long enough to recall its army."

"What?" demanded Stanton, the familiar ugly rasp in his tone. "Well, of all the damn fool performances! Can't you see we must have nothing to do with Rebel legislatures, that we can't?"

"My message was purely a military measure," interrupted the President, gently. "The Confederate troops are subject to recall, until peace is established, by the Confederate legislature. Come, Mr. Stanton, there are fireworks enough outside. Let's not have any within."

"Then you refuse to discuss your fatal act!" cried Stanton despairingly.

"I'll tell you just how it happened," said Lincoln. "I couldn't foresee that Lee would surrender his whole army immediately. I put into Judge Campbell's hands an informal paper repeating the instructions I gave Seward when he met the commissioners at Hampton Roads in February. And I added that if 'the war be now further persisted in by the Rebels, confiscated property shall at least bear the additional cost and that confiscation shall be remitted to the people of any State which will now promptly and in good faith withdraw its troops from the resistance to the Government.' Nothing new in that proposal, Stanton. I've made it many a time. Judge Campbell thought the legislature would do this so I told General Weitzel to let 'em try."

"But it's wrong to countenance *any* Rebel legislature, Mr. Lincoln," said Stanton, very earnestly, "for any purpose. You set a precedent that'll make endless trouble."

"I don't agree with you," said Lincoln. "Good God, what does it matter how it's done, so that this shattered people is restored to normal life?"

Stanton groaned, hopelessly.

Lincoln changed the subject abruptly. "Are you going to get down to Fort Sumter on the 14th when we raise the flag again? I think either you or I should be there and I certainly can't leave Washington so soon again."

"No! No! I'm needed here to unscramble the eggs," replied Stanton impatiently. "And you must stay here under close guard. For many months now, the vindictives of the South are going to be hard after you. I'm going to be frank with you, Mr. Lincoln."

"Do you insinuate that this conversation has hitherto lacked frankness on your part?" Lincoln's tired eyes twinkled.

"I mean that I'm going to tell you, sir, that your attitude on the matter of assassination is pure bravado. No sane man living really courts murder. Look the facts in the face, Mr. Lincoln. Do you *want* to die to-day—to-morrow?"

Something icy clutched at Lincoln's heart. "Certainly not!" he ejaculated.

"Of course not! You're human like the rest of us. Then I warn you again and most solemnly that you must keep away from public places and gatherings. If you don't, *nothing* can save you, nothing."

Stanton was so earnest, Lincoln was so sure of his affection beneath his nerve-racked manner that something of the Secretary's fears crept clay-cold into his brain. He shivered, then laughed at himself.

"I think perhaps, though I'm not sure, that I could shoulder a gun and march into battle firmly enough, Stanton, but you make a woman of me with this question. I promise you again to be careful."

"I suppose that's all I can hope for," grumbled Stanton, rising. "Has Henry Ward Beecher agreed to speak at Fort Sumter?"

"Yes, he's going to drop in here in a day or so to get suggestions," replied Lincoln.

"I like him. He's a great and good man," moving toward the door.

Hill Lamon appeared as Stanton disappeared. "I think," he said, "the only way you'll get rid of that mob outside, Mr. Lincoln, is to talk to 'em. They've been demanding you since breakfast time."

Lincoln glanced at the clock. It was just before nine. So long an hour!

CHAPTER XII

O MISTRESS MINE!

LINCOLN never had felt less inclined to make a speech than at this moment. His relief, his anxieties, so mingled in his weary mind that he desired nothing so much as to be silent. But he knew the persistency of crowds, so with a sigh of resignation he walked through the close packed waiting room, across the hall to the bedroom over the main entrance from the window of which he frequently spoke. He found Tad already providing amusement for the throngs below. The boy was struggling before the window with the butler who was trying to take a large Rebel flag from him. Just as Lincoln entered, Tad broke free and began to wave the flag over the ledge. A mighty surge of hand clapping rose from below.

The President stepped forward and stood with a hand on Tad's small shoulder.

As far as he could see stretched an agitated mass of people. As the crowd spied him, an extraordinary roar of voices rose. Hats were thrown in the air. Handkerchiefs and banners fluttered. The smoke of unheard fire-crackers drifted upward. Bands blared faintly through the Niagara of human clamor. Lincoln could not bear much of it and stretched out his great arm in a faint hope that he might lessen the din. To his astonishment, the silence was instant. The people stood waiting and he knew they expected him to voice everything which they could not express.

But he could not meet their need!

An acute consciousness of all that had happened in the four years just past rushed into his mind with cyclonic force, shook him, paralyzed his tongue. After a moment, he uttered a few broken and inadequate phrases. And then he appealed to the people for help trusting to their sense of humor to give them understanding.

"I see you have a band," he remarked, quietly.

"Three of 'em!" shouted some one.

"Good!" Lincoln went on. "Then I propose that they play a certain tune. I have always thought 'Dixie' was one of the best airs I ever heard. I understand that our adversaries over the way have attempted to appropriate it. I insisted yesterday that we have fairly captured it and presented the question to the Attorney-General. He gave his opinion that it is our lawful prize. But before the bands strike up, I propose three cheers for General Grant and all under his command."

He led the cheers, then proposed three more for "our gallant navy." After these, the bands burst into the tune which had not been heard in

Washington since 1861 and Lincoln smiled at its remembered gayety as he moved away from the window.

"I told you I couldn't make a speech," he said to Hill Lamon.

"It was pretty bad," agreed Hill, "but the crowd didn't know the difference."

"Yes, they did. But they understood and were kind. I must not make any speech I don't prepare first. I'm too tired and I make a botch of any extemporaneous attempt," declared the President, irritated by his own inadequacy.

Mary, who had been standing with a quieting hand on Tad's arm during the short ceremony, exchanged glances with John Hay and said, "Mr. Lincoln, I've asked the Harlans to ride with us this afternoon."

"I hope that includes Mary Harlan!" The President's eyes brightened.

"I hope so!" replied Mary. "You and I must see what we can of her before Bob gets back. But her mother wasn't sure of Mary's plans when she accepted for herself."

They were moving together toward the hall and Lincoln said softly, "Do you really think Bob has a chance there?"

"I have no idea," replied his wife. "She's so demure about him and so friendly with every one! My dear, she's the dearest girl!"

"You're in love with her yourself!" jibed Lincoln.

"I am," very soberly.

"Well, your taste always was good!" with a contented little laugh. "Here, where are you leading me? I've no time for any sitting-room conferences to-day. I've ten days' arrears in correspondence and documents on my desk and look at that reception room!"

The public hall and staircase was packed with visitors. Mary, however, kept his great hand clasped in both of hers, pulling him gently into the pleasant room. "I won't take two minutes. You must hear Bob's letter about Mary which just arrived from somewhere west of Richmond."

"Well, in that case!" He permitted her to tug and push him across the room into his chair before the tiny spring fire. He stretched out his legs with a sigh.

"You must get the true inwardness of this, Abra'm. It's a letter from a boy at the front to his mother waiting in anxiety to learn what's happened to him!" She unfolded the single sheet and read, "Dear Mother, I heard that you and Mary Harlan visited Richmond yesterday. I do think it was foolish. Didn't father realize that the Rebel capital was no place for you two Marys? I shall be relieved when I hear you are safely back in Washington. How did Mary enjoy the trip? Did she enquire for me or were her thoughts all for John Hay? Curse that man! I'm glad you and father see how extraordinarily lovely she is. I wish I could say the things to her that the President does. Can't you give her a hint that *he's* not her most ardent admirer in our family? I hope General Grant and *his* *staff* will be ordered to Washington shortly. Do give a hint to father and old Stanton on that, too. Your loving son—"

Lincoln listened, enchanted. All the world of war and intrigue was for a perfect moment wiped from his mind. He laughed delightedly. "But don't you hint, Mary! The boy must do his own courting!"

"I'll not make any promises," returned Mary calmly, folding the letter and replacing it in her pocket. "You will send for Grant, won't you?"

"He's been sent for, my dear, but scarcely, I am afraid, for the purpose of bringing Captain Lincoln up here to cast sheep's eyes at his lady love! I wish Bob wasn't so bashful! He needs a few leaves from John Hay's book!"

"No, he doesn't! John is delightful but his witty impudence wouldn't suit Bob. Bob's a great deal like you, my dear, and if you wish to understand his state of mind, you must remember your own courting days."

"God forbid he'd be such a fool as I!" protested Lincoln, "and God bless them both. Just think, to be in love again, in April! Lucky Bob! In love in April—What's that thing of Whitman's?

> "When the snows had melted
> When the lilac scent was in the air
> O past! O life! O songs of joy!
> Loved! Loved! Loved! Loved! . . .
> But my love, no more, no more with you!"

"Not that last line! A thousand times, no!" cried Mary. "Abra'm, how can you?"

She flung herself on her knees beside his chair and hid her face on his breast. He looked down on her wonderingly, then bent and kissed her shining braids.

"It's just a poem, darling Mary!" he murmured.

"You always say Whitman is a prophet. Don't quote that again, for God's sake!" lifting her tragic eyes to his.

He returned her look sadly. He must share his thoughts with some one or go mad. He must find some one to whom he could show that shadow which darkened his soul, that shadow which expressed itself in the fateful dream. But what utter cruelty to show it to Mary!

He rose, lifting her with him and said casually, "You know, Mary, Walt Whitman and I have one thing in common and that's a bilious streak!"

She said nothing and he added, "I'm looking forward to that ride this afternoon."

"It will do us both good," agreed Mary, now meeting his effort. "The woods are lovely. Perhaps we'll find some dogwood, wet and cold as it is." She glanced at the timepiece on the mantel. "It's twenty minutes past nine and I am due to leave for the hospitals at half past."

"Jings! Is it that late?" muttered the President, and he rushed into his office.

James Speed, the new Attorney-General, was standing beside the Cabinet table. Lincoln gave a glance half humorous, half irritated at his pile of documents. "No more executions, Speed! The chief butcher is going out of business!"

Speed, handsome, in spite of a heavy beard, laughed and said, "I know how you feel about that!" Then he added soberly, "These are the police detective reports on the alleged illegal activities of Ward Hill Lamon, Leonard Swett, Thurlow Weed and others, in cotton trading. The War Department has asked me for my opinion and you remember you requested me to go over the matter with you."

Lincoln sat down with a sigh. He was utterly weary of the long reports Police Detective Baker was perpetually making. Baker would cast suspicions on the Virgin! As for Hill Lamon! "By jings!" he ejaculated, "I'd answer for Lamon with my life!"

Speed looked silently at the President with fine eyes so like those of his brother Joshua, that dearest friend of Lincoln's youth, that Lincoln actually started. "Speed," he exclaimed, "did Joshua ever tell you what fools we were about women?"

The Attorney-General shook his head.

"I suppose it's as well," sighed Lincoln. "Well, get on with the papers, Speed."

"I think," the younger man rubbed his head in perplexity, "I think, sir, you'd better let me read this to you, skipping the verbiage. The matter has gone out of Mr. Dana's hands into Secretary Stanton's and Mr. Stanton is angry and is hard after the case."

"I see! Go ahead but be as brief as you can." He closed his eyes and listened closely for ten minutes then interrupted to say, "The nub of the thing is that Baker's unearthed a scheme in which I am to be beguiled into issuing a permit to a man named Lazarre to trade in cotton in an illegal contract alleged to have been made with Hill Lamon, Leonard Swett, Thurlow Weed and others. Well, sir, I'll not issue the permit and that jostles the plan, if there is one, to an early and sterile death. What next?"

"The next step is to satisfy Mr. Stanton."

"Mr. Stanton can't be satisfied. He'll have to endure me and my little ways."

The Attorney-General rose. "Ward Hill Lamon ought not to embarrass you this way, Mr. Lincoln."

"He doesn't," said the President, "just to disregard grammar!"

However, as Speed went out, Lincoln pulled the bell rope and sent for Lamon. But he had worried through two hours' work before Hill arrived with apologies. He had been attending court.

Lincoln looked at him for a moment, then said quietly, "Hill, I want you to promise me to stay out of cotton speculations."

"I promise, sir," answered Lamon, readily. "May I know the whyfor of this?"

Lincoln paused. The war with all its forces so destructive of character was over. He believed that Hill had been, always, a man of integrity. If he had been weak for a moment, the cause of the temptation was removed.

"No, Hill, I reckon least said soonest mended in this— Do you know, I had the dream again, last night—that sobbing and the catafalque—"

"It's only a dream, Mr. Lincoln," exclaimed Lamon, "the fancy of an overstrained mind! When it comes, think of the happiest thing you know."

"Bob and Mary Harlan, for example!" smiled the President, turning back to his desk.

But as he ground on through the crowded hours he was always conscious of the shadow and conscious of a growing sense that he must meet and understand that shadow if he was to know peace. Somewhere, somehow, he must find an hour of loneliness and silence. He made a determined effort to cast the feeling of melancholy out of his mind. Mary was not back from the hospitals when he ate his dinner. But she had left strict orders that the sitting room was to be locked during his meal there. He settled himself with a copy of Petroleum V. Nasby propped open against the water pitcher and at intervals for half an hour, Crook, out in the hall, the waiting crowd in the reception room and John Hay in his office three doors away, smiled in sympathy at the peals of laughter which percolated through the sitting-room walls.

Mary came back before he could return to his office and insisted that he go at once for his ride. He protested only mildly and shortly followed her voluminous lavender skirts down the staircase. The carriage was waiting—with the cavalry escort. Lincoln groaned as he lifted his hat to the salute and said to Mary as they whirled with a mighty clatter down the driveway, "Well, this crime against liberty won't be continued much longer, thanks to Grant and Sherman!"

In a few moments they drew up with a noisy flourish before the Harlans' door. Mary Harlan was waiting on the steps and explained that she was substituting for her mother who was nursing a sudden headache. While the President, uttering proper sentiments of sympathy for Mrs. Harlan, was delightedly handing young Mary into the carriage, Senator Harlan appeared.

He was a striking-looking man of forty-five, wearing the monotonous and obscuring beard of the period. But the features left uncovered, the straight nose and the large eyes, were singularly handsome.

After he had received their congratulations and felicitations over the great news from Grant, Lincoln turned his attention to the younger of the guests.

"Mary Harlan, is that your Easter bonnet?" gazing critically at a confection of pansies and apple blossoms.

"I thought you paid no attention to ladies' clothes, Mr. Lincoln!" Mary Harlan's dimple showed.

"I'm not sure as to that," he retorted. "But I do know I always recognize spring when I see it and comment thereon, don't I, my dear?" smiling at his wife.

"Always!" agreed Mary Lincoln. "And it is spring, in spite of the weather! I'm taking you across the Eastern Branch. It's warmer down there and we may see dogwood."

"We couldn't see any if there were hedges of it with this army around us," grumbled the President. "Halloo! They've put guards on the old Navy Yard Bridge!" as they approached that flat and unimpressive wooden structure. "When did this happen?"

"A month ago!" replied Harlan. "At least I was held up then, when taking a ride. I was told that some sort of a vague plot against the Administration had been unearthed in Lower Maryland."

Mary Lincoln's face changed color and the President said quickly, "Senator, when are you going to take over the Department of the Interior? You are badly needed in the Cabinet. I'm going to want men with the long view on capital and labor."

"In May, I shall be able to take the portfolio," replied Harlan. "I heard that Charles Sumner might be Secretary of State." His eyes twinkled. "How, may I ask, do you expect to get any work done with all the sound and fury in the Cabinet? Stanton and Sumner! Whew!"

"I'll pray like the man in the thunderstorm," replied Lincoln. " 'O Lord, if it's all the same to you, give us a little more light and a little less noise!' We've lived through the war, so I'm certain we can weather through even Stanton and Sumner on reconstruction. As a matter of fact, Stanton is not so dangerous a fighter as Charles Sumner. He's not so egotistical. Stanton is all bark and no bite— Well"—as every one smiled—"a little bite!"

"He's fiendish in his office," said the Senator. "But I contribute for what it's worth the fact that I saw him playing mumble peg with Major Eckert, this morning, about six o'clock. Stanton said they were practicing the arts of peace!"

"I'd say his powers of expression were limited," commented Mary Lincoln, eagerly scanning the roadside for signs of spring blossoms.

"Speaking of powers of expression," mused Lincoln, "you ought to read a letter Mrs. Lincoln received this morning from Bob, to assure her he was safe. There wasn't one word—" His wife pinched him. "What have I done now?" he demanded.

Mary Harlan's eyes twinkled. "How is Bob?"

Lincoln began again. "As I was trying to explain, one had to read between the lines to understand that his heart—"

"Now that the war's over, Mr. Lincoln," interrupted Mary Lincoln, firmly, "aren't you going to hurry Bob out of the army and make him get on with his law work?"

"Judging from his present aspirations," replied the President with a broad smile at Mary Harlan and a wink at her father, "we shan't have to do any *hurrying* and *making*."

The young girl blushed from the tip of her chin to the white line of parting in the soft hair under the forget-me-not bonnet. Lincoln eyed her with frank delight. There was to him something infinitely sweet that with the ending of the war's four years' nightmare should come Bob's charming love affair. It renewed one's faith in the legality of happiness. For a long, long time it had seemed as if nothing were legitimate but grief. He looked down at his own Mary. She was far lovelier as Mary Lincoln, the mother of a grown son, than she had been even as a bride. Life with all its agonies had been becoming to her.

He caught Mary Harlan's eye and smiled.

"Bob," she said, dimpling, "has inherited your beautiful teeth and smile, Mr. President!"

"Good gracious!" he ejaculated. "Some one has discovered a good point in this grizzled old front of mine. I'll have to make note of that for the cartoonists—especially those fellows in *Punch*."

"I'll never forgive any of them," exclaimed Mary Lincoln.

"Nor I," agreed Senator Harlan with sudden grimness.

Lincoln was surprised and touched. "Give yourselves no uneasiness over any of those old malignities," he said. "I've endured a great deal of ridicule without much malice and have received a great deal of kindness not quite free of ridicule. I am used to it."

No one spoke for a moment. The carriage was moving slowly up Good Hope Hill and tried to turn out of the heavy clay to make way for two men on horseback. Both were young and elegantly clad, though mud spattered. One of them bowed, taking off his hat. The other glared at Lincoln like a malevolent young tiger.

"Those are the actors, John McCullough and John Wilkes Booth!" exclaimed Mary Harlan, staring excitedly as the two passed and craning her neck to follow them down the hill.

"Which was which?" asked the President. "One of them looked mad about something. I reckon he doesn't share your enthusiasm for my smile, Mary Harlan."

"That was John Wilkes Booth," replied the young girl. "Isn't he lovely? I suppose he was deep in a part and never saw who was in the carriage."

"Let's hope he had some excuse for his insolence," sniffed Mary Lincoln.

Lincoln leaned back and allowed both eyes and fancy to wander over the fields. "Nothing so hits the normal spot in a man as the sight of a farmer plowing," he said. He was silent for a moment, then went on, "I'm trying hard to think of a poem that'll do justice to this occasion. One part of my mind quotes:

> "For God's sake, let us set upon the ground
> And tell sad stories of the death of kings

And then I think of poor Jeff Davis and go on:

> How some have been deposed; some slain in war;
> . . . ; some sleeping killed;
> All murdered; for within the hollow crown
> That rounds the mortal temples of a king
> Keeps death his court and there the antic sits
> Scoffing his state and grinning at his pomp—"

He paused and stared at the Maryland countryside, thinking of Davis and his frustrated dream of glory.

Harlan ventured to break the silence. "Of course, you'll be obliged to hang Jeff Davis."

Lincoln started, turning on the Senator gray eyes in which the reminiscent light suddenly was quenched. He leaned toward Harlan and said quietly but with all the finality at his command, "Not another man from this day forth shall die for his connection with the Rebellion, if I can prevent it. Senator, you spoke as if you *wanted* Davis to hang!"

The man from Iowa stiffened. "If we don't treat the leaders of the Rebellion as traitors always have been treated, this Union never will be safe from attacks within. Davis and his satellites must hang, deeply as I deplore it."

"No, they shall not hang!" Lincoln sighed and observed for the first time that the April wind was cold. "They shall live and suffer what is more painful than hanging; that is regret! The sense of failure will choke their ambitions for the rest of their days. That's punishment enough. That's the punishment of God which no man can escape."

"I believe public opinion will not permit you to save Davis," reiterated Harlan.

Mary Harlan suddenly leaned forward to put a small white gloved hand on the President's knee. "And what quotation is in the other part of your mind, dear Mr. Lincoln? We can't bear to have you look so tragic."

He laid his great palm gratefully for a moment over her little fist.

"The other part of my mind, Mary Harlan, is as festive as a young lamb skipping among the daisies. It says:

"'O Mistress mine, where are you roaming?
O stay and hear! Your true-love's coming. . . .
Trip no further, pretty sweeting,
Journeys end in lover's meeting—
Every wise man's son doth know.'"

The younger Mary looked at the older Mary. "He must have been a wonderful lover."

"He *is* one," returned the elder. "He has improved with the years."

"Hear! Hear!" chuckled Lincoln.

"What other nice thing is in your mind, sir?" urged Mary Harlan.

"A dream of California," replied the President, leaning back once more and closing his eyes. "A dream of a new life in California. I know a poem about California by Walt Whitman."

"Now, no more poems from *him*, Mr. Lincoln," protested Mary Lincoln. "I don't like his implications—"

"There's nothing about California in that poem, anyhow," volunteered Mary Harlan.

"Daughter, are you admitting you've read Whitman? He's an indecent rubbish-monger. I certainly can't permit that!" Senator Harlan's face was flushed.

"But, father dear," began Mary, "he doesn't compare with the Old Testament for—"

"That's enough, daughter! We'll not compare the Bible with 'Leaves of Grass.'"

But she was by no means suppressed. "And yet you swear by Robert Burns, father!"

Lincoln roared with such spontaneity of amusement that even Harlan joined him. But the Senator quickly sobered to say, "Nevertheless, if there were more young people buying the Bible and fewer buying 'Leaves of Grass' it would be better for the state of the country."

"That reminds me of a little story about Bible selling!" exclaimed Lincoln. "A certain Bible peddler was making his rounds through the frontier woods when he came on a poor little cabin chock full of children. The mother appeared to be working hard but it was evidently one of those households where nothing but dirty dishes and unmade beds thrive. The peddler saw at once that here was a field for work and after he'd talked to the mother a little while about her soul's salvation, he asked her if she owned a Bible.

"She was right mad and indignant. She told him they might be poor but they weren't heathen. The peddler urged her to show him the Book. She started at once to search; on the rafters, under the eaves, in the chimney closet, under the bed. Then she called the children in and they rooted the cabin out. At last, the biggest of the young ones dug from the débris under the bed, a few tattered leaves of the Book of Job. The peddler was horrified but the mother didn't budge an inch. 'I knew,' she said, 'that we'd *had* a Bible, though I had no idea we were so near out.'"

Once more laughter filled the carriage. Then Mary Lincoln, testing the weather with her glove off, announced that they must turn toward home at once. During the remainder of the drive, the two men discussed the problems of the Department of the Interior, from the Indian unrest to the opening of new lands in the West.

CHAPTER XIII

FONDLY DO WE HOPE

WILKES BOOTH and John McCullough returned to the city shortly after the President and his friends. As they dismounted before the hotel, Atzerodt, who was waiting to take the horses to the stable, told Wilkes that Mrs. Surratt wished to see him. Leaving McCullough, Wilkes at once went round to the house on H Street. Mrs. Surratt, a big, raw-boned woman of forty-five, closed the door of the parlor and said in a low voice:

"I can tend to that business of yours to-morrow or next day if you'll loan me your horse and buggy. I have to go out to Surrattsville in reference to some money due me on land my husband sold." She picked up a white silk mitt she was knitting and seated herself before the fire.

"I'm sorry!" exclaimed Wilkes. "Atzerodt sold the buggy outfit yesterday. But I'll let you have ten dollars to hire one with."

"Thank you!" She knitted rapidly, a competent figure in heavy mourning. She must have been handsome once but there was something austere and hard about her now which repelled Wilkes. The only touch of softness he'd ever seen in her lay in the fact that she invariably wore at her throat a brooch containing a photograph of her husband.

"Have you heard from your son?" asked Wilkes.

"A telegram. He's in Montreal and has reported to Jacob Thompson. The Canadian helpers left on the 8th."

Wilkes moved impatiently. "Then they may not be here in time. I shall strike whenever the iron is hot. Shoot to kill."

Mrs. Surratt looked up at him. "You've actually reached *that* point?"

Wilkes threw back his beautiful head and thrust his fingers into the breast of his short riding coat. "I have!"

"Do Payne and Atzerodt know?" asked Mrs. Surratt.

"Not the fool of a German, certainly. But I'll tell Lewis Payne. He'll be with me to the hilt."

Mrs. Surratt nodded. "Let me repeat your errand, then. A slip in the slightest detail may cost you your life. John and Atzerodt a month ago placed at our tavern in Surrattsville two carbines with ammunition, a monkey wrench and a rope, telling Lloyd, our renter, to hide them until needed. You wish me to check Lloyd to see that the articles are within quick reach and tell him that it's you who'll demand them."

"Precisely! And be sure you identify me to him."

"Oh, he knows you by sight, I'm sure. But I'll take care. I plan to have Weichmann drive me out and back. It's no trip for a woman alone, these days. He's such a fool that he has no suspicions. Will you stay to supper?"

"Yes, thank you," replied the actor. "But I must leave immediately after to break the news to Lewis Payne."

But after the evening meal, a girl friend of John Surratt called bringing a letter she had received from him and Wilkes delayed to read this. Then Weichmann came down to the parlor demanding music and Wilkes and Miss Ward obliged with some duets. Later Wilkes recited poetry for them and so it was well on toward ten o'clock when he left the house. He felt more desire for drinking than for an argument with Payne so he returned to his room at the hotel and ordered a rum toddy.

While Booth was reciting poetry at the Surratts', Lincoln was receiving a guest whom he was exceptionally glad to see, not so much for reasons of state as for the fact that he earnestly desired to ask this man a question. When John Hay announced Henry Ward Beecher, Lincoln laid down his pen with a sigh of relief. As if, he told himself, the doctor had come at last!

Beecher was a little more than fifty at this time, a striking-looking man, clean shaven in an age of whiskers, with the orator's mobile lips and with eyes of searching intelligence. He wore his iron gray hair, which was very thick, brushed straight back from his forehead. It gave him a very wide-awake appearance, the President thought.

"Well," said Lincoln as they shook hands, "you've ceased cursing me regularly in the *Independent*. What do you do for a staple victim now? I remember the fearful things you said in '62 or '63. They taught me to ignore that kind of criticism."

Beecher's smile was a little twisted as he seated himself on the opposite side of the grate. "We ordinary mortals didn't understand your magnanimity, Mr. Lincoln. You're heaping coals of fire on my head by sending me down to Fort Sumter."

Lincoln grinned. "I wanted the best man for the job! Fort Sumter stands in the public mind as the occasion of this terrible war. That's where the old flag received the first official shot and dropped in shame. I want you to rear it again, Beecher, but not in pride. Rear it in humility. For take it anyway you will, this war has been a humiliating thing."

"I will be humble," agreed the preacher, "but I can't agree that there's been *no* glory in this war. Where in the history of the world has a people ever risen against their own blood to set black men free? Don't tell me that the freeing of the slaves was not glorious, sir!"

"I have no notion of being so foolish," returned Lincoln, looking at Beecher with eyes in which the four years' story of the Civil War was written. "Nevertheless, don't boast down there. Be as chivalrous, as gentle and as magnanimous as the event demands."

Beecher, reading the wordless sorrow in those eyes, said with unwonted modesty, "I wish you'd make the address, sir—you who've borne the brunt of battle. Don't protest, I beg of you. When I think of your unparalleled burdens during these four bloody years, when I think of your patience and fortitude and your disinterested wisdom—"

"Don't! Don't!" begged Lincoln. "The credit goes to Grant and Stanton and to a million others. You must make the speech. I'm not so competent as you and I mustn't leave here anyhow. My job right now is to save Jeff Davis' life—his and Stephens' and all the rest of those mistaken dreamers. Stanton's gone entirely crazy. He's as bad as anybody, hollering that we must hang three or four leaders in every seceded State. Stanton's my chief care, outside Andy Johnson." He watched Beecher keenly.

The preacher shook back his hair with a gesture half of impatience, half of disbelief. "Surely in your long intercourse with Edwin Stanton, sir, you've learned to look behind his bitter tongue! He doesn't mean that."

"He means just that," said Lincoln, quietly and deliberately. He knew there was friendship between the famous preacher and the Secretary of War and he wanted Beecher to use his influence, if he had any.

Beecher resolved his mind of that doubt by saying, "I understand Stanton better than most men do, though I never knew him until a few months ago. I came up Wall Street one day and met a friend who told me that he'd just got back from Washington and that Stanton couldn't hold out much longer. He was breaking down. Well, it struck me all in a heap. I walked into one of those offices in Wall Street and said, 'Will you allow me pen and ink?' And I wrote him just what I'd heard. That he was sick and desponding. But that he must not despond. The country was saved and if he didn't do another thing, he'd done enough. I sent the letter and in a few days I got his reply. If it had been from a woman answering a proposal it wouldn't have been more tender. And when I went to Washington to meet him, he was as tender as a woman, as a lover."

Lincoln's eyes moistened. "Yes, he's shown me that side, too. But don't be deceived, Mr. Beecher. There's nothing tender in his thoughts about the Rebel leaders. He's a wolf!"

Beecher looked affronted for a moment then his face cleared. "I shall go talk to him and try to prove you're mistaken, Mr. Lincoln."

"That's precisely why I brought the subject up. I hoped you'd do just that," smiled the President. He took out the paper knife and ran it through his hair and unbuttoned his vest with a long sigh. "Well, so we've rounded the circle of Hell and have come back to Fort Sumter again! I'll never forget the travail of spirit with which I came to the determination some four eternities ago this month to provision that fatal place." He looked out the window and tried once more to realize that the circuit *had* been completed. But in place of that realization came again the thought that Beecher would give him the help he needed. He turned back to say abruptly, "Mr. Beecher, do you believe in a future life? I've been thinking about that a good deal lately."

"Do you mean you've been thinking about future life or earthly death?" asked Beecher. The indefinable air of the minister of the gospel suddenly changed their relationship. It was no longer citizen deferring to the Chief Executive but pastor instructing parishioner.

"I suppose, as a matter of fact," confessed the President, "I've been searching for 'intimations of immortality.'"

Beecher nodded. "People can no more help being always conscious of the surge of death on the shores of life than those who dwell on the seashore can ignore the sighing of the ocean on the beach. Especially after one reaches forty is one conscious of the other world beating, as it were, on this."

"Then there is another world?" asked Lincoln.

"When a man dies and you go to his funeral you say," Beecher got up and began to stride around the Cabinet table, "you say, a man is dead. But the angels say, a man is born."

"Angels!" ejaculated Lincoln. "Do you believe in *that* kind of an hereafter, Mr. Beecher?"

"Why not?" demanded Beecher. "Does it matter by what name we call the inhabitants of heaven? Yes, I believe in heaven, Mr. Lincoln, and I know how to get there, too."

"I'd give ten years of my life to have that conviction," said the President. "How do you propose to make the transit?"

"By following Christ, Who is perfectly definite. He said, *I am the way.* Christ *knew.* His is the final authority for who but God would say, *I am the road. Press me with your feet.*"

Beecher spoke in tones indescribably thrilling. Lincoln felt his weary pulses quicken. And yet, he told himself, it was only such a thrill as he got when Hamlet spoke through Booth. Was Abraham Lincoln doomed to be only an onlooker at all men's faiths?

"I believe absolutely in God," he said, finally, "but for the rest, Beecher, I reckon I'm caught on a spiritual sand-bar."

Beecher's face lighted. "I know just what you mean! Last fall I was on a huge Government steamer on the Ohio. We were so big that the pilot made no ventures out of the known channel. The water was falling fast and we saw that the craft which had ventured were in trouble, even small boats. In one place several rafts were caught on a sand-bar. But our pilot swung as close to them as he dared and our wake flooded every one of the little boats free! I don't know whether I'm a big enough craft to flood you off, sir! You see these were little fellows and you don't come in that category!"

"I know those sand-bars and snags! There's an infinite number of allegories in them. The Mississippi River enriched my life in more ways than one." Lincoln looked at the preacher thoughtfully. He'd never been able to pin any well-educated Christian down to a definite statement about his belief in heaven. But the folks he'd known back in Indiana who could scarcely write their own names had a concreteness that would defy the pope.

"If you preachers," he said aloud, "could give your congregations an absolute confidence in immortality they'd follow you by any route you'd tell 'em, however hard. That would float me or any man off any spiritual sand-bar."

Beecher jerked his head impatiently. "But don't you see that if you believe in God, the rest must follow? He will give you confidence. No mere man can do that. It lies between you and your Maker, a relationship on which even a clergyman cannot intrude."

Lincoln felt definitely checked. Beecher had nothing for him. His pretty baubles for women couldn't be magicked into red meat for a hungry man. "I'm just naturally a mere onlooker, I suppose. You mustn't take me too literally. I reckon my spiritual curiosity got the best of me," he sighed.

"You belittle your soul-strivings when you speak so," protested the preacher. "Why trouble about heaven? If God were real enough to you, you'd leave all that to Him. And you know, He *is* real. You meet Him constantly, and recognize Him, just as when you pass an open window and hear some one playing the piano, you say, I recognize that! It's a Beethoven Sonata. So in life you recognize strains of God—in a child's innocent affection, in a lover's glow, in a mother's self-denying love."

"Yes! Yes!" stirring uneasily. "You had your mother through your boy-hood, Mr. Beecher, to manhood?"

The preacher shook his head. "She died when I was three, so she's been only an angel to me, all my life until a few years ago. Then I found among a packet of old letters in my father's study a bundle of my mother's letters to him. They began with their first acquaintance and continued into their married life. And as I read those, Mr. Lincoln, at last I knew my mother! What the four Gospels are to the life of Christ, those letters are to my mother's. I remember there was one letter in which she spoke freely and frankly of her love. That to me is her Gospel of St. John's, which was God's love letter to the world."

Lincoln thought of a still, stiff form lying under a buffalo-robe in a log cabin in Indiana, with blunted finger-tips resting on the coarse brown fur. He could recall the touch of those fingers when they had been alive, as vividly as if he were feeling them that minute. But he didn't see how any man could speak of his mother's intimate life as freely as did Beecher. Had his mother left love letters, he couldn't imagine himself reading them. He believed any average man would burn his mother's love letters unread. But perhaps a really great pulpit orator like Beecher must have the temperament which made such an act possible and proper.

He eyed the preacher wistfully. There was no doubt that Henry Ward Beecher had a sublime sureness. Beautiful face— What a family that mother of his and Lyman Beecher had produced!

"You look like your sister," said Lincoln. "She came down to see me, a while back. Had doubts about my sincerity with the Emancipation Proclamation. My stock has never been very high with your family, Mr. Beecher, I'm afraid."

"Don't say that!" protested Beecher. "Harriet came back from the interview your loyal friend."

"I blamed her and her 'Uncle Tom's Cabin' with making this war," laughed the President!

"You told her among other alleged facts," nodded Beecher, "that the war was killing you and you'd never live to see the end of it. Well, peace is here, Mr. Lincoln, and so are you! Your faith has been great save as concerns God's goodness to you."

"I've never doubted His goodness to me," was the President's sober reply. "What I do doubt is my own ability to judge what He means by goodness. I believe He was on our side during the war or we wouldn't have won. But I'm not sure what His attitude is toward me, the human being who four years ago released the spring which induced that mortar shot to drop on Fort Sumter. Is my life completed? Why do I have this inner fear that it may be and why am I not reconciled?"

He knew as he spoke that as Beecher had intimated he was asking a question no human being should ask another, even a minister. Had his own intellectual honesty not given him that knowledge, the expression in Beecher's eyes would have warned him—that look of pained inadequacy which he had seen far, far too often in men's eyes when he gave them a glimpse of his inner starvation.

He relieved Beecher by rising before he could frame a reply, saying, "After all, that's important to no one but myself!"

"If Jeff Davis knew your attitude toward him and his fellow conspirators, he'd hope that your life certainly was not done!" exclaimed Beecher. "The answer is vital to the whole South! The North might fumble along without you, sir, but the South's very existence depends on Abraham Lincoln."

The President put a thin hand on the younger man's shoulder. "You go down to Fort Sumter, my boy, and put the flag back in her place with the sure message for the South that they who sow in tears shall reap in joy."

"I'll try, Mr. Lincoln," said Beecher humbly, and he went out, closing the door softly.

CHAPTER XIV

LINCOLN sat without moving after Beecher's departure. Outside the window, Washington was still celebrating. Band music, firecrackers, blank cartridges and the dull, unceasing roar of many voices floated through the window to his unheeding ears. He was reasoning with himself about his disappointment with Beecher, and he convinced himself shortly that he'd been preposterous in his demands on the minister. But the edge of disappointment did not dull. He was glad when the door opened, admitting the next contingent of visitors.

Fifteen men filed into his office and Hill Lamon, his eyes twinkling, introduced them.

"This, Mr. President, is a Confederate band which left Early's forces a couple of weeks ago, in order to pay its respects to you."

Lincoln now understood the twinkle in Lamon's blue eyes. He walked gravely forward and shook hands with the visitors. Then the leader, with his bearskin under one arm and a tissue-wrapped parcel under the other, cleared his throat, set his heels together and gazing at the President with the glazed eyes of one who with difficulty repeats from memory, made a short speech.

"Mr. President, on behalf of my fellow musicians, I wish to thank you for the great task you have finished in guiding the ship of state through four years of tornado to a safe port. We wish to assure you of our loyalty to you and the Stars and Stripes. And we wish to present you with a slight token of our esteem."

Lincoln bowed and unwrapped the parcel and with difficulty refrained from bursting into laughter. From an enormous and elaborate silver frame a large engraving of his own worn face stared up at the President!

He cleared his throat. "Gentlemen, I thank you for this token of your esteem. You did your best! It isn't your fault that the frame is so much more rare than the picture. And I thank you for your words of praise. It pleases me that you came back to your loyalty to the Union before the Confederacy actually crumbled."

"Mr. Secretary Welles is waiting to come in, sir," said Lamon, and with the skill begot by intensive experience, he maneuvered the drum major and his flock out as Welles came in.

Lincoln thought the old man was looking ten years younger. The two shook hands smiling as the band marched down the hall, playing "Dixie." Then Lincoln said, abruptly:

"How do you stand on Jeff Davis, Mr. Welles?"

The Secretary of the Navy smoothed his beard, thoughtfully. "Try him

for high treason before a civil court and if he's found guilty, let him pay
the penalty. I'm for a speedy trial. But I agree with Seward that the Rebel
State papers must be examined first, preferably by an able economist like
Dr. Lieber. Seward wants a military commission to hold the trial and to
include murder, with conspiracy to burn cities, in the other accusations."

Lincoln smiled sadly. "Poor old Davis!"

"I can't seem to pity him," dryly. "He gasconaded the South into this
trouble. He always was the great I am! Now let him pay." Welles blew
his nose on an enormous silk handkerchief.

The two men were standing before the fire. The evening was cold. The
yellow kitten began to claw her way up the President's leg and he stooped
to loosen her claws and place her on his shoulder.

"We have a very nice tiger-striped cat at our house," remarked Welles.
"She insists on sleeping on my feet at night."

"I've always liked cats," murmured Lincoln, his mind on the picture of
Jefferson Davis fleeing for his life while Abraham Lincoln vainly extended
his arms to stay his executioners. He felt tired and very old. The kitten
sprang from his back to the Cabinet table and after sharpening her nails
on the red felt covering, began to bat with a diminutive paw at a drooping
spray of early lilacs. Tad must have placed them there.

"Davis must be allowed to run away," said the President.

"But why?" demanded Welles. "I don't think even Christianity demands that!"

"Suppose we lay aside any sentimental or ethical arguments," suggested
Lincoln. "We all agree that our sole aim is to restore the Union. Will it
aid or hinder us in that work if we kill off Jefferson Davis and his associates?"

The older man parted his coat tails and warmed his back at the blaze.
"I think he ought to be tried. I'm not as blood-thirsty as Stanton. Cowards
are always blood-thirsty, on paper!"

"I wouldn't call Stanton a coward," objected Lincoln.

"Perhaps not in so many words, sir. But in your heart you know he is.
Do you know, he always carries a seven-inch dagger? I have little respect
for anything about Stanton save his undoubted energy and his devotion
to his job. He is intriguing against your reconstruction policies at this
moment."

Lincoln looked down at Welles in surprise. "Why this renewal of hate,
Mr. Welles?"

"Well," admitted the Secretary of the Navy, "it's the last trivial straw,
I suppose. But a friend of mine went to Stanton at my urging and asked
for a pass into Richmond. Stanton told him to go to hell."

"And your friend preferred Richmond, strangely! You should have sent
him to me. The pressure on Stanton is tremendous and his nerves aren't
his strong point."

"There's no pressure on *you*, of course! The man's an intriguer, sir, as you'll find shortly. He's playing with the radicals while he gives you his approval."

"Well, I'll just have to meet that when it comes," said Lincoln. "In the meantime, Mr. Welles, I want to ask you for a promise. I don't want you to give it now. Think it over. But when Jeff Davis comes up in the Cabinet meeting to-morrow, don't talk hanging."

Welles smiled ruefully. "Does this serve as notice that you're going to put the screws on us as you've been known to do before?"

"I don't want to have to," Lincoln smiled in return.

The Secretary sighed and walking over to the table opened his portfolio. "Here's a proclamation Seward and I agreed upon. It closes those ports in the South we haven't already got our grip on so that the Government may begin as soon as may be to impose and collect duties. Will you look it over, sir, and affix your signature."

Lincoln read the paper and then signed it with the remark that this was the kind of document he liked to issue. Welles thanked him and departed. It was a quarter past ten.

The noise in the White House grounds had been increasing all the evening and as Lincoln again took up his pen to begin work on the speech he had announced he would make on the morrow, Parker, the guard on duty, came in to say that there were a good many Congressmen in the foreground of the crowd, demanding a speech from the President.

"I can't speak to-night, my child," exclaimed Lincoln. "I mustn't try to speak again until my thoughts are written down or I'll be misquoted by the papers."

"Yes, sir," said Parker, respectfully, closing the door. But he opened it shortly to deliver a note from Congressman Hooper saying he thought it advisable for Lincoln in person to dismiss the crowd which was growing unruly. The President reluctantly dropped his pen and followed by Parker crossed the hall to the familiar window in the state bedroom.

It was very different from the morning crowd. He supposed many of its members had spent the day in drinking. There was a maudlin note in the shouts.

He leaned out of the window. And again to his surprise there was instant silence. Very clearly but gently, he explained to them that he must not speak until he had prepared his words. "And I'm very tired," he said. "You will go home now, won't you, and call on me again to-morrow evening?"

"You bet we will, Abe!"

"Hang Jeff Davis on a sour apple tree!"

"We'll bring you Davis' lousy scalp, Mr. Lincoln!"

"Draw and quarter the traitor and hang him in the Senate as a warning!"

Lincoln pulled down the window.

But the crowd was dispersing and he returned to his desk. In two more hours he completed his speech. He read it through, grunted, and walking across the room, threw the paper into the fire. Mary came in a moment later and ordered him off to bed. He obeyed her, gratefully, but he could not sleep and shortly he got up to sit before the window. He knew he could not rest until he had thought out what he must say the next night.

He was fully aware that the people would expect him to make an address of thanksgiving and of gloating. But on these grounds he felt completely sterile; devastated like the country around Petersburg. His soul was the sepulcher of all the dead men North and South on whom four years ago Fort Sumter had loosed the dogs of war. Others could throw off the horror of the Rebellion, even those who had lost those dear to them but he could not now, nor, he knew, would he ever be able to do so. For his had been the final responsibility—his and Jeff Davis'. Before the ultimate judgment of God they must plead their cases.

He did not question the immediate ethics of the Northern cause. He never had wavered in his conviction that slavery was wrong. Nor that he had done his immediate duty in saving the Union. But deep within him was a disillusionment so profound that it had cut his joy in life at the roots.

If democracy had worked, if American democracy were anything more than an increase in material opportunity over anything the world had known hitherto, it never would have permitted slavery to exist, or finding it in existence at the founding of the Union, true democracy would have wiped it out in the writing of the Constitution. And again, though the fathers had proved weak, the sons, had their democracy been pure, would have ended slavery by compensated emancipation long before Abraham Lincoln had pleaded with them to do so.

Nay, democracy, which had been his soul's star, had fallen, leaving him lonely as no human being could endure to be. Democracy had been his mistress and she had turned prostitute. . . . Granted that under God the Union had been saved from immediate disruption, could it be lifted from the dust and blood of men's lusts? Would they permit him to do so? . . . Democracy—the last, best hope of earth and America had besmirched her. Democracy, that yearning of man's spirit to grow to its full, unhampered by tyranny; surely it was the finest flower of human aspirations. But it was only an aspiration, never to be realized. Never! . . . God Almighty! for four years Abraham Lincoln had been head butcher of a slaughter-house! . . . Nay, it could not be so! Not Lincoln! Not the boy, the man, who had hated death since his memory began! Since when? He knew precisely. He had not understood death until he saw his beautiful mother lying rigid in the cabin. Now with eyes wide on the crackling fire he saw again the mud-daubed fireplace, the red-checked table cloth, the bark-covered stanchions of the bed, the red blankets and the buffalo-robe on which lay her hands. Sometimes in his dreams, several times of late, he had seen those hands and had tried to clasp them around his neck as of old. . . . Strange death, so icy, so stiff, so indifferent! Death, the terrible! His first real tears had been shed then when he was nine; a man's tears, for his mother. The great drops were running down his cheeks now.

Here! This was childish! He was as bad as a morbid woman! He wiped his face and came resolutely back to his speech.

The people must do their own rejoicing. For him—the job of putting the Union again on its legs. He would give a plain talk on methods. The newspapers would report it. Folks would say he was disappointing and would talk about the speech to prove that it was disappointing and perhaps one man in a thousand would thus imbibe its purpose. Ought he to speak of his scheme of colonization for the negroes? If he could enveigle the majority of the colored people to move to South America or Africa onto territory bought by America and deeded to them on some plan by which they could take it and self-government over as fast as they made the land support them, would not some such scheme be the one sure road to the negroes' best happiness? They never could be accepted on equal terms by Americans (O democracy!) and no human beings could be happy who were despised socially. Moreover, if the supply of labor were reduced by colonizing the black labor out of the country, by precisely so much would the demand for and the wages of white labor increase. With colonization or the prospect of it, the carbuncle on the social elbow of the South would be lanced and a single generation would see it healed.

The rain had set in again, but gently. He loved the sound of it on the portico roof. Rain on the lilac hedges below—the prairies were flushing green out yonder on the Mississippi.

But he would not mention colonization in to-morrow's speech. No use making folks craw-bound with too many ideas at once! He chuckled suddenly as he recalled Tad stuffing his pet turkey with corn until its neck looked like a red gourd and of the boy's calling in Dr. Stone to aid the bird's digestion. But there was no doctor on earth who could relieve a people over-stuffed with political expedients.

The speech must be merely a plain reiteration of methods of restoring the Southern States to active participation in the Federal Government, the methods he had found most practical, by actual experiment. Perhaps he'd better light the gas and get to work. He struck a match and blinked at his watch. It was half-past twelve. The guard at his door must be changing for he heard loud whispers in the hall. Then the door was thrust open without the courtesy of a knock and Mr. Stanton rushed in accompanied by the guard.

"Whew!" the Secretary gasped. "I had a nightmare about you, Mr. Lincoln. All right, Smith, get out!"

"Must have been realistic to have brought you over this time of night, Mr. Stanton," said Lincoln, gently. "My dear friend, you mustn't carry me on your heart as a woman carries her first born!"

"You're about as irresponsible as a baby," snapped Stanton, crossly.

"I'm behaving in an exemplary manner," protested the President. "Now admit it and have a glass of buttermilk with me. Who's going to chaperon *you* back home through the dark? Shall I?" his eyes twinkling.

"I can take care of myself, because I admit I'm scared, Mr. Lincoln."

Stanton unbuttoned his overcoat, revealing his night-shirt tucked into his pantaloons, and poured himself a glass of buttermilk, after which he replenished the fire.

Lincoln watched him, smiling. Queer Stanton, about whom both Welles and Beecher were right!

"I'm scared, all right," admitted the President, warming thin, bare shanks, gratefully. He'd forgotten the fire. "I suppose neither you nor I would have made good soldiers, Stanton. We'd have been leg cases, sure as guns. I've got a whole file of 'em. Fellows who've run away. I've never had one of 'em executed. Always told myself, it might have been Lincoln —or Stanton—or Seward—or McClellan!"

"You've done your utmost to destroy discipline in the armies, I know that," grunted the Secretary of War. "Why in hell aren't you in bed, saving your strength?"

"I have queer dreams. Bed's no comfort to me," replied Lincoln simply. "And when I'm awake, my mind's no comfort to me either. I suppose it never will be again—'Now farewell, tranquil nights!' "

Stanton's great dark eyes, always difficult to read through his spectacles, studied the President deliberately. "You ought to be the happiest man on earth, Mr. Lincoln. To quote Othello further, 'you have done the state some service and they know't.' To the state, I might add the world and humanity—History will remember! You're tired. Nothing could show me so well how played out you are as this. Your mind fails to take in the fact that the war is over."

Lincoln walked across to the window and listened to the rain for a moment. Stanton set down his empty glass and in his carpet slippers, shuffled over to the President, there, to take his hand and pat it softly.

"Tired! Tired to the very core! Lincoln, I love you!"

Lincoln could not speak, but he clung to the warm hand with an indescribable sense of comfort.

He allowed Stanton to lead him to the bed and to pull off the faded dressing gown and to tuck the bedclothes about him, the humor of the situation swamped by its tenderness. He closed his eyes at Stanton's command and with the Secretary sitting on the bed-edge, held to his fingers as to the one hold on reality. Reality—was death the only reality? . . . Jesus Christ, the one true democrat the world had known?—Stanton's hand was very muscular— Nothing of the woman in this touch—aye but the lover too—rain on the young wheat out there on the Sangamon—'the early lilacs became a part of this child'—

CHAPTER XV

WILKES BOOTH wakened early the next morning in spite of the fact that he'd gone to bed the worse for brandy. He was ridden by an unease so extreme that even drunkenness did not give him rest. He required no spurring from Canada to urge him on with his designs. Whatever may have been Jacob Thompson's suggestions, to whatever degree of criminality the Confederate agent may have been willing to carry the war behind the lines, Wilkes did not require Thompson's promptings to change the idea of kidnaping to murder. Brandy and Booth's own egotism were sufficient motive-forces both to conceive and to execute the crime.

The frustration of all his ill-formed schemes had hurt his vanity. And to hurt the vanity of a nature like Wilkes' was to rouse it to a fury of resentment akin to insanity. The news of Lee's surrender had come to him less as a shock to his Confederate patriotism than as a final reason for punishing Abraham Lincoln. He could not now save the ravaged Confederacy but he could destroy the man responsible for the collapse. And far more important even than this, he could focus the attention of the world on John Wilkes Booth.

It occurred to him, while he was having his pre-breakfast drink, that there was no reason why he could not carry out practically alone the scheme he'd often heard discussed in Canada, that of clearing away not only the President but the Vice-President, the Secretary of State and of the Secretary of War. Grant, he told himself, should be wiped out for good measure.

He ate lightly and went to call on Lewis Payne. Lewis, pale from his long imprisonment, was lying stretched on his bed, fully dressed. He sat up as Wilkes entered.

"Look here, Mr. Booth," he exclaimed, "I've got to get out or go crazy! Can't you do something to help me?"

"Yes, my friend," replied Booth, impressively. "You are to help me play Brutus to old Abe's Cæsar. In other words, I am going to kill the man who has destroyed the nation."

Payne rose from the bed uneasily. "I don't reckon you're called on to take any such step, sir. What good would it do now?"

"Supposing I shoot old Abe, you shoot Stanton, Atzerodt shoots Andy Johnson, and O'Laughlin kills General Grant? Don't you see that Mr. Davis and General Lee can at once take advantage of the confusion resulting, march on Washington and reverse the ending of this hellish war?"

Payne bit his nails and stared at Booth. The actor had never looked handsomer. His face was thin and drawn but his expression was one of complete exaltation.

"Don't try to understand, dear Lewis!" exclaimed Wilkes. "Trust me to see this with a larger vision than is possible to you. Trust me, my one and only faithful friend! Obey me blindly, thinking only of our country and what we are doing for her. I know, I *know*, that God has called me for this work. I strike for my country and her alone. A people ground beneath this tyranny pray for this end. Lewis, help me!"

The cadence of his beautiful voice was unbearably moving. Quick tears sprang to young Payne's deep eyes. "I'll help you!" he said, huskily. "You'll take care of me?—see that it comes out all right?"

"Nothing shall harm you," replied Wilkes very earnestly. "Here, let's drink on it! Then I'll go find Herold and Atzerodt."

They did away between them with a bottle of brandy. A good deal too much for Payne, who admitted he'd had no breakfast. He now declared he was going up to Willard's Hotel and see General Lee whom he'd heard was being brought there a prisoner.

Booth shook his head. "Would you join the Yankees in staring at Uncle Robert's misfortune?" he demanded. "Lewis! No, you go over to Mrs. Surratt's for breakfast and I'll see you there, later. And don't forget you are your father, a Methodist preacher, up from Florida. You look the part in that eary-candle-light coat I bought you."

Lewis grinned boyishly and pulled on the black frock coat which did indeed give him a clerical appearance. Wilkes who had been consistently careful not to appear in public with his protégé followed him now until he saw Mrs. Surratt's door close on his great back.

He found George Atzerodt at the crude stable back of Ford's Theater, currying the one-eyed bay. The roan was saddled, waiting for his exercise and Booth mounted him, bidding Atzerodt to throw the saddle on the bay and come along.

It was still but a little after nine when they rode slowly up Pennsylvania Avenue. The street was for the moment in only a normal state of confusion. Washington was resting while gathering energy for renewing the celebration later in the day. They passed the White House then by a circuitous route reached Seventh Street and ambled out toward the Soldiers' Home. The mud was deep and the going very slow. Booth said nothing of his schemes until they had dismounted at the café at the foot of the hill. But established there at a table he plied Atzerodt with rum and then asked him how he'd like to have a share in a million dollars.

Atzerodt grinned and wiped his curly beard. His bloodshot blue eyes lighted up. "I'd given up hope of that. What's the news?"

"The news," whispered Wilkes, "is this." He leaned close to his fellow-conspirator's none too clear ear and rapidly outlined the butcheries he had planned.

Atzerodt rubbed his chin. "I hadn't reckoned on getting mixed up with any killing," he muttered.

"There'll be only Payne, Herold, O'Laughlin, possibly Surratt and myself to divide that million," whispered Wilkes.

"Is the get-away to stand? Same as Surratt and I worked out? Horses, boat and all?"

"Absolutely."

"When will the money be paid?"

"As soon as we reach the Confederate capitol, in gold," replied Wilkes with blazing eyes as he watched the German mind work.

"What does Herold do?" demanded Atzerodt.

"He acts as my helper because I've got to work against a man with bodyguards. Your job will be simple. I'll get you a room in the Kirkwood House where Andy Johnson's living. You find out his room number and on the night yet to be agreed upon, you stab him in his sleep."

"Well," muttered the other, "I reckon I could do it if I was drunk enough and not too drunk."

"Good boy! Here's my hand on it. Now you continue as my groom until you hear from me. Have another drink."

On returning to the city, Wilkes called at the house on H Street. He found Payne and Herold singing in the parlor with Anna Surratt. Weichmann and Mrs. Surratt were off on their errand for Wilkes at Surrattsville. Payne to Booth's satisfaction already had won David Herold's enthusiastic consent to "do anything to help dear Booth, follow him to heaven or hell!" Wilkes sat down at Mrs. Surratt's desk and wrote to Mike O'Laughlin in Baltimore telling him to come immediately to Washington.

There remained now only to choose the time and place of the various attacks. His imagination at once reverted to the Ford Theater plan and he set off to discover what was the week's program there.

The people were surging up and down Pennsylvania Avenue in vast numbers. Governor Pierpont of Virginia told Mr. Lincoln when he reached the White House about nine o'clock that morning that the only way one could make progress along the main thoroughfares was to join a parade, for all of them sooner or later headed for the Executive Mansion.

"I reckon that's true," smiled the President, "from the sounds I've been trying to ignore all morning. Well, Governor, you can draw the administration of the sovereign State of Virginia out of your breeches pocket and level it now in the face of any man! I suppose you're planning to move out of Alexandria down to Richmond, at once."

"Yes, Mr. Lincoln," drawled Pierpont, taking the chair by the desk and returning the President's smile. "What attitude am I to assume toward the Rebel portion of the State?"

"I'm holding to my established idea, that those who take the oath of loyalty can go on with their interrupted functions of citizenship."

"Good!" the Governor nodded. "I have here, sir, a list of men whom I want you to see personally; Virginians of old family, who left the Union reluctantly. If you can put these men at once in positions of authority, it will do more than an army to restore order in Virginia."

"That's the method!" exclaimed Lincoln, "and we must act before Congress can thwart us. My thought is that the general plan we used in Louisiana and Tennessee is sound but that in each State we must meet the special needs as they arise. We can't go very far wrong so long as our basic philosophy is reconciliation. I told General Weitzel to let the Confederate legislature of Virginia meet long enough to recall their armies from the field." He looked at Pierpont, expectantly.

"Has this been done?" asked the Governor.

"I haven't heard," replied Lincoln.

The Governor spread a great pile of papers on the table. "Anything to get people home again!"

"Peace will carry them back to their cabins—just as soon as they are freed from the army," declared the President.

"Peace—that passes understanding," said Pierpont in a low voice. "The peace of God."

"If we can compass it, we poor mortals," murmured Lincoln.

They spent three hours over the lists of names, not ceasing their labors until John Hay came in to say that the Cabinet members were waiting in the reception room. But by that time, Lincoln told the Governor, they'd about set trembling, frantic old Virginia, on her feet again.

"Come to me next week, Governor, before you make the move to Richmond. I'll have some further ideas for you then." He rose to greet the incoming Cabinet.

All were present save Seward, who was represented by his son, Fred. After a short interchange of felicitations, McCulloch, the new Secretary of the Treasury, brought forward the cotton question. There had been an enormous capture at Savannah and he was "embarrassed how to dispose of it." Lincoln listened without comment to the animated discussion which followed. Cotton had been a running sore ever since the war started but after all it was a minor ill now and would cure itself. He would let his mind sag, a little, while the Secretaries aired their views, with every one of which he was thoroughly familiar.

But Stanton roused him after a while by saying, savagely, "Andy Johnson was drunk again yesterday."

"How can you prove that?" demanded the President, sharply.

The room suddenly was very still.

"Did you see Johnson drunk?" Lincoln's voice was harsh.

"No, but I was told so by unimpeachable authority. You do yourself harm with the country by championing him, Lincoln."

"*Mr.* Lincoln," corrected Gideon Welles, loudly. "Is this a proper subject for a Cabinet meeting, Mr. Stanton?"

"It is, since Mr. Stanton has brought it up!" The President leaned forward over the table, his gaunt face working, his eyes full on Stanton's spectacles. "Andrew Johnson is *not* a drunkard. I've known him for years. He's a first-class man. I'm willing to go on the stand and swear he's not been under the influence of drink since that slip on March 4th."

"I'm in hearty agreement with Mr. Lincoln," said Secretary McCulloch. "I see a great deal of the Vice-President. He lunches on tea and crackers, as I do and he keeps no liquor in his suite. But, after all, as Mr. Welles suggests, the personal habits of a Vice-President are not material."

"Nothing about Andrew Johnson can be immaterial," declared the President clearly, "as long as the threat of assassination hangs over me. But important or no, I want to say that this whispering campaign against him in the official family must cease!" He brought his fist down on the table.

There was an uncomfortable silence which Stanton himself broke by saying, briskly, "I suppose Sherman knows what to do with Jeff Davis when he digs him out from the present Rebel capitol at Greensborough. He should put the traitor in irons and send him up here to us. Unless you've already pardoned him, *Mr.* Lincoln."

There was deliberate insolence in his manner. But last night's memory of Stanton was keen in Lincoln's mind. Before Father Welles' indignation found words, he laughed quietly and remarked:

"Well, that's not in the realm of the impossible, either! Governor Pierpont and I had a debauch of pardoning this morning! It read like a roster of the First Families of Virginia. The old Dominion's almost ready to break bread with us again. I hope every head of every seceded State will come to me the same way. That's the way to handle the Rebels. Reminds me of a little story.

"Years ago a lot of young folks out in Indiana got up a Maying Party. They found an old scow on the riverbank and paddled themselves over to a little island that wasn't much more than a sand-bar and there they fixed their supper, planning to come back by moonlight. Well, they enjoyed themselves and at moon-up went to paddle home. Only to discover that the scow had floated off!

"There was a lot of giggling and gabbling then with some of the girls crying. But the stream wasn't very deep and finally one fellow suggested that every young man hoist the girl of his choice to his shoulder and wade to the bank with her. That tickled everybody and with the girls laughing and protesting, but clinging like wild-grape vines, the crossings were made until there remained on the sand-bar only a very small, puny young man and a very tall and hefty old maid.

"Now, you see that's the way it's working out with Davis and me. The folks with these pardon petitions are going to get one Rebel after another out of this unhappy situation until there's only Jeff and me left on the island. And I'm afraid he won't consent to carrying me over and I'm afraid you people will make trouble about my carrying him, if he consents."

Every one laughed, including Stanton. Then Lincoln added, soberly. "It's more than likely to happen! There are worse men than Jefferson Davis and I wish I could see some way by which he and the people would let me get him over."

"I think we can trust General Sherman to deal adequately with the preliminaries," said Secretary Speed.

"Does any one know Sherman's feelings with regard to the Rebels?" asked Welles.

"His brother's speech in the Senate was clear enough as to how *he* stands," said Stanton. "John Sherman is a statesman. He says there should be no terms granted. That we should not only brand the leading Rebels with infamy but the whole rebellion should wear the badge of the penitentiary so that for this generation at least no man who has taken part in it would dare to justify or palliate it."

Lincoln looked from one face to another while Stanton quoted these sentiments. There was, he thought, not a man at the table who did not in his heart agree with Senator Sherman.

"General William Sherman doesn't agree with his brother," said the President, slowly. "He told me that night on the *River Queen*, before the last drive on Richmond that the South is broken and ruined and appeals to our pity. That to ride the people down with persecutions and military exactions would be slashing away at the crew of a sinking ship. He said he'd fight as long as they fought but when they gave up, and asked for quarter he'd go no further. I'm going to tell you frankly that I'm with the General and not with the Senator in this. Is there more business to come before the meeting?"

Fred Seward remarked somewhat hesitatingly that his father thought he ought to lay before the Cabinet letters which had been received by him during the President's recent absence at the front. They were from the American consuls in London and Liverpool and gave detailed reports of a conspiracy against the lives of Mr. Lincoln, Mr. Stanton, Mr. Seward, General Grant and General Sherman. The revelation of these plots had been made to the consul's secret agents, in Paris.

"How imminent is the danger?" asked Lincoln.

"Well," replied young Seward, "one letter states positively that two desperate characters sailed from Newcastle last month on a ship laden with war supplies for the Confederacy, to consummate the crime. They are to receive $5,000 each for the job. The consuls and my father are convinced that this menace is to be taken most seriously."

"Haven't I been telling you so?" shouted Stanton, his face a greenish-white. "Where there's so much smoke there's bound to be a fire! And you do nothing, Mr. Lincoln!"

"But what would you have the President do?" demanded Secretary Welles, rubbing his handsome nose. "Shall he barricade himself in his office and do business through iron bars and over a loaded howitzer?"

"*You* haven't been threatened, sir," retorted Stanton, "or you'd not be flippant. And if the President had any imagination—"

Lincoln smiled. "I have enough at least to keep the goose flesh roused! You have copies of those letters, Mr. Seward? Then give one set to Mr.

Stanton and the other to Mr. Lamon. I don't know what better action to take."

"I'm sorry to have had to intrude it on such a day as this," said young Seward, "but father thought the report was probably true."

"I don't doubt it's true," agreed Lincoln, the shadow for a moment darkening his vision. "Gentlemen, we'll meet at the same time tomorrow." He bowed and walked over to his desk.

As soon as he was alone, he locked the office door and went to work on his speech. He ate lunch in his office—corn-meal mush and an apple. By midafternoon it was finished and he thrust the close-written sheets into his breast pocket.

Hill Lamon came in the moment the door was unlocked. With him was handsome John Usher, retiring Secretary of the Interior. Lincoln walked across the room to meet them.

"Well, Mr. Usher, I'm glad to see you! I've been wanting to hold you up to Lamon here as a model of relief from the whisker effect," smiling approval at Usher's smooth-shaven face.

He turned to Lamon. "If you knew, Hill, what an improvement it would be for you to get rid of those horse's tails on either side of your upper lip, you'd not sleep till it was done. Or at least, wax 'em and look ferocious!"

The young man smoothed the offending appendages tenderly. "I'll make a bargain with you, Mr. Lincoln! I'll shave when you do!"

"Now look here, Hill, if I shave, the people who've been calling me gorilla will think I've taken the appellation to heart!"

"I'm sure Stanton's regretted giving you that horrible name," protested Usher.

"I wonder if he has!" said Lincoln, thoughtfully. "Well, Hill, are you ready to start for Richmond?"

"Fred Seward—" began Lamon.

Lincoln lifted his hand. "Spare me! You fellows are going to unnerve me yet. Ding dong! Ding dong! You keep it up. If you can, without too much discomfort to yourself, let me forget. Here's your passport, Hill. See Weitzel quietly." He dropped his hand on Lamon's shoulder, slid it down his mighty arm and clasped his palm. "Good-by, Hill! God bless you." He gazed into his friend's familiar eyes, reading there a deep world of anxious affection. "God bless you, Hill!" he repeated. "I'll look for you by Sunday."

Without a word, Lamon wrung the thin hand and walked to the door but hesitated there and looked back. Lincoln waved his hand and then Lamon with dragging feet went out.

Lincoln sat down for a talk with Usher concerning Indian affairs. After the ex-secretary left followed a long interval, during which he shook hands with a stream of callers filing in an unbroken line past his door. At twilight, he went into his room to dress for supper. The Harlans were to be there. Mary followed him.

"My dear, won't you lie down for fifteen minutes? You look so frightfully tired and the evening's going to be hard. Crook is guarding you from interruption in the hall and I'll guarantee no one will break through my door!"

"Perhaps I will," said Lincoln, suddenly aware of his aching nerves. "I'm glad to see you in white again, Mary, like what you have on. But I admit I prefer you in gay colors. How long—"

"My dear," protested Mary, but gently, "after all, I have buried a son and I have lost two brothers in battle, since I came to Washington."

"I know, my darling! I know! But we've been too sad. We must be gay once more!" He looked at her wistfully. Could she out of her fund of wit and former gayety *will* the shadow from him?

She smiled up at him. "I shall get a new pink, *very* pink gown, my dear, for myself, and a red necktie for you! In the meantime!" she led him to the sofa under the south window and when he had stretched out with a sigh, she spread a crocheted cover over him, kissed him and closed the door noiselessly.

The shadow settled deeper. "I know what you are," he muttered, "you're *death-fear*. All these warnings have shown you up. Abraham Lincoln, you're a coward!" He lay for a moment breathing deeply, staring with inner eye at the shadow. Death-fear?—No! only horror, only reluctance to go. Reluctance! A thousand times that mild term! He must not, could not go until his job was done. Four years from now, perhaps—

He jerked his head uneasily. Why not be honest? Would he be ready to go in four years? Hamlet knew the answer.

> "—Who would fardels bear,
> To grunt and sweat under a weary life
> But that the dread of something after death
> That undiscovered country from whose bourn
> No traveler returns. . . ."

He murmured the words slowly. "That *undiscovered* country—" Aye, there was the rub. Whither? Beecher had failed him. Yet Beecher was sure—and Beecher had an intellect as keen or keener than his own. Faith was fact, to the preacher. If only it were so to him! Could he see immortality as Beecher saw it, why then the bare bodkin might pierce when it would and find him content.

Harlan was a strong churchman. Did Harlan believe in heaven? What did the men in his Cabinet, what did all these people he saw daily think about it? Did they carry about in their hearts a shadow like his? He knew that they did not. He knew, had known all his life, that he was a marked man, a man set apart to feel strange influences, to know mysterious agonies of the soul.

What would Harlan say if he asked him the question he'd asked Beecher? Hand out platitudes from a creed of course. If he asked little Mary Harlan? The child would be frightened. It would hurt her sense of security in the scheme of things. No, this had got to be wrestled with alone. And God helping him, he would wrestle with it. He'd meet his doubts head on and conquer them. And thus find peace.

Death. He began by picturing himself as no longer existing, as no longer— He gave a great start.

Mary had come in and was lighting the gas. "I'm sorry to disturb you, dearest, but the Harlans are here," she said.

CHAPTER XVI

IN GLADNESS OF HEART

AT supper, Mary Lincoln wore white silk in full décolletage with a necklace of amethysts. Mary Harlan wore pink tarlatan and a wreath of moss roses crowned her soft hair. Mrs. Harlan, in ivory satin, showed as fine a throat and arms as did her hostess. The President gazed complacently at each charming woman and then said to Harlan:

"Senator, just what did you or I ever do to deserve this?"

"We didn't!" retorted Harlan, smiling. "But men are the fortunate sex."

"You can say that even after the last four years?" asked Mrs. Harlan. "I've been thinking quite the reverse."

"Oh, I'm sure men are the fortunate sex!" exclaimed Mary Harlan. "I'd love to be an officer like Bob and wear the gorgeous uniform. The sword-sash alone is worth the price—almost!"

"To say nothing of the sword!" interjected Mary Lincoln. "Think of the joy General Butler has had out of that enormous jeweled scythe he wears! I saw him walking up F Street on a slippery day this winter displaying all his regalia. Every one was grinning at him. He was too silly, strutting and slipping, his little fat tummy a foot ahead of his enormous nose and the sword behind like a kangaroo's tail! I'll show you."

She left her soup and by a miracle of mimicry instantly became Ben Butler, stumbling over his sword, swollen with absurd pomposity. Her husband and her guests laughed delightedly and the President said as she caught her sweeping train up and returned to the table:

"What a long tail our cat's got to-night!"

Mary twinkled at Mrs. Harlan. "Mr. Lincoln's becoming an absolute connoisseur in ladies' dress. Though I must confess to you confidentially that he's often unfortunate in his choice of metaphor!"

"Come!" protested Lincoln, "you know how fond I am of cats."

"Worse and worse," sighed his wife. "Now when my old black mammy saw me in my first train—I won't say how many decades ago—she exclaimed, 'You-all sho is decked out like de Lawd's little sister!'"

"But she didn't speak so flatteringly about your first hoop-skirt," the President reminded her. "As I recall your story, she insisted you were wearing the devil's umbrella! And she was right. Hoop-skirts are the invention of Satan."

"I'm with you, there!" Senator Harlan agreed emphatically.

"I've heard they are going out in Paris," said Mary Harlan. "How immodest we're going to feel showing our—" She paused with a blush.

"Showing the world we have lower extremities?" smiled her mother.

"Personally I'll be glad to have a silhouette less like a pyramid. Mrs. Lincoln, don't you wish the Directoire styles would return?"

"Not for me," replied Mary. "Only youth could become those slinking skirts.—And doesn't it seem queer to have reached the age where one must make such an admission? I can recall precisely, when I was Mary's age, how I looked on forty-five. I thought that life wouldn't be worth living then. And here I am, being dragged, kicking and protesting, toward fifty yet still finding life worth while."

"Men *are* fortunate," mused Mrs. Harlan. "The mirror holds no terror for them at any age. And after a woman is thirty—"

"Yes, I know," agreed Mary Lincoln, quickly. "What I'm hoping to do is to find a philosophy which will reconcile me to wrinkles and gray hair."

"What *are* these women talking about, Senator?" Lincoln demanded. "Here you and I've been thinking that our wives outshine young Mary when they really get their blood up like to-night and they—"

"They are simply singing a requiem to hoop-skirts," interrupted Mary Lincoln briskly. "Well, let's hope that when crinolines go out, beards will gallantly accompany them!"

"This is an intensely personal conversation," complained Harlan, smoothing his handsome brown whiskers.

"Isn't it!" agreed Mrs. Lincoln, affably. "And such a relief after the topics of the past four years! Did you hear that some newspaper reporter had discovered that dear Mr. Gideon Welles in profile looks like that portrait of Marie Antoinette going to her execution and he's now known among the élite as Marie Whiskerette? What would the dear man say?"

"No one would be more amused than he!" exclaimed Lincoln. "In Cabinet meeting, last winter, he showed us a clipping from one of Orpheus Kerr's stories. It was to the effect that a dying soldier wanted his grandmother to come to see him. But there was no time to fetch the old lady, so some one asked Mr. Welles to impersonate her. The Secretary was very much flattered. Said he'd be glad to oblige but the fact was, he'd just bought Noah's Ark and was too busy fitting it up as a first-class monitor to leave. Welles enjoyed the jibe immensely."

"I'm relieved to learn that Orpheus Kerr has one reader beside my husband!" exclaimed Mary Lincoln. "I insist that a generation from now, Kerr's one claim to fame will be that my husband enjoyed him! It doesn't seem to me he's half as funny as Petroleum V. Nasby."

"Here! Here! I must 'arouze to wunst' on Kerr's behalf!" cried Lincoln, and he plunged into a defense of the peculiar form of humor which he claimed had helped to keep him sane through many a bitter hour. He quoted pages of the nonsense in proof of his point.

"What a memory you have, sir!" sighed Harlan. "I'd give anything for even half your power. I suppose it's a gift and one is born with or without it. Were you conscious of memorizing those excerpts?"

"No," replied Lincoln. "I always remember whatever moves me or deeply interests me. I suppose that we pioneer folks who were starved for literature developed a section of our brains you more fortunate citizens didn't need. When there was only one good book among twenty families, you learned it by heart as soon as your turn came. It's a great blessing. I suppose I could recite practically all of Macbeth if put to it. But I'm not unique. A number of my contemporaries out there on the prairies could do the same."

"I doubt that," said Harlan, smiling. "I wish more people realized with how wide a range of science and literature your mind is stocked."

"Hear! Hear!" cried Mary Lincoln. "Can't you have some handbills printed about it, Senator? I'd love to send some to—well, to Salmon P. Chase, for instance. He's so insufferably patronizing to my husband."

"I was thinking of Chase, myself," nodded Harlan. "He was talking to me to-day about—" The Senator paused awkwardly.

The President laughed softly. "About cotton-trading permits for his particular friends, I suppose, and that led to a few biting generalities concerning my boorishness."

"He's going to make trouble, I'm afraid, about your decision against the trading." Harlan looked embarrassed as well as concerned. "He was asking my point of view, I'll admit."

"No, he won't make trouble," said Lincoln, calmly. "He'll make a lot of loud thunder, then he'll do what he's been told to do. It was always so when he was Secretary of the Treasury. He's like a boy I once saw at a launching. When everything was ready, they picked out this boy and sent him under the ship to knock away the trigger and let her go. At the critical moment everything depended on the boy. He had to do the job by a well-directed, vigorous blow and then lie still while the ship slid over him. The youngster did everything right but he yelled as if he was being murdered from the time he got under the keel till he got out. I thought the hide was all scraped off his back but he wasn't hurt at all! The master of the yard told me that this boy was always chosen for the job, that he did his work well, that he'd never been hurt but that he always squealed in the same way. That's just the way with Mr. Chase. I knew he wasn't hurt, that he was doing his work right and I paid no attention to his squealing. He only wanted to make us understand how hard his task was and that he was on hand, performing it."

"Nonetheless," said Mary Lincoln, when the laughter had subsided, "I can't forgive him for adding so much to the unpleasantness of your position by his incessant screaming. And he's still at it. Mr. Stanton's a good deal like him."

"Mr. Chase was a great Treasurer," mused Senator Harlan, leaning back in his chair as the butler removed his salad plate, "and Stanton on the whole has been a competent Secretary of War. It's strange that Stanton should have been, for he's a narrow-gauge man. He has none of the qualities, for example, that made Jefferson Davis a brilliant success in the same job under President Pierce. A good deal of the success of the North undoubtedly has been due to the military foundations laid by Davis. Providence certainly moves in mysterious ways!"

"Davis wasn't merely a soldier," observed Lincoln. "He had a good many of the qualifications of the statesman. He saw this country with a large eye. Some day people will appreciate the broad scheme of road and railway surveys he put under way in the far West. Our grandchildren will be enjoying the benefits of Davis' broad vision while they scorn him as a traitor. He was the fellow who under the guise of military expediency insisted that a quick land route must be opened to California instead of depending on the trip round the Horn."

Harlan nodded, then smiled. "His camel-corps was a fiasco, though."

"What was that?" asked little Mary Harlan, as the four older people laughed.

"You've heard of General Beale?" replied her father. "Well, sponsored by Davis, he imported camels from Syria and proposed to move military supplies across the desert by caravan. It was a successful experiment. The camels were swifter and in every way superior to horses or mules, but the effort never got beyond the experimental stage."

"How picturesque!" exclaimed young Mary. "Why not?"

"Because something still swifter than those ships of the desert intervened," smiled the Senator. "The steam engine."

Lincoln gave a sudden shout of laughter. "Last time, of the few times I talked with Jeff Davis, he told me the Indians and some of the guides out there on Beale's route swear that the camels which escaped into the ranges bred with the native animals and that they've actually seen a critter that's a cross between the camel and the Rocky Mountain goat."

"Poor Davis!" ejaculated Harlan when the table was quiet again.

"He has a lovely wife," contributed Mrs. Harlan. "I've heard that it is her ambition to be the first queen of the Confederacy which has given her husband certain illusions of superiority and have made real harmony impossible in their Cabinet."

"He was doomed not to succeed anyhow," said the Senator, "so long as he founded his government on slavery. It's his belief in slavery that'll hang him."

Lincoln spoke quickly. "Whenever they've wanted me to have a soldier shot, I've asked myself, Will this man serve his country better living or dead? You must ask yourself that question about Davis, Senator."

"But Jefferson Davis repudiated his loyalty to his country," protested Harlan. "He insists he's no longer a citizen of the United States!"

Mary Lincoln rose abruptly. "From the uproar on the lawns, I'd say that Mr. Lincoln had better show himself before the house walls are crushed in!"

"When we came," said Mary Harlan, "Tad was entertaining them as best he could. He was showing a series of transparencies in the window, of his own make, which he said told the history of the war in a hundred words."

"No!" ejaculated the President. "I must get him to repeat it for us, later."

A group of friends awaited them at the foot of the private staircase and after a moment of handshaking and felicitations, all followed Lincoln upstairs to the familiar north window. He gathered himself together for the effort.

The mass of people was well illuminated by the lamps and lanterns which had been set in every window and along the roof and portico. It was raining and there were many umbrellas, which was disconcerting. But there were also many colored lanterns on poles and many sizzling torches. Brass bands blared.

Lincoln took from his breast pocket the fold of manuscript, opened it and lifting a candle from the sill held it beside the closely written pages. But some one reaching a long arm from behind the window-drapery took the candle and held it steadily for him. There had been an instant's hush as the President appeared. Then there arose such a detonation of cheers as he never before had heard. There was something terrible in this acclaim they were giving him. He endured it for a moment, then wiping the tears from his cheeks with a sweep of his coat sleeve, he began to speak. The moment his lips moved there was silence.

"We meet this evening not in sorrow, but in gladness of heart. The evacuation of Petersburg and Richmond and the surrender of the principal insurgent army give hope of a righteous and speedy peace, whose joyous expression cannot be restrained. In the midst of this, however, He, from whom all blessings flow, must not be forgotten. A call for a national thanksgiving is being prepared and will be duly promulgated. Nor must those whose harder part give us the cause of rejoicing be overlooked. Their honors must not be parceled out with the others. I myself was near the front and had the high pleasure of transmitting much of the good news to you; but no part of the honor for plan or execution is mine. To General Grant, his skillful officers and brave men, all belongs. The gallant navy stood ready, but was not in reach to take active part.

"By these recent successes, the reinauguration of the national authority —reconstruction—which has had a large share of thought from the first, is pressed much more closely on our attention. It is fraught with great difficulty. Unlike a case of war between independent nations, there is no authorized organ for us to treat with—no man has authority to give up the Rebellion for any other man. We simply must begin with and mold from disorganized and discordant elements. Nor is it a small additional embarrassment that we, the loyal people, differ among ourselves as to the mode, manner and measure of reconstruction. . . ."

He read on, holding the attention of his audience but feeling that his hold was through its affections and not through any particular interest he aroused. But he persisted. This problem was one which must be brought home to the plain people. The only spontaneous applause he received was when he said:

"Twelve thousand voters in the hitherto slave-state of Louisiana have adopted a free-state constitution, giving the benefit of public schools equally to black and white and empowering the legislature to confer the election franchise upon the colored man."

Under cover of the applause, Wilkes Booth who, with Lewis Payne, was standing just below the window, snarled, "That settles it, the dirty dog! Shoot him, Lewis, where he stands!"

Lewis gripped the actor's arm. "Too risky here. Control your feelings, sir! I feel as mad as you do!"

"Mad!" Booth's low voice was full of unutterable hate. "If I had my pistol here, nothing could save him!"

"Hush, for the love of God!" pleaded Lewis.

The applause subsided and Booth with it, though he muttered, "It's the last speech he'll ever make!"

Lincoln, as he completed each page of manuscript, dropped it to the floor. Here Tad, scrabbling on all fours, picked up each as it fell and whispered, "More! More!" until Senator Harlan pulled the boy gently but firmly to his side. Here Mary Harlan put an arm over his shoulders and Tad remained contentedly quiet until his father's last word was spoken.

The President returned at once to his office. It was only nine o'clock and there were many people waiting for him. Among others were Representative Daniel Voorhees and Senator Lane. Voorhees caught Lincoln's arm as he passed through the reception room.

"This is a question of life or death within twenty-four hours, Mr. Lincoln."

"Come in," said the President wearily.

There filed in with the two Congressmen an anxious-looking man and a woman in a black silk shawl on whose white face horror struggled with self-control. The look was familiar to Lincoln. He seated himself and his callers, then waited. The story told by Lane and Voorhees was of an aged clergyman in Tennessee who after losing all in the war had sought to save himself and his family from starvation by supplying the Rebels with quinine and ammunition. He was to be shot on the morrow. The clergyman's daughter and her husband were petitioning for executive clemency on the ground that the old man was suffering from senile dementia.

Lincoln listened patiently but found it very hard to bring his mind to bear on the case. He was not unsympathetic but, he told himself, although the day had been an easy one on his brain it had been hard on his emotions and he reckoned that side of him was numbed with weariness. Voorhees was a good fellow and was doing his best but it looked as if the poor old preacher had been guilty as Satan. The daughter perhaps felt a lack in the Congressman's presentation for suddenly clasping her hands she interrupted and began to talk rapidly, though with hard-won calm, of her father's record as a minister of the gospel. As she spoke, something pricked Lincoln's memory. He leaned toward the woman.

"Luckett, madam? You said your father's name is Luckett? Not Henry M.—by any chance?"

"Yes!" she exclaimed. "Yes, that's my father!"

"Why, he used to preach in Springfield, Illinois, didn't he?" queried Lincoln.

"Yes, Mr. President"—the daughter's voice caught—"he preached there."

"Why, I knew him well!" ejaculated Lincoln. "I've heard him preach often. He's a tall, angular man like I am and I've been mistaken for him on the street. He was a man of enormous faith. He could preach anybody into heaven! And he's to be shot to-morrow! No! No! There'll be no shooting or hanging in this case. Henry M. Luckett! There must indeed be something wrong with his mind or he wouldn't be in such a scrape as this! You may rest assured, my child, that your father's life is safe."

He rang the bell and called for John Hay to whom he dictated a telegram ordering the execution of Henry M. Luckett to be suspended until further word came from the President. "And that further word will never be sent," he added to Luckett's daughter.

The three tried brokenly to thank him but he urged them gently toward the door, repeating to himself, "Henry M. Luckett! No! No! There'll be no shooting or hanging in this case!"

During the next hour as he listened to the infinite variety of needs urged on him by his callers, he was thinking of Luckett and of Beecher. Both of them so sure of God and of heaven, yet Luckett so passionately unwilling to test that God and that heaven. Would Beecher behave like this? Or was he doing Luckett an injustice and was the panic all on the daughter's side? Certainly panic was a most natural feeling on her part.

CHAPTER XVII

MARY was preparing for bed when her husband finally quit work for the day. As he came slowly into her room, she turned from the mirror before which she was brushing her long hair and shook her head.

"You poor tired thing! I waited for you in the sitting room until I fell asleep over my book. You must be at least a thousand times more weary than I am!"

He dropped into a rocking chair by her dressing table, clasping his knee with long brown hands. "Mary, do you remember Henry Luckett, the preacher?"

Mary frowned in concentration, the brush following the heavy chestnut strands, slowly. "Um—yes! He was a good deal of a ranter, as I recall. Abra'm, I'm getting gray!"

"Well, he's been in a devil of a scrape. His daughter came to me to-night with a pitiful story." He repeated the tale.

"You let him off, of course," said Mary, beginning to braid the shining locks.

"Yes, I did. But, Mary, these preachers puzzle me. You'd think an old fellow like Luckett would be glad to go to the heaven he's so sure about."

"I don't see why a preacher's life shouldn't be as precious to him as yours is to you or mine is to me. After all, they're human. That's a queer comment for you to make, my dear. . . . Abra'm, just look at the gray around my temples! . . . I'm getting old." Her eyes widened with sudden terror. "Old! Mary Todd!"

Something frantic in her voice roused her husband from his preoccupation with Luckett's and Beecher's states of mind. He looked at her attentively; not in search of gray hairs but to verify the note of terror in her voice. Her distended pupils told him what he wished to know.

"But," he said, earnestly, "you don't expect me to observe that, do you? It's impossible for me to see change in you. I'm too close to you."

But Mary was pursuing her own line of thought. "To lose my lovely skin and my teeth and my hair! It's horrible! Old age is living death."

"After all," groped Lincoln, "the thing that's growing old is just the house *you* live in, your little cabin. It's bound to lose a few shingles from the roof as time goes on and the logs will have to be re-chinked more frequently. But everybody admits that the longer you live in your home the more hallowed it becomes."

"What woman wants to be hallowed?" wailed Mary. "I want to be lovely." She stared unseeingly at him.

NEITHER LET IT BE AFRAID

Lincoln sighed. "I reckon I could understand you better if I hadn't been so ungodly ugly all my life."

But for once she did not protest at his disparagement of himself. "Old age! I'm forty-six. It's coming! It'll be here in another ten years and there is nothing to be done about it. It's as inevitable as the Rebellion was. Your simile fails. Any attempt to patch the roof or chink the walls is futile. 'Summer's honeydew cannot hold out against the wreckful siege of battering years.' Shakespeare faced it."

"And around the dear ruins," quoted Lincoln softly, "each wish of my heart shall entwine itself verdantly still."

Mary did not respond. "One thing is sure! I'll not be one of those dreadful old women who make abortive efforts to look young. What I can do cleverly, I will—" defiantly—"but"—with a sudden focusing of her gaze on his—"what I must and shall do will be to evolve a philosophy that will reconcile me." She gave a little dry sob.

Her husband put out his long arm and catching the flowing sleeve of her eider-down dressing sacque, drew her gently to his knees. "My darling girl, doesn't it do you any good to know that if you were a hundred years old, you'd still be beautiful little Mary Todd to me?"

"Yes, it helps," she said, soberly kissing him, "but, oh, my dear, you can't imagine what an essential pillar of her being a woman's vanity is! I simply can't picture myself as existing without it. I doubt if I have strength in myself to grow a philosophy to take its place. You don't know what it is to find yourself so totally swamped and inadequate."

"Don't I?" demanded Lincoln, grimly. "I'm struggling in my own innards right now with a worse problem. And it's torture."

His words shattered at one blow all of Mary's unwonted concentration on herself. "I'm a shallow-brained fool! What's the trouble, my dear? Tell me."

"That's just what I mustn't do," declared her husband. "It's not fair to you to load you with a problem you'd take too seriously, and it's merely a question in metaphysics."

"How could such a question be torture?" asked Mary.

"That's where my weakness comes in, you see."

"Tell me," urged his wife, a small hand coaxingly on his shoulder. "I won't take it too seriously."

He shook his head. "No, you can't be impersonal about it and you'll be upset. Anyhow, I can't get it into words. I tried to express it to Beecher, yesterday, and got nowhere."

"If you can talk to him you can talk to me," declared Mary jealously. "Sharing helps. I've been eased by sharing with you to-night."

He was sorry that he had brought himself into the conversation. He had no business to pull Mary into the shadow. And yet, as he felt that faithful small hand on his shoulder, the desire to confess to her overcame every scruple and he began deliberately to try to phrase the unphrasable.

"I suppose I'm being troubled as you are by the approach of old age.

I hope that's all there is to it. I'm ten years farther along the trail than you are, dear wife, and the question that's facing me is, what follows old age—at least, that's part of the question."

He felt Mary's fingers tighten. "You mean what follows death! You fear assassination!"

"No, I don't *fear* it," he insisted. Then sighing, he added, "I told you I couldn't mention it without your getting upset!"

"I'm as calm as the church's firm foundation," declared Mary. "You can tell me anything and I won't even *think* hysterically. What did Beecher say when you asked him that, as I suppose you did?"

"Well, you see, Beecher is so sure of heaven, himself, that he simply can't picture the mind of any one who isn't as sure as he is."

Mary returned his gaze steadily. "You never told me you had doubts. I know you have little use for creeds but I thought your deep faith in an all-loving God was unshakable!"

"So it is. But knowing there is God doesn't inevitably include knowing there's immortality. And"—finding an inexpressible relief in opening his heart—"I'm not sure that it's doubt of immortality that constitutes the shadow. Perhaps it's my inability to interpret what may be meant as a warning or even a command. . . . Or maybe it's merely my inability to reconcile myself to going even twenty years from now. You see I, too, need a philosophy."

"You need religion," said Mary promptly. "You need Jesus Christ."

"What could He do for me?" asked Lincoln, gently. "Supposing—mind, I only say supposing—one doesn't believe He was God on earth, what of Christ, then?"

"Even supposing that," she replied sturdily, "He had a sureness about the hereafter which no man ever had in the same way. And His conviction that He knew is comforting to any one even though He seems not God. *Let not your heart be troubled, neither let it be afraid. Sufficient unto the day are the evils thereof.*"

He looked beyond Mary into the fire. Matchless words spoken indeed from a matchless confidence. *Let not your heart be troubled.* To any one who believed Christ was God that admonition must be as soothing as a mother's hand in the dark of a nightmare. So much for faith. . . . But what of the interpretation of the shadow? It was premonition of what? But this he would not ask Mary now.

"You have an inestimable advantage over me," he remarked after a moment, "in your orthodoxy. A mind like mine is a curse to its owner. Mary, my job here isn't done yet. Who'll bind the nation's wounds? Who is left in the North who feels to the South as I do? I feel—" He hesitated, groping again for words.

Mary supplied them. "*Like as a father pitieth his children.*"

"Yes! Yes! Mary, I think Grant feels that way, too, but he doesn't know how to manage the politicians. He's shown that throughout the war. Who'll save poor old Davis and his fellow-failures? Mary, the whole Cabinet has pulled on the black cap! And who'll clinch the victory for the negro by using moderation in the interpretation of the Thirteenth Amendment? Andy Johnson's as bitter toward the southern leaders as a green persimmon. Seward—Seward's—"

"Seward's a mere opportunist." Mary was pale but her voice was firm. "And Stanton will always belong to the man who can boss him as a bully always does."

Lincoln went on: "Charles Sumner might scorn to qualify as a public executioner but there's no doubt he's willing to crush the southern white for the sake of the darkies. Mary, I don't think I'm egotistical when I say I think I still have a job and one demanding peculiar qualities in the possessor."

Mary slipped from her perch on his knees to walk uneasily about the room. When she returned to stand before him she was deadly white and her voice was a little husky as she said:

"I think you're the most far-visioned and most able statesman in America to-day, my dear. But even at that if God really wants democracy to live, if He really is in favor of the Union as we think the outcome of the war has proved, He isn't depending on one man to preserve it. God ultimately will save the Union, whatever happens to you!" She looked at him with unutterable anguish in her blue eyes. "Whatever happens to you!" she repeated, and suddenly clasping her hands before her eyes she burst into tears.

Lincoln put out his long arm and drew her to his heart. She stopped weeping, immediately, and they sat cheek to cheek, watching the leaping fire.

After a moment she murmured brokenly, *"Let not your heart be troubled, neither let it be afraid."*

He drew her closer still. "You comfort me," he said.

CHAPTER XVIII

IMMEDIATELY after breakfast, the next morning, Lincoln went over to the War Office for direct news from the front. The rain of the previous night had passed, leaving only a light mist through which the sun shone warmly. Between the brick path and the wall, tulips and hyacinths were in full bloom but the crocuses which had dotted the lawn had all been crushed by the crowds of the past few days. The oaks and walnuts in Adams' Grove were bursting with rose-tinted buds and the lilac bushes near the turnstile were reeling sweet.

The President walked slowly but lightly, his head up, drawing deep breaths of spring into his winter-ravished body. He could feel the sap rise in his soul.

The telegraph room adjoining Stanton's office was in full swing. Lincoln paused for a few moments to greet his friends.

"Well, boys, what's the news from General Sherman?"

"None yet, sir," replied Major Eckert. "But General Grant will reach Washington to-morrow."

"There is a new letter from Petroleum Nasby just out, Mr. Lincoln," called David Bates. "He has a good deal to say about your visit to Richmond!"

"No! Has he!" The President grinned broadly. "I haven't been to my office yet so haven't seen my copy. Is it good and saucy? That's the way I like 'em."

He sat down on the edge of Bates' desk and took the clipping from the boy's hand.

> Saints' Rest, wich is in the Stait
> uv Nou Gersey
> April 10, 1865.

I survived the defeet uv Micklellan (who wuz truly the nashen's hope and pride, likewiz) becoz I felt assoored that the rane of the goriller Linkin wood be a short wun. That in a few months at furthest General Lee wood capsher Washington, depose the ape and set up there a constooshnal guverment based upon the grate and immutable trooth that a white man is better than a nigger.

I survived the loss of Atlanter and Savanner and Charleston becoz dependin on Suthern papers, I bleeved that them places wuz given up,— mind, given up becoz the Confedrets desired to Consentrate for a crushin blow.

I survived the fall of Richmond tho it wuz a staggerer becoz I still hed

faith that grate and good man Lee did it for strategy that he mite consentrate hisself sumwhers else and when the Ablishenists geered me and
sez "Richmond" and "Go up bald head" to me, I shoke my fist at 'em and
sed Wat and you'll see. I wuz alooken for the blow thet wuz to foller the
consentrashun.

It cum. . . .

Stanton, hearing the President's voice, appeared in the door of his office
and his harsh tones broke in on Lincoln's delighted drawl.

"Good morning, Mr. Lincoln! I have a very troublesome problem here
for which you're responsible."

The President looked over his spectacles. "Hello, Mr. Stanton! You
must listen to this!"

"I'm sorry, but it's impossible at the moment." The color rose in Stanton's tired face.

"You don't appreciate Nasby's genius, I'm afraid," sighed Lincoln, comi-
cally. He rose and after placing the letter in his pocketbook, he followed
the Secretary into the inner office. There he leaned against the high desk
and waited.

Stanton picked up a telegram and said abruptly, "I have censured General Weitzel for not seeing to it that prayers for the President of the
United States were included in the church services in Richmond on Sunday. He replies that the tone of his conversations with you in Richmond
justifies the omission. Will you tell me just what you said on the subject
to Weitzel?"

Lincoln with difficulty held back a contemptuous grunt. Surely this was
too trivial even for Stanton. But evidently not, for the Secretary went on,
"Weitzel permitted the churches to open on the general condition that no
disloyal sentiments be uttered. But the clergy in the Episcopal churches
who had formerly offered prayers for that traitorous Davis prayed only
for those in authority and omitted the President of the United States.
It is a studied affront to you and your office. What order had you given
Weitzel?"

Lincoln felt more annoyance than he cared to show. Nothing could be
more distasteful to him than the empty forms appertaining to his office.
He knew how Stanton delighted in dignities of place and ordinarily he
was willing to take that fact lightly. But the fussiness of Stanton in this
instance was deliberately ungenerous and as absurd as it was unnecessary.

"I don't remember hearing prayers spoken of while I was in Richmond,"
he said, impatiently, "but I've no doubt General Weitzel acted in what
appeared to him to be the spirit and temper manifested by me while
there."

"I can imagine what that spirit and temper were," sneered Stanton.

"Now I will let him have it!" thought Lincoln. He went on, aloud,
"What I ordered Weitzel with regard to the Richmond people was to let
them down easy and I say the same to you, Mr. Stanton. Leave the preach-

ers to stew in their own juice. The welfare of the office I hold is in no degree dependent on the petitions in the Rebel prayer-books. This sort of bullying is particularly unpleasant to me."

"Bullying!" Stanton's voice was outraged.

"Well, you've got the fellow down, haven't you? Good God, would you ask him to pray for you while he's spitting out the broken teeth? They wouldn't stand for that even in a little boys' fight. The important thing at the moment in Richmond is to find out what their so-called legislature is doing. I reckon I'll get a telegram off about that at once."

He returned to the outer office and seating himself at Eckert's desk, wrote a message to Weitzel, ". . . Is there any sign of the Rebel legislature coming together on the understanding in my letter to you? If there is any such sign, inform me what it is. If there is no such sign, you may withdraw the offer."

He handed the message to an operator. "Send the reply over to me as soon as it arrives." Then he stood in thought for a moment. Poor old overworked Stanton! Slowly drawing Petroleum Nasby's letter from his pocket, he went back to the Secretary's desk.

"Just listen, Mr. Stanton! This scratches the itch you can't reach." And quite unrebuffed by Stanton's look of fury he went on with the effusion:

"Lee surrendered. Good hevins! Is this the dyin' in the last ditch? Is this the fightin' till the last man was an inanimat copse? Is this the bringin' up the childern to take ther places, as the old ones peg out under Yankee bullits? Lee surrendered! Why this ends the bizniz. The South is conkered. *Conkered! Conkered!* CONKERED. Linkin rides into Richmond. A Illinois X rail-splitter, a buffoon, a ape, a goriller, a smutty joker, sets himself down in President Davis's cheer and rites despatches. Where are the matrons uv Virginia? Did they not bare ther buzums and rush on 2 the Yankee baynets that guarded the monster? Did they not cut ther childern's throtes and wavin' a Confedrit flag in one hand plunge a meat knife in 2 ther throbbin' buzum with the tother rather than see ther city dishonored by the tred uv a conkerers foot?

"Alars! not wunst. Pir contrary, I reed in the papers that they did rush wildly through the streets with their childern in ther arms. But it wuz at the Yankee commissary train who gave 'em bred and meat which they eat vociferously . . . this ends the chapter. The Confederacy is ded. Its gathered up its feet, sed its last words and deceest."

Lincoln paused to shout with laughter. Stanton eyed him, helplessly, and then gave a delighted titter which grew in a moment to a nerverelaxing guffaw.

"I'll leave this with you as I have a copy at home," said Lincoln. He laid the clipping on the desk, nodded and walked thoughtfully out.

As he moved along the garden wall he pondered on Stanton's lack of a sense of proportion. The Secretary would kick up as much of a fuss, bring up as heavy guns over as trivial a matter as that of prayers in Rich-

mond as he would over the shifting of the supreme command of the army.
He undoubtedly would make more trouble in Richmond over a sentence
in one or two church services than Weitzel would make in imposing Federal control on the whole city.

He paused for a moment facing Adams' Grove, only half conscious of
the rising summer in the tiny world of trees and shrubs while he struggled
to throw off the persisting feeling of irritation toward the Secretary of War.

"I'm not fair to the old fellow," he told himself. "Time and again he's
saved the country by this arbitrary meddling and overzealousness of his."
He reviewed in his mind innumerable crises in which Stanton's dauntless
self-assurance and czarism had pulled the army out of apparently insuperable difficulties. One had only to balance his great qualities as a war minister against his petty qualities as a friend to see how fully the good
outweighed the bad. Mary and Hill Lamon protested often against his
patience with Stanton's tyrannies. Well, they hadn't protested that week
in September in 1863 when Stanton bullied the President and the Cabinet into backing him while he played the brutal czar and saved Kentucky
and Tennessee from the Rebels.

He laughed as he recalled that September episode. Stanton whooped
an orderly out to the Soldiers' Home one night and routed the President
out of bed, with a mysterious request to come instantly to the War Office.
Startled, Lincoln pulled his trousers and coat over his night-shirt and
galloped hatless into the city.

In Stanton's office he found the entire Cabinet assembled with General-
in-Chief Halleck, all more or less in undress and all waiting much alarmed
for the President's arrival. Stanton had refused to make explanations until
he came. But when Lincoln was perched on the high desk stool he announced that the Army of the Cumberland under General Rosecrans was
starving, man and beast, and that its morale was so broken that a sneeze
from the Rebels would destroy it. Even without the sneeze, ten days would
see the Army wiped out by hunger and consequent disease and desertions.

"That will give the enemy the gateway to the West, through the Alleghanies. Reënforcements and supplies must be sent within a week. How
are we to do it? I've called you all together to have the resources of the
country pooled."

"No matter if we do pool everything, Mr. Stanton," the Secretary of the
Treasury protested, "it'll take two months to get adequate reënforcements
up there."

Stanton yelped, "I'll have 20,000 men there in five days if I'm given
power! I'll rob the Army of the Potomac."

"You couldn't get 'em to Washington from Manassas in five days!" Lincoln exclaimed. "What chance have you to send 'em the 1,200 miles to
Chattanooga?"

"It would take a minimum of three months!" General Halleck declared
flatly.

"Three hells!" roared Stanton. "You can all get out of here and go back to bed, except you, Mr. Lincoln. I want you here for authority."

"But, Mr. Stanton"—Lincoln shook his head—"you'll paralyze the country for months."

"Do you mean you'll not back me?" exclaimed the Secretary of War. "Dare you risk the catastrophe? You can't realize—you won't realize—you—" Stanton paused. Articulation failed him. He shook as with a chill. Tears ran down his cheeks.

Lincoln slid from his stool. "Do what you think best, Stanton. What do I sign first?"

The Secretary of War sniffed violently at his cologne bottle. "The rest of you go back to bed," he gulped.

Meekly the others filed out—even Halleck! Then with the President quietly obeying orders, Stanton got to work. For four hours they dictated messages. Within twenty minutes after the first wire, replies began to come in. At 3.30 that morning they were able to telegraph to Rosecrans, "Have arranged to send 16,000 infantry under Hooker. Will have them in Nashville in five to six days."

By seven o'clock that morning, the heads of three railroads which Lincoln had commandeered had arrived in Stanton's office. By eight o'clock, all traffic had been cleared along the route and the first troops entrained at Bealton, Virginia. Every half hour thereafter more troops departed. Stanton commissioned all train dispatchers and station masters along the route as captains, with orders to arrest any soldiers leaving the trains. He ordered 8,000 negroes set at work changing the gauge of one of the railroads. He ordered an acquaintance in Cleveland, in the President's name, to go at once to Cincinnati and take possession of all railroads south of the Ohio and to call on any manufacturer for more rolling stock.

At noon of September 24th, Lincoln left Stanton and went to take care of his own work. He returned at intervals during the next thirty-six hours, to find that Stanton had not slept nor left his office. But on the evening of the 25th, about nine o'clock, when the President put his head into the Secretary's room, he discovered him stretched on the old horsehair sofa, a cologne-saturated handkerchief over his face. Lincoln carefully withdrew and Major Eckert showed him the dispatch that had sent Stanton to sleep. It was from General Hooker, stating that the last man of a reënforcement of 23,000 had entrained that afternoon and that a caravan six miles in length was racing over the Alleghanies.

Within ten days the entire force had reached Chattanooga and the gateway to the West was saved.

As this memory with all its details passed rapidly before his mind's eye, Lincoln's irritation with Stanton gave way to a not unamused gratitude. It was with good humor fully restored that he observed Tad walking slowly across the lawn, with the yellow kitten on his shoulder.

"Tad!" he called.

The boy sauntered toward his father. "Papa day, give me a dollar?"

"That's a good deal of cash this early in the morning," said Lincoln as his hand slipped automatically into his trousers' pocket. "What's up?"

"I want to buy fireworks. A bunch of us kids is going to whoop it up on old Jeff Davis. Come on with me, Papa day, while I buy 'em." He slipped a beguiling small hand into his father's.

"Well, if it won't take too long," agreed Lincoln. "Put the kitten inside the hall and tell the doorman I'll be back shortly."

He forgot that there was such a thing as the necessity for safeguarding himself. A great flush of well-being for a moment crowded every anxiety—his own and other people's—from his mind. With the little calloused palm in his, he strolled through the vegetable garden, lifted Tad over the south fence and for a little while watched the Union Light Guard drilling on the rough ground known as the Treasury Park. Then the two walked slowly east to Pennsylvania Avenue, chatting amiably. But as they reached the door of the Kirkwood House at Twelfth Street, Lincoln's conscience returned to duty and startled him from his preoccupation with Tad's plans for a celebration. Andrew Johnson lived at this hotel.

"I'm going in and call on the Vice-President, son," he said suddenly.

"But you promised to shop with me," protested Tad. "I don't want to talk to old Johnson."

"What grudge have you got against him?" asked Lincoln, looking down on the forage cap which adorned his son's head.

"Him? Oh, he's all right. He's a good old fellow. He bought a dolla's wo'th of lemonade from me the othe' day at my hospital stand on the lawn and he made old Treasurer M'Culloch shell out too. But I'm sick of politics, I can tell you. I'm going to be a farmer when I get to be a man, no matta' how much they tease me to be President."

"What makes you think they'll tease you to take that very unwelcome office?" asked his father. "Anyhow, I reckon they won't want a President who can't pronounce his R's."

"I can too pronounce 'em and you know it, when I put my mind on it!" cried Tad, indignantly. "I've been pronouncing 'em at least half the time lately. And I know they'll want me to be President because I'm your son."

Lincoln, with one foot on the steps of the Kirkwood House, laughed delightedly. "You go ahead and get your snap-crackers, boy, and when you've finished call for me here. Now, don't make a fuss. Here's some hush money!" He pressed a quarter into Tad's palm. Father and son grinned at each other and Lincoln went on into the hotel.

As he approached the desk in the lobby, he observed that the clerk was speaking to a short, heavy-set man in slipshod clothes, with his flaxen hair hanging over his collar. The man slunk away as the clerk turned hastily to the President.

"Get on with your friend," said Lincoln. "I only want to see Mr. Johnson."

"Friend!" ejaculated the clerk. "He's not even an acquaintance. He's hostler, hanger-on or what-not to John Wilkes Booth. He has been skulking around here ever since breakfast and I was trying to find out what he was up to before throwing him out."

He was leading the way up the staircase as he spoke. George Atzerodt had no intention of revealing the purpose of his visit to the clerk. Booth had impressed thoroughly on his henchman's slow mind that he was to get Vice-President Johnson pointed out to him by some one not connected with the hotel. He was to locate Johnson's room, also. Now, in the absence of the clerk he asked several persons if they knew the Vice-President by sight, but by the time the clerk returned he had had no success and he concluded that a short absence would have a salutary effect. He slipped out to the stables.

CHAPTER XIX

FOR OFFENSES MUST COME

LINCOLN found both Vice-President and Mrs. Johnson at home. He had not met Johnson's wife before. She was lying in an armchair before a brisk fire, a bowl of half-blown lilacs on the little marble-topped table at her elbow and a copy of *Harper's Weekly* in her lap. She wore a black merino frock with a flat collar of white lawn caught at the throat by a cameo brooch. A pink knit shawl reflected a little color in her white cheeks. Eliza Johnson was a semi-invalid, for she was fighting against consumption. It had developed under the hardships of the war. Yet, in spite of her delicacy, she was beautiful, Lincoln thought, as he bowed over her hand.

Her eyes, a soft hazel, were extraordinarily large, her nose was pure Grecian, her mouth generous and beautifully curved. Her whole physiognomy was that of a big nature and a keen intelligence.

Johnson had been writing at a table. Now, at a glance from Eliza, he hastily pulled on his coat. The two men then seated themselves before the fire.

"This is homelike," said Lincoln. "I hope the opening weather finds you feeling a little more spry, madam."

"I'm doing well, Mr. Lincoln," replied Mrs. Johnson in the soft drawl of Tennessee. "Mrs. Lincoln, they tell me, is standing up under the strain."

"She's as lively as a humming bird and as cheering. Tad and I would go under if it wasn't for Mother's laughter, I can tell you. She's threatening to come to see you but I don't know when she'll make it. She doesn't exactly have to set the bread to rise but she does have me and the Executive Mansion heavy on those little hands of hers."

"I know," nodded Mrs. Johnson. "Tell her there's no hurry though I'd be delighted and honored to see her"

"You're looking tired, Mr. Lincoln," Johnson's quiet voice broke in. "When do you propose to take a rest?"

"Just as soon as you and the Cabinet are re-tempered—mollified to a softer consistency, as it were. I'm no great shakes as a blacksmith but I'm going to have a try." He laughed softly.

Johnson's black eyes twinkled. He turned to his wife. "My dear, I warned you that Mr. Lincoln was going to try to make me over. You're the one he must consult. Maybe you won't want your magnificent creation tampered with."

Lincoln looked from one to the other. Every one knew that when Eliza McArdle, the young schoolteacher, had married Andrew Johnson, the young tailor, he had been an illiterate, untrained cub and that for all his great natural cleverness as a politician, he owed all that he was to her early teaching and her continued polishing of his rough metal. The Lincolns and the Johnsons had much in common.

"I have only one criticism to make of your work, madam," said Lincoln, at last. "Your husband doesn't realize what a good job you made of him. If he could do that, he wouldn't be so sore at what he calls the aristocrats and half his hatred of the Secessionists would disappear."

"You mean," exclaimed Eliza, "that if he could only recognize the fact that he's the peer of the best of 'em, his bitterness would drop from him! That's true."

"Even my wife or your wife couldn't and can't change the fact that you and I are both plebeians." Johnson spoke quietly but his black eyes glowed.

"That word simply hasn't any meaning in America any more than the word aristocrat has," returned the President. "Personally I don't care what I'm called. God knows I've had my choice of hard titles as you have, Mr. Johnson. You've done more for the Union cause than any one I know, and yet your attitude denies the very bedrock of the Union, that all men are created equal. You say you're a plebeian. You rave against aristocrats. You waste your strength hating weak sisters like Jeff Davis and Judah Benjamin. Hate will hamstring you, Johnson. Vengeance is unworthy of a man of your intellectual caliber."

Johnson folded his arms, compressed his thin lips and said nothing.

A red spot appeared in one of Mrs. Johnson's thin cheeks. "Perhaps you don't understand all my husband's been through, sir," she exclaimed. "He's had—"

The President interrupted her. "He's had the toughest job of the war. Of the public men of the South, he's stood alone against the passions of Secession. He's held old Tennessee to her moorings while she weltered in successive tornadoes; Shiloh, Ft. Donelson, Chattanooga, Lookout Mountain—I needn't count 'em over to you, the battles he's helped her weather. Whenever anybody criticizes your husband to me I tell him no one has a right to judge Andrew Johnson who hasn't suffered as much and done as much as he has for the nation's sake. Yes, ma'am, all that and a hundred facts more I know and appreciate. And yet, I'm going to ask Andrew Johnson to make a still greater sacrifice for the Union. I want him to give up all thought of vengeance, even of punishment for the southern leaders, and turn his great abilities to healing the nation's wounds."

Eliza spoke as if her husband were not present. "You can't change Andrew Johnson's nature, Mr. Lincoln, and after all, it's his nature that's made it possible for him to endure and accomplish what he has. You rule by diplomacy. That's your nature. Andrew rules by force. That's his nature. I remember when Nashville was besieged and the city leaders begged him to give up and surrender, he drew his pistol and said, 'I'm no military man but I know we can hold out and any man who talks of surrender, I'll shoot.' Well, the Union troops rallied and the city was saved. That wouldn't have been your way but it was Andy's."

The Vice-President moved uneasily and interrupted, with a curious expression in his deep eyes. "You think it's the names they've called me that makes me hate the aristocrats. Well, it's not. Do you know what I think of every day of my life and what I'll get even with Jeff Davis for if it takes ten years?" He spoke with impressive dispassionateness. "They threw my sick wife and my dying son into the street and they turned the house I built with my own hands into a barracks."

Lincoln thought of Mary ill and of Willie, dying—Willie in the streets, dying. Sudden tears dripped to his cheeks. He leaned back in his chair and closed his eyes for a moment while he collected himself. The two watching him wore a look of pity not unmixed with awe. The President's expression had the extraordinary sweetness and resignation of a death mask.

"Just what do you want my husband to do, Mr. Lincoln?" asked Eliza Johnson, softly.

Lincoln opened his eyes and said slowly, "I am haunted by a presentiment that I shall not live after the coming of peace. I want to commit my charge into hands that are kindly."

Great lumps appeared on Johnson's lean jaws as his teeth clinched on Lincoln's words. Beads of sweat showed on his upper lip. He leaned toward the President and ejaculated through set teeth, "Assassination! And you expect my blood to remain uncurdled if those dogs assassinate you? *You!* No, Mr. Lincoln, you ask the impossible! By God, I'd hunt them down if it took the entire army! I'd wipe out every damned aristocrat in the Confederacy and hang them if I had to do it with my own hands!"

"Hush, Andrew!" Mrs. Johnson laid a thin hand on her husband's knee. Automatically, his own closed upon it. "Mr. Lincoln," she went on, "you mustn't misunderstand Mr. Johnson. If it's your ideas of reconstruction you're thinking about, don't be concerned. My husband believes in your program."

"But it's a program of conciliation," insisted Lincoln.

She nodded. "I know. It's a healing of the nation as Christ would have healed it. And, as I fear only Christ could do it. But one can try. Can't one, Andrew?" turning to her husband.

But Johnson sat staring at Lincoln with anguished eyes and did not reply. And after a moment, perceiving that he had given the Vice-President more than he could bear, Lincoln made his adieux and went out.

He did not wait for Tad, but leaving word with the clerk for the child, strode out of the hotel.

The misty sun felt good.

George Atzerodt, now in the bar-room, saw him go and made of the fact an excuse for saying to an officer standing at the door, "That was old Abe, eh? Looks like an easy fellow to know."

Colonel Nevins looked at Atzerodt with amusement in his eyes. "He is easy to know. Why didn't you speak to him?"

"I would have," grinned Atzerodt, "if I'd been in my Sunday clothes.

I'm wearing these because I'm trying to see Andy Johnson and he prefers poor folks. A tramp can always get a good word from him. No, I ain't a tramp, if that's what you're grinning at. All you folks'll laugh out of the other side of your mouths yet. I'll admit I'm about broke now but I got friends enough to give me as much as will see me through. I'm going away some of these days but I'll come back with as much gold as will keep me all my days."

"Let me in on the bonanza," smiled Nevins.

Atzerodt returned the smile. "I might, later."

The colonel, who faced the door into the lobby, said suddenly, "There goes Mr. Johnson into the dining room now."

Atzerodt turned eagerly but too late. "Gosh," he muttered, "I gotta see him! Do you know which is his room?"

"Yes, it's near mine. What's the idea, friend?" curiously.

"Well, Andy borrowed money from my old German father, once, and I'm going to get it back."

The officer shouted with laughter. "So that's your gold mine! Well, go after him hard! He's a mean cuss, I've heard. Come, I'll show you his room, for they won't let you into the dining room!"

He crossed the lobby and Atzerodt followed him up the stairs, where Nevins pointed out a closed door to him. Atzerodt muttered the number to himself and then with a word of thanks turned back to the stairs. The colonel went into his own room but later as he left the hotel he saw Atzerodt still lingering before the entrance.

"Well, did you collect?" demanded the colonel.

Atzerodt shook his head. "Haven't even seen him yet."

"He's alone in the dining room now. You can't miss him," chuckled Nevins. "Good luck to you!"

"Thanks!" ejaculated Atzerodt. He once more entered the hotel and peered in at the door of the dining room. Johnson, eating his solitary meal, was quite unconscious of the man's sullen scrutiny. The head-waiter, accustomed to the interest shown by every one in this distinguished guest, allowed Atzerodt a long moment of gaping before he closed the door in his face.

The conspirator was, as he had said, without funds and so had drunk very little that morning. As he walked along Pennsylvania Avenue he pondered, uneasily, on the two famous men he had seen at the Kirkwood. Johnson's face had made no impression on his feelings but as he reconsidered Lincoln's a sensation of uneasiness and vague regret touched him.

"Booth's a blasted fool," he muttered. "There's nothing to hate about that man. He's never hurt a fly, betcha. For two cents I'd cut back to Fort Tobacco and go on with my own job." He bit off a chew from the remnant of a black plug. After all, why did he stick to the actor? Booth was all promise and no performance, as Arnold had said. Here he had been for hours hanging round the Kirkwood House, breakfastless and drinkless, spying on a man he'd been told off to stab although he'd never seen the man and had no possible grudge against him. After all, he didn't *know* that the Confederate government was in on this and would make them all rich. He had only Booth's word for that. It was possible that Booth was lying to them and was merely using them all to make himself famous. What other excuse could Booth have for waiting for Lincoln's going to the theater? Why, any one could shoot Lincoln any time and anywhere! The Richmond government if they wanted to make way with old Abe wouldn't stand for any such nonsense as the theater scheme.

But Mrs. Surratt was a hard-headed dame and she believed in Booth or she wouldn't have him round the house the way she did and let John Surratt do the actor's errands. When John came back from Richmond he always brought gold, so the Secesh government did give money for secret jobs. The stable-keeper had told him Surratt had shown him three $100 notes in his pocketbook. Booth always had big bills with him too. Mike O'Laughlin claimed Booth had borrowed $500 from him last fall but that was probably a lie. Or else O'Laughlin's whining that he was hard-up was a lie.

Ruminating slowly, his thought now turned to Andrew Johnson. The man had broad muscular shoulders and a chest like a blacksmith. "He don't know the meaning of fear," Atzerodt told himself. "They say that out in Tennessee they tried everything but shooting on him and he fought 'em all to a standstill. If he didn't put the fear of God into 'em, I heard a fellow say, he put the fear o' Johnson. You'd need a cannon to kill that Carolina cracker."

He halted, staring unseeing at a plane tree's yellow-patched trunk. This plan of trying to stab Andrew Johnson in the dark—Christ—! Had Dave Herold ever seen him? By God, he'd go tell Herold a thing or two about this job Booth had made them partners in!

He knew about where to find Herold. The boy had made a half-hearted attempt to become a druggist and it was probable he would be hanging around the drugstore at Fifteenth Street and the Avenue. The guess proved correct. A slender, insignificant youth in a short fawn overcoat which had once belonged to Booth and with a little round-rimmed white felt hat pulled low over his gray eyes, lounged idly before the red-and-green-glass druggist's symbol.

Atzerodt shambled up to him. "If you ain't got nothing better'n this to do, come round and help me exercise the horses."

David pulled irresolutely at a small mustache which did not conceal a rather shapeless mouth above his receding chin. "I wasn't going—I was just waiting—"

"Come on, Dave, I want to talk to you. I've just seen some one you're interested in. Come on," jerking his head peremptorily.

"Well, just for a little while." Dave fell into step with Atzerodt. "You see, George"—in a low voice—"Grant's expected in town and Booth told me to locate him."

"You thought you'd meet him in the drugstore buying sulphur and molasses for the spring clean-out, I suppose," grunted George, with heavy sarcasm. "Who's going to tackle Grant, that fighting pup? Not me! I'd rather try to stop Pickett's charge with a broom-straw." He laughed heartily at his own wit. "Haven't got a bottle with you, old man?"

David nodded and when they reached the privacy of the alley behind Ford's Theater, he pulled a whiskey flask from his breast pocket and handed it to his companion.

Edward Spangler was sitting on an overturned water-pail, his back against the stable wall, a corn-cob pipe hanging from his mouth, eyes closed. He was snoring loudly.

"Pretty, isn't he!" giggled Dave.

The two gazed with amusement at the middle-aged face. It was blotched and swollen and discolored with drink and decorated by a stubble which had been growing since his Sunday shave.

Herold uncorked his whiskey flask and held it under Spangler's bulbous nose. The nostrils quivered, the lips worked and with a particularly heavy snort, Booth's confederate awoke. Herold hastily corked the bottle and made great show of putting it back in his pocket.

"Hey!" protested Spangler, "that's no place for good whiskey. Or ain't it good? Hand it over for an expert to test, Dave!"

Again the bottle made a round. David after his own pull examined it gravely and said, "Not enough to be worth saving!" And with a laugh they finished the pint.

Herold and Atzerodt now established themselves on a box close to Spangler and George began to speak with authority on the dangers of his and David's share in the conspiracy. The whiskey had warmed him by the time he had completed his description of Johnson but it had not stiffened his courage. "I say I don't like the job. I don't like any of it," he declared.

"What don't you like, old fellow?" asked a pleasant voice from the rear door of the theater.

The three started. It was Wilkes Booth. He joined them, deliberately flicking his riding whip at his highly polished riding-boots and with the other hand settling the high stock he affected when on horseback. "Aren't you happy, old Port Tobacco?" he inquired, affectionately. "I thought we'd given you the easy job."

"Say, Mr. Booth, did you ever stab Andy Johnson?" grinned Atzerodt. "Now, I never stabbed anything more dangerous than a pig! Did you ever see Andy? No! Well, I have, and let me tell you when I think of sneaking into his bedroom in the dark— Say, how about Mrs. Johnson? Do we stab her too or leave her alone to squeal the news?"

Booth replied coldly. "If you'd attended to your work adequately this morning, George, you'd have discovered that Mrs. Johnson is an invalid and occupies a separate room from her husband. Eddie"—turning to the stagehand—"the President's been asked to attend Ford's day after to-morrow. If you hear through the box-office of his acceptance before I do, let me know for I want to show you about the President's box."

Spangler took a deliberate bite of plug and handed the cake around, all helping themselves save Booth. "I'm smoking, thanks. Eddie, you're going to help me?"

"Yes, I guess so," replied Spangler, good naturedly.

"You *guess* so!" repeated Wilkes. "That's no answer to a man with my responsibilities."

"I told you I'd help and I will," said Spangler, rising.

"Good! Atzerodt, are you out of it or do you saddle my horse for me, this morning? I'd like to know now among just how many the million dollars is to be divided. If Dave does the job alone, he gets your share, that's certain. Hey, old heart of oak?" slapping young Herold on the shoulder.

"Bet your life!" cried Dave, his weak face setting in firmer lines.

Before Atzerodt's mind's eye danced a memory of three $100 notes and of a dozen gold pieces. There was real money to be had, without doubt. He jumped up with alacrity.

"Don't spend that share till you get it, Dave!" he grinned. "Which horse this morning, Mr. Booth?"

"The one-eyed bay," replied Wilkes, gravely.

CHAPTER XX

"FORGIVE US OUR TRESPASSES"

LINCOLN found Mr. Welles waiting for him among the other visitors thronging the White House and had him in at once. He wanted to talk again to the Secretary of the Navy on the matter of assembling the Confederate legislature at Richmond. Welles was still hostile to the idea.

"My thought was," said Lincoln, "to have the men who had done the dirty work come together and undo it."

"They'll use the opportunity to conspire against us," warned the Secretary.

Lincoln shook his head. "They're too exhausted for any more of that. Civil government must be reëstablished at once. There must be courts and law and order in the South or society will be broken up. The disbanded soldiers will turn into guerillas and robber bands. I want Virginians who have been leaders to come together and turn themselves and their neighbors into good Union men. But you're all against me."

"I haven't much faith in negotiating with large bodies of men," remarked Welles. "Each will encourage the other to ask what no one of them would think of asking alone."

Lincoln ran his fingers through his hair. Perhaps it might be as well to give in to the Cabinet on this point. After all he could do almost all that needed to be done through his arrangements with Governor Pierpont. He changed the subject abruptly.

"I've just been having a chat with Andy Johnson and his wife. She's a fine woman. I went over to their hotel to see if I could get her to shut Andy down on his everlasting talk about destroying what he believes is aristocracy, down South."

"Well, his wife could do it where no man could," agreed the Secretary of the Navy. "Any pretty woman can influence Andy."

"Oh, come!" protested Lincoln.

"Nothing scandalous, I assure you!" smiled Welles, smoothing his beard. "He's susceptible, but not too susceptible. I've never heard any one even insinuate that he ever let a neat ankle interfere with his fanatical sense of duty to the Union. On the other hand, he never failed to note one *en passant*, even a Rebel ankle."

"Can't try and convict him of treason for that!" grunted the President.

"His secretary was telling me," Welles went on, "that there was a family out in Nashville, the Hepers, for whom Johnson felt a particular enmity. They had all the characteristics of gentility he despises and they had fought him tooth and nail from the moment he'd been made Military Governor of Tennessee. He finally swore that one more affront and he'd jail the whole family. Not long after this, he was walking along the street in Nashville on which the Hepers lived. As he passed their house Mrs. Heper and her daughter were sitting on the porch. Madam Heper leaned over the rail and spit in Johnson's face and Miss Heper drew her handkerchief through her lips to wet it and flipped it in his eyes—you know the trick. Johnson snatched the handkerchief and without a word tramped on to his office. Then he sent a squad of men and arrested the whole Heper family."

"I'll not say they didn't deserve it!" exclaimed Lincoln.

Welles nodded. "He was purple with rage and rightly. Well, the Hepers as aristocrats had influence and they started using it in every possible way to hound Johnson into freeing them. But they only succeeded in closing his steel-trap jaw the harder. And then, by some hocus-pocus, Miss Heper managed to get herself brought before him. Two weeks in jail had enriched her vocabulary of hate and lady or no lady *bastard Carolinian* was the least of her epithets. Johnson stood behind his desk watching her—she is devilish pretty—and let her talk herself exhausted. When she finished he said gently, 'Madam, here is your handkerchief. I had it washed and ironed for you.'

"She gulped and stared at him. He has a fine, clean, steady eye, you know. And then she began to blush, redder and redder. And then she began to sob, no make-believe, his secretary told me, but shamed sobs like a repentant child. And, be gad, Johnson shook out the handkerchief and walked round his desk and put his arm around her and wiped her tears with it. 'There! There!' he said, 'There! There!' And she put her head down on his shoulder and had a good cry, with Johnson patting her back and looking with a sad little smile first at the girl and then at his secretary. After a moment, she recovered herself and went out with the handkerchief in her hand. That evening, Johnson ordered the Heper family released and he never had a word more trouble with 'em. If it had been Pa Heper who came to his office, Johnson would have knocked the fellow down."

Lincoln was much intrigued by this tale. He chuckled and nodded. "There's great nobility in Andy Johnson. But he's afraid to let people see it. What kind of a President do you think he'd make, Mr. Welles?"

"He might grow to fine heights," replied the Secretary, "if, as you suggest, he didn't stifle his inherent fineness. There's no doubt that he was a great executive in Tennessee. The next four years will tell a good deal. I question very much though whether he could ever be nominated, let alone elected."

"So do I," agreed Lincoln, soberly.

He went over the papers Welles had brought for his signature, affixed his name carefully and went to lunch, turning this new angle of Andrew Johnson's character over in his mind. When the meal was finished, he hurried over to the War Office and found, as he had hoped, that General Weitzel's reply had arrived. "The passports have gone out for the legislature and it is common talk that they will come together."

"Shucks!" exclaimed Lincoln. "It's five days since I talked with Campbell. This delay doesn't show the proper spirit."

"We've received a copy of the call Campbell issued with your permission, Mr. Lincoln," said Stanton, appearing suddenly in the doorway. "If"—with an air of complete triumph—"this doesn't prove everything I've been saying to you, I'm a fool!"

The President took the sheets. They were a telegraphic copy of Weitzel's letter to Campbell and the call to the Confederate legislature. The Southerner had willfully distorted Lincoln's guarded permit. "The object of the invitation," said Campbell, "is for the government of Virginia to determine whether they will administer the laws in connection with the authorities of the United States. I understand from Mr. Lincoln that if this condition be fulfilled, no attempt would be made to establish or sustain any other authority." The call to the General Assembly contained the same distortion of facts. It announced the consent of "the military authorities of the United States to the session of the legislature in Richmond. The matters to be submitted to the legislature are the restoration of peace to the State of Virginia and the adjustment of questions involving life, liberty and property that have arisen in the States as a consequence of the war."

"Weitzel must have lost his mind," grunted Lincoln. "All right, Mr. Stanton, you win." He sat down at Eckert's desk and wrote slowly with long pauses for thought. It was a full hour before he had completed the message to General Weitzel. "I have just seen Judge Campbell's letter to you of the 7th. He assumes, it appears to me, that I have called the insurgent legislature of Virginia together as the rightful legislature of the State, to settle all differences with the United States. I have done no such thing. I spoke of them not as a legislature but as 'the gentlemen who have acted as the legislature of Virginia in support of the Rebellion.' I did this on purpose to exclude the assumption that I was recognizing them as a rightful body. I dealt with them as men having power *de facto* to do a certain thing, to wit: 'to withdraw the Virginia troops and other support from resistance to the General Government' for which in a paper handed to Judge Campbell, I promised a special equivalent, to wit: a remission to the people of the State, except in certain cases, of the confiscation of their property. I meant this and no more. Inasmuch, however, as Judge Campbell misconstrues this and is still pressing for an armistice, contrary to the explicit statement of the paper I gave him, and particularly as General Grant has since captured the Virginia troops so that giving a consideration for their withdrawal is no longer applicable, let my letter to you and to Judge Campbell both be withdrawn or countermanded, and he be notified of it. Do not now allow them to assemble, but if any have come, allow them safe return to their homes."

He took the paper into Stanton's room. "There, sir, does that satisfy you?"

Stanton jerked his head irritably from the mass of papers on his desk and read the telegram. As he read his expression changed. He turned to the President with a delighted smile. "It does the job! Thank God. And clever—! Mr. Lincoln, are you by any chance an opportunist in your policies?"

"Are you?" asked the President, returning the smile.

Stanton said contentedly, "Now we've only to make those rascally clergymen see the light and Richmond will be on the right path. Our friend Number Seven is in Mr. Dana's office, sir."

"Ah!" Lincoln, who had been stiffening himself for another wrestling match with the Secretary, received the abrupt announcement with double pleasure. "Let's have him in."

Stanton rang his bell.

Montgomery looked tired and more nondescript than ever.

"Well, friend, how goes it?" asked the President, shaking hands.

"All well, so far, sir," replied Number Seven. "But I'm glad the war's about over. There's a lot of hotheads up there in Canada. Nobody knows where they'll break out next. They're generous though. They gave me a hundred and fifty dollars for the expenses of this trip. I've credited the cash to my account with this Government!"

"Didn't the hanging of Kennedy and Beall teach them anything?" demanded Stanton.

"Oh, they'll do no more burning of cities or wrecking of trains. But you have no idea of how Sherman's march has infuriated them. Stories of the excesses of his troops are the chief topics of conversation. And I'll admit, it does seem as if Sherman had been—er—excessive."

"Not at all! Not at all!" declared Stanton. "The South asked for it. Who started this war, eh?"

"This policy of an eye for an eye sometimes overreaches itself," said Montgomery, in nowise perturbed. "Some of the stories are heart-rending and I don't doubt they're true. Anyhow, they make the Confederates feel vicious. All of the Confederate commissioners, for example, believe that General Sherman ordered the pilfering and burning of Columbia, South Carolina."

"He didn't," said Lincoln. "He ordered the burning of public buildings and manufactories. All libraries, asylums and private dwellings were to be preserved. Columbia was burned by catching fire from the cotton-bales the Rebels had set the torch to before the Union men entered the city."

"What difference does it make who burned that hell-hole?" asked Stanton. "I'm in hearty accord with General Halleck. He wrote Sherman that if he captured Charleston he hoped by some accident the place could be destroyed and a little salt sowed on its site to prevent the growth of future crops of Nullification and Secession. Sherman told me when I visited him in January that his whole army burned with an insatiable desire to wreak vengeance on South Carolina and he almost trembled at her fate, but she deserved all that seemed in store for her. By God, who can be sentimental about that traitorous State? She's the cause of this war!"

"I'm not pitying her, sir," replied Montgomery, steadily. "I'm only warning you that revenge has unexpected reactions, sometimes. The stories of robbery, insult, bullying and destruction that Sherman's bummers have perpetrated—"

"There's been no rape, as a matter of record," interrupted Stanton.

"But cruelties," insisted Number Seven. "Women in bed with child-birth robbed of their bits of jewelry, old people thrown bodily out of their houses, children separated from their parents; those and a thousand other details inflame the minds of the Rebels in Canada."

"Well, that's the inevitable back-wash of war. And who hollered louder for war than South Carolina?" demanded the Secretary of War.

Lincoln began to pace the floor uneasily. "It's all a mistake. Do you remember last fall, Mr. Stanton, I telegraphed Grant at City Point suggesting that he confer with General Lee and stipulate for a mutual discontinuance of house burning and other destruction of private property? And Grant replied that it couldn't be done or words to that effect. Spoke about burning for retaliation being done only by military order. Burning for retaliation!" Tears filled his eyes.

"It has to be, Mr. Lincoln." Stanton spoke very earnestly. "Don't you see that it's inherent in the very nature of war, if we're to sicken the people of war."

"Jacob Thompson told me," Number Seven's level voice continued, "that the Rebels caught a Union lieutenant and seven of his men foraging. They killed them, mutilated them and pinned papers on their breasts, 'Death to foragers.' The next day eighteen more Union privates met the same fate. Sherman then ordered prisoners to be shot man for man and left by the roadside labeled so that every Rebel could see that for every life he executes he takes one of his own."

"And what did Wade Hampton, the Rebel commander, say to that?" cried Stanton. "I'll bet Thompson didn't tell that. Wade's reply was that he'd execute two for one!"

Black horror swept over Lincoln. All that the last few days had brought of surcease to agony of soul disappeared and he was twisted by such an anguished realization of the depths to which his compatriots had sunk that he could not control himself. Great sobs burst from him. "Stop!" he gasped. "Don't tell me more!" He took a deep breath, fighting for control, and took the cutting from Nasby from his pocket. "Did you read this through as I advised you, Mr. Stanton?"

"Oh, for God's sake!" shouted the Secretary. He turned to Montgomery. "Have you something in particular in mind with regard to Jacob Thompson you wanted to tell us?"

"It is only gossip," replied Number Seven. "I repeat it only to show the extremes to which despair and hate have driven these people. Thompson told me that a proposition had been made him to rid the world of the tyrant Lincoln, Stanton, Grant and some others. The men who had made the proposition, he said, were bold, daring men and able to execute anything they would undertake without regard to cost. He said he was in favor of the proposition but had determined to defer his answer until he had consulted with his government at Richmond. He was only awaiting their approval. He thought it would be a blessing North and South to have these men killed."

"Well, we've received the same kind of proposals about Jeff Davis et al.," said Lincoln. "Such stuff means nothing. Davis will ignore them as I have. . . . Did you see General Barnes' funeral parade to-day, Stanton? He was the vainest man I ever met. If he'd known how big a funeral he'd have he'd have died years ago."

He grinned and shook hands with Montgomery and that keen-eyed personage, meeting the President's gaze, suddenly chuckled and then burst into the only laughter the War Office had ever heard from him. Lincoln went thoughtfully back to his neglected desk.

But the day was destined to be one of curious interludes. As he bent over his letters trying to restore the spiritual balance which he had lost in Stanton's office, John Hay came in to say that the actor James E. Murdock was among the crowd in the reception room. He wanted to thank Lincoln for giving a reprieve to a young relative who had slept on sentinel duty.

"I know how much you enjoyed hearing him recite last year," said John, "and thought we might sandwich him in between Wade and Stevens who are laying for you."

"Murdock! Yes!" exclaimed Lincoln.

A moment later, the handsome, close-shaven actor came in.

"How can I thank you, Mr. President"—he began.

Lincoln interrupted, holding the proffered hand, "How can we pay you for your splendid work for the Union cause, sir? How many thousands of times have you recited for our sick and wounded. The Sanitary Commission ought to raise a monument to you."

"But I've saved no lives, sir," protested Murdock.

"Well"—Lincoln's eyes twinkled—"if you feel that way, you might recite something from Shakespeare for me."

"I haven't been doing much in that line of late," said the actor, "but if you'll indicate something I happen to know—"

"Hamlet's soliloquy!"

Murdock placed his tall hat on the mantel, smoothed his hair, eased his cuffs, folded his arms and began in his matchless voice:

"To be, or not to be: that is the question:"

Lincoln listened with bowed head, drinking in the words which so consummately voiced his needs of soul. When Murdock finished, Lincoln repeated softly:

"The undiscovered country from whose bourn
No traveler returns—"

Then, eyeing Murdock speculatively, he asked, "Do you believe in life after death?"

"Yes, Mr. Lincoln. Simply because I can't imagine time or space without myself within them."

"Hah!" The President's gasp was of surprised pleasure. Here was the sort of reply Beecher hadn't been able to give him. "Is that all?" he urged the actor.

"Yes, Mr. Lincoln, but it's enough."

"Enough?" The President smiled. "You are frugal."

"I've spent a lifetime accumulating even that much spiritual wealth," retorted Murdock.

"That's not wealth," protested Lincoln. "Wealth is a superfluity of what we don't need. And that bit of spiritual manna is an essential for your peace, eh?"

"It is indeed, sir." The two eyed each other speculatively and then Murdock said, "I wonder if you'd permit me to say the Lord's Prayer?"

"Go ahead, my boy, I'll join you."

President and actor knelt by the Cabinet table and repeated the simple, childlike plea. It carried with it the aroma of nearly two thousand years of authenticity and was unalterably comforting.

Murdock was not in his office ten minutes but when Lincoln turned back to his desk and picked up a report from Seward's office, he felt as if he had been gone an hour. He found himself, as he read a statement of the difficulties France was raising in Mexico, striving to picture the twentieth century without Abraham Lincoln somehow being a spectator. He could not do so.

CHAPTER XXI

TWILIGHT came early, stealing in with a gentle rain long before the routine moment for lighting the gas. Lincoln, when he could no longer see, dropped his pen and rose not to call for light but to obey an impulse to get out among growing things. In a garden, new planted, one could forget the devastation and the stench of war.

He rang the bell. "Dunn," he said to the guard who answered, "you go find Anna Dickinson. I'm taking her for a walk in the kitchen garden."

He waited patiently while listening to Dunn calling "Kitty! Kitty!" down the hall and grinned when shortly the man came in, red faced but triumphant. "She was in the state bedroom, in the middle of the silk bedspread, sharpening her claws. Lucky Mrs. Lincoln didn't catch her."

Lincoln placed the purring yellow ball on his shoulder. "Hear that, sister?" he demanded. "If the Missis catches you there, you won't have any tail left. You sharpen your claws on Thad Stevens' shin, after this."

With Dunn beside him he made his way through the back premises to the garden. The dusk concealed all save dim lines of young plants but did not detract from the nameless sense of new life which hung in the air. Out of decay, young growth, Lincoln told Anna Dickinson, purring against his cheek.

He walked along the path just south of the brick wall which separated the garden from the front lawn, drawing deep breaths, his gaze withdrawn. It had been a less crowded day in some ways than he had experienced for a long time and yet it had left him more wearied than he had been for weeks. His unexpected break-up in Stanton's office had left him trembling and he still "felt his insides quivering," he muttered.

"What say, sir?" asked the guard.

"Dunn," said the President, "I reckon there's no doubt but what there are fellows out to assassinate me."

"They can't get you since you let Mr. Stanton put us men on duty, sir." The young man's voice was very firm.

"I'm not really scared," mused Lincoln. "Though I admit that the secretiveness of the thing bothers me sometimes. You see when you join the army and go into a battle you know what to expect and where to expect it. But in my situation, you get suspicious of every place and everybody. At least I do, sometimes. Though, I'll admit, I forget it as far as my callers are concerned. No, it wasn't what he said about assassination this afternoon that upset me so."

"What was it, sir?" asked Dunn, his young voice thick with sympathy.

"It's—part of—it's what Sherman's had to do down South, Dunn. No

doubt but what he's contributed an enormous share toward putting a quick
end to this war and I can't be grateful enough to him for it. But that
march to the sea— My boy, it's a denial of every hope the fathers wrote
into the Declaration of Independence. It's the last shovel of dirt thrown on
the body of our poor raped dream of democracy."

"Well, the Rebels would have done the same to us if Meade hadn't
stopped 'em at Gettysburg. And they were going to try it again when Beall
and his gang went after the steamer *Michigan*. They were going to free
all the Rebel prisoners and march through the Middle States, destroying
as they went. It's only lack of opportunity that's kept old Jeff Davis from
having a Sherman's march."

"That's true and only makes the spectacle worse. Dunn, of all wars, a
civil war is the most inexcusable."

"It had to be, Mr. Lincoln!" The young man's voice in the sweet spring
darkness was serene.

"Youth!" sighed the President, "youth!"

Perhaps Mary's horror of old age was right—if it brought one such griefs
as it was bringing him. Maybe a speedy ending to it—*to die; to sleep; no
more; and by a sleep to say we end the heartache and the thousand natural
shocks that flesh is heir to, 'tis a consummation devoutly to be wished.*
What agonies had wrung Will Shakespeare to bring him to that point?
Life must have rutted and gutted him worse than it had Abraham Lincoln.
For Lincoln wanted to live on and finish his job. A hundred years from
now? Fifty years from now? The sweat started as he struggled to picture
these United States then. He could envisage Lincoln rotting in his grave
and yet he could not, as Murdock had declared, make of Lincoln, *nothing.*
It was a thought worth wrestling over. This sense of individuality, this
entity that was Lincoln; this flesh, these bones, this brain, were they
Lincoln? Were they?

He leaned against the wall, kitten and guard, garden and spring, war
and America, forgotten. Who was Lincoln? Where was his home?—

Light running footsteps did not fully rouse him but when Tad caught
his hand, shaking it impatiently, he emerged with a sigh to say, patiently,
"Yes, son!"

"Mother's waited supper half an hour! Do come this instant!"

"Dunn, you shouldn't have let me be late," said Lincoln, reproachfully.

The guard's voice was indignant. "I have been urging you to go in for
fifteen minutes, Mr. President."

"I didn't hear you! Too bad," apologized Lincoln. "Anyhow, I'm feeling
better. Where'd Anna Dickinson go?" as he moved toward the kitchen.

"She might have climbed up the wall. I couldn't see, sir," replied Dunn.

"I just saw her in the state bedroom, sharpening her claws on the silk
quilt," chuckled Taddie. "I thought maybe you'd gone in there like you do
sometimes to think. That quilt's Anna's favorite place. They say when a
cat sharpens her claws it's getting ready to rain. I hope it won't rain to-

morrow. There'll be another illumination because old Grant will be here. I bet Bob'll say some of the wed fire is fo' him."

"Those R's of yours are sprouting famously, Tad," said his father as they raced up the stairs together.

"Where were you and what were you doing?" demanded Mary, crossly, standing by the dining-room door.

"I was in the vegetable garden, leaning against the wall, thinking."

She looked up into his face, lips compressed, and then as she looked, her lips relaxed, her eyes softened and she said, quietly, "Come in and eat before the meal is ruined. John Hay says Nicolay has got to come home from the mountains, illness or no illness. That the whole contents of the Federal prison camps have moved into the White House since Lee's surrender and Nicolay is the only one with nerve to say no. I don't see why you don't tell them to wait the few days left before peace is declared. You are looking more tired than I've ever seen you, my dear, and that's saying a good deal."

The President began his soup absent-mindedly. "There was a woman in, to-day, who was pitiful. Her seventeen-year-old boy had run away from home in Nashville to join the Rebels, last winter. He was taken prisoner and landed in Fort McHenry. She saw him there and says he's a living skeleton and sicker of war than any boy on earth. She went to Stanton to get him paroled and struck him on an off day. He all but threw her out. So she came to me."

"Of course!" sniffed Mary.

"I'm proud they feel that way," declared Lincoln.

"Well, perhaps I am too," twinkled his wife. "But you do get imposed on. What did you give her—a Post Office job for her son?"

"She had the surgeon's certificate that the boy would be sick for months and would be better off at home. So I gave her a letter to the commandant to permit her to take him where she will, upon his taking the proper parole never to take up arms against the United States again. To remove a boy from that environment and give him to his loyal mother is better for this country than to let him die or to let him get well in a hot-bed of hate."

"And you didn't give either of them a Post Office! You are getting calloused, Abra'm!"

"Oh, come! I'm not that bad, Mary!"

"You're worse, isn't he, Taddie?"

"I bet you'd be glad he was President if it was your son," said the small boy, seriously. He did not join in his parents' laughter but waited in a bored attitude until he could be heard. "Papa day, I want some flags. Will you tell old Stanton to give me some?"

"You've just heard what kind of a temper Mr. Stanton's in," protested his mother.

"He'll give me anything Papa day asks for," retorted Tad, his mouth full of rhubarb sauce.

"We'll put him to the test," said the President. He took out a page from his notebook and wrote:

"EDWIN M. STANTON, Secretary of War. Dear Sir: Tad wants some flags. Can he be accommodated?

"A. LINCOLN."

Tad seized the paper and bolted.

"Tad used to be so unselfish," sighed his mother. "But he never opens his mouth now except to say *give me* or *I want*."

"He's at the hog age," said Lincoln. "Every boy gets there."

"You do say the most disgusting things—more disgusting because they're usually true," groaned Mary.

They eyed each other with amused understanding.

Lincoln was only beginning his heavy evening's work when Tad marched through his office waving a shell-torn Rebel flag. "Here, I didn't know that was the kind of banner you wanted. I don't like the idea!" cried his father.

Tad slammed the door behind him. But the memory of that banner with all its implications was with Lincoln when at midnight he started for bed. It brought with it too a thought of Sherman's terrible job. He went into the little boy's room, retrieved the flag and rolled it up with gentle hands. Then he gave it to Crook who had just come on duty.

"Stow this away where Tad won't find it," he said.

"Where would such a place be, sir?" asked the guard, smiling.

"That's your puzzle," replied the President, laughing as he went off to his room.

He was roused the next morning by the dropping of something heavy on the side of his mattress and delayed in opening his eyes, suspecting that Taddie had come to call him to account for the loss of his flag. But he was undeceived when a rough young cheek rubbed against his.

"By jings! Captain Lincoln!" he cried, sitting up to gather Bob into a bear hug.

"Not much of an officer but a first-class errand boy," returned Bob with a grin.

"This means General Grant has arrived, I hope!"

"Yes, sir! He's at Willard's. He'll appear at Cabinet meeting to-morrow or before if you wish it."

"Can't be too soon, God bless him!" Lincoln sprang out of bed and strode over to the washstand. "Have you seen your mother?"

"Yes, sir! She's dressing. Also Tad. He's running round in his night-shirt, yelping that some one's robbed him."

"Were you present when Lee gave up?" asked Lincoln.

"Yes, I was, sir." Bob's clear eyes left his father's face and fastened on something far beyond the open window. "General Lee could have saved a lot of lives if he'd have seen the inevitable and given up two or three days sooner. One of his own generals told him that. But he had perfect faith he could get his 25,000 men to Lynchburg, then strike south and join

General Johnston against Sherman and prolong the war indefinitely. So he struck out west from Richmond with Grant following along south of his retreat and Sheridan racing ahead to get round in front of him and cut off the road to Lynchburg. Our men did as much as thirty miles in one march, exhausted as they were. It was hopeless for Lee, hopeless."

Lincoln listened patiently. He knew all this but he would not lessen Bob's sense of importance by telling him so. He dressed himself slowly.

"Well," the young captain went on, "on April 7, General Grant sent a note to Lee, asking him to surrender. Lee sidestepped by asking what terms of surrender we'd offer, and kept right on running and fighting. General Grant the next day sent a reply saying he'd meet Lee anywhere he said, to arrange definite terms. Then he moved up close to Lee's rear-guard so's to be handy for receiving communications and the running and the fighting continued. We on the staff and General Grant had cut loose from headquarters trains and had no baggage or camp equipment. The general didn't even have his sword. We slept anywhere, on porches or in any bivouac that would take us in—Grant's a real soldier."

This was the sort of detail Lincoln wanted to hear. He sat down beside Bob.

"On the night of the 8th, we caught up with General Meade and ate at his mess. At least all the staff did but General Grant. He had an awful headache and couldn't eat. He hadn't really slept for a week and ate next to nothing anyhow. He lay down on a sofa in the house Meade was using and we doctored him up as much as he'd let us. I think it was Colonel Porter had the marvelous idea of a mustard foot bath and a plaster for the back of his neck. But nothing helped. He walked the floor with pain. In the middle of the night another letter came from Lee. He wasn't licked yet, by Jove, for he said he didn't think the emergency had arisen to call for the surrender of his army so he couldn't meet Grant for that end. But that as far as his proposals would tend to the restoration of peace, he would meet General Grant at 10.00 A.M., the next day."

"And that's where I came in!" exclaimed the President. "I instructed Grant firmly on the 3rd of March, forbidding him to engage in any political discussion or conference or to entertain any proposition except for the surrender of armies."

Bob nodded. "General Grant wrote back he'd no authority to negotiate for peace. I went out in the yard at four in the morning and Grant was out there pacing up and down and holding his head."

"By jings, the little fellow was crazy with anxiety!" ejaculated the President, "and we all thought he had no nerves."

"Colonel Porter said to him," Bob went on, "that there was one consolation in the pain he was suffering. He never knew Grant to be ill that he didn't get good news and he was getting superstitious about it. We wanted him to ride in an ambulance but he wouldn't. He climbed on old Cincinnati and rode off after having a cup of coffee. About noon, another note came from Lee, giving up and asking for the meeting. General Grant sat down by the roadside and wrote a note telling Lee where he was and to appoint the place, then he moved on toward Appomattox Courthouse. Colonel Porter asked him how his head was then and General Grant grinned and said the pain left him the moment he read Lee's note."

"I told you," said Lincoln, "nerves!"

"We met in the best house in Appomattox, belonging to a man named McLean. Just a usual parlor, you know. Grant sat at a marble-topped table in the middle and Lee at one near a window. Some of the big bugs on our staff sat but the rest stood around. It was quiet like a funeral. After all the days of gun-fire it was wonderful to hear the hens clucking through the window. I couldn't help wishing General Grant was dressed up a little for the occasion. He just had on an ordinary blue uniform with nothing to mark him from a private except a pair of shoulder straps. His coat was unbuttoned. His boots were all red clay and his pants were spattered and he had no spurs and his gloves were an old pair of yellow cotton. He just looked like nothing at all compared with Lee."

The President guffawed.

Bob flushed. "Well, I know what you mean but all the same you should have seen General Lee. He had on a new gray uniform, buttoned to the throat and spotless and a magnificent sword set with jewels and fine spurs, shining like silver and long clean buckskin gauntlets."

"All dressed up to keep his morale!" grinned Lincoln. "How come he was so spotless? No one will accuse Lee of not having been in the thick of battle."

"Well," conceded Bob, "Colonel Marshall, Lee's military secretary, told us that we'd pressed 'em so hard they'd had to burn up their baggage and they'd each chosen their best suit before abandoning the train. It's a pity, by the way, that all General Lee's military papers were burned."

"And then—" the President prompted.

"Oh, it didn't take long. Lee and Grant exchanged remarks about having met each other in Mexico in 1848 and then General Grant said that he hoped their meeting would mean a general cessation of hostilities and he gave quite a little lecture on the subject of peace which I thought bored Lee for as soon as he could cut in, he asked General Grant to put the terms of surrender in writing. So Grant called for his order book and wrote very rapidly without looking up except once, at Lee's sword.

"When he handed the paper to Lee, the general took out his spectacles very slowly and put them on and read while we all held our breaths. You know, I suppose, that Grant in demanding the surrender of the army, said the officers could keep their side-arms, baggage and horses."

Lincoln nodded. "Plenty of trouble that made up here."

"Grant knew what he was doing," declared Bob. "When General Lee read that, he said, 'This will have a very happy effect in my army.' I suppose this concession gave him nerve to ask for more. He said, 'The cavalrymen and artillerists own their own horses in our army, differing thus from the plan of organization of the United States. I would like to understand if these men will be permitted to retain their horses.' General Grant said that the terms in the letter applied only to officers. Then he thought for a moment and added that he hoped and believed this surrender would be followed by all the other armies' laying down their arms. 'I take it,' he said, 'that most of the men in the ranks are small farmers and the country has been so raided by the two armies it is doubtful whether they'll be able to put in a crop to carry themselves and their families through the next winter without the aid of the horses they are now riding and I'll arrange it this way. I'll not change the terms as now written but I'll instruct the officers I shall appoint to receive the paroles to let all the men who claim to own a horse or mule to take the animals home with them to work their own little farms.' Lee looked pleased and said, 'This will have the best possible effect on the men. It will be very gratifying and do much toward conciliating our people.' "

"Grant's the man for me, by jings!" exclaimed Lincoln. "He ought to talk Turkey to the butchers in my Cabinet!"

"General Lee was short on paper on which to make a reply so Grant loaned him some and while the letters were being copied, General Grant introduced the members of the staff to General Lee. Lee didn't speak to any of us except General Williams, who was his adjutant when he was superintendent at West Point. He only bowed, his face very stern. Of course, it was a devilish hard moment for him. But I wasn't sorry for the old traitor, I can tell you."

"You're young," grunted his father.

Bob ignored this slighting comment. "He told General Grant he'd send back the thousand or more prisoners he'd just taken as he had no food for them. His own men were living on parched corn. He was expecting supplies from Lynchburg and would like his men fed from them when they came. We knew those supplies had been headed off so General Grant said he'd turn over 25,000 of our rations, and that about ended the meeting. General Lee went out on the porch to wait for his horse and stood there striking his hands together and looking off at his poor old army."

"Poor old Lee, you mean," interpolated the President.

"No, I don't," returned Bob, stoutly. "But here's something you'll smile at. When we got over to our headquarters we all gathered around General Grant expecting to hear him say something profound for the occasion. Well, he turned to General Ingalls and asked, 'Do you remember that old white mule So-and-so used to ride in the City of Mexico?' And then he went on to tell of tricks that mule used to play. It wasn't till late in the evening he talked about the surrender."

"Grant's easy to understand and easier still to admire," said Lincoln. He sat for a moment watching Bob's tanned face which even these few months in the army had matured markedly, then he rose and began to finish his toilet, thinking of the supremely dramatic moment his son had described so artlessly.

"What happens first, son?" he asked as they descended together to breakfast. "Mary Harlan?"

Bob flushed and grinned. "Well, not until I've eaten, anyhow, father. And I'm not on leave, you know, except I can sleep and breakfast here. Where's Hill Lamon? I've got a souvenir for him."

"He's off on an errand for me in Richmond. I hope he'll get back by to-morrow. Your mother is planning doings and I like to have Hill at my elbow."

"I don't see why you send him away," protested Bob. "His real job is guarding you. Major Eckert is as good at diplomatic errands as Hill."

"Not by a thousand jugfuls, is he!" said his father. "Eckert's a great fellow but Hill's a natural diplomat."

"Nevertheless, I feel uneasy when he's away."

"Hush," whispered Lincoln as they entered the dining room. "Don't get your mother started."

"I've a good notion to," muttered Bob. "She's capable of telegraphing Hill to come back, bless her."

But he did not carry out his threat and the breakfast proceeded with nothing more annoying to discuss than the disappearance of Tad's Rebel flag.

CHAPTER XXII

"O MONSTROUS FAULT!"

T HERE was no word from Sherman when Lincoln reached his desk immediately after breakfast so he went to the telegraph office. There was nothing there. He found young David Bates and Charles Tinker chuckling over the reply General Sheridan had wired to a long series of questions put to him by Secretary Stanton. "No, inclusively," was the laconic message.

Lincoln smiled. "That reminds me of the old story of the Scotch country girl on her way to market with a basket of eggs for sale. She was wading across a little creek when a teamster called from the opposite bank, 'Good morning, my lass! How deep is the creek and what's the price of eggs?' 'Knee-deep and sixpence,' answered the lass. And at that she wasn't as good as Sheridan, was she? He answered twenty-four questions in two words."

He was still smiling as he entered Stanton's office.

"Have you seen General Grant as yet?" he asked the Secretary, who was standing before his desk writing a letter.

"Not yet," replied Stanton. "I suppose you've seen Bob."

"Yes, and got the inside story of the surrender." Leaning on Stanton's blotting pad, he repeated Bob's account, almost verbatim. The Secretary's tired face relaxed and though he grumbled again over Grant's presumption in giving the Rebels their horses, it was evident that he was touched. But not by Lee's tragedy as it turned out!

"Poor Grant! None of us have had sufficient sympathy for his anxieties. But I wish he'd come down harder on the traitor!"

"Grant knew the way out of the woods," returned the President. "We must try to make him ease down a little now the worst is over."

"There'll be no easing down in this Department for weeks to come," retorted Stanton with great energy. "And Grant's got to be on the job. We've got to stop all drafting and recruiting, curtail purchase of arms and ammunitions, reduce number of generals and staff officers and remove all military restrictions upon trade and commerce so far as may be consistent with public safety."

Lincoln heaved a great sigh. "Sing on, heavenly warbler! It helps me to realize I've wakened out of the four years' nightmare. But you must loan Grant to Mrs. Lincoln to-night. She wants him to join her party at Ford's to hear 'Our American Cousin.'"

Stanton's face darkened. "Neither you nor Grant ought to appear in a theater. Underneath all this rejoicing, there's a sinister note, Mr. Lincoln. The bitterness of the South against you and me and Grant—"

The President interrupted. "Well, I'm not honing to go, for a good many reasons. But I've promised Mrs. Lincoln and so my word's out. I hear you're having a reception to-night at your house for Grant. How about the dangers in that?"

"Surely, Mr. Lincoln," said Stanton, "even you can perceive the difference between a small group of carefully invited guests in a private house and a public theater packed with the hoi polloi. Where's your friend, Lamon? Didn't you promise him to keep out of theaters?"

"I promised not to go when my coming was announced. But I don't see how I can get out of this," troubled as he thought of Hill's care of him.

"I'll talk to Mrs. Lincoln," declared Stanton.

"You see, she and Mrs. Grant had a little sort of social misunderstanding down near City Point and this party is to be one of those female diplomatic sessions where all wounds are healed and all scars declared honorable," grinned Lincoln.

"Humph!" said Stanton. "Well, still no word from Sherman! I wouldn't put it past that fellow to make a peace pact with Jeff Davis, if he catches the arch-traitor at Greensborough."

"Oh, he's not liable to do anything foolish!" protested Lincoln, turning away. He looked over a pile of telegrams in the cipher-room. Then he went back to the White House to find a treasure in his mail.

The first letter in the pile on his desk was from his old friend Zack Simpson, telling him that he had found the whetstone precisely in the spot indicated by the President. And above the raucous uproar of Washington, Lincoln for a moment heard the sound of the sharpening of a scythe and the swish of the long blade through the wheat. He would have given his right hand to have returned, a boy again, to that harvest field.

Mary came in toward noon to tell him that she was about to send word to Ford's asking them to reserve the President's box for the following night. And she asked him if General Grant had as yet accepted the invitation.

"Not yet and I don't know but what Stanton'll be over here to persuade you to let both Grant and me back out. He says there's real danger in our going."

"Then you shan't go!" exclaimed his wife, the pupils of her eyes dilating. "I'll call on Mr. Sumner to take your place."

"Don't be in a rush," smiled Lincoln. "To-morrow will bring its own solution of the problems that worry us to-day. I've always found it so. Go ahead and reserve your box and to-night we'll plan how to fill it."

Mary returned to the sitting room uneasily, but she called a messenger and sent him on the errand, as her husband had bade her.

It was nearing the noon hour when the White House messenger reached Ford's Theater. At about the moment he entered the lobby, Wilkes Booth put his head in at the door of the office of the manager of Grover's Theater.

"Do you intend to invite the President for to-morrow night's performance, Mr. Hess?" he asked.

"Yes, of course! I'm glad you reminded me!" exclaimed the manager, picking up his pen.

Wilkes waited while the note was written and placed in the hands of a theater employee. "I suppose the Lincolns will be overwhelmed with invitations," he said, turning to go. "The anniversary of Fort Sumter will be celebrated in a way that'll outdo everything so far."

The manager nodded. "I should have got that invitation in earlier. I suppose you'll be coming here to gape if the President accepts?" laughing.

"Hardly to gape," replied Booth with dignity.

He walked out of the theater and made his way to the telegraph office where he sent a message to O'Laughlin. "Come to Washington, to-day." Then he went to the Pennsylvania House where he had taken a room for Atzerodt on March 27th. The Port Tobacco man was still in bed.

Wilkes eyed the bloated face on the pillow with extreme distaste.

"Look here, Atzerodt, you've got to stop drinking for the next two days. Things are coming to a crisis. We'll need absolutely clear heads."

Atzerodt was sober and very sullen. "You know as well as I do, Booth, they ain't a one of us will do the job sober. And you're a nice one to talk! How many drinks did you have before breakfast this morning? My old father used to tell me that the man who drank whiskey before he ate his breakfast was a fool and a sure-enough drunkard."

"Have you had your breakfast?" demanded Booth.

"No, I ain't. They don't serve meals in bed to this room. How do you know things is coming to a what-you-may-call-it?"

Wilkes told himself that if he didn't mollify this man, he would certainly foil the plot at the crucial moment. He went out and told a chambermaid to send up a meal, then returned to say pleasantly, "This room is pretty bad, I'll admit. I want you to move to the Kirkwood House, tomorrow. I've taken a nice room for you there, directly above Andy Johnson's."

"What sense is there to that?" growled Atzerodt. "Do you expect me to stab him through the ceiling?"

"It's mere coincidence," replied Booth. "It happened to be the only empty room on the third floor. You have to pass Johnson's door to reach it. You'll be very comfortable there and I'll be round to see you, and give you a thorough drilling on details. For God's sake, old fellow, watch yourself! Drink if you must but only enough to keep your courage up."

"Where's Herold?" asked Atzerodt. "Why don't you put him in with me? One to watch the other?" with a sour grin.

"I might," Booth replied thoughtfully. "Dave's a good boy."

"He ain't all there if you ask me. But that makes him all the better for what you want."

"Merciful heavens, I hope they'll hurry that breakfast!" laughed Booth. "I can't talk sense to you until you've eaten, I can see that." He returned to the hall and waited there until the tray appeared when he took it to Atzerodt, himself.

The Port Tobacco man brightened at once but Wilkes did not try to converse further until the last fried egg had disappeared. Then he said, "I suppose a swig of brandy is in order now, according to your wise old father's rule," and he poured a small drink from his own flask into a tumbler and watched Atzerodt take it down.

"Well, you're a pretty good provider for your family of bummers," grinned the carriage painter. "I'm ready for orders."

"Orders are that you keep quiet and moderately sober to-day, and that you study this map of your escape route through Maryland. Look!" He laid a carefully drawn map on Atzerodt's knees. "We must each travel alone. Have a horse outside the Kirkwood House. When you've done your job, walk slowly out to the street, mount your horse and ride slowly for at least five minutes, then break into a trot and start for Georgetown. In Georgetown—"

Atzerodt thrust the map aside. "Why not start direct for Greensborough and see what the folks think of our job?"

"Certainly *not*," was Booth's vehement response. "I'm the one to manage that."

"All right," said Atzerodt grudgingly. "You want to realize, though, that the rest of us are risking just as much as you are. How does this map work?"

"I've indicated with a red dot the towns where we have friends. You memorize those towns, to-day. I'll send Herold over and you can recite the names to each other. To-morrow I'll supply you with the names of the friends Surratt located for us."

Atzerodt nodded, impressed at last by the completeness of his superior's plans. "All right, boss," he said, "I'll get busy."

Booth gave a sigh of relief. Only O'Laughlin was more difficult than this ignorant lout. He went thoughtfully back to his own hotel for dinner and then retired to his room to work out details and wait for O'Laughlin. Much, of course, must stand over until he knew which theater Lincoln would attend.

At five o'clock that afternoon, Mike O'Laughlin arrived in Washington with three companions. On their way up Pennsylvania Avenue they stopped in several saloons and drank but Mike shook them off when they reached the National Hotel and went in quietly to ask at the desk for John Wilkes Booth. He was directed to the actor's room.

Booth, shaking hands with him, said, suspiciously, "Have you been drinking too much?"

"Do I look it, Great Mogul?" demanded O'Laughlin.

Wilkes gave him an appraising glance. His old schoolmate's pale face was a little flushed but his black eyes were steady. He was well groomed, his mustache and little "imperial" carefully trimmed and his black suit pressed.

"You look the gentleman and scholar, old man!" smiled Booth, slapping him on the shoulder.

"Since you admit that fact," laughed Mike, "I'll admit that I've been deliberately trying to convince three convivial friends who came down from Baltimore with me that I am pretty well pickled. We came over, you understand, to see the parade and illumination for Grant to-night and to have a good time. We've called at four bars and one bawdy house since five o'clock. In other words, I'm preparing my alibi."

Wilkes nodded. "Good enough. And it's only six-thirty now. Let's order up supper and get to work."

"I'm agreeable!" Mike took one of Wilkes' cigars and settled himself in a comfortable chair beside the table. "Where's the rest of the gang?"

"Atzerodt's at the Pennsylvania House. Herold's either with old Port Tobacco or at home. He promised me not to go out sight-seeing to-night. John Surratt's hovering round somewhere. I doubt if we can expect him to do any more for us. His mother is too nervous about it."

"Isn't the old lady sympathetic to the latest development?"

"Well, sufficiently for my needs. She's going to do an errand for me, to-morrow. But she doesn't want John mixed up in the actual deed."

"I suppose she expects him to mix in on the loot, though," sneered Mike.

"Up to date, he's done more than any of the rest of you," returned Wilkes, coolly. "And I may be doing him an injustice. He might come in here to-night. But all this is beside the immediate point. I want you to get General Grant."

"Never laid eyes on him!" ejaculated O'Laughlin.

"You will! Old Stanton's giving a big reception for him to-night at his house. You go up there and mix with the crowd and take a good look at him. You can tell 'em you're a lawyer from Kentucky. By God, you'd pass for one, Mike, with your goatee and your black clothes!"

O'Laughlin looked pleased. "Well, they can't do more than put me out. After I've familiarized myself with his mug, then what?"

"Then we work like the devil to-morrow and find out where he'll be in the evening. The blows must all be timed for the same moment. Maybe fate'll be kind and send him to the theater with old Abe. In that case, you and I work together. You can see that we can't lay out a long-visioned program. We must be ready to act rapidly when opportunity arises. In a general way and for your guidance I'll say that we might plan to strike in our several places, precisely at ten o'clock to-morrow night."

"I see," said O'Laughlin, his eyes contracting. "And after striking, what then?"

"We'll have a horse waiting for you wherever you say and you must ride like the devil for Surrattsville. I'll meet you there, if possible. If not, move for yourself and meet me at Greensborough."

Mike nodded. "That takes care of Grant and old Abe. Who has Seward?"

"Lewis Payne. We've been able to work out everything there, because of old Seward's illness. I'd like to have had Surratt tackle Stanton and we may be able to arrange that, yet."

The supper arrived now and the subject of the conspiracy was dropped while the waiter came in and out. After the meal, Wilkes gave Mike a bowie knife and a pistol and Mike went off to trail Grant.

Once more Washington was celebrating. There was an especial illumination of the War building and of the White House. There were bands playing. There were torch-light parades. And there was a gentle mist falling, a gray, wet shadow following the shouting, singing mob, first to the War building, then to K Street where General Grant was receiving his friends and admirers at Secretary Stanton's residence.

About ten o'clock, Stanton's son, David, was accosted in the hall of the house by O'Laughlin, who asked the young man if his father was at home.

"My father is out on the steps, speaking to the crowd," replied young Stanton. "If you'll go out on the porch, you'll see him."

"I'd like to wait in here so as to talk to him," said O'Laughlin. "I'm an old friend—a lawyer." While he was speaking, he was staring into the brilliantly lighted parlor where he could see the little man whose face the past four years had made familiar to every newspaper reader. The famous general was slightly built and round-shouldered and his face was covered by a close-cropped reddish-brown beard. His eyes were blue and very gentle. There was no one in the parlor less heroic looking than Ulysses S. Grant.

"You'd better go out," urged young Stanton. "This is a private affair."

"I'm sorry to have intruded," said O'Laughlin suavely.

He made his way to the porch just as a band began to play again before the door. Shouts came for Grant. O'Laughlin, swaying a little, for he had been drinking heavily, saw the General come out with a lady on his arm, followed by Stanton and Mrs. Stanton, and other guests. Mike touched an officer on the arm and asked him if Stanton was in.

"I suppose you mean the Secretary?" queried the guest, scowling a little.

"Yes, sir," replied O'Laughlin. "I'm a lawyer in town. I know him very well."

"There's Secretary Stanton," said the guest, nodding toward his host and turning his back on Mike.

Mike fingered his pistol and edged back into the hall. "Is General Grant in?" he asked a young man. "I want to talk to him."

"This is no occasion for a talk," returned young Hatter who was one of the War Department telegraph staff. "If you'll go out in front of the house you'll see him, clearly enough."

"But I want to talk to him," insisted O'Laughlin.

Hatter took firm hold of Mike's elbow. "You go out in the street where you belong, my friend."

"Remove your hand, sir," ordered O'Laughlin with alcoholic dignity.

"You remove yourself," retorted Hatter, pushing him firmly out to the porch and down the steps.

Grant had finished his modest little speech and for a moment the crowd was silent. In the delicate mist, each kerosene torch wore a rainbow halo and the mass of faces was iridescent. Then the band broke into a familiar air and thousands of voices took it up as thousands of restless bodies turned and followed after the blaring horns.

"Glory! Glory! Hallelujah! Glory! Glory! Hallelujah!
Our God is marching on!"

O'Laughlin followed, singing also until the parade broke up on Pennsylvania Avenue.

CHAPTER XXIII

IT was nearing eleven o'clock that night when General Grant finally broke away from his admirers and kept an appointment with the President. Lincoln received him in the sitting room where Mary after a moment of conversation left them alone.

"Sit down, General," said Lincoln. "I suspect this has been a harder day for you than any during the war."

Grant smiled as he followed the President's example, and took a rocking chair before the small grate fire. "People worry me with their kindness. This war hasn't been a one-man job. What would my attempts have been worth if we hadn't had Sherman and Sheridan?"

"True! But you were the bulldog who held the Confederacy by the throat and bit and chewed, giving the others their chance at his flanks. And anyhow, thanks to all of you, *all of you*, the war is ended. Yes, sir, the war is ended."

He fell silent, once more letting that fact lave his soul like water after bitter drought.

"What news do you have of Sherman? Where is he now?" finally the President asked.

"I know he's marching toward Raleigh," replied Grant, "but I have no details. I sent a messenger to him, of course, about Lee's surrender, but no reply has come as yet. I miss the Richmond papers since the city burned. I used to get regular news of Sherman's progress through the Rebel reporters! But I'm positive there's no bad news. The Rebels would have seen to it that we heard any such."

"Speaking of Richmond, General, that reminds me of a little story of my own. I went around while I was there to call on George Pickett's wife and baby. I heard about your christening present!"

"George is a good soldier and a fine fellow," nodded Grant. "What's his wife like? He married only a year or so ago, you know. I heard old Ben Butler's gang burned up the Picketts' plantation on Turkey Island, in revenge for my telegram to you saying, 'Pickett has bottled up Butler at Petersburg.'—Their spy system was at least as good as ours! It was entirely unnecessary, that burning."

"Tad attended a circus lately and tells me that one of the side shows had a large hog, labeled Ben Butler, the educated pig," said Lincoln.

Grant's blue eyes twinkled. "I'd like to see that show! What is Mrs. Pickett like, Mr. Lincoln?"

"Lovely! Lovely! Though she looked on me with small favor, I can tell you! I sneaked away while I was down there and found my way alone to their little house. I rapped at the door and a beautiful girl with a baby in her arms answered it.

"I said to her, 'Is this George Pickett's place?'

"She didn't crack a smile. 'It is, but he's not at home.'

"'I know that,' I told her, 'but I just wanted to see the place. I am Abraham Lincoln, George's old friend.'

"'The President!' she said. And then she added slowly, 'My husband loves you.' I could see that *she* didn't have any love for me, however, and it hurt, though I didn't blame her. But her baby didn't know I was an enemy and he held out his arms to me. For a wonder she let me take the little fellow and he and I exchanged kisses. A fine, big boy! Let's see, how old would he be, now? I think he's bigger than any of ours were at that age."

Grant thought for a moment and then said, "He must be about nine months old. Well, I'm thankful his father wasn't killed during the war. I suppose the dear old fellow's ruined. It seems queer for me, of any man out of West Point, to have any money, but I have a little and I'm going to share with George, if he'll take it. Butler's burning his place the way he did sticks in my throat."

The President said nothing to this. The contradiction between Grant, the ruthless warrior, and Grant, the friend, was one of the anomalies of war which was more inexplicable to him than perhaps any other; unless it was Sherman's capacity for killing and destroying contrasted with his private character. His mind on Sherman again, he said, "I wonder how those folks down there like being driven back into the Union by Sherman."

"Coffin, the newspaper correspondent, said that he thought some of them were pretty well reconciled," replied the General. "While he was visiting Sherman, a planter came down the Savannah River with his whole family, wife, children, negro woman and her children of whom he was the father and with a crop of cotton he wanted to sell. He had no complaints. Just wanted to make some money off the Yankees. Glad to accept any situation that would let him get a good price for his cotton."

Lincoln laughed. "I see! Patriarchal times once more! Abraham, Sarah, Isaac, Hagar and Ishmael, all in one boat! I'd like to have seen them."

"If some one would write the history of Sherman's march in terms of the good it's done and going to do, the South might not be so bitter about it," mused Grant.

"They'll never forgive Sherman, General," said Lincoln slowly. "He's earned the undying gratitude of the North and the South will hate him through their children's children. Poor Sherman!"

"Sherman doesn't mind, just so he helped end the war," grunted Grant.

"I hope he'll be as lenient with Johnston as you were with Lee. I was delighted with your handling of that, General. I want you to make an especial point of it when you appear at Cabinet meeting to-morrow. I want you to say how you feel about Davis. How do you feel?" a little anxiously. "Do you agree with me that the wise solution is to let him escape?"

"Yes, sir, I do, except for the fear that he'll go down to Mexico and set up a hostile government."

"Well, let him!" ejaculated the President. "Any man that can set up a stable government in Mexico, even if it's hostile, deserves credit. He'd take all his malcontents with him and thus clean the stables for us himself.—No more bloody assizes, General!"

"Right! No more bloodshed," agreed Grant, heartily. "You'll soon make your Cabinet agree with you."

"I haven't yet, even after considerable effort," sighed Lincoln. "You know the old saying, 'Hell holds no fury like the non-combatant.' Well, you'll hear that vindicated I reckon, to-morrow."

"I know Andy Johnson feels chockful of vengeance," said Grant. "But what does a Vice-President amount to, anyhow?"

"A good deal, if the President peters out," replied Lincoln.

Grant's blue eyes darkened. "I'm glad you brought that up, sir. Are you being *very* careful? I make no bones of saying that I think you're in great danger. Not from defeated soldiers but, in harmony with your quotation, from Rebel non-combatants."

"Do you think my danger is any greater than yours?" asked the President, gravely.

"Yes, sir, I do. You wrote the Emancipation Proclamation."

"So I did!" Lincoln nodded. "So I did! And I'm not shedding any tears over that fact. Well, I'm being careful, reasonably careful, that is." He would have liked to tell Grant that he was sick to the vomiting point of being constantly warned against assassination but he wouldn't risk hurting the General's feelings. So he changed the subject. "Do you know where I'd like to be to-morrow, General? At Fort Sumter, hearing Beecher wind the thing up. No one could do it so well as he. General"—taking out his paper knife—"how does a soldier like you look at the hereafter?"

Grant, who, Lincoln knew, enjoyed nothing more than sitting quietly before his tent and talking all night with a friend, lighted a fresh cigar and crossed his knees.

"I suppose most of us are mere fatalists, Mr. Lincoln. If death comes, it comes. If there is an hereafter—that is, a heaven—fine! If not, well, there isn't and that's all there is to it."

"I think I could work myself into that state of mind," mused the President, "if I were a soldier. But, to get down to cases, if an assassin does get Abraham Lincoln, will it matter to this country?"

"It would be the greatest loss this country could possibly sustain! It would set the Union cause back fifty years. Yes, sir, we'd lag and limp at least that long before the wound healed; over the time it will take under your fostering. I don't believe you have any illusions as to that yourself, Mr. Lincoln."

Lincoln sat thinking with his chin on his breast. If Grant was right and looking at the matter impersonally, looking at himself as a tool in the hands of the Infinite Planner, he knew Grant *was* right, why then, what of Andy Johnson's attitude and what of Lincoln's responsibility for changing it?

"You understand that I'm not trying to add to the strain you're under," Grant went on, "but seeing what you mean to the South as well as the North, I can't help feeling that you've no right to be careless. I don't want to make you nervous—or—or— Well, I'm no diplomat, sir, I know it's a whole lot harder to face the thought of a hidden knife—than twenty thousand rifles on a battlefield but—but—"

"I don't let my mind dwell on that, although I know it's extremely unlikely they'll let me live beyond the making of peace."

"You *know* it?" ejaculated Grant, leaning forward, eyes dark.

"I know it and I'll confess it saddens me, as a soldier wouldn't be saddened."

"But, Mr. Lincoln, how can you know it?" urged Grant, holding a match in his hand till it burned his fingers.

"The knowledge has followed in the wake of a dream," said Lincoln and he told Grant of that rise and fall of a tide of sobs and of the still figure on the bier.

"You can pooh! pooh! at it," Lincoln said when he had finished, "and I shan't blame you if you do. But the fact remains that since that dream first came I've known, and I've wanted to reconcile myself to going. I suppose I have a certain extra amount of self-conceit over the average man of courage and that adds to my difficulty. If a man could dissolve his ego—"

He paused. Grant was watching him with painful eagerness but with something of bewilderment in his blue gaze. The President realized that he was getting beyond the General's depth. The soul of integrity and kindliness but no philosopher was this very great soldier. His simple and direct thinking was part of his greatness.

"I reckon what I mean," Lincoln began again, "is that I'd like to believe in the old-fashioned hell-fire and gold-paved heaven."

"Well," said Grant, "with modern improvements, why can't you? I've often thought that heaven's no harder to believe in than it would be for an inhabitant of another world to believe in this earth. Or for instance for a monkey to believe in the telegraph. What you believe really depends on your mental development, doesn't it? The old fellows believed in hell-fire because they didn't know it was impossible. Now we can't believe in immortality merely because we don't know how a system of immortality could be worked out. But maybe a hundred years from now, folks will know enough. Since the telegraph was invented, I tell you I'm prepared for anything—even flying machines or a real heaven."

Lincoln turned this view over in his mind. "Maybe electricity is the beginning of the answer," he murmured, then his mind went off at a tangent. "Well, I've had a pretty good life on the whole. I used to think it was overhard when I was a boy and I still have an ache in my dry old heart when I think of what I've missed by having no education. I can't say I've had a great deal of happiness, but I've had a great deal of amusement. If I have any complaints to make I'd say the only important one is that I've been lonely a large part of the time. And that the past four years have been curdled by an overdose of agony."

"You're unfortunate in not being able to look on war impersonally," said Grant. But the banality of his comment was outweighed by the quiver of his lips as he watched the President.

Neither man was speaking when, a moment later, Mary came in. "I'm sorry to intrude." She looked hesitatingly from one to the other. "But it's nearly twelve o'clock and I think you'd both be better for a full night's rest."

"I know Mrs. Grant would say the same," agreed the General as he rose.

"Won't you and Mrs. Grant go with us to the theater to-morrow?" asked the President. "Laura Keene is playing in 'Our American Cousin.' They say it's as funny as a Nasby letter."

Grant gave Lincoln a disapproving glance, started to speak, hesitated, then said, "If we're in the city we'll take great pleasure in accompanying you. But I'm anxious to get away and visit my children. They're at school in Burlington, New Jersey, and if I can get through in time, I shall do so." He smiled suddenly. "Unless as my superior officer, you insist!"

"Jings! I've a notion to!" laughed the President.

"Well, I'd obey," sighed Grant. "Though I'll admit I'm so tired of being tied down I'm nearly ready to desert."

"Don't do that! Don't do that!" cried Lincoln in mock alarm.

"Or if you do," suggested Mary, "take Mr. Lincoln with you! I'd like nothing better than to get him out of Washington for a while. Could you start to-night?"

"This, General," said the President, "is technically known as calling the bluff."

"No, it isn't," declared Mary, stoutly. "I more than half mean it. You two go up to Saratoga for a week and then come back and do Mr. Stanton's bidding."

"I don't doubt you and Mrs. Grant could fill our places more than adequately during our absence," grinned the General as he picked up his campaign hat.

"Oh if you think we'd let you and Mr. Lincoln go off to Saratoga without us, you're under a great illusion!" Mary's dimple showed.

The three laughed and General Grant went out.

"If Grant doesn't come, I think we'll ask Noah Brooks," yawned Lincoln.

"Grover's Theater invites us there," said Mary. "But I think I'll send Tad and his tutor, if Bob doesn't care to attend."

Lincoln nodded. "I want to see Laura Keene."

"Abra'm, let's not go." Mary's voice was somber as she took his arm. "Mary, I'm going. I can't live in hiding and I won't. And I need a good laugh." They were crossing the guest-chamber toward her bedroom.

"I can't get my own consent, after what you said, this morning," sighed Mary. "And yet I think the spectacle of us cowering in the White House as a precaution against attack while the whole world tracks up and down these halls is absolutely silly. And I think the Lord will take care of you. He will if there's such a thing as answer to prayer."

Lincoln kissed her and went to bed and almost immediately fell asleep.

Just before dawn he woke up with a start and lay listening. But except for the tentative early notes of a thrush and the hushed fall of rain, he heard nothing. He was under the impression that some one had called him. The door into his wife's room was open. He crept from his bed and listened standing just over her threshold. The regular sound of her breathing told him that unless she had called in her sleep it was not Mary who had roused him. Yet the impression was so vivid that he next opened the door into the hall. The guard was sitting wide-eyed in a chair, facing him.

"Did you speak or hear any one speak, Smith?" asked the President.

"No, sir." A look of alarm rose in the young man's eyes.

"It was nothing," Lincoln reassured him. "I reckon I was dreaming." He closed the door softly and returned to his bed, saying ruefully to himself, "Am I trying to play little Samuel at my age?"

He pulled the covers up to his chin and lay with his eyes on the gray square of the south window, waiting for sleep to return. Softly, delicately, the rain continued to fall. The room was full of the primeval scent of the wet garden— Where had he left off? Ah, yes!—this flesh, these bones, this brain, were they Lincoln? What was individuality? A mere difference in brain-folds? Was an identical force speaking through Grant and Lincoln, through Fred Douglass and Lizzie Keckley, through Jefferson Davis and Robert E. Lee and old John Brown?

Suppose it were true. Suppose this was the key to the scheme: a mighty, conscious, creative entity as subtle and as all pervasive as electricity, but possessed of every capacity men's souls and minds possessed: an entity which manifested itself through all forms of life. If so, why? To what end?

Why Jeff Davis and Abraham Lincoln?

He wiped the sweat from his forehead on the sleeve of his night-shirt and pressed forward into the unknown. Why these two men with their differences which had brought the holocaust? Could it be because that conscious force owed its own expression to the laws it had created? Or that having set in motion the machinery of the Universe it must abide by the formulæ of its own invention? If the law of heredity produced Jeff Davis and Lincoln and Fred Douglass and a slave trader, did it mean that the force deliberately limited by a good or bad or inadequate brain, its own spiritual expression? It looked, yes, by the eternal verities! it looked as if this were true.

It looked, yes, by the eternal verities, it looked as if existence were a stupendously earnest game in which the creator had set himself the task of bringing all life to vivid consciousness of its complete identity with Him. Personality depending on brain-folds which in turn depended on the original law. But within that personality, be it slave trader or Henry Ward Beecher, the creator himself, however hidden by the slaver's lusts or manifested by Beecher's poetic vision. Within both the struggle and the urge toward the light, submerged in the slaver, all but visible in Beecher's best moments.

Perhaps this was what folks would do eventually with the theory of evolution put forth by the Englishman Darwin and so much discussed by Lincoln's friends at the Smithsonian: they'd hitch it up with immortality.

And when as the æons rolled, man became completely conscious that his soul and the creator's were one and the same—Lincoln covered his eyes with his hand, giddy, breathless. For a moment, he lay thus and then again he was conscious of being called. But he knew now that he heard not with his physical but with his soul's ear.

The oblong of the window had turned to palest gray and in spite of the rain, a robin piped in ecstasy.

And so, and so, if he could disassociate himself from this person, this Lincoln, if he could think of Lincoln as Lincoln thought of his hand or his foot, then death, O where thy sting?

The soft, soft patter of the rain, the enchanting odor of the lilacs, the thrilling melody of the robins: all so old, so very old, so natural, so primeval —life—and how much more than life! For it expressed the eternal force that he too expressed—that he *was*.

This call, heard with his spiritual ear, what was it but the wakening knowledge that he was not Abraham Lincoln—save for this moment of existence. Actually he was one with all life forever. The call, did it not mean that that larger segment of himself which dwelt far, far beyond the outposts of human thought, was putting itself in communion with that infinitesimal segment known as Abraham Lincoln: telling Lincoln that all was well.

All was well!

He lay without motion while a flood of peace rose in his soul, overflowed into his mind and saturated his body. It was a sensation absolutely unprecedented in his whole life experience. There was an inexpressible sense of harmony, of serenity, of happiness possessing him to the exclusion of every anxiety. And with an increasing wonder he realized that for the first time since conscious thought began with him, he was not lonely. Never to be lonely again! That which was imprisoned in the poor frame of Abraham Lincoln had envisaged its real identity, had sighted its true home. Happiness! This, then was happiness!— Its other name was God.

CHAPTER XXIV

BY and by James came tiptoeing in with an arm load of kindling. The President watched him build the fire. That black face bending so earnestly over the homely chore, he thought, was no uglier a sheath than Lincoln's for the creator's purpose. James lowered the windows and fell over a chair in his effort to move softly.

Roused from his half trance of felicity by the look of abject contrition in the servant's dark eyes Lincoln exclaimed, "It's all right, James! I've been awake since earliest dawn. So you think I need a fire this morning, eh?"

"Yassir! It's raw, gusty, rainy, cold!"

"All that on the same day! I hope it'll do better than this down at Fort Sumter," said the President.

"This here's Good Friday. Hadn't oughta rain to-day."

"So it is!" mused Lincoln. "So it is."

"Yassir," warming the faded dressing gown, "the Lawd sat in the garden of bitterness come to-night."

"Perhaps that's why it rains," suggested Lincoln.

"It oughta be," agreed James, amiably contradicting himself. "I reckon I'll get the other fires going." He closed the door.

The President rose, dressed absent-mindedly and went to his office. He had recalled suddenly the fact that having had his personal meeting with Grant he could relieve the General of keeping a like engagement this morning. The man was frightfully crowded at the moment. No one could appreciate what a little lightening of the load would mean better than himself. He wrote the General a note.

"LIEUTENANT-GENERAL GRANT: Please call at 11 A.M. to-day instead of at 9 as agreed last evening.

"A. LINCOLN."

Then a line to Fred Seward who was taking his father's place.

"Please call a Cabinet meeting at eleven o'clock to-day. General Grant will be with us.

"A. LINCOLN."

He read through a pile of mail, laying a good deal of it aside to be dealt with later. But a letter from General Van Alen of New York he paused over. It asked him not to expose himself to the fanatic's bullet as he had at Richmond. His first reaction was the familiar rise of sadness in his heart. But almost immediately the sadness receded before the new sense of peace. He drew a fresh sheet of note paper toward him.

"DEAR SIR: I intend to adopt the advice of my friends and use due precaution.—I thank you for the assurance you give me that I shall be supported by conservative men like yourself in the efforts to restore the Union, so as to make it, to use your language, a Union of hearts and hands as well as of states. Yours truly,

"A. LINCOLN."

He told himself he'd show the last part of Van Alen's letter to Andy Johnson. This would be a good man for Johnson to know. He wrote a line to the newspaper correspondent, Noah Brooks, telling him to call during the afternoon. That would let him complete his theater party at the last minute if Grant failed him.

The lilacs on the table were beautiful. He always thought of Whitman now when he was conscious of the scent of these so simple blossoms. Dooryard bushes. The sort of bush your wealthy man was apt to scorn because its foliage turned dusty and flea-bitten as summer wore on. But your plain American liked 'em, had grown up with 'em as well as with snowball bushes and their little black bugs. The first flowers the women took out to the cemetery in the spring were lilacs and snowballs. And Walt Whitman was the plainest kind of an American. At least—Lincoln paused with a frown of concentration—at least the personality the world knew as Walt Whitman was of the essential soil of these United States, of the earth, earthy. But Whitman's soul was certainly an extra large segment of the universal spirit.

Bob came in, smiling. "How about breakfast, sir?"

Lincoln pulled the boy's face down to him and kissed his cheek. "Captain," he said, "tell me what happened after the meeting between Lee and Grant? Some one said a Rebel soldier tried to run Grant out of camp when he called on Lee."

"He did!" laughed Bob. "But you aren't going to make me talk again on an empty stomach! If you'll come along to breakfast, I'll regale you with any number of juicy anecdotes about the hob-nobbing between the two armies."

"I accept the bribe!" Lincoln rose and followed his son.

It was long since breakfast had been disposed of in so leisurely a fashion. Mary, always these days extraordinarily sensitive to her husband's moods, watched him with growing surprise. This mood went back to the early days of their marriage. It was even more singularly happy and tender.

She took his arm as he ascended the stairs when Bob had left them, and looking up into his face she said softly, "You have at last completely realized that your big trouble is over. You show it in your face."

He patted her hand. "Mary! You don't know! I reckon I couldn't make anybody understand how full of peace I am."

"You look to me," she said, "like a good old-fashioned sinner who's got religion!"

"Maybe I have," he smiled. "Whatever name you give it, it's made me—"

He paused. A messenger had touched his elbow. "A note from General Grant, sir."

Mary waited at the stair top while he read. He shook his head with a sigh. "Grant isn't going with us to-night. People are going to be disappointed."

"Let us give it up, too," suggested Mary. "People have lost interest in seeing us. I'll have some nice people here for supper and—"

Lincoln interrupted. "No, let's go on with it. If we stay here we'll not have a moment's peace. People are so excited and pleased that they don't know how to express themselves except by coming here and shaking my hand off. It's almost as bad as a New Year's reception. I sympathize with them but—look at my horny old hand."

Mary gave one glance at his inflamed and swollen fingers and groaned. "You poor thing! Then we'll go. If that's the only way out which pleases you," she added reluctantly.

"I want a gizzard full of laughter. I'll invite some one in Grant's place as the day goes on. Ah! There's Schuyler Colfax! I must see him. He's going out to California on an errand and I want to send a message by him."

He hurried toward the reception room to greet the Speaker of the House. Colfax was a small blond man, looking less than his forty-odd years and with so genial an expression that his friends knew him as Smiler.

"So you're 'bound for Californy, with your banjo on your knee!'" exclaimed the President. "Come into my office! I've got a chore for you to do when you get there. You know this country's going to be flooded with soldiers out of a job in the next few months. It's going to make a bad economic situation, especially in the South where the darkies are looking for employment."

"Why don't you carry out your dream of colonizing the niggers, Mr. Lincoln?" asked Colfax, turning up the tip of his chin beard and nibbling at it.

"Haven't you had breakfast, you poor old Hoosier?" enquired Lincoln, solicitously.

"Sorry, sir!" laughed Colfax, smoothing down the blond appendage. "My dear old mother still tries to cure me of that habit! Just because one effort to colonize failed, you aren't going to give up, are you?"

"No, I'm not. But it's a scheme fraught with tremendous difficulties, and it's only one of many of my ideas about taking care of the black man," replied Lincoln.

"You could take care of the Rebel soldiers by transporting them to Texas, according to Charles Sumner," said Colfax, "and giving their plantations to the ex-slaves. I think myself something like that could be done with the leaders of the Rebellion, unless a miracle should happen and you harden your heart to the point of beheading the whole lot of the traitors."

"There will be no more bloodshed, Mr. Colfax," said Lincoln, wearily. "I've said that a thousand times. I've a good notion to print it and hang it round my neck to save argument."

"Congress will fight you on it, Mr. Lincoln."

"Let 'em. Nevertheless, not another ounce of blood shall be spilled. No one shall be cast into prison. The terrible debt has been paid by the debtors, Northern and Southern— The great job right now is to help the people adjust themselves to the new economic conditions, not only for their direct welfare but to help pay our enormous war debts. And that's where you come in."

Colfax ostentatiously pulled out his purse.

"Don't worry!" grinned the President. "Increased taxation is just the pound-of-flesh idea. You gradually reduce the taxpayer to the skeleton stage. No, what I want to do is to increase the mining of gold and silver. I'm convinced there's an unlimited supply out there in the Rockies and I want to get the disbanded soldiers interested in mining it. There's no reason why we shouldn't pay our debts and one day become the treasury of the world."

"How are the poor fellows to grub-stake themselves, Mr. Lincoln?" asked Colfax. "And isn't it absurd to think of a hundred thousand soldiers, more or less, prospecting in those wilds at your invitation?"

Lincoln interrupted. "I don't think anything so impractical. But I do propose to encourage western immigration with the idea that the few thousands who may respond will naturally increase our gold and silver supply, to say nothing of what homesteaders will do to add to our food wealth. I want you to talk to leading Californians about this. You're an old newspaper man and a trained observer. Look over the field and bring me back a practical report. And incidently," chuckling, "see if you can locate a job that will be open four years from now for an old ex-President."

"Do you think seriously of moving to California, Mr. Lincoln?" asked the Congressman, eagerly.

Lincoln paused. The rain lashed heavily against the window. "I'm only thinking in general terms of the future, Mr. Colfax," he replied with a curious gentle serenity. "But I believe the far West might offer greater opportunities to my two boys than Springfield." He rose and held out his hand.

"But this is not good-by, sir," said Colfax, as he looked pityingly at Lincoln's hand and took it carefully in both his own. "I want to come round later to-day with George Ashmun on some further business."

"Come along," nodded Lincoln. "You'll have to squeeze in when you can."

He glanced at the clock as the Speaker left. It was going on to nine. He must get over to the telegraph office and look for news of Sherman and of Thomas. There was always the chance that Lee's surrender had been contagious clear across the country! As he rose from his desk, however, General Cresswell was shown in.

"Hello, Cresswell! The war's over!" cried Lincoln, offering his left hand. "We're waiting for news from Sherman that he's received Johnston's surrender. Yes, sir, the war is over. But," with a sudden renewal of pain in his heart, "it's been an awful war, Cresswell."

"We needn't think of its horrors any more, Mr. President," said Cresswell, "and may I remark that the ending of the struggle has made a great difference in your looks. You're still tired but no longer agonizing, eh?"

"That's it! That's it, Cresswell. But what are you after? You fellows don't come to see me unless you want something. It must be something important or you wouldn't be here so early."

"Well," admitted Cresswell, "I am after something. But I haven't pestered you for many favors, now, have I?"

"No, you haven't. There isn't a man in Maryland who's deserved more from this administration nor asked for less. Shoot!"

The General brought out a paper. "An old college mate of mine is in prison. He's been a Confederate soldier but he's ready now to be a good Union man. I have an affidavit here vouching for his sound character. I want to get him out."

"That's not such a hard favor to grant. You did right to put it in writing. I don't care to read it, though. I know," with eyes twinkling, "that you know how to make an affidavit. But you fellows are going to get everybody out of this mess except Jeff Davis and me, by your constant petitions; which reminds me of a story." He repeated his oft-told tale of the picnic on the island.

Cresswell laughed heartily and Lincoln wrote on the affidavit, "Do this. A. L.," and followed the General to the door.

But here he was stopped by an old friend from Illinois, Richard Yates, now a Senator. Yates wanted another Illinoisan whom Lincoln knew and respected to be appointed collector of the port of New Orleans.

The President had been deluged with applicants for the post but had found no one who suited him. Kellogg, Yates' applicant, however, he believed precisely filled the bill.

"Yes, you'll do, Mr. Kellogg," he said carefully, "if you'll always keep in mind the kind of attitude I want you to maintain. I want you to make love to those people down there. Do nothing in revenge. Deal without malice. In your every act remember that our only object is to preserve the Union. Promise me always to act on this premise and I'll have no anxiety about you. I've got to send many Northern men south until the Southerners take the oath of allegiance. And you Northerners will keep the wounds festering and disrupt the Union if you go there in hatred. And I shan't hesitate to recall any man I discover with his forefeet in the trough."

Colonel Kellogg flushed slightly. "I am glad to make the promise, Mr. Lincoln."

The President eyed him steadily. Kellogg was the right man now. But how would he stand up under the difficult conditions that now obtained in New Orleans? Well, time must show.

"Time is the best prime minister," he said aloud. "But we'll step on time's tail for a moment. I want your commission issued now." He rang the bell and gave John Hay the necessary instructions. "You fellows wait downstairs until the reply comes from the Secretary of the Treasury," he suggested. "I've got to go over to see friend Stanton."

John Hay waited behind the departing visitors to say, "Our old incumbrance, John P. Hale, is in the reception room. Shall he wait or will you clear him out now, Mr. Lincoln?"

"Incumbrance?" The President raised his eyebrows. "No longer, John! He's our honorable Minister to Spain."

"There never was a more improper appointment, I suppose," grinned young Hay. "But harmless. Do you know that Mr. Welles says that Mr. Seward looks on that old party hack as an abolition leader?"

"Hale will be all right in Spain," said Lincoln. "Seward wanted him to go to France. So be grateful for the situation as it is. And there need be no sour grapes in the Cabinet. I offered the Spanish job to any of them who wanted it and they all refused. Father Welles is sore because Seward wants the Hon. Mr. Hale sent over on a man-of-war. I'm supposed to settle the quarrel but I shan't. I'll see him for a moment."

Standing by the door, he shook hands with Hale and told him a story and then moved with him out to the reception room where he chatted for a few moments with a group of Senators and Representatives. Then he firmly walked out of their reach and out of the house to that so poignantly familiar path to the War Office.

He walked bareheaded through the rain, drawing deep breaths of the fragrant air. Once he paused and laid his hand on the new tendrils of a clematis vine that hugged the wall. "Life," he murmured, "life! Greetings to you, brother." Then he walked on, smiling.

There was still no word from Sherman.

"I can't endure the thought," he said to Stanton, "that Sherman may still be raping that countryside down there. Do you suppose that having received Grant's news about Lee, he'll lay off?"

"Not unless Johnston lays off, naturally," replied Stanton. "What's this about you going to the theater to-night?"

"I invited Grant, but he's refused. Don't pester me, Mr. Stanton. I'm in a most tranquil frame of mind, this morning."

The Secretary of War took off his glasses, wiped them and put them back, staring intently at Lincoln the while. "You are looking very peaceful, Mr. Lincoln. I'm mighty glad to observe it. By God, I'm glad! Nobody wants you to keep that look more than I but you'll have to let me say my say. General Grant was here early this morning. He told me of your invitation and I told him what I thought of it. He said he was only looking for an excuse not to go and so he sent you word that he was going up to see his daughter Nellie this afternoon."

Lincoln sighed.

Stanton sighed in return and eyed the President sternly, and then with a helpless jerk of his shoulders said his last word on the subject. "Since you're set on going, you ought to have an additional and competent guard."

"Stanton," exclaimed Lincoln, "do you know that Major Eckert can break a poker over his arm?"

"No, I didn't. Why do you ask such a question?"

"Well, I think it was in 1862 that your chief clerk, Potts, bought a lot of pokers for the various open fires in your building here. I happened to be in Eckert's office one day and found the Major chaffing Potts about the poor quality of iron in the purchase. He proved them to be cast iron by tensing the muscle of his left forearm and breaking four or five pokers across it. Now, I'm thinking Eckert is the kind of a man to go with me this evening."

"If you think I'm going to encourage the theater project in that or any other way," replied Stanton, grimly, "you're mistaken. I have some important work for Major Eckert this evening and can't spare him."

Lincoln grinned. "Well, I'll ask the Major myself and he can do your work to-morrow." He went into the cipher-room and put his hand on Eckert's shoulder. "I want you to come to see 'Our American Cousin' with us to-night, Major, but Mr. Stanton says he can't spare you. This, notwithstanding the fact that I told him what a guard you'd make with your poker-breaking proclivities. Now, Major, come along. You can do Stanton's work to-morrow and Mrs. Lincoln and I want you with us."

Eckert, who had heard the recent interview between Grant and Stanton, shook his head ruefully. "I thank you very much, Mr. Lincoln, but the work Mr. Stanton has for me can't be put off."

"Very well," returned the President, "I suppose I'll have to ask some one else to guard me in order to pacify Mr. Stanton. But I'd rather have you!" He laughed heartily. "Only because you can break a poker over your arm, of course!"

He went out, still laughing.

CHAPTER XXV

ABOUT nine o'clock that morning George Atzerodt walked briskly into the Kirkwood House and registered. "My room's already taken," he informed the clerk, pocketing the key. "I'll send a friend around with some traps."

The clerk looked after the shabby figure doubtfully. But John Wilkes Booth had taken the man's room so it must be all right.

Atzerodt was to meet David Herold in the lobby of the National Hotel. The young man was waiting for him, his usually stolid eyes bright and uneasy. He took the key from Port Tobacco and agreed to meet him at one o'clock at Naylor's livery stable. Herold went up to Booth's room, and came down carrying Booth's overcoat in which were concealed a pistol and a bowie knife. He took these to the Kirkwood House and left them in Atzerodt's room.

Atzerodt, leaving Herold, made his way to a saloon and took several drinks, after which he went to a livery stable and hired a dark bay mare giving the livery man five dollars for the afternoon. He rode away to kill time until his appointment with Herold was due.

As he moved up Pennsylvania Avenue he saw O'Laughlin coming out of a house of ill repute with several companions. He shouted at O'Laughlin but got no response. "Drunk, already, the fool," hiccoughed Atzerodt.

Wilkes Booth, in the meantime, was sitting with Payne in the latter's bedroom, going over last details. The one-eyed bay horse which Wilkes had bought the previous autumn was to be tied in front of Seward's house shortly before ten o'clock that night.

"I've got Atzerodt and Herold out now, arranging for their horses and Spangler will take care of mine," said Booth. "How are you feeling, Lewis?"

"I'm all right," replied the younger man. "But if the others are drinking as much as you, this attempt will be even a worse failure than the others."

"Don't attempt to dictate to me, sir!" exclaimed the actor. "I'm beyond any human curbing now. My hand is steady and my eye clear. But I am concerned about O'Laughlin. I saw him this morning. He acted like a school-boy out for a holiday. No sense at all of his responsibilities! When I do locate Grant's whereabouts for the evening I'm not at all certain I'll be able to locate Mike's! My responsibilities would overwhelm me if I weren't supported by the glory of my mission. You pay your bill here, to-day, Lewis, and give proper notice that you won't want the room after this evening. We'll leave no debts behind us. This afternoon, I'll send you final word."

He nodded to Payne and strolled out of the hotel.

Wilkes was thinking as he walked, not of the details of his plan, but of himself and of the figure he would cut, that night, no matter what theater the President attended. He, John Wilkes Booth, had access to the stage wings of any theater. If it should be Grover's and not Ford's, he knew the employees. Ten minutes and a few dollars he was certain, would assure him of no molestation from them. He considered what clothing to wear. Black evening clothes?—or why not Brutus' costume? He toyed with this last idea for several moments before he recollected that he had none of his costumes with him in Washington. Dark clothing, then, with a soft hat and a cape. He would enter Lincoln's box from the rear, leap to the stage, pause for the whole house to see him, utter an appropriate phrase and then to horse and away!

He sauntered into Ford's Theater to call for mail. Henry Ford, as he handed Booth his letters, remarked that the young actor was looking unusually well, "which is gilding the lily for the best-looking man in Washington!"

Booth laughed and, taking the letters, seated himself on the doorsill to read them. Ford watched the beautiful face admiringly for a moment, then he said with a grin, "Booth, the President has the State box to-night. He's bringing Grant and possibly General Lee!"

Wilkes looked up from the long letter he was reading and said, angrily, "Never! Lee wouldn't let himself be paraded as the Romans did their captives!"

"Of course, I'm only joking about Lee," returned Ford. "But Lincoln and Grant will be here."

Booth caught his lower lip in his teeth and, folding his letter, rose and started thoughtfully for the Kirkwood House. He was as much worried about Atzerodt's morale as he was about O'Laughlin's. His first move would be to investigate Johnson's quarters and see what he could do to complete the details of Port Tobacco's job. Reaching the Kirkwood he wrote this message on a card:

"For Mr. Andrew Johnson: Don't wish to disturb you; are you at home?
"J. W. Booth."

A boy took the card to the Vice-President's room but Johnson was not in and Wilkes strolled out to the Avenue again where he stood thinking and shivering in the bleak wind. He'd better drop in on Mrs. Surratt and ask her to take his field-glasses out to Surrattsville and while there check up the landlord to see that he would be on the job that night to hand over the weapons and the rope he'd been concealing. The rope especially! It might, when stretched across the road, prove to be more efficacious in throwing horses than pistol shots in the dark. But before he called on Mrs. Surratt, he'd go to Grover's Theater for the rest of his mail.

He moved slowly on, dreaming, and all but ran into Mike O'Laughlin who caught him by the arm and said mysteriously, "Guess who's in town!"

Booth stared at O'Laughlin. "You may not be drunk—but you certainly look it."

"Oh, shut up and listen!" Mike put his lips to Wilkes' ear and whispered, "Surratt's here. He's in Booker's barber-shop. Come in and get a haircut."

"By Jove!" exclaimed Wilkes. "If this isn't like Providence, I don't know what is!" He slapped O'Laughlin on the back and they hurried together to the shop, near Grover's Theater.

John Surratt was lying in a chair, getting a shave. He winked at Booth who slid into the next chair, demanding that his hair be trimmed, while O'Laughlin ordered a thorough face steaming. It was a half hour later when the three emerged refreshed into E Street, before anything of a private nature passed among the three. Then Wilkes said, quietly:

"To-night at Ford's, John, at ten minutes past ten. You be there at ten to call the hour to my watchers in front, as agreed upon. That's all I want of you."

Surratt nodded, carelessly. "I'm going up to Canada to-night, so don't look for me, afterward."

"Good luck to you!" They shook hands and parted.

O'Laughlin said, "We mustn't be seen too often together. I'll drop round to the stable during the afternoon." He strolled away.

Booth, who had been quite unconscious during this short interview of the world about him, suddenly realized that people about him were cheering and he came out of his preoccupation in time to see General Grant drive past. The General's carriage was moving rapidly. He was on his way to the White House.

Promptly at eleven, Lincoln brought Grant into his office where members of the Cabinet awaited them. Stanton had not arrived but Father Welles was prompt as usual. Fred Seward was standing modestly in the shadows.

"How's your father, Fred?" asked the President as Grant and Welles shook hands.

"A little better, I think, sir," replied the young man. "He's really a great Stoic, Mr. Lincoln. I wish I believed I could endure pain half as well as he does."

Lincoln nodded. "Give him my love and tell him I'll get over to see him soon."

"Thank you, sir." Fred moved back to make way for Hugh McCulloch.

The President greeted the newcomer, then walked over to his desk chair and dropped into it a little wearily while Grant held his symposium. McCulloch, he thought already was showing in his keen, clean-shaven face the wear and tear of his few weeks as Secretary of the all but bankrupt Treasury. Eight months of that terrific burden had almost killed Fessenden. Lincoln wondered again how Chase had managed actually to thrive under his long tenure of the office. It was as thankless a job as the Presidency. The general public had no understanding of its technicalities and

always united with Congress in berating and belittling the men who sacrificed themselves to its extraordinary intricacies.

Handsome, whiskered Speed came in, panting, and after him Post-
master-General Dennison, smooth shaven too and with delicate features.
And Usher, also without whiskers. Perhaps Mary's suggestion was pro-
phetic and whiskers were going to accompany the hoop-skirt into oblivion!

Grant looked bored but he was answering patiently all the questions the
Cabinet members were pouring out on him. In a pause for breath, Welles
asked for news of Sherman.

Grant shook his head, as he seated himself near the President. "I'm
anxiously waiting to hear. He ought to be in Raleigh now."

"What is his attitude on peace terms, General?" asked Dennison. "The
same as yours?"

"Of course, neither Sherman nor I make the peace terms," replied
Grant impatiently. "That's not the soldier's job. And I'm glad of it. Although I heartily wish General Lee represented the South rather than Jeff
Davis. In our talk the day after the surrender I said to Lee, 'General,
will you go and meet Mr. Lincoln? I don't know where he is. He might be
at City Point or at Richmond or in Washington, but I want you to meet
him. Whatever you and he agree upon will be satisfactory to the reasonable people of the North and South. If you and Mr. Lincoln will agree
upon terms, your influence in the South will make Southern people accept
what you accept and Mr. Lincoln's influence in the North will have the
same effect on Northerners and all my influence will be added to Mr. Lincoln's.' General Lee looked pleased and said he would be delighted to do
anything in the world he could to bring about a pacification. But he added,
'General Grant, you know I'm a soldier of the Confederate Army and I
can't meet Mr. Lincoln. I don't know what Mr. Davis is going to do and
I can't undertake to make terms of any kind.'"

Lincoln felt very much moved by this sudden statement of confidence
in him from Grant. He waited a moment for comments from the Cabinet
members but only Welles seized the opportunity. The Secretary cleared
his throat. "Mr. Lincoln has been the steady and abiding friend of the
South. No one is better qualified than you are or I am to testify to what
the strength of the President's friendship is, General Grant. We both have
been the recipients of its unchanging qualities for four years." His eyes
were tear-dimmed.

"We have, sir, but," added Grant firmly, "I'm not going to let you put
me off my particular application of Mr. Lincoln's great qualities to the
peace making. I'm going to hammer on that line—"

"If it takes all summer," interrupted the President, laughing a little
huskily. "You do me too much honor, General."

Grant smiled. "And you can't put me off except for the moment, either,
Mr. Lincoln. I'm going to strike again when word comes from Sherman.
The lack of news from him worries me."

Lincoln said slowly, "I have no doubt that favorable news will come soon for last night I had my usual dream which has preceded nearly every important event of the war. Generally, the news is favorable which succeeds the dream. The dream itself is always the same."

The six men now seated with chairs pulled out informally from the long oak table turned curious faces toward him. He was conscious of the varied degrees of skepticism if not of mild derision in each man's eyes. Once he would have squirmed; would have felt keenly this difference from all about him and have withdrawn into his loneliness. But to-day his sense of kinship to that which lay back of the personalities of these men transcended all the old sensitiveness. He could not tell them he was tapping deeps of which they were unconscious but he would share his sense of prophecy with them.

"What was the dream, Mr. Lincoln?" asked Welles, gently as one encourages a child to tell a fairy tale.

"It relates to your element, the water, Mr. Welles. I seem to be in some singular, indescribable vessel, moving with great rapidity toward an indefinite shore. I had this dream preceding Sumter, Bull Run, Antietam, Gettysburg, Stone River, Vicksburg, Wilmington and so on. I had—"

General Grant interrupted, "Stone River was no victory. A few such fights would have ruined us."

The President looked at Grant inquiringly. The General had always acted a little jealous about that battle. But any discussion of course would be worse than useless. "You and I might differ on that point, General—" he said. "At all events, my dream preceded it. I had it again last night and judging from the past we shall have great news very soon. I think it must be from Sherman. My thoughts are in that direction as are most of yours."

The little half smile of derision was on each face as Stanton bustled in. "Well, gentlemen, news at last! Here's a telegram from Sherman, sent yesterday. 'We entered Raleigh this morning. Johnston has retreated westward. If I can bring him to a stand I will soon fix him.'"

"Is that your great news, Mr. Lincoln?" asked Attorney-General Speed.

"No, I don't think so," replied the President. "I don't feel as if it was. However, let us proceed to business. I suppose we must prepare to open free intercourse with the South at any moment, now."

"I propose," said Stanton, loudly, "that I issue the proper orders. The Treasury will give permits to all who wish to trade and I will order the vessels to be received into any port."

Mr. Welles gave Stanton a scathing look. "I suggest that it would be far better for the President to issue a proclamation stating and enjoining the course to be pursued by the several Departments."

Lincoln suppressed a smile as he caught the exchange of glances between these "two old bull-dogs" as he called them to himself. "Stanton trying to hog into the navy as usual. My money's on Welles!" But he did not speak.

"I'd like to be relieved of the Treasury agents," said McCulloch. "They're a continual source of corruption."

"I'm absolutely against them. They demoralize whole sections," declared Grant.

Stanton rose and brought his fist down on the table, his usual preparation for an impassioned speech. There was no longer any necessity for this sort of bull-dozing. Lincoln forestalled him by saying:

"The Secretaries of War, Navy and the Treasury have given more attention to this subject than I have. I'll be satisfied with any conclusion you will unite on."

Stanton grunted disgustedly and sat down.

For a moment Grant, Welles and Stanton discussed the trading matter, then the Secretary of War rose once more. This time he unrolled a manuscript and very politely asked the Cabinet to hear an ordinance he had prepared "with much care and after great deliberation, for reconstruction in the Rebel States."

Lincoln moved uneasily. If Stanton would only tend to his own knitting— However, he'd let him read the paper, and then head off prolonged discussion.

Stanton dealt for the most part with the reëstablishment of the government of Virginia, quite ignoring the fact that Pierpont was already functioning. Lincoln recalled with a warm glow, his session with the Governor of Virginia a few days before.

Secretary Welles spoke the moment Stanton ceased reading. "A proper State government was formed in Virginia when we acknowledged Pierpont as duly elected."

The President rose and walked over to his usual place at the head of the table. "Mr. Stanton," he said, "I suggest that you furnish each member with a copy of that paper for criticism and suggestions. In its general scope, it's substantially the plan we have talked over in the Cabinet at times. I think it is Providential that this great Rebellion is crushed just as Congress has adjourned and there are none of the disturbing elements of that body here to upset us. If we're wise and discreet, we'll get the States functioning and order prevailing before Congress comes together in December. I think this is important. We can do better, accomplish more, without them. There are men in Congress, who if their motives are good, are nevertheless impractical and who possess feelings of hate and vindictiveness in which I can neither sympathize nor participate.

"I hope there'll be no persecution, no bloody work, after the war is over. As I have stated frequently no one need expect me to take any part in hanging or killing these men, even the worst of them. Frighten them out of the country, open the gates, let down the bars, scare them off! Enough lives have been sacrificed. We must extinguish our resentments. There is too much desire on the part of some of our good friends to be masters, to interfere and to dictate to those States, to treat the people not as fellow citizens. There is too little respect for their rights. I do not sympathize in these feelings, either."

He paused, looking from one man to the other with great deliberation. Then he added a few words on the unfair and stupid attitude of Congress in refusing to recognize the new State government of Louisiana and closed by repeating, "I'm thankful Congress isn't in session to embarrass us."

No one spoke for a moment after the President had finished. He hoped that the silence meant they understood that while he was open to suggestions, he proposed to put through reconstruction on the lines he had so many times discussed and that he would override any opposition.

The first man to speak was Fred Seward. "Mr. Lincoln," he said deferentially, "the new British Minister, Sir Frederick Bruce, has arrived in Washington. At what time will it be convenient for you to receive him?"

"At two o'clock to-morrow," replied the President. "Don't forget to send up the speeches beforehand. I would like to look them over."

"If no one has any more business, I must get back to my desk," said Stanton.

"I reckon we're all in the same fix," smiled Lincoln, rising.

For just a moment the men clustered around him, commenting on his buoyancy of spirit and his improved looks.

"That dream of yours seems to have acted like a dip in the fountain of youth," smiled Welles. "You looked a wreck when I saw you yesterday."

"As a matter of fact," said Lincoln, soberly, "I feel as old as the hills, but I'm enjoying the feeling! And you mustn't laugh at my dreams, friend Welles!"

"I'm not inclined to, after the demonstration you gave us this morning," replied the Secretary of the Navy, dryly. He shook hands and the others followed him out of the room, only Grant remaining.

"Do come along to the theater, to-night, General," urged the President. "I can't believe Stanton really influenced you in your refusal."

Grant gave Lincoln an inscrutable look. "I think you take a wrong attitude toward Mr. Stanton's carefulness, sir. We've made all our plans to take the five o'clock train to-day. I think we can make it although I've mountains of work to move first."

"Well, I'm sorry," said Lincoln, shaking the outstretched hand. "Sorry and envious! Good-by, General. Thank you!"

"Good-by, Mr. Lincoln, and thank *you*." Grant went out.

It was one o'clock.

CHAPTER XXVI

"THEY PRAY TO THE SELFSAME GOD"

GENERAL GRANT drove rapidly to Willard's Hotel where Mrs. Grant was awaiting him. As he rushed through the lobby, David Herold observed the small, undistinguished officer and pointed him out to John Surratt. The two were hoping for a glimpse of General Lee. The whisper had gone round Washington that the Confederate general was a prisoner at Willard's. They were unable to verify this but Herold, gossiping with a waiter, heard that the Grants were leaving shortly for New Jersey. He set out at once to find Booth.

He found the actor in a livery stable at the rear of the National Hotel, negotiating for a horse. David, breathing rapidly, paused in the doorway and listened to the negotiations. Booth made no gesture of recognition and the boy, shivering from both excitement and the biting wind, waited with obvious impatience.

"No, I want the sorrel horse I've always had," Booth was saying.

"Can't be done, Mr. Booth," replied the stableman; "that there horse is engaged. I got a nice little bay mare about fourteen hands high, I reckon you'd like."

"Well, let's have a look at her!" returned Booth. "I want a real horse, you understand."

"You always do and I always give you one," retorted the man.

He turned back into the dim aisle between the stalls and David whispered quickly, "Grant leaves Washington late this afternoon."

"Damnation!" muttered Wilkes.

But before he could say more, there was the sound of dancing hoofs on manure-deadened boards and the stableman appeared with the lively little mare. Wilkes examined her shoes and felt of her withers, then nodded. "Saddle her up and give me a tie rein."

"No, I won't neither. She breaks her bridle if you hitch her. Get a boy to hold her." The stableman spat tobacco and eyed Booth, casually.

"She's got to be hitched," declared Booth. "I'll be stopping for a drink, when I leave here and I can't be sure of finding a boy."

"You can't tie this horse except in a stall," insisted the man.

Booth hesitated. The little mare gave every evidence of stamina and he wanted her. "Very well," he said reluctantly, "I've got to go to Grover's Theater to write letters and I'll put her in the stable there."

The liveryman nodded and went into the harness room while Wilkes held the mare.

"Go find O'Laughlin and tell him to follow Grant's every move," he whispered to Herold. David rushed away.

"Where's the best place to take a ride round Washington?" Wilkes asked the stableman as he returned with saddle and bridle.

"You've been 'round here long enough to know all the rides," replied the man, spreading the saddle blanket carefully.

"Not as long as you have! How's Crystal Springs?"

"A good place but it's pretty early for it and even if it's not raining it's certain not a good day for the country."

"Oh, that doesn't bother me!" Wilkes adjusted the curb-bit. "I'll ride out there when I finish with my letters." He swung lightly into the saddle and rode the prancing little horse out onto the Avenue and then at a trot to the alley back of Ford's Theater.

David Herold, in obedience to Booth's order, set out to find O'Laughlin, but first he stopped at Naylor's stable to keep his appointment with Atzerodt. Port Tobacco was waiting for him, having already stabled the dark bay. Herold hurriedly engaged a horse which he had ridden before and ordered it kept for him until four o'clock. He declined Atzerodt's invitation to drink and refused to listen to the older man's reiteration of his fears about tackling Johnson, but set out on a thorough-going search for O'Laughlin. So Port Tobacco went off to brood over a lonely glass of beer.

Wilkes put his horse into the familiar make-shift stable, then sought Spangler. The carpenter was at work with "Peanuts," a stage hand, preparing the President's box. Two balcony boxes on the right hand of the house, facing the stage, had been thrown into one by removing a partition. It would be a long leap from the box to the stage. Henry Ford, who was supervising the preparations for Lincoln and Grant and their party, had had all the usual chairs removed from the box and had had the two men bring in some red velvet easy chairs from the reception room as well as a sofa and chair from the property room.

As Booth strolled in, Ford said to one of the helpers:

"You go up to my bedroom and bring down the rocking chair you'll find there."

"What!" cried Booth, "you are stripping yourself as well as the reception room?"

"Not exactly," replied Ford. "The rocker belongs to the red velvet set in the reception room. But the ushers got to sitting in it and greasing it with their hair so I sent it upstairs to save it. I'll put it in this corner, nearest the audience, for the President. He always prefers a rocker. How do you like my decorations?"

"I'll go to the dress-circle and observe," replied Booth.

A few moments later he was staring at the Treasury-regimental flag, borrowed for the occasion, a blue silk flag with white stars which Ford had hung in the center of the President's box with two American flags above. On the middle pillar was a framed picture of George Washington.

"Very appropriate, Harry!" called Wilkes. "I congratulate you! How long shall you be here?"

"Almost through now! Is there anything I can do for you?" replied Ford. "Later, perhaps," replied Wilkes. "Later!"

He went back to the alley and standing within the door tried to collect his thoughts. His brain felt red hot and his eyes burned. He could not remember just what he had planned to do. Herold's news had driven everything out of his mind like dried leaves before an eddying gust. Supposing Grant got away from them, after all? He could have attended to the General himself, in the theater. But there was no telling what O'Laughlin would do now. It would be necessary to call another conference. Not at the National. Perhaps in the room on D Street. Or in Payne's room. Then he must get word round before four o'clock. Or if not, Lewis had better not give up his key so soon. Had he told David Herold where to meet him? He couldn't remember. *Sic semper tyrannis!* That was the phrase which had eluded him so long. The motto of dear old Virginia. He said it aloud in his fine mellifluous tones. His little mare turned her delicate head to look at him and whinnied. A scud of rain dashed against his hot face. He jumped as if a cold hand had touched his cheek.

"Mrs. Surratt! That's the next business!" He looked at his watch. It was after one o'clock.

The same scud of rain dashed against the office window at which Lincoln stood for a moment after Grant left him. A dreary day. The wind whined through the crack between upper and lower sash. Whine of wind and drip of rain! The old melancholy touched him with familiar pain.

What were these dreams that pursued him? Just to make the case supernatural, suppose that that phantom body on the bier *was* Abraham Lincoln. Even after his supreme experience at dawn, was he any more ready to go? Was he any less wedded to this old machine; this shell, Lincoln; this dear, familiar, ugly vehicle for his soul? Head dropped against the window frame, hands clasped behind his back, he ignored the figures in the doorway, waiting for him. He must seize his moments, to-day, in spite of every one.

Granted the conviction of his real identity with that greater soul, could he be reconciled to letting go of this gnarled old physical being, this house of his mortality? He groaned softly and muttered, "Not yet; oh, not yet! Let me finish this chore. Just this chore. If you can hear me, *wait! Wait!* Hold it back!" He was entirely motionless, eyes closed. And then he heard —was it Mary's voice, or his own or did it come from beyond the frontiers of the conscious mind?—"Let not your heart be troubled. Neither let it be afraid."

And peace once more flooded his heart.

He turned to the waiting visitor, his face serene. It was Major J. B. Merwin of Connecticut.

"Well, Major," said Lincoln, cheerfully, "it's a long time since we stumped the State of Illinois, together! We little dreamed what we'd go through in these four years, eh? I've got another errand for you." He was interrupted by the entrance of James with a tray heaped high with food.

The President laughed. "I see Mrs. Lincoln's given me up. Did you bring extra plates, James? That's right. Now then, Major, show you forgive me for keeping you waiting an hour. Fall to!"

"It didn't matter how long I waited, Mr. Lincoln," said Merwin, shaking out a napkin, "but I should say it was bad for you to take such liberties with the dinner hour."

"Oh, this rush can't keep up forever! People are excited about the coming peace. And so am I. Merwin, Ben Butler some time ago made a suggestion about the disposal of colored troops, after the war, which I think I can appropriate, now the war's over. There really doesn't seem any place for these good colored fellows who have borne arms. They'll get a bad reception if they try to go back to their alleged homes."

"I've heard all kinds of suggestions, sir. What's Butler's?" asked Merwin, spreading a pat of butter on his baked potato.

"He wants the colored men to be carried down to Panama to dig that much-talked-about canal. It's really a good notion, Major. I've gone into it carefully and in some of my free moments recently, I've jotted down my ideas on the subject. I want you to take the paper up to Horace Greeley and Henry Raymond. Have them read it and urge on them the feasibility of beginning to educate public opinion in this direction. It's especially important to interest Greeley because of the wide influence of the New York *Tribune*."

Merwin, eating slowly, said in his thoughtful way, "Whichever of you deserves credit for the idea, it's a good one. I'm not sure, however, that the fact of its coming from you will help it with our Horace!"

The President laughed. "And isn't that precisely why I'm sending it via you? He'll listen to you, even when you are cracking up one of my schemes. Besides, Greeley's got to realize the war's over and get off my back. Yes, sir, the war's over. Have you read what my self-appointed chaplain says about it?" He drew out Nasby's letter and read it with as much joy as if he had never before seen it. Merwin roared with laughter and the two men finished the meal without further reference to Merwin's errand.

But when the Major made his adieu, Lincoln, handing him the papers on the canal project, said, "Merwin, we've cleared up a colossal job. Slavery is abolished. I always believed it would be. In 1842 I predicted that the day would come when there wouldn't be a slave or a drunkard in the land. I've lived to see one prediction fulfilled. I hope to see the other realized."

He shook hands with Merwin and asked one of his younger secretaries, Edward Neill, to tell him who was waiting in the reception room. Neill enumerated a goodly number, among others the Vice-President. Lincoln pulled the bell rope and ordered Johnson to be brought in.

The two men, seated knee to knee, did not speak for a long moment. Johnson finally broke the silence by remarking that the weather had been especially bad for several days.

"Good pasture weather, though," said the President. "How is Mrs. Johnson?"

"Fair, for her, thank you, Mr. Lincoln." Johnson cleared his throat. He looked extraordinarily sallow and his face was drawn.

"You don't look so very well, Mr. Johnson. I reckon you need to get out to pasture, yourself."

"I'm subject to gravel attacks," said the Vice-President. "I had one last night. Damnable pain. Makes a man irritable as a chained dog. There seems to be no cure for them. My wife suggests prayer, as a last resort."

"Do you believe in prayer, Johnson?" asked Lincoln.

"Well, I've said a good many times in my younger days that I didn't. But I'll admit that several times during this war when it looked as if Nashville was going to be pulled out from under my feet by the Rebels, I've got down on my knees and prayed. And it's certain that we never lost Nashville!" He smiled a little wistfully.

The President returned the smile then asked, gently, "What can I do for you, Johnson?"

"Well, my disease is in Dr. Stone's hands so I didn't call to give you a recital of my physical symptoms. But Stone can't do anything for my anxiety over the political situation! I'm in hopes you can reassure me as to that. I'm speaking of the peace terms, in the light of what you said to Mrs. Johnson and me yesterday. I suppose one of the signs of my plebeian blood is that I'm superstitious. You left me with an overwhelming sense of responsibility and loss, Mr. Lincoln. And that, combined with the gravel attack, gave me a night that was as near a foretaste of hell as I think any one could live through. I'm beaten, sir, and I called around to-day to tell you so and that if anything does happen to you, I'll do my utmost to carry out the program of leniency you desire. When I say that, you understand that I'm not as full of the milk of human kindliness as you are. But I'll do my best to act with malice toward none and with charity for all."

Lincoln leaned forward with a hand on either of Johnson's knees. "I knew there was great news coming, Johnson!" he said, huskily. "How am I going to thank you?"

The Vice-President shook his black head. "I don't deserve thanks. But" —with a firm attempt at a smile—"if you really want to thank me, prove to me that I'm a superstitious fool by guarding yourself day and night."

"I will," said Lincoln, meekly. He rose and stared unseeing over Johnson's head, while a wave of nostalgia for this strange business called life deepened the melancholy of his face. He suppressed it, at once, and dropped his hand on the Vice-President's sturdy shoulder.

"God bless you, Johnson. Good-by!"

"Good-*afternoon*, Mr. Lincoln," returned Johnson stubbornly. But his face was working as he moved blindly toward the door.

John Hay rushed in from the secretaries' room. "Mr. Lincoln, did you forget your promise to visit the 'Montauk,' this afternoon?"

The President took an apple out of the fruit basket on his desk. "I must have! Do you suppose they've forgotten?" hopefully.

"Not a chance, sir," replied John, scornfully. "Two admirals, a captain and, from their looks, I'd say seven boatswains, with the ship's cook are awaiting you in the East Room."

"Mrs. Lincoln's supposed to go, too," groaned Lincoln. "I forgot to tell her. By jings, I should have gone down to Fort Sumter for a rest!"

"These vain regrets!" John's black eyes were twinkling. "I spoke to Mrs. Lincoln a few moments ago and she said she'd forgive you once more. She is waiting in the sitting room."

The President heaved a great sigh. "Saved again! John, you've added ten pounds to my weight. By the way," he added more seriously, "I actually do weigh 180 pounds. What do you say to that?"

"I say it's important if true," grinned the young man.

Crook came in and walking carefully across the room said in a low voice, "Mrs. Lincoln thinks you should wash up, sir, before starting."

"Go out and tell everybody I won't be back till three o'clock, John," ordered Lincoln, starting off to obey Mary's orders.

It was only a few moments after two when Mr. and Mrs. Lincoln boarded the U. S. iron-clad monitor "Montauk" and began a careful inspection of its inner secrets.

And at two, young Weichmann opened the door of Mrs. Surratt's house. He was going to the livery-stable for his landlady and he ran into Wilkes Booth with his hand on the doorbell.

"Hello, padre, where are you going?" asked the actor.

"Mrs. Surratt wants me to drive her out to Surrattsville again," replied Weichmann. "I'm going to hire a buggy."

"Where's Mrs. Surratt?" was Booth's next question.

"In the parlor." Weichmann went on down the steps.

He found Atzerodt at the stable. He told Weichmann he was hiring a horse for Payne. They were taking a ride into the country. The horse and buggy would cost six dollars for the half day. The "padre" paid for the rig from the ten-dollar bill Mrs. Surratt had given him and drove back to the house. He tied the horse and went upstairs to his room for his gloves. When he came down he noticed through the open parlor door that Booth was still in close conversation with Mrs. Surratt. Weichmann went on out to wait for Mrs. Surratt and shortly the actor appeared, waved his hand at the "padre" and disappeared.

Shortly his landlady, a paisley shawl over her huge black skirts and a little black bonnet trimmed with jet beads on her head, came down the steps. She rustled across the walk and placed one gaitered foot on the step, then exclaimed, "Stop! Let me get those things of Booth's!"

She hurried back, to return immediately with Wilkes' field-glasses and an envelope of business papers. Then they drove off briskly through the gray April air. The roads were very muddy but the grass by the roadside was green and about an hour out on their way, a group of soldiers was stationed at ease, their horses nibbling the young clover.

"Now what do you reckon those fellows are doing here?" asked Mrs. Surratt. She did not wait for Weichmann's guess but told him to pull up opposite an old farmer, working in a tobacco field, and repeated her query.

"They're pickets, guarding the road," replied the farmer.

"They are *very* particular!" sniffed Mrs. Surratt. "They never said a word to us!"

"And they're called in generally, at seven," grunted the old fellow. "Pretty kind of guards."

"I'm glad to know that," remarked Mrs. Surratt and she told Weichmann to drive on.

While the landlady and the "padre" were pushing through the red mud of the Maryland country road, Wilkes Booth was keeping himself busy in the alley back of Ford's Theater. It was impossible for him to concentrate for any length of time on anything. He chatted for a little while with one of the actresses who was rehearsing for the evening's performance. He chatted with the Ford property man. He sent a scene-shifter to get a rope with which to tie his horse. He took the property man, Spangler, and "Peanuts" into a restaurant which had a rear door on the alley and had a drink with them. He chatted to these men, too, very gayly with now and then a flash of bitterness for the capture of Lee's army. And all this time he was waiting impatiently for the theater to be left alone, that he might prepare the President's box for his evening's work. At intervals, he mounted the mare and galloped up and down the avenue, looking for O'Laughlin. And all the time, he carried on a silent conversation with himself.

"I am going to do what Brutus was honored for and what made William Tell a hero. Only I'm striking down a greater tyrant than either of them knew. My act is purer than either of theirs. One of them hoped to be great himself; one hadn't only his country's but his own wrongs to avenge. I hope for no gain. I know no private wrong. I strike for my country and her alone. A people ground beneath this tyranny pray for this end. God can't pardon me if I'm doing wrong but I see no wrong except in serving a degenerate people. God, try and forgive me. Bless my mother. Do You hear me?"

CHAPTER XXVII

BRETHREN AND LOVERS

LINCOLN rushed back to the Executive Mansion at three o'clock. The lower rooms were thronged with visitors waiting to see him. He passed through the crowd as hastily as he could, offering his left hand which now, however, was nearly as sore as his right. He had promised Mary to ride with her out toward the Soldiers' Home, later in the afternoon and so when at last he reached his office he made a determined effort to grind through the grist of callers with expedition.

One after another, his secretaries introduced the people. Nearly all of them wanted something. He signed a pardon for a soldier about to be shot for desertion, remarking, "I think this boy can do us more good above ground than underground." He wrote on an application for the discharge of a Confederate prisoner, "Let it be done." The Governor of Maryland called, asking a favor. "Anything to keep the people happy!" grinned the President, granting it. One of Sheridan's staff officers entered with dispatches. John Hay had just brought in Secretary Stanton and several prominent army officers who wished to discuss certain details of disarmament. Lincoln broke away from them to shake hands with the newcomer and inquire about Sheridan and "the boys in the field."

He scarcely had rejoined Stanton's group when Neill appeared with a stout, much-flustered woman. Before she could introduce herself Lincoln called to her delightedly, "Why, Mamie!" and gave her his crippled fingers.

She looked up into his face, holding the swollen hand in her hard palms. "Then you remember your old hired girl, Mr. President?"

"I never forget a friend," smiled Lincoln. "What can I do for you, my dear?"

"My husband is in the army and I need him sore. Now it's over, won't you send him back to me?"

"I certainly will. You tell Mr. Neill just where your husband is and come around to-morrow for a pass through the lines. How are things with you, Mamie?"

"Pretty hard, sir. I've supported myself and the children all through the war and I'm about used up."

Lincoln dug some bills out of his pocket and thrust them into her hand. "Give her a basket of fruit, Neill. People keep us overloaded, as a kind of thank offering, I suppose, because the war's over. Good-by, my dear! Come back, to-morrow. I know Mrs. Lincoln will have some clothes for the children."

Stanton touched him on the arm. "You'd better come to my office, later, Mr. Lincoln. I've got a better system than you have. People wouldn't dare to impose on me this way."

"All right!" The President nodded and after a general good-by again turned his attention to the continuing file of visitors.

It was nearly four o'clock before the line dwindled and Lincoln was just wondering if he could slip away to his wife when a soft giggle from the door into the sitting room made him turn in his chair.

Mary Harlan was coming in, wrapped in a bright red cape, her face flushed with wind and mischief. She dropped him an elaborate curtsey. The President came to his feet to make a profound bow.

"Mother was calling on Mrs. Lincoln and they began to whisper so I've come to call on you."

"Be seated, my good lady, and tell me what I can do for you," said Lincoln solemnly.

"I suppose that's the tried and true formula?" Mary seated herself, facing his desk.

He nodded. "Whenever I see you, my dear Mary Harlan, I always think of Walt Whitman. Have you discovered any new beauties in 'Leaves of Grass' or has your respected father made way with the poor little book?"

"If you'll promise not to give me away," whispered the young girl, "I'll tell you that I put it on the top shelf of the bookcase, rather behind the molding and father has forgotten all about it. Yes, I've found lots of new beauties."

"Do you think Whitman is a religious man?" asked Lincoln. "You know your father says he's an atheist."

Mary's eyes deepened. "What does it matter whether he's religious or not? He feels the way we all really feel. Father was outraged when some one told him about Whitman's poem, 'To Him That Was Crucified,' but I wasn't."

"Well, I think Walt is going it pretty strong," mused the President, "when he couples himself with Christ and says they will journey up and down the earth together, till they make their ineffaceable mark upon time. 'Till we saturate time and eras, that the men and women of races, ages to come, may prove brethren and lovers as we are.'"

"I don't care much about that kind of thinking," was Mary's frank comment. "I like the pictures he makes of what he sees and the way he feels about America. Come to think of it, Mr. Lincoln, he *is* religious. You know that long poem on Time? It ends on a very religious note."

Lincoln knew the greater part of the poem to which she referred. But he did not propose to permit that fact to deprive him of the keen pleasure of hearing some of its heartsearching phrases from these young lips, from this young memory which, please fate, never would be haunted by the visions which haunted Walt Whitman and Abraham Lincoln.

"Repeat what you can recall of it, Mary Harlan," he said.

"I learned several lines with which to confound my father, when we come to battle again," laughed the girl. And there was still a trace of laughter in her voice as she repeated:

"I swear I think now that everything without exception has an eternal soul!

"The trees have, rooted in the ground! the weeds of the sea have! the animals!

"I swear I think there is nothing but immortality!

"That the exquisite scheme is for it and the nebulous float that is for it, and the cohering is for it;

"And all preparation is for it! And identity is for it! And life and materials are altogether for it!"

Lincoln sat with his eyes closed while the sweet voice repeated the tremendous credo but he opened them, when she paused, to ask, "And do you call that religion, my child?"

"Well, if you believe in immortality, you have to believe in God, don't you?"

"Yes, I reckon you do," he answered slowly.

Mary suddenly shivered and drew her red cloak closer. "What a day for mid-April!"

Quickly compunctious that he should have cast his shadow even for a moment over the girl's bright youth, Lincoln said, "Well, what do you think of our Bob since he captured the Confederate Army?"

"He's very modest about it," giggled Mary Harlan. "He doesn't lay claim to any such prowess."

"That boy's bashfulness will be his ruination!" with twinkling, tired eyes.

"He's not shy with me!" protested Mary. Then blushing, she said nothing more but looked at the President in her half-wistful, half-shy way, which was so intrinsically young and so intrinsically girlish.

"I'm glad to know that," said Lincoln, slowly. "As I know young men, they don't make 'em any better than Bob. As the saying is, the Lord made him and then broke the mold."

"I think he's very like his father," murmured Mary Harlan.

"He's better balanced than I am," Lincoln replied judicially, "both by nature and by the educational equipment we've been able to provide him with. You see—"

Mary Harlan interrupted, eyes dancing. "You know you sound like a recommendation for a major-generalship! Like some one who wishes to have a friend jumped from a bank clerkship to the command of a regiment."

"By jings!" cried Lincoln, "you saucy little baggage, I've a good notion—" Laughter interrupted him.

"What's the great joke?" demanded a bright voice and Mary Lincoln sailed into the office. "Your mother is waiting for you, dearest child, and I'm going to take this man out for an hour where even cheering little beings like you can't get at him."

"Won't you and your family come to the theater with us to-night?" asked the President.

His wife answered for the girl. "Mrs. Harlan has already declined, Mr. Lincoln. It's strange how difficult it is to make up that party! However, let's excuse ourselves and run away for an hour!"

Mary Harlan made her adieu quickly and the President pulled his wife's hand within his own and patted it.

"Do you want any one to go with us, dear?" she asked, looking up at him.

"No, I prefer to ride by ourselves, to-day," he replied.

A few moments later, as they walked through the lower hall two ladies bowed and the President and his wife shook hands with them. They introduced themselves, Mrs. Hess and her sister.

"Oh, your husband is the manager of Grover's Theater," exclaimed Lincoln. "We're sorry that we couldn't accept your kind invitation to attend the play there to-night." He looked down at Mary. "Did you send word, my dear?"

"Oh, we knew, this noon!" said Mrs. Hess, smiling. "John Wilkes Booth dropped into the theater this noon as he often does. My sister and I happened to be there and he told us that you were going to Ford's. We're heartbroken and jealous!" smiling. "But we didn't come to reproach you, Mr. President, nor to presume on your time. We came to see Mrs. Lincoln's beautiful conservatory."

A lame soldier at this moment monopolized Mary's attention and Lincoln after waiting a moment offered to escort the two ladies to the greenhouses. "I'm immensely proud of what Mrs. Lincoln has accomplished here," he explained, as he opened the glass doors for them. "Look yonder, at the lemon tree they've got to growing. Isn't that interesting?" He beckoned to the head gardener and told him to pick a bouquet for the visitors and then left them.

Mary was waiting in the carriage and he sank down beside her with a sigh of pleasure.

"The sun's come out for our special benefit," said Mary. "Isn't it lovely! A green-and-gold world after all the clouds!"

Lincoln nodded and as they swung out of the gates he touched the little gloved hand which lay on her lap. "Mary, we've had a hard time of it, since we came to Washington. But the war's over. With God's blessing we may hope for four years now of peace and happiness and then we'll go back to Illinois and probably pass the rest of our days there in peace and happiness."

"I'm glad to see you feel so contented, my dear!" Mary moved closer to him. "It's wonderful when you think of all you've weathered through and of your conviction that you never would. Yet here you are! We'll never believe in dreams again, will we!"

"Wonderful!" he agreed. "Everything is wonderful. Perhaps most remarkable of all is that I've found a philosophy."

She did not want him to fall into a serious vein and so she asked with a little laugh, "Is it broad enough to help a female who is facing old age with her knees trembling?"

"Yes," he said, soberly. "It enables one to talk about the future as happily and as surely as Bob and Mary Harlan do. This morning, I woke at dawn and it all came to me. Whether you grow old or I live or die—Your gray hairs—"

Mary gave a soft little cry. "Abra'm, don't spoil the drive! You're going to finish your job. Let's plan what happens when the job is done!"

He gave in to her, though a little reluctantly. "This is the happiest day of my life, Mary. I'm just full of peace. I can't remember a day that even approaches it unless it's that afternoon when you and I came to an understanding after the break in our engagement. Jings, what a day that was!"

Mary laughed. "I wonder if there ever were two men more afraid of marriage than you and Joshua Speed!"

"I reckon there's a lot of them, right now," the President assured her. "That's where the story books are one-sided. They talk about nothing but maidenly modesty and girls' reluctance to tie themselves to a queer relationship when many a lad feels even worse."

"A queer relationship!" protested Mary. "Well! So that's the best you can do?"

"It is queer! Nothing could be queerer than you and I doing team work. And we've done it well."

"Oh, I could mention several couples here and in Springfield who have made a go of it who outwardly seemed even less promising than we. There were—" And she began to enumerate friends of their early married life.

Lincoln laughed immoderately as they recalled the domestic infelicities of early Springfield society and he spoke of some of the cases he had handled in court. "I wonder what shape my old office is in," he added. "Do you suppose Herndon has kept my old green bag and my old copy of Byron."

"Don Juan, it was," said Mary with a sniff.

The President grinned. "I got that bag when I first began to ride the circuit and I tell you I was proud of it. Do you know, Mary, that group of us riding around the Illinois prairies were especially privileged in associating with a man like Judge Davis."

"I guess the privilege was mutual," said Mary. "And I must admit that it always seemed to me that there was as much horse-play in that circuit riding as there was a play of legal wits."

"That reminds me of a story!" Lincoln chuckled delightedly. "Judge Davis was always boasting about himself as a horse trader and I told him finally that I was pretty good in that line myself. Well, we kept that up for several weeks and at last one night we agreed to test each other's ability by making a trade between us, the next morning before court sat. The horses were to be unseen up to that hour and no backing out under a penalty of twenty-five dollars. So sharp at nine in the morning the Judge appeared leading the worst horse I ever saw, all thigh bones and sway-backed, ribs sticking through the hide, hoofs the size of soap kettles and the same shape. Everybody was hollering that I was licked when I came up with a wooden saw-horse on my shoulder and set it down beside Davis' old skeleton. I told the Judge it was the first time I ever got the worst of it in a horse trade!"

When they both had wiped their eyes, Mary remarked, "Well, I don't see but what that story merely proves the truth of my comment!"

"So it does! So it does!" agreed Lincoln, laughing again. "Well, we can't go back to those old days but if we live we'll have some good times. I'm going to see the Holy Land and you're going to see England and we'll visit California and find out if we'd like to settle there. We've laid by some money and I'll get to practicing again."

"That's the way I like to have you look at the future." Mary slipped her hand through his arm.

"We must be more cheerful. Between the war and the loss of our darling Willie, we've been pretty miserable"—smiling at her—"but now we dare to face things with a reasonable amount of hope."

"How differently people greet us now from what they did when we first came to Washington," Mary remarked as a little cheer broke from a carriageload of men and women who passed them. "When I think of the insults we've received—"

"Don't think of them," interrupted the President, serenely. "They understand us better now. That's all."

"You're more forgiving than I am. I can neither forgive nor forget. By the way, shall I ask Charles Sumner to come to the theater, to-night?"

"If you wish. They're going to insist that I have some sort of a guard, so what do you say to inviting Major Rathbone and his stepsister, Miss Harris?"

"Yes, that's a good idea," replied Mary. "There'll be plenty of room for a large party, you know. Bob might like to come if he's not too tired."

"It's turning cloudy again and you'll be cold," said Lincoln. "I must be back by five o'clock." He spoke to the coachman and the carriage was turned although they had not yet reached the Soldiers' Home.

It was cold and gusty again when they reached the White House and they were glad to be back. As the President stepped from the carriage to the portico he saw crossing the lawn two old friends from Illinois, Governor Oglesby and General Haynie.

"Come back, boys! Come back!" shouted Lincoln, waving his arms.

The two men turned and after a laughing exchange of greetings in the portico, the President bade them wait in the reception room while he washed his hands. He was standing before the basin in the little washroom of his office when Charles Dana came in.

"Hello, Dana! What is it? What's up?" he called, soaking his sore fingers luxuriously in the cool water.

"I have a telegram from the provost marshal in Portland, Maine, which

Mr. Stanton wanted you to act on," replied the Assistant Secretary of War.

"Read it to me, my boy, while I soothe my hands," said Lincoln.

Dana obeyed. " 'I have positive information that Jacob Thompson will pass through Portland to-night in order to take a steamer for England. What are your orders?' "

"What does Stanton say?" asked Lincoln.

"He says, arrest him, but that I should refer the question to you."

The President wiped his hands gingerly. "Well," he said, slowly, "no, I rather think not. When you've got an elephant by the hind leg and he's trying to run away, it's best to let him run."

Dana scratched his chin and went out.

CHAPTER XXVIII

FATE

WHILE Lincoln relaxed himself for a little gossip with his old friends, Wilkes Booth went to work in the now empty theater. He first examined the door which opened from the dress-circle into the passageway leading to the President's box. Weeks before the manager had burst the lock when he could not find the key. It had not been mended. Booth wanted to provide for barricading this door against any one who tried to enter from the dress-circle. He had with him a stout wooden bar, provided by Edward Spangler. It was three and a half feet long, the width of the passage. In the wall opposite the door, he dug a mortise to receive one end of this bar. The other end, braced against the door, would hold it closed for the length of time Wilkes required for the assassination. He tested the efficacy of the barricade, found it satisfactory and then concealed it in a corner of the passage.

The next step in his preparations was to loosen the screws on the locks of both doors into the double box. Usually the President's box was locked against intruders, after his entry. Wilkes was providing against this. It was possible that the loosened locks would be discovered. For that contingency he provided another resource. He bored a hole in the door nearest the rocking chair, beginning it with his gimlet and reaming it out with his knife until it was large enough to look through or to shoot through. This completed, he cleaned up shavings and plaster dust from the mortise and returned to the alley. There he took another drink in the restaurant with Spangler, then set out on the little mare to round up his forces.

This last drink made him feel slightly sentimental. The thought of his mother was with him—of her horror and shame. He must counteract that, not only with her, but with all the world which loved him and his acting. He quite forgot the letter he had left with his brother-in-law and suddenly decided to write to the newspapers. He dismounted at the stable of Grover's Theater and went into the office to write a confused explanation of his deed. This letter he signed, "Men who love their country better than gold or life, J. W. Booth, Payne, Atzerodt, Herold."

He sealed, stamped and addressed the statement to the editor of the *National Intelligencer* and mounted his horse, the letter in his pocket. As he rode along the avenue he saw John Matthews whom he had tried to interest in the conspiracy, weeks before. He called to the actor and urged his mare up to the curb. Then he asked Matthews to deliver the letter in the morning unless he saw Booth in the meantime. They chatted for a moment but were interrupted by the passing along the street of a long line of prisoners of war—Lee's officers.

"Great God!" ejaculated Booth, striking his forehead, "I no longer have a country!"

It was consistent with the irony of war that General and Mrs. Grant also should pass at this moment in a carriage loaded with luggage. Wilkes caught the astonished Matthews' hand in a feverish grip, muttered good-by and turned his horse after the Grants' equipage. He followed it up the avenue, now and again riding forward to glare at the occupants until Mrs. Grant's startled and annoyed expression warned him that he was being careless. He then galloped off to find out if possible if O'Laughlin was on Grant's trail. He located Mike with a group of friends watching a parade of Arsenal employees toward the White House and ordered him in a fierce whisper to get to the station at once and take the evening train to Philadelphia.

"Grant is going to New Jersey on it, fool! Why is it necessary for me to do all the work?"

"Well," drawled O'Laughlin, "in order to draw all the reward would be my guess." Nevertheless, he started briskly off in the direction of the station.

With only a half-satisfied expression in his feverish eyes, Wilkes watched him for a moment before going to the drugstore where he would find David Herold. The boy was waiting for him, sober and anxious. Booth clapped him on the shoulder and told him to fetch Atzerodt to Payne's room at the Herndon House. He hoped Surratt would be there too. By six o'clock he was eating supper with Lewis Payne.

Mary Lincoln was having an early evening meal that night with no guests because of the theater engagement. At six o'clock she sent James for the President. He was reading Petroleum Nasby to Governor Oglesby and General Haynie and as usual gave no heed to the first call. James came back at five-minute intervals to repeat the whispered message and finally in desperation appealed to Crook. The guard beckoned Oglesby aside and after apologizing, explained that the President was going to the theater and that it was really necessary for him to go to his supper. The Governor laughed and he and Haynie took their leave.

Lincoln was silent at the evening meal. He suddenly felt very tired and for all his inordinate pleasure in the theater and his long insistence on attending this evening's performance, he was aware of a growing reluctance to going out. He'd prefer an evening secure from intrusion in the secretaries' office, talking to Bob and John Hay. He did not speak of this to Mary but when at the close of the light meal Noah Brooks came in, he expressed his feelings to the young correspondent.

"I sent for you, Brooks, because I'd had a notion of taking you to the theater this evening with Mrs. Lincoln and me to see 'Our American Cousin.' But Mrs. Lincoln's already made up a party to take the place of General and Mrs. Grant, so you can do as you please about coming. I see you've got an ungodly cold and that's why I'm not more urgent. I wish I had as good an excuse myself."

Brooks grinned. "I might give you a cold, though the notice is short!"

"Thank you for nothing," returned the President. "I know we've got to go. We've told the management of Ford's and the place will be filled with folks anxious to feast their eyes on our beauty. It will be bad enough for Grant to have disappointed them without me slipping up on them too."

"I'd like nothing better than to go with you, sir," said Brooks. "But if it makes no difference to you, I think I'd better go home and nurse this cold. I really feel sick with it."

"Wise boy!" Lincoln nodded and after a word or two about the war in the West, they parted.

The President, who had met Brooks in the upper hall, paced slowly toward his office door where William Crook was standing.

"Mrs. Lincoln thinks you'd better get an early start for the theater, sir," said the guard, "and she's asked me to admit no more callers."

"I've got a good many things to attend to before we go and I feel unaccountably blue, Crook." Lincoln frowned in a puzzled way. Where and why had that earlier serenity left him? "I wonder if there's trouble at the front. I'm going to pay a rush visit to the War Office."

It was as if his feet were blocks of lead. Every muscle in his body ached with weariness. He had believed that these sudden moods of acute melancholy had left him forever: vain faith! "Come, Crook," he muttered, "I've got to get rid of this, somehow."

Outside, the world dripped in gray twilight. The familiar bricked path was a miniature canal. The wall was draped with sinister shadows. Lincoln splashed unheeding through the pools, hands clasped behind him, chin resting on his breast. He did not speak until they had passed the turnstile. Then a group of snarling, quarreling, drunken men lurched across their path. Crook quickly stepped between the roisterers and the President.

Lincoln watched the young guard with sardonic amusement. What could Crook do if these bummers really meant harm! They reeled away, however, concerned only with their own ribaldry.

"Crook," said Lincoln, "there are men in the world who want to take my life." He paused and all the mystic conviction of the past months forced him to add, "And I have no doubt they will do it."

The guard's voice was a little panic-stricken as he exclaimed, "I hope you're mistaken, Mr. President!"

The helplessness of Crook's tone roused Lincoln to a moment of contrition. "I have perfect confidence in those who are around me; in every one of you men. I know no one could do it and escape alive. But if it is to be done, it is impossible to prevent it."

Faithful Stanton was at his desk, his beard a curious green under the glass shade of his reading lamp. He looked up as the President dragged his heavy feet over the threshold.

"Are you ill, Mr. Lincoln?" he exclaimed.

"No, Mr. Stanton, I came over to hear of any further word from Sherman." He dropped down on the old sofa and, propping his elbow on the curved head-rest, covered his eyes with his hand.

Stanton stared at him, sympathy and anxiety in his dark eyes. "Nothing special, sir." Then he walked slowly over and sat down beside the President. He had seen him in these moods during great battles. But this was unaccountable. He put his hand on Lincoln's knee. "What has gone wrong since we parted this afternoon, Mr. Lincoln? I never saw you in such fine spirits as you were then."

The President made an enormous effort. "So I was, Stanton. I thought I'd said good-by to this forever, at dawn."

"At dawn?" asked the Secretary, softly. "What happened at dawn, my dear old friend? Come! Don't shut me out in the cold! Aren't we comrades-of-war? Had you discovered some panacea, as you thought, for the blue devils?"

Lincoln's mind returned to that early hour of this long, long day. However ephemeral its beauty might prove to be—nay, because it was ephemeral—was it not incumbent on him to share its perfection with some one who would understand? Curiously enough he felt that Stanton, queer, passionate Stanton, could understand and would bury his confidence deep where no human being could ever man-handle it.

He began the account with infinite difficulty; not because he found it hard to find words but because of that melancholy which clogged the machinery of speech. And yet it was like a miracle—as he struggled on, each sentence came easier! Gradually he sat erect and gradually, Stanton's hand on his knee, the green lamp shade, the fluttering window shade, receded from his consciousness and he was looking out on a vista that compassed the whole of existence. Even the words he was uttering to Stanton were as words uttered by an automaton while he looked on from another sphere. *He* looking on at Abraham Lincoln, whose poor old bodily machine was so ill-adapted to keeping contact with his larger self.

It was only gradually that he realized that a long silence had fallen while Stanton was continuing to pat his knee. Only gradually that he realized that sadness had given way to perfect content or if not content, at least to a serene resignation. He was ready to take up the trivial round again.

"Do you understand me, dear Stanton?" he asked, at last.

"I think I do," replied the Secretary, gently. "You are happier now, are you not?"

Lincoln heaved an enormous sigh. "I'm better than that. I'm at peace with myself."

"Then nothing else matters much," declared Stanton. He rose and took a turn up and down the room.

Lincoln rose with him and stretched himself as if just roused from sleep. He walked over to the desk and glanced at some telegrams the Secretary handed him and they exchanged a few jocose words about the President's leniency to Jacob Thompson.

"What a relief it will be," exclaimed Lincoln, "when all this sort of spying on one another ceases!"

"It will be, indeed! I thank God for your sake, as much as for any other reason in the world, sir. You've suffered too much. But it's all ended now."

"And for your sake, too, Stanton. You've done a great job! A great task. No one knows how great as well as I do."

They smiled at each other. Lincoln dropped his arm over the Secretary's shoulder.

"I—I have a great affection for you, Lincoln!" mumbled Stanton, turning to throw an arm about the President's waist.

They held each other for an instant in a mighty embrace.

When Lincoln came out into the upper room to join Crook, he saw the guard look up at him with an anxiety which immediately gave way to a relieved smile.

"All right, my boy," he said cheerfully. "I must hurry back." He talked to the guard all the way home about the play, his reason for going and his great love for the theater. "I'm making up for all I didn't see in my young days," was his final word. When they reached the White House steps he said, "You go off duty now, don't you?"

"If John Parker is here, sir. He's late to-night," replied Crook.

"He's here, waiting," said Tom Pendel, the door-keeper.

"Then you go home to your wife and baby." Lincoln smiled again. He stood for a moment, wishing that he had not to go in and face more visitors. Then he turned to say, "Good-by, Crook!"

"Good night, Mr. President, not good-by," replied the young man.

"You have two callers in the red room, sir," said Pendel.

The President passed into the beautiful hallway.

Speaker Colfax proved to be one of the callers. With him was Mr. George Ashmun of Massachusetts who had been in Congress when Lincoln had been a member. It was Ashmun who had been chairman of the convention which had nominated Lincoln in 1860. He had shown his friendship to the President in many ways for many years.

"Come upstairs!" cried Lincoln. "There's no chance for privacy here!" He led the way up to the sitting room.

Ashmun was anxious for news of peace terms and to learn if possible what was to be done about trading permits. "I hear Richmond is wide open again," he said, before Lincoln could answer him, "and speaking of Richmond, wasn't it rather imprudent of you to expose yourself there? We were much concerned for your safety."

Lincoln smiled. "I suppose I'd have been alarmed if any other person had been President and had gone there but I didn't find any danger whatever." He turned to Colfax. "Sumner has the gavel of the Confederate Congress. He intended to give it to Stanton but I insisted he must give it to you and you tell him from me to hand it over."

"I have the gavel used in the Republican Convention of 1860," said Ashmun. "I cherish it, I assure you. But, Mr. Lincoln, I don't want to intrude on you as I hear you're engaged this evening. I have a client who has preferred a cotton claim and I want to have a commission appointed to examine the case."

"I've done with commissions," declared Lincoln, vehemently. "I believe they're contrivances to cheat the government of every pound of cotton they can lay hands on."

"I hope you mean no personal imputation, Mr. Lincoln." Ashmun flushed painfully.

"You didn't understand me, Ashmun," exclaimed the President. "I didn't mean what you inferred. I take it back." Then as Ashmun did not speak, he added, contritely, "I apologize to you, Ashmun."

"It is quite unnecessary, sir," returned the lawyer, recovering himself.

"That matter of trading permits is a most vexatious one," Lincoln went on. "I have in my office now a letter from the Attorney-General about it. Wait a moment and I'll get it for you."

He went through the private passageway and began to search through the papers on his desk. He was interrupted by Senator Henderson of Missouri who wanted to obtain an order for the release of a Confederate prisoner.

"I went to Secretary Stanton as you told me to, sir," he informed the President, "but he became violently abusive and would do nothing."

Lincoln took up his pen and wrote an order for release. "I think that will have precedence over Stanton," he remarked.

Henderson thanked him and left.

Lincoln pulled on his overcoat, then turned to his desk, keeping his mind firmly on the moment's occupation: a half-conscious defense against the insistent reluctance to go to the play. He read through the commission reappointing Alvin Saunders as Governor of the Territory of Nebraska, made a memorandum on it and signed it. Then he picked up the Attorney-General's letter and his tall hat. But he did not return to the sitting room by way of the private door. He crossed the hall into Bob's room, where John Hay and the young Captain were smoking.

"Don't you want to go to the theater with us, Bob?" asked his father.

"If you don't mind, father, I'll say no," replied Bob, turning a sunburned face and tired eyes toward the President. He looked to-night like the little fellow whom Mary used to spank for stealing pie. Queer how childhood persists in the face of a good man, thought Lincoln. "I'd rather stay here and get to bed, early," said Bob. "I'm still tired."

"Do whatever you wish, my boy," he said. "Good-by."

He looked at his watch. It was nearly eight. Mary would be along any minute now. He joined the visitors in the sitting room, handing Speed's letter to Ashmun.

"Don't let us detain you, Mr. Lincoln." Colfax glanced at the President's coat and hat.

"Oh, I'm in no hurry!" replied the President. "In fact, I wouldn't care if we didn't go at all to-night."

James came in with Senator Stewart's card. Lincoln picked up a pen and wrote his excuses on it. "I am engaged to go to the theater with Mrs. Lincoln. It's the kind of an engagement I never break. Come with your friend to-morrow at ten and I shall be glad to see you. A. Lincoln."

As James went out, Lincoln said to Colfax, "You'll accompany Mrs. Lincoln and me to the theater, won't you?"

"I'm sorry, Mr. Lincoln, but I'm starting for California in the morning, you know," was the Speaker's reply.

Mary came in, looking very handsome in her evening wraps. "I'm always breaking up delightful conferences, gentlemen," she said as the men rose. "I dislike to do it, but Mr. Lincoln and I are due to go, rather half-heartedly, I'll admit, to see 'Our American Cousin.'"

"No apologies are necessary, Mrs. Lincoln," declared Ashmun, "although I'll admit I'm disappointed in not having a longer interview with the President."

"Oh, that's easily fixed!" exclaimed Lincoln. "I'll fix for you to come an hour before we open shop." And again he wrote on a card, "Allow Mr. Ashmun and friend to come in at 9 A.M. to-morrow. A. Lincoln."

Mary put her hand quietly within Mr. Ashmun's arm. "Help me to get my husband started," she said. "Poor man, I hate to drag him out."

The President and Colfax followed the others to the staircase. There they were halted by two importunate gentlemen who wanted a pass to Richmond.

"You no longer need a pass, my friends," protested Lincoln.

"We've been turned back twice," replied one of the men.

Lincoln bade them wait and returned deliberately to the sitting room and once more wrote a card. "No pass is necessary now to authorize any one to go to and return from Petersburg and Richmond. People go and return just as they did before the war. A. Lincoln."

He was feeling a little languid but quite calm as he again started down the stairs. When they reached the portico, he shook hands with Colfax and told him not to forget the message he had given him for the miners. Then he saw Stewart and his friend near by and he went over to greet them, repeating that he would be glad to see them in the morning.

Mary, sitting in the carriage with John Parker opposite her, watched his dilatory movements with a meager patience won by years of experience. Finally, he put his foot on the carriage step and she heaved a sigh of relief. But it looked as if her relief might be premature for he wavered as Isaac Arnold appeared under the porch lights. She put a firm hand on his and he smiled at her as he called to Arnold, "Excuse me now, I'm going to the theater. Come and see me in the morning."

So at last he seated himself. "I'll telegraph you, Colfax, at San Francisco," he called. The carriage rolled away. "There," he said, "I've comported myself as if I hadn't a care in the world."

"We're going to be a half hour late," sighed Mary.

CHAPTER XXIX

"THE LAST FULL MEASURE OF DEVOTION"

WHILE the President was talking to Mr. Ashmun, John Wilkes Booth was carrying on a low-voiced conversation with John Surratt, who left before David Herold appeared with George Atzerodt.

It was a small bedroom, lighted by an unshaded kerosene lamp on the mantel. The cot-bed was covered with a soiled white spread. Payne sat on this. He was the only member of the fraternity who gave no sign of nerves. His gray eyes were clear and from under his heavy black brows they did not stray from Booth's face. His curiously large nostrils quivered from time to time but this was as habitual with Payne as with a rabbit. His big soft hands hung motionless between his knees.

Atzerodt, down at heel as usual, his short gray coat ragged and stained, his collarless shirt flecked by tobacco juice, his greasy hair hanging on his collar, was the beau-ideal of the assassin. He sat on the edge of a straight, cane-seated chair, chewing violently and swallowing the spit with an audible movement of his enormous Adam's apple. His bleared blue eyes shifted from one to another of his friends, and he constantly scratched his left palm with the dirty, broken nails of his right hand.

David Herold had aged curiously in the few months of his contact with Booth. It was not only that he looked dissipated but that there were deep lines from his lips to his nostrils and his weak chin trembled like an old man's. David was too much excited to sit still. He roamed about the room.

Booth's black eyes were brilliant. His olive cheeks burned. His clothing, a dark morning suit, was of elegant cut and immaculate. He gave his orders clearly although he had drunk double his usual ration since noon.

"You, Dave," he said, "are to do two jobs. First guide Lewis Payne to Seward's house. See him well inside and that his horse is ready at the hitching post, then go to the Kirkwood House, and act as support to Atzerodt when at ten minutes past ten he goes into Johnson's room."

"How do you know Andy'll be there?" demanded Port Tobacco.

"He's in his room, right now," declared Herold, "and I heard him tell a man he could be reached there all the evening."

"That ain't no reason I can reach him," muttered Atzerodt, scratching his palm viciously.

Booth gave him an anxious glance out of his beautiful black eyes but continued to speak, calmly. "After Atzerodt has settled with Andy, Dave, you see him mounted and on his way, then you ride like the devil after me, out over the Navy Yard Bridge to Surrattsville. If I'm not there yet, collect the things Mrs. Surratt has left with Lloyd and wait in the road in front of the tavern for me."

"Yes, little pet!" sneered Atzerodt. "All the glory and cash and none of the bloody work."

"What's the matter with you, old man?" pleaded Booth, keeping a tight grip on his temper.

"You let Dave and me change jobs and there won't be nothing the matter with me."

"Dave's not strong enough. It takes a man's muscles to do this, George, and no ordinary man, either. You and Lewis are each in your way perfect gladiators. Poor Dave's just a plucked chicken. Come, take a drink and cheer up!"

But for perhaps the only time in his life, Atzerodt refused to drink. "I just as soon kidnap but I don't want to kill—not Andy Johnson anyhow. And stabbing's no way for a white man."

"I suppose if you'd been in the army you'd have refused to use a bayonet on the damned Yankees," cried Herold.

"You shut your baby mouth!" snarled Atzerodt. "Using a bayonet in an open battle ain't sneaking into a man's room and sticking a knife in him in the dark."

"Use the pistol I left you then," urged Booth. "Look here, George, you aren't going to ruin everything for me, are you? Andy Johnson is old Abe's man. Not much use in getting rid of the tyrant if we leave his successor to continue the tyranny."

"What do I care about tyrants?" shouted Port Tobacco.

"Sh-sh!" said Payne.

Booth did not raise his voice but it was none the less violent as he whispered, "You dirty, damned coward! I've a notion to force you to do this at the point of my own gun. By God, you do it or I'll see that you hang, anyhow. When I've reached safety in Greensborough, I'll send back the evidence that'll put the rope around your neck. I'll hang you, if you fail me, dirty Atzerodt!"

Port Tobacco's jaw dropped, disclosing his mahogany-colored tongue. "You wouldn't do that!" he whimpered. "God! where's your heart, Mr. Booth? What have I ever done to you except wait on you and take care of you?"

"Nothing that you've done weighs a snap of my finger with me unless you destroy Andy Johnson," hissed Booth. "Come now, we'll go to the stable and see that your horse is in good condition. Lewis, give me your hand, brave friend. I'll see you in Greensborough. And you, faithful David"—patting his shoulder—"will meet me at Surrattsville. At ten, Lewis and Herold, leave here and go direct to Seward. At ten minutes after ten, George, you enter Johnson's room. And at ten or a little after, when I know the stage will be practically empty, I'll finish Abe."

He led Atzerodt down the stairs and to the Avenue, talking at first soothingly. But when they had reached the stable and had found Atzerodt's horse saddled and waiting, he took Port Tobacco back into the street and said in a voice of implacable ugliness, "You do the job, or you hang, damn you!" then he strode off toward Ford's Theater.

Atzerodt started back to eat another supper at an oyster bar. He still was undetermined what course to pursue. Mike O'Laughlin, apparently very drunk, met him on the Avenue. George grasped him by the arm and whispered in his ear, "How about Grant?"

With alcoholic gravity, Mike whispered in Atzerodt's hairy ear. "To hell with Grant! He eschcaped me, the dirty sojer man!" and he walked on with his friends.

"Well, I reckon I'm going to wash my hands of it, too," thought Port Tobacco. And he began looking for a hiding place after first throwing away his bowie knife.

Booth on leaving Atzerodt went to the stable back of Ford's and saddled the little mare. He led her then up to the stage door and said to a stage hand, "Tell Spangler to come out here and hold my horse."

The man disappeared to return in a moment with Spangler. "I can't hold her, Mr. Booth," explained Spangler, "I've got to shift the next scene. Here, 'Peanuts' "—calling to the door-keeper—"you hold Mr. Booth's horse. You don't have to leave your door to do it."

So "Peanuts" sat down on his bench just outside the door and took the mare's reins. Wilkes went into the rear of the theater, crossed under the stage through a passage and so out on Tenth Street and to the front of the theater.

The front door-keeper was standing in the doorway, looking into the house, with one arm barring the entry way. Wilkes quietly took two fingers of the hand on the door frame and shook them. "You don't want a ticket from me, do you?"

The door-keeper smiled in a friendly way. "I guess I don't, Mr. Booth," and lowered his arm.

Wilkes went into the theater and thoroughly surveyed the house. He watched the motionless figure of the President, glanced at the stage to note the progress of the play and went quietly up the stairs to the dress-circle and along the passage toward the state boxes. John Parker's chair was empty. A moment later he had located the guard sitting in a front seat of the first gallery. He sighed with relief and returned to the lobby. The door-keeper was talking with some out-of-town friends and he pointed the famous tragedian out to them, even summoning courage, as Booth remained in the lobby, to introduce the strangers to him. Wilkes laughed and talked genially until they returned to their seats for the next act. Then he asked the door-keeper for a chew of tobacco, which was gladly given.

He was thinking not only of his own immediate task but of Atzerodt and of Payne.

Payne, while Booth was negotiating the chew of plug, was arguing with the colored servant who answered his ring at Seward's door. Payne insisted that the package in his hand was medicine sent by Dr. Verdi which he was to deliver in person with instructions how it was to be taken. The servant was firm in his stand that Mr. Seward could not be seen. But Payne was very insistent and overbearing and the colored man, intimidated, gave way. At the stair top Frederick Seward, the Assistant Treasurer, met Lewis and sternly forbade him to enter the sick-room. Lewis started to go back down the stairs but suddenly turned and knocked Frederick down with his pistol, fracturing his skull. Sergeant Robinson, Secretary Seward's nurse, opened the door and Payne cut him in the face with his knife, knocking him off his balance and rushed past him to the Secretary's bed. He tried to shoot the helpless man but the blow given Frederick Seward had bent the hammer. He then stabbed Seward three times in the face and neck. But the steel frame which held the Secretary's broken jaw deflected the blows and saved his life.

Sergeant Robinson recovered himself and, rushing to the bed, grappled with Payne. Seward rolled off the bed to the floor on the opposite side. There was a desperate wrestling match between Robinson and Payne, Payne stabbing with one hand and using the pistol as a club with the other.

Augustus Seward, the younger son, wakened at last, leaped into the room and together he and Robinson dragged Payne into the hall. Here Lewis freed himself and howling, "I'm mad! I'm mad!" rushed down the stairs, wounding a messenger from the State Department whom he passed.

The colored man had run out into the street, screaming "Murder!" Dave Herold, immediately deserting his post, set spurs to his horse for Surrattsville. Payne mounted the remaining beast and started like the madman he called himself, whither he was not sure.

It was nearly ten minutes past ten.

In the street before Ford's the President's carriage was waiting. Wilkes Booth, sauntering up and down, went into the saloon next door and took a last drink of whiskey. As he came back to the lobby he heard Surratt say that it was ten minutes past ten. Booth went resolutely up the stairs to the President's box.

Lincoln in his rocking chair felt a sudden chill and rose to put on his overcoat.

"Are you catching cold?" whispered Mary under cover of a prolonged laugh from the audience. "It's really very warm in the theater."

"I don't see how you women stand it with your bare shoulders," whispered Lincoln in return. "Still I don't blame you. Your neck and shoulders are lovelier than little Miss Todd's ever were, my darling wife."

She looked up at him with quick understanding. "You aren't going to let me grow old if you can help it, are you, my dear! Are you enjoying the play?"

He nodded and Mary turned her attention again to the stage.

Lincoln was not sorry after all that he had come. The play was extraordinarily funny and still it made no great demands on his tired brain. He was able to enjoy its foolishness and at the same time to ponder serenely on all that had been working in his inner mind during the past weeks.

After all, Mary had spoken truly when she had said that his death would not wreck the Union. If democracy was right, if it belonged in evolution, its persistence in the life of governments was not dependent on any one man. If, as he believed, democracy was one of the qualities essential for the growth of humanity's consciousness of its oneness with its creator, then Abraham Lincoln was only one of an infinite number of tools for shaping man toward that great end.

This tired, rattling old piece of machinery, this Abraham Lincoln—well, what next for him? Had he wrought well enough to go further in what Walt Whitman called the exquisite scheme? Had he?

He caught his breath as again that ineffable call reached his soul; deep speaking to deep. That greater self, beyond the far outposts, was reaching out again to this lonely portion of itself; so lost; so lonely; but now so conscious of its ultimate immortal destiny!

He was conscious of a sudden blow on the back of his head but he did not move.

" 'For thou didst call me!' " he murmured.

And surely, beyond the sudden strange uproar from the audience he heard that superlatively convincing answer:

"All is well!"